Dear Maggie,

Hope you love et!

Best Regards —

Bruce

8-8-23

AN
AMERICAN
RICH GIRL

BRUCE COOK

ARCHWAY
PUBLISHING

Archway Publishing books may be ordered through booksellers or by contacting:

Archway Publishing
1663 Liberty Drive
Bloomington, IN 47403
www.archwaypublishing.com
844-669-3957

Grateful appreciation for the editing talents of Laurie Veitch,
Gus Kane and Archway Editorial.
Cover design by ebooklaunch.com.

ISBN: 978-1-6657-2208-7 (sc)
ISBN: 978-1-6657-2553-8 (hc)
ISBN: 978-1-6657-2209-4 (e)

Library of Congress Control Number: 2022907235

Print information available on the last page.

Archway Publishing rev. date: 06/16/2022

FOR HEIDI MILLER

"Of course all life is a process of breaking down, but the blows that do the dramatic side of the work—the big sudden blows that come, or seem to come, from outside—the ones you remember and blame things on and, in moments of weakness, tell your friends about, don't show their effect all at once. There is another sort of blow that comes from within—that you don't feel until it's too late to do anything about it, until you realize with finality that in some regard you will never be as good a man again. The first sort of breakage seems to happen quick—the second kind happens almost without your knowing it but is realized suddenly indeed."

F. Scott Fitzgerald

CHAPTER ONE

A PRIVILEGED YOUTH

In this age of the independent woman, my father set me up with the man I eventually married. He was doing a business deal with the guy and thought he would also be an ideal husband for me. Sort of a package deal. The semiarranged union, made without the benefit of the internet, became my own modern version of the American love story.

My name is Kate Fairchild. It is a name that sounds just about as Waspy as once can imagine. A true "generation next" girl on the outer cusp of the self-absorbed millennials, I am blonde, of course, and tall. Some even label me statuesque, with a figure that compels construction guys to whistle.

Raised in glittering Beverly Hills, north of Sunset Boulevard on Lexington Road in a fabulous southern colonial home, complete with obligatory pillars, gleaming, white-painted siding, and high-gloss black painted plantation shutters bordering the tall paned windows on two floors, my childhood was the stuff of a Lifetime Channel movie without the drama. Beautiful people, beautiful everything—so ideal you might be inclined to disbelieve the level of privilege. My parents, despite their indulgence in the material pleasures afforded by their financial ability, are truly happy people. Somehow, despite any challenges, they have managed to escape the downside that often comes with a life of not shopping anywhere but Neiman Marcus, not flying any class but first, and never worrying about any expense. While they have not completely avoided life's pitfalls and heartaches, including the loss of loved ones and the trials involved in raising kids in an often-insane world, my parents have kept it together on many levels.

Nancy Fairchild, my mother, might be the original Martha Stewart. Martha would have trained under Nancy. Mother Nancy exudes a strong, over-the-top fashion sense and a real flair for the "only the best will do." Way too much Beverly Hills style. The understated Martha Stewart Connecticut country idiom is a notch or two below my mother's operating current.

At fifty, Nancy has the vitality of a thirty-year-old. She also has the skin, thanks to Dr. Klein, and the hair, thanks to stylist Hugh. Nancy is a five-foot, four-inch velvet bulldozer with platinum-blonde hair and piercing blue eyes, accentuated by just enough eyeliner, always ready for public view, sporting a very pale pink lip gloss to coordinate with her nail polish. She serves on a million committees and takes care of her husband first, her children second, and herself last, but makes everyone in her life feel as if they are treasured, as if each is the most important person alive.

My father's name is Dalton Fairchild, a.k.a. Dalt. At fifty-two, he is one cool dad. Drop-dead handsome and athletic, Dalt plays tennis competitively with ferocious aggression at least two times a week. He is unapologetically positive, always smiling, dressed by Ralph Lauren from head to toe since the time he was in college, and rich. Should I mention how rich? Very rich. Dad came from money and then made more on his own. Making money is an art for my father. And he is generous—too generous with some, me included. He also makes life too easy for my younger brother, Jamey.

I was properly indoctrinated in the lifestyle of the American rich girl over the course of six years at Foxhaven Academy for Girls, tucked away for more than one hundred haloed graduations in a wooded glen off the Philadelphia Main Line. There were so many Buffys and Muffys, and a broad selection of Daisys and Merediths, that it is a wonder I did not rebel and become a latter-day flower child. I grew up with a certain attraction to the liberated 1960s. To my mother Nancy's horror, I redecorated my pink toile sixth grade bedroom in tie-dyed sheets and added a lava lamp found at the Pasadena Flea Market. It was heaven.

As my seventh-grade year dawned, it was farewell to my hippie flashback fantasy and hello to Ms. Ardith Collins, headmistress at Foxhaven Academy. We are talking uniforms, rules, and behavior so foreign to me that I thought I was being subjected to an exorcism. One of my favorite 1960s-era movies that made me think about my mother's childhood was *The Trouble with Angels*, so at boarding school I pretended I was Hayley Mills reincarnated as Kate Fairchild, and I adjusted. Eventually, I rose in status, becoming one of the popular girls at the academy. The Beverly Hills address helped, along with visits from Nancy and Dalt, which created an excitement level more appropriate for European royalty. It didn't hurt that they always brought an abundance of treats.

By the time I reached seventeen, my virginity was in the rearview mirror. Girls' prep school did present its opportunities for boy-crazy behavior. The liaisons were not regular, or often, but I did feel entitled to a share of carnal exploration. Okay, I had sex twice, sort of. It was not romantic, not special, and unplanned, but I did like it. The first time was with a basketball player. My class was on an athletic field trip for a game at an all-boys' prep school in Lower Merion Township. He was Jack-in-the-Beanstalk tall and skinny, and the sweat of his exertion at the winning game lubricated my skin as our bodies met behind the gym on a very cold afternoon in April.

He put his arms around me, pressing his wet and hot uniform against my white blouse and gray pleated skirt. With a strong, hard body, this seventeen-year-old had one thing on his mind. I could feel what was on his mind as his manhood hardened beneath the rayon shorts.

I don't know how he managed to raise my pleated skirt just enough to pull down my white lace panties, but he did, and it happened very fast. I helped, dropping those basketball shorts just enough to release a spectacular vision of a rather significant male tool. He entered me with the speed of a subway entering Pennsylvania Station. I screamed, a controlled sort of pleasurable scream. It felt amazing, and I finally knew just what all the hoopla over sex was about.

As my basketball boy pushed and pulled, making grunting noises I'd never heard, and certainly had not expected to hear during my first sexual encounter, all I could think of was, first, how much I liked it, and second, that this was God's ultimate trick to control mortals: give them immense pleasure that cannot be duplicated in any other pursuit in life, and they will always remain loyal and loving children.

Just like in the movies, or in any number of trashy novels I read, some over and over again, the sex was over almost before it had started. For my own first time, he came inside me very fast, the warm fluid heightening my pleasure. I think I experienced orgasm, but I'm not sure.

"Thank you," he said, pulling up his shorts after removing himself from inside me.

How odd, I thought, *to be thanked.* "Nice meeting you" or "Nice having you" might have been better, at least more appropriate. I laughed at my bizarre thoughts.

I knew one thing: it wasn't love. Yet it was sex that I liked, and I didn't place any super meaning on the moment. It happened. We parted. I did not feel bad or guilty or shameful. It just happened, a life experience for an American teenage girl, probably like the first time for millions of others. I got back to the bus just in time for the ride back to Foxhaven. Everyone had been looking for me, waiting impatiently.

"Where have you been?" Ms. Collins asked.

"Gee, I'm sorry. I was just looking around the school. This is quite a neat campus," I told her.

The bus ride back was something of a challenge. My first-time partner's man juice kept creeping out and running down my leg. With no tissue, I had nothing but my sweater to use as a wipe. With great care not to reveal my situation, I managed to keep the crisis private. As soon as the driver put on the brakes and pulled into the parking lot at our school, I dashed off the bus, pushing my way past everyone in front, going out the door, and heading straight for my dorm room shower. The hot water was magical as I watched the tiny remains of my lovemaking swirl down the drain. No doubt I would ever forget this basketball game. What was the boy's name?

Once Was Not Enough

Almost a year had passed after I'd bid farewell to my virginity, taken by the sweaty and very tall basketball player. I thought about that night a lot. None of the self-analysis revealed any universal truth. There was no epiphany, other than my ability to recount the physical pleasure without any form of regret. Was I just a tramp in training?

Nonsense. I was not a tramp. So many of my good-girl friends from good families were doing it whenever the opportunity arose. Males are not the only gender to pursue the sex act, and they are surely not the only gender to talk about it, brag about it, or share all the juicy details with friends or anyone willing to ask, practically anywhere and anytime.

There had been new possibilities over the past year, yet the setup remained the same: sex by chance, sex in secret and in a serious hurry. I wasn't interested, or not interested enough. Mother Nancy was loud in my subconscious: *Save yourself, my darling. Don't give it away. Wait for the right time, the right place, and most importantly, the right man.*

At boarding school, it seemed to me that there was no right time or right place. How could I possibly know if my suitor was the right man? Why are Americans all so preoccupied with sex? And so judgmental in a double standard kind of way? Often adults take a "Do as I say, not as I do" hypocritical stance. I decided to hold out, take the abstinence road. I suppose it was supertraditional, but my motivation came from my soul. I needed more time to figure out my life without sex.

Never would I be so phony to call myself a born-again virgin. What a concept. What a denial after doing something that is so natural, so real, so human—the absolute core of life and civilization.

Yet, for what it's worth, over the past year, I had taken the path of abstinence. I didn't talk about it. Since I was popular and pretty, my friends just sized me up as private. They all expected that I was doing it whenever and with whomever I pleased. It must have been my aura of confidence.

Right. Well, maybe not, but it was working for me. That is, until the night of the prom. Private school, public school, boarding school, it doesn't matter—prom is another rite of passage for kids who make it a goal to end the dance with sex.

The whole concept is, frankly, trashy. Add to the equation a prom attended by wealthy girls and boys, supposedly raised better than the massive hordes of the unwashed public, and guess what? I realized that we are all members of the unwashed society, regardless of bank balance, especially if that balance belongs to our parents.

My prom was scheduled for the first Saturday evening in December, prelude to the upcoming Christmas season. The tony Glenville Country Club welcomed the onslaught of future business leaders and their soon-to-be debutante future wives.

A magnificent setting exuded old-world taste and screamed traditional values of courtship. Decorated with astounding winter white orchids and pastel cabbage roses overflowing from crystal vases, the club dining room had been transformed into a magical winter garden. Table settings boasted sterling silver candlesticks designed in the fashion of Corinthian columns, with tall eighteen-inch ivory tapers producing a very elegant, subdued spray of illumination.

We were all dressed to impress. Our parents made sure of that. Federal Express boxes had been delivered daily in the days and weeks before our big night. Opening the goods made for quite a frenzy, with plenty of comparison and jockeying for attention and status.

While I tried to rise above it all, I failed, finally succumbing. My first package came on what was a very dreary day in late November. I was with my parents over the Thanksgiving break in the Big Apple, and Mother Nancy and I visited the designer salons with considerable gusto.

I found several dresses off the rack at Saks Fifth Avenue, Bergdorf's, and even my favorite, Bloomingdale's, but Mother wanted me to have my first couture gown. Most girls would kill for my off-the-racks, and I was seriously embarrassed going with Nancy to appointments at the House of Dior, Yves Saint Laurent, Balenciaga, and Carolina Herrera.

At Dior, arriving for our showing at eleven o'clock in the morning, we were ushered into a private salon by a very dapper man who was wearing a gardenia bud in the buttonhole of his lapel. He was joined by two very serious middle-aged women dressed in finely tailored black suits, cream blouses, and low black and cream Ferragamo pumps.

I confess I was really enjoying the entire experience, especially since my dream was still to go to fashion school in Paris. At this moment, the Dior salon on Fifth Avenue was as close as I was going to get.

Mother and I were seated on a settee covered in ivory damask and were each offered a flute of Veuve Clicquot. Accepting with pleasure, I saw that another waiter was entering from a hidden door, carrying a silver tray of canapés and a frosted Lalique bowl of caviar accompanied with the essential capers, chopped onion, egg, and perfectly sliced toast points, no crusts. At least I had learned something about the delicacies available to the few who were very fortunate in life. How many teenage girls know about caviar and capers? That bit of knowledge and one sexual encounter had surely made me into a woman of the world.

After trying on at least a dozen gowns, all amazing, I gathered enough courage to say, "I am so grateful, but no thank you." Nancy was slightly embarrassed, but she let it go and smiled, thanking the Dior staff, never apologizing. Nancy never apologized.

"What was that all about?" she grilled me as we left the salon. Our driver was at the ready, pulling up to the curb just as we had come through the door. The man jumped out of the black Lincoln Town Car, then ran around and opened the rear passenger door with military precision.

"How did he know we were coming?" I questioned rather incredulously.

"Don't be silly, darling. I sent him a signal on my mobile phone," my very much in-charge mother told me, putting out her arm, signaling me to slide in the back seat first.

I followed orders perfectly.

"What would you like to do now?" Mother Nancy asked, taking my right hand and looking right into my eyes.

"How about lunch at Serendipity?" I responded, giving a sheepish grin.

"Fabulous idea," was all she said.

Somehow the driver heard, and the Town Car made a U-turn and headed up Fifth Avenue to Fifty-Ninth Street, where it made a right turn and proceeded toward my dream restaurant. On this day of fashion hunting, we arrived in minutes. We got out of the car and waltzed down the narrow steps, through the well-worn pair of Victorian-era double glass doors, and into the romantic world of the 1950s Beat generation in New York.

"Will there just be two for lunch?" the superskinny black hostess asked. She had a huge Afro hairstyle and wore an African-inspired dashiki-print tunic with a necklace fashioned of dark-stained wooden nuts the size of tangerines.

"What's your name?" I asked the hostess. Nancy sent me a look as if to say, *Are you planning to ask her to join us?*

"I'm Abigail," she responded. Having expected an exotic ethnic name, I tried not to be surprised.

"Please follow me." Abigail grabbed two menus and seated us in the center of the main dining room at one of the small ice-cream tables made of chipped, white-painted iron.

"May I have a frozen hot chocolate?" I asked as Abigail handed us menus.

"Right away, miss." Turning to Nancy, she asked, "Madame, may I get you something?"

"May I have a glass of pinot grigio? What is your selection?"

"Santa Margarita is nice."

"Fine. Thank you."

Mother was not a big drinker, so I was somewhat interested in her request. I feared that I had worn her out on the morning gown hunt.

"Darling, I enjoyed our shopping together. Why did you decline a purchase? That last dress at Dior was superbly perfect. You looked like a princess. If your father had been with us, he would have cried."

"That's just it. I don't want to look like a princess. I just want to look like—well, me. Not that I really know what me is supposed to look like. Do you understand?"

Mother paused, took a large sip of her Santa Margarita, put the glass down, and reached across the tiny table, staring at me with such kindness and love that I almost started to tear up.

"Of course, I understand," she said with slow, deliberate resolve. "Would you like to try Bloomie's after lunch? I saw in the *Times* this morning that they are having a really big sale." Nancy began giggling with an all-knowing sense that her only daughter, a young woman-child, was trying to find her path in a very complicated and confusing world. Since when had my mother cared about a big sale?

We finished lunch, then exited Serendipity, to find our driver waiting curbside. Again, he knew without asking where we were going. Bloomie's was only a few blocks away. I was convinced my mother had mental powers of communication.

At my favorite New York store with the giant alternating black and white gleaming tile floor, and all the special displays that had made the emporium a landmark in the retail world for decades, I felt at home.

My parents had taken me there many times as a child whenever we came to New York. I used to hopscotch on the tile floor and was never stopped by staff, never interrupted.

Funny how little things last in the memory bank. Once I hopscotched right into a big display of some sort of candy and did a header into the cart, sending fashionable multiflavored jellybeans flying like bullets. I didn't get in trouble, even as I sat on the floor attempting to eat as much of the evidence as possible.

Coming of Age at a Dance

I selected a simple navy-blue velvet dress at Bloomingdale's on that day with my mother on the fashion search. It was a short, almost mini, dressy winter frock. High at the neckline, cut low in the back all the way to the waist, my prom dress had long sleeves with a row of about eight or ten pearl buttons from the wrist almost to the elbow. This was not your typical formal floor-length evening gown. I absolutely loved it.

The dorm at Foxy—that's what we called Foxhaven by the time we were in our junior year—was buzzing with electricity as we all prepared for the big night. I slipped on my dreamy blue dress and adjusted the backless bra, so grown-up and sophisticated, and pulled on white silk hosiery. Nancy had sent me a pair of navy-blue velvet pumps she found at one of her favorite Rodeo Drive shops in Beverly Hills. With four-inch heels, I was standing close to six feet. Nancy did not shy away from helping her only daughter tower over the other girls and plenty of the boys as well. I was never afraid of that reality either.

For better or worse, my date for the evening was a boy named Chase Smithson. He stood about six feet one, so we were going to be face-to-face, eye to eye. Chase, or Smithboy as he was called, was one of the lacrosse stars at Boys' Prep, the school sponsoring the prom at the old-line country club. We had met a few times at organized mixers held over the previous year, but that was the extent of our friendship. We had never dated and didn't talk, not much anyway. I liked him; he seemed sweet. And he was extremely handsome in that classic East Coast next-generation male chip-off-the-old-block prep school kind of way. I also liked that he was a star jock. Since I had become a rather formidable tennis star on the girls' varsity squad, it was an appropriate match.

My father, Dalt, was particularly proud of my prowess on the court, a talent that I had not exhibited as a kid back in Beverly. Girls' prep must have brought out some of Father's latent genes in me. I was just a natural player. My stroke was clean, and it came easily to me—no forcing, no struggle. It even impressed me at times. Accolades from fellow players, competitive players, and coaches did not hurt. Nor did the praise go unnoticed.

Smithboy knew all about my talent. So did a lot of the boys across town. When he had asked me to attend prom with him at the last social before Thanksgiving, he confessed, awkwardly, that he really wanted to ask me to join him for a tennis match at the Montgomery Tennis Club, the famous mainline sanctuary of tennis that required all the players to wear white uniforms on court without exception. I told Chase I would accept that invitation as well, and then asked him if his male ego would be damaged if I were to win.

"I am a modern man," Smithboy replied. "I think any woman who could beat me in an athletic contest would be a woman I would like to know better!"

Over the previous couple of weeks, I had talked to my prom date only twice. We talked tennis and lacrosse, and we exchanged a bit of family history. We had plenty in common. His dad was an important Wall Street investment banker, and his mom was another Martha Stewart with the perfect home and the ideal family life in Greenwich, Connecticut. We were two spoiled rich kids with spotless pedigrees—Beverly Hills, meet Greenwich.

My roommate Sara, a "nice girl" from Savannah, finished dressing for the dance. Sara was also tall and slender. Her auburn hair flowed, framing her ultrawhite complexion and accentuating her superseductive emerald-green eyes. Sara had no idea how powerful those eyes were. She could stop traffic with those eyes.

Her prom dress of choice was conservative, as to be expected for a nice southern girl. The gown was one part deb ball, one part church social, and two parts not very sexy or fashionable, unless you were living in 1958. But that's okay because Sara was a genuine sweetheart. In so many ways we were opposites, yet we had each other's backs, 100 percent. Sara and I had been roommates since we had both arrived at Foxy four years ago at the age of thirteen.

"Can I help you with your hair or makeup?" she inquired. Sara looked like a mannequin: flawless skin, hair perfectly coifed. She struggled a bit trying to fasten a simple gold chain necklace sporting a diamond drop.

"I'll get that for you," I said, coming up behind her and fastening the clasp.

"Kate, sit down so I can fix your blonde head of hair. How do you want it?" Sara asked.

"Can you just pull it back into a ponytail and tie it with this white ribbon?" I gave the white ribbon to my sweet Sara.

The conversation then took a serious left turn.

"Are you ready for this prom?" Sara asked with a very different, slightly scared tone of voice.

"What do you mean?"

"You know."

"No, I don't know."

"Ready for what is expected of us."

"I think it is just expected that we have a nice time."

"It is expected that our dates have a significantly better time," she said, pursing her lips.

"Oh, that's just an urban myth started by a bunch of testosterone-driven males in some small corn town in Iowa," I answered, trying to comfort my friend.

"Then we are all in Des Moines, not Philadelphia."

"Seriously? So, the only reason we have been invited to this prom is with the hope and expectation of sex?"

"You've got it right. Tell me, how well do you know your date? Have you been out with him before? Do you share anything special in common other than some surface trivia?" Sara was direct, which surprised me. I thought she was a very smart girl, but very naive.

"I hardly know my date," I responded. "So what? What does that matter? How do you go from hardly knowing someone to assuming that these prom dresses we have all been so preoccupied with are going to be dropped to the floor?"

We both howled uncontrollably, falling to the floor of the dorm room, unable to stop.

"Come on, Sara, I have no plans to have sex with my date. Do you?"

"I've thought about it a lot. I think I'm obsessed." Sara paused, then shared, "I'm a virgin. Is this my time?"

"It's not about time or a place; it's about how you feel about yourself and your partner."

"That's just it. I just want to have the experience. I want to do it. My partner is just one notch above a stranger, but he is a handsome boy. Don't you think he wants the experience too?"

"Oh my God, Sara, you have just undermined hundreds—no, make that thousands—of years of social order and religious doctrine, not to mention the accepted roles of females." I began giggling again over Sara's sarcastic remarks, which set her off and reduced the seriousness of the exchange dramatically.

"You know what, why don't we take a break and agree to be open to possibilities?" I said with all-knowing wisdom.

"Easy for you to say, Doctor Phil. I'm a nervous mess. It's all I can think about," shy, sweet Sara replied, sitting there in her slightly debutant ball gown, perfectly styled hair, and painstakingly applied makeup.

"What time do we get picked up?" I asked.

"In about fifteen minutes," Sara answered. "Promise you will stay near me as much as you can."

"Promise." I raised my hand and did a high-five slap with my roommate. "I'll be right there all the way," I added, again coming close to Sara and giving her a serious hug without compromising her hair and makeup.

We two seventeen-year-old beauties on the brink of putting another notch on our life belts exited the dorm room and made our way down the grand old wooden stairs at Foxy to the foyer, joining a sea of hormones in overly expensive prom attire, all of us waiting for a bus to transport us to the country club and a much-anticipated rendezvous with destiny.

The Big Night

Upon arriving at the Glenville Country Club, the bus turned down the long winding drive bordered on both sides by perfectly manicured evergreen trees.

Suddenly the high-decibel chatter in the chauffer-driven coach fell to a mere whisper. A mix of nerves, adrenaline, and the expectation of what the night would bring silenced the bus full of us girls arriving at our prom. The coach pulled up slowly to the front entrance of the two-hundred-year-old stone structure resembling a European castle more than a club for golf lovers sharing stories from the green over dry martinis. Framed portraits of generations of club presidents lined the walls of the walnut-paneled living room, which was furnished in properly worn leather-covered Chippendale-style furniture placed over antique Persian rugs woven in threads of a deep crimson tone, slightly frayed at the edges. The difference between the rich and the nouveau riche is simply that the really rich feel no compunction to replace rugs frayed at the edge.

Sara and I were among the first to disembark. The night was cold and very dark, but there was no rain and no snow. Nancy had sent me another Federal

Express package that followed the arrival of my blue velvet dress, which had come from Bloomingdale's in New York. It had only arrived the day before my big night. Opening it in my dorm room, with Sara by my side, I moved aside the layers of tissue protecting the contents. Sara saw it first and screamed. It was a scream of *Oh my God. I want one!*

I pulled back the paper and pulled out a sable jacket. It was familiar to me; I realized Nancy had sent me one of her fur coats. Sara reached for the jacket, and I released it. She held it against her torso, stroking the thick, almost black as coal pelts.

"This is exceptional," she said, breathing rather heavily.

"Don't hyperventilate over a fur jacket," I cautioned.

There was a note in the box from Nancy. It read as follows:

> I know that you are an animal lover. And while I do not wish to compromise your principles, I hope that you will understand that this jacket did not harm or endanger any species. The fur was raised on a farm for use by humans, just as a cow is raised to provide food.

I read the note out loud to Sara, who did not appear to be listening at all. She kept stroking the jacket and putting the fur up against her cheek. I continued reading:

> I also want you to consider that it would be fashion suicide to wear your down parka over that gorgeous blue velvet dress, so please, please consider wearing this jacket, partly to please your compulsive mother's fashion sense, and partly to comfort your mother with the knowledge that you will not freeze and catch pneumonia when you decide not to wear a jacket at all.

This was pure Nancy philosophy. I had to smile. Sara finally allowed me to take the jacket from her. I put it on. It was waist length and trim-fitted with a high Mandarin collar. I looked in the mirror and liked what I saw.

"Do you think I am a horrible person for wearing this fur jacket?" I questioned my roommate, even though I knew what her answer would be.

"Are you kidding me?" she came back. "Probably more than half the class will be wearing fur coats. You know that."

"So, nobody will throw red paint on me? No protestors lined up along the driveway of the club awaiting our fur-covered arrival?"

"I don't think so," Sara replied.

She was right. There were no protestors, and just about every girl on the bus was wearing one of her mother's coats. Sara wore a black wool cashmere coat with a mink collar, also sent by her mother. I was going to trade, or at least offer to, but her coat really looked matronly and was long. I wanted to show off my minidress. I figured I was the only one so brave.

As we got off the bus wearing our coats, I was glad Nancy had sent me the controversial jacket. Even more grateful that there was no controversy, I decided I could live with myself for briefly deviating from my principles.

The entrance to the club was adorned with white twinkling lights over the main doors—not too garish, and not strung on every plant, eave, and rafter. Back home in Beverly, if you decided to light up for the holidays, then Southern California Edison would send you a thank-you note for your dramatically increased business. No such concept as restraint. That was the So Cal life, especially in LA. Full throttle ahead; as the slogan goes, go big or go home.

In my years on the opposite coast, I had come to favor restraint. The stuffiness, the inherent exclusion, and the prejudice of old-world values did not offend this California kid. Not too much, anyway. There was an element of comfort and security in the rules and the accepted practices. At least some of the time. I did not totally give up my rebel ways, despite Headmistress Collins's entrenched efforts to reform my uninhibited searching for truth and meaning on the planet.

"You will come to realize that there is great beauty in order," Ms. Collins favored saying. "Life must be lived with diligent purpose. We must conform to the known truths given to us by our forefathers and tested through centuries of trial and error."

I got the message, but I often wanted to say to her, *Are you serious?* Yet I restrained myself.

I had learned the virtue of silence and circumspection when it came to expressing my opinions at Foxy. I worked hard, studied, excelled, and made a real and conscious decision that rocking the Foxy boat would get me nowhere, except possibly expelled.

The Rise of Animal Instinct

Entering the club with the expectedly high anticipation of what would happen on this once-in-a-youthful-lifetime night, we were greeted by a virtual receiving line of extraordinarily handsome men, all in black tie. The sea of gorgeous penguins dispersed into our arriving flanks, hands outstretched, awaiting their respective companions for the evening. A choir of Dickens carolers sang "O Come All Ye Faithful" in the background, making it difficult to hear the greetings from the troop of Prince Charmings. The enormous fireplace, with its baronial carved mantel and raised black marble hearth, roared. We were all thankful for the warmth. The fur coats were quickly removed and spirited away by stately looking women in black and white uniforms overlaid with crisp white pinafore aprons that were ruffled on the border. All the women sported dramatically slicked-back hairstyles and very subtle single-stud pearl earrings.

Smithboy saw me immediately as I crossed the threshold, which wasn't surprising since I had been the first to come through the door. I always liked being first. I was the first to arrive in class and the first to choose to sit in the first seat of the first row.

"You look beautiful," he said, taking me in his arms and giving me a very polite hug, followed by an air-kiss on my left cheek.

"Thank you. Do you like the short dress?" I asked, hoping he wasn't expecting a formal gown. Then again, most teenage guys, even those from rich and formal families, are not particularly focused on the fashions of their dates in high school. Later, when they marry and when they are working on Wall Street, they expect their women to fit a certain substantial and appropriate fashion profile. We had a ways to go before all that kicked in.

"I repeat, you look beautiful. I am proud to be your date. Shall we go into the reception?" He was as smooth as he was handsome, a poster boy, the all-American perfect son of a family with its place within a certain socioeconomic and ethnic hierarchy. I recognized that I was also part of that race by birth, by upbringing, and by association. It was what I knew. It was my comfort zone. He was one of my people.

I took his arm. We left the entrance hall, which was still overflowing with arrivals and greetings. The choir was now into "Silent Night." Sweet Sara was chatting up a storm near the glowing fireplace with her date, a boy named Wyatt Kennedy, but not one of those Kennedys. She had abandoned her mother's long and matronly mink-trimmed cashmere coat and was doing her utmost southern best to charm Wyatt. From the looks of him, I didn't think it would take much. Wyatt was a football player at boys' prep—not a star quarterback, but a utility end, a big bruiser of a fellow. Kind of a stereotype, he was not a mental giant, but he too was handsome, in a goofy way. Tall, broad, and muscular, Wyatt towered over sweet Sara, even though she was a good five feet eight herself.

I turned back briefly to glance at my friend so she would know that I was keeping close and in touch as promised. She caught my glance, which I saw, but never really took her focus off Wyatt. Smithboy and I continued down the corridor toward the reception room. He pulled me in closer to his side as we made a second entrance on this prom night.

The reception hall was more of a ballroom, and it was decorated with appropriate restraint for the holidays. Two ten-foot-tall evergreen trees festooned with identically placed gold balls on both, no tinsel, no ribbon, nothing additional, flanked the roaring fireplace in this room, which was set in the center of a wall of dark-stained raised paneling, which I could see from the opposite entrance portal. A life-size portrait of colonial pioneer and founding Father Benjamin Franklin hung above the mantel, framed in aging gold leaf–painted wood.

Smithboy and I were among the first to enter, thereby keeping my reputation as first intact. Chaperones, including both our headmasters and many of our respective teachers, awaited our arrival. Their greetings were warm but not too familiar. One of Smithboy's teachers, a diminutive woman with dark and stringy straight hair, wearing a rather frumpy black cocktail dress with absolutely no form or style, was especially happy to see him. She gave him a hug. I asked him what was that all about, given the otherwise strict Maginot Line of decorum displayed by the faculty.

"I'm her favorite student," he replied. "She's my French teacher, and she says I have a perfect accent." He continued, "I also participate in class. Most of the other guys sit in silence. She has to drag a response out of them."

"So, you're a pet, a teacher's pet," I joked.

"I don't know. I like French. I like languages. Maybe I'll go to France for college. The Sorbonne maybe."

I had no idea my date was a budding Francophile. This was potential kismet. My fantasy world kicked in, and I envisioned us both in Paris. I would work as an apprentice to Yves Saint Laurent, and he would be studying international relations at the Sorbonne. We would live in a crumbling but romantic eighteenth-century apartment with ridiculously high ceilings, walls adorned with elegant boiserie moldings, and French windows all opening to Juliet balconies framed by hand-crafted iron balustrades. Red geraniums would grow wild in cracked terracotta pots that I would water regularly with my tin watering can hand-painted with yellow posies. I would have to fill it with water in a sink down the hallway in our communal lavatory. This was the life of my dreams.

Sweet Sara and Big Wyatt entered and found us. Sara went for the faux champagne when she saw that I was also sipping. She was shivering and probably preferred cider, but it just wasn't cool. Her dress left her bare across her shoulders and arms, and that flawless white skin was showing some prickly protrusions in response to the cool night temperatures inside the club.

Fortunately, the temperature began to rise as the room filled to capacity with the entire roster of prom participants. The din of conversation rose in direct proportion. The party was certainly off to a successful start. On the eastern wall of the big room, another massive pair of double doors opened, and a duo of men wearing red uniforms resembling the costumes of Christmas toy soldiers raised their trumpets and began blasting a call to prom. There were about a hundred of us girls and boys, and we all, obeying the bugle call to prom, gracefully paraded out of one ballroom and into the next. The dance was to begin.

Dancing into Trouble

Given the austere surroundings, an orchestra playing standards from the twentieth-century *Great American Songbook* would have been a fit for the dancing salon at the country club. Instead, an alternative rock group, part punk, with a little funk, rap, and R & B, headlined the prom. They called themselves the Ice Tongs. Really? They were loud; that's one thing I gave them. I could not envision Ms. Collins booking the Ice Tongs. They must have had an in with somebody. Maybe they were former students at boys' prep, expelled or dropouts to be certain. I thought they were borderline crude, but everyone was dancing bigtime, high on sparkling cider and most likely plenty of smuggled vodka. If it looks like water in the cup, it's not.

Smithboy had his share of the forbidden elixir tucked away in a silver flask in the breast pocket of his not rented Armani tuxedo. We had been dancing and socializing with fellow classmates on the dance floor for nearly two hours nonstop. The Ice Tongs needed a break. So did I. Sara and Wyatt were dancing right next to us at this point, when the band music stopped for a twenty-minute intermission. Recorded rock 'n' roll came over the speaker system to keep the dance going, but just about everyone was ready for a break. Most of the class just milled about the dance floor. Some wandered back into the reception room to find a place to sit. A massive stone terrace wrapped around the outside of the building, accessible through arched French doors from all the public rooms. December had made it a rather impossible destination as an escape from the crowd.

Surveying the terrain, Smithboy took my hand, leading me to his desired private spot. Sara was doing a little making out with Wyatt and seemed to be doing fine without my supervision. In fact, there was a whole lot of making out. God bless the band for having taken a break.

Having escorted me out of the dance, Smithboy led me into the reception room and then out again into the main corridor. There was no one in the hall; it was quiet. We could hear the squeaking of the wide-plank wooden floors echoing with our footsteps.

"Where are we going?" I questioned.

"I have an idea about somewhere we could go to have a little time alone," he said.

Was *time alone* the polite term for sex?

Perhaps a little sex. I knew why we needed privacy, and it wasn't to share another swallow of vodka from that silver flask in his pocket.

Just the same, I did what was expected of me. Following along, holding his hand, I prepared for my second foray into womanhood. At least I thought I was ready. This time it wouldn't be in the back of a gym with a sweaty basketball player. Yet, it probably would be once again fast, secret, and decidedly unromantic. I was prepared for that too. I had no unrealistic expectations of finding true love and meaning at the junior prom. I liked Smithboy, but that was about the extent of my feelings for him. How could this be love?

We came around a corner and found a staircase to the upper floors.

"Are you game?" he asked.

"Game? What's upstairs?" I asked.

"Come on. I'll show you."

Up we went. Again, there was nobody anywhere to be seen or heard. It was a morgue. At the top of the second-floor landing, we encountered another long, wide hallway with rows of doors on either side.

"These are the guest rooms," he said.

"Guest rooms? They have guest rooms in a golf club?"

"Sure. These old country clubs always have a wing of rooms for members who wish to stay overnight."

"Why would they need to stay overnight?"

"Maybe for the use of out-of-town relatives or business guests. Maybe after too much to drink at dinner. Maybe for reasons nobody is supposed to know or ask about." Smithboy gave a full accounting.

"I see," I said, now knowing for certain where we were going and why. About to become one of the occupants of a guest room that nobody was going to find out about or even ask about, I prepared myself.

As we walked down the dimly lit hallway, Smithboy tried several doors, all of them locked. The fourth doorknob he tried turned, and he led the charge into the portal. With his hand behind his back, he clasped my hand with his other, and I followed.

The room was pitch-black with no glimmer of light whatsoever thanks to very heavy fabric covering the windows, pulled tight and overlapping at the center.

After searching for a light switch on the wall beside the door, without luck, he left me standing there with what light was coming from the hallway surrounding my silhouette, which must have created an aura and halo around my body. I was clearly not an angel.

My date felt his way across the room, eventually finding a lamp on a night table beside a queen-size four-poster mahogany bed. He turned the knob, and there was light. I remained in the open doorway, presumably without the halo. He crossed back to me.

"You are a stunning girl, the prettiest and smartest I have ever known," he said in a soft voice.

I said nothing but smiled just a little.

"I am the luckiest guy in the school to be with you tonight," he went on.

I still said nothing.

Smithboy put his arms around my waist and pulled himself up against my body. Managing to shove the door closed behind me, my handsome young man moved up against the closed door and placed his lips on mine, slowly, deliberately, and passionately. A moist tongue entered my mouth, and I felt a tingle that ran down to my toes. This was quite a nice start, but the tingle transitioned to a tinge of remorse, and I suddenly felt, well, regret. I don't know why. I was prepared for sex, better prepared than my first time with basketball boy. And I had no fear of moral accountability. This was a new millennium after all. "Hookups," as my generation labeled sex, were no big deal. That's what I thought until he kissed me and continued to kiss me.

He left my mouth, and his lips and his tongue pursued the nape of my neck, one side and then the other. His soft hands left my waist and were now clutching the back of my neck and stroking my hair.

I believe at this point he could feel my resistance, as I was not participating, not in an equal kind of way. Still, his passion grew more intense.

"Why don't you get comfortable over on the bed?" He paused and pulled away from me, running his hands down from my head and gently touching my breasts under the blue dress. Taking my hand, he led me over to the bed and gently pushed me down, then sat on the side.

"I'll be back in a flash," he said, removing the pillows from under the coverlet, fluffing them, and stacking them against the headboard.

"Lean back and relax. I'll just be a second." He exited into what I assumed was a bathroom through a door next to the night table supporting the lamp. Turning off the light as he opened the bathroom door, he was gone in a flash. I could see some light in the bathroom shining through from beneath the door. What was he doing? Did he need to relieve himself? Maybe he was readying a condom?

Not moving back against the fluffed pillows, I preferred to sit on the edge of the bed and wait. Seconds later, literally seconds, the bathroom door opened with the light still coming through as Smithboy had neglected to hit the switch. He was totally naked.

Gasping, I let out more of a giggle than any kind of noise to signal objection as he came toward me.

"Would you care to join me?" he asked, reaching up to my shoulders, attempting to pull the blue dress down over my arms and to my waist. The dress was very fitted and did not budge. He tried again, not with force, but with more resolve.

I looked at this exceptionally handsome masculine creature. His torso was worked out to perfection, and his arms and shoulders exhibited elegant muscles. He had no body hair except a trimmed section above an exquisite penis—a penis that was at attention, circumcised, with pearl-white unblemished skin and a very large pulsating head. He moved his penis up and down my leg, and that tingle came back with a serious rush.

Now he really sensed my hesitation. I did not assist removing my dress, and while I was into the sex, my response remained unequal to his pursuit.

"Is something wrong?" he whispered.

"No," I said rather sheepishly.

"Then would you like to make love on your prom night—something to remember always?"

Again, I did not have an answer.

Without a beat, Smithboy got the message that this was not happening. Not in the way he had imagined, and not in the way I had imagined either.

He once again reached for my hands and lifted me off the bed, his penis still erect, still touching my body.

Then he did something I had not seen coming. As we were standing face-to-face, he pushed me to the floor. I now was down on my knees. He positioned his penis on my cheek, moving it over to my mouth. Gently, he pushed it toward my lips, between my lips, into my mouth, and back toward my throat. This was a first.

I responded to his desire for oral sex and kissed him with my tongue.

"This is so nice." He hardly got the words out.

I was still not totally committed to this act, but I wasn't pulling away either. Continuing to try to satisfy him, I worked it with more passion.

"Have you ever performed oral sex before?" he inquired in a seriously breathless voice; his words interspersed with moans of considerable pleasure. His joy was a definite turn-on for me.

"No, this is a first," I mumbled, not able to speak with eight inches of rod in my mouth. I wanted to laugh or yell or say anything, but it wasn't possible.

At that moment, probably on the cusp of Smithboy's delivering his male DNA into my mouth, we heard a bloodcurdling scream so horrible that he pulled out of me. We looked at one another.

"What was that?" he asked.

"I don't know, but it came from what sounded like next door."

Smithboy rushed into the bathroom, where he scrambled to find his clothes and dress. I ran out of the room into the hallway. The screams were louder, the crying, more desperate. It was coming from the room next door. I froze for a moment. Should I just go in? Reaching for the doorknob and pounding on the door at the same time to announce my intention to enter, I found the door unlocked.

Entering the room with adrenaline rushing, not knowing what to expect, I was once again in near darkness in yet another guest room without light. In the shadows created by the open hallway door, I could make out someone on the bed against the far wall.

"What's the matter?" I called out, still standing in the open door. "Are you all right?"

There was no immediate answer, just crying that was obviously coming from a female. The deep sadness was reverberating in staccato waves between breathless gasps and choking sounds.

"Please get off me. Please, you are hurting me." Finally, some audible words I could clearly understand.

This was a plea for me to enter and come closer.

I raced across the room to find my sweet Sara pinned under Wyatt. She was hysterical and he was comatose, in another world.

"Wyatt, get off Sara. Don't you hear her? Stop hurting her, you big dumb jerk!"

Wyatt was in a sex act coma. He was paying no attention to Sara's begging him to cease, and he certainly had no conscious awareness of my presence or my words.

"Do you hear me, Wyatt? Get off her," I screamed at him.

Again, nothing. He kept drilling into her, and she continued to cry out for help. All I could see was the broad back of the big football player, who was still nearly fully dressed in his prom tux. Well, at least he still had his jacket on. The pants were down at his ankles, stuffed against a pair of black patent leather oxfords. I could not see Sara at all. Wyatt had fully engulfed my roommate, smothering her beneath his three-hundred-pound manhood.

With no choice but to grab Wyatt by the satin collar of his tux, I yanked him as hard as I could to get his attention. Smithboy came charging into the room to find me pulling on Wyatt with all my strength but having little success. Others followed, having heard the screaming and commotion. Several security guards, two chaperones, and what seemed like a dozen kids from the prom rushed into the room. Finally, Smithboy managed to pull Wyatt off Sara. Then he shoved him with tremendous force and even slapped him across the face to bring him out of his sex trance. Pulling up Wyatt's pants just in time, Smithboy spared him further humiliation as the crowd came on scene.

I ran to Sara. She lay on the bed, burrowed into the comforter as if she were wedged in a trough under the weight of her conqueror. Sara's church social prom dress had been torn in the onslaught, and her perfectly applied makeup had dissolved in the tears running down her face and neck, creating a pattern of rivers going down the front of her gown like the lava flow from an erupting volcano.

"Sara, Sara, can you hear me? Are you hurt? What happened to you with Wyatt?"

Attempting to speak between tears, Sara looked at me and very softly whispered, "Please come closer."

"Tell me what's going on. Do you need a doctor?" I asked, turning around and seeing all the people who were now in the room.

"Can all of you please leave? Wait in the hallway," I said, "This is my roommate, and I will deal with this privately, at least for now."

One of the guards and both the chaperones objected.

"Get out and leave us alone!" I was now yelling at them.

"I will give you two minutes," the guard came back. "Then I am calling the police." He spread out his arms as if to corral the entourage out the door and back into the hallway.

Smithboy had Wyatt calmed down and sitting in a chair. Still in a daze, Wyatt did not fully comprehend the gravity of his behavior. My unsatisfied date came over to me, and I barked at him to retreat and go back to Wyatt.

"Shut the door, Smithboy," I ordered. He did so without question.

"Sara, let me have the guard call 911."

"No. Do not do that. Absolutely not!"

"They are going to do something. He says he is going to call the police too."

"Don't let them do that," she begged.

My two minutes were fast evaporating.

"Smithboy, go out in the hall and tell them all to leave. Everything is okay in here now. Tell them nothing happened and that everything is going to be fine. Just do it."

"Those guards and the chaperones won't believe it," he came back.

"Make them believe it. Sara wants to be left alone. Do you think the Glenville Country Club wants a rape on the front page of the *Philadelphia Enquirer*? Just make them leave."

Smithboy opened the door and went out into the hallway as the noise of the gaggle of geese subsided. He closed the door, leaving Sara and me alone in the room with Wyatt. Wyatt finally got up off the chair, back to some semblance of real-world consciousness, and came over to us on the bed.

"Sara, can you hear me? I am sorry. I did not mean to hurt you. Can you forgive me?" Wyatt was crying now too. His remorse was sincere, and Sara responded.

"It's not your fault. I thought I wanted to be with you, but I just panicked. I wasn't ready, and I didn't know how to stop until it was too late. I am sorry too,

Wyatt," she said. He reached over the bed and put his arms around her, hugging her. Sara put her head on his shoulder and closed her eyes.

The moment of regret and apology passed, and I jumped back into action.

"If you are okay, then let me get you cleaned up so we can pretend that nothing happened and get out of this room and back to the party."

"I can't go back. Can't we just leave and go back to school?" she pleaded.

"How do we do that? We all came on the bus, and we all have to leave on the bus at midnight," I said. "If you really are okay and you really don't want to make a big deal out of this, then you have to suck it up and pretend that nothing happened. We will do the best we can to make them all leave you alone. I will help you."

Sara nodded in the affirmative.

"Wyatt, go out there with Smithboy and help him get rid of the crowd. We'll meet you both downstairs in the dining room in a few minutes. Get a table in the back corner, a dark corner," I said, still barking directions.

Wyatt nodded an affirmative response, then left the room, straightening his tux jacket and bow tie, and running his hands over his tousled hair, pushing it back out of his face and over the top of his head.

Gently, I lifted Sara upright on the bed and began the process of doing my best friend's restoration and repair. I went into the bathroom and found a washcloth, which I soaked in tepid water, and returned to Sara to wipe away the tears and running makeup. I had no luck in removing the stains from the front of her gown.

Sara rose from the bed, went into the bathroom, and closed the door behind her. There were no more tears. I sat on the edge of the bed and waited.

Ten minutes passed, which seemed like an eternity. Sara emerged, her hair combed. Even most of the stains from her running mascara had vanished. She took my arm.

"I'm okay. Really, I am."

"Let's go," I said. "Smithboy and Wyatt are waiting for us in the dining room."

"I can. And I will," she said. The southern girl I had always thought was very naive was in fact iron-willed in her own Scarlett O'Hara kind of way. I was proud of her. She was not some fading flower. Rather, Sara had taken her own share of responsibility for the mess the two of them had gotten themselves into. Wyatt was a jerk to be certain, but as Sara shared, "What seventeen-year-old boy in the throes of what may be his first sexual experience does not exhibit some very unacceptable behavior?"

The incident was not mentioned further when we returned to the prom. Not one word was spoken, not by the guards, not by the chaperones, and not by the four of us. We sat at a table in the back corner of the dining room. Sara was camouflaged by the centerpiece of orchids and hydrangeas; nobody could see her. Our prom night ended with late supper from the Glenville buffet. In truth, we hardly ate a morsel, just moved the food around on the plate, trying to kill the final hour until midnight arrived and the bus would transport us back to the safety of our dorm room at Foxy.

When it was time to depart, neither of us said much of anything to our dates. Both guys clumsily attempted to kiss us each good night, but that was going too far over the edge after what had happened. There would be no midnight kiss to remember.

My second foray into the adult world of sex had been another disappointment. Sweet Sara's was a disaster. But we held it together, for a while, that is. Soon it was Christmas break. Sara went home to Savannah, and I headed west to sunny California. I received word at New Year's that Sara would not be returning to Foxy to complete her junior year. She was with child.

Repeatedly I reached out to her almost daily, month after month. She did not respond. By late summer, again back in LA, I assumed Sara had delivered the baby, but I still heard nothing. I never heard from sweet Sara again. It was heartbreaking. I felt an immeasurable amount guilt for not having called 911 and reported Sara's experience to the authorities. Maybe things would have worked out better. Then again, maybe not. I would never know.

CHAPTER TWO

THE BIG CRUSH AND A BIG BUST

For me, graduating from Foxhaven Academy for Girls was bittersweet. My friend sweet Sara was gone; I hadn't heard from her in more than a year. I was completely conflicted over what I had done that night of the junior prom, or rather what I had not done. I had rationalized my actions with a very clear memory of Sara's insistence that I not tell anyone about the incident, especially anyone in a position of authority. She said Wyatt had not raped her; it was consensual. Yes, she wanted him to stop, but it was not an assault. She, too, was responsible. She had wanted a first time, and she wanted it with Wyatt that night.

Thinking about the night often, I wondered if Sara had the baby and, if so, what the child's gender was. Had she contacted Wyatt? I didn't think so, and I never went so far as to find out, even though I spoke to Smithboy a few times over the year following the incident. At first, he called me almost daily after that night. I didn't call back. The calls became infrequent, but finally I ran into him at a school mixer. We were friendly with each other; I joked with him and made light of the oral sex encounter. I felt stupid for joking with him, but I wasn't interested in any hostility. Kind of like Sara, yet not as drastic as her approach, I, too, just wanted it to be forgotten. Time to move on, grow up.

It has been hard to put the image of that night with Sara in a compartment of my mind reserved for that which is past and forgotten. Many days I wanted to go to the train station and buy a ticket to Savannah just to go there and track her down—partly out of guilt, and partly out of love for the girl. But I didn't do it.

My parents and my brother, Jamey, came to Philadelphia for the graduation ceremony. With them, a small entourage of friends arrived, people I had known for most of my life growing up. I also knew that rich people traveled in packs. They made an occasion special by being together, traveling together, and celebrating regardless of cost. The crew arrived on a Tuesday afternoon in the first week of June on a private jet out of Bob Hope–Hollywood Burbank Airport. My father was a partner in a fractional rent-a-jet charter service for business, so it was a simple arrangement. They checked into the Ritz-Carlton in Center City, Philadelphia, and the party began Tuesday evening with a lavish wine dinner in a private dining room. Headmistress Collins was invited and did attend, along with several school trustees. I had been invited to bring a date but declined. My parents knew about Sara, but they did not ask questions. They also knew that I did not have a roommate my senior year.

Graduation ceremonies officially began the following evening with a baccalau-
reate held in the academy chapel. On Thursday we would don cap and gown and
walk down the aisle to receive our high school diplomas. Listening to the grand
and glorious words of multiple speakers extolling the unbelievable virtues of an
education at Foxhaven and what it would mean for the rest of our lives, I glazed
over. The rest of my life was far away. Now mattered. I did not want to go back to
Los Angeles and enroll at USC. I know I had agreed. I was, despite everything,
still a good girl and still respectful of my loving parents, yet simultaneously I was
unsure of who I was and very unsure of how I was going to discover myself.

I also knew that rich people just transferred their habitual behavior from
place to place. If they dine in Beverly Hills, they will dine in similar fashion in
Timbuktu. It is a moving circus; the date and venue may change, yet the routine
remains familiar. Oddly, this pattern has existed, I think, for centuries—maybe
forever. Regardless of national origin or even the political climate of the times,
whether it be amid a monarchy, a fascist government, or a democracy, it literally
takes a revolution to undermine the lifestyle of the privileged.

The limousines pulled into the driveway of Glenville Country Club just as
our junior prom bus had done. My body stiffened, and I felt a cold sweat across
my back. Being there affected me much more than I had ever imagined. Choosing
not to say one word, I looked out the car window at the lush green evergreen forest
bordered by manicured lawns and trimmed hedges lining the drive to the front
door. The pristine order of the place contradicted the chaos of that night. In the
end, order prevailed, despite the human cost.

Doormen and valets greeted us and opened the limousine doors for the
Fairchilds of Beverly Hills and their friends. Mother Nancy was at her beautiful
best. She glowed. Her graduation suit, a cream and black Chanel creation with a
rounded neckline on the jacket featuring a black silk bow, impeccably tied, was
pure Nancy. Cream and black Chanel pumps and matching cream tufted stitch
bag with the signature double *C*'s on the clasp sent a message of fashion royalty.
Nancy smiled graciously as she welcomed her guests to the country club for a grand
dinner. This was a happy time for her and my father. They were in their element,
and life was good.

Escorted into the club dining room, we were seated, ten of us, at an oblong
table in the center of the room. On this night, the handsome space, paneled in an
old-world style with its tall doors leading out to a massive terrace overlooking acres
of green, was decorated in summer whimsy. Table drapes and florals were coordinated in pastels, with the staff attired in summer uniforms of light blue and white
seersucker over starched white shirts for the men and white blouses for the women,
fastened at the collar with navy blue bow ties bordered with red braiding. It was
the height of conservative gentility. Pure Americana, that is, for the well-to-do.

Cocktails were served. Mother and Father ordered their dry martinis, two olives each. A waiter arrived with petite mushroom puffs and lobster bisque en croûte.

"What are your plans for the summer?" Barbara Von Durah asked. She was mother's best girlfriend, who had come with her third husband, Victor, for the Philadelphia jaunt. A stunning raven-haired former fashion model, Barbara displayed her amazing figure and five-foot-ten frame, just as perfect as it had been when she was on the runway at eighteen. Her high cheekbones, wide dark eyes, Valentine-shaped pink lips, and flawless pale skin complemented her jewelry. Diamonds dazzled on her ears and wrist, and she had one doozy on her wedding finger that could double as an ice-skating rink. Victor, a small man, balding, with a rather large red nose, had found his trophy bride. A wonderful sugar daddy, Victor had made his fortune in the asphalt business. He often told anyone who would listen that he had paved, or at least his company had paved, more roads than anyone else in the USA, including the government. Victor was the unheralded king of hot black goop.

"I don't have a plan," I told Barbara. The rest of the table was listening, including my parents.

"Darling, you don't need a plan," my mother, Nancy, said, adding her two cents. "All in good time, my sweet girl. Your life is just beginning. You have all the time in the world. Your options are unlimited," she added, speaking more to Barbara and the rest of her friends than to me.

So many kids from my kind of family are often at major war with their parents by the age of eighteen. I knew my family had my back. I was loved unconditionally, although I had never done anything so terrible to challenge that unconditional support. My brother, Jamey, on the other hand, had challenged Nancy and Dalt to the limit for at least the past several years, starting at age eleven, when he was in the sixth grade.

Now thirteen, Jamey had come to my graduation. It was just short of a miracle that there was peace in our family orbit given what Jamey had put my parents through. They never lost faith in him or backed away from the problems he had brought upon them. I am certain that unconditional love can and does exist.

"Will you be going home for the summer?" Barbara persisted with questions. I wasn't sure if she was genuinely interested, or snooping, or just making cocktail conversation. After all, the questions were basic. This is what parents ask kids graduating high school.

They want to know plans. They take comfort in knowing the future, defining the road, and, I think, being able to share with their own peers the big plans of their own children. It is a validation of successful parenting, even though deep down, somewhere in the gut, they realize that the big plans of most eighteen-year-old kids are fantasy. They know this because it was the same for them, if they would admit it.

"I am starting USC in the fall and am leaning toward a major in French," I added to the conversation mix.

"That's splendid. How civilized," Barbara said.

Civilized? What a strange way to categorize a French major in college.

"My long-range plan is to work in the fashion design industry, and I would like to someday have that experience in Paris."

"Have you thought about going to design school instead of university? LA is well-known for its programs at the Fashion Institute of Design and Merchandising."

"Nancy and Dalt want me to have a full college experience." I had come back with a very politically correct answer.

Barbara was a close pal to Mother, and I knew she wasn't grilling me to be snide. All the same, I was feeling increasingly uncomfortable. Not to mention that I was facing toward the back corner of the Glenville dining room, staring right at the table in the corner where I had last sat with sweet Sara, Smithboy, and big dumb jerky Wyatt. If only I could share my real thoughts with Barbara Von Durah. If only she knew. If only any of them knew.

The waitstaff took orders for dinner, bringing to our attention the absence of my brother, Jamey. He had excused himself earlier and vanished, presumably having gone to relieve himself. He had been gone far too long.

"I am going to go and check the men's room to see if Jamey is okay," my father said.

"Hurry back, dear. I'll order something for Jamey. I know he likes steak," Mother replied with matter-of-fact confidence. I looked over at her. She did not seem concerned at all. Nancy was in full "let's make the most and the best of this milestone occasion" mode. She was a major believer in holding on to the good times and letting no negative energy interrupt the moment.

"Trust me, life will present its share of trouble," she would tell me, and her advice was strongly ingrained in my consciousness. "We will deal with the challenges when we must. In the interim, do not let the good times slip through your fingers. Hold on. Hold on tight. Laugh as much as you can. It is the only medicine to keep the tears at bay."

Father returned without Jamey. He couldn't find him.

The rest of the guests were oblivious, chatting away, enjoying a third round of exquisitely prepared choice high-octane beverages served in cut-crystal tumblers delivered on a silver tray by seersucker-clothed staff wearing white gloves. I'm not sure why, but I was acutely aware of my luxury status in life afforded me by the accident of birth. Had I chosen my parents, or had they chosen me?

"Where could he have gone?" My father was concerned despite Nancy's insistence on enjoying my graduation dinner with her friends.

"He was bored, dear. I'll bet he went outside to explore. It's still light outside at eight o'clock, and it is a glorious summer night on the East Coast."

"I suppose. Jamey's track record of late is not stellar," Father added. I heard Dalt, and I knew what he meant. For the past couple of years my little brother had spent more time in a series of drug and alcohol rehabilitation clinics than he had spent at home on Lexington. Jamey had become another casualty of the Beverly Hills spoiled rich kid turned addict syndrome, a poster child for self-destructive, self-abusive behavior. The experts fondly label the affliction with all kinds of official-sounding names. I know how desperately my baby brother wanted to please Mom and Dad. For some reason, he always had had this inadequacy chip on his shoulder. It was a fact I never understood since he was never made to feel anything but loved and special, just like me. I also knew at the ripe old age of eighteen that sometimes feeling loved and special is just not enough. All kids are not born equal, in spite of what they tell you. Just who are "they" anyhow?

"Dad, can I help? Let me see if I can find him," I said, also whispering in my father's ear. I was seated to his left side, so I slipped away from the table without any fanfare.

I think I knew why my instinct had led me directly to the staircase leading to the upstairs floor of guest rooms that I had become intimately familiar with on the night of my junior prom. I dashed up the stairs once again to find a very quiet, presumably empty hallway. There was no one in view, and I heard not a soul—not one voice, not a television soundtrack, and no radio sending out a little night music. There were no overnight guests on this graduation eve on a Thursday night in Philadelphia.

With familiar motivation and a very different purpose, I began to try the doorknobs of the guest rooms. All the doors I tried opened. I pushed back the solid panel doors, revealing dark rooms. Calling out for Jamey repeatedly, I got no response.

Then I came to the room that had been the destination of my rendezvous with Chase Smithson. That door was unlocked as well. It seemed that this door was heavier, more difficult to open. I knew it was nonsense, but it seemed that way just the same.

"Jamey, are you in there?" I called out, not wanting to take even one step into that room. Like the others, it was pitch-black. Thankfully, there was no Jamey in the room where I had lived through that humiliating second sexual experience on my haphazard path to maturity.

The room next door was certainly the most difficult. It was the room where my sweet Sara had lost her virginity and ultimately lost her way—a young life taken off course unexpectedly. With a violent shove, I pushed the unlocked door open. It slammed backward against a chest placed against the wall, making a crashing sound. I heard a groan, more a very low and very sad moan, coming from a place deep down inside a person in the darkness across the room. It was Jamey. What had he done?

I scrambled to find light, knowing that a lamp would be on a bedside table next to the four-poster mahogany bed on the opposite wall facing the door I had entered from the hallway.

"Jamey, is that you?" I called out. There was no answer. "Jamey, are you here? Are you okay?"

Then I saw my baby brother. He was sprawled out on the floor facedown with his arms and legs outstretched. His head was turned to the left side as he lay in what was certainly a pool of his own vomit. There was blood streaming down his face, coming out of his nose and mouth. At first glance, it seemed to be coming out of his eye sockets too. I screamed so loudly that surely, they heard me downstairs in the club dining room. On this night, in this same room, there would be no cover-up, no cleanup, no pretending that nothing happened.

Seeing that Jamey was breathing, I bent down and attempted to bring him around.

"Get up. Wake up. Sit up!" I yelled at my brother, grabbing his arms and his shoulders, trying to revive him and bring him back to some sort of state of consciousness.

"Jamey, can you hear me? Please wake up," I demanded. With no success, I kept screaming for help as loud as I could. Getting up off the floor, I left him, running to the door and out in the corridor, yelling again as loudly as I could, *Help! Somebody help!* I'm up here on the second floor!"

Keeping up the call for help for a minute or so, I then charged back into the room. There was no change in Jamey's condition. Shaking him again, then again, I tried to turn him over and right him so he would sit up. It didn't work. As I got up and ran for the bathroom to get water and a cloth to wipe his face, the posse arrived. Dalt, Nancy, and two of the same guards whom I had avoided the previous year in the same room appeared.

"Oh my God!" my father cried.

Nancy ran over to me, grabbed the wet cloth out of my hand, and dropped her Chanel self to the floor next to her child.

"Jamey. Please wake up. It's your mother. I need you to wake up right this instant," she said in her strong, demanding, yet very controlled voice. Nancy never lost it, at least not in front of me—or in front of anyone, for that matter. She persisted attempting to revive her son, wiping his face and removing the bloody discharge.

"Call 911!" my father demanded of the guards. One of them ran out of the room and into the hall and made an emergency call on his walkie-talkie to what was probably the head of club security. He returned a split second later.

"An ambulance will be on its way," he reported to my father, who was at his son's side. Dalt and Nancy lifted Jamey off the floor, away from his pool of vomit, and moved him to the bed, sitting him upright and continuing to try to revive him.

The other guard yelled out that Jamey was breathing, so CPR was not required. Guard number one made the 911 call and came back into the room, discovering evidence of drugs on the floor next to where I had found Jamey spread-eagled. He picked up what appeared to be vials of a white powdery substance.

"I'm going to have to call the police." The guard made his duty clear.

"Can we just get him to the hospital?" my father snapped back with all his conviction.

"Yes, sir." The guard had heard him loud and clear. "But I will have to call the police."

"Do what you must do. Our only concern is getting him out of here and to a doctor at once. If you can't help, please get out of my way." My father was angry, his focus totally on Jamey. It did not take long for the crowd to arrive at the door following all the commotion. Barbara Von Durah broke through to get to my mother.

"How can I help?" she pleaded. "Let me get another cold cloth," Barbara said, dashing into the bathroom.

Nancy was removing Jamey's tie, opening his shirt, and taking off his soiled blazer as Barbara returned, applying the wet towel to Jamey's forehead, his face, and his bare chest.

He was starting to respond as paramedics arrived, bursting through the onlookers in the hallway. In an instant my brother was on a gurney with a clear oxygen mask over his face. The paramedics covered him with a blanket and ran him out the door, down the steps, and out of the club to an awaiting medic truck. Sirens blared as the red and white emergency truck vanished down the tree-lined drive.

Nancy, always prepared for anything, summoned the limo driver. The car was at the ready and waiting. We ran to get in and then sped off, leaving our own dust down the formal cobblestone-paved road, departing the mainline bastion of privilege and heading for the University of Pennsylvania Medical Center in the heart of very urban Philadelphia. My younger brother was possibly dying of a drug overdose on my high school graduation night.

I wasn't feeling sorry for myself. It wasn't that Jamey was ruining the whole thing. It was more that I again had been hit broadside by the fact that life was just not perfect, that things happen and that they happen all the time. The Disney-perfect life I had been led to believe existed in my childhood was pure fantasy.

What could I hold on to? What could I count on? Luckier than most, I knew at least that I could count on Nancy and Dalt.

My silence in the limo did not alarm my dear parents. They were very busy on their mobile phones trying to reach doctors at Penn Med.

The car raced down Montgomery Avenue out of the plush burbs. I was in something of a trance, staring out the window as we sped past beautiful homes surrounded by old-growth trees and emerald-green cut grass that appeared to stretch on endlessly as there were no fences separating these grand homes. Who is the one who said, "Fences make good neighbors"?

I heard Nancy reach Barbara on her cell. "I'm so sorry for all of this. Please tell everyone to finish dinner, and then have the driver take you back to the Ritz-Carlton.

"As soon as we know anything, I will contact you."

Barbara must have protested, telling Nancy that she was on her way to the hospital.

"No, Barbara. Don't come. Please just go back to the hotel. I'm so very sorry," Mother said, then hung up.

Turning the Corner Again

This was Jamey's fourth episode requiring saving by paramedics. Well, the fourth as far as I knew. It was my first time witnessing it, having been away at school for the past six years. I knew the problem was serious, but I had been spared. This was no longer the case.

Doctors revived him at Penn Med in the emergency department. He would live, but we were cautioned that it would take several days or more to determine if there was brain damage or harm to other vital organs.

They told us that Jamey had a lethal level of oxycodone mixed with alcohol in his system. He had been drinking wine at the country club and was not stopped even given his age. I guessed that Nancy and Dalt had thought he was in safe company. The wine had not blended well with the drugs he presumably had ingested earlier in the afternoon, probably when I was walking down the aisle in cap and gown to receive my diploma.

Dalt organized the exit and return to Los Angeles on the private jet for their entourage of friends. My parents and I remained in Philadelphia for the next ten days until the doctors felt it was safe to transport Jamey home. The police showed up at my brother's hospital bed, but at least for now, he was free to go home, most likely thanks to my father's influence or that of one of his Philadelphia lawyer friends.

Even though I feared that the world was unraveling, I did know that, in addition to being able to count on my parents, in life it makes a difference to have connections. Clearly a Philadelphia lawyer had made a call.

Back in La-La Land

The summer of 1998 bestowed upon me abundant warm days and blue skies. LA can be intoxicating. The climate, the palm trees, the majesty of the mountains meeting the Pacific Ocean, all hypnotize mortals living in its midst. I was always somewhat more poetic about all of this than most of my friends. In the fall, when the warm Santa Ana winds blew through Beverly Hills, I would watch the dry leaves fly through the air and imagine I could fly away with them, taken to distant and faraway places. It was my own personal Wizard of Oz complex.

Still, I managed to keep both feet on the ground. Brother Jamey was not so lucky. My first week back on Lexington Road was an adjustment. I had been gone for six years, a veritable lifetime for an eighteen-year-old. One-third of my life had passed living in a distant land, the land of boarding school.

Everything in my bedroom was frozen in time. Sure, I had come back many times for holidays and summer breaks, but this time I was home and not going back to my other life. It was surreal. I was feeling nervous and unsettled. To say I was uncomfortable would be to put it mildly.

I was lying on my pink toile bed. Nancy had removed all my tie-dyed sheets before I left for boarding school. I stared up at my ceiling and connected the glow-in-the-dark stars that I had placed up there so many years before. Madame Alexander dolls stared back at me from the top shelf of a doorless antique armoire across from the foot of my bed. They too were frozen in time, never to age.

Granted amnesty from having to find a summer job, I had been presented with a golden ticket to enjoy my summer. I knew what that meant: days at the beach club in Santa Monica alternating with days at the country club pool and tennis courts. This wasn't so bad. Yes, it was just a part of the life. Not being particularly motivated to change the world or conquer it in any particular manner, I found that a carefree summer was okay with me. Perhaps if I had been more ambitious and more aggressive, I might have insisted on a summer in Paris to explore my fashion dream. Then again, it was just a dream. I had no right to believe that I might find a path to that end or that I would have the talent to achieve some goal that I dreamed of realizing.

Girls with well-connected fathers could certainly arrange an internship. Yet, what would I do, file papers and get coffee? With no training, and no drawing or working in a cutting room, I didn't even know how to sew. Not well anyway. At least I was levelheaded enough to realize that at this point I offered very little as an intern to a Paris design house.

Maybe Barbara Von Durah was right. Should I insist on attending the Fashion Institute in LA and saying adios to the traditional route at USC? Maybe. Well, I would think about that change in direction later. Mother told me, "You have all the time in the world." At eighteen, with no pressure to do anything at all and no need to work and earn money to survive, I did feel like a person who had an eternity to decide her course.

Lazy afternoons sunbathing beside the Olympic-size cobalt-blue-tiled pool with its mermaid mosaic visible on the bottom helped to make the scene at the country club seem as if it had been created for some movie. Superthick terry cloth mansion-size towels with wide green and white stripes were perfectly positioned on a long lineup of plush white canvas-upholstered chaise lounges adjacent to the pool. Pristine oversized white market umbrellas shaded the glistening tan bodies lathered in bronzing lotion. The umbrellas flapped ever so slightly in the summer breeze; like automated crickets, they clicked and clacked.

I found my spot: a favorite chaise by the steps at the shallow end of the pool. It provided quick and easy access for a cooling dip and an unnoticed return to my viewing perch. It was also the perfect spot to keep an eye on my favorite summer crush, a lifeguard named Ricky Robinson. Tall and muscular, his long blond hair streaked with chlorine-green highlights, Ricky had been a water polo star at his high school in the San Fernando Valley. We were the same age and in the same lane of life. Polo guy was going to go to college somewhere on a scholarship in the fall. I couldn't remember if it was Pepperdine or UCLA. He had told me a couple of times, and I didn't want to ask him again. What I did know was that all the girls spending a summer by the pool without the need to find a job found Ricky to be superb eye candy and constant entertainment.

On this Wednesday in late June, LA was seeing an unseasonably hot day. June was usually the month of gloom, as overcast skies off the Pacific Ocean generally kept temperatures mild until the Fourth of July. I did my regular dip in the shallow end to cool off in my black bikini, having left on the chaise my black woven straw hat with its wide brim, which provided the proper look. Ricky jumped off his lifeguard post and dove in without creating even a splash. My summer entertainment emerged from the water right next to me.

"Don't you love the heat?" he inquired.

"It does feel nice, as long as you've got a pool to jump in," I joked.

"There's a great new band playing tonight at Club Z on Sunset. Would you like to go?"

Ricky was asking me on a date. I could feel the jealousy coming from the lineup of pool chaises. I think the eight or ten girls all turned to their right in unison when they overheard him ask me out.

"Sure, that sounds interesting," I replied.

"Can I pick you up around nine tonight? They don't go on until eleven o'clock. We can check the place out. I hear the dancing is crazy. Have you been there?"

"No. But I've heard about it. Everyone has seen all the publicity."

Ricky jumped back out of the pool. He did a flying leap back onto the concrete, again without even a splash of displaced pool water. He was back up on his perch, his flawless skin shining in the direct sunlight as the tiny beads of water evaporated. The official red lifeguard trunks clung to his thighs. He shook them, one leg at a time, to release some of the water. Pushing his hair straight back over his head, Ricky put on his black-rimmed sunglasses and surveyed his pool kingdom. All was right with the world on a ninety-degree June afternoon in Beverly Hills, California.

Dining with Mom and Dad that night at home on Lexington, I shared with them that I had made a first date with Ricky the lifeguard.

"Why are you dining with us if you are going out with Ricky?" Mother Nancy inquired.

"We are not going out for dinner, Mother. We are going to a club to see a new band later tonight."

"I see. What fine club will you be going to?"

"It's called Club Z, on Sunset."

"I've heard about that place. Isn't it where that debutante got so much attention, turning into a celebrity for no reason? What's her name? She is always being photographed."

"That's the place. Her name is Christina Field," I said.

"Do I need to tell you to be careful? Use good judgment. I believe that Club Z is not exactly what I might refer to as a classy joint."

We all laughed. I knew Nancy was right. The clubs on Sunset were just this side of trouble.

"Where's Jamey?" I asked, not seeing him at the dinner table.

"He's in his room," Father Dalt answered.

"Jamey had a rough day. Marta took a tray to him from the kitchen."

"What do you mean, rough day?" I pressed on.

"We have enrolled him in a new day rehab program, and it is not a walk in the park. The adviser uses military training methods that kids like your brother are not used to dealing with." My father added, "We need to give him some space. Hopefully something will turn my son around."

My parents were seriously worried. Jamey had been kicked out of every private school in Los Angeles; there were no more options. In the fall, my parents thought, he might enroll in Beverly Hills High as a freshman, even though he should have been starting his junior year. This fact alone was reason for grave concern. An out-of-control sixteen-year-old in class with fourteen-year-olds at a public high school presented a clear set of challenges. This summer therapy was the latest hope to provide my brother with a sense of purpose so that he might take school seriously and try to apply himself. Staying off drugs was at the center of the challenge.

Somehow, I had avoided the drug scene. It wasn't easy. Just about every kid I knew had tried whatever was popular, from pot, to coke, to meth—even heroin. It was less prevalent at girls' boarding school, but it was there too, especially the pot and the cocaine. I was just part of a drug generation. So many kids were like Jamey, especially within Beverly Hills city limits. Sadly, they were messing with the rest of their lives. And too many kids were losing the rest of their lives. Drug abuse was an epidemic in my generation, and I don't think Americans overall had come to realize just how bad it is.

At Jamey's previous school, the final stop on his journey through every private institution in LA that my parents' money and contacts could provide, First Lady Nancy Reagan's Just Say No Committee from the White House made a visit, as they had done at different institutions around the nation, to push the agenda on ending drug use. An advance team had come to Jamey's school, which was one of the First Lady's LA stops. In addition to securing the school, agents distributed yellow and black pins with the Just Say No slogan printed in black lettering over the yellow background. Jamey went around the school with masking tape covering up the word *No*, writing the word *When* in black felt-tip pen in its place. Dozens, if not hundreds, of kids thought it was a perfectly wonderful prank to wear the more accurate Just Say When pins on the day of Reagan's tour. It made the local news. Jamey was expelled.

A Summer Date with the Pool Hunk

Ricky the Adonis, with the movie star tan, arrived at my home right at nine o'clock at night as promised. He had left his 1970-something Chevy Camaro curbside. The car's paint had peeled; at least Ricky's face hadn't.

Ringing the doorbell, which sounded like the church chimes at Westminster Abbey, Ricky waited to be invited in. It took Marta the housekeeper longer than usual to make it to the door. She was in the kitchen finishing dinner cleanup duties. Marta opened the heavy black-gloss-painted door just as Ricky was about to press the church chimes button a second time. Dressed in her thinly striped pink and white pressed cotton uniform with its white Peter Pan collar and pinafore-style white apron, she greeted the nine o'clock arrival.

"May I help you?" she called out.

"Hi. I'm Ricky Robinson, and I'm here to pick up Kate." Simple enough announcement.

Ricky was fidgeting, moving his body weight from side to side, first one leg, then the other leg. Marta knew that nervous look, figuring he must be a kid from the other side of the hill. Which he was. In LA, what side of the hill you come from matters.

"Please come in. I will call for Kate," she said.

Marta had known he was coming. I had warned her and asked her to let him enter. Otherwise, she would have closed the door and asked him to wait outside.

Ricky proceeded to take a seat in the entrance foyer. It is a two-story room with a double staircase descending from a second-floor landing. A massive antique Baccarat crystal chandelier hung in the center of the hall, which sported a round eighteenth-century inlaid Sheraton-style table displaying an ever-changing arrangement of Mother Nancy's personally grown and nurtured award-winning orchids from her cherished greenhouse.

Appearing at the top of the stairs, I began to come down to Ricky. He bounced up off the bench where he had found a bit of security watching me descend the stairs wearing tight jeans; cute little flats, each with a gold buckle over the arch; a simple white blouse, collar up; and a fitted navy-blue blazer with an embroidered fleur-de-lis on the breast pocket, making my entrance. I didn't want to overdress for Club Z or look like a member of the grunge society. I knew that there would be plenty of those types.

"Hi, Ricky, my favorite lifeguard of all time," I said, teasing him. I went over to give him a hug, followed by an air-kiss on his right cheek. It eased his nerves. He relaxed.

"You look really nice," he told me.

"Well, thank you very much. And may I say that you look handsome in clothes. I've never seen you dressed," I said, giggling. He got the joke and laughed it off.

After I called out good night to whoever might be listening, we left Lexington for our first date amid the unpredictable Sunset Strip club scene. While the Strip was probably less than five miles from my front door, the contrast in neighborhoods was severe. Without exaggeration, I am talking two worlds colliding, divided only by a street sign between Beverly Hills and West Hollywood, including the Strip.

Traffic was backed up as we crossed into West Hollywood, heading east on Sunset. It always was. Club Z was only a few blocks down. Parking was going to be a nightmare. That would be Ricky's issue. I was in the passenger seat, along for the ride.

Since I was far from an experienced dating expert, I kept the conversation superficial and did not say much.

As we approached Club Z, the traffic came to a complete halt. Ricky shouted out a few choice "Oh shits", trying to figure out how to get closer and find parking. I said nothing, just reached over and patted him on the leg as if to say, *It doesn't matter.* Honestly, I didn't care if we never got there. I just liked being out on a date with a nice-looking boy—a little romance on a warm summer night in the life of a free and directionless almost-woman.

We waited in traffic for at least thirty minutes, then it finally started to open up. At one point I feared Ricky was going to pull the Camaro onto the north sidewalk and cut through all the cars to get to the club entrance. Fortunately, that hadn't happened. Once we made it to valet stand, they took the car, which they could have refused, but they had seen young, good-looking kids, the kind that management wanted seen in the club. A bouncer motioned for us to enter, passing over a line of others waiting. We must have really looked good. Ricky's beat-up old car had not stood in our way.

Dark, Dirty, and Degenerate

It was now about ten o'clock as we made it inside Club Z. The place was packed wall-to-wall, body to body. It was pitch-black except for pulsating strobe lights bouncing back and forth in rhythm with the booming rock music that I did not recognize. There must have been a thousand kids dancing, moving their bodies up and down against one another. It was a good thing that this was a ground-floor club; the floor would have given way on a second story.

Waitresses in little more than panties and bra, their version of street clothes, made their way through the crush in five-inch stiletto heels, selling any kind of elixir desired. Was anyone in the place twenty-one? Nobody cared. Where were the cops?

Ricky grabbed one of the cocktail gals by the waist as she passed by.

"Can we order?"

"Sure, kid. What will it be?"

Ricky ordered a Coors beer. I declined. He didn't seem so happy with me for not ordering, but I declined just the same.

"I'll bring you two beers," she said. "I don't know if I will be able to circle back to you again for a reorder with all of this craziness."

"Good idea," Ricky replied. "Make it three, if you don't mind."

"Got it," she said, pushing onward.

So, my date is starting off with three beers, and I'm stone sober. Do I feel trouble coming my way?

"Would you like to dance?" Ricky asked.

"I think we are dancing," I replied. "This is the most space we can have," I added with a grin.

"I guess you're right."

"This band tonight must be hot. What are they called?"

"They are the VDs," Ricky shouted back as the noise level was rising.

"The Venereal Diseases?" I thought that was a real winning name.

"No. The Valley Dudes."

"Oh, the Valley Dudes," I repeated, trying to move to the blasting sound. Ricky followed suit.

His three beers arrived, and since he didn't have a table, a chair, or anything, the waitress handed him one for each hand and put the third in my hand. I took it, to be in the game as it were, but I wasn't happy about being Ricky's beer caddy. He drank one of his beers, downing it in gulps, then he put the glass bottle down on the floor, up against a nearby wall. I was relieved of my carrying duty at that point as Ricky took beer number three from me, holding it while downing beer number two.

"Follow me," he yelled to me, moving on to beer three. After he put the second glass bottle down on the floor, it freed up one of his hands to take mine as we maneuvered through the mass of people, heading toward the back of the club opposite the stage and dance floor.

The farther away we got from the center of action, the darker the place became. Darker and dirtier and increasingly disgusting—not just the club, but also the people. These were not my people, and they sure didn't seem like Valley kids either.

Approaching some sort of back room, Ricky passed a bar. He was still holding my hand as we pushed through the maze.

"Can I order a shot of Cuervo?" he yelled at the barkeep to be heard above the noise. Turning to me, he asked if I'd like one too. I decided to join in. One shot wouldn't kill me.

"Okay. One shot of Cuervo for me," I answered.

Taking plenty of time to finish my drink, I sipped, even though I knew I was supposed to be cool and down the shot in one gulp. Ricky was on a second and then a third shot. Apparently, three was his magic number.

He took my hand again, this time jerking me forward unintentionally, and I dropped my shot glass. It hit the concrete floor with a splat and shattered.

Across from the bar, two huge guys flanked double doors leading to some sort of VIP room in the back of Club Z. Ricky handed one of them cash—I couldn't see how much—and the muscleman opened one of the doors a little more than forty-five degrees, motioning for us to enter.

The aroma of pot hit me like a wave just steps into the inner sanctum. There I was once again surrounded by my peers, members of the drug generation. My thoughts went right to my brother; I was no longer enamored with my handsome hunk lifeguard date. My crush was gone, and I wanted to get the heck out of the VIP room at Club Z on this night debuting the VDs. What a concept.

"Ricky, I don't like it in here. Can we go?" I asked rather sheepishly.

There was no response. Instead, he pulled me farther into the room, still clutching my hand, with his grip feeling tighter, almost hurting me. I tried to pull back and release my hand. It wasn't happening.

The dark, smoke-filled room began to reveal its purpose as I adjusted to the minimal light. People were having sex—all kinds of sex. Men and women, men and men, women and women, in pairs or in groups of three and four, fully dressed, partially dressed, undressed. It was Rome.

"Oh my God!" I screamed to Ricky. "What is this?"

"This is the VIP Pleasure Palace." He could barely get the words out, stumbling somewhat from all the beer followed by the Cuervo shots.

"Seriously, can we please get out of here?" I pleaded as we banged into a couple of gay guys doing a tongue tango. At least they were still in their almost matching tank tops and supertight white Levi's.

Ricky swung me around and maneuvered me up against a wall. Coming right up against me, he forced his wet kiss onto my lips, trying to enter my mouth with his tongue. I wasn't giving in. As I felt his hands come up and onto my breasts, I pushed back against the wall and then catapulted forward, getting him off me. Ricky fell backward and tripped himself, landing on the floor on his butt.

"You are a pig taking me here!" I yelled at him. I pushed my way through the sex crowd, out the VIP door, past the musclemen, through the club, and back onto Sunset. With no car, I began to walk westward on the sidewalk. If I could find a cab, I'd be okay. But the cabs were all heading east, the opposite direction. No luck.

Walking another three or four blocks, I figured I could walk all the way home if necessary. But instead of doing that, I put out my thumb. The first car passing pulled over for me. Boy, was I walking the danger line. Leaning over, I checked out the driver as the passenger window of the car came rolling down.

"Need a lift? Get in," the voice called out. It was a girl's voice.

"Thank you, Jesus," I said, mumbling.

"I'm sorry, what was that?" the driver came back.

"Oh, nothing," I said, opening the door and jumping in. "Thank you for picking me up."

"What are girlfriends for?" she said. "Bad date?"

"The worst."

"Where to?"

"A few miles down Sunset. Just before the Holmby Palms Hotel would be great," I answered.

"No problem. Tell me where to stop," she said.

The girl who had saved my sorry failed-date rear end was kind of a plain Jane. She had mousy-brown hair, straight and cut at the shoulder, parted down the middle of her head, with no bangs. Her skin was white and freckled, almost as if she had a rash, but I knew it wasn't that.

I never asked her name although I should have, if only to be polite. Instead, I let her concentrate on driving. She wore very thick glasses, and the car was one of those huge Ford sedans, probably her dad's. I wondered why this girl was driving down Sunset Strip at eleven o'clock at night in her dad's car. Then again, what did it matter? She was my hero of the night.

Not believing this had again just happened to me, I asked myself if I was sending mixed signals to guys. Why would this handsome, clean-cut lifeguard by day turn into a sex maniac by night? I was not Catholic, but I was considering entering a convent. But would they have me?

Knowing that my father was going to murder me for hitchhiking and not calling him to pick me up, I decided to say nothing about my date. My savior behind the wheel approached the hotel. I asked her to let me off. I would walk up the hill at Crescent Drive to Lexington and home. It was after eleven, but I felt safe in my neighborhood.

The End of Summer

The lazy days of summer in Beverly Hills passed rapidly, turning into weeks. June became August in a flash. I did not go back to the club pool that season, preferring the solitude of the pool in my own backyard. It was time to get orientated and prepped for university; school would begin in less than three weeks. Clearly, I had decided to give up on the idea of challenging my parents and switching gears to attend the fashion academy. I would follow the road most securely traveled. Heck, maybe the fashion passion was just every silly young girl's fantasy. I did look forward to college, hoping to explore new options, fresh ideas. That's what I told myself.

CHAPTER THREE

FIRST LOVE, TRUE LOVE

Graduating Foxhaven with a 4.2 GPA and a nearly perfect SAT college entrance score, my plans for higher education were basically laid out on a silver platter. My dream was to move to France and go to fashion design school. Nancy and Dalt wanted me back in California. They won. I enrolled at USC, in Los Angeles, moved into the Birnkrant dorm, and again questioned my purpose in life. The saving grace—boys. Six years at Foxhaven sans male companionship had created a void. As a child, I had loved playing with the boys, but then they vanished from my universe. Now they were back, and back in full supply.

Wasting no time getting reacquainted, using my East Coast prep school veil of secrecy, I gave off this cool, distant, guarded vibe that was quite simply the call of the wild. Pure sexual friction. Sparks were flying. Having the best time, I learned quickly to ease back on the hype. Not wanting to become the ice queen of Birnkrant Hall, I gave off a little aura of mystery, yet I was still approachable, extremely so.

All the strict rules and the game playing at prep school had somehow tainted my view of life. We were always trying to cut corners, managing to have things follow our own desires, seeing what we could always get away with. The overriding message was that life was and obstacle course and that to succeed and survive, one must play the angles and have a plan or a scheme. Now, looking back, I was certain that this was not the reason why my parents had sent me east. They had done it so that I could be brought up properly.

"Darling, you will have a splendid time learning how to become a master manipulator in life" was not mother's goal, not Nancy's idea of a pedigree for a young woman of privilege. But that is what happened. I had earned an A+ in manipulation.

Moving forward, I found that college was freedom. It wasn't fashion school in Paris, but it was a wonderful time of self-exploration, enhanced by meeting people of all kinds and taking the most unusual classes I could find. I was the only young woman taking Ancient Hebrew 101. Don't ask me why I chose it. Perhaps Madonna's immersion in cabala had led me there. Unprepared for the course, I was forced to either drop the class or receive an F. I chose the less painful route. Just the same, I really loved the exposure.

It didn't take long before I also dropped the cool mysterious East Coast prep school vibe and reverted to my California roots. USC was really all about that anyway. I ended up doing the sorority pledge and learning how to drink too many fruit-flavored daiquiris and still drive home, frequent the local hangouts on Figueroa Street for two o'clock in the morning food binges, and still manage to awake for class at nine.

After a year or more of serial dating and attending endless vapid fraternity parties Friday night after Friday night, I began to think of my life as being a useless mating call and a college rite of passage where the young men lined up checking out the young women to see who would end up with whom, assuming the players were not too drunk to stand up. Then I met David.

David Morgan was not a frat boy, and he had not attended prep school. He was at USC on a scholarship. He was a serious student, a senior with a biology major and sights on medical school. Raised by middle-class parents, he had a father and mother who were both teachers, and his childhood world extended to the outer limits of his birthplace, San Diego. David had never even crossed the border into Tijuana, Mexico.

We met in the cafeteria, sharing a table at lunch on a very busy Monday at noon. His smile was just like mine. How odd to sense something so strange yet so similar in someone I did not know at all.

Our friendship began with the customary "What's your name?" "What's your major?," and "Where are you from?" queries. I answered politely, but I didn't care about his major or his hometown. We were having a love-at-first-sight moment; his eyes seduced me. As I looked at him across the table, I envisioned him naked eating a hamburger. Naked from the waist up, since the table obliterated the view of his bottom half.

My vivid and out-of-bounds imagination figuratively slapped me in the face.

"Do you live on campus?" I asked, mumbling the simple words.

What a dumb question. He will think I'm just another boring blonde coed, I thought.

"No, I share an apartment off campus with three other premed students," he replied.

"What kind of doctor would you like to become?" I said, pushing the envelope and trying my best to be sincere, when all I could think about was how handsome this boy was. I embarrassed myself by imagining asking him if we could go back to his apartment off campus.

"I'm leaning toward pediatrics, maybe even ob-gyn." David had come back with an answer that would certainly capture most women's hearts.

He put down his hamburger and smiled. Looking at me across the table, his penetrating brown eyes behind tortoiseshell-framed specs told me that he was interested. We made a connection that was physical, downright visceral, certainly not based on our scintillating conversation.

I did the unthinkable. "Do you have class this afternoon?"

"Not until four o'clock," he answered.

"Would you like to go for a walk-through campus? I'm headed over to the parking structure to get my car," I told him.

"That would be nice," he answered softly, still looking at me with those brown laser beams.

We got up from the table; dropping my bag, I tripped over the leg of my chair. Not being the clumsy type, I laughed it off. David picked up the bag, handed it to me, and took my hand.

"Everything all right?"

"Just fine. Perfect," I told him.

My hand was tingling. My heart was thumping. I could not believe this was happening to me over lunch in the cafeteria.

"Let's go," he said, still holding my hand. "By the way, I am sorry, but I forgot your name."

"Kate Fairchild," I blurted back like a bullet. "I'm a French major," I added.

"Yes, you told me that. Very nice," he replied.

Yes, it was all very nice.

David did not let go of my hand as we left the cafeteria. We walked down the brick steps and out to the Alumni Park in front of Doheny Library. Less than one hundred yards into our travel, David guided us onto a concrete bench in front of a trickling fountain with water coming from a very old classic bronze figure suspended as if dancing on air. "It is so graceful," I said, looking at the figure, which appeared to be that of a young girl.

"Would you like to go to my apartment?" David followed with an out-of-the-blue proposition.

"Will I meet your three premed roommates?" I asked with coyness.

"Not today," he said matter-of-factly.

"Okay then, let's go. Do we walk or drive?"

"I don't have a car," David answered.

"I do. It's just across the way. I'll drive you."

I couldn't believe what I had just agreed to do. Then again, it had been my plan from the moment I sat down across from him in the cafeteria. My secret plan was now a reality. Was this possible? Was this all some weird delusional thing happening? Or was the universe speaking to me, saying, "Grab happiness when it reveals itself"? *Don't be afraid,* I told myself. I was surprisingly ready to grab this happiness, and a few body parts along with the happiness.

Meeting David Morgan by chance in the school cafeteria changed my life course as if I had run into a block wall. School didn't matter. Career goals didn't matter. Nothing mattered except him. Therefore, I had chosen not to go to fashion school. How could I have met a premed guy who could turn me into Jell-O at hello if I were at fashion school surrounded by ubercompetitive females and very trendy mostly gay young men?

"I know this is crazy," he said. "I have never done anything like this before."

"You've never done anything like what?" I asked.

"You know, ask a girl I've just met back to my apartment. In the middle of the afternoon yet!"

"It's not something I do on a regular basis either—accept such a proposition, that is."

David leaned over and moved in very close, and then he kissed me. First the kiss was slow, deliberate, and very sweet. I shivered; my feet tingled. His kiss was very different from that of every other boy I had kissed, not that there were very many. But there was none like this. I wanted more. I wanted it to go on and never stop. I had never felt this way. Never. Was this what all the fuss was about? Was this love? How could it be love, a first kiss with a young man I had just met?

David pulled away from me gently. We both needed to breathe. I gasped, not just for air, but also because I craved more. He came back with even more passion, pressing his lips against mine. Our tongues danced in perfect unison.

"Shall we go?" he asked. "You want to take your car?"

"Are you sure you want to drive? We could walk. How far is your apartment?"

"About six blocks."

"Walking sounds just fine," I said. I didn't think I could drive anyway. I was feeling very strange. And I also thought it would be unwise to show him my car, a little yellow Mercedes SL Roadster my father had given me for going to USC, seeing as David had told me he did not have a car.

We stopped kissing, much to my regret, then got up off the concrete bench and began walking down the narrow diagonal path bordered by trimmed privet hedges on either side.

"You sure you don't mind walking?" David asked again.

The afternoon sun streaked through the sycamore trees shading the parkway, hitting David's curly brown hair and creating a sort of halo glow around his baby face. My great kisser with a boyish look probably could have passed for thirteen. Wearing a faded light gray sweatshirt and skinny Levi's with ripped knees complete with white threads dangling, he was the best-looking premed. I think it was the penny loafers and no socks that attracted me most. Women always check out a man's feet, or, more to the point, his shoes, first and foremost. You can tell a great deal about a guy by the condition and style of his shoes.

"It's a beautiful day. Walking sounds nice," I told him.

"Okay then, here we go." David took my hand again. There was that tingling feeling. Leaning over, I kissed him on the right cheek, just a quick peck. He responded, stopping in the middle of the narrow path and kissing me with full passion.

Students walking by yelled, "Get a room."

How did they know that was what we were about to do?

Heading off campus down Hoover Street and passing the village at Thirty-Second Street, we turned west on Twenty-Ninth Street and began walking on a sidewalk probably installed in the late nineteenth century. The street still boasted original bungalow houses from that period with their late Victorian architecture having been bastardized over the decades out of economic necessity, the original details replaced by cheap synthetic building materials of the mid-twentieth century. Many of these houses were occupied by families, mostly African American, and many more had been chopped up into rooms for renting to students. Still others had been torn down and replaced with seriously ugly stucco boxes, otherwise known as apartment buildings. Cars were parked bumper-to-bumper on the street; the lawns were poorly kept; and the trees cried out for pruning. The gentility of 1890 had been lost in favor of kowtowing to the requirements of a modern urban world, evolving demographics, and the need for student housing at a major university. This was the place that David and his three premed roommates called home.

Arriving at a funny-looking little yellow house sandwiched between two of those 1960s stucco box apartment buildings, we walked up a few rickety wooden steps with remaining streaks of white paint on otherwise exposed and heavily worn wood to an old-fashioned front porch landing. Most of the wooden spindles of the porch railing were long gone, but the original panel front door with its leaded oval glass insert remained. There was no lock; the door just swung open to a hallway, narrow and barely lit, with high ceilings and walls of shining plaster that glowed like the seat of a pair of well-worn pants that needed to be tossed in the trash.

What once was a traditional floor plan with a living room parlor, a dining room, a kitchen, and more had been closed off with plain hollow-core unpainted veneered doors, each shouting out a number as an address for the student occupants. David resided in number 3, which was once a bedroom connected to an old-fashioned sleeping porch, the porch now being number 4. He and his three roommates shared the two spaces.

"This is it, my whole world in one-half of a room," David joked, unlocking three dead bolts on the flimsy hollow-core door. As I was thinking to myself that one good kick could knock a hole in the door, David opened the door wide and did a flourish gesture with his right arm, very gallant indeed, permitting me to enter. He didn't offer to pick me up and carry me across the threshold; that would have been too much, even for infatuated me.

"Charming," I said. "Who could ask for more?"

David laughed. He knew how dreadful it was. Not to mention messy. Beds were unmade, with sheets hanging halfway to the floor. Pillows were rumpled up against the wall, with clothes piled in various designated corners, which at least meant there was some sort of order to the chaos. Books, papers, and folders were stacked everywhere, mostly on the floor since there was no furniture, except for one old desk and a card table, which served as another desk. The room featured several tall double-hung panes with no coverings. Instead, newspapers were taped to the appropriate spots to assist in reducing the glare of daylight and the superbright security spotlights that came on at dusk, illuminating the apartment building next door.

Not caring about any of the less-than-ideal conditions, I was just happy to be there with him.

"May I sit?" I inquired, pointing to one of the beds up against a wall in the corner.

"That's my roommate Sean's," he said. "Please try the one over there."

What a relief. The one he had indicated was mostly made. At least a blanket was pulled up over the sheets and the pillows were reasonably fluffed and smoothed over.

I sat down, kind of on the edge.

"Tell me more about your life. I want to know everything," I said with a coy grin.

"Everything?" he asked.

"Absolutely everything. Leave nothing out!"

"This could end up being a really boring first date."

"Is that what we are doing, having a first date?" I chided David. "You don't take me to very nice places on a first date. It's a good thing that I am not a girl who needs to be impressed," I added.

"Touché," he came back quickly, then sat down next to me on his mostly made bed.

"I don't know. There is something special about you. Something so special. I was attracted to you on some basic can't-explain-it level the moment I saw you in the cafeteria," he said.

Then he dropped a bomb on my heart.

"And your kiss hit me like a nuclear explosion. I totally lost touch with reality. I couldn't remember my name, where I was, what I was doing. All that mattered was you and kissing you. Do you think I'm crazy?" he asked.

"Crazy good," I told him. "Want to try it again? Maybe the magic is gone," I added, trying to be clever.

With that, David did try again. His first kiss was soft, slow, and gentle. The connection was instant, electric, and overpowering to the senses—all of them. I was helpless, submissive, and oblivious to anything other than David, the scent of his skin and his breath. I could even taste what I thought was his curly hair falling around his beautiful boy face. Where had he come from, the love planet?

Carefully, gently, he pushed me backward on his bed. I fidgeted and squirmed a bit removing my blazer as David unbuttoned my shirt, button by button, from the neck to the waist, opening it to reveal my flesh. My bra was off in an instant, almost mysteriously. Lying back in a love trance, I waited for what would happen next.

David removed his sweatshirt, pulling it up over his head. I was surprised at how muscular his trim frame was. David was worked out, with a superhard chest, shoulders, and arms—my own Arnold Schwarzenegger in miniature. Even better, this flawless male specimen did not shave his chest hair like so many college boys. I never could figure out the whole thing about smooth and hairless men. What can I say, I'm an old soul, I guess, and I like a guy who looks like a guy. David's thick, dark chest hair felt very soft, silky in fact, and the growth made a line down to his stomach, below the navel, and into his jeans.

Those jeans were off in a flash, again to my amazement, as they just went away effortlessly. He was wearing old guy white boxers.

"What cute undies you have," I said with plenty of charm and sarcasm.

"Show me yours," he replied. "And then we'll make a judgment call."

I did just that, as instructed. Removing my jeans, I displayed my plain white bikini panties. Nothing too special. We both laughed.

David's hands were on the elastic waistband of my panties. He pulled them off me so sensuously that I squirmed. In a flash, his plain white shorts were on the floor beside the bed.

The lower portion of my lover was equally worked out. His strong legs wrapped around me, and I drifted into love oblivion as he moved up and down over my body. I could feel the hardness of his manhood and the soft velvety touch of his skin against mine.

David entered me with poetic motion while kissing me in this unbelievable harmony. The pleasure was overwhelming, beyond my ability to describe or comprehend. We made love for more than an hour, our bodies dripping with sweat.

"I'm coming," he whispered as a warning, mostly to see if he was satisfying me and if I was also ready.

"I know," I whispered. "I can tell."

Putting my arms around David, I clasped my hands on his lower back at the moment we came. It was beautiful. I knew I would never again be the same person.

At that moment, I transitioned out of teenagedom and into adulthood, pretty much unscarred and in one solid piece. With my twentieth birthday approaching later this year, I had experienced a milestone in my life. As for David, was he the one? I thought so, but the future was complicated. What would tomorrow bring?

We held one another for about fifteen minutes. It was nearing three thirty in the afternoon. I wanted to stay in David's arms for as long as I could, but our time together was quickly vanishing.

"We need to get up and get dressed," he advised. "I have class at four, and two of my roommates are usually coming in the door just as I'm heading back to campus."

I pulled the blanket up over my head as if to ignore David's warning of impending interruption.

"I don't care who sees us; I'm not ready to let you go."

"Would it help if I say we should meet again tomorrow, same time, same place?" David asked, stroking my hair, looking into my eyes and directly into my soul.

"Not a bad offer. I'll have to think about it though. My schedule is very demanding."

We broke into crazy laughter. David jumped up and found his old man undershorts. He was quickly dressed in those torn Levi's and that gray sweatshirt.

I heard the water running in the bathroom and the gurgle of toothbrushing, then David reappeared in the room in a matter of seconds. His hair had been combed off his face, and he smelled like Crest toothpaste.

"What a great smell," I said.

"Huh? What's that supposed to mean?"

"I love the smell of toothpaste on my man after sex!"

"Okay. Whatever makes you happy. Really, you have to get up and get dressed."

With those words, we both heard the locks turning on the flimsy hollow-core door. David reached for me and pulled me out of his bed, gathered up my clothes, which were strewn about, and escorted me into the bathroom, closing the door before his roommate opened the hall door.

His final words were charming. "Now it's your turn to smell like Crest. I'll be waiting to walk you back to school."

Dressing frantically, then washing my face and other body parts as carefully as I could, I noticed that my hair was acting wild, so I pulled it back into a tight ponytail. Fortunately, there was a piece of ribbon in my jacket pocket to tie the hair back. On the sink counter, a bottle of Old Spice men's aftershave caught my attention. Deciding to use a dab or two as a little personal douche under my arms and between my legs, I finished dressing. Pulling on my blazer, then adding a touch of lip gloss, which I also found in my pocket, I made my reentry into the bedroom.

"Whoa. You sure don't smell like Crest," David said, standing next to one of his roomies. "Actually, you smell like a sailor on leave in port." Obviously knowing what I had done with the Old Spice, he started to laugh again. The roommate didn't know what to make of it.

"Hi, I'm Kate," I introduced myself, reaching out my hand.

"Uh, my name is Bernie," he came back, taking my hand and giving it a strong, yet nervous, shake in return.

"We've got to get going," David said. "I can't be late for Chem 421."

David took my hand and led me out the door. I waved goodbye to Bernie. He stood almost frozen, staring back at us. I took this as a very good sign. Obviously, Bernie was not accustomed to seeing women in his apartment with his roommate.

David and I walked fast in order to make it back to campus on time. Not talking much—indeed, not really saying a word at all—was all right with me. Mentally, I was still lying on David's bed in his arms.

"Can I tell you that you were wonderful?" David told me, speaking softly just as we were about to part.

I said nothing, just smiled at him and looked into his eyes.

"Would I scare you if I said I think I'm in love?" he said.

Leaning into him, I kissed him on the lips. That was my response. He got the message. Turning away, I started walking toward my dorm.

Stopping and turning back, I said, "Same time. Same place. Tomorrow." And then I rushed off in the opposite direction. Without turning around again to look at him, I could tell that he was just standing there watching me, at least for a second, before heading off to class.

I wasn't scared that David had told me he was in love. I knew I was. Or at least it was as close to the real deal as I had ever known. Never mind that I knew practically nothing about this young man. They are correct, whoever they are: love is blind. It is also delicious.

Only One Semester to Dream

The phone rang in my dorm room around eight o'clock. It was David calling. He had tracked me down. I had not given him my number, but not on purpose; it just kind of fell through the cracks.

Can you imagine forgetting to give your number to the most important person you've ever met on a given afternoon?

"How are you?" he inquired.

"Well, pretty good," I said. "I miss you. Can you come by?"

"Right now?"

"No. How about over summer break? Yes, silly, right now of course. Where are you?" My sarcasm got him chuckling.

"I'm still on campus. Just finished my biology lab, and I wanted to hear your voice."

"I could meet you downstairs in the lobby of my dorm." I tried not to be too pushy.

"If I come over now, will we still have a date tomorrow?" he asked.

"It depends on what happens when you come over tonight."

"I can be there in ten minutes, in the lobby at Birnkrant Hall."

"Perfect. See you in ten."

All the so-called rules of courtship were off the table. There would be no playing hard to get, no taking it slow. We broke all the rules. Mother Nancy would just die. Not wanting that, I would not be sharing my first true love story with her. Not yet anyway.

Sitting on the edge of my dorm room twin bed, I knew that there was no going back. I would get to know David, and he would know me in good time.

The thing is, that time was limited. David was in his final semester, awaiting word of medical school admittance, and his senior workload was intense. In that first afternoon together, David had shared bits and pieces of his daily life with me. Realizing that he had no idea what a free Saturday night was like, my new love explained that he studied until the early morning hours, often going all night. Classes and labs wiped out dinner hour. He was lucky to find a vending machine with an energy bar remaining. I wasn't prepared for any of this, having no idea of what was to come in my life.

Just the same, in my state of love euphoria, I combed my hair, dabbed on a little eyeliner and lip gloss, and made my way to the elevator. David was standing in the lobby waiting, concentrating on a calculator.

"Solving the world's economic problems?" I chided him, surprising him.

"No, only trying to solve a math problem for my morning class in physics," he replied, putting the calculator in his backpack.

"This is a pleasant surprise," I said, putting out my arms to give him a hug hello.

"I wanted to come by and properly ask you to join me tomorrow for lunch in the cafeteria." David was oh so charming, even in his worn gray sweatshirt that had experienced its share of life on this day. "Will noon work for you?" he pressed on.

"Noon would be perfect," I told him, even though it wasn't. I had a class that ran through the lunch hour. Too bad. Poli-sci would have to wait. Given that I had no idea how to solve the crisis in the Middle East between the Israelites and the Arabs, the class would not miss my participation.

"Then it's a date," David confirmed. "I'm sorry, but my class schedule tomorrow is like today's. I have an open afternoon, then it's back to the books by four o'clock." He put both arms around the back of my neck and pulled me closer. "Can we step outside for a minute?"

"You're in charge," I told him.

We turned and walked toward the double glass doors leading to the garden.

The night was warm and sultry. February in Los Angeles often presented with summerlike weather, the envy of the nation. The horizon was ablaze with starlight, and a moon serving as the centerpiece seduced any mortal gazing upon the majesty of it all. Drunk with new emotion, I realized my head was spinning.

We were alone outside, at least momentarily. David kissed me just as he had done that afternoon. I surrendered totally. It was crazy, but I knew at that moment that he was the one. I would marry this man. Someday David would be my husband.

Our embrace ended as my fellow dorm residents approached down the garden walk. Oblivious to us, they just kept on walking by and went in the front door.

At that moment, life was exceptionally good, except perhaps for the Arabs and Israelis and for the kids in my political science class, which I would forgo tomorrow in favor of love. It is so easy to rationalize just about anything when you are barely twenty.

"See you at noon tomorrow. My treat. You can have anything at all in the cafeteria line," David joked as he hefted his heavy book bag over one shoulder and headed off into the night, walking through an inner-city Los Angeles neighborhood that once boasted a glorious simple past that had faded decades earlier. The streets were rough; random shootings were not uncommon. I asked God to protect David. I hadn't asked God for anything much in years.

My First Real Date with David

The dorm phone rang again at eleven o'clock.

"Hello," I answered, half in a daze.

Not really sleeping, I noticed the TV was blaring and that lights were on. I had read one hundred pages of a book and couldn't explain anything I had read.

"I just called to say I love you," the voice on the other end of the line said.

"Who is this, Stevie Wonder?" I replied, trying to be funny and not so serious.

"You're the wonder," David came back. "See you tomorrow. Sleep tight."

Right. I didn't think I would ever sleep again.

Finally, at around three in the morning, I fell asleep. The TV was still on, as were all the lights in my dorm room. It didn't matter. I fell into that deep, restful kind of sleep that is amazing, the kind of sleep one hopes for when lying in bed staring at the ceiling and wanting to fall into the perfect sleep rhythm that will take away all stress and restore the body, making it ready to face another day.

Managing to find that kind of sleep, it kept me in its trance until well after ten the next morning. Not only would I miss dealing with the Arabs and Israelis at lunchtime, but also English, French, and bio lab would miss me that morning. It was part of the luxury of being a semiserious college coed. These things happen. Classes are missed from time to time. There will be another one, a time to catch up. Honestly, I didn't worry.

After fooling around for another half hour, then daydreaming, I got up just before eleven o'clock in the morning, then put on my pink terry cloth robe with its white satin appliqué roses and headed down the hall to the women's shower.

Stepping into the small private shower stall, I removed my nightclothes, placing them on the faded wooden bench; pulled open the white plastic shower curtain; turned on the warm spray; and stepped beneath it. I always checked out the shower. It was ugly, tiled from floor to ceiling in basic beige ceramic, but generally always clean. The water poured over my head and down my body. Like a healing tonic or magic potion, the water brought me to life. I loved the feeling of having totally wet hair pushed back over my head and down my back. This was my ritual of being born again on a daily, or sometimes twice daily, basis.

Wrapping my wet hair in a thin white towel, I put on my robe and slippers, grabbed my nightgown, and dashed back to my room to dress for my cafeteria date with David.

Arriving at exactly noon, my hair still a bit wet, pulled back in a ponytail and tied with a large white silk ribbon, I was first to arrive. Having chosen to wear a white blouse with a high collar and a short powder-blue cotton miniskirt trimmed in white piping to match a pair of baby-blue canvas slip-ons with open toes to show off my perfect pink nails, I waited. Back in the dorm room I had put on a pearl necklace and some other jewelry but then decided to leave the gems in the dresser drawer. Didn't want to be too fancy. I figured David would still be wearing his old gray sweatshirt and jeans.

I was wrong. David entered the cafeteria moments later dressed in khakis and a pressed white button-down dress shirt. His hair was combed back over his ears, and he carried a small bouquet of yellow and white daisies tied with a checkered ribbon to match.

"These are for you on our first real date," he said, handing me the flowers.

"They are lovely," I replied, taking them as we both sat down at one of the few available tables.

"You look really nice," he told me.

"You look better, so handsome," I came back at him, reaching over across the table and taking his hand. I put the daisies down between us.

"It's important to make a good first impression on a first date," he offered.

"Well, you certainly did," I said, smiling at him.

"What would you like for lunch? Let me get it while you hold our table," David said. "If we both go, there will be no table and somebody will snatch your daisies," he said, chuckling.

"I would like a small green salad with Thousand Island dressing on the side and an egg salad and olive sandwich," I replied. "On pumpernickel bread." I added, "It is their best sandwich."

"Wow. A girl who knows exactly what she wants. That's rare," David said, heading to the cafeteria line.

I knew what I wanted. I wanted this young man.

David came back about fifteen minutes later. He had doubled the order and gotten the same for himself. He was making all the right moves for a first date following first sex.

"This is really good," he said, taking another bite of the egg and olive sandwich.

"See how much we have in common?" I joked. "We like the same sandwich."

"David, I want to know everything about you. Absolutely everything." I had changed my tone from silly to somewhat serious, hoping I wasn't being too pushy.

"Absolutely everything? Are you sure?" he asked. "There isn't all that much, and I'm afraid that what there is, is not very exciting. I might scare you away with just how boring I really am," he said, grinning, obviously really enjoying his lunch. Who knew a sandwich would open new worlds for a guy?

"Well, I told you that I was born in San Diego, and that I grew up in the Claremont–Mesa area, and that my parents are teachers in the public schools. I have two younger sisters, who share a bedroom in our postwar one-story, three-bedroom, two-bathroom stucco-frame house with an overgrown yard, no gardener, and a two-car garage that holds a Volkswagen and one older Chevy."

David asked if I wanted more. I said, "Yes, much more."

"Let me describe my house and tell you more about my parents. I'll give you the full picture.

"They met in college; both attended Cal Berkeley in the 1960s. That alone should tell you plenty. My dad was a chem major who wanted to go to med school, but life got in the way. Instead, he has taught high school chemistry for the past thirty years. The last time he bought a new suit, lapels were wide, ties were narrow, and pants flared at the bottom," he said, smiling.

"I think they're called bell-bottoms," I interjected.

"You got that right," David came back. "Mom was an English and journalism major, and she planned on saving the world with her copy. Instead, they got married right out of school. Dad escaped Vietnam with a high draft number, and they got pregnant. Mom lost the baby, and then lost another one a couple of years later. Rather than writing a column for the *New York Times*, she became a high school English teacher. And with the miscarriages, they thought there would be no family. Then a few years later, miracle of miracles, along came me. Surprise. Then a year later came sister number one; a year after that, sister number two. The almost perfect little American family in the suburbs of San Diego."

I started to comment that it sounded pretty good, but David cut in.

"Did I describe my family home enough?" he asked, not letting me respond.

"I grew up in a house furnished in college student discards. And guess what? It never changed. Our couch came from Grandma. We took off the plastic covering. The coffee table is an old milk crate with a piece of glass on top. Two beanbag chairs, orange, serve as occasional seating, and our TV, black and white, thirteen inches, is never used, except perhaps for a news flash.

"But we have books. Boy, do we have books. Books everywhere, all stacked on bookcases constructed from cement blocks that support plywood panels. Books in the living room, books in the hall, books in all the bedrooms—even in the bathroom.

"Yes. I learned to read, and I love to read. Books made me smarter than the average kid in suburban San Diego. Smarter in a decidedly left-leaning socialist political sphere, which I have modified to a more centrist and conservative view of the world, much to my parents' horror."

David took a breath.

"I'm almost done," he said, launching into another explanation.

"I've never been to Europe. I've never been to New York, and as I said, I've never been to Mexico—and it's only a half hour drive south. I was always a good student, got mostly A's' played baseball in high school, first base, and was pretty darn good at it, and went to religious school on Saturdays. Oh, by the way, I'm Jewish. Bar mitzvah and everything. My grandmother cried big tears when I read from the Torah."

David went on.

"From the time I was a kid, I wanted to be a doctor. Other kids hated going to the pediatrician, but I couldn't wait to get another shot. Maybe it was partly because I knew my dad wanted to be a doctor but didn't make his goal happen. Maybe, but more so, it was just my goal; it fit. So, here I am, a senior premed, and I think I'm going to get my chance. And even better, but in a whole other way, I have met you. And while I have only known you for one day, it was one day that changed my life. Miracles can happen. I think I am going to go back to synagogue this Saturday. I haven't been back in eight years, since the bar mitzvah."

With that, David reached over and took my hand. I hadn't touched much of my egg and olive sandwich on black bread.

"By the way, where or how did you come to crave such an ethnic lunch special? I kind of judged you as ham and cheese on sourdough with a touch of mayo," he joked.

"Well, that's pretty correct," I said. "I'm not very ethnic. Pretty darn white. Two Episcopalian parents, not very religious, but culturally Christian. From growing up in LA, I have many Jewish friends. I've been to my share of bar and bat mitzvahs.

"*Baruch atah Adonai elohaynu melech ha'olam,*" I said, quoting a little Hebrew, the beginning of the holy prayer.

"Whoa," David said. "Not bad. Not bad at all. Now tell me what it means."

"Another time, perhaps. I don't give away all my secrets at once," I replied.

"Then tell me about you. It's your turn to share," he requested.

"Okay, but it's not as colorful as your story," I told him planning to hold back plenty and only give some vague details. I was not going to scare off my new friend.

"I was born in LA and grew up on the Westside." I did not say Beverly Hills. "My dad is a stockbroker." I did not say investment banker. "Mom is a housewife. I have a younger brother, Jamey, who is in high school." I did not say in rehab. "I went to boarding school in Pennsylvania and came back to USC to please my parents. And someday I think I would like to become a fashion designer."

I had pretty much told the truth, sharing the basics without any embellishment or description. Was I supposed to describe my home as he had his? How could I tell this young man who had grown up with milk crate furniture that I tooled around ten thousand square feet of designer digs kept tidy by a maid? Maybe later. Or maybe not.

We finished lunch, and David asked the important question.

"Would you care to come by the apartment today? We have all afternoon, until class at four."

I didn't answer. Instead, I got up from the table, came around behind David's chair, put my arms around his neck, and clasped my hands across his chest. Leaning over, I whispered in his right ear, "Thank you for lunch. It was the best I've ever had."

David pushed his chair back. I released him.

"Shall we take a walk?" he asked. "I think you know the way."

"I do know the way," I replied.

On the walk back to David's apartment, we hardly said a word, just held hands and made a fast-paced jaunt out of it. I think we made record time. We were even a bit out of breath when walking up the busted-up Victorian steps of his rooming house.

On this our second day of afternoon lovemaking, there was no cat and mouse. The moment we entered the room, David gently pushed me back against the closed door and kissed me with more passion than I had experienced the previous day. Was this possible?

He removed my clothes piece by piece, easily and without distraction. I returned the gesture, unbuttoning his white shirt, pulling it back off his shoulders and down his arms, and dropping it to the floor.

Making our way across the room to David's twin bed, mostly made, we lay down together, body to body, in perfect oneness. We did not make love at first; we simply held one another and gazed into each other's eyes, stroking each other's skin very carefully with our fingertips. David wrapped his strong legs around me and pushed in closer. He positioned his body over mine but did not enter, instead moving back and forth slowly. I began to tremble, quivering sporadically, until I begged him to become one with me.

Our lovemaking commenced as two became one. Every move was in harmony—ecstasy beyond ecstasy. My emotions were bare and raw. I started to cry softly. Tears ran out of my eyes and down my cheeks.

"Is everything okay?" David whispered, feeling the tears on his cheeks.

"I have never been so happy—never felt this way," I said ever so softly.

"Why are you crying?"

"I am overwhelmed with emotion. I love you so much. How can this be?"

"I love you more," David replied.

The Final Months of My Sophomore Year

My relationship with David had begun with my skipping class and pretty much not caring about much else but him. For the first month after we met, I lived in a self-inflicted love trance. I could think of nothing else but being with him. This was easily supported by the fact that I was with him every chance I got. We made love often, always in the afternoon between his classes. My classes, well, those I attended, were few. I managed to keep it all together just barely.

But then everything reversed. I can't tell you exactly why, but I started to take school seriously. We still made love between classes, yet now our time together adjusted to my schedule as well as to his. I think I found new respect for myself seeing how much respect David had for his future and his opportunity to learn and study. He wanted me to have the same level of pride. While I am smart, I was never serious. Perhaps it is the curse of privilege. I knew from an early age that I was "taken care of." I did not have to worry about making a living, making money. Money was just a given.

Now I realized that learning and achieving a level of proficiency in school had nothing to do with money, at least not at this stage in life. Learning was a reward in and of itself, and there was a great deal to learn. I wanted to grab it and hold on to it. David changed my life in so many ways. With gratitude, I was becoming a real person, a whole woman.

Noticing the change in me, even over such a short period of time, David said something very important. He told me he loved me even more for my efforts. David shared his feelings; he was tuned in and in touch with me. I knew this was a special quality in a man.

By the late spring, David and I were in a serious relationship that was all things any adult could ask for. For the first time in my life, I had a real and deep meaning to cling to. The superficial had fallen away.

At home, my parents noticed the change probably before I did. Our time together was filled with good conversation about family and the future. We talked openly about Jamey's challenges, and I even got Nancy and Dalt to open up about their own dreams, their plans for their future as they moved ahead in midlife, and even things in life that they wished they had done differently. We even talked politics; a topic never much broached at the family dinner table.

I revealed my relationship with David at an opportune point. Nancy said that she had known. She could tell. "A mother always knows," she offered. I told her I was in love. She asked how I knew.

"Believe me, I know," I replied.

The tone of my voice must have convinced her of my sincerity. She did not press the issue. Instead, she turned to my father and gave him one of those *Oh my goodness*, all-knowing looks.

"Can we meet him?" she asked kindly.

"I think it would be nice," I said, still worried that I had not been forthcoming about my family with David.

"Shall we plan a dinner date?" Mother inquired. "How about Saturday night?"

I wanted to suggest that we all meet at a restaurant, but I knew they wanted him to come over to the house for dinner, so I said nothing to protest. Besides, it was silly to keep hiding the facts. David and I had come so far together in just a matter of months. Our different socioeconomic backgrounds would not matter. My parents were decent, interesting, intelligent people. David would like them very much, and they would like him too.

It was a Thursday in April, a glorious spring LA day with clear blue skies. The majestic sycamore trees lining the campus walkways were overflowing with new life, the green leaves offering a perfumed scent all their own that was both sweet and musty. I was meeting David at the cafeteria for lunch. No sex today, just class.

"Hi there," I called out, spotting him coming in the far direction from around the old campus gymnasium. He waved a big generous hello and opened his arms as if to send me a hug from a block away. I waited on the brick steps for his arrival.

"I've got a little surprise for you. I hope you will like it," I said.

"I love surprises from you," David came back.

"It's not that kind of surprise," I chided him. "We both have class all afternoon."

"Oh, I forgot," David answered with a sly grin.

"Well, I want you to meet my parents, and they want to meet you," I told him.

"Did you tell them about us?" he asked.

"I did."

"Everything?"

"No, not everything."

"Okay, I would like to meet the people who raised such an amazing woman."

"Can you come to dinner Saturday night?"

"I will rearrange my lab. Yes, I will come."

"Perfect. I will let them know it's a date," I said. "Can you get there? You don't have a car. I guess I could drive you," I told him.

Believe it or not, in the several months we had been together, I never showed my car to David. It was part of that secret—a secret that needed to be let out. But I didn't want to overwhelm him.

"I can get a ride there. You said they live over on the Westside. That's only fifteen miles or so. Bernie can drop me off; he has a car. Just give me the address, the time, and the dress code."

Dinner on Lexington

David had begun the task of applying to medical school the previous fall before I met him. He had aced his MCATs, achieving a phenomenal score, and his grades were straight A's. Money was a major consideration, with most of the top twenty schools requiring tuition approaching or exceeding fifty thousand dollars per year. Among his most ambitious applications were inquiries at Harvard, Stanford, USC, and Penn. David told me that he had also applied to Baylor in Texas, the only medical school in the top twenty-five echelon with tuition under twenty thousand dollars. So far, he had been accepted at all but Harvard and Stanford, expecting final word from the top two any day. Clearly, this week in April would be a tipping point in his life, and I had added the additional stress of dinner with the family on his already full plate.

I didn't see David that Friday; we both had full class loads, and I had a term paper due in English. We talked early Saturday morning and I gave him my address.

"Ten thousand Lexington Road, Beverly Hills 90210," he said. "That sounds very fancy."

"You will fit right in," I told him.

"Do your parents have plastic covers on their furniture?" he joked.

"No, but if it will make you feel more at home, I will see what I can do."

"I'll be there at seven o'clock in the evening as instructed. Bernie said he'd drop me, go to a movie, then come back to get me around ten o'clock. Sound okay?"

"Perfect. If we run late, I can give you a lift back to school."

"You're not spending the weekend at home?" David asked.

"I was thinking about it. I haven't spent much time with my family in months. But that's okay. If you need a ride, I'll take you. Or you can stay over."

"With you?" David was serious.

"With me, but in a guest room," I answered.

"Will you sneak in and visit?" he inquired.

"Possibly."

"I think I'll stay."

"That was a fast decision."

"I know a good offer when I hear one."

"Have you heard from the schools yet?" I asked. David had not mentioned if Harvard or Stanford contacted him on Friday.

"Can I tell you tomorrow at dinner?" he said. I knew it was good news, but I agreed to wait for word.

Following my morning phone conversation with David, I got up and opened my blinds to reveal a perfect Saturday morning. Big white cumulus clouds floated by. It had rained a bit overnight, and the earth smelled very rich. I knew that the trees were thankful since the grass in front of the dorm shimmered with dew in the bright eastern morning sunlight.

What I loved most about Saturday morning was the peace and quiet. It was as if the world had stopped and taken a breath, if only for a few hours. I was glad the week of school was finished. Term papers were a struggle for me, even with my newfound purpose in school. I wanted to do my best, so I wrote and rewrote and reedited again.

Besides being thankful for the peaceful Saturday morning, I was very grateful that I had no roommate. The young woman who shared my dorm room had lasted only a few weeks of the first semester of the school year. She dropped out, and I never got a replacement. This was such a lucky break. Plenty of the kids on the floor were envious.

By ten in the morning, I was in my car. I put the top down on the yellow Mercedes and flew out of the parking garage and up Hoover Street to catch the Santa Monica Freeway and drive west to Beverly Hills. There was no traffic; I made it home in twenty minutes.

Coming in the side door to the service porch was Marta, my beloved house-keeper, who greeted me with a big warm hug. She was doing laundry. I love the smell of Tide in the morning as much as I love the whole Saturday thing.

"Your mom and dad are having breakfast in the solarium," Marta said. "Go see them. They will be so happy."

"And how are you doing, dear Marta?"

"I am fine, missy. Really good. My son Henry is graduating sixth grade next month. Can you believe it?"

"I remember when he was born." I told her, "He is a good boy, I know. And I know you are so proud."

"Yes, very proud. Now go see your parents."

"Is Jamey home?" I asked.

"Oh, Missy Kate, Jamey went away again."

I didn't ask any more questions. Giving Marta another hug, I left her with the laundry and went to see my parents.

"Hello. Any toast and coffee left for an intruder?" I called out upon entering the solarium, to find Nancy and Dalt still dressed in robes and slippers, sharing their usual healthy breakfast of dry rye toast, egg whites, a dash of yogurt, and fresh berries.

"Oh my goodness, we didn't expect you until dinnertime," my mother said, getting up from the table to greet me. She darted over to me and put her arms around me, giving me a lasting kiss on the cheek. Nancy put both her hands on my head and pulled me in close to her. "My precious daughter, it is always such a joy to see you. Can we spend the day together since you are here early?"

"That would be great," I told her.

"Sit down and join us for breakfast. Would you rather have something else?"

"No, thank you. I'm not hungry. Toast and coffee will work just fine."

Sitting down with my parents, I had an instant and somewhat overwhelming realization of what it meant to be a child of privilege. The contrast of dorm life to the setting on Lexington struck me in a way I had never appreciated quite so deeply before.

The solarium was off the main dining room. Its walls were floor-to-ceiling paned French windows positioned in a cut-in-half hexagon, all facing the pool and formal gardens, which were blossoming with incredible first blooms-of-the-season roses, bordered by impeccably trimmed boxwood hedges.

A marble floor of alternating green and white squares, spotlessly polished by Marta and crew, sported an antique white iron table base topped by thick green beveled glass and surrounded by fully upholstered chairs covered in a pastel rose print on a white cotton background. From the white-painted wood rafters, a crystal chandelier descended over the dining table, its candelabra bulbs covered in miniature pink silk pleated shades.

Casual dining in my home still meant fine Limoges china and sterling flat-ware. There was no such thing as a paper napkin, paper cup, or paper anything.

Every meal was an occasion, a chance to celebrate life and our good fortune, our good health, and just being together. My parents knew how to live and live well. I had always known this, but at moments like this morning, seeing them in their glory, I got the message loud and clear.

"You know what I would really like to do, if it's okay with you?" I said. "Could I have some time sitting outside by the pool reading a book? Not a textbook, just a book, perhaps a novel—anything but a textbook."

"Of course, dear. Finish your coffee and toast, and the pool is all yours. We can catch up later."

"That would be super." I turned to my father and asked him about his day. Basically, I knew what to expect.

"It's Saturday lunch at the club with the boys. No golf today. I slept in, as you can see. I'm looking forward to meeting your friend this evening," my father told me.

"I think you will like him," I replied.

"I know I will," he said. "Is this serious?"

"Kind of," I said.

"Kind of serious, or just kind of something else?" he came back.

"We have known each other for a few months, but it was kind of love at first sight. We spend good quality time together, but David is getting ready to graduate and go to medical school. He is a very serious person, so this is not just a casual 'let's fool around' college dating thing."

"That sounds pretty serious," my father said. "Are you in over your head?"

"I'm in completely. If he asked me, I would marry David tomorrow," I told him, instantly regretting my honesty. I knew it would scare my father, and I didn't want him to meet David and put up his guard without getting to know him.

"Well then, I do look forward to meeting this young man. And I promise to be on good behavior." His promise was a major relief.

Nancy and Dalt finished breakfast and left the table with another hug and kiss for me. Sitting for another few minutes, I sipped the remainder of my morning coffee from the rose-patterned cup and saucer, staring out the crystal-clear windows at a garden paradise.

The Dinner Hour Arrives

Cherishing the alone time with my Pat Conroy novel by the pool, I found it to be pure heaven. Nancy returned home after lunch and began working with Marta preparing the dinner and the meet and greet with David. My presence in the kitchen was requested. I was more than happy to participate. It turned out to be one of the nicest times with my mother in a long while. We pored over recipe books, fooled with some exotic ingredients, and finally decided on doing our own version of a trendy nouvelle supper. Nancy and I made a grocery list for Marta, and she ran off to Gelson's Market for the needed supplies. Then Mother and I went to work setting a magnificent table. I chose the Spode Colonel Blue china and Nancy's Francis I sterling. She did the floral arrangements, a real talent all her own. White hydrangeas and blue irises came together, placed in multilevel twin epergnes, in the center of which was a tall Georgian sterling silver candelabra with foot-long pure white tapers. Votive candles in Lalique petal jars were sprinkled about the table. Nancy, with her exquisite cursive handwriting, created place cards written in navy-blue ink, complementing the fine embossed borders.

"How do you spell David's last name?" Mother asked.

"Morgan. It's just as it sounds."

"That's a nice name," she responded.

"He's a nice man, a really nice man," I told her.

Marta charged in, having returned from Gelson's. It was already after four o'clock. Mother was back in the kitchen preparing dinner. This time I stayed out of the way. You know what they say about too many cooks. With Marta there by her side, I knew I could exit stage left. Going upstairs to my pink room and my pink bathtub, I soaked in bubbles for what must have been a good hour in warm water. In my place of total and complete relaxation, I was ready to face anything to come at dinner. In my bubble bath state, I regretted not having clued David in to my wealthy parents and fancy home life. Would he be angry? Would it cause him to question my trustworthiness, my sincerity? Our relationship, while new, was strong. David would understand.

By six o'clock, I was dressed for dinner. The occasion called for simple, classic, and sexy. A sleeveless pale yellow silk sheath worn with a long single strand of pearls, and black patent leather sling-back heels with a pointed toe, made me feel as if I were ready for the cover of *Vogue*. Not too severe, but hopefully a head-turner for David. We were never very fancy together, never had gone on a big date for that matter, not even to a restaurant, or the theater, or anywhere other than places at school. This was all fine with me. I did not need to be taken to restaurants; I had been to them all anyway.

Coming downstairs a bit before six thirty, I found my father in the living room, sipping on a scotch he had poured in his favorite manly crystal barrel glass. Dalt was sitting in an oversized bergère chair, gazing out his enormous living room window at his manicured lawn and beyond, to the handsome street of fine homes on which he lived.

"Everything okay, Father?"

"Just fine, pumpkin. Having a moment of solitude before dinner," he said.

"This is nice of you and Mother to do this," I told him, meaning every word. I wanted them to like David, to approve of him, and even more, to be proud of him and believe in his future—our future. Tonight, was a big deal for me. If I could get through the "meet the parents" without any drama, then our relationship would have a chance to move forward on the proper trail.

The doorbell rang; it was just six thirty.

"Oh my God, he's early," I blurted out.

"Relax, baby, it's just Jefferson," my dad said. "I told him to be here at six thirty."

"Daddy, did we really have to have Jefferson? This whole deal is going to scare David back to his dumpy apartment."

"What do you mean, this whole deal?"

"You know. This house, the table Mother has set, Marta in the kitchen in uniform, and now Jefferson coming to serve."

Feeling guilty and spoiled to be complaining about my life, I stopped myself. Worse, I had known Jefferson for most my life and I adored him. Jefferson was probably well into his eighties, but he looked much younger. He was always the height of refinement, handsomely dressed in a three-piece gray suit, starched shirt, and black silk tie. Jefferson had been a jazz musician, part of the South LA black artist scene in the 1940s and '50s. Today he just wanted to work and be useful. And he clearly appreciated the money he was paid. It took him two hours by bus just to get here from his apartment in Leimert Park off South Crenshaw. When he worked late, I worried about his making it home. Nancy shared with me that Dad would send Jefferson home in a cab, and sometimes he would drive him.

The music man turned majordomo, at family gatherings, was every bit an extended family member, yet I knew little about him. I didn't know if he had a wife or children or if he lived alone in his apartment. For that matter, I didn't know much about Marta either, and she helped raise me. As close as we were, there was a very definite level of separation to our lives within our household. It may have been near the close of the twentieth century, but servants were still servants and masters were still masters.

Marta came from the kitchen and opened the door for Jefferson. The customary pleasantries were exchanged, and my dapper octogenarian houseman entered the living room to greet my father and me.

"How are you doing, sir?" he inquired. "Can I get you anything?"

"I'm just fine, Jefferson. And how are you doing, sir?" my father responded, meaning every word with respect.

"Never better," Jefferson said. He always said that. He could be near death and would always say, "Never better!"

"Big night tonight, Miss Kate?"

"Did Mother tell you?" I asked.

"She did. So, you're bringing home your beau to meet the family? I'll give him a good once-over," Jefferson offered.

We laughed.

"You do that, Jefferson," Father said. "And give me your opinion privately," he added.

Seven o'clock came and went. It was nearly seven thirty when the bell rang. Yes, I was getting nervous. David was never late, always fanatically punctual. Jefferson went to the door. We waited in the living room. Nancy had joined Dad and me for an aperitif. She looked radiant. Was it dangerous for a young woman to have such a stunning mother meeting her beau?

"Come in, young man," Jefferson greeted our special guest.

"Thank you very much," David replied.

"Right this way." Jefferson pointed David in the direction of the living room and led the way.

Jumping to my feet as soon as I saw him, I rushed over to greet David with a hug and a kiss on the cheek. Taking his left hand, I guided him in to meet the parents. They both rose as we entered. Mother spoke first as Dalton stared, as expected.

"Welcome, David. We've heard so much about you and, may I say, all of it extremely impressive," Nancy said with outstretched arms. She took David's right hand and clasped both her hands over his. This was her signature gesture, a warm and gracious hello with two hands.

"It's my pleasure to meet you," David said. "You have an amazing daughter, and frankly, I expected Kate would have an amazing family."

Very smooth, I thought. Then I introduced Dalton. This was new territory for me. I had never brought a young man home to dinner and introduced him to my parents as a boyfriend, instead of just a classmate or one of the gang.

My father was warm and generous too, with none of the grilling I feared would take place. Instead, we all sat down and shared a drink, served by Jefferson and delivered on a silver tray. Each cocktail glass arrived with a small square folded Irish linen napkin with a lace edge underneath and was presented one at a time to each of us. Marta appeared with hors d'oeuvres, Nancy's famous crab dip with a special Italian cream cheese, among other delicious nibbles.

Our initial conversation was typical break-the-ice small talk. We got through the basics, and then I asked the question of the night.

"David, did you hear from Harvard or Stanford today?"

"I did, in fact. I got letters from both, as well as email correspondence." David seemed overly reserved.

"Do you mind my asking?"

"Not at all. We've been waiting for this news together; it's perfect that you are the first to know."

"I can't stand waiting any longer," I said, almost screaming.

"I was accepted, sort of, at both."

"Sort of? What does *sort of* mean?"

"I am wait-listed," David said.

"But it's the end of the acceptance period," I objected.

"That's just it. Both schools are still formulating their classes for the coming year. They are waiting for word from students who, like me, have applied to multiple schools. When the dust settles, it is likely that I will gain admittance to one of them."

"This is so difficult," I said. "So, it's not really settled then, is it?"

"Well, it is settled. I've made a decision," David answered.

"Really?"

"I'm going to accept admittance to Baylor in Texas."

"You said you were impressed with Baylor. What made you decide?" I pressed on.

Mother and Dad were listening quietly, not offering one word.

"You know how I struggled to find the appropriate topic for my application essay?" David asked me.

"Of course, I do, and I believe your essay was inspiring—both thoughtful and brave."

"It is why I chose Baylor," he said.

Dad interjected at this point.

"Would you tell us about the topic of your essay?"

"I am concerned that America is facing a potential crisis in the field of medical care. As the population grows exponentially over the next several decades, the number of physicians will not meet the needs of the population."

"I've read about that recently," Father responded.

"Part of the challenge is the changing demographics of med school applicants. A far greater number of foreign students are taking spots in our med schools, with many taking the education back to their native countries. The second part of that equation is the cost. Too many American students are deciding to follow other careers because the cost of med school is daunting, and they do not wish to graduate with half a million dollars in debt as they face a career that may not provide the level of income it once did."

"I see your point," Father followed. "So, what did your essay offer?"

"I proposed that the United States federal government should cover the cost of med school for qualified US citizens in exchange for a promise to practice in the United States. Further, I suggested additional government support for new doctors who choose to live and practice in regions underserved, remote, and without proper medical care."

"That is a very serious proposal," Father said.

"I know, and I know it sounds extremely socialist in the realm of political dialogue. I am not a socialist. In fact, despite my liberal upbringing, I am rather conservative. But I believe this matter deserves serious attention and possible government oversight."

Jefferson entered the living room and announced that dinner was served.

"Let's continue this discussion at the table." Father instructed us to rise and make our way to the dining room.

Let the Dinner Service Begin

Jefferson arrived at the double doors, intending to open the dining room ahead of us. Standing at the center of the entryway, the dapper old gent gracefully pushed the two doors open to reveal another one of Mother Nancy's triumphs. The elegant table, set to magazine photo-spread-quality perfection, was glowing with candlelight from the tall tapers at the center of the table, joined by the sea of sparkling votives. This fairy tale of shimmering golden rays was enhanced by the gas logs aflame in the grand Regency-design fireplace at the direct head of the dining table, flanked on both sides by nine-foot-tall French doors leading out to a dining terrace surrounded by Nancy's ever-expanding rose garden.

Nancy took over as we entered.

"David, please sit here next to Kate. Dalt and I will sit across from both of you," she instructed.

David pulled out my chair. I sat down first. Jefferson was table side instantly, offering a selection of wine. Even though I was not twenty-one, wine was served at our table, in moderation, since we were eighteen. David glanced at me as if to say, *This does not happen in my house.* I got the nonverbal message.

A first course of very thinly sliced salmon carpaccio carved in a circular pattern and plated on an oversized white china charger with gold-painted rim and boasting the Fairchild monogram was served in front of us. Jefferson assisted, selecting the proper forks and handing one to each person individually.

"David, please finish your explanation about selecting a medical school," Father asked.

"As I mentioned, I decided to attend Baylor in Texas," David announced.

I was surprised; it was not the most prestigious school among all that had accepted him. Honestly, what I was really thinking was what I was going to do in Texas. I said nothing.

"Among all the top med schools, Baylor is the only one with affordable tuition, less than twenty thousand dollars per year than most schools, which are double or triple the cost. My parents are teachers and cannot afford to financially support me in reaching my goal. And I do not want to be strapped with loans, as that may influence my future path. Baylor is a very fine school. So, Baylor, here comes David Morgan."

"Sounds like a very wise move," Dalt said.

I was still thinking about my life in Texas. *Can I transfer to Baylor undergrad and finish my last two years there?*

Marta entered the dining room through the butler's pantry connected to the kitchen. She went to Dalt and whispered in his ear that he needed to come to the telephone at once. Father excused himself and followed Marta into the kitchen.

He returned in a matter of seconds and apologized, telling us that the dinner needed to end abruptly.

"What is the matter, dear?" Nancy asked.

"The clinic requires us there at once," he said, looking very concerned. "The police have been called. We need to go now."

"Daddy, is Jamey all right?" I asked.

"No, he's not all right, but hopefully he will be okay. You and David stay and have dinner. I'll call you as soon as I know anything."

"No. I'm coming," I said. "Whatever is happening, we will face it as a family." I got up from the table with my parents. David stood as well.

"May I come? I don't want to be in the way," he said.

Father and Mother were already out the door. I told him to come, and I told him I was sorry.

"Don't be sorry. I want to be there for you, good times or bad," he said.

I was in love with this man. He was special. And I hoped he knew how much I cared.

Crisis at the Sea View Clinic

We raced west on Sunset Boulevard; Dad ran every red light he could manage without causing a crash. It was another fifteen-minute drive north on the Pacific Coast Highway up to the southern edge of Malibu and the Sea View Rehabilitation Clinic, where Jamey and another hundred or more teens had been placed in the hopes of reversing the curse of drug addiction. Jamey had been there a couple of times before with some improvement, but he always fell short of a clean slate.

The tires on Dalt's black Mercedes came to a screeching halt in the circular driveway of Sea View. The building looked more like some interpretation of a Roman spa in Las Vegas than a drug clinic. Grecian columns lined the front portico, and a rather gaudy fountain was in the center of the driveway, with cherubs spitting water in all directions. Gas lanterns flickered, and the place even had recorded symphonic chamber music broadcasting from speakers in the planters at the front door. Very odd, almost scary, but this was Malibu, and many of the patients were showbiz legacies. The drama had its place, I guess.

We raced in through the front door and found the police waiting for us. They instructed us to follow them to Jamey's room, where we found another half dozen police and other serious-looking people.

"What's going on?" I protested.

I did not get an answer.

That's when we saw what was happening. I screamed so loud that several of the police officers jumped.

David grabbed me and turned me away. I struggled to turn back around.

"Are you sure you want to see this?" he asked sternly.

"I'm sure. What can we do?" I was now crying.

Jamey was holding a large knife at his throat and threatening to kill himself.

"I cannot take this anymore," he called out. "My life is over!"

"Your life is only just beginning," called out the police suicide negotiator. His voice was calm, almost too calm. It made Jamey angrier. My brother was messed up, but not stupid.

"Shut the fuck up," he yelled back at the negotiator. "What the fuck do you know? I'm a prisoner of these fucking drugs, and I can't free myself from feeling terrible all the time. All of you, get out. Get the fuck out and leave me alone!"

Nancy was shaking and holding on to Dalt. He turned her away so she could not see her son. I loved my parents, and I had pretty much always appreciated them for who they were and what they did. Jamey's drug addiction was not their fault, yet at this moment at a life-or-death crossroads, I wished that they were in front of the police, not behind them being discreet.

Jamey lunged forward on the bed. As he moved, the front line of police jumped forward in attack mode.

"Get the fuck back," he screamed, "or you will all be covered in my blood!"

Brandishing the kitchen knife that he had somehow managed to confiscate from the so-called secure kitchen at Sea View, Jamey again taunted the police, threatening to end his life in as gruesome a manner as possible.

The negotiator kept talking, *Blah, blah, blah* ... Jamey wasn't listening, and neither were David and I, as we stood up front and to the side of the talking suicide prevention expert. In this moment of panic, I wondered how many victims had jumped off the roof as this man attempted to calm them. Clearly his training was not working.

I couldn't hold back any longer.

"Shut up," I yelled at the negotiator.

"Jamey, it's me, Kate. I love you so much, Jamey. Don't do this," I pleaded.

"Kate, I am so sorry, but I just can't stand it anymore. I love you too. This is not your fault, and it's not Mom and Dad's fault. It's nobody's fault."

"We can fix this together. We will get you better, I promise. We have our lives to live and be together. We have children to make when we each marry, children who will be first cousins. You and I are all we have. There are no two people in the universe as close as we are as brother and sister."

Jamey was now sobbing hysterically. His hand shook, and the knife wobbled. The police were looking at one another as if to plan a rush, but the negotiator was in charge, and he held them off.

"Keep talking to him," the negotiator directed me under his breath.

"Jamey, you promised me that we would go to Newport this summer and spend a week at the beach house, just the two of us. You promised me a ride on the Ferris wheel at Balboa. You promised me Chinese food on the island. You promised me we would sit on the sand and do nothing together. You promised me all of this." I was crying now and, like my mother, trying to be discreet. Yes, I was like my mother, for better or for worse.

David put his arm around me.

"Jamey, this is David. You haven't met him. I'm in love with David, and you will love him too. Please, Jamey, please put down the knife. You will love David like a brother. He is going to be a doctor. David will be your very own proud doctor brother. There is nothing he cannot cure. He will cure you, I promise. I really do promise. Please."

Jamey was slumped over on the bed, his head down, his chin on his chest. The knife was still in his hand, in his outstretched arm, and pointed at his throat.

"Shall we rush him now?" the head cop whispered to the negotiator.

"Not yet," he replied in a hush. "We are making progress."

"This is not progress," I protested.

At that moment, David got down on his hands and knees and crawled toward Jamey as quietly as possible so that Jamey would not see him or hear him. I kept pleading with my brother to distract him.

David reached the side of Jamey's bed and jumped up like a ninja, yanking the knife out of Jamey's hand, causing it to fall to the floor. David threw his arms around my brother and held him tight. The police, the doctors, the Sea View staff, and my parents rushed in.

David was crying with my brother. I heard David whisper in Jamey's ear, "Can I come to Newport with you and Kate this summer?"

The doctor immediately administered a sedative while aides restrained Jamey, laying him back down on the bed. Nancy and Dalt surrounded him, with Mother practically getting in the bed next to him, as she held him and stroked his head.

The cops and their negotiator backed off, leaving us alone with Jamey and the clinic staff. Taking Dalt aside, the police captain gave him the lowdown on what was going to happen next following the filing of their report. Dalt listened with patience, professional as always, but he didn't hear a word of the *blah, blah, blah.* I think I even heard him say "Whatever" in response to the diatribe.

For the moment, the Sea View staff were moving Jamey to a secure room and placing him on suicide watch. He would remain restrained and sedated until a plan could be decided on to provide him the help he needed, both medical and psychological. Almost immediately, the first strong dose of sedative kicked in. Jamey's eyes closed, and he slept.

Before leaving, the police captain scolded David. "You could have been killed," he said. "And your actions could have led to Jamey's death or possible harm to any of us."

"You are a hero, David. You saved my brother's life," I said, interrupting. Then I called out to others in the area who could hear, "David Morgan is a hero. He saved Jamey Fairchild. We need to get Jamey Fairchild out of this horrible place that clearly cannot protect its patients."

Everyone froze as my tirade had touched a sensitive nerve. I was not sorry for saying what I had said.

"Dad, we must get Jamey out of here as soon as possible. It's not safe."

"We will, Kate. I'm bringing him home as soon as I can arrange it. We will have twenty-four-hour help and security as well. Jamey is coming home, and your mother and I will be on duty as we have never been before."

Dad turned to David and hugged him. "You are a hero, David. We will be forever grateful. Boy, some way to meet the parents. And you didn't even get to finish dinner." The levity may have been a moment of black comedic icebreaking, but it got us all to smile.

Orderlies were moving Jamey to the secure room. Nancy insisted on staying the night with him. They objected at first but finally relented when Dalt joined the protest.

"Twenty-five thousand a month and you won't provide two cots for us?" Dad always knew how to go for the jugular when appropriate.

"Love you, Kate." Dalt hugged me and told me to take the car and go home with David. "I'm sure Marta and Jefferson are waiting for word. I'll call them and tell them you are on the way home. Try not to upset them too much with the news."

David was a gentleman and drove Dad's car. I was still shaking somewhat and breaking into sobs, alternating with moments of relief. We made it back to Lexington. It was now close to the midnight hour. Marta prepared food and Jefferson, still in his three-piece suit, asked us what we needed. I told Jefferson that it was too late for him to travel back to his apartment, and I requested that he stay overnight in one of the staff rooms. He looked tired. Marta showed him to a bedroom and returned to the table.

David and I were nibbling. Neither one of us could really eat much. Marta asked what had happened, and we told her.

She began to tear up.

"I'm so sad," she said. "He is such a sweet boy. Not a mean bone in his body. He'd give you his last peso." Marta was a second mom to us; she had been there from the beginning.

"Thank you for holding dinner, dear Marta, but I don't think we can eat. It's late. You should go to bed. We will do the same. I think I will put my head down on the table and close my eyes if I don't go to bed."

Marta came around and kissed both David and me good night.

"Gracias, Senor David, for saving my Jamey," were her final words before she headed to her room.

"I have to lie down, David. Will you stay with me?" I asked. David nodded and took my hand. We got up from the table. I led him upstairs to my room, where I lay down on my very pink and white four-poster canopy double bed that was raised up so high off the floor that it required a white-painted two-step stool to enter.

Not bothering to remove my clothing, I assumed the prone position and placed my head on two very soft feather pillows. I motioned for David to come and join me, which he did.

We lay next to one another, fully clothed, lights still on, staring at the underside of the white lace canopy atop the bed. Nothing was said. David kissed me gently and put his arm around my waist. We both drifted into sleep.

Despite the tragic circumstance, it was the most romantic night without sex I had ever experienced—something I had never imagined. We both awoke Sunday morning around ten o'clock.

"Good morning," I offered softly. "Now what do we do?" I asked.

David replied, "First, we get coffee. Then, we live life to the fullest, and we thank God for miracles and for the blessings we have."

CHAPTER FOUR

A LEFT TURN IN LIFE

A month had passed since my brother's attempted suicide. He was now home under full watch and with twenty-four-hour care. Nancy and Dalt adapted their lives to save their son. He was making progress—slow progress, painful and challenging progress. There was no room for failure. My parents would never give up, though they didn't accept responsibility for Jamey's poor choices in life. I thought about this a lot.

Nancy and Dalt did not ignore us. I think it is far too easy to blame the parents, especially if they are rich. Yes, we had nannies and a maid who helped raise us, but we were never the stereotypical latchkey kids of the selfish wealthy, who are always taking care of themselves first.

Jamey had gotten into drugs because they were everywhere. At school, at Little League, at church, and at Boy Scouts, drugs were cool and available. Like every kid, Jamey thought it was no big deal at first, figuring he could handle it. But his secret grew along with his addiction. For a time, Nancy and Dalt thought Jamey was going through a rebellious period upon entering his teen years. I was away at prep school, or I would have known and would have raised the roof. I felt guilty about that. I know it's crazy, but I did.

Late spring in Los Angeles is probably the envy of the nation, as I mentioned before. I found it hard to concentrate on school and study for finals. Everything was blooming, especially the amazing jacaranda trees with their periwinkle-blue buds. The sky was another shade of blue, deep robin's egg, with marshmallow cotton cumulus clouds floating by. From my dorm room window, I could see the San Gabriel Mountains in the distance behind downtown LA, so crisp and close that I wanted to reach out and touch them. Where did the smog go on days like this one, and how did it return so quickly?

David and I had grown even closer since the Jamey scare. Our semiregular afternoon lovemaking was the most important time of my life. And we talked more these days—talked about everything. This was love; it was real.

One thing we did not talk about was our future. Our love was in the moment, day to day. David did not bring up what we were going to do next fall when he would be starting med school at Baylor. I knew he was under great pressure finishing his senior year and figuring out where the money would come from moving forward. So, I did not bring it up. All I knew was that I was going with him, one way or another. The details would be figured out later.

Confident of my plan, I did not register for fall classes at USC. Remaining a good student, I studied to ace my finals and end the year with a 4.0 grade point average. David would be proud; my parents would be proud. And yes, I was proud of myself.

The phone rang in my dorm at eight o'clock on Friday morning. I was awake, dressed, and about to leave for class.

"Kate, it's me, David. Can you meet me at our bench in Doheny Park at eleven o'clock?"

"Sure, okay. I'm out of class by then. What's up, David?"

"I need to talk to you about our future, or should I say, we need to talk about it—and we've been avoiding the subject."

"Yes. Okay. We have. I would like to talk about it. The bench in the park by the fountain is perfect. See you at eleven. I love you."

"I love you too."

David hung up. I ran off to class. This was going to be it. We would plan our future in Texas in the fall. I didn't think he would propose. The timing was not right, even though I would say yes, yes, yes. I didn't care if he couldn't afford a ring. I didn't care if we had to live in student housing. I'd get a job and go to school. We wouldn't need to be starving students; I had a trust fund that could support us very nicely. David would never go for that, but I didn't care.

I did not hear one word spoken by my psych professor in class Friday morning. Checking my watch every ten minutes, I felt that the two-hour session would never end. Making matters worse, the teacher asked us to stay an extra fifteen minutes to watch a video. I was dying.

Running out of class the second we were dismissed, I headed back to my room to change clothes, comb my hair, and do all that important female stuff before meeting the love of my life to plan my future. It was nearly ten thirty.

Should I be late, just a little late, on purpose? No time to start playing games. What was I thinking? I left my room at a quarter to eleven and made my way to the park, at most a five-minute walk through the jacarandas, now in full blossom, their wispy flowers falling all over the brick pathway leading to Doheny Park.

Arriving at our bench first, I sat down and put on my sunglasses to avoid the sharp beams of the midday rays stabbing through the old sycamore trees, which were sprouting fresh green springtime leaves. The aroma of the musky leaves mixed with the wafting breeze was enhanced by the cold clear water coming from the central fountain a few feet in front of our bench. It was our bench, David's and mine, the bench where we had spent a few minutes the day we first met in the cafeteria. Now, on this bench, in a few short minutes, we would plan our lives together. It felt so right, so good. I don't think I had ever been happier, more confident, or more at ease.

David was coming around the corner. I saw him walking fast. It was just eleven o'clock.

As I jumped up to greet him, he put his arms around me and kissed me gently.

"Hello, my amazing girlfriend Kate," he said. Not a bad start.

"How was your class this morning?" I asked, being nonchalant. Of course, I wanted to say, *When are we moving to Texas?*

"I have something important to discuss," David came back, his tone serious.

"I know. We need to talk about our future." I returned the serious tone and got right to the point.

"Over the past few weeks, I have thought about little else," David replied, taking my hand and moving in right next to me on the bench.

"Why have you not shared with me?" I said, looking right into his eyes.

"I have thought about that too, but I didn't want to give you any added stress during your finals. You are the most unselfish girl, which, I might add, is saying something given what I know about your life."

We both laughed.

"Which is also why what I have to say hurts. Hurts like I have never hurt before. And considering how unselfish you are, what I am going to say is probably the most selfish thing I have ever said and done."

I interrupted him before he could go on. "David, you don't need to say a word. I do not expect a proposal. I know we're too young and that you have too many years of school ahead of you. I just want to be with you, to live with you at Baylor, to support you and be there for you."

David was silent. The moment was deadly.

"I know," he finally spoke. "But I can't do it. I love you, but I can't make that commitment right now. I want to go to med school and devote my entire life to the experience. I'm afraid I would be a terrible lover and a distant friend, and ultimately it would destroy us and hurt you."

"Are you breaking up with me, David?"

"I am. Our timing is star-crossed. You are just nineteen and I am twenty-one. If we were five years older, and if I were finished with med school and starting residency, and if you were finished with school as well and pursuing a career, it would be different."

"But I love you more than anyone I have ever loved. I don't care about our ages or our place in life. We have something so special, so real, impossible to find. This might be the one and only time we each have this kind of love. I think my heart is breaking. Really breaking."

We were both crying now, holding one another.

"I am so sorry," David kept repeating. "So sorry."

"Can we table this for a few days and think about it?" I asked, trying to hold back my tears. "You have not given me a chance to share my plans, my vision of how this can work."

"Kate, have you not heard all the stories about girlfriends supporting their guys in med school only to be dumped at the end? It's just too stressful, and the stories are many and accurate. I love you too much to do that to you. You are too young. Your life is an open book. I promise there will be another great love, a greater love, when the time is right. You will marry and have beautiful children and the most wonderful life. I promise you this."

"All I want is you, David."

"Let me walk you back to your dorm. We can talk again tomorrow."

David got up. I followed. He put his arm around my waist. We walked back down the brick path frosted with an inch of blue jacaranda blossoms. They were no longer beautiful to me, only dying blooms on the ground that we were crushing as we made our way through.

David held me tight for at least five minutes before kissing me goodbye at the door to my dorm lobby.

"I love you, Kate. I will always love you," he said, turning away to leave.

I ran up five flights of stairs to my room, avoiding the elevator and anyone who might possibly be in it. Fumbling with my keys to open the door, I entered and flung myself onto my bed, facedown, sobbing.

Eventually I fell asleep, coming back to life in the dark of night. It was nine o'clock. My pillow was drenched with tears. I tried to escape my sadness for the remainder of the worst Friday night of my life. Unable to sleep any more, I found a bottle of water in my dorm room fridge, which I drank as if I had spent forty years wandering in the desert.

Staring up at the popcorn ceiling, my thoughts racing, and my mood bouncing between calm/sensible and hysterical/crazy, I picked up the phone and dialed David. The phone rang forever. Finally, the voice mail picked up.

"I love you," I said, hanging up.

Unable to stare at that popcorn ceiling for another minute, I dashed out of my room and went for my car in the parking lot next door. Driving past the guardhouse and over speed bumps, I flew out of the gated garage like Mario Andretti and found myself on Figueroa Street. The convertible top was down, and my hair was whipping against my face in the night air. Heading for Beverly Hills, I wanted to go home like a wounded animal going back to its cave, a pigeon returning to the roost.

Approaching the Robertson Avenue exit on the Santa Monica Freeway, I floored the accelerator and moved into the fast lane. There was no way I could go home. Going home meant failure. Besides, my parents had their hands full with my brother, Jamey. Instead, the Pacific Ocean was calling. A few more miles down the freeway, I would find some peace at the beach in Santa Monica. No one would be on the sand. Coming through the tunnel at the end of the freeway that revealed the ocean, I could smell the Pacific. The shimmering lights from homes bordering the Pacific Coast Highway up to Malibu always enchanted me when our family would take a night drive up the coast. This was familiar medicine, and it delivered a healing effect.

After parking the car in the lot adjacent to the Riviera Club, I jumped out and ran toward the sand. The Riviera Club is a private sandbox for the Beverly Hills and Bel Air rich. By about ten o'clock, the last of the Friday night diners were leaving, well fed and very sedated. I would not be stopped by anyone as I ran toward the shoreline.

Getting closer to the water, I began stripping off my clothes. At the ocean's edge I was wearing nothing but my panties, which I removed and then ran into the surf. It was cold, probably in the sixties. I didn't care. I swam out about twenty feet beyond the soft-breaking waves and began to swim laps south with the current as if I were in the Olympics. Pushing harder and harder, I was heading toward the Santa Monica Pier, a good mile or more down current. The lights of the Ferris wheel on the pier bounced off the dark water in front of me. Beginning to feel numb, the cold water taking its toll, I was also beginning to feel no pain, my mind putting David's betrayal in a closed compartment, sealed and locked.

Suddenly a strong beam of light hit me and a loudspeaker blared, breaking my sense of abandon. The security patrol on the beach had spotted me.

"No swimming allowed after dark. Come in at once. Come in at once or we will have to come and get you and you will be arrested." The loudspeaker was clear. I had my orders.

Swimming into shore, letting the waves guide me, I took my time to float in, albeit still obeying orders. The light shone on me all the way.

Making it to the sand, trying to be as graceful and modest as possible, I stood up in the tide, revealing my state of undress. Placing my left hand over my vulva and my right arm across my breasts, I walked out of the surf, still fully illuminated, toward the beach patrol.

My silhouette glowed with an aura of light around my flesh. Holding my head high, I approached the men in their Jeep.

"I'm sorry to have bothered you," I said. "I really didn't expect to see anyone here. I just wanted to go for a swim. It was a momentary split decision, nothing planned."

"Where are your clothes?" one of the officers asked.

"Just down the beach by the Riviera Club," I answered. "I left them in the sand."

"Are you allright?" another man asked.

"Yes, I'm fine. I'm really sorry to have bothered you."

"Here, wrap this around you." The first guy handed me a blanket. "Hop in. We'll take you up the beach to find your clothes."

The Jeep raced up the sand. My clothing appeared in its strong headlights. The driver stopped the Jeep by the water. Having been first to see my panties, I jumped out and ran to retrieve them.

"Do you need help?" one of the beach patrol guys called out.

"No, I'm okay," I said, slipping my underwear back on, trying to keep the blanket in place.

"We are supposed to cite you," he called out.

"Do what you must," I answered, following the trail of my clothes back up the sand toward the Riviera Club parking lot.

"That's okay. Let this time be a warning. It's too dangerous to swim in the ocean after dark. Are you sure you're okay? Do you have a car to get home?"

"I do have a car. And I am fine. Thanks for being gentlemen" were my final words as I made it to the blacktop and got back in my car.

The ocean swim had been a sort of cleansing, a baptism of fire. I felt renewed. Shivering from the cold water and brisk night air, I pulled my wet hair off my face and drove back to school. Tomorrow would be another chance to talk to David. I was not ready to give up all hope.

Tomorrow never came with the great love of my life. We never talked. I received a letter the following week from David. He had written that this was his only option, adding I would someday understand. The letter ended with his love; he wrote that he had never loved anyone more. And then he wrote, "Goodbye."

CHAPTER FIVE

CHANGING COURSE

The semester ended, and despite my catatonic state most of the time, I did manage to collect that 4.0 grade point average to close my sophomore year. In fact, since I barely left my room, hardly ate, and did nothing but read and study, my success came as no surprise. I'd had no contact with David that final month of spring in Los Angeles. Oh my God, I wanted to call. Desperate to see him, I walked past his apartment one afternoon and waited outside. He wasn't there. That was my only attempt. If I were to repeat the walk-by, I feared I'd join the ranks of stalkers.

Graduation day arrived, and I did the worst possible thing I could do: I went. And yes, I went to the specific graduation ceremony for biology majors following the main ceremony in Doheny Park. David was there being embraced by people who must have been his parents and his sisters. I stayed back so they would not see me. The few brief speeches from the faculty ended, and the crowd mingled over coffee and cake. David was standing alone for a moment, eating a cookie, while his parents talked to the dean. This was my moment to go to him with congratulations. I had prepared my speech, going over my words again and again. I was ready. It was going to be simple and sweet, nothing dramatic. But instead of speaking to him, I looked at him one more time, then turned and walked away. I had been carrying one red rose that I planned to hand to him with my speech. That rose went flying into the hedge as I left the reception.

It was time to face the fact that it was over, time for me to reinvent, change course. Was this my time to abandon security and go to Paris to find a job in the fashion industry? There was one serious obstacle to this plan. It was brother, Jamey. I was filling in on weekends whenever possible, helping my parents with my brother. Nancy and Dalt said he responded to me better than anyone else. I could not leave him now to chase my dream.

So, I did the next best thing I could come up with. Knowing I could not face another year at USC or remain in LA and move home to Beverly Hills full time, I asked my parents if I could move to the beach house in Newport. I would find a job there and eventually enroll in college in Orange County to finish my degree. My telling Dalt I would investigate Chapman University pleased him as he was a big fan of the small private school in the OC.

Given that they were aware of my emotional breakup with David, my parents granted me residence in Newport. I promised to continue coming home often to be with Jamey. I also suggested that when appropriate, he could come down to the beach and spend time with me there.

"That's a wonderful and generous thought, but I feel it's a long way off," Nancy told me. I knew she was right. Jamey remained in bad shape. Making his condition worse, his doctors were predicting that the drugs had triggered either the onset of early Parkinson's disease or a form of bipolar syndrome—or both. It was too soon to be certain. They were monitoring Jamey continuously.

Paris would wait yet again. My substitute destination would be a 1920s-era Cape Cod–style clapboard bungalow on the sand facing the low dunes fronting Newport's Pacific Rim. Nancy had remodeled the cottage to *Architectural Digest* perfection. The operative word was *charm*.

Arriving in Newport on a Monday following the grad ceremony at the end of the semester, I pulled my car into the garage, turned off the engine, and cried. The tears came out of nowhere. I had not cried over David in at least a week. Here I was in this beautiful place at the start of a summer on the beach that any nineteen-year-old American kid would kill for, and I was crying.

My car was packed with clothes and books and just about everything from my dorm room—whatever I could cram into it. Rather than attend to the organizational needs at hand, I got out of the car and went into the house.

I should have known that my mother would do her handiwork in advance of my arrival. Fresh flowers were in every room. The fireplaces, which were throughout the cottage, were stocked with raw cut timber. The panes of the French windows sparkled, and the scent of Windex guaranteed they had just been polished. In the kitchen, the fridge was filled with my favorite fresh pulpy squeezed orange juice, Greek yogurt, berries, pineapple, cottage cheese, salads, and veggies galore, along with a covered casserole of Nancy's chicken and broccoli, my absolute favorite. I opened the freezer and there it was, a commercial for Häagen-Dazs ice cream. Every flavor made was perfectly lined up on each shelf. It was enough to last a lifetime, or at least a summer on the shore.

It was difficult to be miserable and crying in this cottage. The midday sun streamed in through the spotless glass panes of the living room French doors facing the sand. I sank into the down-filled sofa, navy-blue and white stripes, by the fireplace. A painting over the mantel by Laguna Beach, California, impressionist John Botz featured the same blue and white sofa surrounded by blue and white Chinese jars bursting forth with pastel hydrangea blooms. Nancy had placed a pair of Chinese jars performing the same task on either end of the mantel.

Getting off the couch and opening the French doors to the ocean, I allowed a gentle breeze to join me in the cottage. A chandelier fashioned of seashells hung from the center of the white-painted wood rafters in the living room. The breeze set the shells to clinking. I inhaled the sea air coming off the ocean. An unusually strong current provided the music of surf crashing on the beach.

Going back to the garage, I began the task of unpacking the car. The memory of happy times spent in this house as a child overshadowed any fear of the unknown as I set up my room upstairs in the back of the house over the garage. This was the room I'd always wanted but was not allowed to have because it was separate from the rest of the bedrooms upstairs. Kind of a guest quarters with its own rickety wood stairs down the side. The room was enormous with a vaulted wood ceiling, all pained white, of course. There was a used brick fireplace surrounded by an antique carved pine mantel that matched the wide-plank pine floors complete with knots. A Victorian-era white iron double bed boasted at least a dozen feather pillows covered in various Pierre Deux chintz fabrics, and an upholstered chaise lounge placed beside a tall arched window covered in sheer white silk panels was the ideal spot to read my latest book. I was always a reader—two books a week, generally. Placed on the chaise was a bag from Barnes and Noble filled with a dozen current best sellers. The note on top read, "Read on, darling. You are my dearest girl. Love, Mother."

Newport is just an hour south of LA on the Pacific Coast Highway. Coming to the beach for an occasional weekend or an extended summer vacation, I had never connected with the Newport scene. After all, I was a kid on vacation at the beach. What I cared about was sand, surf, boys, and especially the Newport lifeguards in their red and white uniforms. I was also a big fan of pizza on the Newport pier at dusk, watching the lights on the coast come alive, flickering like some very long diamond necklace.

The best part of the day at the beach was catching the bright green flash of light made by the sun as it faded into the ocean over the horizon. We would all gather on the pier and watch, eating our pizza and staring out toward the western edge of the universe, waiting. The one who saw the green flash coming first would scream out as if they were witnessing Santa Claus arrive on the rooftop on Christmas Eve. We would giggle with sheer delight at the fleeting moment, only seconds, when nature would flash that neon-green sight on the horizon over the disappearing sun. This was the Newport I had known and loved as a child.

Arriving here as an adult, moving into my parents' sandbox, about to celebrate twenty years on the planet, I quickly realized that I was not in Los Angeles anymore. It didn't take long for me to face the fact that I was in another world.

June passed quickly. I didn't do much, just checked out the territory. Where I had landed was what I imagined was a 1950s version of LA, even though we were approaching the second millennium. There was no traffic in Newport; parking was free and easy just about anywhere; the only crime was the occasional bike theft at the beach; and the weather was incredibly perfect. When it rained, which was rare, it only rained in the night. I awakened to blue skies and warm breezes and that smell of night rain having washed down the earth.

Most all the buildings in Newport are beige. I call them faux Mediterranean. They are new, with perfectly manicured landscaping. There is no such thing as vintage here, except for my parents' old cottage on the sand. Shopping centers are everywhere, on corners and avenues wherever one turns. The big draws are super-malls called Fashion Plaza and the Hagstrom Center, each competing for the biggest and best names in retail. Rodeo Drive meets Fifth Avenue on the way to Worth Avenue, all under two distinct roofs not far from the beach. I learned quickly that your car can automatically veer in either direction for a little shopping, a bite of dinner, socializing (of which there was plenty), and taking the community pulse.

There was something else unique about Newport. I saw only white people. Where were all the black people? Oh, and another thing: it seemed that everyone went to church. At least they talked about it a lot. In LA, people didn't talk about going to church. I didn't know too many people who went to church on a regular basis. In Newport, Jesus thrives.

The white Christian majority was also largely conservative, and their traditional views were nationally known. As a kid, when I and my family came to Newport on holiday, we were "behind the Orange Curtain." Yet never once had I considered any of this when I decided to run away and leave USC. Why would I care? After all, I just needed a change, and this was a simple solution. Besides, I was not some raving liberal. My parents were Republican. I felt comfortable in a conservative shell even though I liked to think of myself as open-minded and independent of staunch political ideology, strict religious belief, or for that matter labels of any kind. This was the era of the millennials after all. We were changing the world.

Meeting the Neighbor; Making a Friend

I also quickly realized that Newport was a town of families. Most people here were married, looking to get married, or recently unmarried and looking for something new. A single woman barely twenty did not fit right into the mainstream. At least not the adult scene. There were plenty of young people living at the beach. Most were college students, or student dropouts working as waiters, valets, bartenders, or surfboard salespeople. This was not my crowd. I had no interest in the freewheeling drinking and drug-sharing beach party crowd. Frankly, my hair is not blonde enough, my skin is not peeling enough from too much sun, I am not anorexically thin, and I do not favor tank tops and booty shorts as my daily choice of raiment. Oh, and I have not had serious breast enhancement. My God, Newport is the land of protruding mammaries. By young and old alike, the breast is worshipped.

The doorbell rang at around eleven in the morning on Saturday. I was upstairs in my room over the garage, but I could hear the ringing.

I came out onto the landing off my room to peek down and see who was there.

"Hello," I called out. "I'm up here over the garage. Can I help you?"

A cute blonde, the kind that is everywhere, with those special breasts, wearing a tank top, shorts, and high-heel mules, turned and looked up at me. I could see that she was in full makeup, with the big eyelashes and all, even though was eleven o'clock on a Saturday morning at the beach.

"Hi up there. I'm Carrie. I live next door," she called out. "I've come to say hello and bring you a little something."

Carrie was holding a large basket overflowing with treats.

"I'll be right down," I called out.

After undressing, I grabbed my robe and slippers, which were not easy to find in the mess that represented my worldly goods not properly unpacked. Mother Nancy would be horrified that I was still living amid piles and disorder.

Running my hands through my hair, with no time for makeup, I dashed down my rickety stairs to meet Carrie.

"Gosh, how nice of you to come by. You didn't need to bring anything," I told her as I reached the front door of the cottage. I had left it unlocked—something you could do in Newport but that was unheard of in LA. I ushered her in.

Putting the basket down, which was overflowing with wine, cheese, and gourmet breads, I asked Carrie to sit down in the living room as I opened the French doors to the sand and the morning breeze off the Pacific.

"Can I get you something to drink? How about iced tea or orange juice?"

"Nothing. I'm just fine," she said.

"Have you lived here long?" I asked. Carried looked a little older than me, but not much. This was a good sign. Perhaps I might have a friend next door.

"My husband Joe and I have lived at the beach since we married six years ago," Carried shared. I thought she was a lucky young woman living in a million-dollar beachfront home as a newlywed.

"I don't think I've ever seen Joe around," I said.

"You probably have. He's around a lot. In fact, he's out on the beach pretty much every morning either swimming or surfing."

"I hope I'm not being rude, but does he work?"

Carried laughed. "Joe is turning seventy this year. I'm his third wife. We met when I was just twenty-one and got married about a year later. He has three grown sons and a daughter, all of them in their forties. Can I tell you, they're not too crazy about me, but they put on a good show for their dad at least, probably with an eye toward their inheritance?"

This was another oddity about Newport. People were open and friendly, and there was no holding back family secrets. I was not prepared for this. Yet, there was sincerity. Carrie just wanted to lay her cards on the table. It was kind of like, add a little personal drama to the cocktail and mix, and there you go—instant pals.

This was okay with me. Sharing superpersonal stuff was new to me, but I liked it.

"You've been married six years, you said. Do you have any children?" Part of me couldn't believe I was asking personal questions.

"No kids. But I would really like one. At least one," Carrie told me in a quiet voice. "There's a problem," she went on. "Joe is impotent. The most handsome and virile man you'll ever meet, the sexiest guy alive, but he is totally limp. We have not made love in two years since his prostate problem."

"I'm sorry," I threw in sheepishly. "Are you sure I can't get you something?"

"Do you have a bottle of wine in the fridge?" Carrie asked.

"As a matter of fact, I do. I have several. What would you like?"

"Any kind of white wine would be great."

I got up off the blue and white striped couch and went to the kitchen to fetch a glass of chardonnay. I wasn't a drinker, but I decided to join in. I came back with two large goblets of very cold white wine. It was all this talk about impotence and limpness.

"It's five o'clock somewhere in the world. Here's to new friends," Carrie offered a toast, raising her glass. "Joe saw every doctor, every specialist, tried every medicine, and even considered implant surgery but decided he couldn't live with an erection 24/7."

"So, he gave up?" I asked.

"He tried and tried, but eventually it was just no good. I cried the last time he attempted to make love. He never tried again. That was two years ago."

"Are you okay?" I persisted.

"Sure, I'm okay. I have a great life, but I'm lonely."

"You must have friends. Do you work?"

"Wonderful friends, but that's not everything, is it?"

"Friends are pretty important," I replied.

"Yes, they are. I know that. I hope we can be friends," she said.

"Well, we are. I know more about you than just about any friend I have," I told her, laughing in a kind way. I fetched the wine and poured another glass of chardonnay for each of us.

"So, tell me about you, now that you know I am a married virgin saint."

"I'm Kate Fairchild, and I ran away from LA and USC after my sophomore year because the love of my life dumped me."

"You are kidding. That's horrible."

"I was certain he was the one. I was absolutely in love."

"What happened?"

"We were too young. He was going to med school in Texas and didn't want to have me there with him."

"Did he love you?"

"Yes, he did. I know he did."

"God, that's a shame. Life can sure throw some curveballs at you!"

"So here I am, living at my parents' beach house and trying to figure out what comes next."

"Girl, we've got to get you out and about. How long have you been here?"

"Just a month. I haven't done much. You are the first person I've really talked to other than the guy at C'est Si Bon Deli or the makeup girl at Neiman's."

"Well, that's a good start. We can do better. Come with me to lunch next week, Tuesday, at Mariposa, upstairs at Neiman's. You can wave to the makeup gal on your way into the store and then meet some new friends."

"That would be very nice. Thank you, Carrie."

"Don't mention it, kid. Beach neighbors must stick together." Carrie reached out and took my hand. "Come with me. I want you to meet Joe. I'm sure he's back from his morning ocean run. He may not be a great lay, but he makes a fabulous brunch."

"Let me run up and change quickly," I said.

As we left my cottage, Carrie turned to me with some serious morning philosophy.

"Kate, you and I live here in paradise. Don't be fooled by the perfection. Richard Cory lives in Newport as well."

I glanced back at her in visible astonishment. Carrie, apart from not looking like an intellectual, neither acted nor spoke like one either. Had she gone to college? She looked more like Miss July than a student of American poetry. How did she know the poem about Richard Cory?

It didn't matter, because she knew. And the message was clear: Life is not a road without potholes. Sometime the wheels of the car get very stuck. And sometimes you get stuck under them.

I had never had a friend who wore such big false eyelashes and displayed such huge breasts. But I liked her. She was interesting, not to be judged just by what she looked like. This was a Saturday in Newport I would remember, the day I met Carrie Worth—that was Joe's last name, which I would learn over brunch. It was a good last name. I think he was worth millions. Boy, did he know how to cook. I kept looking at him during brunch, thinking about what Carrie had shared. Did he know that I knew? It was very uncomfortable meeting this man for the first time with my knowledge. He was drop-dead handsome at seventy, so he must have been used to having women stare. That's what I hoped anyway, catching myself looking down at his crotch. Oh my God.

CHAPTER SIX

LUNCH WITH THE GIRLS

Having made the lunch date with Carrie at Mariposa, I looked forward to meeting some of her girlfriends. Also, I wanted to check out a new boutique that had opened near Fashion Plaza in Newport's Corona del Mar district called Avenue Foch West, apparently owned by a French couple bringing some European style to the beach. They had been written up in the papers with unusually glowing reviews.

"Dressing" for lunch at Mariposa meant wearing more than a blouse, skirt, and sandals. Seeing as it was almost July and the weather was predicted to be in the high eighties by noontime, I chose a simple white cotton piqué dress, backless, with a coral-colored silk sash at the waist. Putting on the dog, I slipped into white Chanel pumps with the classic bone toe. Nancy had left some beautiful coral beads in her dressing room; I borrowed them for the day. Dressed up a bit, I felt at least twenty-five instead of nineteen going on twenty. In a small velvet pouch on the vanity I discovered a pair of very large faux diamond studs. Oh, why not? I took out my tiny diamond earrings and put in the five-carat stunners. Suddenly, I felt at least thirty. This would work since I was certainly the youngest of the group. I wanted to fit in regardless of the comparison of breast size.

Neiman's was busy as always, even on a weekday morning. Entering the store and walking through the massive cosmetics department, I saw that every counter sported a line of customers. Many of them also had their pooches on a leash. Did you know that dogs shop Neiman's too? You bet they do.

Making it up the escalator to the third floor, I found my way into Mariposa, a wonderful dining room famous for its fluffy popovers with jam and gourmet butter—a modern version of the Tea Room I'd grown up with at the extinct I. Magnin & Co.

Mariposa was clearly hipper with sleek modern décor, but the food and the service recalled those old-world sensibilities. Having done lunch here twice since arriving in Newport, I was certainly a regular.

"Hello, Miss Fairchild. Nice to see you again." The hostess validated my status as a regular in the Mariposa pecking order. I'd made two visits, and now on the third she was calling me by name. Newport was indeed a friendly town.

"Thank you. It's nice to be back. I really love this dining room," I told her.

"Are you meeting anyone?"

"A reservation should be in the name of Carrie Worth," I said, looking around the dining room and not seeing my new friend.

"Mrs. Worth has not checked in, but there is a reservation for four. Would you like to be seated?"

"Yes, please. That would be nice."

Directed to a table by the windows overlooking Fashion Plaza to the west, I took a seat. The dining room was filling up with smartly dressed women in light and loose summer attire, and a few men in the Newport uniform: khakis, a Reyn Spooner Hawaiian-print shirt, never tucked in, and Top-Siders with white soles, no socks. Did all the guys go to work dressed like this? Did any of the guys go to work? I was learning the lay of the land.

Work in Newport was a four-letter word. *Fun* was the operative alternative. Folks in Newport were defiantly addicted to fun, with a whole lot of the fun starting with cocktails at any hour, anyplace. When I first arrived, I began a ritual of walking the oceanfront peninsula for a couple of hours in the late afternoon before sunset. Everyone was walking carrying red plastic cups. Finally, I found the nerve to ask a guy who was seated on a bench by the beach about this red cup custom. He had one in his hand.

"What's with the red cup?" I questioned.

"Huh? What do you mean?" he replied.

"Why does everyone carry a red cup?"

"I have beer in mine. Want some?" he asked politely.

"So, people carry a drink when they go for a walk?"

"Life is a party," he joked.

"Sorry. I'm new around here. I didn't know."

"You can buy these cups at any market. They're big sellers in these parts!"

Carrie arrived about twenty minutes past noon and swooshed into Mariposa like a dove fluttering to its perch. She looked beachy gorgeous as expected, her full head of blonde hair and movie star makeup causing heads to turn as she passed through the now fully seated lunchroom. Carrying a load of packages, Carrie had been doing a little shopping before lunch. She saw me sitting and came right over to the table, greeting a number of women who reached out to acknowledge her as she passed, responding to her admirers with big smiles and lips kissing the air. That was enough given that her arms were loaded down with loot.

Putting down all the goods, Carrie came around the table to where I was now standing and gave me a huge hello hug. I felt her rock-hard breasts against mine; that's how you know surgical from real. God's boobs bounce. Man's are hard and stiff. It was another thing I had learned in my first month in Newport. The knowledge I was acquiring was astounding. Two years at USC and I never knew that man-made breasts were hard; clearly, I was very deprived of real-world knowledge. Given my status as a trust fund girl from Beverly Hills, I found this especially troubling. Destiny had delivered me to the beach to learn about life.

"It is so great to see you, Kate." Carrie was genuinely happy. "I've invited a couple of my close pals to meet you. I hope you'll like them," she continued.

"I'm sure I will. Thank you for brunch the other day. Your husband is a great cook, and even better-looking in an apron, I might add." I was trying to be cute considering everything I knew.

"Here come the girls." Carrie spotted her crew entering Mariposa.

My first thought was that I was going to dye my hair brown to be different. Was every woman blonde in Newport? Carrie's two friends entered, and I could have sworn that all three of them were clones. Maybe the entire town was some kind of science experiment under the control of a mad doctor living high on a coastal Newport promontory in an enormous Nouveau Mediterranean mansion that was in fact a blonde cloning laboratory. Surely, he was turning them out in droves.

"This is Nina Ralston, my dear friend. And please say hello to Grace Villareal," Carrie introduced me. We all sat at our window table. Nina and Grace had been shopping beforehand as well. Surrounded by packages on the floor around the table, I told Nina that her name was one of my favorites. I loved that name, so Nina Ralston got a jump start on likability from me.

"Those ear studs are fabulous." Nina noticed Nancy's big fake cubics.

"I borrowed them from my mother," I told her.

"I think you should keep them. They're amazing. The quality of the diamonds is out of this world."

They are out of this world, all right, I thought. *Right out of a lab factory mold.*

"Carrie tells me that you have recently moved here from LA." Nina wanted the lowdown.

"I finished my second year of college and needed a change. I've been here about a month, and I'm thinking about going back to school to finish at Chapman University."

"Married? Boyfriend?" she persisted.

"No. No on both fronts," I told her, without going into detail about David.

"You won't be single for long. I promise you that," Nina said. "You are absolutely stunning. They will be lining up for you."

Laughing uncomfortably, I thanked Nina for her confidence, but told her dating wasn't a high priority. In fact, it was not on my radar at all. Opening up, I shared that my present goal was to regroup, maybe get a job, and go back to school to finish my degree. Getting too personal, I shared I had broken up with a guy and I hoped that I would find a way to be together again somehow, someday. No other guy could take his place or measure up. No one at all. Not yet, and maybe not ever.

Nina Ralston was in her early thirties, a former Miss New Jersey or Miss Somewhere Back East. Carrie whispered in my ear that Nina had gone to work after losing her crown, at a big construction company in New York as an office girl. She ended up marrying the boss, whom she had met—then dated for a year—while he was still married to wife number one or maybe number two. Big Bill Ralston was the plywood king of the Eastern Seaboard. After his very messy and expensive divorce, Big Bill and Nina moved west. It was time for a change, just as it had been for me. They settled in one of the largest bayfront mansions in Newport, didn't know a soul, just like me, and had a couple of kids, not just like me.

Unfortunately, Big Bill's wandering eye and loose zipper led him to branch out once again. He took up with a barmaid he had met at O'Reilly's Irish Pub on the Pacific Coast Highway. Nina at the time was closing in on thirty with two kids, and the barmaid was just twenty-one and thought that Big Bill was the Big Daddy catch of them all. Nina and the kids now lived in the big house on the water, where she fought with Big Bill for enough support to keep the lights on and the maid coming once a week. Which was not nearly enough help to maintain a twenty-thousand-square-foot re-creation of the Petit Trianon on the water. Big Bill and the new babe took up residence down the highway at the tony Harbor Club, a haven for rich newlyweds and the wealthier nearly dead retirees.

"Hi, I'm Gracie. It's nice to meet you. Carrie says you are the sweetest next-door neighbor."

Blonde number two was effusive. At first, I thought she was really putting on the charm to the extent of overload. After five minutes, Gracie had not stopped chattering. I knew she was either high or wound far too tight. I would learn that Gracie was high—on life. The wife of one of Newport's superstars on the pulpit, Paco Villareal, she was only about twenty-three and was kind of the perfect partner to a man described as a new-generation disciple of Christ. Following in the footsteps of the famous Reverend Robert Schuller, who had created Orange County's world-famous Crystal Cathedral, Paco Villareal was on his way up.

"My name is actually Victoria Grace, but I go by Gracie," she said, continuing to divulge her life story.

"I was born and raised in Waco, Texas, but moved to Garden Grove when I was three," she went on.

"Where's Garden Grove?" I knew of it but wasn't sure.

"Oh, it's about ten miles to the northwest, kind of a middle-class burb. My daddy was a traveling salesman, and he got a territory in the inland part of the county. We didn't have much, and then we had even less when he got fired. But we survived. I got a job as a waitress at Bob's Big Boy hamburger haven, then it, too, went out of business. That's when I met Paco."

"That's your husband?" I asked.

"Yes. He was studying to become a minister at the local Bible college. Paco is from Ixtapa, Mexico, and he could barely speak English. We didn't need to talk much to fall in love. I was sixteen and he was nineteen. We got married when I turned eighteen."

"Paco is loved here in Newport," Carrie threw in. "He has a following of several thousand people who come every Sunday to his services. And he has only been preaching here for a few years. He is amazing. Truly given a calling," she added.

"Where is his church?" I asked.

"It's called the First Community Church of Christ, and it meets in an old converted former Presbyterian church building located in the Back Bay that was sold when that congregation built a new campus. Paco is actually the junior minister, but he is the star, kid you not," Carrie filled me in.

"Don't forget to tell Kate about the prayers on the sand," Nina threw in.

"What's that about?" I wondered.

"Once a month Paco holds Sunday morning prayers on the beach near the Newport pier," Nina added.

"It is a major happening," Carrie said.

"You should see the crowd. When Paco finishes his sermons, Jesus walks on the water." Nina was practically foaming at the month with religious fervor.

"You know what they call him?" Carrie teased. "They call him the Surfer Saint."

"Really?" I asked.

"Really," Carrie and Nina said in unison.

"Oh, come on," Gracie blurted out. "He's wonderful and amazing, but not a saint."

"Don't tell that to his flock. They worship him," Nina added.

Even though I had opened up and shared my story, I was somewhat overwhelmed by all the inside information about the lives of my new friends in Newport. They were all so very different from me, and I always gravitated to women more like me. Just the same, I liked them all. They were real. They were who they were. The glamourous element of their appearance conflicted with their souls, which I was learning to accept as part of the Newport formula. People all wanted to look rich, young, sexy, and carefree. They drove Mercedeses and BMWs even if it took the last dime of their monthly incomes, and they hung out at the right restaurants and bars at the beach. It was just what they had to do to be part of the scene. And being part of the scene meant social acceptance and recognition. This made you somebody, no matter where you came from or if you had any education or pedigree at all. This was a town absolutely invested in living in the moment.

There was one factor that did seem to make a discernible difference: real money. In Newport money was like air in the lungs. It was a life force. This was my sense of things, without concrete proof, at least not after one month here. The reality of all the glitter swirled about in an omnipresent way, enveloping the city limits like an invisible curtain, a walled city without the wall and moat.

Proof of this hunch arrived at our table like a summer rain squall descending without warning.

"Oh my God, Kelly is here," Carrie called out.

"Look at her. Does she look amazing, or what?" Nina added, looking across Mariposa at Kelly Paularino making her grand entrance as literally everyone she passed practically genuflected. Were they kissing her ring? That's what it looked like from my vantage point.

"Who is Kelly?" I asked innocently enough.

"She is probably the most popular gal in town, that's all," Nina filled me in.

"Why?" I questioned, with what was probably a sarcastic look on my face. What makes someone the most popular person in town? Was it their personality, their career, their family fortune? Had they won some big prize like a Pulitzer, or did they have a title like a princess? Maybe they starred on TV or in the movies, wrote a best seller, composed an opera?

In Kelly's case, she was beautiful. Strikingly so. She was married to Dr. Paularino, the most successful plastic surgeon on the coast. Nina told me that he "did" everyone. Ha! There really was a mad scientist cloning women in a mansion high on a hill over the Newport coast. I chuckled silently as Kelly came closer to the table.

Frankly, I was both impressed and surprised by the fact that Kelly was not blonde. She was tall, probably close to six feet, and had jet-black hair pulled straight back and tight up on her head, forming a bun, tied with a yellow satin ribbon. Her flawless white skin and huge sparkling emerald-green eyes were placed perfectly above the most elegant high cheekbones that God, and Dr. Paularino, had ever created. Kelly wore only basic makeup, nothing extreme. Her lashes were her own, and her lips were not inflated, which was another common aspect of the total Newport look. Botox was a big seller. The breasts, however, were a triple P. "Perky, praiseworthy, and pointed." That's what Carrie whispered in my ear.

"If you are a triple P," she said, "then you've been to Paularino."

"Kelly, would you like to join us?" Carrie stood up to greet her stunning friend.

"Oh, no thanks, sweetheart. I'm having lunch with Mrs. A today. Let's get together soon though." Kelly walked on, making a beeline for a corner table looking over the entire dining room. A very attractive middle-aged woman dressed to kill on a summer day was busy looking over papers at her table as Kelly approached.

"That's Mrs. A," Carrie clued me in. The others all knew who Mrs. A was.

"What does that stand for? I mean the *A*?" I asked.

"It stands for Mrs. Absolutely the Most Powerful Woman in Town, that's all," Carrie replied, chuckling. The others joined her.

"Actually, the *A* stands for Adamson. Mrs. A is the wife of Arthur Adamson, local billionaire, real estate developer, philanthropist, and Republican influence peddler."

I was getting the full curricula vitae on all the players.

"If you have only one friend in Newport, make sure it's Mrs. A," Gracie threw in.

"But what about all your other friends?" I said sarcastically.

They laughed. Sort of. I got the message.

All this social maneuvering was over my head, above my pay grade. Frankly, I didn't care much at all; I was amused by it and felt rather aloof or at least separated from such concerns. Sure, I wanted to fit in, have friends, and be among the people, but I still felt mostly like a nineteen-year-old college woman who had lost her one true love. All this stuff was entirely superficial, at least to me. I knew it was real for my newfound girlfriends, so I did my best to be kind and respectful. I wanted to be snarky and sarcastic, suggesting to the girls that if Mrs. A was the most important friend a young woman could have in Newport, then I was going to excuse myself from Carrie's table and go over and introduce myself at the more influential table in town. But I didn't. I thought about doing it just for fun. I controlled myself.

We ordered lunch and proceeded to have a fine time sharing every special the waiter offered. Our conversation never left the areas of fashion, husbands, and August travel. Just as Nina launched into detailing her upcoming summer jaunt to East Hampton, where she'd join some New York pals for the month of August, a male model appeared at our table, literally out of thin air. No one had seen him coming or made a fuss as they had done when Kelly Paularino entered the dining room. And believe me, this guy deserved a major fuss. He was a Greek god in the flesh.

Mr. Adonis kind of slithered around the table and landed behind Carrie. He put his hands on her shoulders and leaned over, kissing her gently on the cheek. She knew exactly who he was. Carrie didn't flinch. No surprise there.

"Tony, darling." She turned to face him and then swung back around with all of us. "You all know trainer Tony Giardello. Oh, you've not met Kate Fairchild. Say hello to Kate."

Tony shot me a wave and a glance. He was right out of central casting for the most handsome male on the planet. Tony was also muscular. Dressed in a white V-neck cotton T-shirt showing off his biceps, tight white Levi's, and spotless white tennis shoes, he wore a thick gold chain-link bracelet on his left wrist. His skin was flawlessly bronzed; his jet-black hair, long on top but cut short over the ears so his locks fell to the right side over his face, covering a corner of his huge blue eye. No actor I could think of had eyes like this Tony the trainer.

"I came to pick you up for our session," he said to Carrie. Oh my, a trainer who picks up his clients at restaurants. This was new and different.

"That's sweet of you," Carrie answered. "We're done here. I was just going to drive over to the gym to meet you," she said.

Looking around the table, I concluded that none of us believed a word of it. Carrie was having an affair with Tony the trainer. Given her husband Joe's problem, I understood. But what was all her moaning to me about being so lonely?

Carrie got up, left a hundred-dollar bill on the table to cover her lunch, and gave us all an air-kiss goodbye. Tony took her hand with one of his and carried her packages in the other, and the pair vanished into Neimansland.

None of the three of us said much of anything following her exit. We divided the bill and said our civil pleasant farewells. The girls picked up their goods and went about the rest of this summer day in paradise. I sat for another ten minutes, drank another iced tea, and stared out the window at the blue sky and white floating clouds. It was time to get a job, any job, and think about enrolling in school for fall classes.

Going Shopping and Buying a Job

This terrific new store that I had read about in the local Newport paper, appropriately called the *Daily Pilot*, or the *Plot*, as locals referred to it, as the voice of Newport, was in another, smaller shopping center just south of Fashion Plaza in a very chic Mediterranean-inspired complex lined with magnificent olive trees, garden walkways, and shops catering to those with very basic enviable life essentials—time and money. It was here in this minivillage designed to make one feel as if she had stepped into a slice of the Côte d'Azur that I found "AFochW"—Avenue Foch West.

The boutique was sandwiched between a real estate office and a pricy cupcake bakery offering cupcakes for as much as eight dollars apiece. I pulled my yellow Mercedes, top down, into a spot right in front of AFochW, noticing the line out the door of the cupcake palace. Walking toward the window of the boutique, I was drawn in by an amazing dress on the mannequin.

Approaching the store window, which was a tall narrow pane of glass arched at the top, I thought I saw the mannequin move, which threw me off-balance, causing me to stumble on an uneven brick paver in the garden walk. Catching myself before landing flat on the ground, I saw that my sunglasses went flying, only to be rescued by a young man coming out of the real estate office next door. He caught them midair, then he caught me by the arm.

"These are dangerous bricks," he said with a smile. "Are you okay?"

"I'm fine. Just a tiny bit embarrassed," I answered.

He handed me the glasses.

"Thanks a lot. I wasn't watching my step—was looking at the mannequin in the store window."

"It is a show," he replied.

"A show?" I asked.

"Look again," he told me.

Turning to face the window, I found that the mannequin had turned completely around with the back of that amazing dress facing outward.

"Is it on a turntable?" I asked.

"No."

"How do they do that?"

"She is not a mannequin. She is real."

"Real models in the window?"

"Pretty neat, huh?"

"Wow. That's different," I said, clearly impressed.

"By the way, I'm Cole Baldwin. What's your name?"

"Kate Fairchild. And thanks again for saving me," I told him, walking to the front door of the store.

"Nice meeting you," he called out as I walked away. Prince Charming made his way to his car parked on one side of mine in the lot facing the store. He drove an old gray Toyota.

I turned and looked again at him as he got into the car. This young man was handsome, almost too handsome, but his clothes were rather frumpy, and the old car stood out in the lineup of shining new metal in the lot. I couldn't quite figure out the package. He looked back at me as I was checking him out getting into the Toyota, and he waved and called out.

"I work here in the real estate office. Maybe I'll see you again when you come back to the boutique?" he shouted. Then he added, "If you need a house or a condo, I'm your man!"

"Okay. Maybe," I answered half-heartedly. This young man with bad clothes and a bad car was trying to sell million-dollar real estate in one of the richest towns in the United States. I guessed he was living the dream.

I went into AFochW and fell instantly in love.

"Bonjour, mademoiselle. I am Honoré Lambert, and this is my shop." A tall slender French woman in her fifties who spoke elegant English with a French accent approached me. I was the only customer in the store. I introduced myself to her and shared my story.

"You've only been living in Newport for about a month? Well, this is kismet.

We have only been open here for about a month," she said. "We will have to be new best friends."

"Your clothing is so beautiful. Who is the designer? I don't think I recognize any of the pieces."

"Everything you see is designed and made by my husband, Lawrence, and me, with our two young girls working in the back room."

"Really? Then this is all couture?" I asked.

"It is. All one of a kind and made for the fashionable Newport woman."

"I have not seen that many fashionable ladies here, just beach glamourous," was all I could come up with.

"Oh yes, there is plenty of that. But women in this town dress to impress when they go out to dinner or to a gala. There are major black-tie parties in this town every night. We have only been here a month, as I said, and business is very good," she shared.

"May I look?" I asked.

Just then the mannequin stepped out of the window and came over to us.

"I would be glad to show you anything you would like to see," she offered.

"This is Lisa," Madame Honoré said, introducing her fashionable live mannequin and salesgirl. We began pulling clothes. I wanted to buy everything she showed me.

Lawrence Lambert came out of the workroom and into the salon. Honoré introduced her master tailor husband.

"Your work is impeccable. The detail is incomparable," I gushed praise, holding a skirt and short jacket that I was coveting. "Can you tell me about this outfit?"

"It is very fine French linen, fully lined in silk, hand stitched of course. You can see the workmanship. Please look at the hemline and the waistband. The cream color is perfect for your skin tone, I might add," the French couturier said, in this tiny shop about nine thousand miles from Paris.

"May I ask the price?"

"Oh, very reasonable," Lawrence replied.

I was thinking, *How reasonable?* but said nothing.

"The skirt is one hundred and fifty dollars, and the jacket is two hundred and seventy-five," Honoré whispered. "You probably could not buy the fabric alone for this price," she added.

Even as a trust fund kid with an allowance, I was not used to spending more than a hundred dollars on an outfit, but I went for it. After all, AFochW was as close to Paris as I was going to get at this point in my life. I was in a French fog, and I loved it.

"Would you like to see the workroom?" Lawrence asked. "Come this way."

The designer took me by the hand. We walked through a portal covered by a rose-colored velvet drape and entered a French sewing room, its walls lined with bolts of fabric, trims, and thread, interspersed with pen-and-ink drawings on torn parchment paper showing off all Lambert's designs in progress.

The center of the room was set up with cutting tables and several sewing stations. Two women, both somewhat pretty, wearing simple cotton print dresses festooned with floral buds, worked diligently, never glancing up to acknowledge me.

"This is our engine room, our war room, as it were," Lawrence shared. "We make everything in here."

"Do you think you might be able to use an intern?" I blurted out. "To learn this trade would be my dream. Could you teach me? I will do whatever it takes," I said, almost not believing my nerve.

"I cannot pay much. Perhaps a part-time wage, or a trade for clothing, something like that?" Lawrence came back.

"When could I start?"

"Do you have any experience?" he asked.

"Not really, but I do know fashion."

"How about Monday after the Fourth of July holiday?" he replied.

"Ten o'clock?" I asked.

"We begin at eight in the morning," he answered.

"Yes, eight o'clock," I said. I threw my arms around him, enveloping my new boss in a major hug. Startled but delighted, he let out a tiny French squeal.

I left the workroom and paid for my new linen suit, which was going to be altered for a perfect fit—another aspect of the unique service at AFochW. Just before leaving the shop, I thanked Honoré and Lisa. Honoré kissed me on both cheeks and told me again that our chance meeting was kismet. I shared the feeling, overjoyed at my new opportunity.

As I walked out, Prince Charming in the faded Toyota was pulling back into the space next to my car. Simultaneously, a guy in a big black Mercedes sedan, parked on the opposite side of my car, was pulling out, and fast. Turning his giant sedan too close to my car, he scraped the rear fender of my yellow baby. Prince Charming witnessed the event, stepping out of his car and yelling at the guy to stop.

The windows of the sedan were tinted dark, and we could hear music blaring. The driver sped off down the parking lot.

My real estate guy jumped back in his car and sped off after him, chasing him and catching up to him at a traffic light on Pacific Coast Highway. Real estate guy was honking furiously, yelling out of his open driver's-side window, with no response from the tinted window sedan, which was blaring a roadside rock concert at full volume.

With no hope of raising this guy's attention before the red light turned green, real estate guy positioned his faded Toyota in front of the big black Mercedes, making it impossible to move forward without smashing into the Toyota. The light turned green, and cars were honking like crazy.

Mercedes guy got out of his car, screaming at Toyota guy.

"What the fuck are you doing?" he yelled, coming over to him, ready for a fight.

"You hit the car next to you in the lot and didn't stop," real estate guy answered. "Look at your bumper. The yellow paint is from my friend's car you smashed."

The guy looked down and saw the paint.

"Do you want to pull over and give me your license and insurance, or are we just going to stay here and block traffic?"

They pulled over. Real estate guy got all the proper information and returned to find me sitting in my car, waiting outside the boutique.

"He said he didn't know he hit you. Here's his name, number, and insurance. He said he would take care of it. And here's the license plate of his car. You might want to report this to the police right away in case he decides to deny responsibility later," real estate guy told me.

"You have saved me twice in one day," I said. "That was dangerous going after him like that."

"Nothing to it for a kid from Reno, Nevada. Facing trouble head-on is what we are made of," he said, smiling. "Would you consider going for coffee or something with me?" he asked.

"Maybe," I said.

"Maybe yes or maybe no?" he asked.

"Just maybe."

"Can I have your number?"

"I know where to find you," I came back. "Don't get me wrong. I am grateful. You seem like a very nice guy."

"Okay then. *Maybe* will have to do. For now."

I got in my dented yellow Mercedes and left. My car had suffered a dented fender, but I had gotten a job and a new outfit, and I had a new suitor I had held at bay. Things were looking up. Life in Newport displayed possibilities I had never imagined, never expected. *I think I am going to like it here.* Running away was not such a bad idea after all.

CHAPTER SEVEN

CARRIE COMES CLEAN

An amazing Fourth of July weekend brought the herds to the beach. It was a totally crazy time, with Newport police on horseback patrolling the coastline. I tried to avoid the free-for-all, even though I lived smack in the center of the bacchanalia. Civilization had been excused; hedonism ruled.

Fortunately, the Fairchild cottage was far enough down the Balboa Peninsula that most of humanity was unable to find a place to park near my piece of the sand. I planted my blue and white canvas beach chair just feet from the ocean's edge, laid out my matching blue and white striped towel, adjusted my dark glasses, and opened my unfinished Pat Conroy novel detailing life in Carolina. As my senses took in the sounds and smells of the Pacific, my mind traveled to an opposite coast and an opposite way of southern life as told by Conroy, like no other. What would it be like to be the proper daughter of southern gentleman Jack McCall and live in an old white colonial house facing the evolution of a lost world at odds with the new morality while family secrets collided with history? Of course, the new morality could not quite let go of the old world's black household help.

I was getting carried away with my beach reading. Conroy's book was appropriately titled *Beach Music*. I felt a lovely cold, wet hand touch my sunbaked left shoulder.

"Hi, friend." Carrie came around in front of me, blocking the glare of the midday rays bouncing off the ocean.

"Happy Fourth," I said. "Have you been in the water?"

"Either that or Joe turned the garden hose on me," Carrie answered flippantly. "He'd have a right," she added.

"Would you go back in with me?" I suggested, getting up out of my chair and putting my book down on the canvas seat.

"Sure. It's really great water today. Not too cold. Clear and calm."

"Let's go." We both ran toward the surf that gently lapped the shoreline, leaving its white bubbly foam lining the dark wet sand, an encoded message from Neptune.

Carrie and I were out beyond the breaking waves in seconds, taking one big dive under the last swell. We swam in the calm ocean, which was sending us southward ever so slowly with the current. I was no longer in South Carolina. I fantasized about drifting south to Mexico. The water was delicious; the salt invigorated my skin; and I felt as if I were being healed of all ills, with all worries washed away. Ocean water always did this for me. In fact, any water—a bath or shower, even raindrops—delivered salvation.

We swam down coast for a good twenty minutes. Realizing we were going to have to buck the current coming back, we turned around before hitting the Newport Wedge, which was crowded with all the surfers, and began to swim back. About halfway, we both stopped and began to tread water, enjoying the peace and sharing some girl talk where only the fish could hear us.

"I'd like to share something with you, Kate." Carrie swam up next to me, almost in my face.

"Sure. Anything," I responded.

"I'm having an affair with Tony. Tony my trainer," she confessed straight out.

"I know," I said simply.

"You know? How do you know?" she asked, honestly surprised.

"I knew that day at Mariposa when he came to pick you up for a session."

"Did Nina or Gracie tell you?"

"They didn't have to."

"Oh." We both laughed, choking a bit on the seawater.

"Joe doesn't know. Part of me wants to tell him, but another part knows that it would hurt him. I don't want to hurt Joe."

"Do you love Tony?"

"I love having sex with Tony. He fulfills me. I feel loved and I feel like a woman. Do I love him completely?" Carrie paused. "No, I don't!"

"Do you love Joe completely?" I pushed on.

Carrie paused again, then answered as a fish flew out of the water and dove back in next to us. "No. I don't. But I do love Joe. And I respect him and appreciate all he has done for me."

"But it's not enough for you to be faithful to Joe?"

"It's not. I need love and attention. I'm only twenty-eight, too young to be a married virgin. There will be plenty of time for that late in life."

We both laughed again.

"Kate, should I tell him?"

"I'd like to think that honesty would be the ideal choice, but I doubt it."

"Tony is getting more serious. What do I do?"

"If you want to stay married to Joe, then you'd better back off. Cool it with Tony and set some limits. Since Tony knows all, he is the one you must be honest with now. Tell him you love Joe, and you are not leaving him."

"I can't do that. Tony would be furious."

"You've got a problem, girlfriend. This is not good."

"There's something else. I think I'm pregnant, only just a couple of weeks."

"Oh my God. Are you sure?"

"Pretty sure. I'm seeing my doc next week."

"Hey, I am sorry to have to say that this is both wonderful and terrible."

"I can't pretend the child is Joe's. He would know it's impossible."

"Will you keep this child?" I asked seriously.

"Absolutely, yes," Carrie came back.

"Then it's time to confess and see if you can work things out."

Carrie nodded and began to swim with her strongest freestyle stroke back toward our point of origin as marked by my identifying blue and white striped chair and towel. I followed her, several strokes behind. Suddenly, life had really complicated my perfect beach day. I was worried for my new friend. Doing the right thing may very well be the wrong thing to do. Wishing that I had kept my mouth shut, I realized my advice came with no expertise—the jilted college coed trying to find her way in life. Good God, I had made some mistakes in my life, but nothing like Carrie.

We walked out of the surf and back up to my beach chair. Collapsing in the chair, I handed the towel to Carrie. She lay down on the blue and white stripes on the sand next to me. Neither of us said a word. She was lying facedown, her face buried in the towel. Putting on my dark glasses, I ran my hands through my wet, stringy, salty hair, pushing it back over my head, letting the droplets of seawater roll down my back. Staring at the ocean, I asked God to help my friend Carrie. Maybe in this awesome setting of natural beauty and power, there was a chance that God, whatever God was, just might be aware of this one woman's conflict, one woman among billions of people on the planet in need of help.

A Surprise Fourth of July Visit

In my room over the garage, I was in bed by nine on a Saturday night with the sound of crackling sparklers and falling fireworks punctuating the silence of my cave on this Fourth of July holiday weekend. An occasional screeching tire outside my window added to the orchestration of the night. Superbly happy to be alone in my nightgown under the down-filled comforter, I was finally finishing *Beach Music* on at least the third try. The cell phone rang. It was nine thirty.

"Hello, darling. It's your mother. How are you doing?"

"Really fine," I replied. "I enjoyed a great day on the sand. Went in the ocean for a swim with my next-door neighbor Carrie. I've told you about her."

"Listen, dear, your father wants to drive down to Newport tomorrow. We're going to bring Jamey. I think the change will do him good. And he misses you very much."

"Wonderful. We can spend the holiday together. Do you need me to go to the market? All that's left in the fridge from your generous welcome surprise is some wine and cheese."

"I'll call Gelson's and have them deliver. Don't bother, dear. We'll see you tomorrow around lunchtime. Maybe we can all take a dip in the tide!"

"Really?" I said, surprised.

"Well, maybe just you, your dad, and your brother. I'll watch."

Nancy was being Nancy.

After reading a new book for another hour or so, I hit the TV remote. *Saturday Night Live* was on. I watched for five or ten minutes, unimpressed. Why did so many in my generation think this show was brilliant and hilarious? Every time I watched; it was nothing more than a stream of mocking jokes directed at public figures. Mostly I found it to be mean-spirited, rather than vital cutting-edge social commentary. The world was becoming so mean, very hostile. I drifted into sleep, lights on and television talking away.

Morning came, announced by a knock on the downstairs cottage door. My TV was still talking, only now it was sharing political news delivered by the Sunday morning panels. I had never paid much attention to those either. I hit the off button on the remote.

"Who's there?" I called out from my upstairs vantage point.

"Grocery delivery from Gelson's Market."

"Can you just leave it there?" I called out.

"Okay. But it's a lot of stuff," the man replied.

"That's fine. On second thought, give me a moment. I'll be right down."

Throwing on some clothes, then grabbing five dollars, I raced down the stairs. The deliveryman wasn't kidding. He delivered ten bags of groceries. I was happy he was bringing them all into the kitchen. Was the family coming for an overnight stay or moving in for the summer? Anyway, I thanked the guy, gave him the fiver, and started to put away the perishables.

Nancy had ordered all my favorite foods, enough for at least a few weeks. Dalt would no doubt be taking us all out to eat over the holiday, so this was just a good reason for Nancy to do something nice for me. I said a silent prayer of appreciation before placing all the fresh veggies and fruits in the Sub-Zero.

At noon the small family entourage arrived. Marta had come with Nancy, Dalt, and Jamey. It was so good to see them all. We hugged and kissed for at least ten minutes. It was especially great to see my little brother. He seemed better, although uncomfortably silent and somewhat detached. Yet, he clung to my side and wouldn't let me go. We sat down on the couch. Jamey told me that he had missed me most of all.

"Will you come home soon?" he asked in a childlike tone, inappropriate for a teenage boy.

"I'm going to live here for a while," I answered. "But I'm only an hour away, and if you ever need me, I am here," I said, giving Jamey another hug.

"I have missed you so much," he said again. "Will you go swimming with me in the ocean?"

"You bet I will. Can't wait."

Mother gave me a look as if to say that Jamey was not 100 percent back.

Marta entered and opened all the French doors at Nancy's request, and then went upstairs to freshen their master bedroom. A warm breeze off the ocean swept into the cottage, setting into motion the clinking seashells hanging from the chandelier.

"Have you had lunch?" Nancy asked.

"No. But there's enough food here for an army," I said, thanking her.

"Your father wants to take us to lunch at the Harbor Club. It should be fun. We haven't been there in a while. What do you say?"

"I say that whatever you want to do is fine with me." I dashed upstairs to change.

"Be ready in ten," Nancy called out.

Saturday Lunch in the Main Cabin

I was holding on to fond memories of playing on the private beach at the Harbor Club as a child, recalling the soft pure white sand in front of the calm bay-front of the Newport harbor. About one hundred feet out into the bay, a floating platform was supporting a waterslide into the salt water. The entire portion of the bay was roped off by swimming pool lines with those football-shaped rope floats attached to the lines every ten feet or so. The roped-in section made us feel safe and secure, as if it kept out any underwater creatures daring to intrude into this privileged corner of the Newport harbor.

Harbor Club was old Newport, a mix of beach casual and conservative snobbery. In its nascence, it was a postwar watering hole for local yachtsmen and returning World War II vets, then in the 1950s it was upgraded to a Newport destination for movie stars and Republican presidents. The ghosts of Nixon, Reagan, Ford, and the elder Bush remained.

By the onset of the millennium, change was in the air. With the tail end of the old guard holding on for dear life, Harbor Club had new owners. The final days of its fading glorious past were numbered. Dalt explained this all to me in the car on the way to lunch. He wanted to have one last meal on the terrace of the Main Cabin before it met the wrecking ball of history. A new and younger crowd, thirty-something, with new values, waited in the wings, ready to take over and take charge.

We pulled into the driveway. The guard at the front gate, noticing the Harbor Club sticker on the windshield of Dalt's charcoal-gray Rolls-Royce, waved us in. Dalt rarely drove his Rolls in Beverly Hills these days; it was too high profile. The beautiful car spent most days in the garage, his driving its replacement, a nondescript black Mercedes sedan. There were unlimited Mercedeses, like insects, everywhere. Dalt loved his gray Rolls, and it was very acceptable in Newport. The bigger, flashier, and more expensive the car, the better. Here the Rolls was still cool.

As we pulled up to the porte cochere, a troop of handsome young valets dressed in the club uniform—logo-embroidered red polo shirts and white cotton shorts—stood at the ready to greet us. There was some sort of commotion at the front of the line of arriving glam vehicles. Dalt's Rolls was only a speck in the crush of Bentleys, Ferraris, Mercedeses, and the few American old-world holdout Cadillacs and Lincolns.

As cars moved forward and we came closer to the front entrance, I could see what all the fuss was about. A woman with a long ponytail of platinum-blonde straight hair to her waist, dressed in a black thong bikini covered by a very see-through short black net cover-up tied in a knot at the top of her bathing suit bottom, was flirting with the boys. This woman was at least seventy, but still with a showgirl figure, albeit wrinkly. Her nails were painted bright stop sign red, and she wore five-inch heels fashioned of sparkling gold lamé leather with heels of clear Lucite.

"Oh my. Look at the lady," I offered, pointing the family in the proper direction of the commotion.

"It's Mamie," my dad answered, recognizing former Hollywood starlet Mamie Van Doren. "She's lived here in Newport for years. I think she's married to a much younger guy. I've met her many times," he told us. "She's actually a sweetheart. Never left behind her sex siren image from the early days."

"Obviously it still attracts attention," Nancy said with a laugh.

We exited the Rolls and walked through the old lobby of the beach building that dated back to the 1940s. It was California midcentury modern optimism meeting with a touch of luau chic. As the social mecca of Newport for fifty years, the place saw some action.

At the far end of the lobby, we walked through glass doors onto the terrace overlooking yachts berthed at Harbor Club. They called it "Battleship Row." The biggest yachts in Newport made their home at Harbor Club docks.

The hostess seated us waterfront at a round glass patio table surrounded by white-painted wooden director's chairs sporting navy-blue canvas seats and backs embossed in white script: "Harbor Club." Drinks were offered and accepted. Inside the dining room, a brunch in silver chafing dishes awaited, backed by a formal kitchen staff in starched white uniforms. The pianist, a man named Bud, who had been playing there for fifty years, sat at the polished walnut Baldwin grand playing Gershwin. Across the room, behind the old Main Cabin bar designed to look as if it had come from an old schooner, was Joe the handsome barkeep. In starched white shirt and black bow tie, he created the best Ramos fizz on the bayfront. That's what Dalt had told me, at least three times before we got up from the table to have our brunch.

After crossing the terrace to the front door of the dining room, a group of people came out the main door, looking very important. At the front, one man, about sixty, bald and with a tan face, dressed in a fine dark pinstriped suit, white shirt, and burgundy silk necktie, was walking with a very sophisticated woman, her arm clutching his. She was quite tall, somewhat taller than her escort, with a major head of wavy auburn hair. She wore really pronounced Jackie Onassis black-framed dark glasses and was dressed in a summer suit of pale-peach-colored gabardine with a cream silk blouse. She carried a cream leather Hermès Kelly bag and walked with a certain determination, forbidding anyone to stop her for any reason. Behind the couple, two very well-dressed men in suits and ties, which I thought was odd for the middle of summer, followed close.

Suddenly another middle-aged blonde woman, this one attired in a white tennis skirt and matching V-neck shirt, rushed the group. She wore a white ruffled visor on her fore, and her tennis socks sported little bells, which jangled from the rear just above the Achilles notches of her Nike shoes.

"Mr. and Mrs. Turnbull, I'm Libby de Benedict, and I'm so happy to meet you."

I'd heard her gush. She held out a hand to shake the hands of both Bentley and Tish Turnbull, new owners of the Harbor Club. They were in Newport from their residence at River Oaks in Houston, Texas. Libby was awkward, trying to be polite and clasp both their hands simultaneously. For a second, I thought she was going to pull Tish Turnbull off-balance and trip her.

"I just wanted to tell you that I am so very happy that you are not going to essentially change this wonderful old club with any plans to remodel and attract new members. I mean, you will be keeping membership restricted and exclusive," she babbled on. Dalt heard her and shot a look at the owners, awaiting their response.

"I'm sorry, what did you say your name was?" Bentley Turnbull shot back.

"Libby de Benedict. My family have been members for thirty years," she told him.

"Of course. We are so pleased to know you," he returned, not having a clue of who she was.

"I'd like you to meet my bankers and business partners who are financing the new club. They've come in from New York. Please welcome Mr. Goldman and Mr. Kaplan."

Libby de Benedict looked as if she were going to throw up. Her face turned white, matching her tennis clothes, as she politely said hello to Goldman and Kaplan. Then she turned away and dashed across the dining terrace toward the beach.

"So much for restricted," my father said quietly, laughing as he opened the dining room door. "It's about time we stopped dividing Americans over race, religious beliefs, gender, and even sexual orientation," he added to my astonishment. When had Dalton Fairchild turned liberal? I had been out of the house and out of Beverly Hills for only a month and here my father was sounding like a Democrat, or as he often labeled them, "a damn liberal."

Growing up in greater Los Angeles, a diverse American melting pot, I had witnessed the once very conservative city of my childhood become largely Democratic as the population of young people and the population of immigrants soared. My hometown of Beverly Hills was always cordial, but very clearly divided between Jew and Gentile, Democrat and Republican, and rich and not so rich, and most demonstrably between the big cheeses and the wannabes. Neighborhoods and streets marked lines of separation. Country clubs were for Jews only or Christians only. Restaurants catered to crowds. I knew all this and accepted it as the way things were, but mostly I was not involved because I always treated everybody the same. I had been raised with privilege, not prejudice. It wasn't in me. Yet perhaps I was blinded by that privilege, by the shelter from reality.

I was proud of my daddy. Mrs. de Benedict's world was yesterday. Dalton knew it, even as a wealthy man fond of driving his gray Rolls-Royce with the softest red leather seats ever made for a car. He knew that a restricted and elitist world that divided people, rather than uniting them for the common good, was not the answer. All this from my father who had railed at Bill Clinton for eight years and recently threw a big party at the house to raise money to get the younger Bush elected. Yes, I was proud, but I was also confused.

Anyway, philosophy of life aside, it was time for brunch. The bacon smelled heavenly. I helped myself to four slices to accompany the Eggs Benedict. I wondered if they had been named after the woman at the door. Probably just a coincidence.

CHAPTER EIGHT

FATE OR REAL ESTATE?

Brother Jamey did not say a word during brunch at Harbor Club. He sat silently in a trance, playing with his food, which Nancy put on a plate for him. Hardly looking up from his lowered chin, Jamey made me very sad as I watched him. At first, I tried to encourage him with attention. Soon it was clear that the attention was hurting him, so I backed off.

At this moment I realized how and why my conservative dad had changed. Jamey's struggle had opened my father's eyes. Seeing his bright son sink into a dehumanized state of fear and isolation, unable to overcome the ravages of drugs on his pubescent youthful body, my hard-driving all-business father had been brought to his knees. He had done everything money enabled him to do, and it just wasn't enough to save Jamey. Dalt had challenged the government, the law, the health-care industry, the drug companies, and the community, looking for answers. He found none. Watching his child slip away, he and Nancy now spent as much time as possible just being with Jamey and letting him know how much he was loved. Their guilt, real or imagined, deserved or unfair, consumed their perfect life, at least on the inside.

Jamey had made possible, in a most unexpected fashion, an opening in my parents' hearts, a deepening compassion for the underdog, the less fortunate, and the lost souls whom they once may have considered life's losing class.

My father was once the president of his restricted club. Now he rarely entered the door, preferring to play tennis at home on his court. He had joined a businessmen's committee in Beverly Hills that was part of the antidefamation council of Los Angeles. This was all because of Jamey. Dalt, entering his sixth decade on the planet, with a life that was nothing but a succession of open doors and silver tray opportunities, had come to know that all men are not created equal. He was no longer complacent with being rich and oblivious, even if it was just so he could take care of his son who needed him.

"Kate, Jamey would like to have some sister time. It is all he has talked about since we told him we were coming to Newport. Could you go with him and sit on the sand this afternoon?" my father requested.

"Are you kidding? I can't wait. Jamey and I are going to have the best afternoon together." I added, "The ocean is calling and we're going in. Don't worry—we'll be safe."

As I put my arm around my brother's shoulders, he moved in closer to me. I kissed him on the cheek.

"Let's get out of here. The beach is calling."

With that, my family got up from the glass table and made a double-time march to the valet station. Dalt and Nancy drove us back to the beach house, and Jamey and I got out of the car. He came to life, if only in a small way, given the prospect of going on the sand with me.

"Mom and I will be back in an hour. Call on the cell if you need us. We'll only be a few minutes away," my father announced. He drove the Rolls back onto the main boulevard, returning in the direction from whence we had just come.

I did not question the move. Jamey and I were going to the sand after a quick change. Marta opened the cottage door, having heard us approach.

"Can you show me where Jamey's board shorts and sandals are, Marta? We're going to the beach."

"Shall I get him dressed?" she questioned.

Taking Marta aside, I asked her if he was unable to dress himself. She nodded her head. I hadn't realized just how difficult things were. Marta told me that he was comfortable with her help, so I stepped aside and went upstairs to change myself.

Crossing the Bridge onto Lido Isle

It was only a five-minute drive from the beach cottage on the sand to the bridge connecting the peninsula to the Isle of Lido. A man-made spit in the middle of Newport harbor, Lido boasted the United States' highest-priced real estate per square foot. This residential haven with some eight hundred homes on tiny lots only feet apart was a bayside magnet for the rich, who inhabited homes on the outer perimeter of the isle with waterfront access valued in the millions.

Dalt and Nancy always admired one residence, a French Regency–inspired minichateau on four contiguous waterfront lots. Built in the 1940s with tremendous old-world charm and character, the residence never had come on the market. But Dalt had seen it advertised in the real estate section of the *Daily Pilot*, and he and Nancy were on their way for a look. The price was ten million, a huge number even for Lido.

Pulling up in front of the elegant old home, Dalt and Nancy admired the handsomely painted facade with its pale shade of dove gray and gleaming white trim. A dark charcoal-gray slate mansard roof blended with enamel, black-painted shutters and entry doors facing the main street. Homes on Lido were directly on the street with no such thing as a front yard.

"It's still a beauty," Dalt told Nancy.

"We've always admired this home," she replied.

"Well, let's take a look," Dalt responded, getting out of the car. He went around to the passenger door and opened it for his wife.

Given that it was a holiday weekend, very few homes were open for inspection.

Dalt and Nancy were greeted at the door by an enthusiastic agent who was all too happy to have a showing on a day most people were out enjoying the Fourth of July weekend sunshine.

"Welcome. Please come in. My name is Cole Baldwin. I would be honored to show you this remarkable home," the young man with movie star looks, a voice that would hypnotize wild dogs, and enough energy to light up the room offered. Dalt was instantly impressed by the young real estate agent as he began the tour.

The agent and his prey entered the formal foyer off the interior courtyard, featuring a European-inspired carved limestone fountain spilling a soft, breezy flow of water into a pond sporting white water lilies. Inside, the entry foyer was two stories tall in an octagon shape with tall paned windows flooding light onto a marble floor. A magnificent old crystal chandelier in a bronze Doré frame hung from the center of the ceiling, which was crafted in plaster to resemble a fluted canvas canopy. In the center of the entry foyer, a gold leaf–painted art deco–period octagonal table held an orange and white Chinese jar filled with stems of white orchids. The scent of fresh jasmine filled the air.

"That scent is divine," Nancy commented.

"It's coming from candles lit in the powder room, just off the entry," the agent said, opening the powder room door wide to give his potential clients a look.

"Are you from Newport?" he inquired. "Do you know about Lido?"

Dalt was circumspect. "We do" was all he said. He gave Nancy a look as if to say, *This is what I expected.*

For the next half hour, Cole Baldwin did his real estate best to impress. He toured the Regency home, pointing out every detail, offering market advice, and talking about long-term value to mitigate the fact that it was the highest-priced home on the isle. A ten-million-dollar sale would set a record in 2000.

"Have you been in the business long?" Dalt asked.

"Only a year. I moved here from my home in Reno, Nevada, and went to work. After studying areas in California, I decided the greatest opportunity for the future was right here," Cole shared with unusual candor.

"For the future of Newport or for the future of Baldwin?" Dalt asked.

Cole laughed. "Both, sir. Both."

He then took them upstairs to view the bedroom suites. There were six. The master was a dealmaker. Once Nancy entered the suite through the double panel doors at the end of the wide hallway, she gasped, but only slightly, so as not to place too much emphasis on her unbridled delight.

Dalt and Nancy entered the sitting room of the master bedroom with its floor-to-ceiling windows on the bay. A charming fireplace with an antique French marble surround burned with a small fire even on this warm summer afternoon.

To one side was an enormous master bedroom, also facing the water, and to the other were his and hers baths fit for royalty, with closets to match.

Dalt looked at Nancy and said, "Should we?"

Nancy replied, "Do we have a choice?"

"Cole, are you the listing agent?" Dalt asked.

"No, sir, I am holding the home open in search of a client. The listing agent is one of the top brokers in my office," he said.

"Son, I think you may become one of the top agents very soon," Dalt said with his sarcastic wit.

"I'm sorry, sir, what was that?"

"We would like to place an offer. Will you represent us?"

Cole Baldwin was dumbstruck. Gathering his composure, he answered, "It would be an honor. Do you wish to think about it? Do you need more information? Will you need to speak to your accountant or lawyer?" Cole shot out questions in machine-gun fashion. He was nervous and excited. In the year since he had come to Newport, he had signed three lease contracts and made one condo sale. Cole was living on borrowed time and walking on thin ice. He was late with his rent. The Toyota needed tires; he was afraid to drive a client around in the car for fear of getting a flat.

"Cole, I'm ready to write an offer. Do you have the paperwork?"

"Darling, are you sure?" Nancy interjected.

"Absolutely. Let's give it a whirl!"

"Let's go into the library, where we can sit and write," Cole advised. "Please follow me." He continued leading his new clients into the walnut-paneled library, then sat down at an enormous mahogany partner's desk crafted in the Sheridan period style, with a leather top embossed with golden fleur-de-lis insignias on its outer border.

Opening a folder, Cole pulled out offer forms, fumbling to find the proper papers. He always traveled with every form required by real estate law. Today he was certainly glad he did.

Going through the basic formalities, he came to the sixty-four-thousand-dollar question.

"What would you like to offer?" he said. "The asking is ten million, and the property has been appraised at slightly more than that," he added.

"Appraised by whom?" Dalt asked.

"The Bank of Balboa–Newport. Here is a copy of the appraisal." Cole handed another paper taken from his folder to Dalt.

"I think this is very aggressive," Dalt responded.

"Sir, this is the highest price ever asked on Lido. It is potentially breaking ground, a new strata." Cole continued, "What do you think it is worth, and what would you like to pay?"

"Are there any comps?"

"No, sir, nothing close."

"Then how can a bank be so bold?"

"This is a rare buy. There is no other house like this. And the value is also in four large bayfront lots that one day will be certainly worth more than two or three million each."

"When will that day arrive?" Dalt questioned.

"In the next decade," Cole answered with authority.

"You seem very sure of yourself, Cole."

"Sir, Newport is platinum property. It will soar in time—a short time."

Dalt hesitated, then looked at Nancy, who said nothing.

"I agree," he came back. "I'll open the offer at eight-point-eight million dollars cash and thirty days."

Cole went on writing, more nervous than ever. In his head he calculated the sales commission at over four hundred thousand dollars, of which he would be entitled to 60 percent of half, or something more than one hundred twenty thousand dollars. Silently he was hyperventilating. Cole had come from a family that barely cleared forty thousand dollars a year, with hardworking parents both bringing in some of the bacon. Could this really be happening?

Dalt and Nancy both signed the offer. Dalt made out a check for half a million dollars as a deposit and handed it to Cole, along with his business card.

"Can I expect a response right away?" Dalt asked.

"Monday by five o'clock as the offer requests," Cole came back.

"I want this kept confidential," Dalt said. "Call us as soon as you know."

"Yes, sir, of course."

"We've got to get back to the family. You have a good Fourth, son."

"I think it may be the best ever," Cole replied. "Only in America," he added under his breath.

"I heard that, son. And you are correct. Only in America could a stranger walk into an open house and change the life of a young man on the spot."

"I'll do everything I can to make this work for you, sir. I am so appreciative for your confidence and your business."

"Call me as soon as you know something," Dalt reminded, taking Nancy's hand, and walking out of their potential piece of the South of France on the Newport bayfront.

They got in the car and looked at one another, both letting out a hoot and a holler.

"Can you believe we did this?" Dalt turned to his wife and gave her a big kiss before starting the car.

"If it's meant to be, then it will be," Nancy said, putting her arms around his neck and going in for a second kiss.

CHAPTER NINE

FACING THE TRUTH ABOUT JAMEY

My younger brother and I crossed the warm sand from the cottage, avoiding civilization, which was invading our corner of the beach and intruding on our bliss on this holiday weekend. Landing at my chosen spot just feet from the surf on the edge of dry sand, we were slightly elevated, up a small berm, which provided just enough protection from the incoming tide. Placing the beach chairs and blue and white striped towels down in the exact spot I had claimed many times before, Jamey and I settled in for our afternoon together at the shore. Marta had prepared drinks and snacks in an ice chest, which Jamey dutifully had lugged across the dune. Placing the chest down between us like a little table, he sat down in his chair, looking over at me as I spread lotion on my face and shoulders. Then he jumped up without a word and ran into the surf.

"Hey, wait for me," I called out, throwing down the lotion and chasing after him. Jamey had been a great swimmer as a kid, but I didn't know how safe he was in water now. Not really understanding what his condition was, I worried that the drug abuse had fried his brain. Why was he semicatatonic, not speaking much, withdrawn?

Catching up with him in a matter of seconds, I grabbed his hand, which he grasped like a clamp. We both entered the surf with a sense of abandon. Jamey let out a big yell. It was loud, almost a scream: "Wow!" His excitement was muffled by the sound of the crashing waves, but I heard it loud and clear. Looking over at him, I saw him smile from ear to ear. The joy was bouncing off his face like the sunlight off the seawater. My brother was happy. I cried, secretly wiping away the tears and pretending they were droplets of the ocean hitting my face, as I splashed my hands in the water, sending the current not only toward myself but also at Jamey. He returned the gesture in double time with exaggerated exuberance. We were both soaked even though we were only in the water up to our waists.

"This is ... the best time ... I've had." Jamey spoke slowly, cautiously, with long pauses between words. It wasn't much, but it was something.

"Me too. The best," I told him.

With that, he darted ahead just as a wave of about six feet approached.

"Dive. Dive under it!" I yelled.

I was not sure that he heard me, but he dove perfectly, missing the crashing tide, going under it, and coming up on the other side. When he surfaced, my heart started beating once again. He waved at me to join him, which I did in haste, before another wave could further separate us.

Reaching my little brother, I found that warm sweet spot in the ocean. We treaded water, floating in place, not moving much in any direction for at least fifteen minutes.

"Can we ride a wave?" Jamey spoke again, this time with more confidence.

"Sure. You keep an eye out for one and let me know so we can swim in with it," I told him.

Seconds later, there it was, the big one was coming in.

"Look!" Jamey yelled.

I looked and thought, *Oh boy.*

"Here it comes," he yelled again.

"Are you sure?" I asked anxiously.

"Sure enough," he said, at which point the surge hit us and we both began to swim on the top of the wave, full speed ahead.

The wave began to crest. We were both perfectly placed at the top as it did its curl under and raced toward the shore. I kept an eye on Jamey as best as I could while trying not to drown myself. He jetted way ahead of me, riding the wave perfectly, landing on the wet sand at the ocean's edge. My ride was slightly less than graceful as I stumbled in on foot, trying to keep my balance and keep an eye on him.

Jamey laughed joyously, lying on his side, rejoicing in his exhilarating triumph, while I tripped and landed on my butt a few feet away.

"How was that?" I called out.

"I think I beat you," he yelled back.

"I think you're right," I said.

"Let's get a drink from the chest."

Jamey and I scrambled up onto the dry sand and threw our ocean-weary selves into our beach chairs. He opened the chest and pulled out a couple of water bottles, handing me one.

"Jamey, can I ask you a question?"

"Okay."

I paused for a moment. "Are you doing okay?"

He looked at me as his expression went from carefree to controlled. "I'm doing okay, but I hate it," he said.

"Hate it? Hate what?" I pressed.

"I can't take the medicine they keep giving me!" he said, almost yelling. "It makes me feel half dead."

"Who gives you this medicine?"

"A doctor comes. Sometimes it's a nurse, but somebody comes every day around ten in the morning. I really hate ten in the morning."

"Did they come this morning before you came to see me?"

"Yes. But guess what? I get to skip tomorrow. Maybe if I move in with you, they will never come back."

I didn't know what to say to my brother. Part of me wanted to say, *Hell yes, move in with me. I'll fix this, and you'll get your life back.* Another part of me was thinking, *I'm not equipped. How can I do this?*

Saturday Night Dinner at the Ritz

Saturday night dinner at the Ritz was a family tradition for us whenever we could all be together in Newport. The restaurant was an old-fashioned dining room with red leather booths, bad art in gilded frames, and Gay Nineties chandeliers complete with those blown glass etched bowls over the bulbs. Father Dalt knew the owner from earlier days in Los Angeles, when he worked at the famous Scandia on the Sunset Strip. Mother Nancy adored the Ritz egg, a hollowed-out hard-boiled egg with a small opening at the top filled with caviar and a touch of sour cream and garnish.

There was no question that the place was the watering hole for the in-crowd. Of course, it wasn't my crowd. This packed Saturday night bistro was not really a family gathering spot. Rather, it was a date night magnet for the cigar-smoking Newport big spender, with a large selection of fancy women sipping champagne cocktails at the bar awaiting an invitation to dine.

Dalt pulled the Rolls up to the valet station. Several young men in red jackets surrounded the car. All the doors were opened in unison, and we got out of the car. Walking down the canopy-draped corridor to the front door, with my brother and I behind our parents, I overheard a superskinny woman dressed in a silver sequin cocktail minidress whisper to another of the red-jacket-clad valets. She handed him a calling card.

"Remember, there's a 10 percent fee in it for you for any business you send my way," she told him as he put the card in his inside breast pocket. The young man nodded and moved to the front of the curb as a jam of more of the most expensive cars on the planet arrived for Saturday night dinner.

Unable to believe what I had just witnessed, I was about to tap my father on the shoulder and share it with him, when a burst of people came out the front door. A couple of the men, the bankers Goldman and Kaplan, we had seen earlier that day at the Harbor Club among the crush. Both men were tall, handsome, and expensively dressed in fine tailored dark blue suits. They recognized my father and approached him. This was just the beginning of a social parade. It would take us half an hour to make it from the hostess, through the bar, and to our dinner table. Everyone in the place knew everyone. It was a family of folks of a certain ilk. And the common denominator was a luxury life—a life of expensive clothes and rich food and service on a Saturday night. There was service at the table for drinks and dinner, followed by service in the boudoir. It was all a package deal, part of the routine, what one did if one was part of the crowd in this corner of the world.

Dalt and Nancy greeted just about half the dining room as we made our way slowly down the long path to the outside dining pavilion, where my parents preferred to sit to enjoy the ideal summer evening weather. I must admit, the setting is magical. The garden terrace was enclosed in lattice bordered by manicured hedges, sculpted trees filled with twinkling white lights, and a forest of tropical plants and gently swaying palms backlit by a nearly full summer moon hanging low in the sky. At the back center of the terrace, a massive stone fireplace was ablaze, filling the outdoor room with that intoxicating scent of charcoal, the kind of odor that reminds one of a firepit burning on the beach at night. At the opposite end of the terrace was a trio of talented jazz musicians, filling the dining pavilion with the sounds of Sinatra.

The hostess seated us at a table smack in the center of the terrace. Every other table was overflowing with people. Dalt made sure his table would be prominent. That is what Dalt did with everything in his life. Our table was large and square, perfect for the four of us, covered in starched white linen with a white orchid plant reaching out of a small celadon vase, sending one stem of huge blooms skyward. Votive candles flickered around the orchid, and each place setting at the table featured formal silver-plated utensils framing an oversized black china charger rimmed in gold and adorned with a gold crest at the center, which was emblazoned with the Ritz monogram. I thought that it was all ritzy—hence the entirely appropriate name.

Dalt and Nancy ordered cocktails and the famous Ritz seafood appetizer, a tall mound of crushed ice layered with an assortment of fresh chilled shrimp, crab, scallops, and oysters in a very large silver bowl. Nancy made certain that the Ritz egg would follow. Jamey wanted no part of the chilled crustaceans and didn't particularly care for the Sinatra vibe, so he asked to be excused so he could take a short walk. Dalt initially requested that he stay and be with us, but he gave in as Jamey became more restless.

"Do you want me to come with you?" I asked my little brother.

"No. I'm okay. I'll just be out front sitting in a chair by the valet station for a minute. I'll be back for dinner."

Jamey had gotten his words out without hesitation. I thought this was a good sign. A day at the beach had done him some good. My parents recognized the change as well. They smiled at me, giving me some unspoken credit for having helped Jamey come out of his depression, if only for a moment.

"He'll be okay," Dalt said as Jamey left the table. "No teenage boy wants to be stuck with his parents on a Saturday night. We'll give him some room. After all, he is under watch pretty much 24/7."

Nancy added, "He can't go far. What harm can come to him at the valet station?"

The image of the call girl handing her card to the valet as we arrived flashed in my brain, and I worried that the valet station may not be safe as my mother assumed.

A waitress came and handed us dinner menus as the jazz trio played "All of Me." Nancy began to mouth the words as the lead singer sang them. She looked over at Dalt and took his hand as if they were teenagers on a date. I always knew somehow my parents managed to keep their spark despite any obstacle thrown in their path. For me, that was the definition of real love, a love that could not be broken, not by anything or anyone at any time.

The waitress was explaining the specials of the night, when we heard some yelling coming from the street side of the terrace.

Dalt jumped up from the table and made a run for the side entrance. He went out to the valet station in front of the Ritz. One of the red-jacket valets was grabbing Jamey by the collar of his blazer and looked as if he were about to pound him with full force.

"What the hell is going on?" Dalt demanded, full voiced. Jamey said nothing, but the valet continued screaming at him and now at Dalt.

"This little fucker tried to steal my stash," the valet yelled.

"What are you talking about?" Dalt came back.

"This is what I'm goddamned talking about," he said, holding up a plastic bag of white powder in one hand while the other still held Jamey in a grip at the lapel.

Dalt grabbed the valet and pulled him off Jamey. The valet tried to throw a punch at Dalt, which my father stopped with ease. The valet was high as a kite, perfect for a driver moving around hundred-thousand-dollar Ferraris at the Ritz.

Trying again to deck Dalt, the angry young man mistakenly threw a punch with the other hand, which was holding his precious bag of junk. The plastic bag ripped open and out came a cloud of cocaine dust, landing all over the front of Dalt's suit. Jamey stared at his father in disbelief. The valet froze for a second, also staring at my father's cocaine-covered suit.

Dalt wasted no time. He reached over and yanked the kid's name badge right off his red jacket. As it hit the pavement, the valet ran off the property through a lineup of more precious metal, nearly impaling himself on one advancing machine pulling up too close to the precious metal in front of the line.

"Jamey, what happened out here?" Dalt wanted an explanation as he tried to dust off his jacket.

"The dude offered to sell me some stuff," Jamey said, again speaking slowly and deliberately, pausing between words.

"How did he know you wanted to buy? Did you ask him?"

"He just came over to me when I was sitting there."

"Why was he about to hit you?"

"I guess I grabbed the bag from him when he showed it to me. Maybe he thought I was stealing it."

"Oh my God, Jamey," Dalt said seriously.

"I wasn't stealing it," Jamey responded.

"Do you realize how serious this is?"

Jamey didn't answer. He just stood there staring at Dalt, who was still trying to shake off the cocaine residue.

"Follow me, Son," Dalt instructed Jamey. They entered the front door of the Ritz and ran into a manager.

"This young man will no longer be employed by this establishment," Dalt said, placing the valet's name badge into the palm of the manager. "You might want to turn over this kid to the authorities for dealing drugs at your valet station. It's up to you."

The horrified manager began apologizing profusely. Dalt wasn't listening. He took Jamey by the arm and took him into the men's room to remove the rest of the white powder. Nancy and I were still seated at the table, waiting, and wondering. I wanted to get up and follow the yelling that we both knew was Dalt, but Nancy asked me to remain with her and let Father handle whatever was happening. I agreed, with considerable trepidation.

Father and son arrived back at the dinner table a few minutes later. The jazz singer was crooning "Our Love Is Here to Stay" as my father took his seat and Jamey took his. I was about to ask the big question, when Nancy sent me that look, the one that meant *Don't say a word*.

"I'm quite hungry for a perfectly charred rare rib eye," Dalt said. "They make them like no other dining room in Newport."

"Do you want to have the waitress explain the specials again, dear?" Nancy played along with her own Do Not Ask routine.

"Jamey, do you want the fettuccini Alfredo that you like so much?" Mother went on.

Jamey nodded. "Can I have it with shrimp?"

At least he had talked. Whatever happened couldn't have been all that bad.

We shared family dinner at the Ritz as if all was right with the world. Nothing was said of the incident. The Fairchilds even managed to make it through dessert, a summer pear cheesecake prepared in flaky, buttery filo pastry and served with a very rare port. People in the restaurant kept coming over to say hello. Most of them knew my parents by way of business connection, as many of Dalt's investment clients lived in Newport.

My father had no intention of allowing anything to spoil his family dinner. At least not anything as obnoxious as a drug-dealing valet.

When we were leaving the Ritz gardens as the crooner belted out "Moon River," the late-night dinner crowd was just arriving, and the valet station was again bustling with departures and newcomers. Not one word was exchanged about Jamey and the former valet drug dealer. It was as if it had never happened. After all, this was a summer Saturday night in one of the richest towns in the United States. Spoiling the carefree mood was not permissible.

The Fairchild family got into the anthracite-gray Rolls-Royce Silver Seraph and headed back to the beach cottage. There would be words between my brother and father in private. After climbing the rickety stairs to my refuge over the garage, I jumped into bed, pulling the soft down comforter over my head. The light of the bedside lamp glowed late into the night before I found the will to move over and reach to turn it off.

CHAPTER TEN

BEACH BLESSINGS

I was up and awake early Sunday morning. The sun rising in the east was strong, piercing through the sheers over the tall clerestory window in my room facing the alley. Putting on spandex walking shorts, a white T-shirt, and tennis shoes, I went downstairs to see if any of the family was up and about. The top half of the Dutch door was open at the cottage entrance, so I figured there was life to encounter. Entering, I could hear Marta singing softly in Spanish as the aroma of coffee came at me. My loving housekeeper was in the kitchen putting together the necessary ingredients for a legendary Marta breakfast.

"Your brother is up," she said, seeing me enter. "He's out on the beachfront patio."

"Good morning, dear Marta. Is the coffee ready?"

"Buenos días to you, my dear girl."

She handed me a large white ceramic mug of coffee.

"I needed this," I told her, and left the kitchen to find Jamey.

It was just before nine o'clock on a clear warm Sunday morning. The beach was deserted except for a flock of gulls searching for their own breakfast in the low sand dune covered in blooming purple ice plants that rose just off our patio and separated the cottage from the stretch of flat sand facing the Pacific.

Jamey was playing catch with himself, throwing an orange Nerf ball in the shape of a football high into the air, catching it, and repeating the motion over and over.

"Hey, Jamey, want to go for a walk with me?"

Jamey turned; the Nerf ball dropped.

"Sure. Okay. Where?"

"Oh, just down the peninsula on the beach toward the pier. Let's walk at the edge of the water," I offered.

I took my brother's hand. We walked over the low sand dune, sending a full flock of gulls fluttering. There were so many of them that we were under an umbrella of flapping wings. Jamey reached up, trying to catch one of the birds. I stopped him in the nick of time. We proceeded to the water's edge and headed northwest up the coastline.

"Jamey, what happened last night?"

"It wasn't anything," he said in a regular voice, without hesitation.

"Dad seemed pretty angry," I replied.

"Some guy was trying to sell me stuff. I didn't get any. Dad came and saw what was going on and lost it."

"Were you going to buy drugs?"

"I thought about it, but … no."

"Well, that's a good thing," I told him.

"I couldn't buy any. I didn't have any money."

"That's a good thing too—and a bad thing, because you wanted the drugs."

"I did."

Hesitating, unsure of what to say, I knew that another lecture from the sister not living at home would be a mistake. I put my arm around Jamey's waist. We kept walking, taking in what was certainly one of nature's most amazing gifts. The stillness of the morning was all around us as the sea softly lapped at the shore. People were beginning to surface on the sand as the sun slowly rose in a cloudless sky. In the distance, over the water, the dark silhouette of Catalina Island protruded, surrounded by a halo of white mist, making it appear as if the island was held afloat by a giant glowing inner tube.

Approaching the Newport Pier, I noticed that the previous absence of humankind on our walk was now a different enormous flock of wingless humans sitting, standing, and huddling in a circle on the sand, facing the water. In front of them, standing on a makeshift wooden riser, was a man in a flowing white robe speaking into a microphone. From a short distance we could hear the echo delay of the amplifier but could not make out the actual words. When the figure in white spoke, the crowd was still. When he paused, there was a roar of response.

"Kate, is that a concert?" Jamey asked. "I don't hear any music. Do you?"

"No. Just people clapping and yelling."

We walked faster, getting closer, and I realized that it was a church service on the sand. At the helm on the wooden pulpit of crates was the reverend Paco Villareal, the preacher husband of Grace, the young woman I had met at lunch. I knew this because his congregation kept shouting his name.

"Paco, Paco, Paco," called out the people on the beach. His name seemed to send them into a frenzy of spiritual fervor. Then music started to play.

"It is a concert," Jamey said.

"Not really," I told him. "It's a Sunday morning church service on the beach."

"Really? I've never heard of that," Jamey said.

"Really, it is," I told him. "And I know who the minister is."

"We don't go to church anymore," Jamey came back.

"We all used to go every Sunday to Saint James Episcopal on Santa Monica Boulevard," I said, recalling my childhood Sunday ritual.

"I don't know. We don't go anymore," Jamey said. "We don't go much of anywhere. Coming here was the first time I have been out of the house."

"Would you like to sit and listen for a few minutes, or do you want to keep walking?" I asked.

"I kind of like the music," Jamey said.

It was rock 'n' roll—the Christian variety, but rock just the same.

We sat down up front, at the far side of the crowd. Nobody noticed us as we joined the congregation. After all, it was just sand seating. Should we have been polite and gone to the back?

Reverend Paco mesmerized. He looked like a Jesus out of central casting, only he was more like a Jesus carrying a surfboard and probably wearing board shorts under his robe. Tall and slender, with long flowing wavy reddish-brown hair parted in the middle of his head and falling to his shoulders, this Mexican surfer Jesus with an accent spoke with a velvety-soft voice. His white robe fluttered in the breeze, and when he raised his arms to bless his flock, the morning sunlight bounced off the ocean behind him, sending an aura of light, creating laser beams off the preacher's fingertips, an effect that added to his already considerable spiritual weight.

"My friends, do you love God?" Reverend Paco called out into his microphone. The word *God* echoed at least three times. The congregation stood without being given orders to do so.

"God loves each of us," came the response. His flock knew this recitation.

"One God is the Creator of all things," the reverend followed.

Then the people shouted, "Blessed be the Lord God, Creator of the universe, King of kings, Lord of lords."

Reverend Paco raised his robed wings to settle the flock, motioning for them to sit back down. They did as requested in relative silence. Looking over at my brother, Jamey, I saw that he was awestruck by the spectacle. This was certainly not the conservative church ritual he'd known at the old Saint James in Beverly Hills.

"As we come to the end of our service together, it is time to ask if there is anyone among us in need of the healing powers of the Lord thy God. Come forward now to confess your sins and beg for forgiveness, mercy, and healing."

A line of parishioners, six in all, formed in front of the makeshift pulpit. A mix of old and young, shabbily dressed, and unkempt, almost homeless in appearance, they waited for transformation. At the end of the formation, my brother, Jamey, somehow appeared without my having realized that he had left my side. He waited for his turn to meet Reverend Paco. I was stunned.

The first individual approached when motioned to come forward. The congregation settled down. There was silence.

"Come forward, friend." Paco's first words once again echoed across the beachfront. "Share with me your challenge," Paco continued.

There was not the expected emphasis on God or Jesus. It was a faith healing without traditional words of faith—a new age spiritual healing, kind of an instant psychoanalysis channeled through a man with a tremendous gift for inspiring his followers. Was this not the mark of all the great prophets?

"I am sleeping with my best friend's husband," the woman began. She continued to tell her sordid story in full detail. The congregation shouted approval after each of the reverend's words of counsel.

"Do you love this man?" Paco asked.

"I do."

"Do you love your husband?"

"I do."

"Do you love God?"

"Oh yes, I do."

"Would God approve of your secret?"

"He would not."

"Do you have the strength found in your love of God to end your affair, to confess your sins to your husband, and to apologize to the man you have betrayed your husband with? And one more thing …" Paco continued.

"What is that Reverend?"

"You must also confess to and ask forgiveness from your best friend, whom you have also betrayed."

"I can't."

"Without a direct confession, an apology, and forgiveness from those you have sinned against, there is no forgiveness from God."

"But, Reverend, I always believed God forgives all sinners no matter what."

Reverend Paco took a beat, then delivered his message.

"Think about this. That belief has enabled mankind to commit the most horrible sins for generations, which is why the world has never changed, never grown closer to Almighty God. If there is absolute forgiveness without real confession and remorse, then the heart is left impure and we repeat our sins, sometimes over and over."

Reverend Paco placed his hands on the woman's shoulders as she knelt before his pulpit of wooden crates.

"May God grant you the will to overcome your desires of the flesh. May God give you the strength to face those you have hurt. May you find the help you need to repair your marriage and once again earn the trust of your husband and share his love in a way that fulfills both your lives."

The congregation rose and began chanting.

"Hallelujah. Praise the Lord! May the Lord give you strength."

The passion was all-powerful as the crowd worked their message of support. Everyone felt the energy, even me.

"I will try, Reverend Paco." The woman burst out crying. "I will do this," she said.

"Say it again so all can witness." Paco put his microphone to her lips.

"I can do this. God is great. I will succeed," she told the flock.

Feeling that I was going to faint, I detected a strange rush of adrenalin surging in my body. I am not a great believer in things supernatural, but I think I had just experienced a touch of remarkable powerful energy, which I didn't fully comprehend.

"Surfer Saint, Surfer Saint, Surfer Saint," chanted the congregation as the woman returned to her spot on the sand. Reverend Paco, part preacher, part healer, and part surfer, raised his arms to silence his flock as the next person approached.

Turning away for a second, I spotted my brother. He crawled, cutting into line behind the woman who had confessed her adultery. Getting up from my place on the outer edge of the beach congregation, politely excusing myself, I pushed through the tightly assembled second row of healing seekers to get closer to my little brother. Squeezing my body between two large women, I sat on my knees directly to the left side of Jamey as he approached Reverend Paco.

From the side angle I could see that his young face was flushed. Jamey trembled as Paco addressed him.

"Young man, how old are you?"

Hesitating, Jamey stared at Paco and did not answer directly.

"I'd say you are about fourteen or fifteen," Paco said, answering his own query. Jamey nodded.

"Who brought you here today, son?"

Finally, Jamey spoke, but with a definite tone of fear in his voice. "My sister. I came with her," he said.

"Where is she?" Paco pressed on.

I stood up, almost falling over one of the women I had sandwiched myself between.

"I'm right here, Reverend," I called out.

"Young man, tell me your name and share with all of us why you are standing here."

Again, there was a long hesitation. The congregation was restless, and chatter grew louder.

"My name is Jamey. Jamey Fairchild. And I am a drug addict."

"Are you taking drugs today?" Paco inquired gently.

"I am not," Jamey responded. "I have been clean for almost six months, but I don't think I can hold on any longer."

"How have you managed to abstain for so long?"

"I am in prison in my parents' house, watched 24/7. Before that I went to every drug rehab in LA. Nothing worked."

"Do you want to change? Do you want to be free of drugs, or do you just want to get high and escape?" Reverend Paco was direct.

Jamey began to cry. "I don't know. I just don't know. Some days I think I can make it. Other days I want to run away and get high and never come back."

"What about this day?" Paco asked.

"This day I want to be free of it. Can you set me free?"

"God can set you free if you ask for help. But you must believe it; you have to want it; and you have to promise not to give in or give up."

Reverend Paco came down off his crate pulpit and placed his arms around Jamey, pressing him against his chest. The congregation was silent as Paco spoke only to Jamey. I could hear some of his words.

"Do your parents love you, Jamey? Would they do anything for you, even give their own lives to save yours?"

"Do you have food to eat and a warm safe bed in which to sleep?"

"Can you attend school?"

"Do you have friends who care about you, as well as a sister and perhaps a brother, too, who would help you in any way?"

Reverend Paco did not wait for an answer. His diatribe was rhetorical, and he knew the answers to his own questions.

"You have been granted great privilege in life, Jamey. Do not throw away these gifts by giving into the evils of drugs, which will only rob you of the blessings you possess. You have fought the demons for six months successfully. Ask God to stand by you, and pledge to make it for another six months—a full year. Every morning when you awake and every night before you go to sleep, talk to God. Ask for help and support and thank God for each day that you get through this fight. You will see what happens; there will be a change in your life. It won't be easy, but change will come—if you don't give up."

Jamey cried audibly now, and the congregation could hear him. Reverend Paco repeated his last words so all could hear him as well.

"God will change your life. It won't be easy, but it will come—if you don't give up on God or on yourself."

I was still standing to the side, crying myself. Running to my brother, I put my arm around him and guided him away, as the next person in line approached, ready to confess with Reverend Paco.

Jamey and I left the church in the sand and walked down to the waterline, heading back toward our home.

"Are you okay?" I asked.

"Okay," he said quietly.

"Did that help you, or was it really hard on you?"

"I think I feel better now." Jamey smiled, turned toward me, and kissed me on the cheek.

"I am lucky to have you, Kate," he told me.

"And I'm lucky to have you, Jamey."

"Do you think I can make it for a year?"

"I know you can."

"If I make it for a year, will I be cured?"

"There's a good chance, little brother. You know, I'm not very religious, but I like what Reverend Paco told you. Ask God to keep you strong every day, and God will do it. You are such a great boy, so smart, so kind. Be strong like Paco told you to be and you will beat this. I promise that you will beat this."

"I love you so much. Want to race back to the house?"

"You've got to be kidding!"

With that, Jamey took off running down the hard wet sand at the waterline. I followed, but never caught up.

CHAPTER ELEVEN

OPPORTUNITY KNOCKS

Jamey and I made it back to the beach cottage. We were out of breath but in great spirits. The surprise session with Reverend Paco had made an impact on Jamey, who only the night before almost traded his six months of drug abstinence for a snort of cocaine provided by a drug-dealing valet.

Dalt and Nancy were up and about, enjoying a Marta breakfast of fresh cut fruit, rye toast and blackberry preserves, and the best coffee brewed by anyone. Marta was the coffee-making queen. Jamey and I found our parents out on the beachfront terrace under the striped umbrella. Dalt was reading the Sunday *New York Times*, and Nancy was just sipping her sublime coffee and looking out at the ocean through her large Jackie O shades.

"Kate, Jamey, come join us for breakfast," Nancy called out to us as we crossed the sand from our waterline jog. We waved back at our always cheerful mother.

Jamey beat me to the table, of course, as I stumbled behind, laughing. We both fell into chairs next to our parents. I sent a wave of sand dust toward Dalt as I slid into place. He put down his *New York Times* and glanced over at us.

"Having a good morning?" our father inquired.

"The best ever," Jamey answered.

"The best ever? Really?" Nancy chimed in.

"Really," Jamey answered without any pause.

Nancy glanced over at Dalt. "The beach life is good for our kids," she said. "We must spend more time here."

"That is the plan," Dalt replied.

Looking at him, I wondered if I was losing my private little cottage to a family invasion from Beverly Hills. Oh well, if it was good for Jamey, then that was all that mattered. Welcoming the idea of my family spending more time in Newport, I thought that at least I would still occupy my own room over the garage.

A Sunday Drive with the Parents

"Kate and Jamey, how about taking a ride with your mother and me?"

Dalt was always delighted to create surprises. He would show up with Nancy at our school and pick us up, and the next thing we knew, we were at the airport boarding a plane to Hawaii, Europe, or Timbuktu—it didn't matter. I remember asking Dalt on one of the first surprise trips what I was going to wear since I had come with nothing. I was probably eight or nine.

"Daddy, I don't have a suitcase," I told him.

"You don't need one," he answered. "We'll buy you anything you need when we get there."

That was how my father operated. As I grew up, I came to appreciate how unique he was and how I had benefitted from this glorious and generous, almost childlike aspect of his complex nature. My father chose to live the dream.

For my junior high school graduation, he landed a helicopter on the soccer field at El Rodeo School and picked me up along with three of my best girlfriends. We landed in front of the main entrance to Disneyland fifteen minutes later. Mickey and Minnie met us and escorted us into the park. I should have grown up to be an incredibly spoiled young woman. Instead, because Dalt and Nancy had made sure, I remained grounded. I knew how lucky I was, but I also knew most people in the world did not go to Disneyland in a helicopter. How had I escaped the obnoxious self-involved teenage girl thing? I guess I was just born to be decent. That's what I liked to believe, anyway.

"So, where are we going, Father?" I asked as Dalt took his final bite of perfect rye toast and blackberry preserves.

"Not far, darling. Your mother and I want to show you both something on Lido Isle."

It was just minutes before ten o'clock, which was early for Dalt and Nancy on a holiday Sunday morning. They both seemed energized and anxious to get going.

"In the car in ten?" Dalt requested.

Marta brought out a breakfast tray for Jamey and me as Nancy and Dalt went into the cottage to prepare for our Sunday surprise drive. The two hungry joggers who half an hour earlier had experienced a Sunday morning revival under the spell of Reverend Paco now gobbled the sustenance placed before us.

"Should we tell Mom and Dad about what happened?" Jamey asked. "I think I want to tell them," he added.

"Sure, let's tell them. Let's tell them all about it on our ride," I answered.

Wondering if I was offering bad advice, I considered how they would feel about my having taken Jamey to a faith healer on the beach.

"Can I have the last piece of toast?" Jamey asked, taking it before I could grant my release of ownership.

"Thanks. I was really hungry. Healing takes a lot out of a person."

We both laughed.

"Better head to the garage. Our ten minutes is almost up," I said. We both jumped up and left the glory of another magnificent morning on the oceanfront at Newport Beach.

Before we could get out the front door, the phone began to ring. Marta picked up the line and called out for Dalt. There was no intercom in the cottage, just the old-fashioned shout-out when the phone rang.

Dalt picked up the phone; I stopped Jamey from exiting to the garage so we could listen.

I heard Dalt say, "You're kidding." Then he let out a holler. "Nan, are you there? Come to the phone." He beckoned Nancy to join him.

"What is it, darling?" Mother inquired.

"We got it. They accepted our offer. Not even a counter. Can you believe it? Is this amazing? We actually got it."

"Darling, did you ever doubt that it would not work out? Of course, we got it. It is meant to be," Nancy said.

"Jamey, what do you think they got?" I asked my brother. He shrugged his shoulders, indicating he did not have a clue.

"Well, I guess we'll find out soon," I told him.

Dalt and Nancy came bouncing down the stairs like teenagers on a first date. My father's arm was around his bride of twenty-four years. He always still called her his bride.

"What was that all about?" I asked. "We heard your end of the call, and I guess you got something you wanted. And from what we heard, you sounded really happy."

"Pretty darn happy, I would say." Dalt gave no details, only instructed us to get in the car.

Crossing the Bridge onto Lido Isle

The remnants of the traditional Fourth of July Lido community parade confronted us as we arrived on this man-made isle in the middle of the Newport Channel. Hundreds of residents, generations of families from grandpas to newborns, lined up, dressed up, and marched the perimeter of the pit of elevated sand that had been developed in the early part of the twentieth century. Lido Isle today boasted some eight hundred homes, all valued in the millions and most erected on lots of thirty or forty feet in width. Dalt and Nancy had always loved the Lido life. They often visited friends on the isle. To them it was like living in a year-round summer camp for entitled adults who, despite differences of religion, politics, and social background, bonded together on tennis courts, on white sand beaches fronting the harbor, and at casual Friday night community potluck barbecues at the island clubhouse.

We lowered our car windows and waved at the parade line, shouting out appropriate Fourth of July salutations. Jamey begged Dalt to pull over so he could get out and join the line. To my surprise, Dalt agreed, and asked me to go with my brother.

"We'll make a circle around Via Lido Nord and pick you both up on Via Lido Soud, then take you to our surprise," Father told me, pulling over. Jamey wasted not a second getting out. My little brother ran toward an old fire truck and attempted to mount it in the rear while it traveled down the route. A man on the back grabbed Jamey as he leaped toward the truck, catching him in midair and swinging him on board. Jamey cheered—so happy. I waved my approval, threw him a thumbs-up, and got in line behind the old red truck. It was probably only traveling at five miles per hour, so the danger of what he was doing was alleviated.

It was almost ten thirty Sunday morning, and I felt as if we had experienced a whole lot of stuff in a few short hours. From Reverend Paco to Fourth of July celebrations, this was turning into a day to remember. How can life be so random and unpredictable? Today was shaping up to be a special day, a day of joy with a touch of wonder. I made a mental note not to take anything for granted on this day.

The parents made the two-mile drive around the perimeter of Lido in a matter of minutes, then pulled up beside Jamey and me and the old red fire truck. Dalt lowered his window and called for us to get back in the Rolls. With some reluctance, Jamey obeyed and jumped off his magical red horse. I clasped his hand as he leaped off. Dalt stopped his car. We both jumped in the back seat.

"Here we go," Dalt said. "Are you ready for our surprise?"

"Ready," we both said, looking at one another with puzzled expressions.

"What is it?" Jamey whispered.

"Got me," I replied.

Not long after departing the Fourth of July parade, we pulled up in front of a very handsome large home on the harbor side of the isle. I recognized a car parked in front at the curb. It was the old Toyota that belonged to the guy who had come to my rescue, right in front of us. What was his name? *Cole something*, I thought.

As Dalt pulled up right behind the car, the guy got out. It was the man who had chased down the guy who had dented my car in the parking lot.

"I know him," I said. "What is he doing here?"

"How do you know him?" Nancy asked.

"His name is Cole, Cole something, and I think he is a real estate agent," I shared.

"That's right, he is an agent, and he just sold your mother and me this house," my father told us. "This is our big surprise."

We all got out of the car as Cole came toward us. "Kate is that you?" were the first words he spoke.

"Yes. It's me. This is my family," I said.

"I think I now believe in fate," Cole responded under his breath, but we all heard him.

"Cole, this is my daughter, Kate, whom you seem to already know, and my son, Jamey." Father made his proper introductions.

"Sir, I met your daughter recently in a parking lot next to my office," Cole began to explain.

"Father, Cole came to my rescue when some guy dented my car."

"Well then, he is a double hero," Dalt said. "He saved my precious girl, and he made me the deal of the year, representing us in the purchase of this house."

Dalt turned to Cole and asked, "How did you do this without a counteroffer on the price? I was certain we would have to come up."

"I can't take too much credit," Cole replied. "The sellers are several heirs who have been squabbling over the sale, and I found out that they really want the money. I told them it was a onetime and final cash offer—take it or leave it. And they took it."

"Bold move, kid. What if they had refused?" Dalt asked.

"You can always go up, right?"

"I admire your guts, kid," Father told him. Cole continued to stare at me.

"Can we all go inside?" Nancy asked.

"Let's go," Cole answered, walking into the entry courtyard behind my parents and brother and next to me.

Getting the distinct feeling that I would be seeing this young man again, I figured that the next time he would most likely be driving a much newer car, thanks to my father.

CHAPTER TWELVE

A NEW DAY AND A NEW JOB

What a challenge rising at six o'clock in the morning the day after the Fourth of July holiday weekend. My parents celebrated the new house with Cole Baldwin, Jamey, and me with decidedly too much French Champagne—out of respect for the French architecture, naturally. We dined in the Shell Room at the Harbor Club, which was practically deserted on this Sunday night. It was a sign that the day of Fourth revelry was clearly over, or at least on hiatus. Calm had returned to the Newport scene. Admitting that I preferred it that way, I found it very curious that citizens here were always on celebration overload, surely a direct correlation to having too much money and plenty of time to enjoy it.

The lack of pressure to be productive put me in a very happy place, but it also lacked inspiration to motivate. Worried that I had run away from Los Angeles, a knee-jerk reaction to losing David, I tried to wipe my Monday fears away by jumping into a tepid morning shower. Due at my new job at the salon by eight in the morning, I planned to arrive by seven thirty, a demonstration of my seriousness about becoming an apprentice to Monsieur Lawrence. This was my entry into the world of fashion, a starting point that I had created by myself, for myself, without any connection to my family's influence.

When sharing the news about the job with Dalt and Nancy over Sunday supper, I had gotten the distinct feeling that while they were proud of my pursuit of work, they would have preferred that I enroll at Chapman. Promising them that such a move was next on my radar, I told them that I really wanted this job at AFochW.

Getting out of the shower, I towel dried my hair and wrapped it in a turban, then began rummaging in the closet for the perfect outfit for the first day of a fashion career, hoping to impress my mentors. Frustrated, I began tossing clothes about. Nothing seemed right. Everything I owned was too spoiled rich girl. I needed to look creative and individual, even slightly bohemian. Cutoff shorts with a fringe hemline and a T-shirt was the extent of my bohemian street urchin apparel.

The bedroom looked as if a tornado had hit it. I put on my standard raw silk straight-leg beige slacks; a starched white blouse, collar turned up at the neck, sleeves rolled up at the forearm; and simple beige Ferragamo square-toed flats, adding a black satin ribbon to my blonde hair, which was pulled back in a bun. Coco Chanel would be proud, so I fantasized, checking myself out one last time in the mirror and then making a dash for the car.

There was no traffic on the peninsula or on the Coast Highway. I arrived at the salon just before seven thirty. The center was a ghost town. Pulling my dented Mercedes into a parking spot right in front of the boutique, I turned off the engine before having second thoughts about parking in front of the store. It would be presumptuous. Moving the car down to a distant corner, out of view, out of the way, I walked back to the front door. It was locked. I knocked gently on the glass. Honoré appeared. She unfastened the latch and welcomed me graciously on my first day.

"My husband is waiting for you in the workroom," she said in her thick French accent. "Are you ready?"

"Very ready. This is such an opportunity," I gushed.

"You are lovely. We shall see. One day at a time. I think you are not a young lady used to work. This may be an adjustment."

"I look forward to the adjustment. And I hope you will give me the chance to prove myself to you both. I am not afraid of work, and I want to learn."

"That you will certainly do, my young friend. You will learn if you listen and commit yourself. Now go on. You do not want to be late with my husband on your first morning."

I passed through the shop and parted the heavy velvet drapes lined on the edge with tiny balls of fabric that framed the entranceway to the workroom, also known as Lawrence's revered and private sanctuary. There he was, the master, at his sewing machine surrounded by piles of fabric, cursing in French as he struggled to stitch something in the manner desired. Lawrence looked up, saw me, and halted his tirade.

"Bonjour, mademoiselle. It is good to see you so bright and early." Lawrence made a point of recognizing that I was early, then he instructed me to go to a worktable across from his, where bolts of fabric were stacked almost to the ceiling.

"I need you to do an inventory and measure each bolt on the machine there at the end of the table. Make notes of the amount of each bolt of fabric. Do you know how to use the Measuregraph?"

"Can you show me?" I answered rather sheepishly.

"I can, and I will," he said, leaving his sewing machine, adjusting the black horn-rimmed glasses on the top of his full head of wavy salt-and-pepper hair, the envy of every man over sixty, French or not.

After a quick demonstration, I shouted, "I can do this!"

"No need to shout, young lady."

"Oh, I'm so sorry. I was just excited."

"I can see that. Please start measuring. I must go back to my machine."

For the next three hours I measured and measured again without stopping. Nearly finished with the mountain of goods, I glanced over at Lawrence. He had finished working on the machine and was now adjusting an amazing hand-tailored gabardine suit he was fashioning on a headless mannequin.

"Do you approve?" he called out to me, noticing that I was staring.

"Very much. It is beautiful," I told him. "Is that for a customer, or is it for the rack?" Using rag industry lingo, I thought I had finally arrived.

"We do not call it the rack," he chided me, bursting my bubble of big girl confidence. "Nothing we make, or sell is off the rack."

"Of course. Please accept my apology."

Finishing the final six bolts of fabrics to be measured, I asked what my next assignment would be. It was close to eleven o'clock in the morning. The store had been open since ten. Customers were starting to arrive.

I was instructed to go on the sales floor and assist Madame Honoré. "Follow her lead," I was told. "When the store's empty of customers, study the garments. Learn the inventory, the pricing, the sizing, and the style."

Madame Honoré was working with a very trendy-looking woman, perhaps in her late thirties. She was elegantly thin with cerulean-blue eyes and dark brown hair, which fell to her shoulders in major waves. She resembled the actress, Marisa Berenson.

With great care and a very serious demeanor, this handsome customer examined every detail of a skirt and blouse being displayed for her approval. I watched with fascination, trying to be invisible and unobtrusive, studying the sales technique of a master.

It was more than that, though. This was a morning lesson in human nature, and I realized just how personal shopping for clothes can be for a discriminating woman. Every detail mattered. There was no such thing as simply trying on clothes for this woman. A T-shirt must be the correct T-shirt. The bracelet must be the proper adornment.

When she turned, around I noticed she was wearing a Hermès *H* belt around the waist of a perfectly fitted straight leg cotton jean that showed a slight *V* incision on the outer hem of each leg. Yes, her cotton jeans were specifically tailored to suit her taste. Growing up around women who dressed in major fashion, I surprised myself that I was zeroing in on what defines real style. The proverbial light bulb flashed in my brain. It was not just about spending the most money for the latest trend; real style was an outward extension of one's personality. I made a mental note, one I would not forget.

The bell tingled at the front door of the salon, signaling the entrance of another customer. Turning my attention away from my study, I walked toward the entrance to greet the arriving guest. Was I ready to help someone in my new environment? Probably not, but I was anxious to try.

But this would not be an opportunity to prove my worth. After the door swung open, Cole Baldwin entered. The drop-dead sexy Cuban Italian real estate guy looked very handsome in a navy-blue suit that sported exaggerated pointed lapels. A red silk necktie against a starched white shirt framed his chiseled face with its high cheekbones, narrow Roman nose, and flashing dark chocolate-brown

Latino eyes lined with the envy of many a woman—thick dark lashes. Cole looked more like a male fashion model than a real estate agent, one who had just opened escrow on my parents' nearly nine-million-dollar purchase. Seeing me immediately coming toward him, he extended both arms, offering a hug.

I accepted. Cole did not release me as one would expect in a typical hello kind of hug. His body was totally against mine; I could feel the definition of his chest against my breasts. He smelled like fresh laundry on a clothesline drying on a warm summer day with just the perfect breeze.

"How is your first day at work?" he asked, pulling back with a slightly awkward facial expression since he had held on to me for so long.

"It's great. I am loving being here and learning so much," I told him, smiling at the nine-million-dollar man.

"It's almost noon. Do they give you lunch around here? Can I take you across the street for a break?"

"Gosh, I don't know. I'm rather afraid to ask seeing as it's my first day."

"Of course, you may take a lunch break," Madame Honoré chimed in. She had overheard Cole's proposition. Turning away from the elegant customer, she added, "Can you make it quick, say, forty-five minutes?"

"Perhaps I should not go today," I responded.

"It's not every day that such a handsome young man comes in the store. You must go," Madame went on.

"You see, Kate, she says you must." Cole was very smooth.

"Then I must. What have you got in mind?" I asked.

"I think you look like a gourmet-salad-for-lunch girl," Cole said.

"Well then, you would be a little bit wrong. I hear they have the best fresh roasted turkey sandwiches on French rolls at Bristol Farms across the parking lot."

"If you wanted octopus for lunch, I would make that happen—in forty-five minutes or less," he said with a big grin.

This was beginning to feel like a date with the young man who had rescued me from the runaway driver who dented my car. The young man was now in business with my father, and he held onto hugs too long and smelled like clean laundry. I thought I could deal with all of it.

"Let's go to lunch. Are you paying?" I inquired, just being obnoxious.

"I am," he said.

"Then maybe I'll order something to go for dinner. I am a working girl on a limited budget."

"That would be fine as long as I can come over and share it with you."

"Oh, really? I'll have to give that a little thought."

Cole took my hand. We started to leave the shop. I turned to reassure Madame Honoré that I would be back soon.

We made it across the lot without being mowed down by any of the many black cars with tinted windows. The line at the turkey sandwich counter inside the Bristol Farms market was at least five deep. We took our place in the queue. Cole promised we would be served and have our sandwich in time for me to return as directed.

Ten minutes passed before we made it to the front to order. Time blew by as Cole kept talking, and yes, I was charmed. This man was not anything like David or, for that matter, like any of the kids I had grown up with. He wore his ambition on his chest, which was decidedly more aggressive than on the sleeve. This young man came with plans for his life, big plans. He was going to be somebody, stand out from the rest. I sensed this about Cole. It was a good thing. He reminded me a little of Dalt.

The deli man handed us our turkey sandwiches. The aroma was amazing, possibly even better than Cole's fresh laundry scent. I had asked for cranberries on mine—Thanksgiving on a roll in July. Cole and I gathered up our food and found a small cafe table in a section of this rather wonderful market famous for stocking foods not found anywhere else. This was another of the Newport magnets for the rich and the wannabe rich. Being seen perusing the aisles was a sort of status symbol. Shopping here made you part of a crowd—that crowd, the important crowd.

My family and I shopped Jorgensen's Market in Beverly Hills, also kind of a status emporium. But it wasn't the same. Nobody really cared in Beverly Hills if you shopped for groceries at Jorgensen's. In Newport, people cared. I didn't care. Would this mean a second-class future here? I decided to concentrate on more important matters, such as Cole Baldwin making the moves. Did I care? Did I like him? I hadn't been on any kind of date since my breakup with David. This lunch was sort of a date, I thought. Was I doing okay, or was I too snarky with this young man, keeping up my guard? I was a good guard, a real expert—especially as of late as a runaway from USC, from Los Angeles, from David, and from my family. I was just a spoiled rich girl trying to find my place in the world. Did I really think that? Boy, what a concept. Who was I kidding? Certainly not myself.

"Kate, will you go on a real date with me? Maybe a nice dinner and a movie?" Cole was direct.

I paused, not because I had known this was coming, but because I really wasn't sure this was such a good idea. The pause was a little too long, kind of like Cole's hug. Finally, I answered him, throwing caution to the wind: "Yes, that would be nice."

Cole beamed. His gorgeous face lit up; his cheeks blushed red; and those eyelashes of his fluttered.

"Tonight? Are you free?"

"Would you mind if we wait until Friday or Saturday, Cole? I have this new job, and it's only Monday."

"I don't know if I can make it until the weekend, but I will try."

"That's sweet of you," I told him. "If you wish, you could take me to lunch on Wednesday again—that's halfway through the week. We could try the roast beef sandwich here and talk about life. I need to know more about you." Pausing again, I delivered the zinger. "I need to know that you are not simply interested in me because you are doing business with my dad. Is that fair?"

"I wanted to date you the first time I saw you, when the guy hit your car," he told me. I believed him.

We finished the last bites of the best turkey sandwich in Newport, then Cole got me back to the salon. It had been thirty-nine minutes.

Getting to the door, he put his arms around me and again pressed his body against mine, kissing me with a passion I had not expected to experience.

"See you Wednesday," he said, opening the salon door for me, then leaving to go back to his real estate office next door.

Standing in the doorway in a state of mild shock—or was it just confusion? —I didn't know what to think or, worse, what to feel. I knew that I liked the kiss. It was that good.

The Second Half of My First Day

Madame Honoré was darting between several demanding customers, trying to charm them all with equal attention, as I reentered the salon, having taken just thirty-nine minutes for lunch, not the allotted forty-five.

She caught my eye and sent me a clear directive to get involved, tilting her head in the direction of a striking blonde woman, probably about forty with the figure of a Las Vegas showgirl. The woman was holding one of Lawrence's signature shift dresses up against her body as I approached.

"Hello, my name is Kate, and I would love to help you if I can," I said.

"Well, hello back. I'm Sofia, and I really like this dress. Do you think I have the right size?" she asked.

"Sofia, is it okay if I call you by your first name?"

"Don't be silly. Of course, it is."

"Everything in this store is made to measure. If the garment needs to be altered to fit, then it will be made for you and only you. The samples on display are just that—samples." I took the shift from Sofia and examined the silk tag. It was a size 6.

"This particular dress is a basic American six," I told Sofia. "Would you like to slip it on?"

"Honey, I may be a six on the bottom, but I'm a definite eight to ten on top," she said with a charming giggle.

I could see her point very obviously, yet I was very proud of my sales discretion. I found the sample dress in a size 8 and handed it to Sofia.

"Try this one. The dressing room is over here."

While Sofia went in to slip on the shift, I checked the sample to find a 10 if necessary. I also deciphered the price from the code, as I had been taught by Honoré. None of the garments displayed visible price tags. Instead, there were codes on the labels that translated into prices. Those codes were colored threads of gold, silvery pink, and violet fashioned in a manner indicating cost. It was very French, and I loved being on the inside of the pricing secret. Next stop Seventh Avenue, so I fantasized. Already I was planning my big New York to Paris future in the industry and had been employed for only about five hours.

Sofia came out of the dressing room wearing the linen shift. She looked like a model, stunning. The rounded neck hit her shoulder line perfectly, and the short cap sleeves accentuated her long, slender arms.

"It's a little tight in the breast area," she said, holding her breath to make the point.

"That can be let out just a bit, but the rest is perfect," I replied.

"Does the dress come in other fabrics?"

"Indeed, you can have it made to order. What do you have in mind?"

"The linen is great for daytime, but I would like the same dress for evening in something dark, short, and sexy."

"Not a problem. Our dressmaker has an outstanding selection of fabrics. I will get him."

With that, I left Sofia and made my way back into the workroom to greet Lawrence with the news.

"Marvelous, my young charge. And on your first day you may be making a nice sale," he said, patting me on my shoulder. "Tell your client I will be right out with a selection of fabric."

Returning to Sofia, I found her looking at a selection of very fine gowns. She was fondling the fabric on one, a kind of simple floor-length sheath fashioned in fine gold lace with appliqué gold sequin florals. Monsieur Lawrence had made this dress, with a team of seamstresses hand-applying the floral sequins. I had noticed the gown immediately when I arrived that morning. It looked like a dress Grace Kelly or Catherine Deneuve would wear to the Oscars.

"May I try this on?" Sofia asked.

"Of course." I checked the label and saw it was also a sample size 8. The gold and silver thread design indicated a price of fifteen thousand dollars. I gulped.

"I think this will fit," I told Sofia, taking the gown off the hanger, and following her into the dressing room, saying nothing about the cost.

Sofia slipped out of the linen shift, and I helped her into the delicate gold gown. She wore a slip, so she glided into the dress with ease. Fastening the back, I concluded that the gown fit as if it had been made for her—a Cinderella moment. Sofia looked as if she was going to cry.

"Is everything all right?" I was concerned.

Sofia hesitated. "Oh my God. Yes. It is just so beautiful. I love this dress, and I must have it," she gushed, never asking the price.

Madame Honoré entered the dressing room—perfect timing, as if on cue—and took over to make the sale. She had brought a selection of evening fabrics from her husband's workroom. Sofia selected a black silk brocade for a copy of the linen dress made for evening wear. The three items came to a sale of just under twenty thousand dollars. Madame Honoré winked at me, which I took as both a sign of success and a directive to go back to the showroom.

My first day in the world of high fashion was turning out reasonably well.

As Sofia finished her business, she came over to thank me.

"I understand this is your first day," she said. "Well, I am so happy to be your first customer. I hope I bring you much luck and success." Sofia handed me her calling card. It was a very cream-colored card in heavy stock with a bit of a ragged paper finish. Her name was in pink script, reading Sofia Berns, along with a phone number. That was all.

Taking the card and looking at it, I said her name out loud.

"Thank you so much, Sofia Berns. It was lovely to meet you, and I hope to see you again soon," I told her.

"I have a daughter about your age. We will all have lunch one day," she replied, turning to leave the salon.

"Good job, my dear." Honoré turned to me with a compliment. "Sofia Berns was in the store several times looking, but this time she purchased."

"She seems very nice," I answered.

"Nice, yes. But a very troubled marriage," Madame shared. "Sofia is married to Arthur Berns, a major East Coast financier who sports as many girlfriends as he can handle. His exploits are legendary around here. Another 'well-kept' everybody-knows-it secret in Newport."

"Seriously? Why does she stay with him?" I asked.

"Because she is trapped. Trapped by a lifestyle she cannot duplicate without him, and afraid to break it off. Trapped by an image of family and marriage that is not real but binding just the same. Her oldest daughter, the one she mentioned, is engaged and planning a fall wedding at their waterfront mansion."

"This sounds very complicated and rather sad," I said rather naively.

"It is life," was all that Honoré came back with. Repeating herself, she went toward the workroom. "It is life."

CHAPTER THIRTEEN

UNEXPECTED MOMENTS

Leaving the store at around five thirty on my first day, feeling elated and responsible, at least in part, for a twenty-thousand-dollar sale, I felt my self-worth had risen demonstrably. Perhaps I truly was cut out for a career in the fashion world. Avenue Foch West was not exactly Avenue Foch Paris, but it was a start. Anyway, it was my start.

My Mercedes with the dented rear fender was still capable of going topless. On this summer evening in Newport, the warmth of the sunset beckoned. It was a glorious intoxicant as I made my way down Pacific Coast Highway back to the peninsula and my parents' beach hideaway.

Part of the peaceful satisfaction on the drive was thinking about my after-lunch kiss from Cole. That kiss almost made me think there might be hope for love after David. It scared me because I was still certain that David remained my true love, and one kiss from a near-stranger surely could not derail that love.

Pizza would be the only remedy for my inner conflict about the kiss. Conveniently, this incredible pizza parlor called Z Pizza was right in my driving path on the way home to the cottage. The car simply stopped right in front, and I got out, then dashed inside, following the aroma of pepperoni and mushroom, which beckoned. I ordered an extra-large pizza to go just as my cell phone sounded its buzz.

Fumbling through my bag and locating the electronic marvel, I managed to spill all the other contents onto the pizza parlor floor.

"Hello," I answered.

"Kate, is that you?"

"Yes. Who is this?"

"It's Cole."

"Cole? Did I give you my cell number?"

"No. Your dad did. I called him in Beverly Hills, and he said to call you."

"Really? About what?"

"I have the escrow papers for the house, and he wanted me to drop them off with you rather than faxing them."

"Oh, I see. Can I get them tomorrow at the store?"

"You could, but I have them with me now. If you don't mind, I'd like to drop them off this evening at your house." Cole added, "I think your dad may want to go over some of the clauses with you over the phone."

Really? That does not sound like my father, I said to myself. "When do you want to come?" I decided to take a chance.

"Whatever time is good for you. I can be there in twenty minutes."

"Make it an hour. I'm not home yet."

"Your dad gave me the address on Balboa Boulevard. I'll see you in an hour."

Upon hanging up my phone, I was feeling somewhat uneasy about the delivery rendezvous. My pizza was ready, so that helped to sidetrack the fear. The man behind the counter asked me if everything was okay with the order. My facial expression must have reflected anxiety over Cole's pending escrow paper delivery, which I suspected was a ruse he'd created to see me. Dalt never asked me to go over his financial documents.

"Oh, it's just great," I told him, paying for the pizza. "This is the best pizza, and I'm celebrating my first day at a new job."

"This is a really big pizza for one. I hope you'll have company," he said with a grin.

"It seems that I will, although that wasn't the plan," I replied. "There's nothing better than a girl getting to eat pepperoni pizza alone in her PJs with no sense of guilt or control. Pure indulgence."

The man laughed, nodding in agreement. I took my pizza and returned to my car, then headed down Balboa Boulevard to my sanctuary. I would save the pizza until after Cole left to relish it alone in pure selfish indulgence.

So Much for a Quiet Night Alone

Entering the Dutch door entrance on the side of the beach house, I could see the silhouette of a person sitting with his or her back toward me on the oceanfront patio outside the living room. With the sun lowering over the ocean horizon, I could not make out my unannounced visitor.

Placing the pizza down on the entry hall console, I entered the living room, opening the French doors leading to the patio.

"Kate, it's me, Carrie."

"Carrie, what's up? Are you okay?"

"Not so okay, Kate."

Walking over to her, I sat down, putting my hand on top of hers on the arm of the wicker chair between us. She began to cry.

"Oh no, is it the baby? Did something happen? Have you seen a doctor?"

"I am pregnant, Kate, and I have seen a doctor. But that's not it. The baby is fine and normal for a month-old fetus, according to the doctor."

"What's wrong? How can I help?"

"I told Joe," she shared, letting out a deafening sigh. "I told him everything. About Tony and me, that is."

"What did he say?"

"He was really hurt, Kate. I think he started to tear up, which I had never seen before."

"Did you tell him how much you love him and that you were so lonely for physical intimacy that you strayed?"

"I did. But he felt betrayed. Joe could hardly speak. He just looked at me as I stammered on, trying to explain, trying to ease his pain, trying to make sense of all of it."

"Really?"

"Yes, really. I know I made it worse."

"What did you say?"

"I told Joe I loved him and that I wanted to stay married to him but that I wanted to keep the baby even though it was not his child."

"That was brave. How did he take it?"

"He asked me to leave. I begged his forgiveness. He walked me to the door. I came over here. You were not home, so I took refuge on your terrace."

"Well, you'll just have to stay here until we can figure this out."

"I have no clothes, not even my toothbrush."

"It doesn't matter. You'll stay here for now. Oh, I have the largest pepperoni pizza ever made. We'll eat. We'll drink. We'll talk and find some answers."

Carrie got up out of her chair and came over next to me, putting her arms around me, kissing me on the forehead.

"You are the best girlfriend I have ever known for less than a month."

We both hesitated for a split second and then laughed. Laughter and pizza are indeed the best medicine.

The Evening Plot Thickens

Carrie practically devoured my pizza, along with more than one bottle of Nancy's chardonnay over ice, not such a great idea for a one-month-pregnant woman. The sun was now low in the sky, but the day was far from done. It was almost seven o'clock at night, and Carrie could no longer keep her eyes open. Putting a throw blanket over her that I had grabbed off the living room sofa, I went back in the house to get out of my work wardrobe. The evening of solitude and pizza had not evolved as planned or hoped for.

The doorbell chimed before I could make it up the back stairs to my perch above the garage. I had forgotten that Cole was coming over with Dalt's papers. Turning around to go and meet him, I wanted to make the transfer quickly.

Since I was not inside the main part of the cottage, I surprised Cole by coming up behind him outside.

"Did I beat you here?" he asked.

"No. I've been home for a while. I live over the garage; it has a separate entrance," I explained. Cole reached out and put his arm around me, intent on kissing me hello. I pulled back.

"Gee, I'm sorry. Did I offend you somehow?"

"Oh no. I'm not offended. I guess I'm just a little surprised. And a little worried."

"Worried about me?"

"I guess so."

"Because I'm doing this deal with your parents?"

"I guess so."

"If I weren't doing this, would you still be worried about me?"

"Probably."

With that answer, Cole took my hands and pulled me in toward him. He slowly and carefully planted his moist lips on mine, and his tongue entered my mouth. It was that same amazing kiss that had caught me off guard earlier in the afternoon, with the same reaction, namely, shivering from head to toe. After a few moments, I kissed him back with equal interest and more passion. We broke the embrace. Cole stepped back, looking at me dead in the eyes.

"Are you still worried?" he said softly.

"More than ever."

"Good. Then we're on the same page."

"Are you here to deliver documents?"

"I am."

Cole placed his briefcase on the brick stoop. Reaching down to retrieve Dalt's escrow papers, he handed them to me.

"Can I come in? Maybe you'd like to go over them with me so you can answer any questions your dad may have over the phone."

I knew this was a handy excuse to steal another kiss. I was tempted.

"No, that's okay. I can read," I offered in protest, playing it at least a little cool.

"I'd sure like to see the house, look at the ocean view as the sun goes down. I promise to be good."

"Well, if you promise, I suppose I can oblige."

I knew I was asking for trouble, but so what? After my encounter with Carrie, who was still sleeping on the terrace, what else was in store?

Opening the Dutch door, Cole and I entered.

"This is really sweet," he said, admiring the living room facing the ocean.

"I agree, and I hope you are not talking to Dalt about selling this cottage." I was direct.

"Gosh. I don't know. Your parents didn't say anything about this house. Nothing about selling it or anything like that."

"I think I would never speak to you again if you made them sell, even after that second kiss."

With that response, Cole changed the subject, noticing the back of Carrie's blonde head resting on the top of the patio chair.

"Is somebody out on your patio?"

"It's my neighbor Carrie. She had a little too much wine, and she's taking a little nap."

"Okay."

"She had a really hard day. I didn't want to disturb her."

"Do you have any wine left?" Cole asked, smiling at me again, staring into my eyes.

"I'm not sure that's a very good idea."

"Share one glass with me sitting here on the couch as the sun sets. Then I'll go home."

"Is that another promise?"

Cole sat down. I went into the kitchen to get the wine. I'd already finished a couple of glasses with Carrie, more than my usual. I returned and handed Cole a goblet. He raised the glass to toast our friendship, new as it was.

"To the most beautiful girl with a dented Mercedes who I have ever known."

We clicked glasses. I gave him a look and sat down on the couch beside him, but not too close. Just close enough.

As the eight o'clock hour approached, the Newport sky was ablaze with hues of orange and purple as the giant ball of flame was about to melt into the sea.

"Oh my God. Look, Cole. Look. It's about to start. The green flash is going to happen any second."

Cole didn't know what I was talking about.

"The green flash?"

"Look west, Cole. There it is!"

We both saw the green flash, which lasted only seconds.

"That was awesome. How did you know?" he asked, moving right next to me.

"Just something I know," I replied a bit smugly.

"I bet you know many things you could teach me." Cole was serious.

"Maybe. But that will take some time," I added with caution.

Cole hesitated no longer. Kissing me once more, he was serious this time, and he wanted more. His passion was convincing. I was trying to use my head, not my heart, to rationalize engaging in the moment. Having been with only three other men in my life so far, with just one of them being a true lover, I was seeing this as an opportunity for comparison. Yes, I was being coldhearted, but I was not in love with Cole. I hardly knew him. This was all about sex, pure animal attraction.

As I continued to evaluate, Cole made advances. He was unbuttoning my blouse, still kissing me as his hands cupped my breasts, stroking one of them gently. Somehow his suit jacket was off, his tie unfastened, and his white starched shirt unbuttoned. I wasted no time helping him remove the shirt. Cole's chest was perfection. He was slim, defined, and tan. I ran my hands down his cheeks, moving down the sides of his neck, across the tops of his shoulders, then over his chest. Cole's nipples stood at attention. I moved my head down, placing my lips on the right, then the left, sucking very softly. He squirmed, then our eyes met again. I knew there was no turning back.

Tempted to pull the plug and ask Cole to stop, I gave in to my carnal pleasure. I whispered to him, "Am I going to regret this in the morning?"

"Not if I can help it," he came back.

We made love, hot, sweaty, wild love, on Nancy's blue and white couch facing the French doors of the patio, where Carrie still slept in a wine-induced semicoma. In fact, we did it twice, both times climaxing. Cole was a wild man, unstoppable. He wasn't David, but he was a remarkable lover. Trying not to compare him to David, I thought of how I didn't love Cole and how I still loved David. Yet, Cole, the real estate guy doing a deal with Dalt and Nancy, rocked my world. Oh my God, I was confused, but I was also euphoric. Words escaped me; I could hardly speak.

"Are you hungry, Cole?" was the only lame thing I could muster. "I have two slices of Z pizza left that I brought home. Carrie ate the rest, but I do have two slices I could heat in the microwave."

"That's sweet, but I'm not hungry. I may never need food again after you."

Laughing a little, I wondered, was I food for the heart, for the soul? I had crossed the line of female decency with a man I really didn't know. Perhaps this was just a onetime thing. I could pretend it never happened in the light of day. On the other hand, his real estate office was next door to my new place of employment. And I had promised him a roast beef sandwich for lunch on Wednesday. *I am in big trouble. Huge trouble. Beyond huge trouble.*

"May I spend the night with you, Kate?"

"What if my dad calls to discuss his escrow papers? Do I tell him I'm busy making love to his agent, then suggest he call him in the morning?!" Cole howled and made me smile. "Not a good idea? Can we hold off on the overnight?"

"I'd rather not. I want to make love to you again and again."

"I think you already did," I came back, grinning.

"Was it good for you?" Cole joked.

"Oh yes, it was good for me," I told him.

"Good enough to try it again, maybe tomorrow night?"

"Good enough for sure. Tomorrow night maybe."

We turned toward the French doors as Carrie started to rally. She called out, "Where am I?"

Cole and I dressed in a split second, as best we could. Carrie was now standing up, looking in at us. She appeared to be dazed. I went to the French door and opened it, motioning for her to enter. She followed my lead, surprised to see Cole and me.

"Carrie, this is my friend Cole. He's a real estate agent working with my parents." I never went further than that. Cole smiled at her and put out his right hand to shake hers.

"I'm just leaving," he said. "Nice to meet you. Hope to see you again another time." Then he reached over to me and shook my hand. "Thank you for your help with the papers. May I call you tomorrow?"

"That would be fine," I said, showing my secret lover to the door.

"Carrie, I'll be right back. I'm going to walk Cole out to his car."

Carrie was still in a trance. She plopped herself down on my lovemaking couch as Cole and I left the cottage.

As we made it to Cole's Toyota, which was parked illegally in the alley behind our house, he kissed me again with that same killer kiss. I went weak in the knees.

"I'll call you tomorrow," he said, releasing me. He got in his car.

"I have something to confess," he continued. "I faxed the documents on the sale to your father. Bringing them to you tonight was an excuse to see you. Will you forgive me?"

Saying nothing, I was in my own trance, different from Carrie's, but a trance just the same.

Going back in the cottage, I went right over to my new friend with the big dilemma and told her she was spending the night with me. Tomorrow would be another day, another chance to figure out what to do, another day to reconcile my feelings for, and my actions with, Cole.

CHAPTER FOURTEEN

REMORSE OR REBIRTH?

I had gotten little sleep following my sexual encounter with Cole. Adding to my complicated mental state was the situation with my new roommate Carrie, who was pregnant with the child of trainer Tony and was also wife of the handsome, impotent great chef Joe Worth.

Just about every hour I rose from my sleepless bed with its sheets, pillows, and comforter thrashed from turning left to right and back again. I went in the cottage to check on Carrie in the guest room. She had slept like a baby while I remained in a state of mild panic.

The sunrise came with great relief. Dressing without fuss, I left my over-the-garage sanctuary to make morning coffee and once again check on Carrie. Enveloped in Nancy's monogramed Egyptian cotton sheets, I saw that Carrie remained sound asleep, perfectly content, even appearing to smile.

Drinking a cup of coffee by myself, I went out on the oceanfront patio and took in some very deep breaths. The ocean air was medicine. I began to feel stronger and less stressed, albeit still tired.

It wasn't so much that I had given in so quickly to sex with Cole. Rather, it was an overwhelming sense of betrayal to David. How could I claim to be so in love with this man but then give myself to a virtual stranger? Was this just an act of rebellion or some stupid selfish impulse? Cole was a masterful lover. He made me feel something, but what was it?

With Carrie still asleep, I left her and went to work on my second day in the world of high fashion in a relatively small town of very rich white people. Arriving early, I knocked on the door. Madame Honoré greeted me cheerfully. She directed me to the back room, where I found her husband waiting to instruct me on cutting more fabric for one of his latest designs.

Having been given a specific and difficult task, I was learning a trade, a skill. It was also an artistic pursuit. I concentrated with every ounce of my focus as Monsieur Lawrence taught me the craft of the scissor. The lesson would turn out to be the bulk of the morning immersion.

As the lunch hour arrived, my teacher asked if we could order in and continue working. Madame Honoré had been busy all morning with customers in the salon. We could hear the constant tinkling of the doorbell and plenty of conversation with clients. Now, just after noon, the salon was silent. Monsieur Lawrence called for his wife and requested a lunch order to be delivered. She obliged with her customary deference to his command and dashed to a phone to collect our midday sustenance. Curiously, she never asked what he, or I for that matter, wanted for lunch. Just as well since I had no appetite. Remaining in the store was something of a blessing because I did not want to run into Cole next door if I were to step out to get lunch again at Bristol Farms.

While Madame was on the telephone ordering food in French, which I did not understand despite years of studying the language in school and receiving mostly top marks, that tinkling doorbell began to ring. Madame finished her call and went to answer. It was Cole.

"How pleasant to see you again, young man. Are you here to see Kate?"

"I am. Is she available? I do not want to intrude."

"Wait here. I will check."

My heart sank. I buried my head in the stack of silk gabardine fabric Monsieur was teaching me to trim and pretended to be extremely occupied.

"Master Cole is here to see you. Can you take a moment?"

"Would you please ask him to come back later, perhaps at the end of the day? I must keep at my task."

"You are a very dedicated young lady. I think I may have judged you wrong as an American rich girl."

I thought that she was not so far off, yet I was enormously relieved to avoid Cole, while at the same time impressing Madame Honoré.

Facing the End of the Day

At five o'clock sharp, Cole Baldwin stood outside AFochW waiting for my exit. I could see him from inside the shop. Avoiding him was childish. Putting on my big girl happy face smile, then saying "Good day" to my fashion mentors, I opened the door. Cole rushed toward me; his arms outstretched. Before we could say hello, we were kissing. Well, he was kissing. I was trying to respond in kind but was not feeling the joy. He could tell.

"Is something wrong?"

"Oh no. I'm just tired and preoccupied."

"I am so happy to see you. All I thought about all day long was seeing you."

I think it's pretty much the dream of every young woman to have a drop-dead handsome man thinking about her and waiting to see her all day long.

"You are so sweet," I told Cole, perhaps a lame response given our intimacy the night before.

"Can I take you to dinner?"

"Really? Gosh, I don't know. I'm not very hungry. It's kind of early."

"We can wait and go later whenever you say."

"Cole, I need to go home now and check on Carrie. She spent the night, and I'm worried about her. I left her this morning still sleeping and came to work."

"I will go with you," he offered without hesitation. "You may need some backup."

"Probably not wise. Can I explain later?"

"Can I call you in an hour?" Cole persisted.

"Yes. Absolutely, call me. Maybe we can go to dinner."

I went to give Cole another hug, this time without the kiss, and jumped into my car. Of course, it wouldn't start. This never happened. It always started. Cole came over and quickly assessed the problem: a dead battery.

"Let me drive you home. We can call the auto club and fix the battery later."

"That would be nice," I told him with a sigh. I got out of the yellow Mercedes. Cole took my hand as we walked down the parking lot toward his Toyota.

"Did you have a good day?" he questioned politely.

"I did. Monsieur Lawrence is teaching me the art of cutting fabric. And you? How was your day?"

"Also, very good. Besides thinking only of you, I was on the phone with your dad about the Lido purchase. He is one great guy."

"I can agree with that," I said, again worried that I had leapt off the cliff with Cole too soon, especially given his business connection with Dalt. Feelings of guilt and fear were clashing in my head and heart.

Traffic was very light on the Pacific Coast Highway; we arrived back on the peninsula without delay. Cole pulled up and parked parallel to the garage, again illegally, in the alley, and I jumped out to see if Carrie was still there. Cole followed.

Opening the Dutch door, I called out for my new friend. She answered almost immediately.

"I'll be right down. I'm upstairs in my room," she called out.

Carrie appeared down the stairs, surprising me by looking happy—her beautiful, smiling, big-chested blonde self. Her makeup was flawless; her hair, flowing and falling free to her bronzed shoulders. Wearing an off-the-shoulder loose T-shirt and those little booty-favoring shorts, the woman with the major crisis seemed unfazed just twenty-four hours later.

"Carrie, you look really good," was all I could say without being too obnoxious, given my shock and disbelief.

"When I feel good, I look good," she came back, uttering the Newport Beach philosophy of life shared by the average beach chick. What about Joe, her husband, who had thrown her out over the confession of her sexual needs resulting in pregnancy?

"Kate, Joe came over this afternoon, and we talked. He apologized for his tirade and for throwing me out. He wants time to think."

"Think about what?" I pushed.

"Think about if we can handle this and still stay together."

"Is that what you want?"

"It might be."

"And what about Tony? Is that what he'll want?"

"Tony doesn't know."

"Don't you think you'd better talk to Tony?"

"I do. I will."

"You are having his child."

"Kate, I don't think Tony wants a child. He'll want me to abort."

Sitting down on the couch, amazed and upset over our conversation, Cole was silent, sitting down beside me. My mind raced. Was this the same situation I was potentially facing with Cole? Our one-night stand was amazing, but I did not love Cole. What would I do if I were to get pregnant? Of course, I wasn't married to someone else, so at least I wouldn't have to face that moral dilemma.

"Kate, can I stay here for a few more days until we work this out, one way or the other?" Carrie asked.

Not answering right away, I looked over at Cole. He took my hand.

"I suppose it's okay," I finally replied.

"I promise to be no trouble. You are an amazing girlfriend. Can I take you both to dinner? We won't talk about anything that's not fun. I promise."

Cole spoke up, seconding the idea for a fun dinner.

"Let's go to the Cannery for some amazing sushi," he offered. "I'll buy."

"No way," Carrie came back. "This dinner is on me."

Carrie went next door as if nothing was different and found Joe in the kitchen. She invited him to join us for sushi. He declined. Grabbing her car keys off the kitchen counter, she went to the garage and got in her white BMW convertible, put the top down, and came to pick us up in the alley, where Cole and I had found ourselves leaning up against his car and waiting.

Strange, but Cole seemed unfazed by the situation. I was in a fog. We got in the BMW. I sat up front. Cole jumped in the back. Carrie stepped on the gas and sped off down the alley.

After Dinner, I Was Dessert

I tried to stop Carrie from drinking more chardonnay and from eating sushi. She was unstoppable, though.

"Oh, all that stuff about pregnant women not drinking wine or eating raw fish is just a scare tactic," she protested.

Cole and I held back, trying to set a respectable example. We each drank a couple of glasses, and I was feeling the buzz but was still in control. Nobody asked me for ID at almost twenty. Cole was older, but I didn't know his age; I'd never asked. We'd had sex, but I didn't know his age or much of anything else about him.

After dinner, Cole insisted on driving the white BMW convertible, with Carrie and me sharing the tiny back seat. The top was still down, the night air, crisp and pungent. We welcomed the wind blowing through our hair as Cole made our way home down Balboa Boulevard.

Using Carrie's remote to open the garage door, Cole pulled in. The noise of the door lifting summoned Joe. He appeared in the doorway of the garage leading into the house. Staring at Carrie, looking very sad, but only for a moment, Joe turned away, closing the door. We got out of the car and walked out of the garage and down the brick walkway next door to my front door.

Carrie seemed perfectly fine with seeing sad-faced Joe. She was still high from the wine, ready to make her way back to the soft down comforters in Nancy's guest room. Running away from home can be far less traumatic when you only go next door.

"Good night, my new best girl pal and her friend Cole." Carrie was almost singing. "I had a wonderful time with you both. Thanks for being my friend."

With that, Carrie floated up the narrow stairs to her hideaway. Cole and I looked at one another, saying nothing. Then, without warning, Cole embraced me with both his strong arms and picked me up off the floor in one big swoop.

Carrying me out the door and back down the brick path to my rear staircase, Cole lifted me up the wooden incline with great ease, arriving at the door to my bedroom over the garage. He pushed the door open with his backside. We entered. Still holding me tight, Cole crossed the room and gently deposited me on my bed.

In something of a romantic haze, I looked up at Cole. He was very happy, smiling ear to ear, eyes watering as if almost crying. Clearly, I was in over my head. This boy was in love. I still didn't even know how old he was. What was his favorite color? Did he like a certain kind of music? Where had he gone to school? Had he gone to school?

Despite my concern over the formidable unknown, I gave in yet again to the primal desire for love and attention. Cole began to undress me as I leaned back on my bed. He was very gentle, stroking my flesh. He unbuttoned my shirt. It was simple carnal pleasure. I began to respond to his desire.

We made love three times that night and slept in each other's arms naked. I was holding on as Cole's chest rested firmly against my back, as if we were one. Cole was my blanket; his body heat made me feel protected—safe and secure. I kept resisting the thought that this was love. It couldn't be. It was just sex. Okay, it was very good sex. Cole wasn't David, but Cole was special. He made me feel special.

As we rose with the summer sun pouring in through my east-facing window, Cole refused to let me out of his arms. I squirmed a bit as he held on tighter.

"I'm never letting you go."

"Never?"

"That's right, never. You are mine, and we are just going to stay like this forever."

"Forever?"

"Have you got a better idea?"

"Gosh. Never and forever are rather serious time commitments."

"Kate, I'm in love with you. I know you are not in love with me. Not yet anyway. But I plan on changing that. Do I have a chance?"

I was surprised by Cole's love confession. I had known it was true, but I didn't expect him to say it.

Trying not to pause too long and hurt his feelings, I returned the passion with a deep, long kiss. That was my response.

Cole took it as a good sign.

"I need to get up and shower before work," I finally spoke.

"I will let you go if you promise to see me tonight after work."

"I have another date. Maybe we can catch up some other time."

"Really?"

"No, not really. Yes, I'll see you later after work," I said, laughing at him. "You can sleep in if you wish, but I need to be at the salon by eight."

"How are you going to get there?"

"I'll drive as always."

"Oh. But your car is already there, with a dead battery."

"Cole, time to rise and shine. I need to get to work on time."

With that order, my lover whom I knew nothing about jumped up, his amazing naked body standing at attention on top of the bed.

"Do I have time to dress, or shall we just go now?" he said.

"You look fine, very fine, just as you are. We can go now."

Cole leaped off the bed and embraced me. The stiffness of his manhood indicated he wanted morning sex. I wanted to give in, but instead I insisted that we get ready for work. When had I become so practical?

"You know what, Kate?"

"What?"

"I do love you. Yes, I do."

We parted. Cole fetched his clothes that he had thrown on the floor by my bed the night before. Dashing into the bathroom to dress for work, I would sort out my feelings later. Maybe, just maybe, I would also find out Cole's age tonight before we made love for the third night in a row.

CHAPTER FIFTEEN

REALITY CHECK

Back at work under the command of Monsieur Lawrence, continuing my education in the art of cutting, I was instilled with a greater sense of pride and purpose given my goal of becoming someone of consequence in this industry. Maybe I'd never get to Paris, or New York, or even back to Los Angeles. Perhaps my future was right here in the workroom with my French tutors.

These feelings conflicted with everything my parents had taught me. *Aim high,* they always advised. *Anyone can aim low, but if you wish to accomplish anything to be proud of, you must set your sights on the greater goal.*

For me now, the greater goal was simply to learn. The "aim high" would wait. I feared, seriously, that I was not meant to aim high, certain to become an eventual disappointment to my parents or, worse, to myself.

Working diligently, cutting as instructed by the ever-watchful Monsieur Lawrence, I was overwhelmed by another feeling that threatened my fragile composure. I needed to cool it with Cole, at least until I could reconcile my feelings for him. It was unfair to pursue a romantic involvement with such imbalanced motives. Cole would not understand, but I decided we needed to become friends. I wanted to know his age and everything else about him before we slept together again—if we were ever to sleep together again.

This was not going to be easy. I already had demonstrated my lack of sexual control. It was something of a foolish rationalization that my generation pretty much accepted, our having grown up in the latter years of the twentieth century, after the sexual revolution of my parents' youth. The concept of holding out for the perfect union with the perfect person had kind of gone out with so many other social givens and standards of the recent past, despite my mother's warnings to the contrary.

Interestingly, all this so-called sexual freedom available to my nineteen-year-old self engaged in self-exploration was in direct contrast to advice from the parents I adored who had lived so happily under the old order, going to considerable lengths to instill within me a constant and reliable moral compass, a compass based on a time-honored view of life and the importance of the choices one makes. I was certain that they would be surprised and probably dismayed at my choice to have slept with Cole so soon, so freely, as if the sex were not important, just an experience, like going to a controversial foreign film or skiing down a steep mountain for the first time.

I couldn't help it; that's what it was for me: just another experience. I read no great meaning into it, just as it had been in boarding school. Still, I knew it was time to backtrack. Taking a break would be the right move for me, at least for now.

Wandering sex thoughts apparently had sidetracked me as I was trying to concentrate on cutting. Monsieur Lawrence strictly admonished me, claiming that I had lost focus.

"It is essential to follow the exact pattern," he said sternly. "The art of the scissor is the foundation of the garment. If the cut is sloppy, then the result is sloppy."

"I'm sorry. I will be more careful."

"See that you do. There is no room for error or excuses."

Putting Cole in the back of my thoughts, I concentrated on my task. Monsieur and I once again worked through lunch. Madame Honoré arrived with midday energy in the form of a quiche created with gruyère and mushrooms that she had prepared at home, warming our lunch in a microwave in the rear of the workroom. It smelled divine.

Working diligently throughout the afternoon, I managed to improve my cutting skills to the satisfaction of my mentor. The pieces were now ready to be formed on Lilly. That was the name of Monsieur's mannequin used as a model for his creations.

Cole was again waiting outside at the five o'clock hour, just as he had done yesterday and the day before that. I was not surprised to find him, although I was extremely pleased to find him standing outside next to my car talking to the AAA man who had come at his calling to charge my dead battery. I could hear the engine running.

"Kate, you have a car once again thanks to Bill here," Cole called out as I left the salon.

"Oh, thank you so much, Bill. Cole too. What a wonderful surprise." I gushed a bit; glad I hadn't had to figure it out myself. Dead batteries were not my strong suit. After all, as a bona fide daddy's girl, I was used to calling for a little assistance. It was just another one of the perks of a rich girl. Sound elitist? Not really, just lucky. I may be spoiled, but I am never unaware of my good fortune. Not all girls—or boys, for that matter—are born equal.

"Can I follow you home, Kate? Maybe dinner again tonight? We could talk, get to know each other better."

"Perfect idea, Cole. I would really like to talk, just the two of us, no Carrie tonight. At least I hope not."

"Okay, then, I'll follow you home. Or should we avoid going to your house and just go out together somewhere?"

"That's probably a good idea, but I think I'd rather go home first and check on her."

"I'll meet you there in about half an hour. I have to check out a house coming on the market on my way over."

Arriving home, I found Carrie out on the oceanfront patio with a large goblet of chardonnay and smoking what looked to be the remains of a pack of cigarettes, given the large assortment of lipstick-marked butts in an ashtray at her side. She had claimed to want her baby very much, yet she did nothing to curtail her bad habits, which just about every doctor in the world cautioned against during pregnancy. I don't know if it was just plain selfish or stupid. Beautiful young people often think they are invincible. Either way, I wanted to tell her to stop, but I didn't. After all, I hardly knew her. Then again, I also hardly knew Cole, yet I was sleeping with him. Maybe it was the whole Newport thing, instant close relationships.

"Carrie, how are you doing?"

"Okay, I guess. Kind of had a tough day. Joe and I went at it, and it ended badly. He threw me out again."

"What happened?"

"I told him there was no way I would give up this child. He wanted me to have the baby then give it up for adoption."

"Have you talked to Tony yet?"

"That didn't go well either. As expected, he wants me to have an abortion. Then he asked me to fool around. He said pregnant women turn him on."

"That's really nice."

"I told him it was his baby. Can you imagine? He seemed he could care less."

"Carrie, what are you going to do?"

"I'm going to finish my wine and think about it tomorrow. Can I stay over again tonight?"

Courage of Resistance

Cole arrived as promised, on time and ready to share the evening. He wanted to talk. So did I. He also wanted to stay over. I was planning to resist. Carrie would serve as an excuse.

"Would you like to go to Billy's restaurant for dinner, Kate? I closed a deal on a small lease, so I can take you to a decent dinner."

"You should save your money. The big escrow on Lido has yet to close. We can just grab something easy and cheap."

"No. I insist. You deserve a white tablecloth and candles."

Cole took my hand. We got in his car, destination Billy's for a white tablecloth dinner. The Hawaiian-themed bistro on the bay was probably a good place to talk. We could get a quiet table away from the body-to-body action-packed mai tai bar.

It was still early, so we found the restaurant not full. The hostess took us to a back corner enclosed booth surrounded by tropical-looking rattan walls.

An antique painting of a native Hawaiian woman on the beach at Waikiki hung behind our cozy booth. Candles flickered, and a starched white tablecloth sported silver flatware fashioned in a bamboo pattern. Soft hula music filtered through the dining room. Cole and I slid into our booth, sitting close and facing the floor-to-ceiling windows on the bay, as the evening lights from boats bobbing on the water began to replace the sunrays of another summer day on the Pacific coast.

"Cole, I have a request."

"Tell me. Ask me. Whatever you want."

"I want to date. I want to date and get to know you before we have sex again."

"We can do both," Cole came back with a smile and a giggle.

"We could," I said, laughing with him. "But I'd like to wait, at least for a while."

"Is there a reason you'd care to share?" Cole was direct.

I hesitated. Was honesty the best route?

"Because I'm not in love with you. Because I still have feelings for my former boyfriend. Because you are doing business with my parents. Because I don't know anything about you. Well, I take that back. I know you are an amazing lover. But I don't know how old you are, or if you like brussels sprouts, or if you will vote for Gore or Bush in the next election. And, Cole, I need to know all these things. Mostly, I need to know if I have feelings for you before we share our bodies."

Cole was silent. He smiled at me.

"How long do you think we need to date and talk and have me answer all of these questions?"

"Forty-eight hours," I came back sarcastically.

We both laughed again, relieving some of the tension caused by my diatribe.

"I can do that. Shall we start talking now?"

"It may take a little longer than forty-eight hours."

"I can talk fast," he replied. "Here we go: I was born and raised in Reno, Nevada. My dad is a keno dealer at Harrah's Club. My mother is a hostess in the casino steak house. My sister is a dancer in a seminude revue down on the Strip in a place called the Boom Boom Room, and my older brother is a Reno cop. We don't talk to him much.

"I have two years of community college and got the real estate bug. I have no family connections, in a business sense, and I want to make real money. I want a life of my own, not that of my family. And I'll have to do it on my own.

"I don't like brussels sprouts. I hate them. I'll vote for Bush. I'm turning twenty-five next June second.

"Can we make love now? I do love you even though it's only been a couple of days."

"Wow." I didn't know how to respond. "That's a great start, Cole."

Something came over me, kind of an evil suspicion. The name Cole Baldwin seemed incongruous with his confessed family background. It was a little too patrician—East Coast preppy sounding.

"Is Cole Baldwin your real name?" I asked point-blank.

He didn't miss a beat. "No. I made it up. Thought it sounded like a successful name that successful people would want to associate with."

"So, who are you then?"

"I am every inch Cole Baldwin, even legally since I paid a tidy sum to file the paperwork. But I was born Sal Costa. My father is 100 percent Cuban, a Castro refugee first-generation American, and my mom is from Naples, Italy, also first-generation American. Both of my parents came from working-class families. They have no real education, but they made the most of their lives here. They are good people. I am proud of them, and I love them. And I will always be Sal Costa, but to make it in America my way, I will also be Cole Baldwin."

"Now I know where you get those incredible eyes and eyelashes and that thick wavy hair. You are my Cuban Italian stallion lover with a phony name!"

We both nearly fell out of the Billy's booth with our howling. The waitress arrived to take our order at the peak of our hysteria. She stood and waited until a much-needed recovery of our composure so we could sit up erect in the booth.

Cole and I shared a wonderful dinner, talking and sharing our life stories over Billy's smoked Hawaiian fish. He finally agreed to date me until further notice while I was taking time to decide if I was falling in love. I knew it sounded cold, even cynical, but it was the truth. I now felt so much better about him and, more importantly, about myself.

It was still early, not even eight thirty, on our way home, when Cole turned up the alley behind the cottage. We were blocked by the flashing lights of a dozen police cars, several fire trucks, and an ambulance.

"Oh my God. Is that my house?" I yelled out.

"I don't think so. It looks like it's next door at Carrie's house," Cole replied.

Cole pulled over; we were unable to drive closer. Two Newport police officers stopped us as we got out of the car.

"I'm sorry, you cannot go any further." The cop held out his arms to indicate we needed to halt.

"I live there," I protested.

"Where do you live?"

"Right there, the white house with the black shutters."

"What is your name, miss?"

"Kate. Kate Fairchild."

The cop made a call on his wireless and, a minute later, came back with approval to let us pass.

"I will escort you home," he told us.

"What's going on?" Cole questioned.

"There is an incident next door to you," he said.

"An incident? What's that mean?"

"There has been a shooting," the cop replied. "I don't know anything more at this time."

"Oh my God. Was it Carrie?"

I was shaking, feeling sick to my stomach.

Cole put his arm around me. We followed the cop down the alley.

As we got closer, I saw Carrie in the street, surrounded by police. She was sobbing, with two female officers holding her on either side. I broke from Cole and ran toward her.

"Carrie, Carrie, what's going on?" I yelled, coming up behind her. Cole was following me.

Carrie turned around as the officers released her from their hold.

"Kate, oh Kate. Joe killed himself. It's all my fault. My news killed him. It's just as if I had taken the gun and shot him myself."

"I don't understand, Carrie. What happened?"

"Kate, Joe came over to your house and asked me to come back home and talk.

"I thought it was a good sign, so I went with the hope that we could figure something out.

"As soon as we got in the kitchen, he pulled a gun out of a drawer and pointed it at his head.

"Joe started crying. He told me that if he could not have me as his wife, he had no reason to live.

"I started crying, begging him to stop. I told him I would do whatever he wanted, even give up the baby.

"Joe said it would never work, that he had failed me as a husband, as a man. There was no way it could ever be the same.

"As I told Joe that I loved him, he pulled the trigger."

CHAPTER SIXTEEN

LIFE TURNS UPSIDE DOWN

Joe's death affected me in ways I had never imagined. I hadn't known this man, even if he did live next door, a fact I found very odd since I knew the intimate details of his failure to perform sexually and the infidelity of his wife. Still, I was haunted by his death. It was the element of violence, the act of shooting himself in front of Carrie.

Several weeks passed. The feeling of an idyllic summer on the beach was demonstrably tarnished. Carrie temporarily moved in with me, afraid to go home, even for a change of clothing.

Doing my best to be a loyal, caring friend, I did much more in fact. I served her tea in the morning, bringing it to her bedside. I made lunch and left it in the fridge before I went to work, then came home every night to make her something for dinner. Not that it made much difference. Carrie finally got out of bed midday and began drinking chardonnay and smoking packs of cigarettes throughout the afternoon. By nightfall, she was comatose. Scared for the health of her child, my caring nature was turning to disgust.

One aspect of this tragedy, which I'd been forced into by way of my proximity, is that it gave me the time and space I needed to keep Cole at bay. We had not made love, or rather had sex, in weeks. The young man still wanted me. He came to the salon every day, either at lunchtime or closing time, to see me, talk to me, kiss me. I did miss him. At least I missed the passion; I was a silly romantic girl and Cole made me feel like a desired woman. Doesn't every young woman long for that? Desire is a very potent love calling. It trumps all those practical elements of a good relationship, things such as a sense of humor, conversation that connects, shared moral values, and whether your lover sleeps in pajamas or nothing. Desire can be blinding.

For now, however, with Cole, my desire remained on hold. He told me he understood but expressed frustration over my earlier request for a forty-eight-hour reprieve.

"Forty-eight hours turned into forty-eight days," he moaned. "I've got nothing else to share with you about my life. You know it all." He even told me that I could call him Sal, his real name, if it would make me happy.

I didn't care about his real name. The fact that he wanted to be Cole Baldwin and conquer the world, at least business-wise, was a concept I could embrace. My father, Dalt, was my hero after all, and I saw a little of Dalt in Cole.

Apparently, my dad did as well. During my weeks-long absence from intimacy with Cole, he became closer to Dalt and Nancy. Their business arrangement was moving full steam ahead, and it required multiple conversations daily, as well as frequent meetings to negotiate every detail. Buying a nearly nine-million-dollar house required skill and finesse on the part of the agent. Cole was green, but more than anything, he wanted to prove his worth.

He also wanted to make a killing. Cole's commission on the closing of the sale would finally exceed one hundred twenty thousand dollars, a fortune for a young man of twenty-five from Reno with nothing—proof positive for his family that the runaway Cuban Italian with the phony name knew exactly what he was doing. I was happy for him, no longer fearing that his interest in me had something to do with the deal. Maybe I was naive, but I let that little obstacle float away.

My father shared that he was also talking to Cole about more business. The powerful local land baron the Weston Company was starting to develop major sections of the old Weston Ranch land, and Dalt smelled an opportunity to get in on the ground floor. This kind of opportunity would also elevate Cole's career, taking him to the top level of real estate producers in one of the United States' richest enclaves.

Meanwhile, I was earning twelve dollars an hour as an apprentice for Monsieur Lawrence and fulfilling my other duties as caretaker of Carrie. Something needed to give.

After I'd shared the Carrie horror story with Nancy and Dalt, they offered understanding but were certain that she was taking advantage. They implored me to speak to her about seeking help and getting her life on track. Making my guilt worse, my baby brother was showing signs of improvement in rehab and was anxious to come to Newport and see me again for some summer relief. I kept putting him off, promising to make good as soon as possible.

On this Friday in early August, a very hot day made even hotter by blowing Santa Ana winds coming up from Mexico, turning the southland into a bone-dry desert, I agreed to have lunch with Cole and leave the salon for forty-five quick minutes. He met me at the door at exactly a quarter after noon. We braced ourselves against the devil wind and headed to our regular rendezvous at the Bristol Farms counter. The wind had kept the crowd away. We walked right up to order, totally windblown, and requested a pair of their amazing turkey sandwiches on sourdough.

"Kate, I would be happy to help you talk to Carrie. She needs to get her act together." Cole was serious.

"I know."

"You know, but look what it is doing to you and, may I say, what it is doing to us."

"Us? What do you mean, us?"

Cole hesitated, taken aback by my cold remark.

"Is there no us? Do I mean nothing to you? How often must I tell you that I'm in love with you?"

"Cole, I told you I am not ready to fall in love. Not yet."

"Let me help get Carrie out of your house. I want the girl I fell in love with back. Carrie is sucking all of your energy."

"I appreciate the offer, but this is something I need to do. It would be wrong to turn it over to you. I have to be strong and just tell her."

"Make me a promise that you will talk to her this weekend."

Stumbling over my words, I said, "I will try. I don't want to make things worse."

"I don't know how they could be much worse."

"Okay. I get it."

We were finished with our sandwiches. I had eaten only a bite. Cole hadn't eaten much of his either. He took my hand, and we walked back in the wind to my workplace. Upon our arrival at the door to the salon, he put his arm around me and kissed me beyond anything I had ever experienced before.

It broke the moment, which was crazy.

"I love you, Kate. I want to spend my time with you. I want to be there for you, help you, support you. I believe in you," Cole said. His words touched my heart like no others spoken. It was a meltdown moment.

"I will talk to Carrie, I promise." And with that, turning away from my suitor, I returned to the sewing room. Cole stood outside the salon and stared as I walked away.

Was I now falling for this young man? Maybe.

Confronting Carrie

When I got home Friday night, Carrie was outside on the terrace, half conscious from her overdose of chardonnay. It was a warm night; the wind had settled somewhat. Nancy's awning overhead bounced furiously with every gust, not fazing Carrie. Deciding to avoid confronting her, I asked her how she was doing, also asking if she was hungry for a little dinner. There was no response. I asked again, this time coming around in front of her and kneeling at her lap. I looked her in the eyes.

"Carrie, what are you doing to yourself?" I asked as calmly and as quietly as possible.

There was still no response. She took another sip of the chardonnay and sent me a weak smile.

Pausing for what seemed to be an eternal amount of time, saying nothing, I took her hand and held on until she pulled away in order to take another drink.

"Can I get you something to eat? You must eat, if not for you, then for the baby."

Again, no response.

I stood up and walked away. Leaving her, I called out that I would be in my room if she needed me. Another gust of wind pounded the beachfront awning, which made a loud boom and a crackle. I jumped. Carrie didn't move an inch.

Cole was right; I had to talk to her. But it wasn't going to be tonight. Maybe tomorrow, before she started drinking.

Going into the kitchen, I made a salad for my dinner, taking a tray up to my room over the garage. It was the best I could do.

Everything Always Seems Better in the Morning

Saturday morning arrived with that strong eastern Newport sun pouring into my room. The morning light made me happy, even in bad times. I never closed the blinds to the morning sun, wanting it to pour in and wake me no matter the circumstances. Even if I had been up all night, I thought, *Bring on that healing ray of morning light.*

On this day, the sun was exceptional. Everything in my room flashed and flickered, bouncing light from ceiling to floor. Pushing back my comforter, I sat up against the at least six down pillows behind my back, squinting and stretching. Feeling strong, I would find the courage to confront my circumstantial roommate. Today would be the day.

The bedside clock told me it was nearly ten o'clock. Putting on my pink chenille robe with the white appliqué rosebuds, I found my flip-flops halfway under the bed. Going down the wooden stairs, running my hands through my hair, I looked to see if I could find Carrie.

Entering the main part of the cottage, I figured would wake Carrie if she was still sleeping. No more waiting for her customary noontime arrival on the planet. Coming in the front door, I smelled coffee. Did I have an angel on my shoulder? Was she awake? Was she sober? The coffee was a sign of hope.

I found Carrie in the kitchen, sitting on a stool at the counter. She was nursing a giant mug of coffee that she had managed to make herself. I smiled.

"Good morning, friend," I said sheepishly.

She came back at once. "Good morning to you, Kate. I owe you so much. You have been so kind."

I thought, *OMG.* How was I going to tell her my help was over? How cruel would that be?

"Kate, I spoke to my older sister yesterday. I told you about her. She's married to a zillionaire entertainment agent and lives in a massive house in LA on Bel

Air Road. She offered to take me in and let me live there until I can get myself together."

I knew then that I really did have a guardian angel.

"How does that sound to you, Carrie?" She paused. "I think it could be really good."

"Will she get you help? You have to see a doctor," I said.

"She says she will, and she can."

"And your brother-in-law the zillionaire won't mind?"

"They kind of live separate lives in the massive house. She says he won't even know I'm there."

"And how about the baby?"

"I'll get a doc in LA. She says I can stay there and have the baby if I want to."

"Will you promise me that you will try to stop drinking and smoking?"

"Do you think it's a problem?"

Carrie always resorted to a wicked sense of humor.

"It's a big problem," I said. We both laughed.

"My sister is sending a car for me today. Will you miss me?"

"Like an earthquake," I replied, choosing a bit of honesty. "I really want the best for you, Carrie, but I can't give you what you need. I pray that your sister can. And I pray that you get the help you need. You must think about the baby. It's not just you anymore."

"I know."

"Please try."

"I will."

"You must keep me posted on your health. I will come and find you on Bel Air Road if you don't straighten out."

"You know, it is so hard to be responsible when you have always been a coddled blonde beach girl who gets everything she wants based on her looks."

"Time to break that habit. Try getting everything you want just by being a decent person. A good girl with your amazing looks will be an amazing package. Who knows, you might even eventually find a good guy who will love you for the right reasons."

Did I just say that? How does a barely twenty-year-old come to speak such philosophy about love, especially when she has no clue about the whole thing herself?

Carrie stared at me and finished her coffee.

"I'm going to take a shower and clean up. They are coming for me around noon. Will you miss me?" she asked again.

"Yes, friend. I will miss you."

CHAPTER SEVENTEEN

PICKING UP THE PIECES

A black Cadillac limousine pulled up in the alley behind the cottage at precisely noon on this summer Saturday in Newport. For a spectacular day, the peninsula was still relatively calm. The crowds must have slept in on this weekend morning. Given what I had come to know about the importance of Friday afternoon barhopping on the coast, if you weren't part of the happy hour hoppers from saloon to saloon, then you just were, well, not with the beach life vibe. So many of the people I had met in my short stint in Newport were literally addicted to happy hour, an intrinsic aspect to the routine of the fancy-free life. I didn't get it. I thought it was, frankly, rather lowlife.

I kissed Carrie farewell. We embraced in the alley as the driver placed her bag in the trunk of the Cadillac.

"I love you, Kate. You are a true friend. Will you call me? We could have lunch at La Scala in Beverly Hills when you come to town to be with your family."

"That would be nice," I said quietly.

Smiling her big blonde smile, Carrie hugged me again. "We'll do it. Promise?"

"Yes, I promise."

As the driver closed the door, I barely got in my final words: "Please take care of yourself and the baby."

Carrie waved at me through the glass as she opened her purse to locate and light a cigarette.

I guess she hadn't heard me; she simply wasn't going to change. Not for me anyway. Sadly, not for her unborn child either.

Amid my Pollyanna mindset, my God voice spoke to me, assuring me that this child would be protected despite Carrie's bad habits. What sort of mother would Carrie be to this fatherless baby? Seeming to have zero maternal instincts, she would perhaps come back to the beach with the child in a stroller and rejoin the Friday afternoon happy hour brigade.

Feeling a strange chill come over my entire body, I shook it off as I left the alley. As the car drove off, Carrie turned around and looked at me through the rear window. I waved a final goodbye.

The cottage was once again mine, responsibility lifted. My worry had blown away in a black Cadillac limousine. I was free. The month with Carrie had been very difficult. Feeling some guilt over having kept Cole at bay, I remembered that he had repeatedly told me that he understood, that he would wait if I needed him to wait, no matter what. Being honest with myself, I mused that as much as Carrie had been a worry, she also had served as a buffer, giving me the excuse to hold off furthering a relationship with Cole. I still needed more time.

My first free weekend delivered some of that time. This glorious day was warm, and the sky was clear. Hearing the gentle waves breaking, I took a deep breath, listening to the little laps of water as they rushed ashore. The sea was so calm that the surfers were out of luck. Taking advantage of the peaceful moment, I went for a long walk along the shore. Starfish and clamshells washed ashore in abundance as I zigged along my path, avoiding crushing all.

The cell phone rang. I checked the caller ID and saw it was Cole, the third time he had called this morning, all of which I had avoided. It was not very nice of me, but I didn't want to talk. Since I had promised Cole that I was going to speak to Carrie, he wanted to follow up and see how it had gone. Little did he know that the miracle happened with her sister's rescue and that I was off the hook regarding the "you need to move out of my house" conversation.

After my walk back to the cottage I prepared a salad for lunch. Sitting with my salad on the terrace, I planned to take the entire day, grab a beach chair and umbrella, and plop myself on the sand and read. Heaven on earth.

Heading to the shoreline, I created my own cocoon on the sand. I sat in my folding chair with book in hand, shielded by Nancy's beach umbrella. A crowd invaded the quiet perfection of my heaven on earth. My mind wandered off the page. I could not stop thinking about my high school roomie sweet Sara, the girl who'd gotten pregnant after her first and only sexual encounter at the prom and then vanished from my life.

Carrie, my new friend, had just done the same—different circumstances, but same result. Both women had given in to their natural sexual selves, pleasing their own carnal desire and that of a man. And in each case, the man really didn't care all that much. For the man, it was just sex. Maybe it was that way for Sara, and probably for Carrie. Yet, both now faced the consequences of their life-changing choices.

Swearing I was not going to put myself on a similar path, I still had had sex with Cole, which was great, love or lack of love notwithstanding. I vowed to be careful—careful with my body, but even more careful with my feelings. I wanted to be a woman in control of my life, not a woman whose biology forced her to compromise to do the so-called right thing just because of sex.

Was I kidding myself? It was still a man's world, despite the many advances made by people of my gender. How much of the cause and effect of sex was just biology, the fundamental difference being in the physical, sexual, and emotional constitution of human beings? I simply did not want to turn my life over to a man, not yet anyway, and maybe not ever. Had I not learned that with David leaving me? Was Cole the antidote to my fear? Or was he just the next chapter of the same story, but with a different character?

My cell phone buzzed again. This time it was Dalt. I answered.

"Hey, Pops. So great to hear from you."

"I'm glad you answered. Everything okay? I mean with your friend. Did you talk to her?"

"Carrie moved in with her sister. She just left this morning."

"It's for the best, kitten. You do not need that kind of responsibility. Are you sure you're okay?"

"I'm fine, Dad. I am taking the whole day and doing nothing but reading a book on the beach."

"Your mother and I have a little surprise for you. We thought it would be a welcome diversion."

"Really?"

"How would you like to go to Hawaii for your birthday at the end of the month? Your grandmother Gertrude wants to throw a party for your twentieth year on the earth. And when Gertrude throws a party, it's a party."

Dalt's mother, standing at five feet two and weighing barely one hundred pounds, was Auntie Mame, Eleanor Roosevelt, the Unsinkable Molly Brown, and Joan of Arc all rolled into one modern twentieth-century woman. She was my role model, a standard setter, a rule breaker, and an unconventional woman with an unwavering sense of fair play and a rather liberal and visionary global view of the human condition. We shared the same birthday, August 23, so I was Gert's special present. She was turning eighty as I was leaving my teenage years. Perhaps Dalt was right, this would be a great diversion. Even more important, sharing this birthday would be a once-in-a-lifetime kind of thing.

I loved Gert; we shared a special bond. She had moved to Honolulu full time after my grandfather Burton passed almost ten years ago. I was a little girl at the time, and my memory of him has faded. Such is not the case with Gert. I feel her presence often. She always sat with me, so close to me that we were not two people but one. She looked into my eyes with such intensity that it seemed she was looking right into my soul. These are the childhood connections that never leave me. They are stamped on my psyche forever.

"I think that sounds pretty wonderful, Dad. But I don't want her to do a big deal. Are you and Mom coming too?"

"Kate, this is your special weekend with your grandmother. Your mom and I can't make it this time. We will celebrate your birthday later."

"I'll have to see if I can get off work."

"Please try to work it out. And speaking of work, have you thought about going back to school in the fall?"

"I've thought about it, yes. But I've not moved forward on it. I am loving working for Monsieur Lawrence, and I am learning a trade."

"We'll discuss that later. See what you can do about some time off and make some time for your mother and me next week. We'll be in Newport for the closing of the Lido property deal. And your brother is anxious to see you. All he can talk about is his time with you at the beach."

"I love you, Dad. I'll work on the time off, and I guess I'll see you soon."

"Oh, and by the way, your friend Cole has done a remarkable job for us. That boy has a great future. I am planning to invest in more properties with him. I also think he is very smitten with you."

I hesitated. "Well, you are certainly right about the later."

"Love you, sweetheart. Let's talk Monday."

Folding Nancy's umbrella and chair, throwing my towel and book in the matching blue and white canvas bag, I trekked back on the sand to the cottage, dodging what had become an avalanche of humanity on the shore. At the end of a wonderful afternoon, I now faced Saturday night without plans, which was just fine with me. Perhaps a movie ticket at the old Lido Cinema would be in order. Going to a film alone was sometimes my choice. That's how I really got involved with the story without needing to be conversational with whomever I was with. I admit that I am part recluse and loner, a strange combo for a basically social creature who does love to be with people I like.

Back at the cottage at almost four in the afternoon, I stomped the sand off my flip-flops and dusted off my legs, taking refuge under the awning, lying down on the chaise. Closing my eyes, I realized that the afternoon in the sun had drained me. Immediately, a knock on the Dutch door echoed through the living room and out into the terrace.

"Who's there?" I called out, not rising to go to the door. No reply.

I called again, thinking that whoever it was had not heard me.

"Hello, who's there?"

Turning to get off the chaise, my legs hit the stone floor. I looked up to see Cole standing a few feet away, his arms bearing a massive bouquet of pink peonies in full bloom.

"The Dutch door was open, so I came in. I hope you don't mind."

"I guess you already have. Come in, that is."

Flustered, I was making no sense.

"Are you okay?" he asked, coming over to me. "These are for you. I know they are your favorite. You said so one day at Bristol Farms when we passed the flower display. I hope you like them."

"They are my favorite. They make me happy."

"Are you happy?"

"I am happy to see you. I'm sorry I didn't call you back. I know you've left messages."

"I was worried."

"No need. Carrie moved in with her sister."

"That's good news. Are you relieved?"

"I have to say that I am. I couldn't help her, and she needs to find some help."

"That's very grown-up of you."

"Well, I am turning twenty in a couple of weeks."

"That has a nice ring to it."

"Yes, it does."

"Could I ask you on a date tonight, that is, if you're free?"

Giving In, but Not Giving Up

My telling Cole that this was one Saturday night when this young woman was not interested in a date had deflated his ego and his mood.

"Before you showed up, Cole, I was going to go to a movie alone and just fade into the darkness of the theater, think about absolutely nothing, and concentrate on the story."

"What were you going to see?"

"Well, I haven't looked to see what's playing."

"Would company be out of the question? I could sit two seats away, and we could use the seat between us for popcorn and candy. I'll buy."

"You are the sweetest man, but I think the concept defeats my need to be alone."

"Forget being alone. Be with me. I promise I'll not say one word. I just want to look at you."

"Really? Just look at me? You've got to be kidding!"

"I'm just a romantic Latin man disguised as a WASP businessman."

"That's quite a confession."

"Now I confess that I'm hungry. Do you think we could get something to eat? I won't talk to you, just eat."

"I could go for that. I'm hungry too. Where shall we go to eat and not talk?"

"You make the call. I don't care. What do you want to do after we eat?"

"Don't push it or I'll go to the movie alone."

"I'd never push it."

My Cuban Italian stallion disguised as a WASP real estate comer took me to a little Italian restaurant on the Lido Peninsula the locals love. Sabatino's was famous for its Italian sausage and for an old gent sitting at an electronic keyboard next to the front entrance singing along to Sinatra tracks.

Cole and I shared a table for two on the awning-covered patio, sitting at the table covered with a red and white checkered cloth, drinking full-bodied Chianti, and waiting for our spicy sausage and peppers to be served.

Getting over my demand for silence, I opened to Cole about my fear of falling for him and my greater fears about my future. Mostly, I laid out my panic over sex with him. I told him about sweet Sara and now Carrie. Getting pregnant was not what I considered to be the ideal plan at this stage in my life, unmarried at barely twenty, with just two years of college and a twelve-dollar-an-hour apprentice job in a boutique.

"There aren't too many twelve-dollar-an-hour apprentices living in a million-dollar oceanfront cottage." Cole was direct, but his comment revealed more of his perspective based upon the experience of his youth. Was I making a mistake with him? Were our worlds just too different?

"Don't get me wrong, Kate. I just want you to realize how lucky you are. The world is on that silver platter for you. Your options are unlimited. You can do whatever you want with your life. You have something I don't have, something most people our age doesn't have. You have family backing. They will never let you sink, let alone fail. Your parents are there for you, 100 percent, 24/7. With that kind of security, there is power. You have nothing to fear. Nothing."

Wow. That was some speech. I was surprised by Cole's candor and his honesty. He was right, I had nothing to fear. Yet, rich girls are insecure just like poor girls. Family money is not the entire enchilada. It has nothing to do with how a young woman feels about love. Well, at least it shouldn't. I struggled with the concept.

Cole and I finished our wine and the last bites of that tasty Sabatino's sausage. He reached across the table and put his hand over mine. I did not retreat.

"Do you still want to go to a movie? It's early. We could do that."

"Can we just go back to the cottage? Let's go out on the terrace and watch the sun go down over the ocean."

"Perfect."

Inadvertently I had just asked for trouble. Not wanting to be a cold you-know-what when Cole started making the moves in time with that ball of fire sizzling in its final burn over the horizon, I decided I would take my chances. *Whatever will develop, will develop.*

We were back home just before eight o'clock. It was clearly the magic moment. The sun was just over the water in its full magnificent glory. The beach was pretty much deserted, and the temperature remained in the midseventies. Pure Newport bliss.

Making it to the outdoor sofa at just the right time, Cole and I sat down with our hands clasped together and witnessed nature at its most awesome.

"Can I kiss you?" he asked politely. "Okay, I know it's not in the 'leave me alone' plan for tonight, but it seems like a pretty good idea."

Saying nothing, I leaned over into him. Our lips met like a magnet on refrigerator metal. I felt that same chill run down my entire back. Cole's tongue entered my mouth, and we did the dance. The sensation grew stronger. I grew weaker.

His soft hands enveloped my breasts, which were still covered by a slightly sheer cotton summer blouse. Cole began to unbutton the top, slowly and deliberately, as we remained locked together. The tongue dance escalated.

With my top around my shoulder, falling down my arms, Cole gently stroked my neck, running his hands across my shoulders then down each arm. It felt wonderful, loving, and sincere. I gave into his passion totally and completely.

We were both removing our clothes as our long kiss broke. My tongue was a little raw from the prolonged passion, but it was that good kind of raw, like when a cat's tongue licks your face—a little rough and prickly, but the sandpaper feeling adds to the sexual arousal. I had never told any of my cats that secret.

In seconds, Cole and I were naked on the terrace sofa. It didn't matter, no one could see, and frankly I didn't care much if they could. I was totally into Cole. There was nobody else in the world.

Staring at this perfect specimen of manhood, I concluded that he was the most beautiful man I had ever gazed upon. As much as I loved David, he did not look like Cole. My new lover could have been a model for Greek or Roman statues. Michelangelo would have preferred Cole to his model for the statue *David*.

As I looked at Cole intensely, I wondered what he was thinking about me. I didn't care. I just wanted to take all of him into my view. Cole's body had been proportioned exquisitely by his Creator. With a classic swimmer's A-line build and with broad shoulders tapering to a slim waist, Cole showed no fat, only muscle, and a workout-defined chest and abdomen, totally smooth, no body hair. I think he shaved.

Why? Because his pubic hair was too perfectly trimmed. Did he do it himself, or did he have a pubic stylist? What a concept!

The chill of his kiss turned to ecstasy. I was drunk. Uncontrollably drunk. Placing my arms around Cole's neck, I pulled into him as tightly as I could possibly get to him. Our bodies were one, moving in total unison.

Would I finally have to give in and admit that this was the real thing, love? How could I not know that now?

One thing was certain: I was not afraid. I had never felt this way before. This was why so many girls gave in to sex. There is just nothing like the real deal. Nothing. The consequences do not trump the passion. Again, my God voice spoke to me, telling that this was God almighty's plan. Why else would there be so many souls on the planet? There simply was nothing else more powerful, not even peace on earth.

"Kate, I love you," Cole said.

"I love you too," I told him.

I think I had just crossed the threshold. Now what?

CHAPTER EIGHTEEN

THE BIG PAYDAY

August was slow in the salon. Over the past two weeks since Carrie had left for Bel Air, I had settled into a regular routine at the shop. Monsieur Lawrence had begun to teach me his skilled couture draping on the mannequin, and I was eating it all up. I don't think I had ever enjoyed learning anything as much in my life. My not getting enough of his teaching and asking a great many questions did not deter his enthusiastic instruction. Rather, he relished in the queries, taking time to explain and go over every detail, no matter how minute. This was serious mentoring, and I realized it was special. How fortunate I was to have a patient and caring tutor.

Our project for the past week had been to create a dinner suit for Mrs. A. When we had seen her at lunch at Mariposa, Carrie filled me in on her Newport status and prestige. She came into the salon when I was on the floor and recognized me from that brief encounter across the dining room. Mrs. A apparently never forgot anyone or any detail, and she was gracious as if we were old friends. I liked her; her friendliness was genuine. Another aspect of this unique Newport social life—everyone was always "nice." Nothing like the competitiveness of the social women in LA. They could kill you with one of those stares if they chose to do so. Mother Nancy always joked in a warning tone that women in LA could be so competitive that they would stab you in the front. That always made me laugh. If the viciousness existed in Newport, and I guess it must have since people tended to be the same everywhere, it was most definitely hidden below the surface.

Mrs. A wanted my opinion on fabric and on the overall look of the suit, which gave me confidence to speak honestly. She asked about a traditional velvet for winter, and I showed her some alternatives that the Monsieur had just imported from his source in Milan. Once I had explained that the fabrics were the very latest trend in Europe, Mrs. A responded with affirmation.

We had spent at least two hours talking, only a limited amount of it about fashion. Once I'd given her the edited version of my life, she responded in kind.

Her candor surprised me. Sharing stories about her husband and children more appropriately reserved for a counseling session, she was so real that I could not help but like her even more.

Madame Honoré returned from an errand, ending our girl talk, and closed the deal on the suit. Another milestone in my fashion career, albeit a career that was only several months old. But it was progress; a several-thousand-dollar sale was nothing to fool around with. I figured the profit would pay my twelve-dollar-per-hour wage for a good amount of time, earning my apprenticeship with Monsieur Lawrence. For that, I felt good, even worthwhile.

Meanwhile, Dalt kept checking in on a regular basis, both on the phone from Beverly Hills and in person while in Newport, as he was getting near to closing his deal with Cole on the Lido property.

"When are you going to enroll at Chapman University and finish your two years of undergrad work?" he questioned as kindly as he could without being overbearing. His seriousness, however, was not diminished by the friendly tone. "Baby, I am going to call President Doti and see if he will enroll you for the fall. I took the liberty of sending your USC records to Chapman's admissions office. I was told with your high SAT scores and a 4.0 GPA at USC, there would be no question."

"Daddy, you didn't do that," I replied with a degree of indignation.

"All I did was get the ball rolling. It is up to you to take it forward."

"That's some ball you've got rolling," I told him. "I told you that I would think about it, but I'm not ready. I love what I am learning here at the salon."

"You have all the time in the world to study fashion. First you should get your degree."

"Spoken like a good father."

"Father does know best."

"That TV show has been off the air for thirty years."

"How do you know that? You've only been alive for almost twenty."

Dalt got off the Chapman subject and dove into the plans to send me to Honolulu for my birthday with his mother, Gertrude Fairchild.

"Are you ready for the trip? It's next week."

"I am ready, and I'm looking forward to being with GiGi. I miss her terribly. And yes, I was given a few days off work, so I can spend three days over the weekend with her."

"She's planning a wonderful birthday dinner for you at Michel's. Remember, that was one of your favorite spots at the Colony Surf."

"It's probably the most romantic restaurant in the world."

"Too bad you'll not have Cole there with you." My dad was moving into uncharted territory.

"What does that mean?" I replied with more than a hint of *It's none of your business.*

"I know the two of you have been seeing one another. I've been meeting with Cole almost daily. He's not sharing personal information, but he is obviously crazy about you. Is it fair for a father to ask how you feel about him? Does that mean you may have resolved your feelings after the breakup with David? Remember, it was that breakup that led you to leave USC and run away to Newport. Maybe this means you might also be ready to come home."

Boy, that was way too much directness for me to handle in one swoop. I was silent on the phone   , the uncomfortable kind of silence, unable to begin to offer my point of view. I finally mustered the courage as Dalt repeatedly asked, "Are you there? Are you okay? Did I upset you?"

"No, you didn't upset me. You just threw me off a cliff. Daddy, I have been seeing Cole, and I think it's the real deal. We have gotten close, but I am still in hesitation mode. One step at a time."

I told my dad that Cole had helped me heal the wounds from David not at first, but after some time together. Sharing that initially I was afraid because of his family business connection, I mentioned that I had overcome that too. Not at first. Yet, I said, I still wanted to take it slow, not move into uncharted territory too quickly.

Going to Hawaii to be with GiGi was a blessing, a chance to have a little extra separation from Cole. I chose not to share with Dalt that Cole and I had spent every night together over the last couple of weeks since Carrie had moved out, and I certainly didn't share that we had made love in every corner of the cottage in every way possible. Cole was insatiable, and I was love crazed. There were mornings when I stumbled into the salon, walking as if I had spent the night riding a horse. Madame Honoré gave me that look but said nothing. How very French of her to be so discreet.

"Daddy, I'll keep you posted on what I decide to do about school, I promise. But for now, just trust me that I will do what's best for me."

With that, Dalt told me how much he loved and adored me, which I knew and always liked hearing. He ended our little talk by informing me that the Lido deal was due to close on the coming Friday and saying that he wanted to take Cole and me to dinner with Nancy and my brother, Jamey.

"That would be great," I told him, hanging up the phone.

The Day Cole's Life Changed

Friday came fast, but not fast enough for Cole Baldwin. I had never seen a young man so nervous. His cell phone rang constantly whenever I was with him, which was every night after work. Escrow kept alerting Cole to last-minute hitches in the Lido deal with Dalt and Nancy. This paper or that paper was missing. Signatures were missing. The seller wanted more proof of funds before closing. A discrepancy in the title report had delayed transfer of title insurance. Cole shared every problem with me, while I kept reassuring him that it would all work out. But neither my reassurance nor even my body alleviated his panic.

Cole had refused sex on both Wednesday night and Thursday night. This was a first. I figured that whenever I needed a sex break, I could just ask Dalt to buy another property. Then again, maybe not; it would certainly complicate our relationship more.

Even though I had given Cole all the loving support I could, including lots of long hugs and even more "Don't worrys", he ate nothing for most of the week. On Thursday night, I forced him to have one of my famous grilled cheese sandwiches, made in a frying pan with the sourdough bread totally saturated in pure butter.

By eight o'clock Thursday night, the constantly ringing cell phone fell quiet. Funds had cleared in escrow. The title had been transferred, and the deal was set to close the following day.

"What if there is an earthquake and the home suffers damage?" Cole was serious.

"Really?" I came back at him. "How about an electrical fire?"

"Oh my God, I never thought of that. The house is old by Newport standards. There could be a fire, and since nobody lives there, who would stop it in time?"

"Cole, you are so silly."

"These things happen," he replied.

"Yes, they do. But they won't happen to you. Not tonight and not to any of us. And not to Dalt either. Have a little faith, a little confidence. You have worked hard for this success."

Cole put down the grilled cheese, not an easy thing for anyone to do. I must admit that my grilled cheese is, well, the best, impossible to ignore. Most of my victims require a second serving.

Cole did put it down on his plate and stood up, coming around the counter in the cottage kitchen to put his arms around my waist and deliver a very strong kiss.

"That's more like it," I said as our embrace broke.

"Now I must finish the grilled cheese," he replied, not kidding.

I knew he really loved me and my grilled cheese. Did it get any better than this?

Finishing dinner—I'd had only one grilled cheese and had made a second one for Cole per his request—we went upstairs over the garage to my room, jumped into bed, and turned on the TV. Within minutes Cole was sound asleep. After reading for an hour, I also fell asleep soundly next to him.

While reading, my wandering mind had focused on what my life might be like with Cole working in real estate. It is such a difficult profession. No payday until a deal closed, and I knew that they didn't always close. Even my rich dad could not continue buying property to keep Cole in nice suits and keep us with a roof overhead. This was silly, but real. We were nowhere near a position to worry about our future. Maybe it was just a female thing since I was falling in love with him. Women plan their futures; I think more than guys. And guys didn't realize it most of the time. That was the female advantage. Maybe it was also a curse.

The amazing bright Newport summer sunlight poured in my bedroom window around six thirty Friday morning. Cole moaned and turned over on his stomach to avoid the light, pulling the comforter up over his head.

"Cole, it's Friday morning. It's your big day," I whispered softly in his ear.

Throwing the comforter back, Cole sat up with military precision.

"Oh my God. It's Friday. What do I do now?" he asked rhetorically, still half asleep.

"You've done everything. Your deal will close today."

"Was there an earthquake or fire?" he asked, smiling.

"No, I don't think so. You should be okay!"

"Do you know how special you are? You guided me through all my nervous panic. You kept assuring me it would all be okay. How can I ever thank you enough? All of this is because of you, because I met you that day in the parking lot outside of the salon when the guy hit your car. Do you believe in fate, in destiny?"

"Cole, you are a sweet man. You deserve the success. Yes, it was a bit of a miracle. Call it fate, call it luck, call it being in the right place at the right time."

"I'll call it love. I am so in love with you. Everything you do makes me love you more and in so many ways."

"Boy, that's what a girl likes to hear."

"Would you care to make early morning love before we face the day?" Cole moved over next to me and began kissing me down my neck.

I began to shiver. His morning man unit hardened in an instant, rubbing against my thigh. How did men do that so quickly, so effortlessly? It was more sex magic.

Of course, I gave in. We made incredible morning love.

"This is definitely my lucky day," Cole said gently as we climaxed together.

"I think that's a safe bet. However, did you feel the earthquake?"

"What?"

"Oh yes, I felt the quake just as you entered me. It was at least a 5.0, or maybe even a 6.0."

Cole finally got my message.

"No, it was over 7.0," he said. "I think the Lido house might be leveled."

"Do you care?" I asked.

"Not at this moment, but I think I will care later."

Cole kissed me again, then we both got out of bed to dress for the big day.

Dinner with the Family to Celebrate

To be sure, it was the longest Friday of my life, and certainly Cole's as well. He dropped me off at the salon by eight o'clock in the morning, then headed next door to his real estate office. He was dressed in his best suit, with a white shirt and red silk tie. He had placed a white starched hankie, folded perfectly, in the breast pocket. Correction: it was not just his best suit; it was his only suit.

My day was spent mostly with Monsieur Lawrence as we continued our tutorial on sketching. He was very kind to me, encouraging me, praising my burgeoning talent as a fashion sketch artist. In his French accent, he kept the accolades coming, putting me in sketch heaven. Never had I experienced such reinforcement of my dreams.

At midday, Mrs. A stopped in to check on the progress of her suit. So proud, still basking in that glory, I felt it didn't hurt that Mrs. A also bestowed a heaping amount of praise on me. Since she was one of the most important women in Newport, this was surely a vote of confidence, which I accepted wholeheartedly.

Cole checked in constantly throughout the day. He did not call; that was forbidden. Instead, he just poked his head in the door, offering the simple words "Not yet!" to clue in Madame and Monsieur. They were understanding, and congratulatory to Cole.

At four o'clock in the afternoon, Cole burst in the door. "It closed," he yelled out. "It really closed!" He ran to me, arms outstretched.

Madame Honoré was between Cole and me, so Cole grabbed her first, hugging her, then lifted her up off her feet and swung her around. She let out a squeal. Monsieur Lawrence came out of his workroom just in time to see his wife flying through the air.

"Oh my goodness" was all he could say as he peered out over the top of his glasses.

Cole put Madame back on solid ground and started running to me.

"I am so happy for you. So proud of you. I told you it would all be okay."

"I have a surprise for you, Kate!"

With that, Cole ran back to the door of the salon and swung it open. "Look who's here," he called out. Dalt, Nancy, and my brother, Jamey, entered.

Cole Makes Major Points

The Fairchild family celebrated their good fortune in the salon as Monsieur Lawrence locked up the shop for the night on this Friday in the summer of 2000. Madame Honoré excused herself and went into the workroom to locate a special bottle of chilled Veuve Clicquot in the back of the old Frigidaire that on any given day was the receptacle for lunch in the shop.

A loud *pop* rang out, and a corresponding burst of laughter echoed the sound of celebration. Madame dashed back into the showroom with crystal flutes on a silver tray, champagne bottle in hand. She stumbled, and the approaching toast was almost just that—toast. Our future real estate mogul Cole managed to grab the tray of glasses and stabilize both the clinking flutes that were beginning to topple and Madame.

She thanked Cole profusely, apologizing for the momentary clumsiness. The toast had been rescued.

"I am so excited for you all," Madame offered in her lovely French accent.

"And my family is so pleased to finally meet you and your husband. Kate has told us so many wonderful things about how you are mentoring her. We could not be more in your debt." Dalt had used his golden tongue, creating instant rapport with Madame Honoré.

Setting the tray of flutes down on a display table, Cole carefully moved an assortment of silk blouses aside. Madame noticed his effort and smiled.

Coming over to the table with the bottle of Veuve, Madame poured, filling each flute. Nancy stepped in to assist, passing out each glass as Madame completed her task. Sharing the golden touch with Dalt, my mother was always the epitome of graciousness.

Each of us held a glass of champagne, except Jamey. I offered him orange juice. Cole spoke.

"Here's to you, Mr. and Mrs. Fairchild, for trusting me with this remarkable business opportunity when you really had no reason to do so."

Dalt answered almost before Cole could finish.

"We were impressed by you at our first meeting in the house. You have earned this success. We hope the commission will start you on a career path of many accomplishments."

"I would like to go with all of you over to the Lido house now and officially open the front door and hand you the keys," Cole replied. "And I would love everyone to come. And that means Madame and Monsieur too. After all, it is a French manor house."

Cole then asked Dalt and Nancy if they objected, hoping he had not overstepped his authority. They both nodded in total agreement.

The family Fairchild left the salon with my fashion mentors. Everyone was able to fit in the limousine Dalt had waiting out front. Fearing that the limousine and the French mansion might overwhelm my tutors, I launched into fashion small talk with them, trying to reinforce my seriousness as a fashion student. Both Madame and Monsieur knew I was a rich girl from Beverly Hills, but I had overcome the obvious doubts and prejudice—a prejudice, by the way, that was well deserved. So many of my rich girl friends had not one serious bone in their bodies.

The limousine pulled up in front of the Lido house, an imposing Regency structure that was something of an anomaly in Newport. Classically designed and built several decades earlier by a definite Francophile, the home sat in contrast to its neighbors, which were designed in a more contemporary architectural style.

The front of the residence spanned some one hundred twenty feet directly on Via Lido Soud, one of the main arteries on the isle. The precious dirt was considered platinum waterfront property. For this reason alone, the sale was record-breaking, approaching the nine-million mark.

Getting out of the car, taking my father's arm, I told him how lovely the new house looked. The dove-gray and stark white mansion boasted touches of elegant wrought iron painted a polished black in front of tall French windows framed by black shutters. It was a beach version of the color scheme of my parents' home in Beverly Hills.

As we entered a gated courtyard on the west end of the property, the central fountain delivered a stream of fine flowing water. White cement urns adorned with carved cement wreaths were planted with exquisite white gardenias.

Cole moved to the front door, handing Dalt the key. "Congratulations," he said, putting out his hand for another shake. Dalt responded in kind, then reached over and gave Cole a man hug. I had never seen that from Dalt except with close family.

We started to applaud as Dalt put the key in the lock. He summoned Nancy to join him. He did not pick her up and carry her over the threshold, but instead leaned over and delivered a gentle kiss, taking her hand in his and opening the door. So romantic. They walked in together.

I held back my tears, my eyes focused on the blessing of my perfect parents. None of my friends were lucky enough to have the perfect family. How had I gotten so lucky?

"What's all this?" Dalt called out as we trailed behind the lovebirds checking out their new beach home.

Directly ahead of Dalt and Nancy, through the handsome two-story entry gallery with its curvilinear French staircase, then through an elegant archway forming the hallway into the waterfront main living room, a round dinner table was placed in the center of the massive room, draped to the floor with a tablecloth of silver peau de soie. Crystal candlesticks sported silver tapers, which were flickering in the glow of the summer light pouring in through the wall of windows on the bay at sunset. White hydrangeas and roses were centered on the table as waiters in white starched waistcoats and silver bow ties scurried about.

Then a maître d' appeared in a tuxedo.

"Welcome, Mr. and Mrs. Fairchild and family, to your new home. A dinner has been prepared in your honor to mark this very special occasion. My name is Luis, and my staff and I are at your service. May we offer you a cocktail?"

Dalt looked at Nancy. Luis continued, "May I introduce your host this evening?"

"Yes, of course. It is the seller?" Dalt asked.

"Your host is your agent, Cole Baldwin."

Cole moved up next to my parents. I let out a gasp, more of a screech. Madame Honoré was next to me.

My parents were overwhelmed by Cole's gesture. I wondered how he had arranged for all of this. Saying nothing, just enjoying the moment, I thought it was an amazing once-in-a-lifetime kind of thing.

I hugged my little brother, Jamey. We were all escorted to the beautiful table in the middle of the otherwise empty baronial living room. Dinner was served. What a night.

CHAPTER NINETEEN

A WEEK NEVER TO BE FORGOTTEN

Dalt and Nancy checked into the Four Seasons Hotel with Jamey after having drunk too much Veuve Clicquot in the middle of the living room of their empty French manor. Cole and I went home to our love cottage on the beach. We didn't make it past the entry hall. Our clothes littered the floor from the door to the staircase. As we made wild love on the second step, my back was jammed into the third riser. Cole thrust into me so strongly that I felt the indentation across my back, no doubt leaving a long red line from side to side—a backside hickey.

Our lovemaking kept repeating through the night and continued every morning and every night for the rest of the following week. Monsieur noticed that my usual concentration on his tutelage was lacking. Not objecting, he worked harder with me, critiquing my fashion sketching. Monsieur Lawrence was so talented that I wondered why he was not a famous couturier. Why had he and Honoré left France? And why on earth had they ended up in Newport Beach as opposed to, say, New York or LA?

By the middle of that week of Cole's new life of success, I was exhausted from his joy and appreciation. Barely keeping my eyes open at the salon, I had let my guard down. Losing the adherence to respect that had stopped me from getting too personal with my mentors, I asked Monsieur Lawrence the big question.

"Why did you leave France, and what brought you here?"

Monsieur Lawrence did not look up from his table. He continued to ply the gabardine fabric he was shaping into one of his designs for the fall/winter collection. There was a moment of awkward silence. About to ask again, I stopped, thinking better of it. Best to leave it alone and go back to drawing. Then he spoke without looking up, without stopping his task.

"We left France in 1941, my dear. Madame and I were just children. Our parents were close friends, and each managed to pay for passage to New York, getting us out. We escaped the eventual Nazi takeover of Paris and found ourselves safe with relatives in New York."

"I did not know you were Jewish," I responded rather stupidly.

"Yes, Kate, we are. And we made it to New York with a small amount of money and a few items of gold jewelry sewn into the lining of my coat, thanks to my father, who was a master tailor. His name was Israel Avedon. I never saw him, or my mother, Leah, again."

I felt an overwhelming sense of shame; I was embarrassed for having asked.

How could I be so ignorant, so insensitive? Tears welled up and began to flow. I tried to cover them up, acting as normal as possible.

Monsieur Lawrence stopped my tears.

"Come. Come, my dear. Do not cry. It was a long time ago. We survived. So many millions did not."

"I am sorry. I feel rather foolish for not having some idea given your age and French background. I also must confess my further embarrassment because I asked you about your life, thinking that you and Honoré are so talented that you both should be famous designers in New York or Paris, instead of shopkeepers in Newport. Can you forgive my boldness?"

"Kate do not be embarrassed. I could sense your thoughts by the look on your young face. My dear child, even you, a young lady of privilege, will discover that life often takes you down an unexpected path. It is not always our choice which path rises before us."

Monsieur Lawrence continued, "You see the world as a platter of infinite possibilities. It is how it should be at twenty. Our course was dictated by our time, just as yours will be influenced by the world in 2000. In the end, we all do the best we can. For Madame and me, we have made a good life here in California. It was not our plan, but we made it our plan. Honoré and I got off a bus in Santa Ana and found work at a local department store. Would I have rather been an intern at the Paris salon of Chanel?"

"How did you ever end up here, opening the salon?"

"We arrived in New York only aware of some very distant cousins in America. A Jewish relief agency caring for refugees came to our aid. We were introduced to a family named Morris. They were New Yorkers in the garment business who gave us a home, seeing as we were starting over in the United States. The first year was very hard. We were lonely; we were afraid for our family; and we lost all contact. Arriving without speaking the language, and despite everything, with the help we received, we grew up, survived, and made a life.

"Honoré and I were in love as children, and we got married on July 12, 1952, at city hall in Manhattan. We were both not yet twenty, so young, so raw."

"Oh my," I said sheepishly. "When and how did you come to California?"

At this point in our little talk, Monsieur Lawrence moved from his workstation and came over to sit next to me, pulling up a stool right next to my chair. He looked at me with great care, almost as if I were the daughter that he and Honoré had never had. I felt the great passion and love in his faded gray-blue French eyes, which were surrounded by so many lines of life experience at the vibrant age of sixty-seven.

"Our dear mentors Mr. and Mrs. Samuel Morris had family in LA, and they were launching a major clothing line downtown. LA was becoming a fashion capitol, next to New York and Dallas. And it was 1958, the war long over. We were now in our twenties without children, and we said, 'Why not?'"

Monsieur Lawrence explained that he and Honoré had come to California in the back seat of a 1950 Ford courtesy of another cousin of the Morris family making the journey west across the United States. He confided that the free trip was less than ideal. The cousin, who was with his wife, tried to make the moves on Honoré somewhere outside Albuquerque, New Mexico, one night in a shabby roadside motel off Route 66. Monsieur Lawrence said he had gone to a store at a nearby gas station to buy some aspirin. Meanwhile, the man's wife was taking a long, cold bath, washing away the heat and dust from the road. It was a horribly hot and humid night, and Cousin Morris made his advance on Honoré in their shared motel room.

"Suffice it to say, I stopped his advances, having come back from the store at the gas station just in time. It was the end of the line for us in the back seat of the 1950 Ford. We had enough money for bus fare to LA.

"In 1958, once again, both of us twenty-five-year-olds found ourselves strangers in a strange land. We decided that seeking the help of the Morris family would probably not be wise given the situation with the cousin, so we got off the bus in downtown Santa Ana, California, about fifty miles southeast of LA. It was a magnificent late summer afternoon; the warm air was intoxicating, and the blue sky seemed to be infinite in its scope and reach. There were palm trees, thousands of palm trees, and the scent of oranges filled the air. This was paradise.

"Before I bore you to death, let me say that Honoré and I found work at a department store called Buffums. We worked very hard; we saved every penny; and in 1968 we were transferred to Buffums's new store in what was called Fashion Plaza in Newport Beach. That is our story as it happened, my dear."

"When did you open your own salon?" I pressed on, figuring I needed the whole story.

"In 1979 we took a major chance. Using every penny of our savings, almost fifty thousand dollars, and approaching fifty years of age, we opened our first shop together down on Via Lido not far from your parents' new home. The rent was five hundred dollars a month. I designed and Honoré sold. Slowly the ladies came. Mrs. A, your customer, was one of the first. She has been our angel for twenty years. You should know this about her. She didn't just wander in to buy the expensive suit that you sold her."

Feeling foolish now, I was not the brilliant young saleswoman after all. Monsieur Lawrence could see I was deflated.

"Do not discount your effort, my dear. Mrs. A is a very discriminating woman. She bought from you because she liked you, respected you, and believed in you. It was your sale."

With that vote of confidence, I threw my arms around Monsieur Lawrence and hugged him with all my strength. He pulled back at first, ever so gracefully, but then gave in to the moment. As the hug broke, I kissed him on his left, then right, cheek.

"I am so honored you shared your life with me. So honored."

"Let us get back to work then," he said, grinning as he rose from the stool. He returned to his table and the gabardine awaiting his touch.

I sketched like crazy the rest of the afternoon. Monsieur told me it was my best work to date. As five o'clock came, with anticipated certainty, Cole came bounding through the salon door.

The Big Check

Cole marched into the salon with more enthusiasm than usual. In the same fashion that he had lifted Madame Honoré off her feet and swung her around the showroom the night Lido escrow closed, he picked me up and swung me around.

"Wait until I show you!" he shouted.

Putting me down on the ground, Cole pulled an envelope out of his inside breast pocket. Opening the envelope with extreme care, he pulled out a check.

"Take a gander at this little doozy!" He shrieked again.

I reached carefully for the check in his right hand. Cole held on tight, not letting go at first. I pulled back, and he laughed, releasing the check.

Fixing my eyes on the amount, I saw the certified check was made out to Cole Baldwin for $122,812, his share of the Lido commission, less broker split and expenses. It was my turn to squeal. All I could say was, "Oh my goodness."

"This is a life changer," he said quietly. "For both of us."

I was caught off guard.

"Cole, this is for you. You and you alone. It is your chance to make a life and the career that you dreamed of. Have you called your family in Reno? They deserve a call," I told him with total sincerity.

"I have not. I wanted you to be the first."

"Go call them right now," I came back.

"Really? Now?"

"Yes, really. Now," I said, telling him to get his cell phone and dial.

Following my order, Cole dialed. Madame, Monsieur, and I watched with childlike anticipation. This was Christmas morning in August, and we awaited the revelation of a very special present.

"Hi, Mom, is that you?"

"Yes, Son, it's me. How are you? We miss you something terrible. Can you take a few days off and come on up to Reno?"

"Mom, is Dad home yet?"

"He just walked in the door, Son."

"Can he pick up the extension line? I have news to share with both of you."

"Father, pick up the line in the bedroom," Rose directed her husband to oblige.

"What's the big news, Son? I miss you too," Cole's father said as Cole put them both on his cell phone speaker.

"Mom, Dad, I just closed my first big real estate sale."

"That's wonderful. Did you make a little money?" his mom asked.

"A little," Cole replied with a definite smile in his voice.

"How much is a little?" his dad questioned.

"Well, it's enough to buy a new car," Cole replied.

"You're kidding. That's fantastic," his dad said.

"And it's also enough to buy a nice house in Reno," Cole added.

"What?" his mother screamed.

"Mom and Dad, I made over one hundred twenty thousand dollars today."

There was silence on the line, and it persisted.

"Hello? Are you there?" Cole inquired. Still silence. "Mom, Dad, are you there? Are you okay?"

Finally, a response.

"Oh my God. Did you sell the First National Bank?" His dad was trying to be funny, but his voice was quivering and breaking up.

"No, not exactly. I just sold a really nice house to some really nice people."

"You sold one house and made that kind of dough?" His mom was recovering from her shock.

"Listen, I want to send you guys ten thousand dollars to help out. Okay?"

"No. Not a chance, Son. This is not our money. We are proud of you, boy. How about using some of that cash to come home for a visit?" Cole's dad went on.

"Will do, Dad. Can I call you both later? Right now, I've got to go."

"We love you," they both said at once. And the call was over.

I turned to Cole and gave him a kiss.

"I think you scared your parents," I said.

"No way. They're tough. But I'll bet they are sitting at the kitchen table staring across at one another in total disbelief."

"Are you going to send the ten thousand dollars?" I pushed on.

Cole did not miss a beat. "No, I'm not sending it. Kate, I'm taking you with me to Reno to deliver the check and meet the family. How can they turn me down when they meet you?"

"Whatever you say, my newly rich boyfriend. Whatever you say!"

Money to Burn

I was getting ready to fly to Honolulu on Friday for my extended birthday weekend with GiGi, thanks to Papa Dalt. Cole really didn't want me to go. He put on a happy face, though, telling me he loved the fact that I loved my grandmother so much.

Truthfully, I was excited to go. I had not seen GiGi in a long while. She was getting older, and when I was a young girl, she was a very important part of my life. I think I was closer at times to her than even my own mother, Nancy. Often telling me that we were kindred spirits, Gigi said I was the daughter she'd never had, as Dalt was her only child. Yes, she spoiled me, I guess, but not in an obnoxious way. I was the kid who never took advantage, never crossed the line. Funny thing, in spite of the family wealth, I never thought about money, and I was always kind of frugal. Among my friends, I was the one who saved my allowance. I was the one who never charged anything to Dalt and Nancy. My friends would go into Saks Fifth Avenue or Neiman Marcus in Beverly Hills and just buy whatever they wanted, even at the age of twelve or thirteen. I would never do that. Once Nancy told me she was worried that I wasn't her child because I was so conservative with money. "Where did you come from?" she would joke.

I would answer that GiGi had shared stories of her childhood growing up in the Depression years in New York, and it had really sunk in.

Nancy would come back stating that the Depression ended seventy years ago, adding that GiGi and Grandfather Burton Fairchild had gone on to do quite well in life.

Somewhat precocious, even pretentious, I answered that the lessons learned in the Depression when they were both young obviously had served them well later on.

My newly successful boyfriend arrived at the salon exactly at noon; he was always annoyingly exactly on time. Cole came in sprinting, hugging Honoré, and asking for me. Hearing him, I excused myself, leaving Monsieur Lawrence to slip away for a little bite. I only hoped that Cole would not want to make lunchtime love. I was spent.

"Can I take you to the Harbor Club for lunch? It's our last day before you leave for Honolulu after all," he asked coyly.

"I don't want to be gone too long. Can we eat and be back in an hour?"

"I promise I'll do my best."

"Very well then, Harbor Club it is. I'm craving one of those 'power burgers' at the beachfront café."

"Sounds perfect to me."

"A power burger for Newport's newest power agent!"

We hopped into Cole's dented and faded Toyota and headed up the Pacific Coast Highway. It was only a few miles to the club. I had the feeling that this would probably be my last ride in the Toyota.

A windswept August day showed skies punctuated with billowing fat cumulus clouds floating east over the ocean, heading inland on their way to the California desert to deposit summer rain in the "monsoon" season.

The Harbor Club hostess Willie showed us to a table on the terrace, shaded by a giant white market umbrella. Settling into the navy-blue and white canvas director's chairs, Cole and I ordered our power burgers, extra grilled onions, a side of Thousand Island dressing, and extra thin-sliced dill pickles. The crispy beer-battered thin french fries were my new guilty pleasure.

Cole ordered a mai tai, which I thought was odd for a lunch quickie, but I didn't comment. After all, he was still in major euphoria over the deal. He asked me if I wanted one. I declined but told him I'd have a sip of his to be a sport. No rum was going to spoil my power burger and fries.

Willie arrived with Cole's mai tai, complete with a tiny paper umbrella floating in the large barrel glass filled with crushed ice. Toasting with my water, then taking the promised sip, I thought it was delicious. Cole inhaled the drink and went for the question of the hour.

"Shall I buy a Porsche or a Mercedes?"

"Excuse me?" I said, not totally surprised, but faking it a little.

"Kate, I need a better car. What do you think?"

"I think your money is burning a hole in your pocket. Isn't that the expression?"

"Well, it's been a whole day since I got the check."

"Really? A whole day?"

"Is getting a car a bad idea?"

"No. But don't you think you should take a breath and really do some research and make a plan of how to budget your money overall?"

"That's why I love you."

"Cole, how about talking to a financial guy? You need some good advice. Or just talk to Dalt. He can help you."

"I feel funny about talking to Dalt."

"He would welcome it, Cole."

"So, what do you think, a Porsche or a Mercedes?" Cole laughed, getting back to the heart of the matter.

I changed the subject back. "What about the ten thousand dollars for your parents?"

"I'm saving it for them. It's not forgotten."

"Have you thought about taxes?"

Cole hesitated. "No."

"You'd better."

"So, you think I should wait on the car?"

"Wouldn't be a bad idea. How about waiting until I get back from Hawaii next week, then we can talk about it more. And please, talk to Dalt or somebody you can trust."

Out came our power burgers—pure heaven on a lunch plate. The money talk stopped, and we dined in our piece of paradise.

"What will I do when you are gone?"

"You will work hard. You will plan a budget. And I'll be back in a few days."

"I will be so lonely and sad."

"Really? In just three days?"

"Really."

I had to admit that I would miss him very much. Taking his hand across the table, I reluctantly put down my power burger.

"Cole, I love you," I told him. This was the first time I had said those three words without doubt.

"Oh my God," he replied. "I am loved. My life is perfect."

"So, you'll be okay for three days without me? You're not going to find another girl to celebrate with?"

"Three days of abstinence. I might explode. Did you ever consider what might happen when you come back?"

"I think I'm afraid. Very afraid."

"Kate, I don't think I've ever been in real love before. You are my everything. I love you so much."

On the drive back to the salon following lunch at Harbor Club, Cole pointed out every fabulous car we passed on the Pacific Coast Highway. He was possessed.

CHAPTER TWENTY

ALOHA

Cole drove me to LAX to catch my plane to Honolulu. I tried to talk him out of doing me the favor. Driving to LAX on Interstate 405 North at six o'clock in the morning put us in major morning rush hour traffic, even in the carpool lane. Then he had to drive back, facing the traffic going the opposite way. I had told him the airport shuttle would be fine, but he would have none of it.

"I'm taking you and there is no more discussion."

The early morning ride in the Toyota sans air with the worn-out passenger seat stuck in an upright position was not the perfect way to be transported to the airport. Knowing he meant well, I tried to display an overabundance of appreciation. Rich girls know how to put it on when required. I suppose all women know that.

We made it to LAX in a little over an hour. Cole pulled up to the United terminal, jumped out of his car, and came around and opened my door, putting out his hand.

"So gallant," I chided him.

Taking my carry-on bag, he escorted me to the terminal door, where he threw his arms around my waist and pushed me up against the glass, delivering a kiss for the record books.

"Get a room," a man who was trying to pass and enter yelled. We'd heard that before and ignored him. The kiss brought on those Cole shivers that I had become addicted to.

"Maybe I should just miss the plane." Finally, I'd gained the ability to speak as Cole ended his romantic farewell.

"Fine by me," he replied. "There are plenty of hotels right here on Century Boulevard outside the airport."

"Very tempting," I said, moving in to give Cole another kiss, only this one just soft, sweet, and brief.

"I guess that was a kiss-off to the hotel hideaway on Century Boulevard?" he came back coyly.

Lots of people were now crowding the United terminal door, trying to pass us.

"I'd better say goodbye for now. Be back in just three days."

"Oh boy, I will miss you so much. I love you, Kate."

"I love you too. Be good. Call Dalt or someone for that financial advice!"

"Okay, will do."

"Promise?"

"Yes, I promise."

With his promise, I took my carry-on bag off his shoulder, gave him a second kiss-off kiss, and headed inside for my flight. Fortunately for Cole, we had ended our long goodbyes in the nick of time. Running back to the Toyota in the no parking zone, for drop-off and pickup only, he found an airport policewoman was beginning to write a citation. Cole jumped back in the Toyota, yelled out to the officer that he was sorry, and sped off as fast as his cutting into the morning LAX traffic would permit.

I was taking the morning flight from LAX to Honolulu on United, leaving the mainland at eight in the morning and arriving in paradise at ten. It was a five-plus-hour flight, but the three-hour time difference made the travel time pass, since then one had the entire day on the island after arriving.

The best part of all was disembarking the plane and getting hit with that air. Intoxicating humidity infused with the aroma of plumeria blossom was nothing less than a euphoric experience right up there with, well, you know what. Never disappointed, I made my way off the flight full of island dreamers already in their hula shirts and muumuu shifts. The first timers with no idea what to expect when that air enveloped their senses I watched with genuine glee. Grabbing my bag—I never checked luggage—I saw Gert in the terminal lobby. Waving furiously to capture my attention, she looked radiant from my vantage point some one hundred yards away. There was an aura around her; she glowed.

Standing at five feet two, Gert always appeared taller than that to me. For one thing, she always wore heels, even on her casual sandals. "It makes my legs look so much sexier," she always said. And then there was her platinum hair. She had a mass of platinum hair worn full and high off her forehead, pulled back in a very elegant bun in the back. Gert's bun was always surrounded by a silk ribbon tied in a large and noticeable bow—her signature. She went to bed wearing that bow.

"Darling, over here," Gert called out. Everyone on the departing plane could hear her. She cared not.

"Kate, Kate, your grandmother awaits," came the next call of the tropics. Of course, it was a very melodic call. Gert was, after all, a born and bred New Yorker with a remarkable past and an earned and developed pedigree. Not coming from money or social standing, she just evolved into a life of bounty with her supersmart husband, along with, as she put it, "perfect timing, plenty of luck, and unrelenting work ethic."

Grandfather Burton Fairchild had put himself through college and started working on Wall Street post-Depression as a ticker tape runner boy for one of the big firms. He was lucky to find the job; most Wall Street houses would not hire a first-generation immigrant boy. Over his fifty-year career in the market, he would build one of the first and one of the richest funds, which father Dalt carries on today. Burt died young, just seventy years old, when my dad was a young broker with the firm after graduating from Stanford with an MBA. I never knew my grandfather; Gert was ten years younger than Burt. She had never remarried and was now entering her eighties as I was crossing the line from teenager to a woman of twenty.

Gosh, I was so happy to see her, so happy to be with her in Hawaii. After Burt passed, my father moved a major part of the fund from New York to Los Angeles, where he wanted to live and raise his family. Dalt was raised in New York, a Park Avenue kid, but had come west to Stanford for business school and was seduced by California, especially the weather and the ocean in Southern California. My parents moved to Beverly Hills the year I was born.

Gert had followed her children's migration west, only she kept going. She and Burt had discovered Hawaii years earlier. Burt enlisted in the navy in 1940 prior to the onset of World War II to be eligible for college funding after service. The navy interrupted his rising career as a fifty-dollar-a-week ticker tape messenger boy. Sent to Hawaii, he survived the bombing of Pearl Harbor as he was not on the *Arizona* at the time of the attack. Years later, after the war, and after he and Gert had started to make their way in New York, they came back to Honolulu. That was in the early 1960s, and they returned every year thereafter.

When Grandfather passed, Gert, against the well-meaning advice of everyone in the family and the firm, said she was buying a home in Honolulu and exiting her beloved New York.

"It's time for me to start act 3 of my life," she said. "And I will be charting my course alone." Gert and Burt were a team. Now it was her time, her adventure.

When I was ten, the family flew over to Hawaii for a major holiday. Gert was settled, having lived there for some five or six years. An amazing compound on a beachfront three acres, built in the 1920s in a Moorish Mediterranean architectural style, had become her refuge and residence. Creating a new life as promised for herself, she had accomplished much more. Gert had made a name for herself in Hawaii. Patron of the arts, political activist, she became famous for her "salons" of important guests who would come to the estate, which was named La Mamounia II, to solve the problems of the world. This was de rigueur for my grandmother; her inquisitive nature was boundless.

Gert wanted the family to stay on the property. "There are three guest houses," she protested as my father, Dalt, politely and persistently declined. Instead, we checked into multiple adjoining suites at the Royal Hawaiian Hotel on Waikiki Beach.

"Mother, we will spend every meal with you. We will see you as often as you can stand all of us invading your life. But believe me, with the kids, the hotel will work better for all of us," Dalt had said.

Gert eventually agreed.

By the second day on that trip, I had become a hotel deserter and ended up moving in with Gert. I will never forget the amazing time this ten-year-old girl had for the next ten days with her grandmother. I really think it changed my life. Every year for the past decade of my adolescence, even when away at boarding school in Philadelphia, I had made the summer pilgrimage to Gert. It was just part of my life, an important part. I was hoping she would live past one hundred. This planet would just not be as rich or as full without her.

Approaching Gert in the terminal, my temporary fear of eventually losing her faded.

At eighty, she looked sixty, maybe even younger. More than her looks, her spirit was fully intact. Running to embrace her, almost knocking over a couple of first-time tourists in their hula outfits being greeted with airline personnel handing out leis of small purple orchids, I threw my arms around her.

"GiGi, where have you been all my life?" I cried as I embraced her, kissing her repeatedly.

"Right here, my dear. Just waiting for your return," she replied.

"Well, here I am. Maybe I'll just never go back."

"Perfectly fine with me. We won't say a word to Dalt and Nancy. It will be our plan. How long can we get away with it before they catch on?"

"It may take a little while. They are very busy, you know."

"Yes, I know, Kate. Your father has plenty of me and Burt in him. And that mother of yours is a champion. Nothing gets in her way!"

"What an expression for Mom!"

"Don't you think it's accurate, dear?"

"It's perfect."

Gert's driver Kimo and her houseman Raul offered to take my bag and bring the car around. Both men had worked for Gert for some time. I knew them both. I gave them each a hug when handing over my luggage. They ran ahead, and Gert and I made our way through the terminal. I kept taking deep breaths of that air. Even inside the terminal in Honolulu, the air permeated. Gert put her arm around my waist as we walked down the highly polished corridor of old terrazzo flooring toward the front entrance.

"I know what you're doing," she said with her fabulous smile. "You're smelling what you always call 'that air.' You've been doing it for years."

"You've got that right, GiGi. Can I ask a favor?"

"Of course, my darling girl. What?"

"Can we make a couple of stops on the way home?"

"What sort of stops?"

"How about a malasada stop, a Hawaiian ice stop, preferably for grape-flavored ice, and then a stop for a slice of Hawaiian pizza!"

"It's only ten twenty, darling. Did you miss breakfast?"

"No, GiGi. I missed you, and I missed Hawaii and all the things we do together."

"Malasada, ice, and pizza, here we come."

Kimo and Raul were front and center awaiting our terminal exit, parked in the loading zone. Kimo was the driver of GiGi's 1970s-era Mercedes-Benz 600, and Raul jumped out to open the rear door for us to get on board. The old steel-gray machine had belonged to Burt, the last car he purchased before passing. GiGi had shipped it over to Honolulu from New York. The car reminded her of her lost mate. She would never part with that car. It was just who she was.

We got in the back seat and off we went to La Mamounia II, with three stops. This was going to be an amazing birthday, probably the best ever.

Turning Around

On the drive back to Newport Beach, Cole hit the bumper-to-bumper backup. After more than an hour, he had traveled only about halfway, passing Long Beach. It was almost eight thirty in the morning, a little early for a business call, but he grabbed his cell phone, which was resting on the passenger seat beside him, and dialed Dalt Fairchild. The number was indelibly etched in his mind.

"Good morning, Cole. This is an early call." Dalt was pleasant but direct.

"Did I call too early, Mr. Fairchild?"

"No, son, you know I'm up at five for the market. I told you that you could reach me when you needed to do so. So, what's up?"

"I need your advice. I mean, would you be willing to give me advice on how to handle the commission money I received from the sale of your new home?"

"Wouldn't it be better if you consulted your own dad and mom?"

"I've told them about my good fortune. They are not the right people to offer financial advice." Cole wanted to be kind when explaining his parents' lack of business savvy. Dalt got the message, which he probably had already ascertained.

"Cole, I would be happy to help. How about coming up to Beverly Hills to meet me? I'll take you out to lunch, and we'll come up with a strategy."

"When can I come, sir?"

"Well, today is fine if you can make it. My Friday calendar is light. The market closes at one o'clock, and I have no afternoon meetings today."

"That would be really great."

"How about the Sunset Lounge at the Holmby Palms Hotel at one thirty?

I'll reserve a table on the patio. It's a perfect summer day to sit outside and plan a bright young man's financial future."

"I'll be there. Thank you so much."

Cole ended his call. The traffic remained at a standstill on the 405 just north of Long Beach. It took him another twenty minutes to reach the Carson Boulevard off-ramp so he could swing back around and head north to Beverly Hills.

Not exactly sure how long it would take him to get to Beverly Hills, and not exactly sure where the Holmby Palms Hotel was, he finally managed to get back on the 405 going north. It was after nine o'clock on that Friday morning.

After another hour and a half in hot summer traffic in the Toyota without air-conditioning, Cole reached the promised land. He passed the Santa Monica Boulevard off-ramp, then Wilshire Boulevard, and then Sunset Boulevard. That registered. In his prior explorations of the glamorous homes of movie stars and moguls, he knew that the Holmby Palms Hotel, which he had passed by but never entered, was on the famous Sunset Boulevard. He forced the Toyota into the far-right lane, cutting off two panel trucks and one Cadillac limousine to make the sharp off-ramp turn onto Sunset.

Reaching the stop sign at the end of the off-ramp, he was faced with a serious choice: right or left turn? He had no clue, choosing left. It seemed to be the proper choice since going left would be to go west toward the Pacific Ocean. After a few minutes down Sunset, Cole reached Brentwood Village and realized he had made the wrong choice. Doing an illegal U-turn in the middle of crazy Sunset, he was back on track, heading east toward Beverly Hills. Immediately he knew his bearings were correct, as the homes became larger and grander as he drove the winding tree-lined boulevard. It was now after eleven in the morning. Surely it wouldn't take two and a half more hours to reach the hotel in order to be on time for lunch with Dalton Fairchild.

Minutes later, he passed the Beverly Hills sign on Sunset, announcing to drivers that they were crossing into hallowed land—Oz, as it were. Cole let out a sigh of relief. Soon he would see the Holmby Palms pink palace looming on a knoll over the road, the early twentieth-century landmark of American dreams created by a daring new industry called cinema that had revolutionized the planet.

Cole pulled his Toyota into the left-hand turning lane at the light on Crescent Drive, and when the signal changed to green, he turned up the long narrow driveway leading to the hotel. Both sides of the drive were bordered by huge hedges of red blossoming bougainvillea. A line of the world's most expensive automobiles was parked bumper-to-bumper up the far-right side of the drive, barely leaving enough space for Cole, or anyone else, to make his way up to the hotel's grand porte cochere.

"Geez," he said to himself out loud, looking at all the fancy cars, "I don't think they are going to let me park here."

They did. In fact, they treated Cole as if he had arrived in a Ferrari instead of a dented Toyota. Beverly Hills valets in their pink oxford shirts and forest-green short pants welcomed the future real estate mogul and advised him on how to find the Sunset Lounge. It was barely eleven o'clock in the morning. He had more than two hours to kill before meeting Dalt Fairchild.

The hotel doorman, in his pink, green, and gold maharaja costume with a Punjab-style puffy hat, making him appear to be seven feet tall, stood at attendance by the glass entry doors of the hotel at the top of a slightly inclined path leading from the valet station. With military precision, the very tall majordomo reached over to open the glass doors, permitting Cole to enter without any delay in his step.

"Oh boy, this is something," Cole said to himself under his breath. The lobby was a vision of old Hollywood deco glamour—a fantastic exaggeration and an understated slice of sophistication at the same time. Cole had never seen anything quite like it, certainly not the many casino hotels in Reno or Tahoe where he grew up. His idea of wealth and glamour resembled a ringing slot machine pouring out coins into the lap of an overweight woman in a housedress, chain-smoking while attempting to finagle placing the magic coins in the proper slot.

The Holmby Palms Hotel was very foreign territory for Cole. He had never eaten out at a nice restaurant at any time growing up.

Looking around the lobby, he thought there were surprisingly few people, and those who were there seemed to be talking to one another in hushed tones. It was eerily quiet for a late Friday morning in August. Directions from a passing bellman sent Cole on the path to the Sunset Lounge. Making it to the restaurant, which was tucked away in a corner of the lobby, Cole thought better of entering and taking a table. It was just after eleven o'clock, and his lunch with Dalt Fairchild was still two and a half hours away. Instead, he would do a little exploring.

Finding a helical stairwell going down to a lower level, the young man from Reno descended the steps, arriving at a lower floor of the old grand dame of a hotel. Passing by an informal lunch counter, noticing one older woman with a pageboy haircut and enormous, black-framed round glasses sitting alone at the counter reading a book, Cole was sure she was somebody important. She just had that look.

The lower corridor took him past an array of posh hotel boutiques and eventually outside, where he landed in front of what is arguably the most iconic Hollywood pond, the Olympic pool at the Holmby Palms Hotel. Cole let out a rather loud guffaw, saying to himself, "Oh my God. Who are these people, and what are they doing here? Does anybody work in Beverly Hills?" The newly flush real estate agent admired a lifestyle that he would not mind duplicating.

The enormous rectangular pond, surrounded by thick-cushioned chase lounges in turquoise and white, as well as a lineup of matching canvas cabanas that would bring a smile to any VIP type visiting, bustled with hot women and equally hot men. All of them were young, tanned, fit, and supremely confident. This was a parade, a beauty pageant by a pool on a workday in a very unusual place.

Naturally, Cole assumed all the beauties were rich, some even famous. Never once did it occur to him that perhaps, just maybe, some of them might very well be dreamers just like him.

Well, not all. Cole passed by a young family just arriving at the pool. They were a poster family for privileged American tourists. The handsome thirty-something dad and drop-dead raven-haired mom had just come off the hotel tennis courts, appearing so cool as never to have chased a single ball. Their two children, a boy about eight and a girl about five, wore matching bathing outfits, gender-appropriate, overlaid with crisp white terry cloth pool jackets emblazoned with the forest-green coat of arms of the hotel on the breast pocket. Cole overheard them talking about their grandmother back home in Highland Park. Was that in Texas or outside Chicago? Cole had heard of the town but wasn't exactly sure of its locale. He was sure it was a good place to be from either way.

Finding himself taking a stool at the poolside bar, he settled down under another spread of turquoise and white canvas, shaded from the already strong August sun. From this vantage point, turning around, away from the barkeep, he could watch the ongoing parade of beauties availing themselves of the soothing blue waters.

"Can I get you something?" the barkeep inquired. Cole hesitated.

"I'm not a hotel guest, sir. Meeting someone for lunch at one thirty in the Sunset Lounge. Can I order if I am not a registered guest?"

"We prefer room charge. No cash accepted. You may use a credit card."

"I don't have one on me. Maybe just a glass of water then?"

"With pleasure, young man."

One of the handsome tanned men sitting on a barstool down the counter overheard Cole's plight. He moved over next to him and offered a solution.

"Hey, man, let me buy your drink," he said.

"Really?"

"Why not? Can't a guy help out a fellow traveler?"

"That's very nice of you." Cole was liking the whole Beverly Hills vibe even more now.

"What'll it be?" chimed in the barkeep, overhearing the offer.

"What are you having?" Cole asked his newfound buddy. "And by the way, I'm Cole. What's your name?"

"Just call me Charley. I've having a margarita with a shot of Patrón."

"Sound pretty good to me," Cole responded.

Charley launched into some very friendly small talk, delivering a pretty good line of Hollywood BS. The bartender rolled his eyes. He had heard it all before, and he'd heard it from Charley and scores of other wannabes sitting at his bar.

Cole clicked his margarita glass with Charley's, having picked it up just as the barkeep placed the pair of drinks on the highly polished mahogany bar.

"Here's to you," Cole offered. Charley accepted and continued to extol the virtues of his budding acting career. Cole listened in a state of Charley worship.

They enjoyed a second drink, even though Cole had thought better of it, at least for a moment. He would buy some breath mints in the shop he had passed by on the way to the pool before having lunch with Dalt. Besides, it was only eleven thirty, so he had two more hours to sober up.

"Can I show you something, Cole?" Charley asked, putting a hand over Cole's hand on the bar. Charley looked right into Cole's eyes and continued, "I'd like to do something special for you. Come with me and I'll show you. It will just take a few minutes. This will make your day, Cole."

The two young men got up off their barstools. Cole followed Charley around the pool into what was the men's locker room, which was off the pool. Charley guided Cole into a private changing area, behind a closed door. "What is this?" Cole asked, not getting the picture.

"This is where I'm going to make your day. This is where I am going to give you something special." Charley put both his hands on Cole's shoulders, looked at him again right in his eyes, then moved his hands down to his waist. Cole flinched, but he didn't stop Charley. He said nothing and did nothing. Charley took it as a signal to proceed.

In seconds, Charley was on his knees. He unfastened Cole's belt, opened his pants, and dropped them to his ankles. Cole wore no underwear. His large and perfectly formed male unit delighted his suitor.

"Brother, you are nicely packaged," Charley said taking Cole's penis into his mouth.

Cole jerked back, not out of surprise or objection, but instead because he liked the sensation. Charley knew what he was doing, and Cole was responding. Charley continued. Cole said nothing, only groaned as the pleasure rose. Cole put his hands on Charley's head and massaged his scalp, but he failed to get hard. Charley pulled off his dick and looked up at him.

"Is something wrong?"

Cole finally spoke. "Charley, I'm sorry. I don't want this. I can't do this. I feel bad and guilty. You have to stop."

"Are you kidding me, man?"

"No, I'm not. Please stop." Cole pulled back, raising his pants as Charley turned away after shooting an expression of disgust at Cole, not saying a word.

Finally, Charley spoke.

"This is sure strange. I was sure we had that connection. I could see it in your eyes. You are one messed-up dude." Charley dumbfounded Cole with his final words. "So, I guess you aren't going to pay me my usual hundred-dollar fee, man?" Charley put out his paw.

Cole stared at him in disbelief. "This was for money?" he finally spoke.

"You think I hang around this pool for nothing? This is prime territory."

"I couldn't pay for my drinks. You think I have money to pay for sex?"

"Shit. I'll make it up the next time." Charley turned and walked out the door, but not before turning back and shouting at Cole. "Man, get some help. You need to get your head on straight. And that's no pun intended."

Charley exited the private changing chamber while Cole stood in a catatonic state. He was shaking, immobile, and confused. *How did I bring this on? What did I do or not do? Why did I not stop it before it began? Am I gay?*

Coming out of the room, Cole was instantly and totally sober—and scared. *How can I be gay?* His head spun in thought. *I'm supposed to be in love with Kate. We make love over and over, and it's always great. How can I be gay?*

With about an hour to pull himself together before lunch with his lover Kate's father to request financial advice, Cole headed out of the hotel to walk it off. He practically sprinted down the hotel driveway and out onto Sunset Boulevard with the pace of an Olympian. Heading up Crescent Drive to Lexington, he made a complete circle around the hotel property. Unaware of the fact that he was passing the Fairchild mansion on Lexington, Cole did his best to clear his head. He would face the sexual demons later. Or maybe never. On this day, they would be banished from his memory and his mind. These were not his values, or so he thought. He justified his abhorrent action by remembering that he had not followed through with Charley and made him halt the full-on fellatio.

Getting back to the pink palace on Sunset, a hot and sweaty Cole made the walk up the hotel entry driveway, past the uniformed doormen, who once again offered the standard welcome greeting, through the lobby, and straight to the men's room to wash his brow and clean up his act. Spending the next half hour before his lunch meeting with Dalt sitting in a dark, obscure corner of the lobby, Cole attempted to erase the perspiration from his underarms and the chest area of his shirt. Watching people pass by in the distance, he spotted Charley going through the lobby and walking up to the front desk. He panicked. It was no use trying to control the sweat; his forehead was dripping as if he'd just been caught in a rain swell. All he could do was to try to stop shaking. This young man had never felt so much anxiety.

Keeping an eye focused on Charley at the front desk, while at the ready to move at a moment's notice if spotted in his dark corner, Cole saw the desk clerk hand Charley a room key card. The handsome male gigolo and part-time actor shook the clerk's hand, then turned and went for the elevator bank. *Where is the pool hustler going?* Cole questioned himself, realizing that Charley probably had made a connection with a horny guest, male or female, poolside after Cole fled the scene. Charley was just providing his own brand of room service.

The gold-toned elevator doors closed on Charley, giving Cole the final respite needed to compose his sweating, shaking self. Then he spotted Dalton Fairchild entering the double glass doors of the hotel, presumably making his way to the Sunset Lounge for their lunch meeting. Dalt was dressed in a very finely tailored charcoal-gray suit with the jacket sporting notched lapels. A small pin of the US flag was visible from the distance on his left upper lapel, the symbol worn by a most successful financial adviser for Cole.

Mustering the nerve, Cole rose from the peach-colored velvet chair in the dark corner of the Holmby Palms Hotel lobby and made a dash toward Dalton Fairchild, meeting him halfway to the Sunset Lounge.

"Sir, I am so thankful you agreed to see me. How has your day been so far?" Cole questioned as politely and positively as he could.

"It's been a good day, Cole. How about you? You look a bit hot. What's with the sweating?"

"It's nothing. I got here early and went for a walk. I didn't realize how hot it was outside today," Cole answered, trying to offer a reasonable explanation.

"The patio of the Sunset Lounge is shaded, and there should be a nice breeze. You will get comfortable fairly fast," Dalt remarked.

"That will be great," Cole said with appreciation.

"Follow me, Cole. We'll get a table and order some lunch so we can talk."

Armand, the maître d' at the Sunset Lounge, stood at attention just inside the door to the legendary restaurant. He greeted Dalton Fairchild with obligatory kindness and recognition, escorting him and his young guest through the dining room with booths upholstered in rich forest-green fabric—indeed, the room was forest green from floor to ceiling, including the tables—out the glass doors and onto the interior courtyard patio, which was surrounded by trimmed ficus hedges and more manicured red-blooming bougainvillea. Private booths lined the perimeter, with elegant old-world wrought iron tables and chairs in the center of the famous al fresco dining room.

The entire space was bustling with wealthy-looking patrons who were sampling the infamous chopped McQuithy salad and sipping Schramsberg sparkling wine at midday in slender frosted flutes of crystal.

Armand escorted Dalt and Cole to Dalt's regular booth in the far-right corner, totally enclosed and private, yet with the perfect vantage point to see everyone coming and going. It was all about prestige and power placement. In the best Beverly Hills bistro, this was the name of the game.

Dalt motioned for Cole to take a seat. Cole slid into the booth, his back to the comings and goings.

Then Dalt took his usual place. Armand handed the men menus. A busboy arrived with lemon water, asking if they needed anything right away. Another waiter arrived with the signature lavash crisp cracker bread in an overflowing silver wire linen-lined basket.

"Try this bread, Cole. It's the best. Lightly seasoned with parmesan cheese, garlic, and butter and baked to a crisp."

Cole helped himself, immediately taking a second and then a third slice. The lavash was that good. The rapid-fire eating was also Cole's nervous response.

The waiter returned to take the order. Dalt requested his customary McQuithy salad, light on the dressing. Cole ordered lobster.

"Shall we talk finances?" Dalt dove right into the purpose of their lunch together.

"Yes, sir, that would be really appreciated."

"How much was your commission after the split?"

"Just over one hundred twenty thousand dollars."

"How much exactly? My first lesson when it comes to money, be accurate to the penny."

"One hundred twenty-two thousand and eight hundred twelve dollars."

"That is before or after tax? Did your real estate company withhold tax?"

"No, sir. I am an independent contractor, responsible for my own tax."

"Okay. Then, you may keep and spend twelve thousand eight hundred twelve dollars of your commission as you please. The rest of the earnings, one hundred ten thousand dollars, should be held as follows: Thirty thousand goes in an account for potential tax payments. Could be less or more depending on your overall return. Second, you will open a Roth IRA account and begin saving money. I have arranged for my accountant Zach Zimmer to meet with you to discuss that plan. The balance of your funds will be invested, partially in tax-free bonds, partially in stocks. For this you will meet with a young broker in my firm, Jack Craig, the most talented young man I could recommend."

Dalt finished by asking Cole if he could live on the $12,812 until his next commission. Cole said he could but added that he needed a new car. Dalt reduced the amount he had suggested for investment, advising Cole to spend no more than twenty thousand on a car, new or used. He could write off much of the expense as a realtor and independent contractor.

"May I set up appointments for you with my guys?" Dalt asked, respectful of Cole's novice position.

"Absolutely. Yes, sir," Cole replied. He added, "The sooner, the better."

Lunch arrived, and the two financial planners ate, sharing small talk, mostly about the Lido house that Cole just had closed on behalf of Dalt and Nancy. The small talk conversation shifted when Dalt inquired into the seriousness of Cole's relationship with his daughter.

"You seem very close to Kate. How long have you been seeing her?"

Cole choked a bit on his lobster lunch, not having expected the change of subject to his personal life.

"Not long, sir. Only a few months over the summer."

"My daughter seems to be very fond of you, son."

"Yes, sir. And I am fond of her." Cole hesitated, then to his surprise, he revealed, "Sir, I love Kate."

Dalton smiled but did not overreact.

"Really, Cole? How do you know?"

"I know, sir. I think I fell in love with Kate the moment we met. Now I'm sure of it."

Dalton thought about Nancy. He too had fallen in love with his her the moment they met. To him, this was a very good sign, so he left it alone, not pressing Cole for more information.

Rather, Dalt came back with some advice, not of the financial variety.

"You are young. Kate is very young, just turning twenty tomorrow, in fact. Love can be a funny thing; it can be deceiving and fleeting. Solid relationships often take a little time. That is not to say I don't believe in love at first sight. It happened to me with Nancy."

Cole smiled, finally relaxing somewhat. He had found a connection with Dalt.

"I just ask that you take your time to get to know one another. You are just starting your career. The big world lies at your feet. Kate is still trying to figure out her path."

"Yes, sir, I know. But I do love her, and I would never hurt her. Never."

Cole meant his words in spite of the betrayal in the pool dressing room only hours earlier. That transgression was already wiped from memory.

Dalt reached into the breast pocket of his suit jacket and pulled out an envelope, handing it to Cole.

"What's this, sir?" Cole asked.

"Open it, son."

Opening the envelope, Cole removed a round-trip coach airfare ticket to Honolulu dated for departure the following morning at eight o'clock on United out of LAX. There was also a prepaid receipt for a room at the New Otani Hotel in Waikiki for two nights in Cole's name.

"I don't understand, sir?"

"Cole, Nancy and I are treating you to a little trip to the Islands, partly to thank you for all you have done for us on the real estate transaction, and mostly because we thought it would be a wonderful birthday surprise for Kate," Dalt said. "My mother is giving Kate a birthday dinner tomorrow night at Michel's restaurant in the Colony Surf, which is next door to the New Otani. Show up at seven o'clock."

"I think this is the nicest thing anybody has ever done for me, sir."

"I think you can drop the 'sir' and call me Dalt."

"How can I ever thank you, Dalt?"

"Treat my precious Kate well, Cole. That is all any parent can ask."

CHAPTER TWENTY-ONE

UNEXPLAINABLE ACTIONS

Cole lay awake in his bed alone most of Friday night. Confused, even unraveled, by his encounter with the male prostitute at the Holmby Palms Hotel pool, he was even more perplexed by the generous action of Dalton Fairchild over lunch in the Sunset Lounge. Stretched out on top of the covers, not having removed his clothes, Cole had his right hand clutching the airline ticket meant to deliver him to Hawaii and to the young woman he thought was the love of his life.

With major stars in his eyes, Cole thought over the sum of his life experience as a traveler, which extended from Nevada to California. Cole never had traveled on a plane. There was no money for travel and no reason to travel. Before he parted Reno for greener pastures in California, McDonald's was the extent of his fine dining. He had graduated to lobster for lunch at the Sunset Lounge, a meteoric rise.

Now at this remarkable juncture, Cole was flying off to Honolulu on a ticket paid for by his girlfriend's father—the girlfriend he had just betrayed, albeit somewhat unknowingly, with a handsome phony-baloney sometimes actor / sometimes hustler. Even more incredible was the fact that he was flying off to paradise with a bank balance well over six figures. He asked himself, *Why is this happening? Do I deserve this? Who am I?*

The eight o'clock morning flight from LAX to Honolulu Saturday morning on this day in August was full, every seat taken, with standbys having been turned away. Cole had made it with minutes to spare. Breathless, he had run through the airport down the Jetway and into the main cabin, jumping in just as the stewardess began closing the door.

Nudging his way down the crowded aisle as passengers jockeyed for space in the overhead compartment, Cole found his seat, which was almost at the back of the aircraft. Relieved, he'd gotten an aisle seat, no doubt booked by Dalton to give a degree of comfort to Cole's six-foot-two frame.

As he reached up to place his carry-on in the bin, someone passed by, knocking into him, and he lost his grip on the bag, letting it fall into the lap of a young woman seated in the middle seat of the three-person row. The petite brunette with sparkling blue eyes and rather prominent breasts nicely displayed in an unbuttoned silk hula-print blouse let out a small squeal, more like a high-pitched tickle.

Cole sprang into action, grabbing his bag before it could do damage, and apologized with earnest sincerity.

"Oh, it's nothing. I'm fine," responded the girl, who looked as if she were no more than seventeen or eighteen. "Don't be silly. These things happen on a full flight. At least it wasn't your hot coffee."

Cole laughed, then apologized again and took his seat.

About an hour into the flight, a continental breakfast was served, and Cole struck up a conversation with the young woman in the seat beside him. Her name was Nicole. Turns out Nicole was also a first-time flyer and a first timer to make her way to Hawaii. At twenty-two, the perky brunette had not attended college, instead going to work as a bank teller out of high school in Riverside, a town like Reno—not too big, not too small, and not too hip.

The two of them had all this in common, plus she had outrageous sparkling blue eyes. And sparks were flying. The pilot banked the plane to the right over the Pacific and the blazing morning sun filtered through the cabin. Passengers in the window seats began lowering shades. That was all it took to encourage Cole to reach over and take Nicole's hand.

Moments later, the bank teller from Riverside discreetly followed the real estate agent from Reno down the aisle and toward the restrooms at the bulkhead. Somehow, they both ended up in the same one, even though all were unoccupied.

Clothes hit the lavatory floor as Cole pressed Nicole up against the tiny sink. He watched himself make the moves in the mirror behind her. The plane jolted, and he used the sudden jerking motion to lift Nicole up on the sink, her legs apart. Grabbing his package, she guided him inside her, rocking back and forth until the tiny sink began to creak and crackle. Cole never left her mouth, his tongue whipping the insides of her cheeks and moving down her throat. Pulling at his thick black wavy Cuban Italian hair, Nicole screamed as Cole came. Their passion came with the banging of another variety on the door.

"That's enough in there. Come out at once. Come out or I will be forced to enter. Do you understand?" One of the copilots had been informed of the mile-high adventure by a nosy passenger. The pair of lavatory lovers got their act together quickly. Cole came out first, closing the door behind him as if nobody knew that there was a partner in crime still inside.

Seconds later, out came Nicole, fluffing her hair, buttoning her hula blouse, smiling ever so sweetly as she walked bowlegged down the aisle and back to her seat.

"Excuse me" was all she said to Cole, stepping over him to sit in the middle seat.

Cole stood up halfway and smiled as she passed over him, saying nothing but grinning wildly, an animal in heat. Soon the pair of sexual addicts fell asleep, awaking three hours later as the captain announced the approach to Honolulu International. A stewardess passed out warm hand towels, which helped to revive the sleeping beauties. As the seat backs were returned to the upright position, the big bird made a perfectly smooth entrance into paradise.

Nicole handed one of her business cards to Cole; it had her personal phone number scribbled on the back. He took it politely with zero intention of keeping it. Once off the plane, the two parted nonchalantly, and Cole discarded Nicole in a trash receptacle on the main corridor, heading to the outside world.

Flagging a Yellow Cab, Cole jumped in, the driver barely having come to a complete stop. At only a little past eleven in the morning Hawaiian time, Cole wanted to get to the beach.

"Where to, son?" inquired the native Hawaiian cabbie in broken English.

"Can you take me to the New Ottoman Hotel?"

"New what?"

"New Orlando?"

"No such place."

"New Aloha?"

"Nope."

"Wait, let me check my notes. How about New Oregon?"

"I think that one is in Portland," joked the cabbie. "Do you think you want New Otani, the Japanese hotel on the gold coast?"

"Is that near a restaurant called Michel's?"

"That's the one."

"Is it far?"

"Only about twenty minutes without traffic."

"Great. Let's go there."

Mesmerized by the natural beauty of Oahu, Cole practically hung his head out the window of the cab like some retriever.

"What's with this air, man? It's like being high." Cole had discovered the magical Hawaiian air infused with plumeria blossom and ocean trade winds.

The Reno kid, so enthralled with being in Hawaii, totally erased his guilty pleasure with Nicole. Once again, he had betrayed the love of his life, the young woman whom Daddy had sent him to Hawaii to surprise on her birthday. His sexual wandering did not faze Cole, not as much as it should have.

In a strange way, Cole felt relieved, even vindicated, by the sex. It was proof, at least to him, that he was not gay. The Charley thing had been a weird transgression, nothing to be worried about. With Nicole he was pure hetero male, testosterone in high gear. He'd been cured of the homo demon despite having cheated on Kate, not once, but twice in just two days being apart from her. He'd taken her father's money for the trip to see her also with no regret and had no remorse about his sexual dalliance. After all, he wasn't married to Kate, not even engaged. He was a free man.

The cabbie pulled up in front of the New Otani. Cole jumped out, almost forgetting his carry-on.

"Thanks, man," Cole called out, paying the cabbie but not handing him a tip.

"Thanks to you too," the cabbie shot back, driving off.

Checking into an ocean-view room with a balcony over the water reserved by Dalton, Cole figured that the hotel was probably the nicest he had ever known, although not deluxe like some of the famous gold coast establishments. Dalton clearly wanted to be generous, but not overly so.

Cole stripped then put on his bathing suit. He opened the glass doors to the ocean view and pounded his muscular chest like some hula-crazed Tarzan. Looking down from the tenth floor, he could not find a beach, only rocks. Where was the beach?

Calling down to the front desk, Cole learned that a public beach was just steps up Kalakaua Avenue, a five-minute walk from the hotel. Alternately, he could hike in the opposite direction and find a small beach in front of a building called the Colony Surf, which was where the restaurant Michel's was located, on the ground level facing the beach and the ocean. Cole chose that option. This way he could scope out his dinner surprise destination.

With little effort, Cole found the beach behind the Colony Surf. Leaving a towel and his flip-flops on the sand, he dove into the ocean. The warm water enveloped him—pure ecstasy. Not only was the temperature around eighty degrees, but also the sea was crystal clear turquoise with visibility to the ocean floor. It was all he imagined it would be. He began swimming out to sea. A long shelf of shallow water spread out before him. Soon he was swimming clear out to the breakwater a mile away. Passing sailboats overflowing with mai tai–impaired yachtsmen, outrigger canoes with bronzed crews competing, and even a school of porpoises, Cole thought about growing up poor. Perhaps it had not been such a blessing of simplicity after all. You don't know what you are missing when you don't know what you are missing.

The Reno kid now knew. He swam for at least two hours, then headed back to the hotel to find some late lunch and take a nap before the big dinner surprise, feeling as if he had never been happier. Never.

Lunch under the old hau tree on the Otani's oceanfront terrace turned into an afternoon of drinking. The après swim in the ocean had given way to too many Corona Extras and more than a few shots of Patrón tequila. Two o'clock became four o'clock and faded into six. Cole was flying high. Indeed, he'd never been happier, or so he told himself—and never more drunk. This fact he could not admit, for his ability to discern drunk from sober had long passed with the four o'clock shot of Patrón. Cole fell into a self-inflicted trance.

He was drunk, not just with alcohol, but also with a sense of self-righteous power. He was the master of his universe with money in the bank, more than he ever dreamed possible; sex with whomever he desired, anytime, anyplace; and a mentor of substance paying his freight to paradise.

Around six thirty in the evening, the Otani staff were lighting the sunset tiki torches on the terrace. One of the waiters found Cole snoring as he sat slouched in a wicker lounge chair with his feet propped up on the stone seawall.

"Sir, can you please wake up? We are setting the terrace area for dinner and cocktails. Sir, please, it's time to go to your room."

Cole began to rise slowly—very slowly.

"Huh?"

"Sir, you fell asleep. Are you okay?"

"Huh? What? Who are you?"

"I am Yuki, a waiter. Can I help you back to your room?"

Cole came to with a startled look on his face.

"What time is it, Yoko?"

"Six forty-five, sir. And it's Yuki."

"Shit. Six forty-five. I've got to go."

Jumping out of the wicker chair, Cole made a run for the elevator. His vision was so impaired that he ended up punching all the floor buttons before hitting his tenth-floor level. Naturally, the slow-moving lift seemed to take forever, stopping at each floor. All Cole could do was scream out a succession of very audible *fucks*. Fortunately, no one got on the elevator on its slow journey to ten.

Fumbling with his room card key, dropping it several times, Cole was relieved when the door finally permitted entry. He tore the clothes off his back and bolted into the shower, slipping on the marble floor, and leaping toward the side of the toilet, narrowly missing a bloody concussion by banging his forehead. The flow of warm shower water afforded him a modicum of upright stability. Holding his head under the nozzle for a good five minutes, he figured he now had enough composure to dress for the big dinner surprise. Of course, he was fooling himself. The booze was seeping out of every pore of his body. Not the scent of a perfect gent's cologne, the aroma closely resembled a frat boy post–*Animal House* bacchanalia. It would have to do.

The Birthday Surprise

Cole made it to the Colony Surf, just next door from the Otani on Kalakaua. It was almost eight o'clock, the surprise clearly behind schedule. Cole was dressed in his best, his only, navy-blue suit, white shirt, and Republican-red silk tie. His hair was perfectly combed and dabbed with far too much Old Spice aftershave, which he'd used in an attempt to disguise the expulsion of liquor via his pores.

The cheating love of Kate's life, the master of his own universe, appeared in the posh formal dining room known all over Oahu as Michel's, one of Condé Nast's lauded top restaurants of the world. He had come to the mythical land of Aloha traveling further then he had ever gone in his life to surprise his lover.

"Oh my God, Cole, you're here," I blurted with considerable joy and surprise. "This is so wonderful. What's gotten into you?"

I rose from the large oblong dining table positioned in the middle of the dining room facing a windowless wall in front of the ocean. Cresting waves gently came ashore, illuminated by spotlights at the shoreline. An August moon hung low on the horizon, shining ever so brilliantly a mile out to sea.

Running to Cole, I embraced my beau, throwing both arms around his neck. Smelling the obvious, I said nothing. Cole kissed me passionately as Gertrude's dinner guests looked on, applauding their approval. Nothing like superbly good-looking young lovers embracing in the shadows cast by moonlight.

"Come meet my grandmother and her amazing friends." I took Cole's hand and moved toward the table.

"I'm sorry to be late. I meant to arrive at seven," Cole whispered in my ear.

"What does it matter? You're here. That's what matters. Besides, we haven't ordered dinner. Your timing is perfect.

"GiGi, I'd like you to meet someone special. This is Cole Baldwin, my boyfriend."

Gertrude put out her right hand, a triple row of platinum and diamond bangle bracelets blinding the kid from Reno.

"A pleasure to meet you, Cole. Kate speaks very highly of you."

"She is a very special girl, and she also speaks of you with great love and admiration."

"Indeed. We have always shared a special bond. She is my first granddaughter and first grandchild.

"Cole, won't you join us for dinner? Allow me to introduce you to our guests. Sit down right here next to Kate. I'll bookend her on the other side."

I was glowing. Showing off a day's worth of golden Hawaiian bronzing, my porcelain-white skin had taken on a mirrorlike reflectiveness. I had tied my head of blonde hair in a severe bun with a pink satin bow, matching Grandmother GiGi's to the limit. We both wore similar white cotton piqué A-line summer dresses with bare shoulders and arms, had stocking-free legs glowing with lotion, and wore two-inch-heeled pink leather mules with one thin strap across the toes of each, accented with a classic bow.

"Cole, please share with us the story of your surprise arrival. I'm sure everyone, especially Kate, is anxious to hear." GiGi was pushing Cole, testing him. She, of course, had known all about it because Dalton had called her. GiGi also smelled his liquor-laced aftershave and was not a fan from the get-go.

Before Cole could speak, GiGi continued, "Cole, please say hello to my very dear *ohana*. Going around the table to your right, meet the legendary Don Ho. Don't ask him to sing 'Tiny Bubbles,' because he will do ten verses. Next to Don is one of Hawaii's most iconic couples, Mr. and Mrs. Lyle Guslander. They own the Coco Palms Hotel. And Lyle is one of the major developers here on the island.

"Next up is society band leader Del Courtney from the Royal Hawaiian Hotel with his beautiful Eurasian lady Choo Choo, and to my left are my very best friends and neighbors Mrs. Doris Duke and her man Friday, Bernard Lafferty, then my other close friend and neighbor Richard Smart, heir to the Parker Ranch on the Big Island. There you have it, Cole. Kate is surrounded by brilliance, talent, and love on her birthday."

GiGi was laying it on thick on purpose. She wanted to see his reaction. How would Cole handle meeting her famous and wealthy friends?

"Cole, now it's your turn to tell us about yourself. We all want to know more. How did you arrange to come on such short notice?"

Cole stumbled, knocking the table, and sending the china and crystal clanking inharmoniously as he attempted to stand in place. He was obviously somewhat disoriented and totally above his pay grade.

"My name is Cole Baldwin, and I came here because I am in love with Kate Fairchild. She has been gone for two days, and after the first night I knew I could not miss one of her birthdays. I work in real estate, and Kate is an apprentice at a designer salon next door. We met over a hit-and-run, a man who dented the fender on her car. I caught the crook attempting to flee the scene and met Kate."

There were a few ahs and oohs at the celebrity table. Cole was managing to impress those who were not so easy to impress. Unfortunately, he didn't know when to quit, going farther down a dangerous path.

"I just closed an escrow and made a little money, so I thought I could afford a trip to Honolulu to surprise Kate on her birthday. I missed her that much. I could not wait another day."

Cole sat down to the polite applause of the crowd. GiGi was not clapping. Instead, she glared at the young man. Now he was both a drunk and a liar in her eyes. She would have no choice but to tell Kate to be careful.

Dinner orders were taken as the party blossomed. Guests at the table jockeyed to change places, extending the conversation. Dom Pérignon flowed. With the musical chairs, Bernard Lafferty, Doris Duke's 24/7 butler, secretary, and shoulder to cry on, ended up next to Cole.

Lafferty was not your typical Englishman Friday in waiting. His dyed blond hair was long, but he was balding on top, the length tied in a ponytail at the back and falling halfway down to his backside. Overweight with a distinct beer belly, he had the buttons of his wildly multicolored shirt open at the waist. Clearly, he preferred eye makeup to enhance his blue Irish lenses. On his fingers, all of them, were incredibly garish rings in all sizes, colors, and designs. Bernard had been at Doris Duke's side for years. They were inseparable. He was her very own Rasputin of another age and another sensibility. Chatting up Cole, Bernard had his own charming way of grilling the young man to get the dirt. Cole was all too happy to oblige, which seemed odd to Bernard. Most people were more private, even standoffish, when he came in for the kill.

Satisfied with the lowdown he had sought, Bernard rose and kept moving around the dinner table, coming up to GiGi and whispering in her ear. "He's gay. At least bisexual. And he doesn't know it."

GiGi looked aghast. "What? Are you sure?"

"Of course, I'm sure. Takes one to know one. You'd better go to work, Gertrude. Trouble lies ahead." Those were Bernard's final words.

GiGi leaned over to me and whispered, "Darling, can we talk later tonight?"

"Sure, GiGi. Is everything all right?"

"Perfect, darling. I just want to share some thoughts with you on your birthday away from the crowd, just the two of us."

"It might be quite late, GiGi. I will want to be with Cole for a while after dinner."

"Kate, when did I ever go to sleep before two in the morning?"

"I'll see you then to say good night."

"I can't wait. Our time together is limited, not often enough for me. Darling, why don't you consider moving to Hawaii for a year?"

"GiGi, what a wonderful idea, but you know I need to stay in Newport. I have a job I really love, and I think I'm in love with Cole. If things work out, I want to get married on your beachfront lawn. Would that be possible, GiGi?"

"Indeed, my darling girl. Very special."

With GiGi's final words, her sarcasm concealed with expert grace, Cole tipped over backward in his chair, crashing to the floor. Managing to hold on to his champagne flute, his umpteenth refill in this long evening of awkward discomfort and posing for the celebrity guests, he remained on the floor.

"Cole, are you okay? What happened?" I jumped into action and came to his side on the floor. I removed the flute from his right fist, grabbed both his hands, and pushed him forward in the lotus position, with only the top of his wavy black hair visible at table height. Everyone was silent.

With perfectly terrible timing, the Michel's staff entered with a lavishly ornate orchid-encrusted cake, candles ablaze. Waiters lined up singing a French version of the birthday song. They didn't seem to notice that the birthday girl and her boyfriend were on the floor.

Now at table side, the cake was placed in the center. GiGi encouraged all to join in singing to lift the mood. I rose first, sending a series of air-kisses to GiGi's friends. I blew out the candles, then hugged my beloved grandmother.

"My prayer for you, GiGi, is that you have blessed health for at least another twenty years and that we will celebrate together often and again soon. I love you so much. You are my true love always. Thank you for this amazing birthday dinner."

Gertrude started to tear up as I hugged her.

"Now, GiGi, I must go and take care of Cole. I will get him back to the hotel and hopefully get him feeling better. Then I'll be home for our early morning girl-to-girl talk."

I said a quick farewell and helped Cole up, then he and I made our way out of the Colony Surf.

"Cole, where can I take you? You never said where you are staying."

With considerable effort to get a clear word out, Cole answered, "It's a Jap hotel down the street. I can never remember the name."

"Is it the Otani?" I asked.

"Yes. The Salami," Cole came back.

"Salami, here we come." I giggled and took Cole's arm as he stumbled the short walk down Kalakaua Avenue.

A Tipping Point at the Otani

A few well-meaning silent prayers and a strong arm to hold on to had kept Cole upright on my arm back to the Otani. He couldn't remember his name, let alone his room number. The kindness of a night clerk breaking hotel policy translated the room and floor from the passkey card. Seeing Cole, he took pity on me. I confided that my friend had celebrated a bit too much at my birthday. The clerk bowed, understanding.

I managed to get Cole into the room and to the bed as quickly as possible. He went facedown on the mattress in his best blue suit and was out in seconds. Deciding not to try to make him comfortable, I didn't attempt to take off his clothes and get him under the covers. Choosing to lie down opposite Cole for a while to see if he would awaken, I hoped he would begin to sober up. Figuring that a tall order of coffee and a double dose of some Tylenol would help him, I ordered room service and waited at his side for an emergency bathroom run if necessary.

Lying down on the hotel bed, I saw the enormous moon over the Pacific staring in through the sliding glass doors right at eye level. The open panel of glass transmitted the lulling sounds of the tide lapping at the seawall below. Despite all the birthday drama, I was grateful for all the bounty of nature surrounding me. Somehow it made the bizarre behavior of Cole more tolerable. I convinced myself that it was just an aberration, a lapse of good judgment brought on by nerves and a feeling of intimidation among some very famous people, people not on Cole's radar. Although Cole reached for the heights and wanted all the recognition, it was early in the game. His people skills needed work.

An immobile and silent Cole let out the occasional belch, which amused me, because his anatomical grunts seemed to be in time with the crash of the surf. I dozed off in a half sleep, trying not to drift fully away.

The peace broke suddenly. I came to, startled by Cole, who now lay on top of me and was trying to kiss me, his champagne breath choking the life out of this birthday girl. Pleading with Cole to stop, to get off, I quickly realized it was no use.

I didn't know Cole like this, a predator, not a lover, insatiable. He managed to unfasten his pants and shorts, which both hung on his legs, unable to get past his shoe-clad feet.

Still refusing to stop kissing me, he had his tongue permanently lodged in my throat, his hands pulling at my breasts. Trying to drop the A-line dress below my bosom and failing to do so, Cole yanked up the dress, exposing my panty-free private parts.

In his drunken stupor, Cole retained the skill necessary to get and maintain an erection, which easily found its way as he jammed it inside me, oblivious to my screams to stop. As a predator, he was pushing in forcefully. I screamed. There was no stopping him, no reasoning with him. The more I protested, the more he came at me with aggression and force. Cole was having his way with me no matter what.

I pounded on Cole's back with both fists and all my strength to get him off. With one final thrust, he climaxed, sending an enormous stream of his DNA into me, onto me, everywhere. Finally, it was over. Cole went limp all over his body and slid off back onto the bed. He was disheveled, still with his pants below his knees, returning to a silent fetal position on the opposite corner of the bed.

Crying tears of deep sadness, I realized that the man I loved had just raped me. I was emotionally and physically spent. My first coherent thought was to get into a warm bath. Soaking for at least an hour, hurt, and confused, I wanted to pretend it hadn't happened. Happy twentieth birthday.

Finally, out of the bath, wrapped in a terry hotel robe with a towel around my hair, I went to check on Cole. He was still in the same spot, snoring loudly. I lay down on the bed facing away from him and fell asleep.

An early sunrise poured in through the glass doors, illuminating the room and bringing me to life.

Oh my God, it's almost seven. GiGi must be worried silly, I thought, jumping out of bed, looking for my clothes.

Dressing with the pace of a fireman called to duty in the dead of night, I was up and out of the room and hailing a cab in front of the hotel to return to GiGi's estate. It was only a couple of miles down Beach Road. I arrived minutes later to find GiGi sitting on the ocean-facing lanai sipping coffee. GiGi was never up at seven o'clock in the morning.

"GiGi, are you okay?" I called out, seeing my grandmother from behind as I approached.

"Kate, I should ask you that question," Gertrude replied, turning around to see her girl coming home safely.

"GiGi, I am so sorry. I meant to be home after midnight, but I fell asleep and didn't awaken until a few minutes ago, horrified that I left you hanging and waiting."

"My darling, I have not slept all night. Yes, I was very worried." She continued, "Please come sit by me. I must talk with you."

"What is it, GiGi?"

"It is your boyfriend. I have a bad feeling about him. He came to your party drunk and proceeded to drink more. He was not honest and forthcoming with some of his stories and was rather rude to my guests. Most importantly, I did not like the way he treated you on your birthday. It was all about him, his needs, his feelings, his desires."

"Oh, GiGi, he was just feeling overwhelmed, intimidated, I think, by your roundtable of the rich and famous, and maybe by you, too, since I've talked about you to him so much."

"Perhaps. But I'm worried. He is not right for you. Will you promise me that you will be careful, watch for signs, take nothing for granted? Most importantly, as a young woman do not let sex, good sex, get confused with real love. They are not the same.

"When there are equal partners, life can be very rich, but that is rare. If you must, you can live without sex, but a life without real love is empty, lonely, and deadly. You are so young; the future is unlimited. Do not give it away. Do not throw it away. Be smart. Discriminate. Keep on looking over one shoulder and asking yourself, 'What would GiGi do?'"

Coming over to GiGi, I wrapped myself around my beloved grandmother. I spoke not a word of Cole's betrayal, instead promising GiGi that I would always keep her close.

"Darling, you have a noon flight to LA. Why not take a morning swim and freshen up for the trip? We'll take you to the airport around ten or ten twenty this morning and wish you aloha."

"Great idea, Grandmother. Will you join me for the swim?"

"You bet I will. Let's change. I'll meet you on the beach in twenty minutes."

"That's a deal."

An hour of slow and steady laps in the ocean erased more of the demons. I was feeling better. Our entourage left for Honolulu International, once again in Grandfather Burton's 1970 Mercedes-Benz 600 Pullman limousine. Choosing not to check on Cole, I figured that he was on his own. Assuming we were both booked on the same noon flight to LA, I reckoned I would see Cole on the plane.

"If he makes it, he makes it. If not, he will figure it out," I said out loud to myself. Anyway, I needed time to think. Boarding began around a quarter after eleven, and I was one of the first on board, taking a seat in first class, the perfect vantage point to watch all passengers come aboard. One by one they passed, but there was no Cole. At noon the cabin doors closed, and the jet taxied for takeoff to Los Angeles. I now had five hours alone to think. Knowing it would not be enough time to figure it all out, I thought that at least it was a start.

CHAPTER TWENTY-TWO

QUESTIONING EVERYTHING

Monday, then Tuesday, passed with deafening silence. Nothing from Cole. Returning to work with newfound seriousness, I was not the same young woman who had left days earlier. Monsieur Lawrence and Madame Honoré knew something was wrong. My spirit had taken flight. On the other hand, my work was never better. With my demonstrable attention to the smallest detail, my mentors made frequent comments about the change. Monsieur confided in Honoré that such a transformation must be the result of falling in or out of love.

Late Wednesday afternoon, a florist came through the door with two dozen long-stem red roses in a tall clear glass vase. The note simply read, "I'm so sorry. Do you still love me?"

I burst into tears. Monsieur Lawrence assumption was correct. A major pothole on the love road had brought on the change. Madame Honoré ran to hug me, holding me tight.

"Madame, what do I do?" I cried.

"My dear girl, what did you do about what?"

"Cole was so drunk. His behavior was horrible."

"Is that all?"

"No, not all."

"Then what?"

"I have told no one, not my parents, no one."

"What did he do?"

"He forced himself on me. I tried to stop him, but I couldn't. He was a predatory animal, a wild cheetah attacking helpless prey. Oh, I know this sounds crazy, but I felt like prey. He never treated me in a violent aggressive forceful way before. I was falling in love with Cole, and now I am afraid."

"This is terrible, Kate, but you must talk with him, hear him out. We may live in a new age of feminism and equality, but it is something of a mirage. Men, even the best of them, can fall off the pedestal. Sometimes it is best to forgive. But only you can decide. And you can only decide after confronting him with your feelings. Clearly, he knows he has failed you."

"Madame, I don't think I can talk to him. Not yet anyhow. Why has he taken three days to contact me? Especially with red roses. I don't even like red roses. Why didn't he call? Why didn't he show up? His office is next door."

"He is very young, Kate. Young men are still very much little boys. He is afraid you will reject him. That's what red roses are for—baby steps of reconciliation. Don't forget, we have seen this young man's affection for you since the beginning. It can't all be fake. Wait for his call. It will come next. Maybe he will find the courage to come through our door. Maybe."

"I think I need to talk to my mother. This is a call for Nancy. I can't tell my father. He will be devastated at first; he likes Cole so much. Then he will want to kill him."

"The day is nearly done. Go home, have a glass of chardonnay, and call your mother."

"I think it would help."

"Of course, it would. So, make sure you follow through. Just don't be tempted to call Cole. Do not do that."

"That's one thing I will not do, you can be sure."

"Be here by ten o'clock tomorrow morning. Mrs. A is coming in. She wants to wish you happy birthday."

The Mother-Daughter Bond

I called Nancy around eight, finding it odd that the phone just rang and rang. Finally, Jamey picked up.

"Kate, is that you?"

"Jamey, how the heck are you? I miss you so much."

"I'm doing great, big sister. Really good."

"Tell me all about it, Sweet Baby James." I used my affectionate nickname for my little brother, borrowed of course from James Taylor, a 1970s music icon from Nancy and Dalt's younger years.

"Kate, I've been clean now for a couple of months. I feel good. The doc thinks I might be able to go back to school, regular school, in September."

"That's the best news."

"Can you believe it?"

"I sure can."

"Dad says he might even consider allowing me to go to Beverly High, a real school."

"I sure hope it works out for you." I continued, "You'd better come see me soon, or I'll come up to you. Is Mom home?"

Jamey explained that Nancy and Dalt had gone to dinner, and he was home with Marta. I thought the fact that they had left Jamey home with Marta meant real progress. Previously, they would never have allowed that scenario, even though they trust Marta.

"How was your birthday with Grandma?" Jamey changed the subject.

"*Interesting* would be an accurate word choice."

"Did that boy you like, the one who sold Mom and Dad the new house, show up?"

"Jamey, how did you know about that?"

"Dad wanted us all to go, but Mom said no. I heard Dad tell Mom that he was going to pay for a trip for that boy to surprise you since we were not coming."

"Really? I didn't know that."

"I'm pretty sure that's what he said. Did he show up?"

"He did, but it wasn't too great. Jamey, I must go now. Somebody is knocking at the door. I love ya."

"I love you too, big sister."

Hanging up the phone, I dashed for the door. Who would be knocking after eight? From across the front hall, I saw him. Having a Dutch door has its advantages. Behind another large floral arrangement was the face I hadn't been able to get out of my mind as he drilled his manliness into me, ignoring my pleas that he stop.

I came up to the glass window on top but did not open the door. Instead, I raised my voice, half shouting at Cole.

"No flowers wanted here. Not tonight. Maybe not ever. I am not ready to talk, Cole. Please go."

"Kate, please believe me, I am so sorry. I'm not even sure of what I did. I was so drunk that I got sick and couldn't get out of bed for two days. I missed my flight and just got home today. Maybe you don't believe me, but I don't remember much of anything. I know whatever happened, it must be terrible."

"Terrible is just the beginning."

"Won't you let me in? We need to talk."

"Not tonight. I need more time. And don't try to come by the store. I will call you—maybe. I'm confused. I need time."

"Please know how much I love you. I will never forgive myself if I lose you. Please …"

With Cole's final plea, I turned away from the door, walking out of sight. He remained for a moment, staring into the beach house. He was crying. Putting the flowers down on the landing, he finally left. I went into the kitchen, made some tea, and headed upstairs to my room over the garage.

At around ten o'clock at night, the phone rang. It was Nancy.

"Hello, my doll. Jamey said you called."

"Mother, I need some advice. You are the only one I can confide in. Promise you won't share with Father."

"This sounds serious."

"It is. Did Father pay for Cole to come to Hawaii?"

"Why, yes, dear. He thought it would be a surprise for you."

"Mother, it was horrible. He got very drunk—drunk like nothing I have never seen. He turned into a monster. He insulted GiGi and all her friends and made a scene at the table. But it got worse."

I began to sob as Nancy tried to console me over the phone. The tears kept coming; my breathing was more strained. Nancy feared I was going to have a stroke.

"Mother, I took Cole home from the dinner to his hotel a block away and tried to get him settled. Becoming violent and abusive, he suddenly was on top of me, both of us fully clothed, and then his pants were down at his feet, and he was pushing up my dress. Mother, he forced me to have sex and I couldn't make him stop. Before this, I had thought I was falling in love with Cole. Now I'm afraid, confused. I don't know how I feel or what to do."

"Oh my God. This is horrible. You must come home at once. Right now. Get in your car. You can be here in an hour."

"No, not a good idea. I don't want Father to know. I need time to figure out how I feel."

"I'm coming down there first thing tomorrow."

"Can you come at lunch?"

"Lunch it is. What can I bring you?"

"Just come. I need my mother. I'll wait for your arrival in the store around noon, and we'll go out together and talk."

"Deal. You're sure all is okay tonight?"

"I'm sure. I'm under the second blanket of my own bed in my own room. I'll be okay."

"I love you, darling girl."

"I know. I'm so lucky to have an amazing mom. I'm sorry if it seems that I sometimes take you for granted. You are a formidable force and have always been there for me. Always."

Making the Appointment with Mrs. A

I was hoping to do some business in the morning with Mrs. A, my best client, thanks to Madame and Monsieur. She, one of the most prominent women in Newport, did not come for a fitting, but rather to ask me a favor.

"Kate, we are having a cocktail party tonight at the house, and I am hoping that, at the last moment, you would accept an invitation to come and be a friend to my young nephew Wyatt Adamson, who just arrived from the East Coast to go to law school at Loyola. Wyatt is my husband's favorite nephew, a smart, good-looking young man your age. He knows no one here except us. I would be grateful if you would consider making him feel welcome—not a date, just friends at a party. He is a perfect gentleman, I assure you."

I was rather dumbfounded. Of all the times I had been asked to perform escort service for a stranger from out of town, this one took the cake. I would rather have jumped into a river of snarling gators. There was no way I was going to be rude to Mrs. A. I owed her. Or so I thought. Without much hesitation, I said I would do it.

"What time shall I be there? What is the preferred attire?" I asked politely.

"My driver will pick you up around six o'clock. Please give me your address. And dress for a summer soiree by the bay!"

Mrs. A hugged me. She turned and practically skipped out of the salon. What a mistake; instantly, I regretted the whole silly thing. I took a deep yoga breath, counted to ten, exhaled, and went into the workroom to face my task for the day. Fortunately, Monsieur Lawrence had prepared plenty for me to do. As I had done all week long, I dove into the work with the seriousness of an army approaching battle, making my mentors very pleased with me—showing another side to the American rich girl sometimes one-dimensional spoiled stereotype.

Nancy Arrives at Noon

Relieved to see my mother come through the salon door, arriving exactly at noon, I greeted her with a hug and a kiss on both cheeks. Madame welcomed Nancy, who politely requested an hour for lunch with her daughter. Permission was granted. Mother suggested that we just go across the lot to Bristol Farms, where we would have more time. I told her it was not such a good idea since Cole often ate lunch there too.

"Got it. Then get in my car and we'll go to the Harbor Club Grill down Pacific Coast Highway. We'll get seated quickly."

Ushered in and seated at a bay window table overlooking the main channel of Newport Harbor, we watched the constant parade of boats, large, small, and very large, drifting by.

Feeling foolish and guilty for troubling my mother with this, I was sitting in a posh dining room, ordering fine food, looking out at a magnificent view, and ready to pour my heart out, burdening my mother. Did I expect her to just make it all go away? Wave her powerful wand and heal my heart? Or would my privileged life just cover up the pain with another layer of privilege, like so many drugs or bottles of wine consumed to dull the reality of life? At twenty, I was still pretty much a child. Would I be strong enough to face the truth? Was I ready to be responsible for my own choices and for my destiny, whether good or bad?

Nancy was spoiled, but also wise and tough. Getting right into it with no small talk, she came right out with the bottom-line questions.

"Had you been sleeping with Cole prior to the incident?"

Hesitating, I eventually answered honestly, "Almost nightly since we met three months ago."

"Are you in love with him?"

"I thought I was beginning to fall in love, but only recently."

"Then what were the other two and a half months' of lovemaking?"

"Experimentation?" I answered sheepishly.

"Oh, come on."

"Okay, it was great sex. I liked it."

"Do you think you know him well? I mean, really know him—inside, that is, his core, his heart?"

"I thought I did. I believed he was genuine. He was a little rough around the edges, a poor kid trying to make something of his life, but he seemed honest and real. Mostly, he seemed to be in love with me from the first moment we met."

"Was that uncomfortable?"

"It was. Your daughter grew up fast in the big city. I don't think I suffer fools, and I am not a pushover for people who tell sob stories, or losers with ulterior motives. You taught me well."

"That's good to know."

"I just don't know what happened." I continued, "It was Dr. Jekyll and Mr. Hyde."

"What do you think happened?"

I took a moment of silence.

"I think Cole got scared. I think he was intimidated by GiGi. And I think he was feeling guilty about accepting the trip from Father. In fact, he lied about it and did not tell the real story when asked how he had come to join the surprise. Cole felt small, inferior, so he drank to excess to bury the feeling of inadequacy."

"Go further. You're on to something."

"By the time he attacked me, he was out of his mind from alcohol poisoning. I can't even tell you how much he consumed. Cole even fell over backward in his chair at Michel's, hitting the back of his head on the floor."

"Dear girl, you have just solved your own dilemma. The choice is yours. Forgive Cole for his abhorrent behavior and talk it out, or don't forgive him and move on. It's just that simple."

"Oh my God, you are so right."

"One thing I will agree to is that we are not going to discuss this with your father. Not until you have reached your conclusion and the time is right—and even then, maybe not at all. Give yourself a few more days. Analyze every bit of the experience. Then call me and let me know your decision."

The weight of the world, make that the universe, had been lifted. Nancy got me back at the salon by a quarter after one, a little late, but I had no regrets. My mentors, noticing that my spirits had risen, commented on the positive change.

An Evening at the Adamsons' with Wyatt

Surprised to find that the Adamson compound on the bay was literally two blocks from my beach house, I found it strange that Mrs. A hadn't mentioned the proximity when I gave my address for her driver to fetch me for the party. At six o'clock sharp, there he was in a black Bentley, standing at attention by the car in front of my garage. Ringing my cell phone, he let me know that he was out front, advising that there was no hurry; he would wait until I was ready. Anyway, I was ready. I had chosen a simple summer dress with big yellow appliqué daisies. Bare shouldered, I put on a little yellow jacket with a Mandarin collar that happened to have buttons fashioned as daises. Quite chic if you ask me, as I had been fishing for unrelated items, pulling them out of the closet. Little makeup, just some lip gloss, with my hair down at shoulder length, brushed back over the forehead, and strappy white sandals completed the image.

As I came out of the cottage, the driver opened the rear passenger door for me to enter the car. Two minutes later we pulled into the motor court of the compound. Having passed by the property a great many times, I admired the expansive grounds and the stately home crafted in early twentieth-century Mediterranean-style architecture, featuring a gracious third floor of Palladian windows looking west at the Pacific Ocean and east at Newport Harbor.

Funny, I had never really thought about who lived there. I admit I was excited to see the interior of this unique home.

Mrs. A had summoned handsome young men in page uniforms from the Cartier boutique at the Hagstrom Center to stand at attention and greet guests at her front door. The tall young men in their red uniforms were a touch of class. Mrs. A did everything with class and taste; it was what she had a reputation for. Someday I wanted Nancy to meet her. They would be friends.

As I entered the home, in the center of a magnificent great hall with a vaulted ceiling of hand-painted ocean-themed images, Mrs. A glided in. I do mean glided, as if she were on a magic carpet. Wearing a stylish pale peach full-length summer gown, not too fancy, just right for a cocktail party at home on a warm August night, she greeted me with gracious attention, making me feel special and very welcome. She took me by the hand. We walked out onto the bayfront terrace. Directly in front of the massive entry tower, some one hundred guests, mostly young and very upmarket, sampled hors d'oeuvres and clicked glasses of summer wine.

Mrs. A located her nephew Wyatt, who was chatting up not one but two very pretty young women, both cooing and giggling like teenagers on a first date. He seemed to be quite at ease in a crowd of young beautiful strangers. Why had Mrs. A needed my assistance?

"Wyatt, excuse me. I have someone I'd like you to meet. This is the girl I've been bragging about, Kate Fairchild."

That was uncomfortable. Clearly the two young things thought so too. They faded into the party without much prodding. Wyatt turned his attention to me.

"Kate, I have heard so much about you. My aunt calls you the catch of a lifetime."

I looked at Mrs. A. with an embarrassed grin.

"I do, Kate, because you are. And I think my nephew is one too. So, you see, you had to meet."

Oh my God, I was being set up. It was a date, not just a friendly "welcome to California" party. Mrs. A began listing Wyatt's credentials.

"Wyatt is a recent graduate of the Wharton School, following four years of undergrad business study at Tulane. He has recently been hired as an intern at Franklin Investment Fund with headquarters here in Newport to specialize in international money trading and the world bond market before heading to law school. More importantly, you can see he is drop-dead gorgeous—a fine young man with solid values, definitely going places."

I nodded my appreciation for the résumé rundown, starting to feel like one of the wenches at Disneyland's *Pirates of the Caribbean* ride awaiting purchase from a future swashbuckler in need of comfort. Wyatt suggested we go for a walk on the Adamson grounds. He wanted to show me the rose garden and the glasshouse growing orchids on the property. This sounded quite civilized. Then he flagged down a waiter and took two glasses of chardonnay, handing one to me.

"This is for our sunset garden adventure," he said.

Indeed, he was a charmer. Beginning to feel less cynical about the setup, I realized Mrs. A had arranged this meeting with good intentions. On the surface, Wyatt seemed to verify everything she had mentioned about his qualifications. More important than any of this, though, I needed to step out of my torment over Cole and get some perspective. A date with another guy might be a blessing. I snapped out of my cold defense, perfected over years of experience, and tried to be charming in return as Wyatt turned up the volume.

Wandering through the rose garden, following a path created by a maze of manicured privet hedges, I saw that the summer blooms were still bursting forth in profusion. This was a special place, to be sure. We ended up in front of the glass orchid house. Wyatt opened the door for me, and we entered yet another fairyland. The array of orchids was simply enchanting, one plant more beautiful than the next, as we walked down the center aisle. Taking my hand, he sat us down on an antique wrought iron settee at the end of the orchid rainbow. He took my wine-glass and set it and his own down on the small matching iron table in front of us.

Then the worst happened: the young man with the perfect credentials leaned into me and started kissing me passionately, tongue in mouth and all. His free hands, without the constraint of wineglasses, reached under my yellow jacket and cupped both my breasts. I managed to break away from the kiss. Even Wharton boy needed air.

"What are you doing?" I protested.

"What do you think I'm doing?" he answered rather snottily.

"Wyatt, I don't know you. We just met. This is a mistake."

"No mistake. I'm attracted to you, and I want to be with you."

"You don't think your behavior just might be out of line?"

"I've never had any complaints."

With that, he lunged back at me, trying to insert his tongue into my mouth. Slapping him hard, I got up and left the glasshouse and the Adamson compound without a goodbye, soon finding myself standing on Channel Road. At barely seven o'clock, the sun was still bright. Thanking God that I lived only two blocks away, I began walking home as fast as I could.

CHAPTER TWENTY-THREE

A LIFE CHANGER

Minutes after I got home, the cell phone began buzzing. The caller ID showed that the number was blocked, but I knew it was Mrs. A. I didn't answer; I had no intention of explaining myself or even talking about Wyatt. The phone buzzed every ten minutes for at least an hour, then it quit for the night. Thank God.

What did she think I would say? The young man who was such a catch had tried to catch me. What silly woman could resist the advances of a man like that, a man with pedigree, credentials, and such a promising future?

Would I tell my friend Mrs. A that her nephew Wyatt was a rotten pig? Should I tell her that I, too, was a catch? A pretty young woman from a loving family who was well educated, well traveled, and cultured, and who came with a trust fund of her own. Who was the catch now?

What a week. First the horrible, forced sex with Cole, now this. I could not help thinking that I was somehow at fault. Yet, it didn't take very long for me to snap out of "blame the victim." Instead, I screamed "Bullshit!" at the top of my lungs into the white-painted rafters of my bedroom. The *shit* part even echoed. Perfect.

My life experience with men had shown me all sides, from loving to lechery. I knew the drill, or at least thought I did at twenty years old. In the millennial year 2000, my coming of age had dawned in a conflicting era of moral ambiguity relating to sexual relations and the feminine role.

Women my age were raised to pursue independence and equal treatment. We were encouraged to pursue careers. At the same time, we all dressed like mini hoochie mamas and told ourselves that it didn't matter, we deserved respect regardless. We still expected to be treated like ladies—have men pay for our dates, open the door, tell us how beautiful we looked—all while competing with the guys in school and at work.

No wonder guys started acting out sexually. The closer girls and guys became, the more sex became the reward for guys for putting up with all the confusing signals. Perhaps most bizarre of all was my generational preoccupation with the perfect wedding—the best dress, the most romantic location, an amazing party. The groom was only a stand-in at a childish Barbie-infused fantasy.

Sorry, girls, but we are off track with all of this. In fact, we are in some ways less independent and far less realistic than our mothers and grandmothers, who were and are equal partners, although with different roles and talents than our fathers and grandfathers.

What a mess.

Lying in my bed alone on Saturday, I was miserable and even more conflicted. If nothing else, Wyatt strangely had taught me that I needed to give Cole a chance to explain, to repent, to start over. Pulling the comforter up over me just under my chin, I made a promise to think it over in my dreams. Good advice always came to me around two o'clock in the morning, just about the time Grandmother GiGi went to bed. I wanted to believe she was sending me love telepathically—a very comforting concept for a young woman who had been attacked by a guy twice in one week.

A Difficult Sunday Morning

Awaking with the sun streaming in, I didn't feel my usual healthy self. Maybe I was getting a summer cold. Or maybe the stress was getting to me. Either way, I was kind of achy and feeling off-kilter.

Up and out of bed by eight o'clock, I showered, feeling a little woozy under the water. I dressed quickly in white shorts and a polo shirt, put on my tennis shoes, and left for the twenty-four-hour pharmacy to buy some Tylenol and vitamin C.

Looking for relief, I passed the section featuring do-it-yourself remedies, including instant pregnancy tests. Since I was a couple of days late, it did not cross my mind that I could be—I can't even say it. Cole and I had used no protection in Hawaii; it was not planned. That couldn't be right; I was always so careful. Had I not sworn repeatedly that I would not turn my life inside out with an accidental pregnancy? I had never stopped wondering about the fate of my prep school roommate sweet Sara who had gotten pregnant on her first prom date. Then there was the recent nightmare with Carrie, impregnated by the trainer she used to make up for a lack of sex with a loving but impotent husband. Rumors persisted that Carrie had shot her husband, rather than the official explanation of suicide, in the heat of emotional confrontation over the revelation of her condition.

Carrie had left town to go live with her sister in Beverly Hills, her whole life having been turned upside down. This was not going to happen to me.

Buying the tester, along with the Tylenol and a few other items, I went home posthaste. Minutes later, sitting on the toilet, I began to cry as the test strip turned a bright pink.

No Choice Now

Fooling around in the cottage, cleaning like a maniac, I managed to avoid facing my situation for most of the day. Two or three loads of wash later, with polish on every surface of furniture, the linens changed in every bedroom, and the vacuum sucking up the last vestige of lint on the carpet, I was about to wash down the patio and Windex the French doors.

Instead, I finally sat down and hoped that all the exercise had exorcized the pregnancy. It hadn't.

At three o'clock in the afternoon, I picked up my cell, checking a half dozen missed calls from Mrs. A—number blocked. Trying to phone Cole, I nervously misdialed several times. Subconscious fear to be certain. Finally, I got it right, but not before reaching two sex lines on my misdials. Can you believe it, phones are programed to direct misdialed calls to all sorts of lowlife connections? Our technologically advanced society is in the gutter.

Cole answered, thrilled to finally hear from me.

"Baby, is that you?"

"It is I, Cole. We need to talk. Can you come here for dinner—just dinner, no dessert—tonight?"

"I can't wait. What time?"

"Six o'clock. And no flowers."

Arriving without flowers, Cole had brought a personally selected pound of Scotchmallows from See's Candy. A step in the right direction in my opinion. What girl could refuse a See's Scotchmallow?

Sitting down on the terrace following a kiss on the cheek and a hug, I did not pull away, doing my best to be kind. The table was set for dinner, even though it was early for us. I wanted to have something to do when sharing my feelings and the news. If we were sitting on the sofa, I would probably be uncomfortable, especially if he were to move in to embrace me. Strange—about to tell the man who had fathered my child that he was becoming a daddy, I didn't want to be embraced.

I was also afraid of the opposite. What if Cole's reaction was to suggest abortion? I would throw him out for good. It was the initial reaction Carrie had gotten from her trainer boy toy—an easy out for the man not in love. Got an unwanted pregnancy? Just get rid of it—pretend it never happened.

Anyway, we sat down to another glorious day at the end of summer facing the sand. The ocean sparkled with those flickering diamonds created by the last rays of the sun. I had prepared an antipasto of Italian meats and salads, which made Cole smile. Even though his name was now a preppy Episcopalian East Coast phony-baloney calling card, he was, in his soul, still the Latin kid from Reno. The cliché expression applies—you can take the kid out of Reno, but you can't take the Reno out of the kid. Of course, you can substitute the name with that of any town to fit the circumstances.

For dinner I had prepared chicken piccata, lightly breaded and sautéed in butter and extra virgin olive oil, with capers, serving it over mushroom risotto. This had kept me busy most of the afternoon. The maternal instinct had kicked in with the knowledge of my condition. First, the major cleaning fit, then the cooking in the kitchen. Oh brother, this was new and different.

The antipasto and the piccata turned Cole into a marshmallow of sweetness, not unlike the candy he had come forth with at the door. Smiling from ear to ear, devouring every morsel on his plate, and then mine, he knew it was now time to talk seriously.

Beginning with some hesitancy, I told Cole he looked handsome, which he did—one good-looking male specimen. I asked him if he was feeling okay, if he had recovered from his hangover and all that had happened in Hawaii. That led me into the territory I wanted to face head-on.

"Cole, do you have any idea what you did to me in Hawaii?"

Looking directly at me, he answered, "At first, I did not remember, but now I do. And I will never be able to say I am sorry enough."

"What came over you?"

"I have never drunk so much; I think I got alcohol poisoning. I was literally out of my mind."

"What made you drink so much? I've never seen you like that."

"I was nervous showing up at your dinner unannounced. Your father had given me the trip, telling me to be good to his daughter. Maybe it was nerves, or maybe fear of the unknown, and maybe guilt for accepting the trip. I should have paid for it myself."

Telling Cole that I had talked to my mother, I shared her advice with my beau.

Forgive and move on or quit. Nancy's voice reverberated in my head. *Two choices dear. Two choices. Select carefully.*

"Cole, yesterday I decided on the former choice—forgive and move on. But I want to keep my distance for a while and make you plead a little. It's a girl's right."

Cole smiled. "We are okay then?"

"Well, maybe. Things changed today."

"I don't understand."

"Cole, we had no protection the night you attacked me in Hawaii. And you know what they say—it only takes one time."

"Are you pregnant?"

"We are. I took a test this morning. I will go to the doctor on Monday to be sure."

Cole was silent, trying to come to terms with the shock. Suddenly, he jumped up and screamed, "That's the best news I've ever heard! This is wonderful! Will you marry me after you see the doc tomorrow?"

Wow, that wasn't expected. Beginning to tear up, I opened my arms to him, and he came around the table to embrace me, delivering one of those Cole kisses that had won me over when we first met. My Cuban Italian stallion was back on the white horse. I breathed a sigh of relief.

"So, will you marry me tomorrow?"

"I accept your proposal, but not tomorrow. Soon though. Soon."

Changing the mood, I joked, "So, where is the ring?"

Seriously, I thought, *First Sara, then Carrie, now me. This wasn't going to happen to me.*

CHAPTER TWENTY-FOUR

TURNING THE CORNER

At eight o'clock Monday morning I checked in at the Hoag Hospital outpatient clinic. Wanting a doctor to verify my over-the-counter pregnancy test, I had no time to drive into Beverly Hills to see my regular gynecologist. Besides, Nancy went to him too, and Nancy and Dalt deserved to hear the news from me—and hopefully from Cole as well.

By eight thirty I had my verification. The $19.99 test strip kit was right on the money. Funny, I felt relieved, even somewhat elated, euphoric. Must have been the maternal instinct kicking in; I don't know. But I felt like a different person, different from the twenty-year-old woman I was only yesterday.

Wasting no time, I called Cole to share the news. He let out a holler. That helped even more. Cole loved the idea that I was pregnant. The way it had happened didn't bother me anymore. I had forgiven and purposefully forgotten. I just wanted us to be happy.

Leaving the clinic, I drove straight to the salon. Madame Honoré and Monsieur Lawrence were there, always in early, always working on any number of projects. Admiring their work ethic very much, I wondered if I would ever have that constant and consistent purpose in my life. Maybe rich girls from nice families never understood. Comfort can be a curse. At least I knew that much.

As if the news of a baby were not enough, there was some additional big news to share with my mentors. My baby euphoria propelled me to open up and share my idea to create a line of superchic casual separates from drawings I'd created under Monsieur's tutoring. In hand, I had a book of my sketches to present, with a large dose of nerves.

Strolling into the salon as if floating on a cloud, I encountered my trusted employers, who were arranging new items on display. Running over and surrounding both for a three-person hug, I shared all.

"I have wonderful news," I said, almost shouting.

"Yes, you seem very happy, my dear," Madame responded.

"Never, ever have I experienced this level of joy."

"What is this wonderful news?"

"Would you both care to sit down?" I asked.

"Oh my. Sit-down news. Did you win the lotto, dear?"

"I'm pregnant. Only just found out. We're having a baby!"

"That's marvelous. Who is we?"

"Cole! Cole and I are having a baby!"

"My, my, my. That is news."

"We are going to get married fairly soon. Plans will be made."

"Yes, that will be wonderful too."

"And then we will live happily ever after," I said. "And I still plan on working. You cannot fire me because you do not sell maternity clothes, promise?"

"Of course not. We would not think of such a thing. You have become like a daughter to us in only a few short months. Kate, we see your potential; you have talent. More importantly, we see that you are a genuine and lovely young lady."

I was taken with Madame Honoré's emotional words. She was rarely so forthcoming. Another major hug was necessary and appropriate. Then Madame followed with a kiss on both my cheeks. Swearing them to secrecy, I felt it was time to present my portfolio of drawings and make the pitch on my plan to create a line of separates.

"I have something else I would very much like to show you before the salon opens," I said, opening my sketchbook. I suggested that we go into the workroom and sit at the large worktable so I could display my sketches. They agreed.

Once at the table, opening the book, I began explaining the concept.

"What I am about to show you are what I will call high fashion casual separates, to be made of the best cotton fabric available from either France or Italy. These are clothes that can be mixed and matched and worn for just about any occasion, from day to evening. They will be made in pure white cotton, which may have a monochromatic pattern or not, depending on what we find. The appeal will be in the cut, the design, and the detail." Boldly continuing, sounding like a pro, I said, "Quality of stitch will be very important. I want to do several jackets, tops, skirts, shorts, and pants." I paused again. Monsieur interrupted my pitch and asked to look at the drawings more carefully.

At his request, I removed sketches from the portfolio and spread them out on the table. There were no words as both mentors passed the pages back and forth between them. Madame's glasses balanced on the tip of her nose as she examined the drawing of one of the short Eisenhower jackets very carefully.

Their silence was deadly. I had to say something.

"I even have a name for the line, and a logo. It will be called Fair Child, and in between the two words will be a signature pink pansy with a blackish border. The pansy will be embroidered on the garments as the icon of the line."

"Kate, this is very impressive." Monsieur was the first to break the awkward silence. Madame followed.

"You know, this reminds me of the beautiful line back in the 1960s and '70s by Courrèges. It is a modern interpretation."

Then Monsieur said the magic words: "Why don't we search for the perfect fabric, then construct a few pieces?"

"Really? You would do this and help me?" I said, almost tearing.

"Why not?" he replied. "I think you may have a winner. Let us see."

Boy, life can turn a corner in one day. A baby and a career move in less than a full morning. Could this be happening to me? With all the excitement, we opened the salon that Monday morning at ten o'clock sharp, and it was business as usual. Consistent and committed to the routine in good times and bad—that was their creed. I was learning the value of one step at a time and one foot in front of the next, and most significantly, of the long-distance runner often takes the race.

Cole Gets More Good News

Receiving the "father" news on his cell phone, Cole was rushing to get his act together to make a listing presentation on a potential twelve-million-dollar home. The call to participate had come to him because of his newfound notoriety as the agent who had sold the big Lido listing to the Fairchilds, clients he assumed would soon become family. It was the ultimate package deal. Not only was he potentially marrying rich, but also he was getting rich on his own. For Cole, this was everything. There was much to prove to the folks back home in Reno and even more to prove to himself.

Now, as fate shined upon him, the world was in the palm of his hand. Silently he vowed to make the most of his remarkable good fortune. The Catholic schoolboy instinctively made the sign of the cross on his body, thanking Jesus out loud, his head turned upward toward the heavens. Having not set foot in a church in at least seven or eight years, and having left home and changed his name, he felt that God clearly had forgiven his abandonment.

With the money from the sale of the Lido house burning a hole in Cole's proverbial pocket, he wanted a new, or at least newer, car. His present transportation did not send the proper message to a potential twelve-million-dollar client. Still, it was either drive or walk to the listing appointment. Cole chose to drive. He would park a block away, just in case someone might see him.

It was just a ten-minute drive to the residence located at One Pacific Island Drive. Cole made it without incident. He parked at least six houses down the drive, checking out his hair in the rearview mirror.

I'm going to make this happen, he said to himself, crossing himself again. That youthful religious indoctrination had not been wasted after all.

Once again dressed in his one good navy-blue suit, white shirt, and Republican-red silk tie, Cole walked up to the front gate of the waterfront mansion and rang the bell.

Several minutes passed. He rang again. Still no response. The ornate iron gate was locked electronically; somebody needed to buzz him in. He rang a third time, holding down the buzzer.

Checking his watch, he saw that it was exactly twenty after ten in the morning. Cole was ten minutes ahead of schedule for his ten thirty appointment. *Is no one home?* he asked himself. *Maybe they are meeting me here at ten thirty?*

Deciding to walk around the perimeter of the property as best as possible given the limestone wall and fully manicured hedges, Cole got a glimpse of the enormity of the place. Set on a prime peninsula overlooking Newport Bay with views of the Pacific Ocean, this was unquestionably a trophy listing.

"If I land this one, I will make a name for myself," he said to the trunk of a massive ficus laurel tree trimmed like a giant green lollipop. The tree did not respond.

Ten minutes passed. At ten thirty a male voice came over a speaker at the gate. "The Carondolet residence. May I help you?"

Cole made a dash for the speaker. "This is Cole Baldwin. I have an appointment with Mrs. Carondolet."

"One moment, please."

The gate buzzed. Cole entered, walking across the limestone courtyard toward the formidable front entrance.

One of the tall double doors opened, the one on the right side. A slender, tanned bald man in a white Nehru jacket greeted him.

"Please come in, Mr. Baldwin. Mrs. Carondolet is expecting you."

Cole assumed the man was the butler. He couldn't be the husband. The boyfriend? Not a chance.

"Please come this way. Follow me."

The tall thin man escorted Cole into a formal living room. Cole noticed the man was wearing velvet slippers.

"Can I get you anything, sir? Coffee, tea, champagne?" he offered.

"Champagne?" Cole replied with a laugh, more of a question than a response.

"Mrs. Carondolet starts each morning with her glass of champagne. Perhaps you would care to join her?" he said.

Cole was intrigued. Who was this woman? Was this real? And who was the guy in the Nehru jacket and velvet slippers?

Just as the man left Cole in the salon, Mrs. Carondolet appeared.

He was expecting an old woman, an eccentric older woman, perhaps in a kimono with her hair done up in chopsticks. His imagination had run the gamut.

How can I possibly close this deal? he thought. *I think this is a very strange house. How can I fit into this puzzle?*

Mrs. Carondolet far exceeded Cole's wildest imaginations. A drop-dead gorgeous thirty-something blonde bombshell with a Playboy centerfold figure swooshed into the drawing room in an all-black spandex exercise leotard and sneakers. Her long, thick blonde hair was pulled back in a ponytail and tied with a rubber band. There was one oddity—she was fully made up, fake eyelashes and the works. Mrs. Carondolet would stop traffic on the Pacific Coast Highway, a pure vixen sex machine.

"Hi, Cole. I'm Mrs. Carondolet. Thank you for coming," she said, extending her hand.

Cole jumped up, taking the hand.

"My business manager told me to interview you," she continued.

"Really?" Cole replied awkwardly, thinking to himself, *What's a business manager?*

"Yes, really. Are you as good at selling houses as you are at looking like a million bucks?"

"What?" Cole was thrown off his game.

"I've interviewed at least a dozen agents for this house, and most of them looked like graduates from Ghoul University. Cole, you're more like it."

"Thank you, I think." Cole was uncomfortable being on the receiving side of the sweet talk.

Skinny Lurch made his reentry into the living room with champagne and two flutes, pouring a glass for Mrs. Carondolet and handing it to her.

"Care to join me, Cole?" she inquired.

"Yes, of course," he replied, delivering his share of the sweet-talking charm. Cole wanted her business and felt that there was an opening, a chance. Needing to play the game, he accepted the morning flute of champagne and offered a toast.

"Here is to meeting a beautiful woman in her amazing house that I will sell for more money than she ever thought she could get!" He was really pouring it on.

Clicking flutes, they drank. She never took eyes off him.

"Did you bring a proposal?" she asked.

Cole reached into his breast pocket and pulled out an envelope. "I did. Please open it and take a look."

Mrs. Carondolet followed Cole's instruction. Silence ensued as she flipped through the pages.

"You think I should ask fifteen million? Everyone, including my banker, my business manager, and all the other agents, say no more than twelve million."

"They're wrong. We can do better. We will do better. Maybe not fifteen, but not twelve either," Cole came back.

"Where do I sign?" she asked.

Cole pulled out his pen, showing his new client where to sign.

"We can fill out all the other papers later, okay?" she asked.

"We can. It's your call. Whenever it is convenient," Cole answered.

"Well then, we're done. Let me show you out."

Caroline Carondolet took Cole Baldwin by the hand and walked him out through the massive two-story entryway to the front doors. At the portal, they stopped, Cole facing his new client.

Reaching over to him, she kissed him on the mouth. A short kiss, it was nevertheless a wet and sensual one.

"Our business has been sealed with a kiss," she said coyly as Cole stared at her. "Now you'd better get going on selling this house. I expect you will report to me daily, if not more often."

Cole turned and exited through the right side of the double doors just as he had entered. The electronic gate buzzed, and he left the property letting out yet a "Thank you, Jesus!" at the top of his lungs.

He had landed the big one.

CHAPTER TWENTY-FIVE

FACING THE FAMILY

I arrived at my parents' home around seven thirty on Tuesday evening, having maneuvered the northbound traffic on Interstate 405 from Newport in about an hour and a half—not bad for a weeknight in LA. Dinner was planned for eight o'clock to reveal the news I had shared in confidence with Nancy. She had promised to act surprised. Hoping that my father would be happy, with part of me prepared to defend my situation if faced with his lack of support, I would remind him that he had sent Cole to me in Hawaii and unwittingly had become the recipient of a modern-day arranged marriage—shotgun style.

Dalt would never accept my twisted logic, but there was some truth to all of it. Whatever my father's reaction, I knew where I stood. I would marry Cole and have the baby.

Coming in the front door, I discovered Nancy working her magic. An amazing spread of her roses filled a clear crystal vase on the entry table. Votive candles, slightly scented, flickered around the vase, and Andrea Bocelli's voice provided the background.

My childhood home was as warm and welcoming as it was elegant and formal. Soft light from crystal chandeliers bounced off cream-colored damask-covered walls. Fine highly polished antique English Regency furniture supported family photos framed in sterling silver, strategically placed Limoges objets d'art, and books as thick as encyclopedias on Joan Miró, Pablo Picasso, and Jasper Johns, which were stacked in carefully placed yet seemingly random order.

Jefferson appeared and greeted me with a big hug. I introduced him to Cole as he was a member of the family, an important part of my entire life. Nearly eighty, a very proud and dapper black gentleman, Jefferson was always perfectly dressed in suit and tie, his white hair cut short, and his snow-white thick mustache always trimmed to exacting standards. Jefferson spoke with a charming lilt in his voice as if he were about to recite a poem or deliver a monologue from Shakespeare. Then there was his walk, or should I say dance steps. As a girl, I had imagined Jefferson could break into a tap dance as he crossed the floor. Nancy told me he had been a dancer and a jazz musician as a young man.

"Kate, your parents will be down in a minute. They know you have arrived. Jamey is coming to dinner as well. Would you and your young man care for something, perhaps a drink? Your mother has put out some hors d'oeuvres in the living room."

Turning to Cole, I asked him if he wanted anything.

"We're just fine, Jefferson. Don't need anything."

"Then I will go into the dining room and finish helping Marta get ready for dinner."

Jefferson danced his way into the dining room as Cole and I sat down in the living room and did a bit of nibbling on the cheese platter Nancy had prepared.

"Are you nervous?" Cole asked.

I hesitated. "Well, sort of, I guess. But not really. No. I would say no, I'm not."

"That sounds confusing."

"I'm really not. It's just not the way I planned this moment in my life."

"You had it planned?"

"Well, every girl has a plan, or at least many do. I was not going to be the girl to invert the sequence of milestone events. My plan brought love first, marriage second, baby third. And I also thought the marriage and baby parts would come when I was at least thirty."

"I guess I spoiled that plan."

I turned to Cole on the couch and leaned in to kiss him. "Yes you did. But I love you for it."

"But will your parents feel the same about the situation?"

"You know what, I bet they will. And even if they don't, they will support me—and you. That's just who they are."

"I think I know that, even from only knowing them a short time."

Nancy and Dalt entered the living room with their usual perfect timing. They both looked like the happiest, best-dressed couple on the planet.

"This is certainly a pleasant surprise having you both come to dinner." Dalt knew something was up.

Rising and coming over to my father, I gave him a proper hug. Cole was right behind me with his handshake at the ready.

Nancy, in her usual motherly fashion, asked if we were hungry and if the drive up from Newport had been bearable, while managing to discreetly rearrange the cheese tray into a display more to her liking.

"Sir, I wonder if I could have a private word with you before we have dinner?" Cole was direct and quite manly. I thought he was off to a good start.

"That would be fine, Cole. Is everything all right?" Dalt asked.

"Everything is perfect," Cole responded.

"Follow me into my study, Cole. Nancy, Cole and I need a moment. We'll be right back."

"Fine, dear. Kate and I will catch up."

Dalt escorted Cole into his walnut-paneled library and study. Nancy had decorated the room with a thick wool plaid carpet in greens, golds, and tones of red. In the center of the study, a red leather Chippendale divan sported coordinated plaid pillows and was flanked by oversized wing chairs in green and gold striped fabric. A massive English library table, no drawers, with a pair of red leather tufted chairs on either side, served as Dalt's desk. Dalt invited Cole to take one of the seats, himself sitting down at the library table so they were facing one another.

Cole was more than just a little nervous.

"What did you want to discuss, Cole?" Dalt launched right in.

"Sir, I came here, or rather we came here, tonight with some really important news. I wanted to tell you in person and ask you something as well." Sweat droplets were beginning to show on his forehead.

"I'm all ears, son. This can't be too earthshaking since you told me earlier that everything was perfect. Those were your words, correct?"

"Yes, sir, those were my words."

Dalt reached over to pour a drink from a crystal decanter sitting on a silver tray at the corner of his desk.

"Would you care for a shot of J&B scotch?" he asked, inviting Cole to join him. Cole accepted without hesitation. "So, tell me the news," Dalt continued.

Cole took a beat and took a large swig of the scotch.

"Sir, we are pregnant. I've come here tonight to ask for your permission to marry Kate."

Standing up, Dalt came around the table. Cole rose as well. He wasn't sure if Dalt was going to punch him or hug him.

To his relief, it was the latter. Dalt gave Cole a man-to-man embrace.

"That is big news. Very good news as well," Dalt spoke in a slow and deliberate tone. "I knew you were in love with my Kate, and I thought she felt the same about you too. I guess I was right."

"Yes, sir, we are in love. Getting pregnant was not part of the plan, but we are both very happy about it. And we hope that you and Mrs. Fairchild will be too."

"Kate is very young, Cole, but she is smart and worldly, and we trust her judgment. If this is right for her, then it is right for us. You have my permission." He paused. "And you have our blessing."

Ushering his future son-in-law out of the study and back to the living room, Dalt found his wife and daughter laughing hysterically. Cole interrupted the comedy scene.

"Kate, did you tell her?" he asked sheepishly. His query sent both women into a deeper state of hysteria. Finally able to compose myself, I explained.

"Cole, yes, I've told her, but that's not what we are laughing about."

Nancy chimed in, "Why don't you men sit down and have some cheese? How about another drink?"

Dalt and Cole accepted the invitation.

"Nancy darling, I assume you are up to speed. I'd like to propose a toast to Kate, and to Cole, and to our first grandchild. May you all be blessed with health and abundant happiness for all time."

Jefferson entered the living room with Jamey, announcing that dinner was served in the dining room. Nancy and I were still laughing, with Dalt and Cole remaining clueless. Jamey joined the party.

"What did I miss?" he said, looking at me.

"Jamey, you are going to be an uncle."

"Huh? I'm only in the ninth grade. How can I be that?"

"Because Cole and I are getting married, and we are having a baby who will be your nephew."

"You're kidding!"

"You'd better start practicing your best uncle skills."

Nancy gathered the family together, herding us in to dinner.

A Most Unusual Dinner Conversation

Thrown off-kilter by the dinner conversation at the family engagement and celebration after the pregnancy announcement, I selfishly wanted the dinner to be all about the bride and the mother-to-be. Instead, it was all about Cole. Dalt took the lead, directing the dinner talk into business mode in support of Cole's future. Perhaps if I had not been hormonal, I would have been less upset, realizing that my father, the modern-era matchmaker, was extending himself to Cole in order to provide for his daughter's future.

Just the same, I wanted to talk about wedding plans and baby preparations, not real estate deals. Nancy put her hand over mine under the table, giving me the *Don't worry, dear; Mother has this all under control* look. Nancy always had it all under control, whatever it was.

"Cole, I've been meaning to call you to discuss a business plan with you. This would be an ideal time while we are all together," Dalt said.

"Yes, sir, what are you thinking of doing?" Cole asked.

"Son, you will be the doing, and I will be providing the financing. I'm putting together a small group of wealthy investors who believe that the residential real estate market in Newport Beach is about to take off with the development of Newport Coast and Shady Canyon. We are going to put together a development fund with an initial twenty-five million dollars cash and another twenty-five million in financing to build and sell semicustom homes. We believe the market is about to be influenced by a significant influx of foreign buyers seeking US residency in a secure location. This could easily end up becoming a multibillion-dollar project over the next decade."

"Boy, that sounds amazing."

Cole was dumbstruck by the enormity of Dalt's proposition. I asked Cole to pass the rolls, with no response.

"I'm sorry, what was that?" he asked.

"The rolls. Could you pass them?" I came back.

"Oh, sorry. I was trying to digest your father's business plan."

"Yes, I can see that," I told him with a smile, slightly forced.

Dalt came back into the conversation after my brief interruption asking for the rolls.

"Cole, I want you to be my point man for the deals. You will be the man to find and negotiate the land deals to buy the right lots at the right price in order to build our custom homes. You will earn commission on each closed deal, and you will draw a salary over and above that. Within a year, if this works as well as I believe it will, you will also share in the profit structure—you, Kate, and my grandchild-to-come."

"Dad, are you serious?" I blurted out, not having expected Dalt to put my future husband in business. Part of what I loved about Cole was his drive to make it on his own. Dalt not only inadvertently had set Cole up for marriage and family but also was now setting up his entire life. Had he not done enough by giving Cole the Lido house deal and earning him a huge commission? Was I supposed to be grateful, thrilled? Was I supposed to feel relieved that we would have financial security? I didn't want to appear ungrateful, but on the other hand, I felt funny about the whole thing. Really funny as in not funny at all.

"Dad, that's an incredible offer. Are you sure?" I managed to respond.

"Of course, I'm sure, Kate. What could be more important than helping my children?"

"Kate, you know your father always has your best interests in mind. He would not make such an offer lightly."

All I could do was to ask Nancy to pass the veggie platter. Cole shot me a strange look as if to say, *Aren't you happy?*

Taking an inordinately large helping of broccoli, I sent Cole another smile.

"Now that we have resolved the financial future of our family and have also seemingly developed the entire Newport Coast as well, could we talk about our wedding plans?"

"Of course, darling," Nancy was quick to interject. "Now what do you have in mind?"

CHAPTER TWENTY-SIX

CHARTING A COURSE

It had been a rather remarkable week. My happiness quotient was off the charts. Cole had made the most passionate love to me every night since announcing the baby and marriage plans to my family. He also was just about the happiest guy on the planet. He had landed a multi-million-dollar listing on his own; Dalt had put him in business with fifty million in investment dollars behind him; and he was marrying the young woman he loved and was having a child. Doesn't get much better than that.

As for me, well, I felt loved and was in love. It was different from when I loved David in college. Maybe a couple of years of life experience had created a whole other conception of what love was.

With David, I hadn't cared about anything else but David, including caring about myself. At the time, he was my whole world. When I lost him, I was broken, truly and completely broken, and searching for a way to come back and rediscover myself. It was different with Cole. He was not my whole world. I loved Cole, but I had not turned over my life to him. I was now finding that I was my own unique person. And while I was thrilled to be marrying Cole and to be having his child and be a family—a family like the loving family in which I was raised—I also knew that I wanted to continue pursuing my own dreams.

This confidence and self-awareness had propelled me to be even more serious, and more ambitious about creating the fashion line. I don't think I had ever worked so diligently at the store before. Odd, I was not overly distracted by making wedding plans or even finding the right ob-gyn in Newport. I knew I could manage it all and still move forward with creating my clothing line, that is, with the help of Monsieur Lawrence and Madame Honoré, who were totally behind me. After completing the daily tasks in the store, we spent at least a couple of hours each afternoon, working past seven each evening, fabricating the line. Every day, the project became more exciting, more enticing, more real.

Monsieur Lawrence had found a perfect high-thread-count cotton in a small French mill he knew in the village of Ville France just south of Nice on the Mediterranean. Samples were on a plane. In the meantime, I kept drawing and my mentors kept editing. With any luck, we would be cutting and sewing in a month's time. So far, the only expense involved had been shipping a bolt of cotton fabric, which I readily paid for.

The week was ending, and so was the summer of my twentieth year. I could feel a slight difference in the weather, offering a hint of change to come, even though September in Newport was often the hottest month of the season. Fall always meant renewal to me, a chance to start over, make new plans, get a fresh look at life. I looked forward to the change in seasons, even in Southern California, where the palm trees neither changed colors nor dropped their fronds once October arrived.

As the workday in the salon was ending and our time in the back room, set aside to work on the new line, was about to go into full swing, the bell at the front door of the shop tinkled. Mrs. A entered.

I had not seen her, nor spoken to, her since my "date" with her nephew at his "coming to California" party at the Adamson estate. She had called me repeatedly, but I never called back. I knew it was wrong on so many levels, including because Mrs. A was such a good customer of Monsieur Lawrence and Madame Honoré.

"Mrs. Adamson, can you please forgive my rudeness in not calling you after your party?" were the first words out of my mouth as I greeted her with a handshake that she turned into a caring hug.

"Sweetheart, not to worry. I know what happened, and I wanted to apologize to you."

"You know?"

"Very little gets past me. I have spies everywhere."

"I really felt awful for just leaving without a proper goodbye, but under the circumstances, I just had to bolt."

"Trust me, I had words with my favorite nephew. He got the message. Perhaps you would care to give him a second chance?"

I could not believe what she was saying. My response at first was silence; I was speechless. Then I found the courage to be tactful. Nancy would have been proud.

"Mrs. A, I am engaged, and I am also pregnant. I don't think a second chance with your nephew would be in order," I said with a giggle.

Mrs. A was silent, maybe even a little shocked.

"Oh my dear, I had no idea. How are you feeling? Who is the lucky man?"

"I am doing great. My fiancé is Cole Baldwin. He works in real estate; I don't think you know him."

"Well, all the best, my young friend. You must allow me to throw a shower for you."

Not having expected such an offer, I accepted gracefully.

"That is so kind and generous of you," I replied.

"Let's set up something soon. Is Monsieur here? I need him to do some alterations for me."

"He is in the workroom. I'll go and get him," I said, leaving Mrs. A in the salon to look at the new arrivals.

When I returned a moment later with Monsieur, the bells at the front door began to tinkle yet again. In walked Cole, carrying flowers and champagne.

"I thought I would end our first week of engagement with a little toast," he announced. Madame Honoré had heard the clarion call and came into the salon from the workroom to join the group.

Running over to Cole, I gave him a kiss hello.

"I didn't expect you until much later," I said, taking his hand and walking him over to meet Mrs. A.

"I couldn't wait to see you," he whispered.

"Mrs. Adamson, I'd like you to meet my fiancé, Cole Baldwin." Cole extended his hand.

"It's a pleasure to meet you, Cole. Kate just told me about your news."

"We are very excited," he replied, turning to me. "Can we open the champagne? I have a surprise," he said to me and all. Madame Honoré once again performed the hostess duties and went for the crystal glasses, while Cole popped the champagne cork.

"I certainly came in the store at the right time," Mrs. A joked.

Madame Honoré set the glasses down on the display table in the center of the salon. Cole poured and passed out the flutes to everyone.

"To my beautiful future wife. I want the whole world to know how much I love you," Cole said, melting the hearts of all the women in the room, including mine. I was a sucker for sentiment. We raised our glasses, taking a sip of the champagne. Looking in my glass, I saw something shining at the bottom. Had a piece of the metal covering the cork landed in my glass?

Putting my index finger in the champagne, I discovered the shining object was not a segment of the *muselet*, but rather another form of metal. It was a ring. My engagement ring had not arrived in a robin's-egg-blue box, but instead had come with a pouring of Veuve Clicquot.

Reaching in, I removed what appeared to be a simple gold band with tiny diamonds.

Putting the ring on the ring finger of my left hand, I held it up for everyone to see. They all clapped. Madame Honoré held back a tear.

Cole came over to me and kissed me on the cheek.

"Is it okay? I know it's just a band, not a fancy diamond. I hope you don't mind. Someday I'll buy you the diamond you deserve."

"Cole, it is stunning. Absolutely perfect. I couldn't have chosen better."

"There is another matter your parents shared with me, but it is only okay if you agree per their wishes?"

As I was waiting for the other shoe to drop and ruin my liquid engagement surprise, Cole proceeded with more news.

"Your mom and dad suggested that we move in together as soon as possible before the wedding so I can be with you throughout most of the pregnancy. They offered that I should share the beach house with you until we can afford a house of our own."

Well, at least there was no shoe dropping. It was what I had in mind as well, although I had never discussed the idea with my parents. How could I be upset? I lived a life with total love and support from my family.

The engagement ring surprise was enough excitement for the end of the weekday at the salon. Forgoing a late session of design on the new line, we all parted. Cole asked me out to dinner and suggested that we go to the Quiet Woman, a bistro down the Pacific Coast Highway in the village of Corona del Mar. We loved their hamburgers and the music in the bar. Not exactly the Ritz for an engagement dinner, but I agreed that it was a great idea.

Dinner at the Quiet Woman was fun, but the after-dinner celebration back at the cottage was even better. Our lovemaking lasted until daybreak. I couldn't remember falling to sleep, and I didn't rise until noon on Saturday. Fortunately, I had the day off following the ring ceremony in order to celebrate with Cole over the weekend.

A Saturday Surprise

Cole went to his office to plan a strategy and the marketing for the twelve-million-dollar listing on Ocean Drive. He was very excited, and I was thrilled for him. This was a big deal for a twenty-five-year-old without long-term connections in a very tight-knit town of mostly millionaires and wannabes. Besides that fact, every other person in Newport was licensed to sell real estate, so the competition for the big listings and big sales was cutthroat at best. Apparently, Cole was getting a reputation as the hot new kid in town.

Taking advantage of the quiet downtime to catch up on hasty wedding plans, I figured I had at best only a couple of months to set a date for the ceremony before beginning to show my condition. Nancy had made it very clear to me that a maternity bridal dress was not a great idea for a white wedding.

The morning after our dinner with the parents, I called my grandmother in Honolulu to tell her the news. I received the recorded "Aloha" message again; we had missed each other all week. GiGi needed to hear this news from me, not from Dalt or Nancy. They both had promised me that they would say nothing.

As the time was approaching one in the afternoon, I thought I would try her again since it would be ten in the morning in Hawaii, which was early for GiGi since she often slept until noon. Dialing the number, because I just couldn't wait any longer to talk to her, I thought that maybe the housekeeper would pick up and

I could at least leave a message with a real person. The connection went through, and the phone began to ring. Funny, it was a deep-throated ring, not a ding-a-ling ring. The hoarse, throaty ring was, I thought, perfect for GiGi, the tough yet gentle New York transplant in hula land. On about the sixth ring I was ready to give up, but then she answered.

"GiGi, is that really you, or is it your voice mail?"

"Yes, darling, it is I. You've been back in California for only a short time, but I miss you terribly. Why don't you just fly the coop and come back to me? After all, I am eighty and I desperately need a twenty-year-old sidekick to keep me young and in the know. The world is changing so fast."

"Oh, GiGi, no twenty-year-old could possibly keep up with you, including me."

"Well then, how are things? It didn't end so well with that young man who came to be with you at your birthday party. Are you okay?"

"Yes, I am okay. I am very okay, which is what I need to talk to you about."

"I only hope that you took my advice to heart, my darling girl. That boy seemed wrong for you, and you have so much to offer."

"Yes, I did take your advice to heart. I also took your offer of having my wedding at your home in Hawaii to heart."

"Well, of course, dear. That's a given—a standing offer for when the time is right."

"How would you feel about, say, two months from now, around Thanksgiving or possibly sooner, like Halloween?"

"You are a funny child. So, tell me, what's really going on?"

"That boy you didn't like who got drunk at your dinner party and fell off his chair—his name, by the way, is Cole, Cole Baldwin—is going to be the father of my child, due in May of next year. We are hoping to marry as soon as possible, and I only want to marry at your home with your blessing and with you standing at my side. GiGi, I know Cole made a very bad impression, and I hope you will forgive him and get to know him, but I love him and I'm truly happy to be having his baby."

GiGi was quiet.

"I will always support you, Kate, no matter what. What I think about Cole is not important, as long as you are sure that you are in love."

GiGi was quiet again, then continued, saying, "May I come to California to meet with you and with Cole? We can make plans in person. More importantly, I want to share with you some of your family history that I know you are unaware of. A young lady about to get married and have her own family should know where she came from. Your legacy is far more interesting than one generation in Beverly Hills and Newport Beach."

"I would love that. Are you sure you want to come?"

"I am sure. I think there is some urgency. How about early next week? I'll call you with details once I've made plans. Is it all right if I talk to your parents about this?"

"Of course, it is. They know, and we have their blessing."

"I can't wait to see you, darling. We will have a smashing time. We will plan a gorgeous wedding to your liking. And I want to hear all about your fashion line that you mentioned briefly to me when you were here. That's one of the reasons I need to share some family history with you. You may not know it, but the rag business is in your DNA, dear."

"Seriously?"

"Indeed. Wait until you hear. You will be mesmerized."

"Promise?"

"Cross my heart. I'll be in touch."

CHAPTER TWENTY-SEVEN

A LESSON IN FAMILY HISTORY

GiGi arrived in Newport the following week as promised, checking into a suite overlooking the bay at the Harbor Club. It was late afternoon Sunday when my cell phone buzzed.

"I'm here. When can I see you?" GiGi spoke with her usual loving enthusiasm.

"We were waiting for your call. I wanted to pick you up at the airport, but you refused," I answered.

"No need, darling. This old gal knows how to flag a cab. Don't forget where I came from, dear."

"Cole and I are at home sitting out on the beachfront terrace and taking advantage of this beautiful day. Would you care to join us? There is a large chair with blue and white striped cushions that has your name written on it. It's not your Hawaii view, but it is looking out at the Pacific in that direction."

GiGi laughed. "That would be a splendid idea. I could get to know Cole as well. Shall I come now or later? It's almost three thirty in the afternoon."

"GiGi, Cole can come pick you up in fifteen minutes."

"That's sweet, but I'd rather have the hotel drop me off. I know where the house is located. I'll try to arrive by four o'clock so we can all enjoy the sunset together."

"Perfect. We'll be waiting anxiously. I must tell you, I have been obsessed with your mysterious pronouncement of sharing past family history. Am I descended from royalty or horse thieves?"

"Oh, it's far more interesting than that, darling. See you very soon."

Cole looked exceptionally handsome on this warm lazy Sunday afternoon. I thought he would look hot in a paper bag but dressed in his white polo shirt with the turned-up collar over blue and white seersucker shorts and those navy-blue boat shoes tied with thick white leather laces, he was my personal Cuban Italian stallion. The Versace shades finished the look.

"Where did you get those sunglasses?" I had to inquire.

"I found them on the floor in my office. Nobody claimed them, so I figured they needed to be put to good use. Do you like them?"

"Rather flashy for an upstart real estate agent, don't you think?"

I loved to tease Cole. He took my jibes in good spirit, even though at times it deflated his formidable self-confidence. I knew that at least a part of it was pure bravado. Cole was a creation of his own ambition. I would say that he most likely looked in the mirror as a kid growing up and, seeing a strikingly handsome face, told himself that someday that face would matter. Someday he could be someone beyond his beginnings.

For me, this was instinct. Growing up privileged in a big city with a father in a tough business, I had learned early how to read people. More importantly, I learned how to read myself, to know my pluses and minuses. I did not live in a dreamworld. I didn't need it. Instead, my world was already rather exceptional. For me, I just wanted to be happy, be in love, and find a path to do something creative to express my worth in breathing rarified air on the planet. My privilege did not trump my goal of becoming a successful designer. It was just part of the picture.

This was not the same path for Cole, and I knew it. He was driven to make it. Which ultimately meant making tons of money. For Cole, money was the measure of a man's worth. I understood that. Part of me respected it, whereas part of me feared it. My father was a very influential role model in my life when it came to making and investing money. Growing up, I had witnessed plenty of Dalt's associates taking on too much risk and going down the drain. Dalt used to quote his dad, saying, "Every day is not Sunday in the world of finance." I suppose I learned that lesson well just by absorbing my surroundings. I dealt, and I hoped I could help Cole realize to do the same in time. Frankly, I could see him going off the cliff in pursuit of his dreams. But for now, it was not important. I was in love, and I was having a baby, and that was that.

"Kate, do you want me to do anything before your grandmother arrives?" Cole asked thoughtfully.

"I'm going to make some lemonade and put out some crackers, cheese, and veggies. Can you just straighten up the terrace and pick up all the Sunday papers thrown about?"

"I'm already on it," he replied. "You do want me to be here too, don't you?"

"Yes, of course," I practically shouted back.

"I just thought you might want some alone time with your grandmother."

"We'll have that during the week. I want her to get to know you. Your first impression was, shall we say, marginal."

"Got it. I'll be on my best behavior."

GiGi arrived on schedule. The bell rang at four o'clock. Cole answered. She was supergracious, giving him one of her gigantic hugs with her petite stature.

Taking Cole by the arm, she walked with him to find me in the kitchen. I dashed to my grandmother for an embrace; there was nothing like it in my world. Pleasantries were passed over rapidly, and the three of us landed on the terrace to sip lemonade, experience the late Sunday sun dropping toward the Pacific horizon, and talk.

Talk we did—nonstop. GiGi asked Cole a barrage of questions, all very polite, but also very direct. I didn't mind. He handled them extremely well. Cole was forthright and direct back at her. I could tell that pleased her. A good sign.

"Cole, are you ready to be a married man and a father? You are so young, just starting out," GiGi said, looking him square in the eyes.

"Mrs. Fairchild, I love Kate. I loved Kate the first day I saw her, and I will love our child. Yes, I am ready. I will do right by them. I hope you will give us your blessing as it means everything to Kate."

GiGi was coming around. I could tell she was still worried, but at least her facial expression appeared more positive. Deciding to change the subject, I took the laser beam off Cole, at least for a while.

"GiGi, will you share some of the family history you mentioned?" I asked, catching her a bit off guard.

"My dear, are you sure? I planned to talk to you, just the two of us. No offense, Cole; please do not think I am excluding you. I simply thought that this is rather personal, and it would best be coming to you from Kate, if she chooses to share."

"No problem. I totally understand. You know, I can take a jog on the beach and leave you both for now," Cole answered.

I interrupted, "No way. I want you to hear, Cole. If you are marrying me, you are marrying the family tree, so you might as well know. I already know that there is neither royalty nor thievery involved, so how shocking could it be? Right, GiGi?"

"My girl, it's not shocking. Surprising, perhaps, but very real and ultimately revealing. I am proud of this heritage, even though it is rarely discussed."

"Does Dalt know?" I asked.

"Of course, but your father has no use for past stories. It is just not his cup of tea."

"So, I guess that explains why I have never heard anything much about the family before. Funny, I never even thought to ask. My whole family world was complete—Nancy, Dalt, Jamey, and you."

The three of us settled into the cushions on the chairs, watching the last segment of beachcombers on the sand in the distance pack up their goods and depart for points inland. My grandmother finished a bite of Havarti cheese on a pumpernickel cracker topped with a slice of pimento-stuffed green olive, one of my appetizer creations, which were admittedly a bit odd, then began to tell the backstory of the Fairchild family.

The first thing she said did come as a surprise. Apparently, our family name was not originally Fairchild. As least not back three generations. My great-grandfather emigrated to the United States in the latter part of the nineteenth century, at nineteen, leaving family behind in Warsaw, Poland, to make a better life in the New World. His plan was to find work, which was scarce in his native land, especially for Jews, unbeknownst to me, and eventually bring his parents and his sisters to the United States. My great-grandfather's name was Jules Daltonovitz.

Arriving at New York's Ellis Island terminal in the winter of 1892, the young man from Poland who had traveled across the great ocean as another number on the steerage manifest disembarked, to be met by government officers charged with admitting or denying entrance to the throngs of poor seeking a better life. Great-Grandfather Jules spoke no English, apart from a heavily accented "hello" and "yes, please, sir."

GiGi was passionate sharing the story. Cole was listening to every word, mesmerized. I think I was rather like my father, Dalt, interested but not really fixated on a past to which I had no connection. How did this matter to me? I wondered if I was being selfish, spoiled, or uncaring. Was I so insulated in my own life? Could I ever imagine traveling across the ocean in steerage, not knowing a soul, not knowing where I would land or what I would do, with only pennies in my pocket?

GiGi continued sharing what she had known from a very early age when she first met my grandfather Burton just at the start of World War II.

"The immigration officer motioned for Jules to come forward to his table. Jules was confused. He froze, and another officer had to take him by the arm and move him forward," she said. "'Do you speak English?' the officer asked. Jules hesitated.

"'Hello,' he replied in his Polish accent.

"The officer got the message: no English.

"'Your name, sir?' He repeated the request several times, finally handing Jules a pen and motioning to him to write his name on a card. Jules took the pen and slowly wrote in cursive, 'Jules Daltonovitz,' which the officer could not read or decipher.

"'Do you have family here in America?'

"It was no use. Realizing he would get no answer, the officer instructed Jules to take a seat and wait for another officer to come and attempt to interpret for him. There were several hundred people in line.

"Jules sat down on a bench; he often recounted the feeling of total bewilderment experienced on his first day in America. There was a newspaper beside him that had been left behind. It was the morning *New York Times*, and one of the headlines read, 'Fair Child Program Approved,' next to a picture of seemingly immigrant children roaming a New York street. Jules stared at the paper and the photo.

"The next officer appeared and motioned for him to follow. They went to another table, where he was asked his country of origin, in English. 'Poland? Russia?' the officer repeated.

"Jules was able to say, 'Poland.'

"He then pointed to the newspaper he had clutched in his right hand, showing the officer the poor children in the photograph. The officer read the headline out loud: 'Fair Child Program Approved.'

"Jules came to life. He repeated the words *Fair Child*, thinking he vaguely understood. Then something rather amazing happened. Jules, who spoke no English, managed to speak. He said, in very broken English, 'In America, fair child.'

"The immigration officer responded, 'Then that will be it, young man. Your name will be Fairchild.' And he wrote it down on the card and sent Jules to be examined for health clearance."

Cole blurted out, "This is incredible. What a story."

"GiGi, you are telling me that my great-grandfather was a poor Jewish boy who came to America in 1890 with nothing and was named after a newspaper headline?"

"Indeed, my darling. But that is just the beginning. The best is yet to come."

"Really?" I said slightly sheepishly.

"Yes, really. This is the part that you will gravitate to. This is the part that is in your DNA, as I told you!"

"Oh my goodness," I said in response. Was I ready for this?

"Jules passed the physical exam and was admitted to the new world of New York City as the Gilded Age and the industrial might of the modern world demanded labor to generate new wealth and power. Like his father, Asher, who was a tailor, Jules had been an apprentice in the trade. It was one of a few options available to young Jewish men without pedigree in a very segregated Warsaw. He would make his way to the Lower East Side, looking to find a lonsman who would speak his language and help him to find a rotten place to stay and ultimately a low-wage slave job in a garment factory sewing men's trousers and suit jackets."

Life was hard. GiGi described the hardship in great detail. The facts were chilling: the filthy living conditions, the lack of food, the fourteen-hour days six and seven days a week. All of this was commonplace for thousands of men and women just like Great-Grandfather Jules. But apparently, he was tireless and stubborn and refused to fail. He would sew and produce more suits in a day than any other worker. Jules would be noticed. He would rise. The ascent came slowly and painfully. But he would rise.

He had just turned nineteen when he disembarked at Ellis Island. Ten years of labor followed. Jules was twenty-nine at the turn of the century. He managed to save enough of his small salary to eventually bring over his aging parents and two sisters, the sisters now in their twenties and still unmarried.

Living conditions improved. His home was a fourth-floor walk-up flat, two bedrooms with a kitchen and one bath, shared with his family, a rarity, in an old brownstone on the Lower East Side. As it were, he was living the American dream and was appointed to a managerial post in the factory. Then, his life took an unexpected and radical turn for a young Jewish man from Poland. He met a young Catholic woman who worked as a secretary in the office. Her name was Rose Walsh, an Irish woman of just twenty from the poorest part of East London. Rose had come over alone just as Jules had done. With ten years under his belt, Jules would show Rose the lay of the land. Almost thirty, he never had had a romance. There was no time and no money for dating. And certainly not with a non-Jewish woman. He didn't even know any Christian women, for that matter. Both in Poland and in New York's Lower Manhattan, he only knew Jews. Exposure to Christians extended to Irish Catholic cops on the beat, not any real form of social interchange or friendship.

One year later, Jules and Rose would marry, and seven months later a son would be born. His name would be Burton Fairchild. "He was your grandfather," GiGi said, reaching over and taking my hand.

"Seven months later?" I questioned.

"Yes, seven months," GiGi came back with a smile. "Sound familiar, my child?"

"Oh my God. I'm repeating my family legacy," I said with a tear spilling down my right cheek. Cole got up and came over to me. He put his arm around me. He and I shared the large canvas chair as GiGi shared the family saga.

"Your grandfather Burton was born in 1903, and he was named Burton as an homage to Jules's Hebrew name, Baruch. Being the child of a Catholic mother and a Jewish father in the 1900s in New York was uncommon and largely unacceptable to both faiths. It didn't matter to them, as they were in love and were devoted to one another. Both worked like dogs not just to survive, but also to succeed. They wanted the American dream for Burton, more than anything else.

"And they got it. It took a good twenty or more years, but they got it. Jules and Rose ended up owning their own factory and employing more than three hundred people, providing both men's and women's clothes from noted designers, with goods shipped all around the globe. They finally moved into a fine home on the Upper East Side as Burton was readying for school. They never had any other children. Work was all-consuming, and all their attention was devoted to their one child.

"There would be no garment factory work for that boy. He was going to college. Burton entered New York University, finished in three years with a degree in finance, and headed for Wall Street. The year was 1926, and the Jazz Age had turned New York into the center of the social universe. Opportunities abounded; money was being printed because of the stock market.

"While the economy was robust, Wall Street, with a few notable exceptions, was closed to Jews. This was pure Anglo territory. But Burton 'Baruch' Fairchild, of mixed heritage, passed. He found work and prospered. The Great Depression came, sending the world reeling, including the young Burton Fairchild, who was turning twenty-six on the eve of the crash in 1929.

"His parents, Jules and Rose, would eventually have to close their factory, letting many people go. Yet, they all survived and fought back. It was in their makeup not to give in. Unthinkable.

"I met Burton in 1933. He was thirty and I was twenty-two, a dancer with big Broadway dreams. We met at Sardi's late one night when sitting at the counter. I had come from a rehearsal, and Burton had escorted Jules and Rose to a show. Jules and Rose were tired and had gone home. Burton wanted a corned beef sandwich. I ordered turkey and swiss on rye with coleslaw, and that was that. We courted for a few years, during which time we were inseparable. We married in 1938. Your father came along in 1942 at the dawn of the war. We named him Dalton after the original Polish family name, Daltonovitz.

"Your grandfather Burton, in his forties when Dalton arrived, was too old for service in the war. He went to work with a vengeance to do his part for our family and for his country. Burton always felt guilty that he had avoided service. He often commented that brave people endured challenges beyond imagination."

Cole and I held onto one another tightly. We were silent.

CHAPTER TWENTY-EIGHT

COMING TO TERMS
WITH MY REALITY

On the next morning when we arose, I turned to Cole in bed and asked him if he loved me more now that I was an Espiscajewalic. He smiled.

"When you marry me, we will be a couple of Episcajewalics."

Cole was unsophisticated in a poor kid kind of way, but he had his share of undeniable charm. I kissed him good morning.

"You know, our child will probably grow up to be either a Muslim or a Buddhist, or anything else just to rebel against us," I chided him. He looked at me with the puzzled look he often formed when one of my zingers had come out of nowhere.

"This is all my father's doing," I quickly added. "It's his fault we got together, since he had to go and buy that house and discover you as the superbroker and perfect potential beau. His fault for not telling me that I am a Protestant with a Jewish great-grandfather and Catholic great-grandmother who made their way in America as garment workers. And it is also his fault that I never knew that my grandfather Burton was conceived before marriage, translating the trait to me through some mystical generational voodoo causing me to repeat the pattern."

Cole didn't know what to say.

"I guess it just means that it is all meant to be. We are meant to be," he came back, giving me a hug.

I was having a psychotic moment and burst into tears.

"My life has been preordained. I am not the master of my destiny," I protested.

Cole came back with another hug. The warmth of his bare chest warmed my heart.

"Kate, you're being silly. It's the hormones," he explained.

"That's what men always say. 'It's the hormones,' for goodness' sake."

"Well, whether it's hormones or divine intervention, we are all good. It is meant to be either way. No tears."

"Are we doing the right thing?" I asked.

"What does that mean?" he replied.

"Maybe we are rushing. People don't have to get married just because they are pregnant. That was yesterday's morality. What if we end up hating each other?"

"Oh, come on. Now I know it's the hormones, Kate. Get a grip," he said.

I didn't answer. Getting out of bed, I put on my robe and headed for the bathroom. Slamming the door behind me, I sat down on the edge of the tub and cried.

Cole knocked on the door until I asked him to let me be.

"Cole, I'll be fine. It's just the hormones," I said. "Go to work. You have that broker's open house to prepare for your new listing. I'll call you later. Really, I'll be fine."

By midday I was fine. The tears had stopped. The feeling of bewilderment had evaporated, and I was back to being a hopeful and cheerful six-weeks-pregnant woman engaged to my handsome lover. I thought I had come to terms long before with the influence of Dalton in my relationship with Cole. Yet, truthfully, my father had played a significant role. I loved my father. I trusted him unquestioningly, and he had picked Cole not just as his real estate broker but also as my boyfriend. Dalt saw the raw potential in Cole to be a success in life, to provide for his daughter, to keep me safe and secure, and to remain loyal and steadfast.

Subliminally I had gotten this message as well. Anyway, as they say, the cards were already on the table. Still, was I having doubts, second thoughts? Could I have Cole's baby and not get married to him? Was that so unthinkable in the year 2000? Not really.

Later that morning, the fabric Monsieur Lawrence had ordered from Europe arrived at the salon. I could not wait to remove the packaging. All three of us left the showroom and went into the workroom, where I placed the heavy bolt on the large cutting table. Madame Honoré was the first to attack the wrapping, with her large scissor. As she cut the package down the center and pulled away the gauze covering the fabric, we all let out a small squeal.

"Is it not perfect?" Monsieur Lawrence was the first to comment.

We pulled off the wrapping at one end as if we were stripping the casing off a giant salami. There it was, my fabric, my future. My dream of designing something of my own creation lay on the plain wooden table in Newport Beach in a tiny salon run by two runaway French expatriates who had gotten off a bus one day in California with no place else to go and no money to get there anyway.

Recalling once again my grandmother's story of my great-grandfather Jules Daltonovitz, I thought of how strange life could be. Was there some mystical connection to one's life, something one cannot comprehend?

The doorbell in the salon began tinkling, so we left the excitement of the fabric arrival behind and went back to work. For me, the rest of the afternoon was a blur. I could not wait until closing time to pull out my forms and begin cutting.

The Fifteen-Million-Dollar Real Estate Man

Cole was in his own personal state of glory, a state of glory he had dreamed about but probably never expected to become reality, at least not in a record six months' time. Calculating his amazing good fortune on one hand, I recalled that five months ago a chance meeting over a hit-and-run fender bender of a stranger's car in the parking lot would start the wheels in motion to change his life forever.

The fender would lead him to me. A job would lead him to a chance meeting with my father. Dalt would take him under his wing, providing business opportunity beyond his wildest imaginings. And now he was engaged to be married to me, a beautiful, kind, smart woman who also came from one of the wealthiest families in Beverly Hills and Newport Beach. Finally, Cole was the father of the family heir apparent. All this on the fingers of one hand in five months.

I knew that the words of Cole's very hardworking Italian mother echoed constantly in his inner ear. "Only in America," she would often say, her expressive arms raised toward the heavens, whenever anything seemingly miraculous would happen. "Only in America!"

Cole was due to meet his new client Caroline Carondolet at her fifteen-million-dollar home that he had just registered on the multiple listing service. The manager of Cole's office was his new best pal. The guy never had had a newbie land two multimillion-dollar deals within months of starting in the business, especially when the newbie was basically new in town without connections. Newport might be one of the wealthiest cities in the county, but it remained a small town in so many ways. It is a place where who you know matters. The real estate manager kept pounding the three-letter initialism into Cole's brain: "SOI," he would practically shout at every office meeting. "You must build upon your SOI."

Cole nodded in obedience, but had no idea what SOI meant, and was too embarrassed to ask. Finally, one of the agents used the phrase *sphere of influence*, and Cole was able to nod with confidence at his manager's next insistence upon building SOI.

The real estate business never turned me on. Not surprising, since I had been raised in about the best home anyone could possibly dream of living in.

It seemed to me that people who loved real estate were always thinking about the next house—not just the next sale, but the next house to buy and live in, before selling it and buying another. Modern-day nomads. Just the same, I was marrying my own real estate nomad, who had just left his studio apartment to move in with me at the beach. And my plan was to be the ever-supportive real estate wife. This was going to be my husband's future, so it would also be mine regardless of whatever else I accomplished. This was another lesson I had learned well from my parents. They were the ultimate team, always. Nancy had her own life, but at the same time she was right there with Dalton every step of the way. For me, this was how a couple managed to have a long and happy marriage.

It was clearly instinctive. Even though the world was sending my generation a different message, namely that women were not just boosters, partners to their men, and not just supportive adjuncts to their husbands' respective careers. They needed to stand strong on their own merits. Was I supposed to focus on my design ambitions and let Cole focus on his real estate? Sounded like a selfish and ultimately lonely sort of marriage.

I was proud of Cole for landing the big listing. Maybe it was a fluke, just luck. Or perhaps it was his charming, good looks that had won over the client. He had shared with me that she was a very beautiful woman going through a big divorce. I knew that looks and personality were a factor in real estate, especially in Southern California. Both the men and the women in the business all looked like specimens for the next Ken and Barbie plastic mold series. Okay, that was a bit rough. When I told Cole not to use his good looks as his calling card, but rather his brain and his work ethic, my handsome husband-to-be grinned. How could he help himself? He was so gorgeous.

Then, totally off subject, I flashed on the possibility that we were going to have one good-looking baby. Overanalyzing everything was one of my major faults.

Cole's Second Meeting with Caroline

Cole straightened the stiff collar of his white dress shirt as he rang the bell at the massive iron gate in front his new client's waterfront mansion. This time the butler answered right away, buzzing him into the front courtyard. Meeting him at the main door, the butler, whom Cole had named Lurch, opened the portal to admit Cole, directing him to walk down the long-inlaid marble floor of the main corridor to a set of tall French doors leading out to the garden.

"Mrs. Carondolet is getting some sun by the pool. She is waiting for you there," he instructed. Cole obliged, heading down the hallway, briefcase in hand with all his papers at the ready to share with his client. Cole was pumped up. A fifteen-million-dollar listing did not come every day, not even for the seasoned expert with connections. Cole did not fully understand the rarity. After all, his very first two deals were megadeals. He figured it could and should always be like this. *Why not?* he thought, passing through the French doors and entering a formal garden planted with manicured topiary trees lined up like lollipops in a row fronting a stone pathway leading to the pool. Cole walked the path, attempting to look for Caroline Carondolet while still peering out at the ocean between the lollipop trees. This was a special place.

Mrs. Carondolet was just ahead of Cole. She lay on an oversized lounge chair, her back to him as he approached the pool. She was talking on her mobile phone. Cole could hear, even though he had not yet come face-to-face with her. Celebrity gossip magazines were strewn about the glass table beside her lounge, the table also supporting a silver wine chiller shimmering with droplets of ice water, which were flashing in the sunlight. A large crystal goblet lay on its side on top of some of the magazines.

Coming up behind Mrs. Carondolet, Cole turned to greet her. She caught a peripheral glimpse of him to her right side and immediately grabbed for her plush pink pool robe to cover her exposed breasts. Mrs. Carondolet was not fast enough for the task. She dropped her phone midconversation on to the stone patio and let out a quiet "Oh shit," but it was no use. Cole had seen the forbidden fruit. He chuckled. She responded in kind.

"Well, they tell me homeowners eventually develop close personal relationships with their agents," she said, smiling.

"Then I suppose we are off to a good start," Cole responded.

"You might say that," she came back. "You've had a tour of the house, and now you've had a partial tour of its owner!"

"So I have," he said, flirting a bit more.

"So you have." At this point Mrs. Carondolet dropped her plush pink robe, got off the lounge chair, and dove into her pool. Cole looked on, surprised, amused, and confused. Caroline Carondolet surfaced, then swam to the deeper end of her pool. She pushed her wet hair back off her face and wiped the water from her brow and cheeks.

"Would you care to join me, Cole? We can do business together in the water."

Cole hesitated, saying nothing. He stared at Mrs. Carondolet. Then he began unbuttoning his white shirt. Slowly and methodically, he unfastened each button, finally unfastening the sleeve buttons. Then he pulled the shirt out of his pants and off his back, letting it fall to the stone pavement.

Caroline Carondolet watched very carefully. "Surely you don't want to get your pants wet," she called out.

Cole unlatched his black leather belt, and his pants came off. He kicked off his black loafers, removing his socks. Standing at attention poolside, wearing only his black bikini briefs, Kate's Cuban Italian stallion fiancé, the father of her expected child, removed his briefs by stepping out of them. Then, twirling them above his head, he threw them onto the lounge and finally dove naked into the pool.

Cole swam to Caroline. They embraced, exchanging a long, wet kiss, which turned instantly into the sex act. There was no lingering sensual foreplay; it was straight business. Cole's erect masculinity stroked between Caroline's legs as the warm pool water pushed their bodies back and forth in a sort of water ballet. They both kicked their legs, treading the eight feet of water, permitting their deep kiss to linger in oxygenated territory.

Cole had no trouble finding his way into her lubricated vagina as they became one body, suspended in clear blue liquid.

As they danced the sex dance, Cole thrust harder. Waves began to form on the previously calm waters. Soon the waves were splashing over the edge of the pool. The commotion, coupled with intermittent howls of pleasure, attracted the attention of the butler.

Cole sensed Lurch's presence somehow, even as he remained in the house looking out at them from a living room window directly opposite the pool. Turning his head slightly to the right toward the house, Cole never let his tongue leave Caroline's mouth, in which it was firmly planted. He saw the butler and winked at him. The butler did not flinch. He did not look away, nor did he leave the window in an act of deference to his employer and her guest.

"I am coming," Caroline whispered in Cole's ear, finally breaking away from his kiss.

"Me too," he answered. "Let's do it together on the count of three."

"One. Two. Three," they said in unison.

Grabbing Cole around the neck, Caroline pulled him to her as tightly as she could. Cole remained inside her, not moving. Some minutes passed. Then the pair of pool sex mates were on dry land, finding themselves wrapped in blush-pink towels next to one another on adjacent chaise lounges. Caroline righted the tipped-over crystal goblet and poured a fresh cold glass of the chardonnay, which she'd left waiting in the ice bucket. There was only one goblet, so she took the first sip, then handed the wine to Cole for the second. They drank. "Well, here's to a successful real estate partnership," she said. "You may call me Caroline."

Cole looked over at her, saying nothing.

A Late Night in the Workroom

I had prearranged a late night in the salon to work on my designs. Cole would have to fend for himself at dinnertime. GiGi was also invited to drop in after hours to watch me at work and to share a little wedding planning in Hawaii over Halloween, or perhaps as late as Thanksgiving. That was my cutoff date.

It had been a long and busy day at the salon. I was tired, as were my mentors.

"Would you like us to remain with you to assist in the cutting?" Monsieur Lawrence asked.

"I would love your careful eye, but no, go home. It's been a long day. My grandmother is coming by to keep me company," I replied.

"Very well. As you like it. But do not fret if you make a cutting error. This is all about practice—trial and error. There is more than enough fabric. We must get it right. Samples must be perfect, flawless."

"Your advice and your confidence in me make me want to do my best. I am so grateful for both of you." I crossed the salon to give my mentors a hug. "Never enough hugs for you both," I said quietly to them.

"We accept," Madame Honoré replied. "Then we will see you tomorrow. Lock up carefully when you are finished."

Going straight to work at the cutting table, carefully laying out my tissue paper forms, I began with one of my favorite pieces, a short-waisted Eisenhower jacket. I wanted to design the jacket with a tall Mandarin collar, epaulets, and oversized pockets concealed on the sides. Each section of the jacket would be built in pieces—the back, sides, front, shoulders, and collar, and the lining as well.

My hand was not as steady as I would have liked at first, but it got better. Within an hour I was feeling as if Coco Chanel was looking over my shoulder. Finally, I was making something real. It was no longer just a goal, a dream, or a fantasy. I was cutting the pieces to turn a drawing into a real item of clothing. For me, this was amazing. People had been cutting and sewing cloth since early humankind decided that being naked all the time was not ideal, especially in wintertime, but now this was my turn.

The doorbell tinkled. GiGi entered. Coming out of the workroom, I greeted her with my total love and appreciation. How lucky I was to have GiGi. I thought about other young women lacking GiGis of their own.

"Come into the workroom and check out my first cutting of the new line. Did I tell you I'm calling the line 'Fair Child'? What do you think?"

"I love it. So classy. So adorable," GiGi said, taking my hand as we entered the workroom. We took stools on either side of the worktable.

"Do you mind if I continue cutting while we talk?"

"Of course not, dear."

"Are you hungry for dinner, GiGi?"

"No, darling, it's early for me. You know I prefer to dine at nine. If you're not too tired, may I take you to dinner after we work and chat?"

"Love to."

After cutting the additional pieces of the short-waisted jacket and ironing each piece carefully by following the bit of extra trim on the jagged edges, I laid them out on the table on top of the parchment model cutouts made with Monsieur Lawrence. GiGi looked on with pride as we talked about planning my wedding on her Hawaiian lawn.

"What would you think about having a traditional island ceremony with fire dancers, drums, and fabulous orchids lining a white-silk-covered path over grass leading to a wedding canopy festooned with palm fronds and island blooms at the edge of the lawn meeting the sand?"

"Oh my, that sounds rather amazing!" I said, cutting yet another piece of my jacket.

"We could have an orchestra and lovely Native girl singers performing melodic island music on the sand behind you both as you take your vows," GiGi continued. "Do you want a religious ceremony? Perhaps your family pastor from Beverly Hills Episcopal Church? What is Cole's religion?"

"He is 100 percent Catholic," I told her. "His father is Cuban; mother, Italian."

"Really? His name is rather, well, Waspy sounding. Not very Catholic and not very Latino, or very Italian at all."

"That's because his real name is Sal Costa. He changed his name to lose the ethnic connection."

"I thought we were living in the age of 'be proud of who you are.' Your great-grandfather, I assumed, was part of the last generation to change their names in order to assimilate into the American milieu."

"Well, I guess not the last," I replied.

"Does that bother you?"

"At first I thought it was odd. I'd never known anyone who changed their name, other than some movie stars we all are familiar with. Even that has changed. Now that I know that our name is not really Fairchild, how can I possibly object to Cole's reasoning?"

"Fair point, darling." GiGi paused, then got extremely personal. "I am still worried about you. Are you sure you want this? Do you love him unconditionally? Tell me you are not marrying just because of the pregnancy."

I did not need to think about my answer.

"GiGi, I love Cole, but I cannot say it is unconditional. I'm young, but I'm street-smart for a girl from a privileged upbringing. Don't forget, a kid, even a rich kid, maybe even more so, grows up fast in LA. I have seen a lot and done a lot. I never planned to be married or pregnant at twenty. But it happened, so I am fully on board. Cole loves me. I've known that from almost our first meeting. I love him. So that's enough. It will have to be enough for now, and hopefully it'll last forever!"

"I am so pleased to hear you say that. It gives me great comfort to know that you are doing the right thing. I will try very hard to let go of my first impression of Cole. And I will adore him as you adore him. He will be my second grandson."

"Thank you, GiGi. That is important to me. I want you in the picture, part of the plan, close to both of us—and to your soon-to-arrive great-grandchild."

"It's all a blessing. The Fairchild né Daltonovitz clan is blessed. We now shall add the name of Baldwin to the triumvirate."

I finished trimming the last of two sections of the jacket, directing the conversation back to my wedding plans.

"GiGi, I do want a Hawaiian wedding on your oceanfront. But I want it simple. No fire dancers, no orchestra, no choir. Yes, to the amazing orchids. Yes, to the wedding canopy of palms. No to flying in Pastor Reynolds from Beverly Hills. Cole and I prefer a civil, but spiritual, nondenominational ceremony, and we will write our own vows."

"No music?" GiGi protested.

"No orchestra. Yes, to music. How about a ukulele or two and a really mellow vocalist?"

"Whom shall we invite, dear?"

"Family and really close friends only. How about, say, fifty people? You, Dalt, Nancy, and Jamey are my only close family. Cole will want his parents and sister and brother, plus a few close friends."

"May I suggest a wedding dinner at my home following? Would you like a luau on the beach with torches—oh, there I go with fire again!"

"A luau with torches sounds romantic, and yes, I would love that."

GiGi let out a little scream of joy. She got up off her stool and came around the worktable to give me a kiss.

"We did it," she said. "And so painlessly."

"Yes, we did, GiGi."

"One more thing: when?"

"Can we pull this off—or, should I say, can you pull this off—in a month? It's September fifteenth today. How about October—the second Saturday in October? I really don't want to wait until the end of the month and Halloween. And Thanksgiving seems like a year away."

"Absolutely. GiGi can pull together any event with any notice. It will be my great pleasure to give you a simply elegant, warm, and wonderful Hawaiian wedding for as many or as few guests as you desire. If we are only a month out, you must get on the invitations at once."

"Done," I said, hugging GiGi again. "Shall we go to dinner?"

"Do you want to keep working? I can wait or do dinner alone. It's up to you, dear."

"Let's celebrate. I plan on working every night after work for a while on my line. Tonight, is our time."

GiGi placed both her soft hands on my cheeks. She looked into my eyes with unconditional love. I may not have had that yet with Cole, but it was solid with my GiGi.

Pulling her hands off my cheeks, GiGi began to cough.

"Is everything okay? Do you need some water?" I asked, making my way to the fridge to get a bottle.

The coughing got worse. It was louder and more pronounced.

"Are you choking on something, GiGi?" I asked with a growing sense of concern, opening the bottle of water and handing it to her. Not taking the bottle, she instead buckled over, grabbing the stool to keep from toppling to the floor. The coughing became extremely deep in her throat, and she began gasping for air.

"Oh my God, GiGi. What's wrong?" Making sure she was not going to fall off the stool again, I carefully moved her to Monsieur's chair and sat her down. She was unable to speak; the coughing continued. Tears ran down her face. Her breathing became more difficult.

"I'm calling 911," I blurted out, then ran to the phone, looking over my shoulder at her as I dialed. The operator answered immediately. I left my message of panic with details and the address of the shop. Assured that help was on the way, I ran back to GiGi. She was now turning a shade of gray, and it was getting worse.

I panicked. Did she need mouth-to-mouth? I had never done that and had no idea what to do. Her tears were now streaming like a river, and her lips were gray as concrete. Fluid oozed from the side of her mouth. She was totally unresponsive. I began screaming for help, as if anyone could hear. A moment later, the coughing and wheezing ceased. GiGi's head dropped to her chest. She was silent.

"GiGi, GiGi, don't leave me. Hold on. Hold on, GiGi, 911 is coming. Please, GiGi, hold on. I love you. I love you. Don't do this. I love you."

The paramedics burst in the front door of the salon. Hearing my screaming and crying, they came charging into the workroom. They rushed to GiGi, pulling her out of the chair and placing her on top of the worktable on my pieces of the jacket.

As one of the EMTs checked GiGi's vital signs, another covered her with a blanket. Both men shook their heads.

GiGi was gone.

I collapsed to the floor, inconsolable.

CHAPTER TWENTY-NINE

PICKING UP THE PIECES

Dalt, Nan, and Jamey left Beverly Hills within an hour of hearing the news. I was catatonic, unable to stop crying, afraid to move. The family arrived at the store within an hour, around eight, followed almost immediately by Monsieur Lawrence and Madame Honoré. I don't know how they knew; I certainly did not call them as I was barely able to call my parents. Misdialing my home number three times, I finally had hit all the digits without breaking down into hysterical sobbing. Finding the strength, I called Cole next, but his voice mail answered. Trying to temper my emotions, I had left a simple message: "Call me soon. I love you."

GiGi remained on the worktable, her body covered with a large piece of the Italian fabric from my samples. The paramedics notified the police and the coroner's office. All of them descended onto the scene within minutes. Monsieur Lawrence introduced himself to the Newport Beach police officer and thanked him for the call to alert him. That explained that.

Being surrounded by family and the security of authorities, I calmed down. The convulsing ceased; the tears eased. I was able, at last, to rise from my fetal position, crumpled in a corner of the workroom.

"We were making wedding plans for Hawaii one moment, and the next GiGi was coughing uncontrollably, —and then suddenly, instantly, she was gone." I cried in Nancy's arms.

"Was she able to speak at all?"

"Not a word. Her facial expression was blank as well. She never got to say goodbye," I said, breaking down in tears again.

"Kate, I'm so sorry and so sad, but I know she loved us all, especially you, darling, with all her heart. You must know that you were her very special girl."

"I know. I loved her so much. GiGi will never meet her great-grandchild. It's not fair." I continued weeping.

"It's not unfair either, Kate. It's life. There are inevitable endings just as there are blessings of new beginnings. You carry that blessing."

"I so wanted her to stand up with you and me at our wedding," I confessed selfishly at a totally inappropriate time.

"She will be there, I promise. GiGi's spirit will always be with you," Nancy said, releasing me from her embrace. "Now go and give your father some attention. He just lost his mother, whom he also adored, more than you may know."

Cole came rushing in the salon door as the coroner's team was rolling GiGi out on a gurney. Before seeing the body coming toward him, he had witnessed the assemblage of police vehicles and the white coroner's van in front of the store, which had sent a clear signal of trouble.

"Oh my God, who died?" Cole blurted out upon entering. "Was it Monsieur Lawrence or Madame Honoré?" he asked the police, following the deceased on the gurney.

Hearing Cole, and leaving Dalt and Nancy in the workroom, I ran to him. "Cole, thank goodness you're here," I said as he threw his arms around me and kissed me on the forehead.

"Are you okay? What happened? Who died?" he asked in a rapid-fire manner.

"It was GiGi," I told him, crying again.

"GiGi? What?"

"We were having a great time talking and making wedding plans. She suddenly fell ill—and died."

"What can I do?" Cole asked with genuine concern.

"You can love me. You can hold me. You can take me home and hold me close all night. I don't know how I will get over this. I have never felt so sad, so hopeless. Never!"

"Can we go right now, Kate?"

Cole was ready to get out of the salon as soon as possible.

"Let me tell the family and we can go," I said. "Come with me, okay?"

We went into the workroom, where we found them, all consoling one another, even Monsieur and Madame, who did not know GiGi. It was no surprise; they were now my family too. I loved both of them.

"Cole is taking me home. I want to go to bed and bury myself under the covers. Do you want to come over and spend the night in your beach house with us?" I asked my parents.

"We will check into the Harbor Club since the Lido house is not ready. We'll call you first thing tomorrow morning," Nancy answered, taking charge. My father was trying to be brave, but I could see he was crying just like me.

"Madame and Monsieur, I love you both. Thank you for being here so quickly. May I check in tomorrow with you? I don't think I am able to come to work."

"Do not be silly, my dear. You take care of yourself and let us know how we can help," Madame answered with genuine care.

A New Day Brings a New Perspective

Cole held me close all night long as I had asked him to do. There was no lovemaking, just tenderness. The warmth of his body, and the unique smell of his skin and his hair, comforted me. I was secure in my time of great loss. Intellectually I knew I would recover, move on, and compartmentalize my grief, turning it into good memories of GiGi for the rest of my life. Emotionally, I was not so strong. My passion for the design task at hand was evanescent, like raindrops falling on warm concrete sidewalks. Would I get it back? Would I get over seeing GiGi pass away on top of my samples and covered with the fabric from which I wanted to build a career? Somehow none of it really mattered. They were just sample designs for clothes. *Are there not enough clothes on the planet? Who really cares anyway? More to the point, will I ever care again with the same passion that I thought I once had?*

Cole kissed me good morning as the warm Newport sun rose toward the east over the Pacific Ocean and streamed in like lightning through the clerestory window in our loft bedroom over the garage. One particularly strong ray of gold hit me smack in my face. I squinted, yet for a moment I felt warm, and all was right with me. I was embraced by the promise of a new day and was loved by the man at my side.

"Should I take the day off and stay home with you, Kate? Will that make you feel better?" Cole asked, delivering his offer with sincerity.

"You know, I would love that, but I am okay, and the family is here to be with me. I don't want you to miss work. You have a fifteen-million-dollar house to sell, and we're having a child coming whom you'll need to support," I said half-heartedly with a grin, knowing that Cole knew well I never cared about money—perhaps because he knew I had always had enough.

"You're right, Kate, I need to be a good provider for our child. I will keep in touch all day. Call me anytime you need to talk. Anytime, got it?"

It was only seven thirty in the morning. Cole got up, showered, and dressed for work. Pulling the covers up to my neck, I fluffed the pillows and put myself back to sleep. Dalt, Nancy, and Jamey would wait until at least ten in the morning to call. My family had manners to a fault, which I appreciated beyond words, especially on this morning when being alone in my bed with the morning sun flowing in was the healing I needed most. There would be plenty of talking and sharing yet to come.

Making Plans

As expected, Dalt called at ten o'clock in the morning to check on me first and foremost and to let me know they were on the way over to the beach house. I had coffee ready when they arrived, and tea for Nancy. We hugged; we shed tears; and we proceeded to talk for hours.

My father had already planned for GiGi. She would be cremated, per her final instructions, and it would take place in Newport following the coroner's release of the body next week sometime. Dalt would fly his mother's remains to Honolulu and place her ashes in a temporary urn in her home, as she also conveyed, in a prominent place with an ocean view, until final arrangements for a memorial and burial at sea in front of her estate could be finalized. GiGi's attorney in New York would do a formal reading of her will via teleconference for her beneficiaries, also later.

Dalt shared that he was fully aware of the details as he would serve as GiGi's executor.

"I really shouldn't reveal this until all are informed, but I want to tell you how much GiGi loved you. Right after her birthday, she called me to let me know she had instructed her lawyer Lewis Avedon to set up an additional one-million-dollar fund as her investment in your start-up clothing line, to assist you in launching your dream." Dalt surrounded Nancy, Jamey, and me, and we hugged once more. I cried.

"I don't know what to say. I am overwhelmed," I came back. "Dalt, do you think it would be terrible not to go to the memorial? I don't want my last memory of GiGi at her home to be sad."

"There is no right or wrong. You will do what is best," Nancy chimed in. "GiGi will always be with you, as I told you before."

Nancy went into the kitchen to toast bagels and slice some fresh fruit. The family had arrived at the cottage bearing a ripe pineapple and fresh berries in honor of GiGi, along with her cherished onion bagels and salmon-infused cream cheese.

Sitting down on the oceanfront patio, we shared in a little nourishment and some memories. Plenty of "Do you remember when's" crossed back and forth until I cut to the chase, asking Dalt about the family heritage I had learned of from GiGi. Previously, Nancy and I had talked following GiGi's revelation, and Mother told me she was going to share the news with my father. He wasn't surprised when I brought it up. Jamey, however, was all ears. My kid brother was at full attention as I had never seen him before. He did not question, only listened.

"We are just another American family of immigrants who, over four generations of hard work, hardship, and luck, and with the unique blessing of this republic, in spite of its many faults, roadblocks, bigotry, and unfortunately worse for so many, finally achieved the proverbial American dream."

Dalt went on, "It was a dream that once reverberated around the world. Former president Reagan called America 'the Shining City on the Hill,' but I fear that dream is fading, and it worries me."

"Oh, Father, you can be so serious," I responded.

Nancy joined the chorus. "Dalt, this is not the time for doomsday predictions. For goodness' sake, the market is robust, and acceptance of a diverse society has never been more embraced by so many. The dream is not fading, just evolving," she said.

Dalt came back with his customary wit: "For a Beverly Hills and Newport Republican, you sound like a progressive Democrat."

"There's a little progressiveness in every thinking person. The world now changes by the literal minute. One must be open to change and be able to analyze its effects on each of us."

"Wow, Mom is like a philosopher or something," Jamey said, entering the family conversation.

"Or something," I added with a smile. At least I had stopped crying.

Cole entered as it was now approaching noon.

"Hello, everybody. Good to see you all smiling," he said. "I'm sorry about your mom, Dalt. May she rest in peace."

Dalt motioned for Cole, his new soon-to-be son-in-law, to come sit next to him.

Changing the Subject

Nancy asked Cole if she could toast him a bagel or get him a fruit plate. We had long finished ours.

"I'm fine, Mrs. Fairchild. I'm just happy to see Kate smiling."

Dalt caught Cole up on plans for GiGi's memorial in Hawaii, sharing with him my reluctance to attend.

"I go where she goes," Cole answered. "Whatever she thinks is best, is best for me too."

Nancy entered the fray.

"I know this is perhaps insensitive, but I'm asking anyway. What about your wedding?"

"Do you think a combined memorial and nuptials would be out of order?" I asked with full sarcasm.

"That's one for you," my mother replied.

"Seriously, I cannot see getting married in Hawaii now. I don't want to cry hysterically while walking down the aisle pregnant. I think it might send the wrong message to our family and guests," I added with a chuckle.

"Okay. Then what?" Nancy persisted.

I turned to Cole. "Would you marry me right here on this beach in Newport?" I asked.

"Of course," he responded.

"Would you take our vows the following Saturday?"

"In less than two weeks?"

"I want to get married right away. Nothing extravagant. Just warm, wonderful, and loving."

Cole nodded his agreement.

"Then we will get started tomorrow. I will ask Monsieur Lawrence if I can work part time for two weeks. I'm sure he'll understand."

"Perfect," Nancy replied. "I'll go back to Beverly this afternoon with Dalt and Jamey, and I'll return tomorrow to help plan. Are you sure you'll be okay?"

"I am okay. Cole is here to make everything all right. He was an angel last night. I don't think I would have made it through without him. Losing GiGi was a life changer for me. I went from pretend adult to full-fledged adult in one day."

"It happens that way," Dalt said.

"A week from Saturday it will be," I said.

"Really? A week from Saturday?" Nancy hoped she could convince me to give it a little more time.

"Yes, really, Mom. I promise it will be okay, and I will not drive you crazy. But I need your help. Will you stay here in Newport and take charge? There is a reason I always have called you 'the general.'"

Nancy saluted. Dalt applauded. Jamey yelled, "Hooray."

Cole and I looked at one another, then kissed.

"Save that for the 'I do's,'" Dalt interjected.

"A girl can never get enough great kisses," Nancy said, throwing in her two cents.

Cole jumped in and bid farewell to the family.

"Since you are okay, Kate, I'm going back to work. I'll be home early, and we can go to dinner and share a glass of wine. Let me help in whatever way I can with our barely-two-weeks-away wedding. Can I call my parents?"

"Absolutely," Nancy said. "I want to call your mother as well, Cole. Get me her number."

"Will do."

Cole headed out. We returned to the patio to continue sharing more "Do you remember when's".

Life moves on, fast. Get on board or get out of the way. My head was spinning.

CHAPTER THIRTY

MOVING FORWARD

It was now twelve days until the wedding. I know it was an insane idea, but I was actually very happy about it. Losing my GiGi, being pregnant and hormonal, to say the least, and trying to create my fashion line—my dream goal—amounted to three life roads too many to follow.

Pregnant and hormonal took first place. Everything else had been put on hold. Knowing very well that my DNA carried "Bridezilla" genes, I thought it best to suppress them and spare every one of their impact, especially Cole and Nancy.

Monsieur Lawrence gave me space, allowing me to work part time. We packed away all my fabric, cuttings, drawings, and plans, to be tackled later. At first, I thought I should throw myself back into the process full speed ahead. But going into the workroom and looking at the table upon which GiGi had died, lying on top of my first sample cuttings, I knew I had to take a break, create some distance, and return with a clear perspective.

Nancy moved into the beach house with Cole and me, which we liked. My mother, the ball of fire, was a total blast of positivity. Her boundless energy gave both of us a kick in the pants. There was nothing laid back about Nancy from Beverly Hills, a major contrast to the much more casual Newport vibe. I liked Newport; I was comfortable here. Even the weather was more laid back than in LA, only some fifty miles to the north. When it poured rain in LA, it drizzled in Newport, and it did so at night, leaving most days sunny and mild. The sky here was bluer, the clouds puffier, the palm trees greener. Newport people were just as competitive, just as money and success driven, yet their outward aggression was reduced in scale.

Anyway, Cole and I reflected and deflected the constant glow of my incredible mother. On her first day, she had created an invitation list, which I thought unnecessary since it was only going to be family. She attempted to convince me that we had to invite a few close friends, including some of mine from my growing-up years, along with some of Cole's. She lost that battle.

By midweek a caterer was on board for the prenuptial dinner, which would take place in their new Lido house, as well as for the prewedding cocktail reception and postevent candlelight dinner at the beach cottage.

By Thursday, Nancy had researched, interviewed, and hired a wedding planner to gather all the design elements such as the actual setup on the beach, rentals, music, and décor. She's also hired a floral designer, Andrew Gromek of Couture Flowers, one of the best on the California Riviera.

Just three things remained: the dress, the officiant, and the vows. Cole and I were going to be taking care of the vows and the officiant. We decided we would ask Paco Villareal, the man known as "the Surfer Saint" who preached Sunday morning on the beach. As for the dress, I was designing it with Monsieur Lawrence. In a week's time, we had pretty much gotten it in the final stages.

With Nancy at the helm, my totally uncomplicated wedding went up a few decibels, but I didn't mind. She was keeping it simple by her standards, and I knew she was making it special. My dress was going to be sublime, no lace, no sequins, no beading, no nothing, just a floor-length column gown of cream-colored satin.

I wanted an Asian-style high-necked A-line gown straight to the floor, sleeveless and with a slit up one side to show a little leg and beautiful pumps. Monsieur, who knew exactly what I wanted, had done some drawing, found the perfect fabric, and went to work. More importantly, I wanted the dress to be an homage to GiGi and the Island style she loved. It was what I would have wanted to wear on her beachfront if things had been different.

On Friday, when I was working in the salon with Madame Honoré, Mrs. A came in for a look. She greeted me warmly and inquired about my pregnancy and the upcoming wedding plans. I explained that we had moved up the date, adding that the ceremony was planned for next Saturday.

"Kate, don't forget, I want to throw a wedding and baby shower for you as soon as you feel ready. I will invite our neighbor ladies on the peninsula, along with others I want you to meet. If you and your man are going to settle in Newport, you must start to meet the neighbors."

"That would be great. Perhaps we could set a date a little later in the year or, better yet, maybe in January after all the holidays."

"Excellent. Just tell me when and I am on it," she said.

Madame Honoré began pulling new items for Mrs. A. She liked them all, spending more than five thousand dollars in a matter of twenty minutes. Madame Honoré whispered in my ear, "Kate, take Mrs. Adamson up on the shower. She is sincere. And besides, you won't need a thing for your baby." She laughed quietly upon finishing her advice to this mother-to-be.

Smiling at my mentor, I winked my understanding. Honoré was a hard-driving woman, a trait created by circumstance and necessity, but was also pure of heart.

At the close of business, I met Cole, and we drove home together to share Friday dinner with family. My father and brother had returned that afternoon to bring Nancy home for the weekend, so we all relished an evening together over Italian delivery. Nancy had ordered from Villa Nova, one of Newport's old Italian restaurants that was a transplant from old Hollywood decades earlier.

"Your father and I used to go on dates to the Villa Nova in Hollywood." Nancy shared stories of their courtship while serving chicken piccata.

Cole Delivers News

Cole requested a second serving of the piccata, which Nancy readily supplied. Jamey was seated next to Cole, clearly impressed by his new brother-in-law-to-be. Giving Jamey full attention, Cole talked sports, high school girls, video games, and surfing. Jamey had started surfing on the Santa Monica beach when he was about ten. Recently, Dalt had hired an instructor and chaperone to drive Jamey to the beach and "give him lessons." I think it was more to keep him safe, off drugs, which were a major factor in the beach culture of Southern California. Surfing gave Jamey a healthy athletic outlet to boost his confidence. It seemed to be working.

Taking his full attention off my little brother—not so little, now fifteen years old and six feet tall—Cole thanked Dalt for offering to assist his family in coming down from Reno for the wedding.

"Dalt, it was really nice of you to offer to bring down my parents, brother, and sister and put them up at the Harbor Club." Cole was sincere.

"It is our pleasure. As you know, they politely declined, preferring to take a short vacation in the form of a road trip down the California coast. Your mother wanted to stay in Pismo Beach for an overnight at a motel on the oceanfront they once visited years ago and remembered fondly."

"Dad told me," Cole said. "He was grateful for your offer of the Harbor Club but thought that the Holiday Inn would be a better fit for all of them. My dad is a good man and a very proud man. I hope you like him, Dalt. He's never had money, but he is the hardest-working guy I have ever known."

"I believe your unchecked ambition may scare him a bit, son, if you don't mind my being frank."

"I think you're right. And I know that Newport will be a little intimidating."

"We don't want that, Cole. Nancy and I will do what we can to make them comfortable and feel like part of the family."

"I really appreciate that, Dalt. Maybe part of my ambition is just to show them that they were great parents. I don't know, that sounds crazy, I guess."

"Not at all, Cole. It sounds honest. You know we believe in you. All you need is a little leg up to get going. You will reach all your goals."

"Your confidence in me is more than anyone, except my folks, has ever shown me. I hope I deserve it."

"It has already been proven."

Nancy brought out the dessert she had ordered in LA, having instructed Dalt and Jamey to pick it up on their way down to Newport from Beverly. She marched out of the kitchen with the well-known white box, and I let out a scream of pure joy.

"Oh my God, a Hansen's cake."

"That's right, dear, your favorite chocolate chip cake with pink buttercream icing and a field of pale pink roses."

I was in Hansen's heaven. The greatest bakery in the world had made the perfect cake sitting in front of me and I did not have a care in the world, at least not for a sugar-inspired moment.

"Mind if I take a discreet finger to a rose?" I asked Nancy.

"Go for it, dear. By the way, I ordered your wedding cake from Hansen's as well."

I started clapping. Cole looked amused.

"Wait until you take a bite. You'll get it," I told him.

"Before we cut the cake and all go into a sugar coma, can I share some news?" Cole asked.

Everyone was at attention.

"Did you get an offer on the house?" I blurted out.

"No, not that kind of great news, but I'm giving that my all," he said.

"Okay, we're waiting," I followed.

Cole stood up at the table as if he were about to deliver an address to Congress, or at least a graduation speech.

"How do I look?" he questioned.

Nancy answered, "Quite handsome, I would say."

Cole said "Thanks" and proceeded to tell the family that he had completed his first TV commercial to promote his real estate career. Explaining that an agent making a real estate advertising video was uncharted territory, he added that he was proud of how well it turned out.

"You didn't tell me about this, Cole," I said.

"Because I wanted to see if it was good enough before telling. If it didn't turn out, I was just going to forget about it."

"What did you say?" I asked.

"It's only a minute long. The producer called it 'a stand-up shot' with 'B-roll,' which basically means, I learned, that I am standing up talking to the camera, and in the editing process they are cutting in various images of properties I might be representing."

Cole continued to explain that he had spoken well, having introduced himself and told the viewer that he could be trusted to handle the most important financial and lifestyle transition of their lives.

"'From modest homes to megamansions, I will work for you. I will make money for you. And I will do it with discretion and with style,' I said. And at the end I gave out my phone number and email contacts."

"Sounds very impressive, Cole," Dalt spoke up.

"Was it expensive, Cole?" I questioned, ever the practical rich girl.

"It cost just under two thousand dollars. I used some of the commission money from your parents' sale."

"Money well spent, Cole," Dalt added.

"I'm proud of you, Cole," I offered. "This shows initiative and creativity. I don't think I have ever seen an agent do a commercial. When and where will it air?"

"Just on local cable TV here in Orange County, which is very inexpensive. I'd love to have it on network TV, but it doesn't make sense. And we can't afford that right now anyway. Let's see if this gets any traction."

With that, Nancy cut the Hansen's cake. Dalt popped a bottle of champagne for a toast, and our evening of family celebration came to a close. Of course, I skipped the champagne. Nothing was going to harm this baby.

CHAPTER THIRTY-ONE

THE UKULELES PERFORM

The final week before the wedding was a blur. Nancy and Dalt had come back to Newport with my brother, Jamey, on Monday, and they checked into the Harbor Club's Presidential Suite and went to work on all the final arrangements.

Cole's family arrived in Newport, checking into the Holiday Inn across the street from the Harbor Club on Thursday. We all met at dinner for the first time that evening. Thankfully, the gathering of in-laws went well. Despite their obvious differences, I think they all liked one another. Conversation flowed; laughter was loud and often.

Dalt really got a kick out of Cole's dad, Joe. They had a good deal of common ground in terms of politics; both were Republicans with much to say about the progressive movement of the liberal Democratic Party in the United States—this coming equally from a blue-collar wage earner and a country club Wall Street millionaire. I took it all in silently but with maximum curiosity.

Seated next to me, Cole held my hand under the table through most of the meet-and-greet dinner. I stroked his leg and squeezed his package not once, but twice. Each time he jumped an inch or so out of his chair. I managed to hit the bull's-eye each time Cole was in midconversation, accentuating the point germane to the political discourse. His voice rose to a falsetto for an instant, everyone looking over in amazement. Managing to cover by clearing his throat, he somehow turned the awkward seconds into humor. My soon-to-be hubby was a master charmer.

To my relief and pleasure, Nancy and Cole's mom, Rose, got on well. Rose wanted to do whatever she could in the two days remaining until the wedding, and Nancy was happy to get her involved and make her part of the team. Of course, Nancy had already done it all. As we dined early that Thursday evening at the Captain's Table in the Harbor Club, Nancy's crew was laying the platforms on the sand adjacent to the beach cottage lawn to make a firm aisle for me to parade down with Dalt to the wedding arch. She even managed to persuade the Newport Beach City Council to issue the event permit on the sand without the customary waiting period. Cole's mom asked if she could prepare a Sunday brunch at the beach house for the family. She wanted to do an Italian feast appropriate for a wedding. Nancy said yes, even though she and Dalt had made brunch reservations for everyone at the Four Seasons Hotel.

Despite my mother's repeated requests for me to extend more invitations to close friends, I chose not to do so. Perhaps it was selfish or foolish, but I was still feeling

GiGi's loss in a major way, and it just didn't feel right to throw a big party. Cole went along and did not invite childhood friends at my request. So, in the end, it was just family plus Monsieur Lawrence and Madame Honoré, a total of thirteen people, including Pastor Paco Villareal and his wife, Gracie.

I guess I should also include the two ukulele players that I wanted as an homage to GiGi. Nancy found them, and we invited them to stay for dinner after both the rehearsal and the wedding ceremony. That would make the total count fifteen.

Believe it or not, I chose to go to work Friday morning and spent a half day in the salon. Monsieur Lawrence did a final fitting of my dress, which was total perfection. Working with Madame Honoré, I made a few sales for good luck. By noon, Nancy picked me up and we were back at the beach house, where she had arranged for our hairstylist Hugh to come down from Hollywood, along with his makeup artist Farid, to work wedding magic. She also had asked the caterers to prepare a wonderful lunch of grilled salmon salad with capers over fresh greens, drizzled with a wine vinaigrette dressing. In one of the upstairs bedrooms, a masseur was at the ready for an hour or so of therapy before the big event.

Outside, a crew put the final touches on our wedding, following Nancy's directions to the utmost, with no detail forgotten. So much effort for fifteen people. Maybe an elopement would have been the right choice, but I couldn't do that to my parents.

Cole also worked a half day on Friday. After dropping me off at the salon first thing in the morning, he went to meet his client Mrs. Carondolet. A possible offer was circulating in the real estate wind. She wanted to meet with Cole to discuss the possibility. I asked him if he had told her that this was his wedding weekend. The response was odd. Cole said he didn't share his personal life with her and would meet with Mrs. Carondelet, then spend the remainder of the afternoon with his family.

"Did you buy a new suit?" I asked. It had slipped my mind to ask earlier, what with so much happening. I would have liked to have gone with him and find something nice for him to wear.

"You bet I did. It's the nicest suit I've ever owned. I will make you proud."

"I just want you to be proud, Cole. This is your big day too. I want it to be special, something we will never forget."

"If we were sitting on the beach alone sharing a peanut butter sandwich and exchanging vows, that would be special enough."

"You are the most amazing person. I love you."

The charmer melted me once again. Cole had a golden tongue in more ways than one. I confess this was all rather foreign to me. We the Fairchilds were a warm and loving family, but there was no gushing on Lexington Road.

A Terrible Choice

Cole arrived at the Carondolet mansion, once again admitted by "Lurch," only this time with a warning: "Mrs. Carondolet is very upset. She is running around the house smashing things, throwing objects against the wall," he said.

Just as Cole was about to ask why, his client appeared at the top of the second-floor balustrade of a sweeping staircase in the massive double-story grand entry hall of the mansion. She was clearly distraught, her blonde hair appearing to have suffered electric shock. And even from the vantage point below, Cole could see that her red lipstick was streaked across one cheek as if she had tried to put it on properly in her state of rage. She was wearing only a see-through leopard-print robe tied haphazardly at the waist, her right breast not quite having found secure placement, appearing to pop forth at the slightest movement.

"Has she been drinking?" Cole asked her man Friday.

"Perhaps, but I don't think that's the problem," he replied.

"Then what? She can't be this upset because we don't have an offer yet. It has only been a few weeks," Cole offered.

"It's Ricardo," the butler continued. "He's cut her off."

"Who's Ricardo?"

"Her estranged husband, a French Argentine German polo player, playboy, and heir to a vast mining fortune in South America. He is twenty years older than she, married twice before with many children, including one girl with Mrs. Carondolet," he said, revealing all the family history.

"She has a daughter?" Cole followed up.

"Yes. Her name is Alexis, and she is in London at boarding school. Did Mrs. Carondolet not share that with you the other day in the pool?" he said with a distinct tone of disdain in his voice.

Cole replied in similar fashion: "No, she did not mention it. We were busy doing other things."

At that point, an oriental ginger jar vase came hurtling over the balustrade, hitting the marble floor below like a bomb. Cole and the butler ran for cover. Mrs. Carondolet yelled for Cole to come upstairs.

"Get up here, Cole, now. Right now. I need to talk to you. Now!"

Cole followed the order and ran up the stairs. She grabbed him by the arm and told him to come with her. Leading Cole down the baronial upstairs hallway, which ended at double doors with gleaming golden hardware, she kicked open her master bedroom entryway and pulled Cole in. Slamming the doors behind them, she then grabbed Cole's crotch and began pulling off his clothes. Her sheer leopard robe fell to the floor, and the real leopard underneath took her prey, staking her territorial claim.

Cole didn't resist. The two naked creatures fell into the disheveled sheets of the master bed and began the act. It was not love, just opportunity—momentary release, sexual satisfaction, escape from reality. For Cole, it was also business. He was messed up. Unable to separate his unyielding ambition to succeed and to make money from his desire not to be his father, he was not deterred from the idea of using sex, if necessary, to achieve a goal on his unconscious road to hell. Cole rationalized that his love for Kate was not compromised by sex with Caroline—or anyone else for that matter. There was no meaning, no love, no commitment. As a teenager growing up in the Clinton 1990s, Cole had learned that lesson from the president. One of his high school history teachers at Reno High even had told his class while discussing the Monica Lewinsky / Bill Clinton peccadillo that "most successful powerful men have enormous libidos and seek sexual satisfaction whenever and wherever possible." Cole remembered that admonition, especially the "successful and powerful" part.

Their sex on the Friday morning before Cole's prenuptial dinner was quick, hard core, and wild. They fell off one another, taking deep breaths, lying naked on top of a massive heap of crumpled linens, the pillows having been tossed to the floor. Even a bedside lamp had overturned and was now precariously hanging over the edge of the table, about to crash to the floor and shatter like most of the rest of the fragile ornamentation in the suite that had destroyed by Caroline in her rage prior to sex with Cole.

Without turning to look at Caroline, the naked stud, still erect with his flag-pole standing tall, asked, "Can you tell me what's wrong?"

Caroline did not hesitate. "Oh my God. That bastard is cutting me off. I mean totally. No money. Nothing."

"You mean your husband? How can he do that?"

"He can do whatever he wants. Ricardo is not an American citizen. He lives between homes in Monte Carlo and Buenos Aires. He is a billionaire. I was a sec-retary he met in Dallas at a big oil company he was doing business with."

"But you have a daughter together. Is he cutting her off too?"

"Of course not. It's just me. I am suing him for divorce, and this is his way to leverage me to stop fighting him, take less, and disappear from his selfish life."

"Were you ever happy?" Cole asked sheepishly, thinking about his own con-cept of marriage.

"We were at first. Then the cheating started, and there was plenty of it. I looked the other way but finally could not take it any longer and asked for a divorce."

"How did you end up here?"

"Ricardo asked me to try again and told me he would buy me a house any-where in the world. We fell in love with California, Newport in particular. This house became available, and that was it."

"I'm sorry to hear all this," Cole said, feeling foolish.

"Cole, now you must sell this house fast. I will run out of money fast."

At that point, Cole faced the music. It was no surprise: sex for business. He was nothing but a male prostitute for Caroline, a boy toy, revenge sex to get back at Ricardo.

Cole got out of bed, his johnson finally limp. Dressing, he left Caroline's boudoir. Turning back toward her, he said, "I will bring you an offer in the next thirty days."

"See yourself out, Cole. Keep me up to date," she replied, still lying naked in the crumpled linens.

The Rehearsal Dinner

Arriving back at the cottage by four that Friday afternoon, Cole planned to spend a couple of hours with me before we got dressed together for our prenuptial family gathering at the Lido house.

Nancy had gone back to the Harbor Club to get ready with my father and Jamey. The crew had wrapped up outside, the hairdresser and makeup artist having performed their miracles, and I languished in a hot bath for at least an hour following my massage.

Cole found me resting on our bed, totally relaxed and at peace. He kissed me hello passionately and asked me if I wanted to make love before dinner.

I did. And we did. It was the best it had ever been. Cole was amazing. For the first time since David, the stroke of Cole's penis reached my heart, emotionally speaking. He was not only my master charmer; he was also my master lover. How did he know so much about making a woman feel ecstasy? We never talked about past sexual relationships. I assumed he had learned from considerable experience.

After climaxing together, as we always attempted to do, part of our ritual in lovemaking, Cole rose to shower. I followed him in shortly thereafter.

We held one another under the warm water just long enough to wash the sex down the drain. Then we got out, dried off, and dressed for dinner. I slipped into a smart black and white shift with black satin bows resting on the shoulders of white satin straps, which were attached to the dress, which was cut straight across the bodice. The dress looked like Chanel, but it wasn't. I had picked it up on the sale rack at Neiman's. This was the sort of dress I would design, so it was perfect for my prenuptial dinner.

Due at the Lido house by six thirty, we arrived fashionably late by half an hour. The rest of the two families had converged at six o'clock, per Nancy's invitation, and were now sharing cocktails and hors d'oeuvres. We made an entrance to the sound of two ukuleles strumming the Hawaiian version of "Somewhere Over the Rainbow." It instantly became our wedding song since we had not selected anything. Cole's mother rushed to us, gushing praise over Nancy. "Your mother is an angel," she said, giving us both a kiss and a big loving hug.

"Yes, I know," I said with a smile.

"Do you know what this angel did?" she continued.

"Just everything," I answered.

"Do you know she prepared an Italian wedding dinner for all of us tonight? It is authentic right down to the last bite of ravioli," Mother Rose gushed.

"Yes, my mother is a dream," I added, not surprised at all that she was so thoughtful to have created an Italian dinner for Cole's family.

After we had sat down to the Italian supper at a large, rented table to accommodate all fifteen guests, servers brought out trays of Italian antipasti and baskets of fresh, hot buttery garlic toast. A wine sommelier filled oversized handblown goblets of green glass with the best Italian pinot money could buy.

Nancy had even found authentic Italian pottery made in Tuscany for the table, which impressed Joe and Rose. The ukulele music was not exactly Italian, but it didn't matter. Following a glass or two of wine, except for pregnant me, the toasts began, with Cole's dad delivering an emotional showstopper. We all cried. The toasts and the tears continued through the next four courses of dinner, which Cole's mom declared to be the finest Italian food, the only exception being her sainted late mother's cooking.

My father gave the sweetest toast of all, at least to my mind.

Raising yet another green goblet, Dalt pronounced, "First, to my wife, whom I love every moment of each day. Without her, I have nothing.

"Second, to the memory of my dear late mother and father, who sacrificed for me and to whom I owe everything I have ever accomplished.

"Next to my children, Kate, twenty, and Jamey, fifteen, who have given my life meaning, substance, and connection to a divine purpose that God grants to human beings.

"And now to the blessing of marriage between Kate and Cole. May your love reign for a lifetime and may you both know the happiness in life that Nancy and I have known. If you have that, you will be the luckiest couple on earth."

Cole's mom and dad stood and shouted "*Salud!*" with glasses held high.

We all cried some more.

Then Cole's parents made a follow-up toast of sorts, still standing and holding their goblets of wine. His father spoke, "We could not do much for you both in preparing this wonderful wedding weekend, so, Cole, your mama and I want to give you a honeymoon like we never had."

Cole's mother took out an envelope and handed it to Cole.

His father continued, "Inside that envelope are two round-trip tickets to Hawaii and a hotel reservation at the Hilton Hawaiian Village for a week."

Cole and I looked at one another. We both knew what to say and what to do. The table was applauding and sending love to his parents. I caught a glimpse of Dalt and Nancy applauding in appreciation, well knowing as we did that this was not such a great idea, although Cole's parents would have no idea why. To them, this was the greatest gift they could give, especially because it was a financial stretch and something they had never been able to do in their long marriage.

Cole spoke first: "Mom and Pop, this is the most generous gift of all. I can't believe you. You shouldn't have done this."

I cut him off.

"And there's more. First, I love you both for doing this. It is beyond generous—so thoughtful. With my having said that, Cole and I want to go to New York for our honeymoon. He's never been there. We have tickets to a couple of Broadway shows, and then we are renting a car to head into New England to see the fall leaves." I made it all up on the spot.

Cole came back in the game. "So, you know what, my wonderful mama and papa, Kate and I want you to take the honeymoon you never had and go to Hawaii for a week."

Cole gave the envelope to Kate. She walked it over to Cole's dad, placed it in his hand, and gave them both a hug.

"We love you so much. You go. Have a great time, and think of us on your belated honeymoon," I said.

Everyone cheered. We were still crying.

Dessert was served, a selection of every Italian delicacy from imported cookies to cannoli, to spumoni ice cream, and finally an Italian layered wedding cake. Departing Lido house around eleven, everyone went their own way for a good night's sleep in anticipation of the wedding day to follow.

CHAPTER THIRTY-TWO

A RITE OF PASSAGE

Few dates resonate more during a lifetime than one's wedding day. I am told that it is every girl's dream. Or it once was, I suppose. It was not my dream, although I did plan to one day fall in love with a man and have his children. Having a family was a dream for my future life, but I had never fixated on the whole white gown and veil thing. No wonder I was wearing a cream satin sheath, no veil, for my walk down the wooden platform over sand tonight.

Taken by a twinge of irony, which is neither ideal nor permitted on a girl's big day, I laughed at myself, envisioning the wooden plank set up as a makeshift aisle pointed in the direction of the Pacific Ocean. Kind of a walk down and off the plank.

Was I still having doubts? Not really. I had crossed that line weeks ago, confident that marriage to Cole was the perfect idea. I did truly love him, and I wanted us to be a happy family.

Then there was the other aspect of my self-inflicted irony. In this young life, I had witnessed two young women become pregnant in unplanned circumstances, with the timing totally upending their lives. Neither one got married, not having loved their partners. It was just sex. I swore this would never happen to me—swore it up and down. And here I was, rowing that same boat, telling myself that I was different because I was in love with Cole and that, because we had a relationship, our sex was about making love. That was what made my situation totally different to my mind.

Still, I was pregnant at twenty. I had not finished college. I had only begun to follow a dream pursuing fashion design, and I knew it was all going to change. Could I be a devoted wife supporting Cole's career, follow my own dream career, raise a baby, and hold it all together?

Millions of women were able to do so, and they did it in past generations as well as today. *Can I do it all?* I wondered. *Am I ready for the challenge?*

On a certain level I knew neither my husband-to-be nor even my parents seriously cared about my pursuit of a design career. Cole had his eye on making it big and being the provider. Dalt and Nancy just wanted me to be happy, live a comfortable life, and produce wonderful grandchildren. Not that they would be against my going after a career. They would be proud and even supportive. But they wouldn't care if I chose not to do so.

Over four generations, my family had gone from being dirt-poor immigrants to joining the elite class of the American affluent. Dalt often quoted the famous response by J. Paul Getty when asked by a reporter, "How much is enough?" Getty replied, "Always a little more."

Dalt worked every day in the market and always did make a little more. Yet he also knew that enough was enough. My father achieved wealth but was not obsessed by it, and he also knew that he provided for the security of his family well into the next generation if none of us were ever to make a dime on our own.

That is something that most people just don't understand. Many people wish for such good fortune, but they will never quite understand how this kind of security molds a child. For some it is a catalyst to moving mountains, seeking major discovery, pushing the envelope, using a great fortune to amass even more wealth and alter the human condition by virtue of their ambition. For most, like me, the security removed the hunger to break out, break through, make money, and make a name for oneself. How many people would give anything to remove the stress of having to put food on the table and provide a roof overhead? Such things would never be my worry. I was free to worry about more esoteric matters, such as the meaning and purpose of marriage, the essence of true love, and God's plan for me on earth. People living day to day have no time to concern themselves with such wondering. I knew this partly because of my privilege and partly because I am sensitive and care about others.

Sitting in my bedroom at the beach cottage, being pampered by stylist Hugh and his assistant Farid, who were preparing me for the wedding, my bridal thoughts wandered. Not exactly normal. Hugh asked if I was having regrets, as I seemed rather glum to him.

"Oh no, my friend, no regret, no remorse. I guess you might call me a serious bride, not a giddy one all wrapped up in the excitement of the moment. I know the ceremony will be beautiful and memorable. And I'm so happy you are here. Did anyone ask you both to stay for dinner?"

"No, but that's okay. Not a big deal."

"Ridiculous. Please excuse me for not asking. I insist you both stay. I'm sure Nancy would agree. I was emphatic about no guests; she clearly obliged."

"We'd love to," Hugh replied instantly, putting a final comb through my hair, which he pulled back in a French bun. Farid applied false eyelashes and accentuated my eye makeup, applying an amber shadow on the lids. A final touch of a very pale lipstick was carefully administered. Real diamond earrings on loan from Nancy dazzled. I stood up to have Hugh help me step into the dress Monsieur Lawrence had so lovingly created, fitted to my two-months-pregnant body. It was not terribly challenging as I was not showing.

As it was approaching five thirty Saturday evening, with the family due to converge at six o'clock for a cocktail and appetizer reception, Cole was in another bedroom getting dressed in his "amazing" new suit. He had finally shown it to me after I'd asked at least ten times. He wanted it to be a surprise. After we had made love before the prenuptial dinner the previous night, he gave in and proudly modeled his choice of wedding attire.

It was perfect. A simple exquisitely tailored Armani suit in jet-black gabardine silk with thin lapels, hand stitching, and straight-leg pants, no cuffs. He planned to wear a white shirt with a spread collar and French cuffs with a black satin necktie.

Earlier, Dalt had presented Cole with gold cufflinks that once belonged to his father, Burton, as a prewedding gift to welcome Cole into the family. Truly honored, Cole had purchased a shirt with French cuffs, a style he had never owned or worn before. This was truly a badge of honor, another sign of his moving up the ladder of success. He was yet another step away from his childhood in Reno and his blue-collar existence, a way of life he had known from a young age that he wanted to leave behind.

There was no rehearsal before the prenuptial dinner, mostly because I didn't want one, but also because we didn't need one. Nancy had covered everything. Our vows were written. The guests would have no trouble knowing where to go and where to sit. The Surfer Saint was at the ready to perform the ceremony. The caterers were catering, and the designer was lighting candles and torches. The florist Andrew fine-tuned the amazing orchids, which were perfectly placed everywhere, and the ukuleles were set to strum on cue. Nancy had cheated, hiring a violin quartet as well, finally confessing to it only about an hour ago.

As for me and my role, I would simply appear, and Dalt would walk me down the plank, or rather the aisle. That's why no rehearsal was necessary.

Remaining in my room with Hugh and Farid while the family gathered, adhering to the old wives' tale that the groom must not see the bride, I hid until beckoned. Funny, being so modern and open-minded, I did not want to take a chance on not adhering to that superstition.

Hiding out with Hugh turned out to be a small blessing. Having known him for years, I adored him. He always made me laugh with stories about his Hollywood celebrity clients. As I was coming out of my introspective seriousness, we shared some joyful tears and hysterical laughter.

"Look at you, you're smiling," he said.

"Don't let me ruin the makeup," I replied.

"Oh, not that. Never that. We don't want Farid following you down the aisle for touch-ups," Hugh said.

Six thirty came quickly, and my cue was delivered. Waiting outside my door was my father, front and center, ready to escort me to the ceremony. The family, after finishing a cocktail or two, were now finding seats out on the beach as sunset approached on this balmy Indian summer Saturday on the California Riviera.

Nancy certainly had created magic. Torches had been lit in memory of GiGi as a nod to the original plan to marry on her beach in Honolulu. My supercreative mother had designed the ceremony in a most unique way. The guests took their chairs, which were arranged in two semicircular rows placed upon wooden platforms on the sand, which were covered with a plush cream-colored pile carpet to blend in with the sand. And get this, the seating was set up behind the pop-up pulpit, so the family could see the bride and groom face-to-face rather than watching our backs. The family's backs would be to the ocean, while Cole and I would face the Surfer Saint, allowing us to look behind him and watch the sun lower into the Pacific as we exchanged vows.

Escorting me down the back stairs from the bedroom over the garage, Dalt walked me through the house and out onto the beach-facing terrace to find my wedding aisle. It was a straight shot on the plank on our way to the wedding canopy. Cole and his dad, the latter serving as best man, were already in place, waiting for us. For an instant, I felt bad that I had not asked any of my childhood friends to stand up with me, but the felling passed.

As Dalt and I took our first step on the platform aisle, the violins commenced. Nancy had instructed them to perform selections from Rachmaninoff, GiGi's favorite romantic composer.

Looking over at my father, who was tearing up, I whispered to him to stop. I would soon be crying too if he didn't cease.

"Imagine that everyone out there seated is nude," I joked. Dalt chuckled; the tears stopped.

Making it down the aisle without incident, managing not to trip over my cream satin sling-back Dior heels, I felt beautiful in my Asian-inspired dress. The family applauded as we reached the wedding arch festooned with orchids glowing in the light of the torches surrounding the pulpit. The Surfer Saint opened with an original prayer, beautifully composed—spiritual, not religious in a traditional sense.

"Loved ones, we come together on this evening of God-given magnificence, warmed by the late day sun, touched by a gentle breeze off a vast and mysterious ocean, to participate in the union of two loving souls given life by the Creator of all life, and blessed by God's graceful loving direction. Human beings should have the capacity to love one another and to live full lives in harmony with the Creator's purpose for humankind."

The Surfer Saint continued, "We welcome the bride, Kate Elizabeth Fairchild, and the groom, Cole Baldwin, and we pay tribute to their respective families, who have nurtured their children and brought them to this spiritual union on this day, at this time, in this place, in the year 2000. Let us mark the very moment in our memories, so we remember it always with joy, hope, and peace for Kate and Cole and for all witnessing this sacred promise."

The Surfer Saint directed Cole and me to join hands as he continued with his prayers. The ukuleles strummed gently in the background as the sky began to fade to black.

Looking into Cole's eyes, his serenity alluring, I was totally at peace, completely in touch, intoxicated by the simplicity and beauty of this perfect moment. As the Surfer Saint finished his prayers, we read our own vows, sharing them quietly and privately as the family looked on trying to make out the words, yet respecting our desire to hold the feelings to ourselves.

"I sincerely hope you both promise to love, honor, and cherish one another till death do you part," the Surfer Saint followed. The family cheered.

"We must keep some traditions; we are not exclusively new age. We are eternal, all age," he offered, which made everyone applaud enthusiastically.

"With that, it is time for another time-honored tradition," the preacher said. "Kate, do you take this man to be your lawfully wedded husband?"

"I do."

"Cole, do you take this woman to be your lawfully wedded wife?"

"Yes, I do."

"Do you promise to be kind, generous, faithful, understanding, and—most important—always loving and considerate of each other's unique and special gifts, needs, and desires?"

Cole and I both spoke at once: "We do."

"One more thing. Marriage is not a promise of never-ending bliss. There will be challenges. Will you face them with strong resolve to conquer the bumps in the road of life in a manner that is in keeping with the loving-kindness you commit to on this, your wedding day?"

We looked at one another and made the promise. Cole kissed me before the Surfer Saint could pronounce us husband and wife in the eyes of God and the laws of the state of California.

I called out, "We did it!"

Our families stood and cheered, and the violins began to play once again. This time, it wasn't classical music. Instead, Nancy really surprised us by having requested that they play a full-on rousing rendition of "Hava Nagila," the classic Jewish celebration song. Cole and I looked at one another, not knowing why this song was playing for us as we left the altar.

As we entered the beach house, Nancy came over first to kiss us both and then explained that the song choice was another nod to the long-lost family history that had resurfaced in my quest to discover our family's roots.

"We are a blended family of many religions, many cultures, and many remarkable ancestors. This was for the generations who came before the two of you, and mostly was meant as a call for you both to embrace everything in your pasts so you may build for yourselves your very own special future. Live, love, make beautiful babies, and always be true to yourselves and to one another. My last piece of advice, today, that is, is always to laugh. Find humor in life, even in the direst of circumstances. Without laughter in a marriage, well, it can keep two people apart, especially in the hard times."

We sat down to a wedding feast right after the ceremony ended. Nancy had placed one long rectangular table on the cottage terrace to seat everyone. After her last-minute seat adjustments to add Hugh and Farid, more toasts followed. It was a nonstop love-in; never had I experienced such kindness. Everyone was crying with each toast. It was even more emotional than at the prenuptials the previous night. Cole's parents were the most emotional. Both his father and his mother were overcome with loving feelings bordering on melancholy. This was a significant rite of passage for their handsome son, who despite his desire to surpass the standard of living afforded him as a boy, which his parents were fully aware of, was loved unconditionally by this close-knit Catholic clan.

Standing up to make a toast of gratitude to Dalt and Nancy, especially Nancy for all she had accomplished in less than two weeks to create my wonderful wedding, I raised a glass of water in their honor. Just then I felt a terrible pain in my back, radiating around to my stomach, sudden and sharp as a knife stabbing me. Doubling over, I screamed in agony and fell back into my chair. Cole, Dalt, and Nancy rushed to my side.

Barely able to talk, I said, "Call 911." Within ten minutes, I was on a gurney and being transported to Hoag Memorial Presbyterian Hospital in Newport, only a ten-minute drive from the cottage.

Cole reached my ob-gyn Dr. Grimes, who in turn called ahead to Hoag to arrange admittance, which allowed me to avoid the emergency department. Dr. Grimes told Cole she would leave her Saturday night dinner to make it to Hoag before we arrived.

My pain lessened in the ambulance but remained strong with intermittent jabs of lightning that were at least not as severe as the first jolt. Following the EMTs, the family drove in several cars and formed an entourage of support heading to Hoag.

After being checked in, I was rushed into an examining room and was met by Dr. Grimes, along with a team who hooked me up to monitors and checked all my vitals. Everyone waited in silence in the hospital lobby, awaiting word. Cole wanted to stay with me, but Dr. Grimes requested he wait with the others. An hour of testing produced no serious results. I was moved into a corner room with a view of the ocean under Dr. Grimes's instruction to remain for at least twenty-four to forty-eight hours for observation and more testing. At this point I was alert and relatively pain-free. She administered a mild pain suppressant that would not harm the baby. My first question to Dr. Grimes was whether the baby was okay. She assured me that everything looked fine—not to worry.

Cole, Nancy, and Dalt had received the good news prior to my being moved into the hospital room with a view. In Newport, even the hospital has an ocean view. Nancy did another incredible Nancy thing: she had called the caterers at the cottage and told them to pack up the dinner, deliver it to Hoag, and serve it to everyone in my room.

Dr. Grimes hesitated giving approval but ultimately agreed because of the circumstances and mostly because she believed that the incident was a momentary aberration and nothing serious.

It was approaching nine o'clock when the caterers came in with Nancy's wedding dinner. A few people managed to get a chair. Others sat on the floor. Nancy and Dalt took the wide window ledge, and Cole got the edge of my hospital bed.

There were no more toasts, only plenty of relief and gratitude that it was nothing serious. Everyone was hungry at this point, enjoying every bit of Nancy's fancy dinner on plastic plates using plastic utensils. Wine was poured in paper specimen cups, the only thing available.

"I'd like to thank you all for coming and sharing my wedding to Cole. This is going to be one wedding none of us will ever forget."

The Surfer Saint had come to the hospital along with everyone else. He offered a prayer for my recovery and blessed the doctors, nurses, and staff at Hoag. After our picnic in the hospital, we all said good night, with me getting too many kisses. The family departed. Cole remained and snuggled up on the bed next to me. Fortunately, our union had been consummated many times prior to the ceremony.

"This is the best wedding night I could have ever imagined," he said. "I love you, and I am so glad you're okay. How are we going to repeat this experience on our anniversaries?"

"I bet we'll think of something," I said, putting my arms around him. I was dressed in my very attractive hospital gown, while Cole was still in his Armani. "We are some pair," I said.

"You looked unbelievable in your wedding dress, and you look even more unbelievable in your hospital gown," he added.

He was absolutely my very own Cuban Italian stallion charm machine. And so, it was indeed a wedding for the books.

CHAPTER THIRTY-THREE

MOVING ON

The next six and half months proved to be a very happy time for Cole and me. We had missed our chance to see the fall leaves on an escape to New York and New England after the wedding, yet it didn't matter. There would be other chances to travel.

Our after-the-wedding months, as pregnancy bloomed, ended up being probably the most peaceful and simple time of our lives. Dr. Grimes had ordered a month of rest following my release from Hoag. The diagnosis was just stress—no serious complications with the baby. Just the same, I stayed home, not ordered to bed exclusively, only advised to keep a low profile.

My dear fashion mentors insisted I take leave for as long as necessary. Arranging for Cole to bring home all my sample drawings, the fabric, and the first cuttings, along with some important tools such as the fabric shears and measuring instruments, Monsieur Lawrence even had offered to come by and assist, or at least check in as needed. The dear man came at least twice a week after the salon closed for the evening. Each time I was more amazed by his talent, his eye for detail, and his knowledge of style and design.

Even better, my success-driven new husband made an effort to come home for dinner almost every night, other than when dining with a client to solidify a deal. Cole's television commercials were also working. About two months into the TV run, sales calls began coming in. The calls led to meetings, and within a few more weeks Cole had landed a new buyer and two new sellers offering to list their properties with him. All the deals were modest by Newport standards, in the one-million-dollar range for a decent fifteen-hundred-square-foot, three-bedroom, two-bath ranch-style home on an average seven-thousand-square-foot lot. Just about anywhere else in the nation, such a property might bear a price tag of closer to fifty thousand dollars, or about 5 percent of the down payment required to become a homeowner in one of the wealthiest communities in the United States.

Cole's career continued to rise. He closed deals on all three of the clients, earning commission in excess of one hundred thousand dollars. On top of that, he courted six more potential clients in his pipeline. On the flip side, Cole shared a bit of the nightmare he faced with the fifteen-million-dollar deal with Mrs. Carondolet.

He did not like to share his business with me, instead keeping the details close to his vest, preferring to leave all the real estate drama at the office. Part of me appreciated that, although sometimes I felt I wanted to be more involved, as Nancy was totally involved with Dalt's brokerage business. Nancy knew the ins and outs of every deal, every client, every challenge, and every triumph my father faced and achieved. This was my model. Still, I understood that it was not the same with Cole, and I accepted that fact.

He did open up somewhat more about the Carondolet situation, telling me that she was becoming very difficult to deal with, often belligerent and more often drunk when he came to do business. On his most recent showing with a very wealthy Chinese family from Beijing arriving with an entourage and an interpreter, Mrs. Carondolet was so high and so abusive, they were forced to leave.

Asking Cole what he thought was the reason for her behavior, he said, "She is divorcing her husband. He cut her off months ago. She is running out of money and is very afraid of landing on the curb of her fifteen-million-dollar lifestyle," he explained. "I have the listing coming up for renewal. Foolishly, I had promised her a fast sale when we first met. She continues to berate me for failing to deliver as promises. Kate, I've spent thousands on marketing, and I've gone the extra mile to keep her happy. I am doing everything I can to keep that listing for us."

"Cole, that is sweet of you to say that it is for us. Truly sweet. I love that. But seriously, if you lose it, so what? You are doing so well, and your star is on the rise. Losing this client will not damage your reputation, just your pride and your motivation to have a significant payday," I said sincerely.

"Kate, I could lose upward of seven hundred fifty thousand dollars in commission if I don't sell this house controlling both sides of the transaction. I know that money is not your God, and it's not mine either, at least not totally, to be honest, but I just can't walk away without a fight. Besides, this money could be the funds we need to buy our own house."

"Do you have a plan to keep her happy so she stays with you?"

"I'm doing everything I can," Cole said, repeating his earlier answer to me. I let it go. I had nothing more to say.

What I did know, despite Cole's confessed stress over his big deal, was that we were extremely at ease in the first months of marriage. One night at dinner I asked Cole if he appreciated how lucky we were. He said that he did.

"We pay no rent; we have no debt; we live in paradise, there is always great food on the table; we are healthy; and our baby is coming. We don't even need much money to live on. And that doesn't even consider the amazing money you have made in less than a year since we met, or the fact that I get a monthly allowance from a family trust. There aren't many young couples with that kind of security in their twenties," I said to him. We really did survive on love, not money, but our situation was about to get more complicated as I was to receive the one-million-dollar gift from GiGi to support my fashion dream.

Making Progress

In our desire to share all the holidays with family, Cole brought his parents and siblings down for Thanksgiving, and they stayed with us in the beach cottage. His mom, Rose; sister, Maria; and I prepared Thanksgiving dinner with an infusion of Italian joy, while his dad and Cole deep-fried the turkey, managing not to set the house on fire.

Next stop, Christmas. Christmas was a special sight to behold in Beverly Hills, as Nancy always made it so. The arrow on the electric meter spun wildly because of the display of twinkling white lights, which rivaled the work of Disneyland artists at holiday time. Most importantly, we were all very happy together. My brother, Jamey, was doing better in school and was very relieved to be at Beverly High rather than at some drug rehab continuing ed institution. His surfing had become more passionate, as well as providing him with an emotional release. It mattered to him, giving him self-confidence and pride of accomplishment.

Dalt and Nancy traveled to Honolulu before Christmas to have a memorial service for GiGi and to spread her ashes over the ocean. They had asked us repeatedly to go, but I remained unwilling, preferring not to remember my beloved grandmother by way of a memorial service. Finding my own closure, I did not need the tradition of a formal farewell. Even though GiGi wanted to be cremated and have her ashes scattered over her beloved ocean, I just did not want to see that. My parents understood.

With arrival of the New Year, I had been away from the salon for a month and a half, making some progress on the line at home. Yet, it was time to go back to work. Having been cleared me after my checkup and having learned from the sonogram that Cole and I were having a boy, I ventured back to the salon. Again, the doctor had advised me to take it easy and demanded no stress, even asking if I could work part time for the first month to see how it went. After agreeing and promising to check in with her regularly before my next visit to her office, I received the green light.

Spending New Year's Eve at home, ringing in the year at nine o'clock with a cable TV preview of the midnight ball drop in New York, Cole and I toasted with Dick Clark. Cole held a flute of Veuve, and I had apple juice. Then we went off to bed. We spent a special New Year's evening in the bedroom over the garage, making exquisite love for hours. Dr. Grimes had given us the go-ahead at four months, and our lovemaking was the best ever.

The truth is our simple and uncomplicated life was totally wrapped in unbelievable sex. We had fallen into a lovemaking rut. Can you imagine that? It was dinner at seven most nights, then lovemaking by ten o'clock. We never stayed up long enough to watch any of the late-night talk shows. I don't think we watched Jay Leno once in months. Our lovely rut didn't include going out to dinner or attending parties, and there were plenty of parties. Newport is undoubtedly the party capital of the

USA. With Cole's rise, he was getting noticed by the local elite, and invitations were coming in to join a myriad of charities, support groups, and civic endeavors—and so much more. It would all have to wait. Cole was ready to mingle; I needed more time.

Dalt continued to advise us to get involved in the community for the sake of Cole's career and so I could make a few new girlfriends. My father was seriously bothered by the fact that I had not invited my childhood friends to the wedding. But Cole and I didn't need friends, not now anyway. We had each other, and that was enough.

By March, I had completed my first set of samples of Fair Child with the input from Monsieur Lawrence. Extremely pleased, he offered me more confidence than I deserved. We created a line of ten pieces of luxury sportswear. I knew it was special and unique. I asked Nancy to come down to Newport to check it out because I wanted her honest review. Blown away by the samples, she could not stop praising the results.

"This will fly off the rack," she repeated over and over.

Monsieur Lawrence interjected, "First we must get it on the rack. LA is not an easy market to launch in. And it can be costly."

Not knowing the process, foolish me thought that you just took the samples into a store and offered to sell them pieces, them someone took the order. Monsieur explained that it once was that simple, but not so much anymore.

"Fashion is all business today. And it is big business. There are many factors and forces involved in launching a line, especially an unknown line. Even the established brands struggle from season to season, year to year," he said.

Nancy put her arm around my shoulder.

"Monsieur is right, my darling girl. You have the ability to cut through the barriers because, first and foremost, you have a brilliant product. Second, you have the funds to launch this business properly. You can hire a publicist to get a celebrity to wear an outfit and make some noise in the media. You can hire the right jobber/manufacturer to create multiple samples of the line to display to buyers. You can hire a sales rep to travel to the shows in LA, Dallas, New York, and Miami to meet all the big players in US and foreign markets. In short, you can do this. You have the talent, you have the tools, and you have the support of this wonderful mentor Monsieur Lawrence to make this a reality."

Hugging Nancy, I thanked her.

"Have you made an arrangement with Monsieur Lawrence?" Nancy inquired. "An arrangement of financial profit sharing, dear?"

"Oh my, I never thought about it."

"It is time you did. Just because you've never worried about money does not mean you can keep your head in the sand. If you want to be a successful businesswoman, you must think and act like one," Nancy advised.

"You sound like Cole, Mother," I threw in.

"You married a young man with ambition who probably always worried about having enough money."

"Did I marry down, Mother?" I said, laughing.

"On the contrary, dear. The only way is up for both of you."

Turning to Monsieur Lawrence, I asked him what would be fair. He replied by requesting that I make him an offer.

"Okay then, how about sixty/forty?"

"Sixty for me, forty for you?" he answered slyly.

I thought he was kidding, but I wasn't sure.

"Oh, Kate, I am joking. I will accept a 10 percent fee for my tutelage. This is your dream, your design. May you be enormously successful. And if you are, 10 percent will be a great deal of money."

Once I held out my hand, we shook on the deal—my first deal in the business arena. Nancy glowed with pride.

Our baby was due soon. I had decided to put fashion design on hold again, planning to resume later in the year. Monsieur Lawrence gave his blessing.

As it was nearing the end of the workday, the salon door tinkled and Mrs. A sauntered in, greeted by Madame Honoré. Bringing Nancy out of the workroom to meet Mrs. A, I knew they would hit it off. Which they did.

Mrs. A came to collect a cocktail dress she wanted for one of her upcoming charity dinners. Madame Honoré carefully wrapped the dress in fine tissue and placed it in one of the salon's exclusive garment bags, which were custom made of soft yellow cotton imprinted with a black and gold monogram of the salon's name, Avenue Foch West.

The garment bags, a great marketing tool for the salon, were noticed all over town, having become a status symbol.

"Kate, I am coming in next week to plan your shower as promised. Can we make a date to meet now? Perhaps your darling mother will join us?" Mrs. A asked.

"I'll be working all week," I replied.

"How about next Wednesday at noon? If Nancy can join us, we'll go to lunch at the Harbor Club. You must have that shower soon; you will be a mom before you know it."

"Next Wednesday at noon it is," I said, turning to my mother. "Can you make it?"

"I wouldn't miss it. Count me in."

Mrs. A gave me a hug and Nancy too.

"See you next week," she said, dashing out the door with her new cocktail dress.

"Wow, this has been one interesting day, my child. I am so happy for you; it seems you have your world by the tail. Make sure you enjoy every moment," Honoré said with heart.

CHAPTER THIRTY-FOUR

THE CHOICES WE MAKE

Cole's commercials had created an opportunity he had never planned and never expected. Not only did these one-minute sales pitches provide client leads, but also they were extraordinarily helpful in building his business and earning him a reputation. As a result, Cole became something of a minor local sex symbol and TV celebrity.

My husband had what was called telegenic appeal. He looked like a star and sounded like someone one just had to know—charisma extraordinaire. A fledgling television cable company launching a real estate channel, something new and untried in an expanding world of reality video, had answered his call to action on the commercial and requested a meeting. Given little information on the phone, Cole accepted the meeting, which was to be held in an office tower in LA's Century City. Leaving no potential opportunity on the table when it came to his career, Cole ramped up the aggression.

The meeting in Century City in the Twin Alcoa Towers turned out to be a game changer. Two guys, in partnership with unknown financial backers, were launching their real estate channel and calling their first program *The Dream Home Search*. They had been auditioning potential hosts for weeks, making no decision. Then someone had seen Cole's local commercial and sent them a link. After meeting him in person and engaging in twenty minutes of talk, they offered him an audition. Cole couldn't say yes fast enough.

"Do you mind doing some videotape takes right now?" one of the guys asked.

"Sure, why not?" Cole replied.

Taken into an adjacent office set up as a mini studio with a camera, lights, and a makeshift set that consisted of a large photo backdrop of a beautiful Cape Cod–style house on a tree-lined street in fantasyland in the United States, Cole was given a short script and was told to memorize it. An attractive young female assistant applied some facial makeup on Cole to eliminate glare from the lights when he went on camera. Loving the attention, Cole flirted shamelessly with his attractive makeup girl.

A few minutes later they were ready to shoot the tape. The makeup girl turned into a wardrobe mistress, smoothing out any wrinkles in Cole's suit jacket and pants, then adjusting his collar and red silk tie—the ideal uniform for a future real estate tycoon on TV.

As Cole was standing on set at the appointed spot in front of the dream home backdrop, the director counted down: "Five, four, three, two, one. And action." He pointed at Cole to deliver.

Cole's performance was flawless, every word delivered as written, with exceptional emphasis and flow.

They all clapped.

"Would you please do it one more time?" another of the partner/producers asked.

Cole did it a second time following the countdown to action. Again, his delivery was perfect.

"You're hired," the men shouted in unison, looking at one another for confirmation.

"Really? Are you sure?" Cole was surprised despite his bigger-than-life confidence.

Going back into the other office, the team spent the next hour with Cole going over plans and details and negotiating the preliminary points of a contract. Cole would be contacted by an attorney to finalize the deal. They assured him this would not interfere with his personal objectives in real estate regarding time or reputation. It would only enhance his business beyond his ability to predict any outcome.

"The power of television will change your life," they told him.

Before departing, Cole shared that he was having a baby soon and that he was busy with ongoing transactions. He wanted to be sure he could do this job, please the partners, and cover all his responsibilities.

They would not begin a shooting schedule until midsummer, promising to give him plenty of notice.

After shaking hands, Cole left. He rode down the elevator to the parking garage in a state of semishock. When he attempted to call me on his cell phone in the elevator, the call wouldn't connect. He tried again in the underground garage, and again it wouldn't connect. Finally, on the drive home back to Newport, he got through to me.

"You're not going to believe the news, Kate. Are you sitting down?" Cole was jubilant.

"I just came from a random meeting in LA and—" The phone died again. This time it was low battery. Cole threw the phone down on the passenger seat. The big news would have to wait until he made it home.

Mrs. A's Shower of Power

The baby shower long promised by Mrs. A unfolded on the first of April, of all dates. Certainly, this was not intentional, with no hidden meaning. Mrs. Adamson had gathered some thirty of Newport's female power brokers, all the women who were socially prominent and successful both and by virtue of their successful men.

Many of them were also longtime friends of the hostess, as well as neighbors on the Newport waterfront, living in enormous and extravagant homes on small lots nestled side by side but facing world-class vistas of the bay and the ocean, and some also incorporating the Oz-like background of Newport's Fashion Plaza Towers. In the distance, snowcapped mountains in the winter season framed this spectacular residential enclave.

I knew none of the guests, except of course my mother and Madame Honoré, who were my security. With my having been once before to the Adamson estate, which was just down the beach road from the cottage, we arrived, meeting handsome valet attendants who took the car and then escorted us across the porte cochere. The boys in blue blazers and Republican-red ties with their arms outstretched to steady the female guests, most of whom were in high-heel shoes traversing the stone driveway, made quite the scene.

A jovial butler with thinning gray hair, a shining forehead that could light the night sky, and a grin that reminded me of one of my favorite old comic actors, Ed Wynn, whom I loved to watch in classic movies on TV on Saturday mornings when I was growing up, welcomed us to the party.

Offering each of us a glass of wine or champagne on arrival, a housekeeper in a formal pink and white uniform with the obligatory ruffled peplum led the way into a solarium room with a spectacular ceiling of glass in a dome configuration facing the Newport harbor. The ceiling rose to a height of some twenty-four feet, with a grand crystal chandelier centered in the room, suspended from the crisscrossed metal bracings that held the glass panels of the ceiling in place. Twenty-foot-tall palm trees spread their fronds out gracefully in strategically placed positions in the solarium, planted in massive stone urns filled with blooms of pink, white, and baby-blue delphiniums around the trunks of the palms. Four round glass tables, each seating eight, were centered in the room and positioned around an antique stone fountain that was topped with a whimsical child figure fashioned in gilt bronze holding a water pitcher that poured forth a stream, replicating a child watering her garden.

The tables were festooned with beautiful vintage epergnes, no two alike, with small delicacies on the lower glass trays and a blush of pink and pale blue roses on the upper level. I don't think I had ever seen baby-blue roses. Nancy whispered that they were white blossoms dyed baby blue.

"Kate, did you ever tell Mrs. A that you were having a boy?" Nancy asked quietly.

"Oh my goodness, I didn't, and she never asked. Is that why we have a pink and blue theme?"

"You've got that right, my child."

As the solarium filled with the invited guests, and as waiters circled with treats on silver trays, we introduced ourselves with the help of the hostess, Mrs. A.

First, we met Adrienne Arnold, a raven-haired beauty married to an international businessman in the world of import–export, then in came Sally Cox, sophisticated in the real-deal way, married to a paper-manufacturing king. Sally got on very well with Nancy.

I got a kick out of Eve Summers, a vivacious blonde who apparently ruled the roost among the glitterati. Then entered Sharon McFarland, a stunning green eyed Irish beauty. She came with her exquisite daughter Lauren, who was my age, thankfully.

The who's who crowd continued to converge. Mrs. A introduced Susan Simon, wife of a tech mogul; then Marta Bentallini, wife of a sports franchise owner; Harriet Van der Gelder, wife of an inventor billionaire; Idit Avedon, wife of an international diamond broker; Newport society editor Donna Maria Bellamonte; Vera Oxblood, the Avocado Queen, with the largest avocado ranch in California; fashionable women Maralou Hamilton, Carole Parsons, Elizabeth Swanson, Kathy Harrison, Joan Isman, Beverly Abramson, and Patti Exeter; and another of her neighbors on the harbor, the very glamorous Caroline Carondolet.

Place cards had been specifically placed at each table. I searched for our spot and found it. Nancy and I were seated together. Mrs. A was next to Nancy. I was in the middle, with Caroline Carondolet to my side. It surely was Cole's client. There could not be two Mrs. Carondolets.

Did Mrs. A know Mrs. Carondolet was working with my husband? How could she know? Mrs. A was the boss; she knew all. Maybe Mrs. Carondolet had told her she was selling her house with Cole Baldwin. Mrs. A had met Cole in the salon, and she knew he was in real estate.

What surprised me more was the fact that Caroline Carondolet had it all together. She was another over-the-top middle-aged Newport *Venus de Milo* beauty. Her hair, makeup, and wardrobe, total perfection. She spoke with confident charm and laughed easily and warmly, even taking my hand and giving me a gentle embrace as we sat down for lunch.

This was certainly not the woman given to rage, the abusive-mouthed alcoholic mess Cole had shared a few details about. I didn't know what to think. As the rest of the tables settled down, Nancy was involved in conversation with Mrs. A, while Caroline Carondolet turned toward me.

"I believe I know your husband," she said. "Cole is selling my house, did you know?"

"Yes, I know. Only recently Cole shared with me his working relationship with you, and I put the pieces together when we were introduced." Then I decided to lie, which I rarely did, even to be socially polite. "Cole speaks very highly of you, and I understand you have an exceptional home," I said, crossing my fingers in my lap.

"Did he?" she came back.

"He told me he's trying everything possible to make the sale for you."

"Did he?" she said again.

"I may be speaking out of turn, but Cole is concerned that he has not delivered on his promise fast enough to bring you a qualified buyer."

"It has been challenging, Kate," she replied, changing the subject. "Cole never mentioned he was married, let alone having a baby."

"My husband does not like to mix his personal and professional lives. He tells me very little about his clients. How did you find out he was married and going to be a father, by ending up here at the shower?" I asked with some trepidation.

"I've known for some time, Kate. Mrs. A is my best girlfriend, and we talk almost daily, sharing every detail of our lives. I told her I had listed with a very handsome young real estate agent new in the business and gave her his name. She remembered meeting him with you at Madame Honoré's salon, and we put one and one together to make two."

"You can count on Cole to make you happy," I told her. This was the only thing I could think of saying to assure Caroline Carondolet that Cole would do a good job and satisfy her every demand.

We hardly spoke another word for the rest of the lavish shower. Caroline turned away to her other side, chatting away with Madeline Zinc, a powerhouse PR agent with Fortune 500 clients in Orange County.

Opening the final gift, I had been showered with the most expensive layettes and baby necessities money could buy, all from women who did not know me. I offered my sincere thanks. All the gifts were in neutral colors, including shades of white. No pink. No blue. Nancy told Mrs. A we would send a van to pick up the gifts as soon as possible to clear them from her home.

Walking out the door, I again thanked one and all. We exchanged kisses on both cheeks and promised to keep in touch and get together for lunch after the baby was delivered. Then Nancy, Madame Honoré, and I headed for the valet to retrieve our cars.

"Did you get a chance to talk to the lady next to me, Caroline Carondolet?" I asked Nancy.

"No, dear, I did not. Was she nice?"

"I suppose so. She is Cole's big client with the fifteen-million-dollar mansion for sale."

"That's quite a coincidence," Nancy replied.

"I'm not sure," I said in my streetwise tone. "I'm not sure."

Back at the Villa

Cole had set a late afternoon meeting with Caroline at her mansion. She had just returned home from the baby shower when Cole arrived. This time Caroline answered the door, her butler nowhere in sight. Cole entered, surprised to find her greeting him without the intermediary staff.

"Come in, darling Cole," she said gracefully, throwing open the massive door with a swoosh.

"Am I darling?" he asked. "The last time we met, you were throwing vases at me."

"That was before I knew you were soon to be married to a lovely girl pregnant with your child, who is very definitely far too good for you."

"What?" Cole said, raising his voice, but not too much. He never lost sight of protecting his business goal.

"I just met Kate, and we had a lovely little talk." She came back with a sly smile.

"You attended her shower?"

"I did, and I sat next to her through the entire affair."

"What did you tell her?"

"It's not what I told her, Cole. It's what she told me."

"And that would be …?"

"She said, and I quote, 'Cole will do anything necessary to make you happy.'"

"So, she does not know about us?"

"There is no us, Cole. There never was, never will be. There is only my sexual gratification, which you willingly deliver in order to keep this listing and in order to keep me happy—just as your beautiful wife promised."

"Oh my God," Cole muttered.

"Let's not play games, Cole. That's the bottom line. Your listing is up next week. If you want to keep it, make me happy. Make me happy now."

Facing the reality of what he had created, Cole felt slapped across the face. He rationalized the clandestine sex as a premarital rite of passage. He was not technically cheating on his wife; they were not yet married. So, it had been with the random young woman on the plane to Hawaii, and even with the actor by the pool at the Holmby Palms Hotel. There were other quick and dirty encounters that Cole also rationalized as something every young man does, a period of growing and experimenting. He was sure he loved Kate, but he also loved sex, as much as he could get. Telling himself it would stop after marriage; he now faced a moral challenge that could not be rationalized away as merely horny bachelor predatory behavior. With his decision at this moment, Cole would make a life choice.

"I want it now, Cole. What are you waiting for?" Caroline persisted, beginning to remove her clothes with slow and seductive moves right there in the entry hall of her home. Cole stared at her, then lunged forward, pulling her toward him and placing his lips upon hers and his tongue deep in her mouth. The sex dance was in full throttle once again.

Cole had made his choice. He was a weak and flawed man with great potential to be otherwise. With all his bravado, talent, ambition, and skill, Cole's large amount of confidence was not enough for him to realize, to know, that he was good enough and was man enough to make it and become successful based solely on his intelligence and hard work. Instead relying on primal instinct, he realized that the power of flesh was what ruled him.

Cole and Caroline went up the grand circular staircase, dropping articles of clothing along the way as they headed for her boudoir to finish the dance of sexual pleasure. Cole would secure an extension of the listing, and Caroline would receive her momentary pleasure and escape from her own misery. Both would forfeit so much for so little in return.

If our lives are the result of the choices we make, then Cole changed his life by making this choice on this afternoon following his wife's baby shower, less than two months before the birth of his son and heir.

CHAPTER THIRTY-FIVE

AN ATTEMPT AT REDEMPTION

Dr. Grimes was concerned that my baby's position was a sign of a possible problematic delivery, so she ordered me to a month of bed rest prior to my due date. I was feeling very tired and even experiencing some pain, which made this request for bed rest a welcome one. Nancy immediately hired a nurse. She wanted the woman to spend the night, or if that was not possible, she planned on hiring two. I told my mother that this wasn't necessary; Cole would be with me at night. Nancy accepted that premise with the caveat that she was coming down to Newport as often as possible, adding that she hoped she would be welcome to stay over if required. I assured her that she was always welcome.

After I'd given Cole the news over the phone concerning Dr. Grimes's order of bed rest, he promised to be home every night before the nurse ended her shift.

"You don't know this about me, Kate, but I'm a really good cook. I will make us dinner, and we'll eat on trays in bed," he offered.

"Really? Where did you learn to cook?"

"At my mama and grandma's side. Plus, I and my siblings often fended for ourselves because both my mom and dad worked long hours at their jobs, so if we wanted to eat, we cooked."

Coming home after Dr. Grimes's diagnosis, climbing into bed, I propped myself up on the pillows and began turning the pages of the latest edition of *Vogue* magazine. A stack of glossy fashion magazines rested on my bedside table, so there was plenty to keep me busy. Just the same, I dozed off in less than fifteen minutes, sleeping soundly for several hours in the afternoon until Cole arrived home early as promised.

Entering our bedroom, Cole walked silently over to the bed, trying not to wake me. He kissed me gently on the forehead, and I opened my eyes.

"Cole, I'm so happy you're home," I told him, putting both arms around his neck, pulling him closer in for a real kiss. He obliged.

"What would you like for dinner?" he asked. "I told you I am a good cook. If I fail at real estate, I could get a job as a cook, maybe at Denny's, to support the three of us."

Of course, my studly jokester would suggest cooking at Denny's. Knowing him well in just a year of our relationship, I knew he was only partially kidding. If Cole needed to get a job cooking at Denny's, then he would go to work cooking at Denny's. In his desire for success, I also knew he would prefer to own a Denny's.

However, he always knew the pressure of earning a dollar, something that would probably never leave him no matter how successful he might someday become.

The last month of the pregnancy went well. I was perfectly at ease in my bedroom, waited on during the day by the nurse and by Nancy, and at night by Cole, who had never displayed such sweetness or been so attentive and reliable. He was never late once, never ran out for a client appointment, and never discussed work at all, not even a peep about his troubles with Caroline Carondolet. And I didn't ask. Was I being selfish? Yes. However, this important life experience, awaiting the birth of our child, would be a time just between the two of us.

Taking advantage of the opportunity to talk, we made plans and dreamed together. I got to know Cole better, deeper, and more intimately in that month than ever before, which was remarkable given the fact that sex was forbidden. For Cole, no sex for a month was asking plenty. He didn't seem to care. Instead, we talked about planning a future together. He wanted ten kids. I said, "How about two?" He negotiated with me, settling on four. I said, "One at a time. Maybe."

He especially wanted to buy a home, our own house. Living in my parents' beach house was a great favor, not to mention quite special as we were able to live on the oceanfront as newlyweds.

"As soon as we can, I really want us to find our own first home," he shared more than once.

Telling Cole that I loved the idea, I also said it would come to be in good time.

He asked me more about my dream to create a fashion line and become a real designer, creating real clothing that we would see people wearing as we walked down the street.

"The passion is there," I explained. "I will develop my line and do what I can to see if it can be marketed. I know it's not easy and that it will take total devotion. I'm afraid I may not have that devotion. I made a choice to marry you, to support your career, and to have and raise our baby. Can I be devoted to a career as demanding as fashion? Cole, I don't know, and I am really afraid that I will fail."

Sitting down next to me on the bed, Cole put both his hands on top of mine.

"You have my total support. If that is what you want, then we will make it all work. Forget about it for now. We'll revisit this after the baby is born. What's important now is choosing his name!"

Cole was a master at changing the subject, and this time it did the trick. Laughing, I blurted out a name I had in mind, which I had not yet shared with him over the days and hours of tossing boy names back and forth. Some of them were real doozies. Cole wanted an aristocratic name such as Preston, Chandler, Gregson, or Baron.

"Really, Baron? We're having a boy, not a German count," I joked. He howled.

"Cole, would you agree to consider my preferred name?" I proposed coyly.

"Of course."

"Can we name our boy Burton after my grandfather? We could call him Buddy for short, or Burt, whatever you like."

Cole didn't miss a beat. "I love it. Perfect. It will be Baron Burton Baldwin—BBB monogramed on his shirts." He smiled with a devilish grin.

"Oh, stop," I said with a tone of frustration.

"Okay, Burton Baldwin it is. We'll pick a middle name when we see what he looks like."

"He's going to be the best-looking baby in the nursery," I said.

"Then we'll name him Burton Hunkster Baldwin."

"Whatever you say, my husband. Would you mind getting me a cup of tea?" I asked.

Cole jumped up, at the ready, and went off to the kitchen for hot tea.

Later that night I started having pain. Worried that the sharp jabs might be signs of labor, I called Dr. Grimes. It was after ten o'clock.

Once I had explained the symptoms as best I could, the good doctor inquired about what I'd had for dinner.

Cole had made a very spicy and delicious pasta with lots of garlic and olive oil, fresh basil, and tomato. I think there was also pancetta in the recipe. We had sat in bed watching TV and eating his pasta and every last piece of the most amazing buttery garlic and Parmesan toast.

"And you're wondering if you are having labor pains? You are having gas pains, and so is your future son. Drink several glasses of water; use the bathroom before you go to sleep; and call me in the morning. Obviously, if anything else happens, call me at any time during the night. Good night, Kate."

She was correct. I drank the water and went to sleep, and by morning the pains were gone. Of course, there was the residual effect of an inordinate amount of gas at intermittent intervals through the night. Each time it came, Cole and I looked at one another in horror. I covered my mouth with one hand, then exploded with more laughter. The Surfer Saint, my parents, and my dear GiGi had all told me that laughter was the glue that held together a good marriage. On this night, it was certainly the case for us.

My delivery date came and went with no little Buddy in the world. At this point, Dr. Grimes was checking on me daily, and Nancy practically moved in. During the more than a month of bed rest, the baby had moved into proper delivery position. No need for a C-section. Dr. Grimes was still very cautious. However, Buddy, estimated to be just over seven pounds, did not raise a red flag.

"I don't think C-sections run in my family," I said to Cole.

"Everything is going to be fine. You're just a little late," he answered. "We'll call him Burt the Fashionably Late!"

As it turned out, I was given another week to have a natural childbirth, then Dr. Grimes was going to induce and possibly have to perform a C-section. The calendar moved from May to June 1. That night Cole prepared another pasta dish that was even spicier, an *arrabbiata*. At midnight, I went into labor.

I had managed to stay home until three o'clock in the morning with Nancy and Cole by my bedside, but now it was time to head to Hoag Hospital. After calling Dr. Grimes to alert her, Cole fetched the car as Nancy grabbed my bag, and we were on our way.

Baby Burton Baldwin entered life without complications and with ten fingers and ten toes at five twenty on the morning of June 2, 2001.

CHAPTER THIRTY-SIX

AND BABY MAKES THREE

Cole and I adapted to new parenthood with relative ease. It helped to come home with a baby and a baby nurse, the latter courtesy of Dalt and Nancy. Belinda the doula joined the family as if she had always been my aunt, big sister, and best friend all in one.

Belinda took over like a drill sergeant with a big heart. Everything worked as if on a military schedule, to the minute. Cole and I got to know Buddy, and he us, relatively stress-free. Belinda gave us our duties, and we both obeyed. She handled all the late-night rocking and changing so I could receive the blessing of sleep and recovery and so that Cole could get a good night's rest, enabling him to pursue a full day of work without a baby hangover.

There was one other benefit. After a month, the headboard was banging, and so were we. Lovemaking returned after a dry spell. It was better than ever; Cole was on fire. The sexual deprivation had clearly released him in ways I never imagined. He became an explorer, and he surely did explore more positions than any version of instruction offered by the Kama Sutra.

The bliss continued throughout the summer. I took three months off from the salon, with blessings from Madame and Monsieur. Cole came home for dinner every night, turning into a real chef. He loved creating dishes almost as much as he loved exploring sexual positions. Thinking that my days in the kitchen might be over, or at least limited, I found that the result of the trade-off was a phenomenal love life. Quite a trade-off indeed.

Summer 2001 delivered a mild season on the sand with daily temperatures rarely surpassing the low eighty-degree mark. The normal June gloom in Newport never materialized; instead, we had crystal clear blue skies and warm breezes, ending in blazing orange sunsets to the west over the ocean. I spent most days with Buddy, Belinda, and a baby encampment of paraphernalia on the sand just beyond the lawn of the cottage. Belinda had the baby rocker, a porta-crib with umbrella, and all supplies at the ready. I will never forget the image of Buddy taking a bottle while in Belinda's arms, smiling up at her. After a certain interval, she would pass him over to me to finish. He was a darling baby who looked like Cole, with sparkling blue eyes and strands of dark hair.

Pinching myself for having such good fortune, I was still haunted by having placed my dream on hold. I wondered if I was serious about following through with the fashion line. Flashes of guilt haunted me. While Belinda was with us,

I wondered if I could find some time to get back to work. There was so much to accomplish. Only the dedicated, unrelenting, and persevering person had even a slim chance of making it in the design world. My tutors, my parents, and just about everyone else had made this fact clear. Not GiGi, though. She had told me over and over I could do it, and she left me a whopping sum of money to pave the way.

In a way I owed it to GiGi as much as I owed it to myself to get back on track as soon as I could. Looking over at little Buddy and Belinda, I also knew I did not want to miss my son's childhood by working 24/7 pushing a rack of rags and convincing stores and women across the United States that they had to have garments from the Fair Child line. Somehow it sounded trivial compared to having time with Buddy.

On one of our idyllic summer afternoons on the sand, Belinda dropped her military formality when I asked her about her life. A black Puerto Rican woman in her midforties, almost six feet tall and built like a brick wall, she had her hair cut very short. She wore no jewelry and no makeup, and she always had on a green hospital scrub uniform—V-neck top and drawstring pants with spotless white sneakers. Belinda had flown out to Newport from New York, where she lived with her husband in Brooklyn. He was a construction foreman, and she traveled around the country as a baby nurse. Recently she had finished a position in Boston, and the agency Nancy contacted had recommended her with five stars. So had the letters of reference from previous families. Wondering how she became a baby nurse, I asked Belinda to share her story, which she did, speaking perfect English in a deliberate, matter-of-fact tone.

"It is not so much a matter of how I became a nurse, Miss Kate, as it is a matter of why," she said, opening up. "I came to America from Puerto Rico when I was twenty-five. My parents died in a car wreck in San Juan when I was seventeen, leaving me and seven younger brothers and sisters. We had no one and nothing. I became both parents, taking a job as a maid in a hotel, along with my sixteen-year-old sister. She and I managed to feed the family and keep everyone all together. We lived in a very rustic shack my father had built out of discarded construction materials. The tin roof did not keep out the rain—so much rain—and it retained the heat on account of so much humidity," she said. I sat silently, holding Buddy.

"Do you wish me to take him?" she asked.

"Oh no, he's fine. Please continue," I requested.

"We all worked hard. We went to school, all eight of us, and we survived. By the time I reached my twenty-fifth year, all my family had reached eighteen, even the youngest boy, and all of them were self-sufficient, hardworking, and responsible. I told them I was going to America to find a better home for all of us, with the promise that I would send for them all when I was able. It was a very hard decision. We cried," Belinda finished.

"That's a remarkable story of devotion to your family," I told her. "I am in awe of you," I added, wanting to know what happened next.

Belinda hesitated, then agreed to go on.

"Arriving in New York with little money, I searched for a job and moved around, taking shelter from Puerto Rican people I would meet who were very kind to me. As a Puerto Rican, I had American rights, but work still proved hard to find. Then I met a woman on the subway who worked in a factory in Brooklyn, a place I had never been. She told me that they were always looking for workers. I got the address and went there immediately.

"It turned out to be a bagel factory, a big bagel factory. I didn't know what a bagel was. It didn't matter. They needed people and I was there, so I was hired. Minimum wage, graveyard shift—ten o'clock at night to six o'clock in the morning—Monday to Friday. I would earn just under four hundred dollars a week, more than I had ever dreamed. This was America.

"I made bagels overnight for five years, saved every penny, and one by one brought my brothers and sisters to the mainland. I enrolled in junior college and began to earn a degree in nursing. I met my husband, Alfredo, on the bus one morning leaving the factory at six in the morning, and built a life," Belinda shared, still serious and direct.

"You are amazing," I said rather stupidly. But she was amazing.

"One day I was attacked coming out of the factory on a dark street. It was a cold Brooklyn morning. I fought the man off. Probably scared him because I smelled like a giant bagel. Maybe he decided he didn't want to force himself on a big bagel woman. I decided that morning I needed to quit the factory and find another job. Alfredo agreed. Raising kids seemed second nature, and I had the beginnings of a nursing credential, so I applied for a job and landed my first position in Brooklyn as a baby nurse for an Orthodox Jewish family. I loved my job, and I loved the family. Their reference started my new life. That was almost fifteen years ago now, and that is why, Kate, I am here with you."

Summer was ending as the final days of August came upon us. Belinda had another family to report to after Labor Day, in Chicago. We had become very close, but begging was no use. She had completed her task. Buddy was thriving, healthy, and adjusted. She told me it was now my turn to bond with him without her. Belinda would remember us with great fondness, and she would miss Mr. Cole's cooking.

Learning about her life's journey, I felt more spoiled and superficial for worrying about managing a family with one child and an involved husband while still pursuing my own career goals. I made a promise to myself that I would try to go after the dream, not only for GiGi but also now because of Belinda.

The day after Belinda left for her next job in Chicago, I went to my regular appointment with Dr. Grimes. She came back into the examining room following some routine tests with an announcement.

"Kate, did you know that you are about two weeks pregnant?" she said.

"Oh my God, really?"

CHAPTER THIRTY-SEVEN

THE WORLD SLAMS ON THE BRAKES

Indian summer arrived in Newport, as it most always did, just as September dawned. Temperatures were reaching into the nineties, which was unbearable for the beach crowd. They started to drip and moan by eighty-five degrees. Inland from the ocean, the numbers were into the low hundreds. Consequently, it was bumper-to-bumper traffic as a migration of the inland people invaded the beach.

On this September 10, not only was it ninety degrees, but also there was no breeze off the ocean. The beach house was not air-conditioned, so I had all the windows flung open, which I think made things worse. Little Buddy was having a tough time, so I kept sponging him with a cold cloth and providing cool water in his bottle. Eventually we gave up inside—no nap for this hot boy—and went out on to the terrace, which was covered by a large canvas awning. Bringing out a couple of portable fans and a pitcher of ice water, I got us settled in for the afternoon. Finally, Buddy fell asleep in the porta-crib, the hum of the whirling fan serving as music to his little ears and mine.

Cole left the beach house around noon. He had worked all morning preparing a presentation for Ricardo Carondolet, the estranged husband of his client Caroline. Cole had shared that Caroline's last days in the house arrived at the end of August. Her husband had won the money battle, offering her an unknown sum to sign the papers finalizing their financial arrangement prior to ending the marriage in court.

In the end she had no leverage. All the big money was in a family trust, including the house, to which she had no claim. The gravy train had ended. Taking what she could get and packing her ten pieces of Louis Vuitton luggage with designer clothes that she would likely never wear again, thinking that she might even have to sell them at some point, Caroline got on a plane for Dallas. The built Texas blonde secretary formerly associated with big oil was headed back to where it had all begun, her future unknown and uncertain.

Cole also shared that she had kissed him goodbye and apologized for all the tantrums and drama. He, too, apologized for not having kept his promise to get the house sold.

"Cole, you know what, baby, it probably wouldn't have mattered anyway, because Ricardo would never sign the deal. The bastard always gets his way," she had said.

The sale commission on the Carondolet mansion had become an obsession for Cole. He wanted that money in order to buy a house. He wasn't giving up.

Ricardo had arrived in Newport a few days earlier to put his property in order and find a new agent to market the house. Apparently, he was aware of Cole. Caroline must have shared details with him while Cole worked the listing. Cole figured Ricardo had let her move forward with the listing, playing along while knowing that he would not allow her to sell and demand the lion's share.

Having tried repeatedly to reach Ricardo over a few days with no success, Cole decided to try again. Still with his calls unanswered, he prepared the best pitch he could and headed in person to the waterfront mansion, planning to sit at the property's front gate until Ricardo answered or appeared. Not the best strategy, but it was the best Cole could come up with. No one in Newport knew Ricardo Carondolet. He was a ghost.

Front-Door Stalker

Preparing to wait in his car all day if needed to meet Ricardo, Cole's good luck once again tapped on his shoulder. Ricardo opened the gate on the first ring and then opened the grand double door entry himself. There was no butler. "Lurch" had been dismissed along with Caroline; Cole assumed.

Noticing an extra-large moving van parked in front of the mansion, Cole witnessed a crew of men in white overalls covering furniture, packing boxes, and getting ready to move everything out of the home. Ricardo was barking instructions in his loud yet lyrical French Argentine voice.

"May I help you?" he asked as Cole entered. "Are you the moving company manager Mr. Vincent?"

"No, sir. My name is Cole Baldwin."

Before Cole could make his pitch of explanation and purpose, Ricardo stopped him, ordering him to follow into the study. They crossed the entry hall and went into the library room of very fine walnut paneling, now empty, and Ricardo slammed the doors shut, having ordered the movers not to enter. Cole was puzzled. How much did Ricardo know? Was he going to beat him up? Cole tried to speak again and once again was shut down.

"Do not say a word, Mr. Baldwin. I know very well who you are. And I know what you want," Ricardo said sharply.

"Then, sir, may I make a pitch to relist your home?" Cole got that much out before Ricardo barked at him to stop.

"You think I do not know that you want this listing? Do you think I do not know what you did to please my former wife in order to get and keep the listing? I know it all, every sordid detail, right down to the size of your penis. Caroline used you to get back at me just as you used her to make money. So, you see, it is all equal. One large exchange of use for selfish purposes." Ricardo took a beat, and Cole tried to enter the dialogue with something like an apology to change the direction of the conversation.

"I am really sorry, Mr. Carondolet. I didn't know at first that Caroline was still married."

"Oh, please, Mr. Baldwin, do you think I give a goddamn? Do you think I lost sleep over Caroline's sexual exploits with you or, for that matter, anyone else? And yes, there were others, many others. You were hardly special—just another bad boy toy."

Ricardo went on, "So, was it worth it, Mr. Baldwin? More to the point, what will you do to keep this listing with me? What can you offer Ricardo?"

Cole stared at Ricardo Carondolet, unable to find the words. Before him stood a slender, muscular, classically handsome sixty-five-year-old world-class polo champion with a six-foot-four frame, wavy jet-black hair pushed back off his forehead, and piercing green eyes resting above chiseled French Argentinian cheekbones, his face ending in a perfect jawline with a deep cleft in the superwhite skin of his chin.

"Sir, I can sell this house if you will stay with me. I have worked the property for months. I know it inside and out," Cole managed to say in a mild panic.

"Yes indeed, you do know it inside and out," Ricardo responded.

Cole stood in silence as Ricardo made him an offer. Dressed in a white Lacoste polo shirt, collar up, and white short-shorts, Ricardo unzipped his fly and yanked out his man-sized shaved dick. He wore no underwear to stall the reveal. Cole was frozen.

"You want this listing? Then you please me like you pleased my former wife," he said. "I suggest you get down on your knees and start sucking."

"Really?" was all that Cole could say. "Really?"

"Blow for dough, Mr. Baldwin. How badly do you want that major six-figure commission? You were ready to do it with Caroline, so why not a little extra something for me as well?" Ricardo was stroking his dick and bringing it to full erection. Cole was still frozen.

"Last chance, Mr. Baldwin. Blow for dough or get out and I will have to take care of myself," the polo player demanded.

Cole moved closer, starting to kneel as if ready to perform.

"Very good boy. Smart move. Make certain you take it all the way in. All the way," Ricardo said, reaching over and placing his hands on Cole's shoulders. Just as Ricardo touched him, Cole jumped back, then stood up and turned around, darting toward the door of the library. The door was locked; he had trouble opening it. Finally, the lock clicked, and he ran. Ricardo stood in the middle of the empty walnut room, still erect with one hand on his unit, laughing a loud, deep, sinister laugh.

Cole made it out the front gate, breathing heavily and trying to avoid bumping into the stream of moving men loading the van. *Is this a crazy test?* Cole wondered. *Did Ricardo really want a blow job to sign the listing, or was it a test? But a test for what?* If he had leaned in to perform, would Ricardo have wanted it, or would he have beaten him up?

More troubling for Cole was the deeply suppressed feeling that he would have done it—done it for the listing and because he might have liked it. Or at least had no moral problem with it, so he thought. Worse, Kate and Buddy had not even entered his mind. It would have just been another form of sex, not love, not commitment. Sex for business.

Cole did think about his experience at the Holmby Palms Hotel with the male hustler in the locker room. For Cole, he knew the sensation of a male blow. This would be another incident in his life to be compartmentalized in his psyche. Already moving on, forgetting the whole thing, Cole got in his car and headed back to his office.

Now the task at hand was to figure out another way to sell that house and make the commission. Life could be so strange, almost never the way it appeared. Cole had figured that out as a kid in Reno. He was setting out to create a specific reality for himself. Nothing, especially not the shaved erection of a crazy French Argentine polo player, would set him off course.

A Morning Wake-Up Call

The phone rang like mad around six o'clock on the morning of September 11. Its consistent ringing finally forced Cole and me to rise. We tried to ignore it all, but it was no use. Cole had told me over dinner the night before that he had lost the listing on the mansion. We had made up for the loss with a night of love, Cole, the baby-to-come, and me.

He leaned over and embraced me, kissing me on the neck. I managed to reach for the phone.

"Kate, are you awake? Turn on the TV." Nancy was almost out of breath.

"What is it?" Cole asked me, sensing trouble.

"Nancy says turn on the TV." Cole followed my orders. Within seconds, we saw that every channel was exploding with terrifying images showing the destruction of the World Trade Center in New York.

"Oh my God, Mother, what is happening?"

"America is being attacked," she replied. I could hear her trying to hold back tears. Nancy did not cry easily. I tried to offer words of comfort with no idea about what I was saying. The newscasters kept saying "terrorist attack." What did that mean?

Cole started yelling at the screen.

"Oh God, I just saw somebody jump out of a window," he blurted.

In a state of semiconscious panic, I flashed on four-month-old Buddy asleep in the other room while the world was coming to an end. Even worse, I was thinking about bringing into the world an innocent child to face a very uncertain future. Lying naked following a night of passion on our warm and cozy bed, Cole and I watched in terror the collapse of Tower One, which was three thousand miles away.

"Mother, are you okay?" I focused my thoughts.

"Kate, your father is in New York with Jamey. I have been trying desperately to get through, but the phone lines are all jammed. Nothing is getting through, not landline or cell."

"Mother, I didn't know. Why are they there? When did they go?" I begged for information, moving into a real state of panic.

"Your father took Jamey with him on a quick business trip. They left yesterday and are due back late tomorrow," Nancy said.

"Don't worry, I'm sure they are okay," I said with little faith. Nancy knew it, then dropped a bomb.

"Please don't worry too much, Kate, but I have to share that your father had an eight o'clock meeting at the top floor of the World Trade Center with the Kantor Fitzgerald firm."

We both let go of our phones and began screaming. With a horrified expression on his face, Cole grabbed me and held me tight, unaware of the news Nancy had just relayed.

CHAPTER THIRTY-EIGHT

GUT PUNCH

Cole and I left Newport with Buddy minutes after hanging up with Nancy, as soon as we could gather Buddy's stuff and get in the car. We were now facing the morning traffic north on Interstate 405 from San Diego into Los Angeles. The carpool lane was unusually open. Cole punched the accelerator. We were flying. I didn't even try to make him slow down. My level of fear was at a pitch it had never been at before. Were Dalt and Jamey okay? Were they in the tower?

I was manically switching radio channels, searching for news. Every channel was on high news alert, anchors and reporters breathlessly delivering bits and pieces of largely unverified information.

Cole told me to turn it off. His suggestion was a good one. It was making me crazy. Not taking his advice at first, I finally punched the power button of the radio. Cole tried to make light of things, which I did not appreciate. "Hey, kid, I'll need that radio after we learn that Dad and Jamey are okay." Cole rarely called Dalt "Dad." To me, this meant he cared maybe as much as I did. That made me relax, but only a little.

Making it to Beverly Hills in a bit more than an hour, we arrived just after seven o'clock in the morning. The Lexington house was ablaze with lights. Finding the front door ajar, I could hear multiple voices inside as we approached. Cole carried Buddy as I charged in to learn if Nancy had news. As I crossed the threshold, seeing Nancy surrounded by neighbors who had come to offer support, Marta hastily served coffee, trying to hold herself together. She was more visibly shaken than Nancy.

Mother saw me enter and broke through her ring of support. She ran toward me, arms outstretched. Cole and Buddy were right behind. We met midfoyer and embraced, all four of us. Cole and Buddy politely stepped back so that Nancy and I could share a moment.

"Have you had word?" I asked, trying not to cry.

"Nothing, darling. I've tried everything."

"Did you call Dad's New York office?"

"Of course. No connection."

"How about your cousin in Larchmont?"

"Still no luck."

"I suppose it's useless to call the police, hospitals, his hotel?"

"Useless. We just must wait. Your father will call. That's right, there is no doubt; he will call as soon as he can. We will stay here and pray, and he will call."

"Mother, we are here for as long as it takes to find good news. Is that all right?"

"That's what family is all about. We stay together in difficult times, and we celebrate together in the good times. There are plenty of rooms upstairs, including your own. Move in; make Buddy comfortable. Your father and I set up a nursery in the small room adjacent to your bedroom. It is fully stocked. If you wish, you and Cole can share your former bed."

Mother returned to her friends as we went upstairs to get Buddy settled and fed. His schedule had been compromised but was not totally thrown off; everything we were doing was working toward finding a routine. Neither Cole nor I had packed any clothes.

Downstairs, every television blared, each one on a different network. The phone rang, and Nancy jumped. It was just shy of eight o'clock.

"Yes. Hello, Dalt?" Nancy was certainly not her otherwise always composed self.

"This is Westside Pest Control calling to remind you that your technician will be there later this morning."

"Are you kidding me?" she blurted out. She managed to add, "Since when do you call before eight o'clock?" Then she hung up with a slam.

That was pure Nancy. First horrified by such a badly timed call, and then annoyed by its timing and saying so.

Morning turned into evening. Still no word. We watched replays over and over as the first tower fell and then the second. Broadcasters were given to reporting that the United States was on the brink of war. All air traffic and rail traffic were suspended. Hospitals overflowed with the injured. First responders were faced with the ultimate challenge and ultimate sacrifice.

The crowd on Lexington Road swelled, then diminished. Everyone was facing their own fears, needing to be close to their own loved ones.

Cole had suspended all business, not that anyone was serious about buying or selling luxury real estate when war loomed. He devoted himself to Buddy so I could be with my mother. Cole even chipped in helping Marta in the kitchen, preparing sandwiches and snacks for all the friends and neighbors, and Dalt's business associates who also arrived.

By ten o'clock, everyone was gone. Buddy was asleep. Cole and I sat with Mother in the library. The phone was not ringing, and the televisions were temporarily shut off. Nancy required a break from the omnipresent news yet did not want to stay uninformed for too long.

"We'll have to turn it on soon," she said. "Maybe we will catch a glimpse of Dalt or Jamey as one of the cameras covers the people in the street."

"Mother, it's one o'clock in the morning in New York. How could we possibly recognize a face in a flashing second?"

"I would recognize," she replied firmly.

Regretting my comment, I knew that she would recognize Dalt or Jamey if such a miracle were to happen.

Sitting on the leather library furniture all night, never going to bed, but dozing off and on, Nancy had provided cashmere throws. Marta had delivered feather pillows. She also stayed up with us all night, fetching hot tea with lemon and honey. Nancy poured a jigger of schnapps into our tea. We needed it. Yes, I refrained, being pregnant again, unbeknownst to Nancy. Undoubtedly it was the wrong time to bring this up, regardless of the great news.

Still nothing the following morning. Buddy had managed to sleep through the night in an unfamiliar crib. Feeding him a morning bottle, I was still sitting on the library couch, wrapped in two throws and using a pillow to prop Buddy in my arms. Cole was in the kitchen making breakfast with Marta. Nancy was curled up in a deep sleep at the opposite end of the sofa.

At two in the afternoon on the following day, the phone rang. A man from Dalt's New York office finally had managed to get a line through. He told Nancy he had tried calling for hours.

"Oh my God, are my husband and son all right?"

"Mrs. Fairchild, they are alive."

"Thank God. Is there more?"

"Yes. Both Mr. Fairchild and your son are in the hospital."

"In the hospital? What hospital? Do you know what happened? Is it serious?" Nancy begged.

"I'm told they were taken to New York Presbyterian, but that could be false. Information is very unreliable at this time."

"How did you get this information?"

"When the ambulance took both, your husband was able to tell one of the EMTs to call you or his New York office. Apparently, the lines were down across the nation, but the first responder did get through to this office, but not by phone. He came in person this morning to the office. We are only blocks away from the World Trade Center on Wall Street.

"The man did this between making runs to and from the site, darting in and out with no time to spare. I didn't even get his name," the caller shared.

"Did you try to call New York Presbyterian?"

The man explained that he was the only one in the office building. He had been asked by management to try to make it in to handle any emergencies. He was not a broker but rather a security officer. Consequently, he didn't know Dalt, but he had been there to get the message from the EMT. Nancy praised him profusely and went to her computer to begin emailing every hospital in Manhattan. Telephones were still impossible. Air travel remained on hold; however, the news began reporting that limited service would hopefully resume in days. Between sending distress messages to hospitals, Nancy managed to make an online reservation for one ticket from LAX to Kennedy on American on a flight leaving just shy of a week later on Saturday. The internet cautioned that the flight could be canceled.

Mother turned to me and threw her arms around me, hugging me harder than I ever remembered her doing.

"Darling, I'm sorry, I could only get one ticket."

"Are you kidding me? At least you got one. That's all that matters."

"Besides the fact that you're my girl, I really don't want my new mother of a four-month-old in New York with all that's going on. I'm sure your father would agree, bless his living soul—and that of your dear brother."

"We know that they have survived. At least we have hope," I said rather lamely.

"No, darling, we know that they have survived without any doubt."

Cole and I, along with little Buddy, stayed in Beverly Hills for the remainder of the week. My future real estate mogul husband was attentive and caring when not on his cell phone. Fortunately, the entire world was pretty much on hold business-wise. Still, Cole moved full speed ahead working on his TV show, also trying hard to land a purchase client for the Carondolet mansion, along with laying plans for negotiations with the California Ranch Corporation, which was developing a new section of spectacular untouched hillside coastal land on the Newport coast being called Society Hill.

By week's end, communications began to flow. Phone connections remained hit-and-miss, but some calls were getting through. Nancy also received emails from many of the hospitals. Some five responses that she had opened relayed negative information. Three others were still to come.

"Maybe they are not in a hospital. Perhaps they're in some other facility or a clinic. Who knows?" Nancy confided just as she got a response from Mount Sinai Hospital. It was short. "Dalton Fairchild and James Fairchild are patients at Mount Sinai. For more information, please call or email Dr. Lewis Silver."

The message included information on how to contact the doctor. Nancy hit send before she could speak. Checking with American Airlines, she found that her upcoming Saturday morning flight was still scheduled to depart LAX. Cole came up behind Nancy at the computer and put his arms around her, kissing her on the cheek.

"You always knew it would be okay," he said. Nancy turned her head to her side and nodded a thank-you, saying nothing. Marta was standing behind us, and she began to sob. As I was comforting her and hugging her, she wiped her tears with a kitchen cloth in her right hand.

It had been a remarkable week at my childhood home. The 9/11 drama and fear for my father and brother's safety would not affect the young life of baby Buddy, who slept through it all. He took his bottle on schedule and had his diapers changed without awareness of the world-changing events taking place. I was particularly struck by the eerie silence of the previous days: no airline traffic above, very few cars on the roads, the familiar noise of daily life coming to a halt. The stillness and quiet was something I had never experienced. Surely it had been the norm in centuries past. I time-traveled to colonial times in the United States, then to early California before the gold rush. This was the quiet of daily life. How strange. Imagine only knowing the vibration of modernity, never to experience the peacefulness of an uncomplicated planet. We'd had a fleeting image of the past for two days, unexpected and unprepared for, even amid numbing worry over my father and brother and the future for my child and child-to-come. Not to mention the rest of the planet.

The unique moment in time was short-lived. On Saturday morning, Cole, Buddy, and I drove Nancy to LAX for her morning flight, and the real world resumed. I could hear the planes again, and traffic was flowing on the 405 freeway.

As we were exiting the freeway at Century Boulevard, Nancy's cell phone buzzed.

"Mrs. Fairchild, this is Dr. Silver." Nancy put the phone on speaker. I let out a controlled gasp.

"Yes, Doctor, thank you so much for calling. Please tell me about my husband and son."

"It is good news, Mrs. Fairchild. Both are doing well and will fully recover from their injuries," the doctor said.

"Thank God," Nancy said with serious relief. "Can you tell me the diagnosis?"

"From what I know, your husband is another hero of the 9/11 emergency. He and your son were on the street beside the North Tower as it began to collapse. They stood beside a group of several people who had just fled the building, covered in dust and attempting to shake it off. Your son apparently saw a large piece of the falling building coming down in their direction and yelled at your husband to look out. There was little time to do anything. Your husband threw himself on top of James, also covering and protecting several of the others, taking them down onto the street under him. The block of flying debris managed to avoid a direct hit, but it did wound your husband's shoulder and arm. It also crushed your son's left arm and scraped the side of his head. The blow knocked the wind out of all of them. Yet, all survived and were transported by EMTs to multiple facilities.

"Mr. Fairchild and your son were originally taken to New York Presbyterian but were transferred here to Mount Sinai's orthopedic clinic. Both were given morphine for the pain and arrived partially conscious," Dr. Silver said. "Given the extreme nature of the many casualties, their treatment was not deemed emergency status, so both were kept sedated on feeding tubes for a couple of days, being fully monitored until we could arrange surgery. As we speak, both are out of surgery and going into recovery."

"Oh, Dr. Silver, that's the best news. I can never thank you enough, but I will do my best when I get to New York later today. I'm on the way to the airport as we speak."

"Safe travels, Mrs. Fairchild. I look forward to meeting you when you arrive. I can tell you that New York is a very different city today."

"I'm sure of that. God bless you, Dr. Silver."

The phone clicked off. We all sat in silence for a moment, then burst into joyous chatter.

Dropping Nancy off at the American Airlines Terminal 4, we kissed goodbye and promised to do everything possible to communicate. The airport was busy. The quiet world had indeed vanished.

Cole maneuvered the car around the airport concourse, and we made our way back onto the 405, traveling south back to Newport Beach. Buddy was beginning to stir in his car carrier, with me sitting in the rear seat next to him and stroking his little forehead. Feeling incredible relief over the good news about my father and brother, my mind began to focus on Dr. Silver's words to Nancy.

"Your husband is a hero," he had said.

I had always known that my father was a hero—my hero, and now a hero who had placed himself on top of others at his own peril, especially to protect his son and my brother.

CHAPTER THIRTY-NINE

THE NEW NORMAL

Nancy made it to New York without drama. A car waited for her at Kennedy. She arrived at Mount Sinai Hospital and found my father's room within the hour. Learning that Jamey was in surgery for a second round of orthopedic adjustment on his crushed left arm, she also learned that the falling cement had hit his left side and splintered his left elbow into small shards of bone. Doctors advised that Jamey would require at least two more operations, followed by a month of traction in rehab. Without a full recovery, he could lose his arm.

Under mild sedation, Dalt was sleeping when Nancy found him. At first, she wasn't sure if he had any idea of her presence. Taking his right hand, she squeezed. Dalt responded. Practically jumping over him and onto the bed, Nancy kissed him wherever flesh was available to kiss. Father apparently did not awake, yet Nancy reported that he had a slight smile after she'd kissed him on both cheeks, his forehead, the tip of his nose, and finally his lips. Pulling up a chair, she waited, still clasping his right hand.

At eight o'clock that evening on her day of travel and worry, Dalt began to rally, if only slightly. A nurse came in to check vitals. Seeing that Nancy had not left his side, the nurse asked Nancy if she wanted something to eat. The hospital kitchen was closed for the night, but the nurse had plenty of snacks. She pulled out packages of peanut butter crackers, tubes of string cheese, and even Lorna Doone cookies. Nancy accepted, taking all the items. The nurse finished her routine, assuring Nancy that Dalt was coming around nicely. Nancy pressed for more information, knowing nothing about his injury and condition. Responding that Dr. Silver would appear shortly, the nurse excused herself, recounting the exhaustion experienced by everyone in the hospital over the past week. Releasing Dalt's hand, Nancy rose to her feet and moved toward the nurse to hug her and bless her for her selfless service and care for both Dalt and Jamey.

Dr. Silver entered, passing the nurse and almost running into Nancy in the doorway. He looked worn out, his thin gray hair standing on end as if he either had been electrocuted or was running from a hurricane. His glasses precariously clung to the end of his nose, and he emanated a faint odor of perspiration resulting from days of undoubtedly wearing the same clothes, never leaving the hospital.

"You must be Mrs. Fairchild. I'm Dr. Lewis Silver." He put out his hand.

"Forget the hand," Nancy replied, grabbing the good doctor and giving him

313

a kiss on the cheek. "Doctor, can you update me? How is Jamey? Is he out of surgery? May I see him?"

"He is in recovery now and shall be in his room in a couple of hours, maybe by ten tonight."

"Did you perform the surgery?"

"No, I am your husband's primary doctor, and I am also overseeing Jamey as I am the chief of surgery here. Let me assure you that your son is in the care of one of our finest orthopedic surgeons, Dr. Barad."

"Please tell me about my husband?" Nancy continued.

"Mr. Fairchild will make a full recovery, but his injuries are serious. He suffered a collapsed lung, a damaged spleen, a severely bruised spine, and four broken ribs, and as a result, he had considerable internal bleeding. We have been running multiple tests to clear him of other potential problems, especially infection. Currently, he is on heavy antibiotics to fight infection, along with strong painkillers for the extensive pain resulting from the number of broken ribs, which as you know cannot be operated on or braced. They must heal. It is very painful and will take at least two months' time. We are recommending that both your husband and Jamey check into a rehab facility in New York for at least a month following release from the hospital. I do not recommend any travel, not for some time. I want them here for follow-up."

"This sounds very serious, Dr. Silver. What can I do?" Nancy replied.

"Being here for them is the best medicine. My staff will help you make arrangements for rehab and will also help you with hotel accommodations close by, when you make a decision on the proper place to go."

Turning to face Nancy, Dr. Silver asked if she had made a hotel reservation for the night. She said that she had not, adding that she planned to stay in the room with Dalt, if permissible.

"I can sleep in a chair," she advised. "May I stay here as long as my husband remains?"

"You may, Mrs. Fairchild. Let us know how we can make you more comfortable."

With that, Dr. Silver excused himself to check on Dalt's labs and collect his vitals. Then he performed a quick exam on the patient, who was only beginning to wake up.

Finishing the routine, Dr. Silver gently patted Dalt on the leg, telling him he was doing fine. Dalt opened his eyes slightly, fixing them on the doctor, who was blocking Nancy from view.

As Dr. Silver turned to leave, Dalt saw Nancy. Out of his dry mouth, with a tube protruding from one corner, he let out a muted cry, more like a joyful grunt of recognition. Nancy dashed to his bedside, carefully placing herself back on his bed just to his left side, away from the tubes that were providing lifesaving medicine.

"Darling, I'm here. You are going to be just fine," she said, holding back tears.

Before leaving, Dr. Silver asked Nancy if he could speak with her in the hallway. Nancy carefully moved off the side of Dalt's bed, whispering to him that she would be right back. In the hallway, Dr. Silver presented some news that was difficult to hear.

"I do not want to alarm you, but I have some concerns about your son. He has been seen by trauma specialists, and we are very likely to advise further treatment for what appears at this time to be posttraumatic stress. Jamey was hit very hard by the concrete and perhaps hit even harder from the mental impact of witnessing the towers fall. Surely, he also witnessed people jumping to their deaths and so many other incidents making up the overall warlike terror of the experience."

"We will do whatever it takes, as long as it takes, to bring my Jamey back to normal." Nancy feared her false optimism was transparent.

"Our lab tests show that Jamey struggles with substance abuse and is currently on prescribed medications to counter his cravings and offer a sense of balance. I'm afraid we may be in for challenges," Dr. Silver added.

"Yes, Doctor, it is so. But Jamey made real progress over the past year. He lives a drug-free life, has returned to school, and has been adjusting with success," Nancy informed.

"This may set him back, Mrs. Fairchild. Again, we will do all we can. Let's just wait and see. But I wanted to prepare you."

"Will someone come and get me around ten o'clock to see him when he comes out of recovery?" Nancy asked.

"Either I will do so, or I'll send someone," Dr. Silver responded. "I'll be around all night if you need me. For now, stay with your husband and try to get some rest. The nurse will bring you blankets and a pillow, as well as some toiletries. Welcome to New York, Mrs. Fairchild, the greatest city in the world."

Nothing Will Stand in His Way

I gave Cole credit, a great deal of credit, for standing with my family in a time of trouble and uncertainty. Before, I had never counted on anyone other than my parents, and now I relied on Cole's support. My father and brother had been lost in a city reeling after an unforeseen attack. This was unimaginable for most Americans, especially those my age raised in a time and place of coveted and unappreciated security. Cole reinforced that feeling of security in me. In part because of him, I had been able to believe Dalt and Jamey would be located and safe.

The minute after dropping off Nancy at LAX to go find my family in New

York, my husband was back to work. For days he had silenced his cell phone, only discreetly making business calls as much out of my presence as possible and away from my mother and others. He was working on details for his television show, which was being reinvented from the half-hour real estate advertisement running on brokered time on local cable and being turned into a reality pilot for potential network syndication. Cole shared that the new show would be called *Living the Dream*, a title he was proud to have created. The focus would be an insider's look at the luxury homes of the rich. Cole would host, narrate, and do an interview and home tour.

And if that weren't enough, Cole had confided that Ricardo Carondolet had given the listing on his waterfront mansion to another broker in Cole's office. The new agent had been given a sixty-day window to bring an offer. Cole knew the guy; they were office friends. He also knew that this guy had bluffed his way into the listing with no chance of bringing a buyer within sixty days. Cole did have a potential buyer but clearly needed to stay out of the deal. So, he made a deal of his own, turning over the buyer for a 50 percent silent referral fee of the commission, which would essentially net him the same commission amount if he still held the listing and had to deal with an outside broker bringing in the buyer. Many times, he had told me that with this money we could buy our first home together. Funny thing, I was happy in our beach cottage with no urgency to be a homeowner. I knew it was Cole's dream, something he had never known as a child growing up in a rented house in Reno.

His silent partner would present the offer at week's end, following some additional negotiation and signatures from the potential buyer. Cole was amazed that his buyer had offered the full listing price of fifteen million dollars, a figure Cole had thrown at Caroline to entice her, knowing it was probably three million over market price.

Anyway, the calls had come nonstop over the next days and into the following week. In between all of that, my husband ran back and forth to Los Angeles, working with partners on the TV project. I hardly saw him for what seemed like a month. As September rolled into October, I enjoyed many visits on the phone with Dalt, and fewer with Jamey, who was having a rough time. My mother remained in New York on duty full time with husband and son. Progress was being made. Relieved, I mentally focused on Buddy and taking care of myself, now three-plus months pregnant and feeling the change.

Every day I also thought about my clothing line, or at least the beginning of that dream. I spoke to Monsieur on a regular basis. He calmed me down, assuring me that it would be there when I was ready and able. More importantly, he and Madame would be there as well to support me, help me, and guide me, promising that they would lead me to some kind of progress and to realization of the demanding plan to market my clothes in a real store somehow, somewhere. It was unrealistic, I was sure, but I still wanted to be in the window at Neiman's and even more so in the window of Bergdorf's on Fifth Avenue in New York. Okay, every twenty-year-old woman has dreams. Life did not yet present roadblocks I could not handle. Knowing that my life's umbrella was based largely on being a woman of privilege, I was neither spoiled nor greedy. Never spending money foolishly, I was not a Beverly Hills princess brat.

Given all that had happened on 9/11, I considered turning over the one million in inheritance I had received from GiGi to Cole as my share of an investment in a possible new home for our family. Perhaps it would take some of Cole's self-imposed pressure off his back to make the big commission on the sale of the Carondolet mansion. For that matter, I never had shared with my husband any facts pertaining to my trust. Cole knew I received a monthly allowance of five thousand dollars. What he did not know was that the five thousand dollars was a small portion of the actual interest on the trust, paid monthly. The majority was reinvested. My trust was valued at ten million dollars. Maybe it was time to be transparent.

Why? For the obvious reason: Cole loved me, and he loved our son and our future child. He knew my family had wealth, and this fact made him want to work harder. He took it as a challenge to prove himself worthy of this rich American girl—his own self-imposed challenge.

What mattered to me was to be real and in the present. I did not live in the past or in the future, for that matter.

Despite having this ten-million-dollar trust and a monthly income, I was a practical rich girl, a "one day at a time" woman. This I had learned from my mother. "Take each day as it comes. Make the most of the daylight. Laugh, love, and do not be distracted by anyone or anything that enters your life in a negative way." Such advice from Nancy was always followed with, "Face your challenges. Solve them. Move on. Adversity is an education on the path to success."

Facing the reality that my fashion career was definitely on hold, I made my choice to focus on family, including my young child and the one to come. I wanted to be with them every day, to experience it all. I wanted to make the most of the daylight with them and, as it turns out for mothers with infants, most of the dark of night too.

Financial security can hamper ambition. Hunger is a powerful motivation. Looking in the mirror, I was captivated by the concept of personal creativity, including conquering a task and building a business. This partially validated the fact that I am my father's child. As a role model, especially in business, Dalt was on a pedestal I had put him on.

Making the decision to offer my treasure from GiGi to my husband, I planned to tell him tonight when he came home. We were scheduled to go to the home of one of Cole's new potential clients on Lido Isle for dinner and to meet new friends. Arranging for a baby nanny to stay late, I planned to dress for dinner early and present Cole with a bit of champagne and a few hors d'oeuvres before going to dinner. I would tell him about the money after our twilight toast.

Big News and Big Boobs

Cole came through the cottage door at five on the dot. He was never one minute late. I, on the other hand, was not so punctual. The small celebration I had created was waiting on the beachfront terrace. Dressed for our first couples' dinner party in Newport as married adults, I wore a bright orange sleeveless fitted flared dress that was fastened at the neck and free and loose at the waist. Matching black patent sling-back pumps and my standard uniform look, a black satin bow tied around my thick blonde hair, which was pulled back in a ponytail, completed the look. It was October, with Halloween just around the corner.

My husband laughed when he first saw me.

"You look like a very hot-looking hundred-pound pumpkin that is capable of feeding a baby. Do you offer pumpkin-flavored milk?" he joked.

"If I were breastfeeding, I could offer multiple flavors," I responded. "I would have grape with a purple dress, lime with lime, lemon with lemon, and best of all, chocolate with brown. And I'm sure your son would love the chocolate."

Cole came and sat next to his family on the wicker settee. He stroked Buddy's forehead, then mine.

"I'm not a poodle," I offered with a smile. So, Cole leaned over and kissed me with all the passion that had made me fall for him.

"I'll be your Great Dane if you'll be my poodle," he said.

After breaking away from his kiss, all I could say was, "Woof, woof."

Cole howled like a hound. We laughed. I poured champagne for him and the usual water for me, and we shared a few Hawaiian-style BBQ chips, some olive tapenade, and some sliced hard salami and cheddar cheese. Then I laid it on him.

"Cole darling, I have something to share."

"Uh-oh, I don't think you've ever called me 'darling.' You're already pregnant, so that can't be it. Your fashion line isn't ready, so Bloomingdale's can't be calling with an order. You look very healthy, so I know it's not your health. Okay, give it to me bottom line, no sugarcoating."

"That coming from the prince of sugarcoating," I joked.

"Touché."

"It's just my small contribution to keeping you grounded. Only so you won't fly away because of too much hot air."

"My hot air is all for you, my love."

"Cole, I want to open up with you about something."

"Okay," Cole said, looking perplexed.

"How about another champagne?" I inquired.

"Do I need one?" he replied.

"Might be a good idea."

Cole held up his flute. I poured. He took a large sip.

"Cole, I want to share with you a million dollars that GiGi left me when she died."

Cole sent the champagne in his mouth spraying out over my Hawaiian BBQ chips. "I think you just created a new brand of chips—salt and champagne," I said. Cole laughed.

"I'm sorry, darling. Yes, I can use that word too. What are you talking about?"

"Just what I said. GiGi left me money to help me launch a fashion line. I've decided to launch our life together. Use this money to buy us a home. It's your dream, and I want to make it happen."

Cole teared up. I followed. Buddy kept playing with his dinner. He wanted none of the interruption. Pausing for a minute, Cole came back and told me he didn't want the money, saying that it was his job to buy us a home.

"I love you for offering. But no," he said.

"Really? I am serious."

"Yes, really. Can we talk about this later? It's time to go to dinner at the Murphys' house. I love you. Okay, I'll think about it," Cole said, giving in. "But I doubt I'll change my mind. I'm a stubborn macho-ass Cuban Italian stallion."

Buddy finished dinner, and the nanny took him as Cole and I left the cottage for our grown-up dinner party.

Arriving at the Murphys' home on Lido Isle, apparently the last to do so, we were greeted by Tom Murphy, a real estate investor Cole had met at a seminar on buying and flipping single-family homes in the high-end market. The strength of the upward climb in prices for coastal California property was now bringing in foreign investment as Dalt had predicted; values were escalating into the mind-numbing digits.

Cole wanted part of that action. In the perfect place at the right time, he knew that this new area of spectacular untouched Newport California coastline was developing. Named "Society Hill" with unobstructed views of the Pacific Ocean, and with gently rolling hills and cypress and palm trees dotting the landscape, this was the American version of the French and Italian Riviera.

Tom Murphy had come from a family with money. Cole had formulated the right pitch. A bond was created between Tom and Cole, with my husband looking for the right deal to launch the business venture. Dinner tonight was important to Cole. The wives needed to bond as well to help seal the deal.

"Are you sure you want to bring a pumpkin to meet your potential business partners?" I chided Cole as Tom Murphy and his wife Daisy welcomed us at the front door.

"You are my pumpkin," Cole whispered. I gave him a strong pat on his arm with the back of my hand.

"Ouch, that hurt," he protested. "I thought *pumpkin* was a term of endearment—as in, 'Hello, my pumpkin.'"

"You've been watching too much TV," I replied.

"I hardly ever watch TV, except my commercials," Cole came back. "It's just something people call one another, like honey bunny, or lovebug, or babycakes ..."

"Really? Who are you?" I gave him that grin.

"I guess you can take the boy out of Reno, but you can't take Reno out of the boy," he said. Cole was nothing if not disarmingly self-deprecating when it was called for. For a guy with a huge ego, his self-deprecation was another reason I loved him. He made me laugh.

Tom and Daisy Murphy were characters out of the central casting look book, Ken and Barbie in the flesh. Both were tall, but not too tall. Both were blond, but not too blond, and perfectly dressed. They even smelled good. Tom was scented with an ocean breeze, and Daisy smelled like her name.

Tom spoke first. "Cole, so glad you could make it. This must be Kate. May I say you look stunning in orange?"

Cole giggled discreetly.

Tom's voice was deep, more like the voice of a big burly football player, which contrasted with his rather slight physique and fresh-faced good looks.

"Do you like the orange? Is it too much the week of Halloween?" I asked.

Daisy answered, "Never too much, Kate. It's fabulous. Tell me where you got that dress. I'm Daisy, Tom's wife, by the way. Won't you both come in? We don't want to spend our evening standing in the entry hall, do we?"

As we were walking through the main rooms of the Lido residence, Tom filled Cole and me in on the Murphys' recent million-dollar remodel of the Mediterranean villa that was once owned by a famous movie star from the golden age of Hollywood. Tom mentioned the guy's name several times, but it didn't resonate with me. Besides, I could have cared less, having grown up surrounded by movie stars. They came and went—just people.

Getting over myself, trying not to be too obviously not caring or aloof, a quality or lack thereof that I have been called out for, for all my life, I had to say that the Murphy home was exquisite. It was elegant, classic, and refined, not trendy or glittery—just rich without being pretentious. And even with all the expensive good taste, I still felt that I could plop down in a chair or on the sofa and curl up with a book and a blanket. Maybe the Murphys weren't so bad and one-dimensional, or maybe they just had a great decorator.

Every October in Newport extended summer on the Pacific coast. The coming of fall was in the air, yet the tree leaves hadn't yet turned red and gold. Still, one could smell the aroma of the seasonal transition. That so-called aroma only began on this day, even though the temperature had reached eighty-two degrees.

At twilight, with an earlier-setting sun, the temperature remained in the low seventies. Daisy Murphy had chosen to throw her dinner party in their amazing new conservatory sunroom constructed of glass doors and a white lattice domed ceiling. It was a junior version of Mrs. A's solarium.

All their guests were sharing cocktails and hors d'oeuvres as we entered. At first glance, I counted eight people. In addition to us and our hosts, that made twelve for dinner. In the center of the conservatory was a long dining table set for twelve. Each place setting boasted a place card, with such formalities being de rigueur at Newport parties. Nothing had been left to chance. Tom and Daisy introduced us to all their friends. Yes, I was charming with no aloofness. Since I was not drinking, I slipped away to snoop at the dinner placements and found our seats. Tom had placed Cole at the opposite end of the table across from him at the head. I was next to Cole at his left. Every other placement appeared to be man–woman. This gave me some sense of relief. I had feared all the couples would be mixed up to create conversation, which was not my thing with strangers. The only thing worse was going to the dentist.

Dinner was ready to be served. We took our places. The chatter never ceased. When all twelve of us were at the beautifully set table about to dine off glistening vintage floral Haviland china, with complementary polished sterling fashioned in a coordinating floral pattern, accompanied by a striking lineup of Baccarat crystal awaiting water, wine, champagne, and an after-dinner surprise, I realized that we were are all clones of one another.

The women were all blonde, pretty, slim, and dressed perfectly, each sporting formidable jewelry, carrying a small clutch with a big label, and talking pretty much nonstop about where they had gone on summer holiday. Other topics of note included what big events they were attending on the fall social calendar in Newport; the challenge of finding and keeping good help; dinner at the latest restaurant; and what A-list charity groups were essential to join this season on the coast.

Becoming instantly depressed, I buried my despair and carried on, doing my best to chatter away too. With no other choice, I knew my involvement was all for my husband, who was doing his best to win over business connections. Dalt had advised him to join social groups, meet the players, and view every major social opportunity as an entrée to creating a business connection. Cole had taken my father's advice to heart. At least I knew that, and on a certain real level I did admire him for it, even though I thought, make that *knew*, I wanted to run out of the Murphy house screaming, "Take me, Jesus! I've had enough." I suppose that is dramatic for a woman barely twenty-one. What can I say? While I may not be so smart, I do know myself pretty darn well.

After the Murphys' catering staff removed the third course entrée dishes, a palate cleanser of lemon sorbet was served in a hollowed-out lemon half on a crystal dish. Tom and Daisy stood up at the table, where she was seated to the left of her husband in a similar fashion to Cole and me at the other end. Daisy took her spoon and clinked on the dish of sorbet.

"Tom and I hope you have enjoyed our dinner so far tonight. May I ask for a round of applause for Chef Milton?" she requested.

The chef peered out of the swinging door leading to the kitchen and saluted his employer.

"Now I have a little surprise for all of you gentlemen here at the table tonight," Daisy said, beginning to slur her speech. It had been an evening of nonstop drinking to support nonstop chatter. I feared that Cole, too, was halfway gone.

Daisy said, "We girls have planned a little surprise tonight. Some of you know that five of us here tonight made a little pact. Sorry to leave you out, Kate. You're the new girl on the block," she said. I waved my acceptance. Daisy continued, "Girls, please stand at your places, and on the count of three, let's all display our gifts. One ... two ... three ... go!"

At "go," all five women dropped the tops of their dresses to the waist, revealing their breasts. I have to say, one was more beautiful than the next. They giggled; they posed; they even swung their breasts around. Their husbands howled and hooted. The liquor flowed; champagne corks popped like bullets.

Looking over at Cole, I saw that he, too, was hooting. I think I was shocked. What was going on? Would an orgy follow? Was this a prelude to a remake of *Bob, Carol, Ted, and Alice*, a movie from the 1960s that I had discovered as a teenager because I had loved Natalie Wood ever since I was a child watching *Miracle on 34th Street* every Christmas?

Daisy raised another glass and cleared up my confusion.

"So, dear men, your wives have all visited Doctor Klein. At your request, I might add. Are you pleased with the results?"

The hooting turned to screams of primal sexual obsession the likes of which I had never heard. Then the topper took the cake, before the cake was served. The perfectly conservative Daisy Murphy, with the house exquisitely decorated, who had just served an elegant dinner, stripped down to her panties and, wearing high heels, proceeded to parade around the table, then through the house, requesting all her guests to line up and follow her in a conga line. This could not have been improvised; it must have been planned. The bare-breasted blondes lined up first behind her, with the men at the back of the line. Looking at Cole, I could tell that he knew we were not lining up. Taking my hand, he led me toward the back rather sheepishly, although he was certainly curious. Where the heck were we going? Cole noticed that Tom had vanished.

Next thing we knew, the chorus line, led by our mostly nude hostess, was out of the classic Mediterranean villa's front door and onto the street. They were out and walking down the middle of the street. The men all had fallen back and were watching from the sidewalk.

Then, Tom appeared driving his Jaguar convertible, top down, high-beam lights on, aimed behind the chorus line of wives, sending ethereal beams of light skyward into the black night. Music blared from the radio; he was honking his horn. Neighbors on both sides of the street were gathering at their windows.

The parade disbanded at the dead end of the street upon reaching a white sand beach on the Newport bayfront. A small pier jutted out from the beach into the bay. Daisy was the first to leap into the water. The rest dropped the remainder of their clothing and joined her, one by one, diving off the pier.

Sirens were heard in the distance.

"Cole, I think it's time to go home. Are you ready?"

Cole nodded, not saying a word. We made a dash for our car.

"Just another fun night in Newport," I told my husband. He still said nothing. I drove home.

CHAPTER FORTY

LIFE IS GOOD

As Christmas neared, I took stock of my blessings. Never religious, I instead chose to embrace the concept of God as an overwhelming and mysterious force of good in the universe. Needless to report, I had not been the pet in any of my Sunday school classes at Beverly Hills Episcopal Church. As early as I can remember, maybe by the time I was nine or ten, I had asked so many questions of my youth ministers and teachers that the only thing I vividly recall was the familiar look of eyes rolling back into heads. Eventually, at thirteen in the eighth-grade class, I became a Sunday school dropout.

To my relief, and to my surprise, Nancy and Dalt never objected. We had a little talk. I presented my case, or views I guess would be more accurate, and my parents accepted. Nancy told me the church door would always be open and welcoming. Dalt said that I should come to him anytime to discuss religion. My father never seemed religious, so this was a curious offer, even to a precocious eighth grader.

Pressing for meaning, not understanding his offer, I asked my father if he knew God. Dalt took a step back, staring at Nancy.

"That's quite a question from a thirteen-year-old," he said.

Nancy jumped in. "Darling, now you know why Kate is a Sunday school dropout."

"Well, I would think if she asked questions like that, then the church fathers would welcome giving the child more in-depth study, rather than let her drift."

"Seriously, Father. If you know God, does God know you? Tell me," I asked.

"Kate, for now let me share this. I believe that God is everywhere and in everything living and inanimate. God is here with us in this house. God is inside of you, my daughter. Every move you make, every thought you have, and every question you ask has God right there in all of it. God is in every rose in your mother's garden. Who or what else but God could make a rose?"

"Is God in an elephant?" I blurted out, not knowing where that thought had come from.

"Yes, Kate, God is in every elephant. Who or what else could create such a beautiful creature with such a trunk?" Father answered.

"So, roses, elephants, and all of us are all part of God? That is how you know God?" I came back.

"I know God for all those reasons and so many more. Mostly I know God because he gave me your mother and she and God gave me you and Jamey."

I often remember that talk with Dalt and Nancy, but especially and always at the end of the year when lights are twinkling, Christmas music fills the shopping malls, and the bells are rung by Salvation Army volunteers standing on corners, holding out their red buckets.

For me, this Christmas month in Newport was low-key, quiet, and peaceful. My second pregnancy had been an easy one so far. I was closing in on five months. Buddy was reaching eight months and was just a remarkable baby. Every day he was changing as he approached his one year of life on the planet. I could already see he was not an infant but a pretoddler for sure. No doubt Buddy would be walking and saying words by his first birthday.

The greatest news of the season was that Dalt and Jamey were ready to come home with Nancy. I had been in constant communication with all of them over the previous ten weeks while the nation continued to lick its wounds over 9/11. My own family had survived and recovered and were coming home right after the New Year.

There would be no big Christmas celebration for the Fairchilds in New York this year. Nancy planned a small family dinner at the rehab center. She'd bring in food from some great New York bistro. She shared that Dalt was nearly 100 percent, but that my brother, Jamey, would need some more care back in California. I had spoken to my brother several times each week; he sounded pretty good to me. Jamey only wanted to come home and stay with Cole, Buddy, and me at the beach.

"Your bed is ready when you are, Jamey. We can't wait to see you," I told him on every call.

On the Cole front, you might say that we both had fallen for fall. Our sex life over the past two months after breast parade at the Murphys' was rather record-breaking. On that night, watching five women march down the street, being followed by the high beams of a Jaguar blasting the music of the song by Lady Marmalade "Voulez-Vous Coucher avec Moi?" I had been somewhat offended.

When we got home to the cottage, I had made the first move on Cole in the kitchen. We were naked by the time we reached the stairs and had full on intercourse at the top of the landing. Making it to bed after the first climax, Cole cupped his hand over my mouth to prevent me from screaming and waking Buddy and the baby nanny. That was the first of three orgasms. The evening ended with morning sex in the shower just after the sun had risen.

We both sank to the white marble floor of the shower, still being rained on by the showerhead, lying down, totally wrapped in each other's arms.

"Do you really want to go to work today?" I said in a whisper. Cole hesitated for a moment.

"If I don't go and we keep this up, we might end up making Buddy an orphan. When the coroner comes, he'll have to list the cause of death as sex overdose."

Making It on His Own

Dalt had offered Cole that large financial backing when we got married. Before the 9/11 tragedy, Cole and I had met with Dalt and Nancy in Beverly Hills for one of those financial future kind of talks. The proposed fifty-million-dollar investment fund came up, and Dalt told Cole that the ten investors were lined up, each willing to guarantee five million dollars for a fund set up to purchase exclusive land in the new Society Hill development on the Newport coast to build luxury villas overlooking the Pacific.

Clearly excited, Cole had seen the opportunity of a lifetime in front of him. Then he said something to Dalt and Nancy that shocked me.

"Your offer is the most generous proposal ever presented to me—the chance for big success, a major home run for me, for us, laid out on a silver tray. But I am going to decline respectfully," Cole had told Dalt. Nancy looked as if she had just swallowed an onion.

Turning to my husband, I put my hand on his and smiled, saying nothing.

"Really?" Dalt responded. "Are you sure?" he added.

Cole came back immediately. "I have tasted success on my own, in great part thanks to your first deal, which set me up. I like the feeling of independence. I think I can do this on my own. I have much to prove to myself," he said.

Dalt looked impressed yet surprised, asking, "Cole, do you have a plan?"

"Yes, sir, I do. It's not in cement. Can I share it and ask for your advice?"

"Of course, son."

"I have met a new friend in Newport with access to financing, and he is willing to work with me to buy a first lot, then build a house and sell it. Over the past year I have sold ten properties, beginning with yours, and have earned net commissions of around three hundred thousand dollars. And this week it just got much better. I delivered a buyer on a bayfront estate that I previously listed. It closed Friday at a price of fifteen million. My commission after expenses and split will come to around two hundred thousand dollars. My plan is to use this income to invest with my friend Tom Murphy to buy a lot and build a house to sell."

Cole spoke with such a professional demeanor, a side of him that impressed me. I knew his drive, his ambition, and his talk, but this was different. He had just laid out a genuine plan that made sense. Yet, part of me felt left out. Why had he not shared this with me? All we had talked about lately was finding a house of our own. I knew he had not given up on the Carondolet sale since losing the listing when Mr. Carondolet took over from his wife. Cole had shared the fact that the guy was a big jerk.

But he hadn't told me that he found a buyer. I was getting used to the secrecy, not because I liked it or because I believed he was hiding anything. Rather, Cole was this macho guy who figured his wife didn't need to be involved in the man's business. Pretty old-fashioned for a millennial.

When Cole confided in my dad, I tried to interrupt and tell him that I wanted to be a part of the plan. I wanted him to know that I could be trusted and could offer a valuable opinion or an alternate idea, or at least serve as a sounding board. I wanted to be his true partner no matter what.

Still, I had kept my mouth shut, showing a failure to act. This was Cole's moment. Dalt seemed very proud of him. Nancy, I was certain, was thinking what I was thinking. Strong women, especially close mothers and daughters, share mental transference bigtime. We finished each other's sentences. We laughed at the same time without saying a word. I think they call it *simpatico*. Whatever it is called, it was the real deal.

On the drive back to Newport, I sat in the back seat next to Buddy, who was buckled in his car seat. Cole did not talk. Traffic south on Interstate 405 was moderate. The radio played a Madonna song. Buddy was kicking his feet and moving his little hands to the beat. I broke the silence.

"Cole, you never mentioned that you were doing business with Tom Murphy."

"Baby, I can't hear you from behind. What did you say?"

Unlatching the seat belt, I leaned up against the back of the front seat. After a quick blow in Cole's ear, I repeated my question.

"It's kind of a new arrangement, nothing formal, just talk," Cole said. "Was it a mistake to turn down your father's offer?"

"Not a mistake, but I wish you would have shared this with me. I felt really left out of our life," I told him, massaging his shoulder from behind.

Cole did not reply right away. I think I had touched a nerve, or perhaps he had just never considered my feelings about his business deals.

"I'm sorry you felt left out. It was not my intention. To be honest, I've never thought of you as my business partner, Kate."

"That's pretty clear. Strong marriages are made of equal partners."

"Kate, you never cared about real estate. At least I never thought so."

"I care about you. I care about us and our family, so yes, I care about real estate or anything else you do."

"I hear you, but this is going to be hard for me. I was not raised like you. My parents were partners, but not like Dalt and Nancy. When I was growing up poor, my dad had the last word, pretty much the only word. Mom was the traditional wife and homemaker; she always did what my pop asked."

"I can't believe your mom never had any opinions or ideas of her own. She is a very strong woman, Cole. I've seen her take charge in the kitchen."

"Of course, she had her own ideas, but she always assumed the backup role. They talked about money plenty because they never had any. But Mama never talked business with Pop, never told him what to do or not do to bring home the bacon."

"Cole, you've always said that you wanted a different life from that of your parents."

"For sure, but it is still hard for me to escape everything from my past, especially the example set by my pop. Is it any different for you?"

"I understand, but I'm going to work on this with you. I hope someday you will understand as well that I can help you reach your goals and make that we can reach our goals. I want to be part of your dream, your journey. Cole, I may be extraordinarily attractive, but I am no trophy wife."

We both laughed.

I sat back in the seat next to Buddy. Cole kept driving, turning up the radio.

CHAPTER FORTY-ONE

DANGEROUS MIDNIGHT MOVES

I was never much for the forced hoopla required for the New Year's Eve celebration. Forget the pointed hats; the strings under my neck hurt me when I was a kid. I would pull the elastic string from the hat so I could pretend it was broken. "No thanks, I don't need a new one."

The broken hat trick did not spare me from doing the New Year's Eve thing as 2002 arrived in Newport Beach. Cole really wanted to do the black-tie thing, something not in his repertoire. His new partner Tom Murphy and Tom's wife Daisy had asked us to join them for the annual formal midnight revelry at the Harbor Club.

Total old-world formula. Cocktails on the bayfront terrace at eight, white glove wait service dining at ten, dancing to a big band until the bewitching hour, and then breakfast at one in the morning. I did love eggs Benedict, but there was no chance this pregnant woman was going to be hanging around in a black satin maternity cocktail dress past midnight. I would barely make it through the salad course at dinner.

Cole promised we could leave whenever I wanted to go, so I agreed. He said it would be good for business, reminding me of Dalt's advice to him to get involved in the community. Oh brother, I wanted to tell Cole and Dalt that such a strategy was simply not in my repertoire. Of course, I shut up and said nothing. Even though I had been raised to believe that men and women were equal, I knew that such philosophy was incomplete. Men and women were separate and sometimes equal. In certain things men dominated; in others, women held the upper hand. Dalt had built his business on relationships; I had grown up watching him with his clients. Perhaps some of his business instinct would help my husband, which thought justified my silence.

After feeding Buddy, I put him to bed with our new nanny, Bonnie, who had recently arrived from the cornfields of Iowa. Bonnie was just eighteen, fresh out of high school, and had never traveled beyond the borders of her state. One of ten children, she was an expert with kids, and I loved her at the first Buddy bathing.

Cole was upstairs getting ready for the big night in our new bedroom facing the oceanfront. With the upcoming arrival of second son Brady, we had moved from the apartment over the garage with Buddy into the main house, taking over my parents' former room. Buddy, and eventually Brady and nanny Bonnie, would be all right down the hall. The perfect little family at the beach.

Life was wonderful. While I did not feel any sort of pressure to find a home for us to buy, Cole still itched to buy a house we could call our own. It was a regular topic of conversation, or should I say debate. "Don't put yourself under so much pressure," I kept saying. "We can stay here as long as we want."

My husband knew that, but I think it made him feel unworthy, emasculated, a poor provider. This was another one of those man–woman "separate but equal" things. I didn't push the subject, figuring it would work itself out one way or another.

Joining Cole and leaving Bonnie with the Baldwin heir, I pulled myself together in ten minutes. Cole was ready and dressed to kill, waiting in a chair and looking out the window at the beach.

"It's almost eight," he called out as I entered.

"No worry, I'll be ready in a flash. Besides, do we need to be on time for a two-hour cocktail reception? What can I talk to Daisy Murphy about for two hours?"

"You'll think of something. You're good at that. Talk to her about her new body. You set people at ease; they like being around you," he replied.

"Talk about her new body? You've got to be joking. Don't certain people realize that I don't like being around them?" I answered sarcastically.

"Please don't say that, especially about Daisy Murphy. Our future is partially in the hands of my business with Tom. Hopefully, we will close escrow on the land for our first building project in the next couple of months."

"I get it. Don't worry. I will be the perfect wife of a future real estate mogul. I know just what to do."

"I knew I married the perfect girl."

"You had better believe you did."

A New Year's Eve like No Other

Doing the whole New Year's Eve thing every year growing up with my family, and never being a fan, I was resigned to the fact that it was just a part of the Fairchild program. Dalt and Nancy celebrated every occasion in life. Birthdays lasted a month, anniversaries, an entire year. In the Fairchild family, December 31 was always black tie, even if the New Year was celebrated at home. As children, we too dressed in our finest. If we behaved, a sip of champagne in a crystal flute awaited us at nine o'clock, if we had remained awake up to that point.

Although I made the West Coast midnight hour by about the age of ten or eleven, my brother, Jamey, then six or seven, would be asleep, his head in my lap by eight thirty, having tried to make it until nine to have his own sip. Stroking his long wavy blond hair, I would cover him with a throw blanket, placing it over his boy's tuxedo with bow tie and short pants that had been his holiday uniform for many years. I think he refused to wear the shorts by the age of nine. Mother cried.

The years when we ventured out of the Lexington homestead, we usually attended a formal dinner at the country club. I don't remember ever seeing other children at any of these parties. Dalt and Nancy would never celebrate without us, so there we were, standouts in the fashionable Beverly Hills crowd of moguls, movie stars, and yes, wannabes too.

Of course, I didn't know about any of those distinctions as a child, but I did have my big eyes wide open, watching everyone. I didn't miss a detail. Fascinated by how the people dressed, how they moved about, their manners, and their quirks, I still remembered it all.

Famous faces were often there. I knew them as if they were members of every American family with a TV set. And then there was Mr. Mullen with those huge ears. I couldn't help but stare. Once I asked him where he had gotten those ears. Nancy was horrified. Dalt tried to cover his laugh. My favorite was a woman from New York, Mrs. Gordon. I stared at her too. She was tall and thin and always had a very dark suntan as if she had just returned from the islands, regardless of the time of year, winter, summer—anytime. Mrs. Gordon dressed like a rich woman, and her major jewelry sent out beacons of light that always seemed to be pointed at me.

These experiences were unique for a kid. I watched and absorbed. I think my fascination with design was born on any one of these journeys out on New Year's Eve with the family.

I had not done the black-tie, glittery pointed hats, and blowers with streamers thing since my college years at USC. Okay, that was only a few years back, but it seemed like a lifetime ago. I promised Cole I'd be the perfect, supportive, happy New Year wife with his new business partner and bride, even though I still had not gotten over the bare-breasted parade down Via Genoa on Lido Isle, that little after-dinner surprise with the Murphys and friends when we first met.

Arriving at the Harbor Club, we were greeted by klieg lights crisscrossing the night sky. An army of valets in red jackets and black ties ushered us out of the armada of gleaming black cars, the occupants stepping out on to a red carpet and being guided into the reception foyer of the Harbor Club ballroom. A jazz band, fronted by a sultry female jazz singer in a ruby-red sequined strapless minidress and five-inch sequin-adorned heels to match, made the most of her long bare legs while moving to the beat of Burt Bacharach's "What the World Needs Now Is Love."

The crowd was robust, their conversation bouncing off the granite floor and walls of glass looking out over the Newport Harbor. Cocktails flowed, and the decibel level of conversation grew. By around a quarter to nine, Cole spotted the arrival of Tom and Daisy. Once he waved at them, they responded, moving through the crowd in our direction.

I thought, *Gee, only an hour and a quarter to fill until dinner is served. Would it be totally horrible to fake a headache or, better, pretend a call from nanny Bonnie summoning us home? I could be the sacrificing martyr and tell Cole to stay and have a wonderful time with Tom and Daisy.*

No, that was not going to happen.

Making the Best of This Night to Remember

Giving up on the idea of a fake reason for a fast exit, I put on my most charming face to act like a new best girlfriend to Daisy. Figuring she was harmless, not the winner-take-all woman on the upward climb, I made the necessary effort. I was aware that plenty of women were on the hunt for upward mobility in Newport. This shocked me as I thought that such a breed flourished only in 90210 territory. Now that I was living full time in Newport, instead of just being a summer guest, it made a discernible difference. I got it, and I didn't care. I loved my new life here, and besides, pregnancy brought me scary emotional swings. Weird thoughts such as social-climbing women just popped into my head, and then such thoughts would vanish as fast as they had come.

Anyway, Daisy was cheerfully boring. This night, she seemed regular, very traditional, so sorority girl–like. All I could think of was the visual of her parading down the street butt naked in her high heels, flipping her bleached blonde hair from side to side and then running her fingertips up her scalp on both sides of her head, pushing the hair up, then letting it fly. Who was this woman with two very different sides?

The Harbor Club maître d' opened the tall double ballroom doors to announce dinner as a full orchestra took their cue, welcoming the crush of the now seriously happy New Year's Eve cocktail crowd. Two hours of martinis was surely one hour too many. It was very hard to be sober in a drunken crowd, even when the health of my unborn child was the factor. I managed, and Daisy kept congratulating me with each of her "only one more" lemon drop martinis. How odd. Why was she congratulating me? Daisy and Tom had no children; abstaining from alcohol during pregnancy was simply not within her sphere of concern.

Tom somehow managed to seat all of us at a table front and center just off the dance floor. As the captain guided us through the crowd to the A-list seating, Cole, holding my hand, leaned over and whispered, "Tom told me he arranged for us to sit with the chairman of some fancy bank, his wife, and their guests, and said we'd have a chance to make some progress on our business plans!"

Smiling at Cole, I let go of his hand and gave him a big goosing on the left cheek of his bottom.

"What was that for?" he asked quietly.

"Just don't confuse the pimp and the client," I replied sarcastically.

Cole said nothing, somewhat amused, as the captain arrived with us at the prize table. People were watching, probably thinking, *Who are those young people, and how did they get such a prime seat?*

The banker and his bride were already seated. Now they stood to greet us. Cole had not met banker Jack Weston; he was Tom's business connection. We shared that awkward first air-kiss as we were introducing ourselves with big New Year's hugs. Jack Weston, of average height, balding at the temples, and rather, well, ordinary-looking, and his wife Diane, same age and basic profile, but of the female variety, seemed okay enough. Preparing myself again for the ultimate boring night, I turned on the charm as directed and required.

"Kate, how are you feeling? What month are you in?" Diane inquired after we had introduced ourselves.

She seemed genuine, so I took that as a good sign. "I'm about halfway there," I told her. "And I'm feeling pretty darn good."

"You look fabulous. I'm so happy for you." Diane continued getting personal as she spoke in a soft, confidential tone: "Jack and I don't have children."

Not knowing how to respond, and ever mindful of my role as supportive wife, I stopped myself from saying *I'm so sorry,* or something dumb such as *Kids are not for everybody.* Instead, I simply said, "Then this New Year's Eve will be all about the six of us here together tonight."

Diane smiled. She was sweet and had a sexy silhouette in a superconservative way. I wondered what her bedtime life was like with old Jack. He didn't look like a lot of fun.

It was odd, but we ended up seated with men together and women together. Daisy Murphy, dressed like a shimmering Christmas tree with two of its major branches well accented, dove in, chattering with Diane Weston in high gear. Sipping sparkling water in a champagne flute, I pretended to hang on to every word.

The guys were into serious "impress each other" mode. Tom and Cole were on either side of Jack Weston, and at one point it looked as if the two of them were both pitching Jack in opposite ears simultaneously. When I started choking on my sparkling water, Cole shot me the *Are you okay?* look. I smiled and nodded. He turned back to his position, facing Jack Weston's left ear.

Dinner was served. The orchestra played on as the people overflowing on the dance floor moved in rhythm with the cocktail service. With each round, the real estate pitch got louder in order to be heard over some band singer's rendition of Sinatra's "New York, New York."

As the staff cleared our entrée plates, our table was the only one in the ballroom not on the dance floor. Daisy was still yapping at Diane. Tom and Cole continued to try to impress the banker.

Suddenly, Tom and Jack rose from the table, cocktails in hand, excusing themselves to go out on the terrace to puff on a cigar. Cole stayed behind. I hoped we could share a few moments together. Instead, Diane broke away from Daisy and asked me if she could ask Cole to dance. "Of course," I answered, being the supportive real estate wife, whose husband wanted a loan from Jack's bank.

"Oh, that's awfully nice," Diane said, "You're sure you don't mind?"

"No, really. I'm not in my dancing shoes tonight," I came back, patting my pregnant belly.

Turning to Cole, I asked him to dance with Diane.

Obliging, he stood up and came over to pull Diane's chair out, allowing her to rise. She may have been a little prune-faced earlier, but now she was beaming. Perhaps she had no children because she never had done much dancing.

Daisy didn't bother to pick up the chatter with me. She was concentrating on her Pouilly-Fuissé. I stopped counting wine pours at number seven. We watched the revelers doing their darned best to be deliriously happy, ever so sophisticated, worldly, and rich, proud to be in one another's company as 2002 wiped away the horrors of 9/11 from all our lives.

Refraining from my innate snarkiness over the swirl of pointed hats and blowers circling the floor, I said a silent prayer, thanking God for protecting Dalt and Jamey in New York. They were home safe. That was my New Year's wish and my New Year's blessing.

Carried Away

At Diane's request, they were starting a third dance. Cole was feeling a little uneasy. One dance was polite. Two was being friendly. But three? Three was pushing it. Worse, all the three were slow dances, and the couples all around Cole and Diane were beginning to dance even closer. Diane was clearly in no rush to return to the table. Besides, Tom and Jack had not come back inside from their cigar break. Cole kept glancing over at me, and I kept sending my sign of approval, so he and Diane kept dancing.

Diane moved in and was now up against Cole as the strings in the orchestra reached their crescendo. Clasping her hands together around his neck, she nuzzled her head up against his throat. I watched as the fifty-something banker's childless wife made the moves. Surprising myself, I imagined my Cuban Italian stallion lover wanting to bed down with boring Diane. *It's just about playing the game,* I said to myself. *Business is all about relationships and connections.*

I watched as Cole began to move Diane around on the dance floor with some demonstrable manly leading. At one point, he swung her out away from him, holding her at the waist with one arm, then bringing her back toward his strong physique. Again, she clasped her hands together at the back of his neck, then leaned in and whispered in his ear. I could see Cole flinch backward.

Danger on the Dance Floor

Cole knew he was in trouble. The music continued. Cole was in dangerous territory. He knew enough about himself to realize that he had always compartmentalized the act of sex in his mind. Sex with Kate could be about love. But sex with others was just about sex. Sometimes it was about getting what he wanted. Sometimes it was about momentary physical pleasure. Sometimes sex was just about nothing. Cole knew, however, that he was not intending on having sex with Diane, even though it might be about getting something that he wanted—a construction loan to start his business with Tom Murphy. Cole did ponder, *Would I do it if it would seal the deal?* At that moment, Diane leaned in, nuzzling Cole's ear and said, "You can tell how a man is in bed on the dancefloor."

With no time to respond to Diane or to formulate a plan, Cole turned slightly with her, and saw Tom coming back in the ballroom, following Jack Weston, who was charging toward the two of them on the dance floor.

Weston was yelling something, which Cole could not make out, and Tom seemed to be chasing after him to stop him. Jack then threw his scotch, which he held in his right hand, to the floor, where it crashed, creating a small earthquake. The ballroom was so loud that the noise was ignored by nearly all except me at the table, who was watching the men returning from the terrace to the party, one chasing the other.

"Get your fucking dirty hands off my wife," Jack Weston yelled, coming at Cole and Diane, who were still locked in an embrace on the dance floor.

"Did you not fucking hear me?" he yelled even louder. Cole heard what was coming.

Diane was oblivious, still with both her arms around Cole's neck. By the third "Take your fucking dirty hands off my wife" coming from Jack, she turned and saw her husband in a red-faced drunken rage coming at them. Releasing Cole, she stepped back just as Jack made it to the dance floor, sending his best right hook to Cole's abdomen.

Swinging at this fantasy suitor captivating his woman, Jack tripped, his punch missing Cole completely, as he fell flat on his face on the parquet flooring. The orchestra paused. The crowd gasped, but only for two seconds, and then everything resumed as if nothing had happened, with the black-tie, pointed hat, and blower crowd simply dancing all around and over Jack Weston, who was lying on the dance floor. An embarrassed Diane tried to revive her man. Tom and Daisy came to her aid as best they could, given the fact that neither one could possibly have spelled their own names if questioned. Cole took Kate's hand and left the ballroom, and simply vanished into the midnight Newport air on the first morning of the year.

CHAPTER FORTY-TWO

APOLOGIES AND CONFESSIONS

Several weeks had passed since the fiasco. Apologies were exchanged with less than enthusiastic reception. It was back to business, the confrontation in the past forgotten. Cole and Tom worked tirelessly supplying financial projections, spreadsheets of building cost breakdowns, and written bids from contractors, all at the request of the bank. They were certain a decision on their one-million-dollar loan was forthcoming in days.

The New Year had brought a fresh start following the serious life-altering experience of 9/11 that had rocked the Fairchild family to its core. Cole and I were young, with everything in life ahead of us, so many dreams still incubating. Despite everything that had occurred, we lived a charmed life. I knew it; I always had. But privilege was new to Cole. He was learning to be grateful, yet he was very hungry to prove his worth. With the instincts of youth fighting for his attention, his reaching for an identity above the fray had complicated his journey. In a very personal and slightly drunk moment, Cole shared with me words of his hard-working father, who had never gotten a break of any kind. "That's how the world works, Son. Take what you can get because nobody is gonna do you any favors."

His father had given him another piece of advice that was buried in his sub-conscious: *You can fall in love with a poor girl or a rich girl. Rich is better.*

As a kid growing up in Reno in a lower-working-class neighborhood, Cole also shared with me that he didn't know any rich people. The only rich girls were on TV or in the movies. He said that he paid no real attention to his father's words about rich girls. Girls were not about money; they were about sex. Just the same, the subconscious message had become reality. Cole had fallen in love with and married a rich girl, me.

Another Deal To Chase

Waiting for word from Weston and the bank, Cole remained cool. He believed it was going to work out, so he forged ahead with business as usual. Lining up a new listing appointment for a waterfront home on tony Linda Isle, a gated enclave of 1970s-era stucco mansions just feet apart from one another on the California Riviera, Cole went into his high sales gear best.

The property was a potential two-million-dollar deal, and if it were to sell, that would be another one hundred thousand dollars in commission. For a guy in his midtwenties from nowhere, this was mind-blowing. He had tasted the candy and was getting used to its flavor.

Making it to the appointment on time, racing back from a morning television shoot for another episode of *Living the Dream*, which had managed to stay on the local airwaves for almost a year, Cole took a deep breath to relax as he crossed the bridge to Linda Isle. The TV exposure had given Cole recognition in the market, but it had not made him the big reality TV star as he had imagined he would certainly be. Still, the call to present a sales pitch on Linda Isle had come from a potential client who had seen Cole on TV.

The would-be celebrity was puffed up in his fancy Calvin Klein suit and new Gucci loafers. He rang the buzzer at the tall arched iron gate. The gate clicked and released; Cole entered a courtyard facing an open front door. Calling out, "Entering!" Cole found himself inside the home at the edge of a large interior swimming pool. An open two-story atrium topped by a metal-framed pitched roof of glass permitted the southwestern midday sun to stream in and hit the still water of the pool. At the far end, opposite the front entry where Cole stood surveying the unusual architecture before him, a steaming spa gurgled, and in it Cole could see the silhouetted heads of what appeared to be a man and a woman.

"Is that you, Cole Baldwin?" a male voice called out from the spa.

Cole could not make out a face to put with the voice. "Yes, sir. I am here for a listing presentation," he responded.

"Well then, come on over here. My wife and I are in the spa," the voice beckoned.

Cole followed the stone path on the side of the indoor pool toward the spa. Thinking, *Oh brother, this is different,* he did his best to act nonchalant, stepping up to the edge of the spa. In his hand was his briefcase, filled with his presentation papers, meant to impress. The man stood up in the spa, wiping water off his brow and pushing his salt-and-pepper hair back off his face. He looked to be around sixty, with skinny legs supporting a belly enhanced by brew, and was wearing a black Speedo.

"My name is Walter Benheim—call me WB—and this is my wife Candy," he said. "We have seen you on TV and want to talk to you about selling our home." Candy said nothing, smiling at Cole. She was at least half WB's age.

"Did I come at a bad time?" Cole questioned.

"Hell no," WB came back. "How about taking off that suit and coming in here so we can talk business?" Cole was sure he was in trouble again. Was this another Carondolet mess about to happen?

"WB, I came prepared with everything except a bathing suit," Cole responded, trying to be funny and break the ice.

"The hell with that, just come on in. if you want to be modest, wear your underwear. Or not. It's up to you. We don't care."

Cole didn't waste a moment. Undressing as WB and Candy watched, placing his Calvin suit and Gucci loafers on a lounge to the side of the spa, the real estate agent who had proven before he would do whatever it took to get a listing stood in front of his potential clients wearing only his black bikini underwear and showing off his muscular physique.

Tempted to drop the briefs and display his formidable package, Cole thought better of it since WB was in his Speedo. He stepped into the spa, put out his right hand to shake WB's hand, and smiled back at Candy, settling down on a ledge opposite what he hoped would become his new two-million-dollar clients.

In the spa, which was gurgling and bubbling, Cole prepared for whatever was coming. What did come was plenty of silly small good-old-boy talk about football and the upcoming Super Bowl game. WB had his arm around Candy's shoulder. She nuzzled into the base of his neck. Cole remained on the other side of the spa following WB's lead, trying to bring up real estate and make his pitch, but always dominated by WB's football stories.

Twenty minutes later, spa time was over. They were all cooked enough in the hot water. WB stood up, again in his Speedo, displaying a demonstrably larger unit than that initially viewed upon Cole's arrival.

"Son, you've got the listing. You're my kind of guy. We'll do business well together." Cole stood up, again reaching out to shake his hand. WB did not oblige, his right arm still touching Candy's shoulder under the water. Then Candy rose out of the spa water, revealing her naked breasts, while a black bikini bottom covered her lowers. At least her attire matched her husband's spa wear. Cole flinched but remained cool. WB took Candy by the hand and helped her up the steps and out of the spa, taking a large towel from a nearby table and wrapping it around her.

"Call me tomorrow, Cole, and we'll meet to finalize details and sign your papers," WB shouted out as they left the indoor spa together. "See yourself out, kid. Nice meeting you. Let's do this again" were WB's parting words at noontime on this Wednesday in January.

Cole exited the spa, having taken another towel from the table to dry off. He removed his wet bikinis, wrung out most of the water, dressed in his Calvin suit sans underwear, and left.

Driving back to the real estate office, Cole laughed out loud, thinking that life in Newport was nothing like what he had imagined. How very strange some rich people acted. Daisy Murphy had paraded down the street nude after a dinner where six women all had dropped their tops to display their breasts, and total strangers, a married woman with her husband, had stepped out of a spa seminaked, her beautiful, enhanced bosom pointing the way.

Am I in heaven, or is this hell? Heck if I know. Cole's silent words rattled his brain. He did admit to himself that if it was hell, he was having a hell of a good time.

The Decision Arrives

Almost a month had passed. March was approaching, but there had been no word from Weston and the bank. Cole finalized the Linda Isle listing with WB and was aggressively marketing the sale. He had signed the deal with WB at a desk fully clothed. The spring selling season required more advertising, and the TV show continued to generate leads. Cole's fame was spreading in the Newport social world.

Tom Murphy, who, Cole finally realized, never really worked at any job, kept assuring Cole that their business plans were on track. "Be patient," he said, repeating it continuously. "This is how money moves in Newport. You must build relationships. You have to talk the talk, do the schmooze thing."

Cole could not help but wonder if the relationship building hadn't faltered from the start that New Year's Eve night on the dance floor at the Harbor Club. If Tom Murphy was such a formidable guy, financially strong and well-connected, then what was the holdup?

The answer finally came. Their loan had been turned down. Little information was given other than that the application did not meet the appropriate benchmarks of underwriting that would have given financial security for money requested. The truth, between the lines, was that Tom Murphy was a big talker and that Jack Weston was not going to lend either of them ten cents after Cole's dance with his wife.

"Tom, I've decided to take a different course," Cole told his now former real estate development partner. "I am going to go out on my own. We can still be buds, right?" he said. Tom Murphy acted as if nothing had changed in their relationship. He slapped Cole on the back, laughing and carrying on, talking about nothing. Murphy lived the good life at the beach, holding a Heineken in one hand while sitting behind his oversized black granite slab-top desk wearing the Newport business uniform consisting of a Reyn Spooner Hawaiian-print collared shirt, khaki pants, and scuffed Top-Sider slip-on shoes.

The meeting with Tom had reinforced Cole's fear that he was still green when it came to business and was even greener when it came to sizing up people. He admitted that to himself. But he also realized that Tom was just another spoiled trust fund kid living on a comfortable allowance from daddy or mommy, or perhaps granddaddy, and really had no significant business clout of his own.

Sitting across the granite-topped desk, Cole zoned out as Tom blabbed on. His mind was focused on his task. How was he going to make it big in real estate? Should he go back to Dalt and ask for support? Cole knew that just being a successful sales agent would never set him apart from the rest. He could make a great living but not a killing. Cole wanted to be the master. He had to be somebody.

It wasn't enough to make a good living, have a good marriage, raise children. Already he had compromised his marriage, having cheated on his wife to make a deal. How far would he go?

"No problem, man. There are many other deals to make," Tom said to Cole.

"Sure thing, man. Lots more deals. I'll call you," Cole replied. He and Tom shared a man hug before Cole left the fancy office, where no papers, no files, and nothing of a business nature existed on the granite desk—or anywhere for that matter. Cole grumbled under his breath, "Bullshit. Nothing but BS."

Beginning to face his unchecked ambition honestly, Cole also faced his personal demons, including his sexual promiscuity and the resulting secret betrayal of Kate. He did love her; she was like no other woman he had ever known. And for him, it was love at first sight the day they had met in the parking lot. Never having been in love before, he knew Kate was his first and only. He wondered if Kate would still love him if she were to find out about the secret part of his life. Cole was smart enough, or at least honest enough, to know what that answer would be.

Following the revelation of Candy's bare breasts at the listing appointment on Linda Isle, Cole had made a promise to himself to try to change. It was a promise he had never made before. Kate was due to give birth to their second child in only a few months' time. With mountains to climb to follow his business ambition, Cole worried if he could make the journey without becoming a lowlife cheater, which clearly was part of his initial road map to money and success. And if he was going to have even a prayer of making it to the top of that fantasy mountain, he also realized he would have to be the catalyst. Any number of Tom Murphys would not be there to back him up, and he did not want to ride on the Dalt Fairchild caboose either.

After leaving Tom Murphy's office and returning to his own, Cole pulled into his parking space in front of the real estate office. In just a little more than a year he had transformed from a nobody from Reno into a Newport agent handling multimillion-dollar deals. His name was stenciled on the cement parking bumper, a sign of progress indeed. Looking at the lettering of his made-up name in cement, and parking his new to him, but used, luxury BMW sedan in the spot, Cole made his plan.

It was time for his family to move out of the Fairchild beach house and purchase a house of their own. It would be a fixer-upper that Cole could buy below market value, repair and remodel, live in for a year, and flip at a profit. He would do this multiple times until he acquired enough cash to become the developer he aspired to be. Deciding that he would share his plan immediately with Kate, he went to seek her blessing. Upon turning twenty-seven, Cole was certain he had found his path and that time was on his side.

CHAPTER FORTY-THREE

EASY MONEY

By the spring of 2002, banks were anxious to lend money on real estate as prices were rising at meteoric pace. With good credit and a strong appraisal, loans with no down payment were now possible, and the market was hot. Cole was ready to act.

Over dinner that night, Cole pitched me on his plan to start buying property with little or no down payment. He had anticipated my concern, particularly over the need to buy a home and leave the beach cottage.

"Cole, we don't need to rush on this. Nobody is putting a gun to our heads. Besides, have you noticed that I am almost five months pregnant?" I was being intentionally sarcastic. Cole's intense preoccupation with work had classified him as missing in action. We had not made love in days, unfamiliar territory for me.

"I'm sorry. Of course, I know you are almost five months pregnant. That is more reason I want to do this now, for us. For all of us. Kate, I don't want to live in your father's house. Can you understand that?"

Cole had made his point. I respected him for it. Still, moving now was not in my plans.

"Can we at least wait until after the baby comes? Maybe at least six months after?" I pushed.

"Babe, you got it. But I want to look now, even buy now if the right deal comes along. I promise we don't have to move until you are comfortable with all of it. Besides, we will need to make a few moves over the next couple of years to build a financial footing. Eventually, we can settle into our own permanent house."

Knowing the plan made sense, I was cautious. This was new and unfamiliar ground for me, what with my having lived in one house for most of my growing-up years. *Am I ready to live the life of a house flipper with two kids?* I asked myself.

Abruptly shifting gears, I looked at my husband. "Do you want to have sex?" I was blunt.

"I thought it was off-limits. Didn't the doctor tell you at your last visit to be careful?"

"When did I tell you that?"

"A couple of weeks ago, after your last visit."

"She never said no sex. She just said to be careful."

"So, no chains or whips, but the rest is okay?"

"Funny. Cole, you've been absent from our bedroom since our New Year's Eve 'welcome to 2002' lovemaking. Do you want to talk about it?"

"No talking." Those were Cole's last words as he took me by the hand, kissed me up and down one side of my neck and then the other, pulled my chair back from the table, and with arms around my waist slid me out of the chair and moved me up and next to him, as close as the two of us could be, side by side. Moments later, the door to the master bedroom clicked closed. It was nine o'clock and the house was silent. Buddy and nanny Bonnie were asleep down the hall.

Unfastening Cole's tie, giving it a good strong yank, I then unbuttoned each button of his white dress shirt. Cole flipped off the light switch by the door, which operated the table lamps in the bedroom. The oceanfront master chamber on the second floor of the cottage had no window coverings on the paned windows, which lined the wall facing the beach and the ocean beyond. Moonlight, bouncing of the water, cast its mystical glow through the glass panes.

"Maybe you'd better turn the lamps back on, Cole, so you can find the whips and chains."

Cole, now with his shirt open and his pants falling, picked me up and shuffled across the room to our marriage bed.

"You can pretend to be in chains, and I'll deliver the whip," Cole whispered, putting me down gently.

A piercing cry burst out from down the hall, and both Cole and I jumped up. Cole quickly sat back down on the edge of the bed and pulled up his pants. Out the door like a bolt of lightning, I went to check on Buddy.

A few minutes turned into ten, I could not calm him. The crying did not cease. Ten became twenty, and finally there was silence. Still, I did not return to Cole drifing into sleep cuddling with my Buddy and his giant stuffed black and white Panda bear.

Cole Takes Care Of His Personal Business

Staring at the ceiling, waiting and again naked on the bed, Cole was restless. It was early, not even ten o'clock. His mind raced, focusing on zero-down real estate. He wondered, *Should I try to buy more than one property with little or no down payment and start to build an income portfolio rather than look for a personal home? Maybe Kate would be okay with that. How important is it to buy a house of our own? Rental property is a better plan.*

Alone with little hope of being with Kate, Cole began to stroke the hair of his lower groin above his dick. His mind was off real estate as he began to pleasure himself. An erection instantly followed his private pubic message. Cole's right hand had been a steady sex partner since the onset of puberty. The practice was routine, and he engaged in it often. It was a form of tension release and recharge for Cole. On this day, the episode would be third time, the first being in the morning while showering, and the second being in the stall of the men's room in his office around two in the afternoon. This was his third, in his bed alone, without Kate.

Cole always accompanied the act with mental sex fantasy, which was often abstract. As the moonlight danced around him, Cole stroked harder. His sex fantasy did not include his wife, but rather was a threesome with his Linda Isle spa clients.

For a moment, he stopped himself and his dick went semilimp in his hand. He had just realized that his promise to change, to be true to his wife, had not lasted very long, at least in his mind. How easily his pursuit of sexual pleasure compromised him. Cole returned to complete his masturbation, climaxing with a controlled grunt while thinking about intercourse with Walter and Candy Benheim in the spa on Linda Isle. In his abstract mental state, Cole was doing Candy, and Walter was doing Cole.

A New Day and Another Chance

The dancing moonlight that had set the mood for Cole's solo sex was replaced by the rays of the morning sun streaming in through the paned windows of the cottage. Upon awaking, Cole found Kate in bed with him under the covers, totally hidden by the pink paisley Pierre Deux sheets and comforter. He had remained naked on top of the bed through the night. Quietly sliding off and making his way to the bathroom, Cole headed for a warm shower. Telling himself there would be no morning jack-off to begin this new day, he was haunted by his mental anal sex with Walter Benheim, a sixty-year-old man whom he didn't know and didn't think he was attracted to sexually. It had put him in a state of bizarre confusion.

The warm water pouring from the waterfall showerhead above him ran down his body, relieving some of the weirdness. Kate knocked twice on the bathroom door to let him know she was coming in.

"I hope the shower didn't wake you," Cole semishouted through the clear glass enclosure surrounding him.

"It's okay, I needed to get up. I've got plans today, and I want to be sure Buddy is feeling better."

"What was the matter last night?"

"Probably nothing. He just seemed anxious, wanting to be held before he finally fell asleep."

"Are you okay?"

"I guess. Tried to rouse you when I came to bed around two o'clock, but you were out. I even tried a little kissing down there, since it was a very available option. You turned to your side; I went to sleep."

"Boy, I guess I blew that," Cole offered, getting out of the shower. I handed him a towel and gave him a look.

"I tried, but you turned away," I said, grinning.

"Copy that." Cole returned the look, continuing, "So, what are your big plans today?"

"You don't remember? I'm going to the Newport Charity Foundation luncheon at the Four Seasons Hotel because you asked me to go. Then I'm stopping by the salon to visit with Monsieur Lawrence. He asked me to come by. How about you? What are your plans, my future real estate mogul of Newport Beach, or should I say America, or the world?" Sarcastic, but sweet. I wanted Cole to succeed, to have his dream become reality, but teasing him about his ambition was routine.

"I've got an eleven o'clock client showing at Linda Isle, then I'm meeting with a mortgage broker recommended by the Linda Isle client Walter Benheim. He tells me this guy can help me finance property with very little cash."

"Sounds risky, Cole."

"I don't see why. It's just taking advantage of a strong market flush with cash to lend for properties in high demand," he countered as he finished dressing for his day to conquer the Newport real estate business.

"Have you spoken to your parents? What's up with Jamey?" changing the subject.

"Nancy called me yesterday. Jamey is not doing well. They are worried. Jamey's specialist at Cedars-Sinai thinks the 9/11 experience may have given rise to serious neurological defects, in part associated with drugs, but also possibly from latent genetics."

"Seriously, what does that mean?"

"They fear that Jamey may be showing very early signs of bipolar disorder, which usually does not surface in people until they are in their early twenties."

"He's only sixteen," Cole said, stating the obvious.

"That's what makes it so bad," I said, my voice breaking. "The family is coming down for some time together this weekend at the Lido Isle house. Maybe on Sunday we could all get together? Can you be around, or do you have to work? It would mean a lot if you could be here."

"I'll make it work," Cole promised, remembering that he told me of plans for a tennis game with Walter and Candy at the Vista Del Mar Country Club. Cole never played tennis before. He was athletic, so he could fake it. How hard could it be? It was only the middle of the week, with plenty of time left to buy a racquet, white shorts, and a polo shirt.

Cole was dressed, ready to go. I required more time to properly prepare for the society luncheon I had been requested to attend by Cole to get my face out in the crowd "for business reasons." Buddy was just awaking. I could hear him stirring, along with Bonnie's voice greeting him on this new day. Not having to head to the Four Seasons Hotel until eleven o'clock for unwanted cocktails and totally unwanted chitchat, I had plenty of morning time to spend with my son. Breakfast with Buddy was so much more important.

"Here's to the Ladies Who Lunch"

I made it to the Four Seasons Hotel close to the noon hour, having spent a little extra time with Buddy over breakfast, which had turned into a follow-up hour of reading his favorite clothbound book all about farm animals. Bonnie joined the magical hour, impersonating animal sounds and movements as we turned each page. Buddy's favorite was the cow. Bonnie was an expert at mooing.

Being the perfect wife and mother in the twenty-first century had its challenges. Add to that equation career woman, and I was honestly scared. Confident me, scared. I was feeling guilty about having allowed so much time pass after Buddy's birth before getting back to my career goals. And then with my dad and brother's 9/11 trauma, the career woman clothing designer part of my personal Superwoman trifecta was, well, pretty much dysfunctional. At least one element was perfect, or so I would like to think: I was a good mother. That was my priority. Playing the part of the good supportive wife was about to earn me points at the charity league luncheon.

The over-the-top glamour of the 1980s Reagan era had faded during my teens in the 1990s. Society women were dressing down. Black was the color of choice for everything in the 2000s. It may have been expensive black, but the new uniform was less pretentious in the society circles of LA where I grew up. Such was not the case in Newport.

Style remained king. On this day in the middle of the week, the luncheon crowd was nothing less than spring dazzling. I was not dazzling, especially in my baby-blue maternity dress. Let's just say I was "classic." With a string of ten-millimeter pearls at my neckline and Nancy's diamond studs (I had kept them after the wedding with her blessing), I was ready to meet and greet and make Cole proud. Having grown up in a pretty business-savvy family, I knew that connection did matter. "People prefer to do business with people they know," Dalt was famous for repeating. "Especially when money is changing hands for an investment," he'd add. I suppose it was just human nature to know this. Cole was learning this well without the benefit of a business-savvy family.

The ballroom doors opened following the clinging of bells, and the crowd of high-fashion competitors crowded together, passing through the two sets of double doors. The bells continued to cling as the line narrowed. Waiting to be among the final group of heifers entering the prize pen, I had no intention of competing with these women for recognition. For one thing, most of them were older. A group of twenty- and early thirty-somethings were also intent on being part of Newport society. I assumed I would be seated with some of them, probably in the back of the ballroom. For that reason, I thought it odd that my table number was 1. Surely, the lower numbers were in the back, rising to the larger numbers up front. That much I knew about ladies' luncheons for charity. Every attendee gets a moment to feel special, even if she is not a big fish. Special, that is, until reality finds her seated at the rear. Nancy chaired many a charity event, and I had learned from the best.

All that wisdom proved faulty. I went to the back of the Four Seasons ballroom and found the table numbers were all in the twenties. Smiling and nodding hello, sidestepping through those still standing and chattering beside each table, I made my way to table 1. It was front and center. No one was there. Standing uncomfortably and wondering what sort of error had been made, I noticed that each place at the table was marked with a formal place card with hand-applied script announcing the seating. Trying not to be too obvious, I started around the table, recognizing no names. Practically back to my point of departure, I read the place card: "Mrs. Cole Baldwin." I kept going. Next to me was the card for Mrs. Alexander Adamson III, and on the other side of Mrs. A was Ms. Heather Adamson, who, I presumed, was Mrs. A's daughter. Surprised, but somewhat relieved, I thought, *At least I am in familiar territory.*

Mrs. A appeared with her daughter Heather, followed by a flurry of fans, some of them filling the places at her table. I had not met Heather; she was away at college when I first met Mrs. A in Madame Honoré's showroom. Heather was not the typical Newport Beach deb girl, at least not by appearance. Instead, she seemed to be a regular, unpretentious college coed. Her clothes were plain—a navy-blue V-neck sweater over a white-collared shirt, with cream-colored slacks and black penny loafers, no socks. Heather's figure exhibited signs of too many midnight foodie runs, and the curls of her dark, slightly auburn hair flowed freely, on the wild side.

As Mrs. A approached, she held her daughter's hand. Seeing me, she broke free and stretched out her arms. A generous hug and a kiss on both cheeks preceded my introduction to Heather, whom I liked instantly. She seemed genuine. You know how you can sense that just looking at a person's face? Heather was a good girl, a smart girl, and I could tell she was close to her mother regardless of their generational differences—just like me and Nancy. Mrs. A, having noticed our instant bonding, switched place cards, putting Heather next to me. Perhaps I would make a new friend. Clearly table 1 was not so bad. I would make it through the charity league luncheon.

It had been quite some time since I had made a new friend. Upon my realizing that I missed girl talk, Heather became my instant narcotic. The fast-track friendship lifted my spirits. We talked through every luncheon speaker and every round of applause, even ignoring the waiter who was attempting to serve lunch. Was there anyone else at the table? in the room?

Turns out Heather was finishing her senior year at USC, an accomplishment that might have been mine too at this very same time. That coincidence brought on a dose of melancholy. What if I had not met and fallen for David? Everything changed in my life after David. Heather was free to chart her course. I was a wife and mother. Cole's career came first; my personal goals were on hold—possibly forever.

Such realization did not overwhelm my joy in having a new friend. Sure, it was in the back of my mind, but it always was anyway. Besides, I was going to check in on my fashion mentors later that afternoon. Perhaps I would find new inspiration to get back on track. Always trying to be the realist over the dreamer, at almost five months pregnant with child number two, I was grounded enough to know my priorities and how they stacked up. Heather planned on heading to law school, having shared with me her dream of becoming an advocate for women's reproductive rights. Prochoice was not a popular theme in conservative Orange County. I found her fascinating. She allowed me to open up and talk with a stranger about a subject that I believed controlled my destiny and that of most women. The sex factor, I called it. Nothing else affected any woman's life more than sex.

I had fallen in love and made love with David and left school. I had fallen in love and made love with Cole and got pregnant, leaving my fashion career goal on the cutting room table. And the trouble was, my whole journey had been foreshadowed by the experiences of girls and women close to me, beginning with my high school roommate sweet Sara. That wasn't going to happen to me. I had sworn it wasn't going to happen to me. Still, the sex factor had gotten me.

How ironic to be thinking about this as my new friend Heather was presenting her passionate focus on women's rights and her fear that *Roe v. Wade* may be overturned. Impressed by her dedication and her directness, nodding to send my approval, yet only halfway there, I was thinking selfishly of my own feelings.

Both of our serious thoughts were interrupted by an ear-piercing scream. A very pretty young woman, older than me, thirtyish, with perfect shoulder-length blonde hair and stunning blue eyes adorned with major eyelashes and too much mascara, rose from her seat at table 2 right across from me, crying at a pitch that silenced the room.

"No, no, you can't do that!" she screamed, repeating herself multiple times, then breaking into sobs.

Turning to Mrs. A, I asked what had happened. Heather and I had missed the lead-up to the drama. Mrs. A had no clue.

The live auction was going on, raising money for the foundation. As I turned away from Mrs. A, the auctioneer shouted, "Sold. The golf package is sold to the man with the gold tie holding up the number two in the middle of the room. Sold for two thousand dollars." The crowd cheered, drowning out the loud cries from table 2.

At this point, the frantic woman with the stunning blue eyes, her excessive makeup now streaming down her cheeks, stood and told the now silent ballroom, "You can't do that. I need new clothes." She cried hysterically, falling back into her seat. The women on either side of her took an arm and escorted her out as fast as they could. Mrs. A discreetly filled in the blanks for Heather and me. "Girls, her name is Victoria Daniels, and her mother, Regina, is an acquaintance of mine. My guess is that Victoria has enjoyed too many chardonnays with lunch. The guy in the gold tie is her husband, Mark Daniels. A bunch of the husbands volunteer every year to sell the raffle tickets going around the room during the ladies' lunch. Mark clearly decided to bid on the golf trip in the auction. Victoria clearly wants new clothes over golf for Mark. There you have it," she shared with a devilish grin.

Heather chimed in, "It's just a slice of the Newport society scene. Clothes are important here. Looks are important. My mother is the queen of the fashion patrol, which is probably why I don't care all that much. How do you like my hair?" she asked, laughing. I responded by giving her a hug, feeling a little awkward that I hadn't shared my love for fashion design with my honest new friend.

Deciding to duck out after the drama, I exchanged numbers with Heather, promising to stay in touch. She wished me good luck with my pregnancy, as did her mother. After sharing a three-way kiss, I made a beeline for the valet station in advance of the social crush departing the charity luncheon for an afternoon of leisure. Most of the women in Newport did not work. Nor did they want to. That's what rich husbands were for.

Much-Needed Inspiration

My mentors' shop was down the avenue from the Four Seasons Hotel in a newly developed Mediterranean Riviera–inspired retail center. Manicured olive trees and tall skinny cypresses, standing like so many Roman soldiers at attention, lined stone-paved walkways shaded by specimen pineapple palm trees, which surrounded gurgling tiled fountains. Handsome iron furniture upholstered in sunflower-yellow canvas offered a quiet place to revive oneself between exhausting shopping expeditions in carriage trade boutiques.

I found a parking spot directly in front of Madame Honoré's front door, the first space I had parked in when I came to work there, surely a sign of destiny. Silly, of course, but pregnant women are entitled to a bit of mental escapism. Madame saw me pull in, recognizing the yellow Mercedes Roadster, a perfect match with the cushions on the outdoor furniture placed in front of her store.

"Darling, I am so thrilled to see you," Madame called to me, approaching with her arms extended. Her signature eyeglasses attached to a golden chain were perched on top of her head, held in place by a giant bun of slightly frizzy salt-and-pepper hair, which was tied with a satin ribbon.

Getting out of my car as gracefully as possible given the fact that my belly was now almost touching the bottom edge of the leather-wrapped steering wheel, I took Madame's hand as she gently lifted me upright and out of the car. I was showing in a major way at five months, which was unusual for most pregnant women at this stage.

"Phew, this is getting to be more of a challenge," I said with heavy breaths.

"You are large, my dear, but you look fabulous," she replied sincerely.

Hand in hand, we entered the shop.

"Slow day?" I asked, seeing no customers.

"It will pick up. Late afternoon, just before cocktail time, proves to be fruitful. But you know that, darling," she continued.

"How is Monsieur Lawrence?"

"He is in the workroom awaiting your arrival. He has a little surprise for you."

"Really?"

"Yes, really."

"What is it?"

"You will see."

Monsieur Lawrence had heard us talking—his cue to make an entrance. He carried a hanger supporting a garment covered by a cloth bag.

"Hello, my girl," he gushed, coming to me as I rose from a chair to meet him.

As we hugged, the garment bag fell between us awkwardly. Monsieur pulled it back up, concealing what was hidden within.

"We must not crush the fabric," he said seriously. "It must be perfect for the reveal."

"The reveal?" I asked with a happy grin.

"Oh yes, the reveal. A most special reveal."

With that, Madame motioned for the two of us to sit on the settee in the middle of the salon. Monsieur stepped up onto the cylindrical platform used to model their couture to clients.

"My dear wife, will you please provide a drumroll?" he requested.

Honoré obliged. It was a French snare drumroll. I laughed, and she took my hand and squeezed it tightly.

"Are you ready?" he said loudly.

"Yes, of course we are ready," Honoré blasted back. "We are also ready for the Second Coming, but hopefully your reveal will arrive momentarily."

Methodically and on purpose, Monsieur Lawrence began pulling up the cloth bag covering the garment from the bottom.

"Your pace is killing us," Honoré shouted.

With a swoosh, the bag was off the hanger. Monsieur Lawrence stood erect, silently holding his reveal.

"Oh my God" was all I could say. I jumped up as best as I could from the settee to hold the garment. Examining it, feeling it, and caressing it, I realized the big reveal was a completed sample of my first blazer design with its Mandarin collar and military accents, including gleaming gold and pink enamel buttons imprinted with my signature pansy icon sewn onto a sexy ice-white silk shantung fabric imported from Italy.

"So, what do you think?" Monsieur asked, beaming with pride.

The waterworks flowed as I continued touching the blazer. It was very soft and lightweight, yet very strong, with a feminine military structure.

"I love it, but how did this happen?" I could barely speak.

Monsieur Lawrence confessed that he had been working on the blazer for some time, building several samples using different fabrics and then modifying the cut, which was first too long, then too short, then finally perfect, at least to his trained eye.

"I did this to inspire you, my child. Yes, your hands are very full as a new mother and wife, but you must not give up your dream."

"It is so beautiful. You are an artist, Monsieur; I always knew that. You have made a blazer far above my talent," I told him, meaning every word.

"Nonsense. This is your exact design. I just called on forty-plus years of tailoring experience to perfect it."

"You have no idea what this means to me, especially today," I said. "I came here today from a ladies' charity luncheon where most of the women do not have careers. They live lives of plenty and endless leisure, courtesy of marriage."

Madame Honoré interrupted me. "So, you were lunching with our best customers," she chided.

"Yes, in fact, I was. One was Mrs. A, but that's not my message. Rather, a young woman had a meltdown when her husband won an auction bid for a golf trip. She stood up screaming for him not to spend the money on golf because she needed new clothes."

"Seriously?" Madame questioned.

"Are you that surprised, Honoré?" Lawrence followed. Honoré just shook her head, not answering.

Explaining that I had found the scene sad at first, I realized with a little help from my new friend Heather, that fashion was essential to most women. Not all women, but many women. And especially women in Newport Beach.

Yet Another Chance Meeting

Cole believed that the remarkable good fortune in his life was all due to a chance meeting with Kate. And that meeting had happened because he put himself in a place, or rather a town, where chance meetings specifically led to amazing life changes. That had not happened for Cole in Reno. It was Newport Beach that had delivered the magic.

On this, another spectacular clear and sunny morning on the California Riviera, Cole left Kate to do his bidding at the charity luncheon and maneuvered his pristinely polished black BMW sedan through light traffic on the Pacific Coast Highway, turning into the guard gated entrance to Linda Isle. Asking himself, as he often did, pretty much daily, why he deserved such good fortune, Cole knew the answer, but he camouflaged his reality with bravado. The money he had earned justified his failure to be honest about himself. Big money would make him a man of importance, a proper husband and father. Newport Beach was all about big money; Cole knew that much as well.

Pulling up once again in front of the Benheim residence, Cole saw that a gray Chevy sedan with darkened windows stripped of all chrome ornamentation was parked in the driveway. It looked like a police car but had no sirens or painted symbols of authority. Cole pulled in next to the car, got out, and attempted to look inside, finding nothing.

Entering the courtyard, he approached the front door. A tall and handsome man built like a bodybuilder, dressed in a black T-shirt and black jeans, stood at attention.

"Can I help you?" the man spoke as Cole came closer.

"I have an appointment with Walter Benheim. My name is Cole Baldwin."

"Please wait here. I'll be back," the man directed.

Cole waited, wondering who this guy was. Certainly not another butler, like the one he called "Lurch" who guarded the Carondolet mansion. This guy was more like a bouncer, standing at attention like the ones he recognized outside the bars and casino clubs in Reno.

Cole didn't have to wait long. Walter Benheim came bounding out the front door. At six feet six, WB was a sixty-something-year-old jock who had put on a good fifty extra pounds in his gut. His thinning, stringy gray hair was slicked back and pulled together at the base of his skull in a tiny ponytail, which was fastened with a rubber band. His hair was so thin and short that it stood erect, jutting out an inch or so from the back of his head. Cole laughed, thinking, *I wonder if his dick looks the same.*

"Hey, man," the ever-jovial Benheim called out, opening his arms to give his real estate agent a hug. Again, Cole amused himself, thinking, *It is now the age of hugging. Everyone is always hugging. Men didn't hug this much when I was a kid, and I am from an immigrant family! The world is falling apart, the Twin Towers have fallen, yet everybody is hugging. What does it all mean?*

Surprising himself with his psychological meandering, Cole thought that this kind of thinking wasn't his style.

"Cole, man, you seem distracted." Benheim had noticed Cole's introspective look.

"Heck, it's nothing. Who's that man at the door?" Cole asked.

"Heinrich? Oh, he is my wife's bodyguard," the former jock responded nonchalantly.

"Candy needs a bodyguard?"

"I just hired him. She's been feeling creepy lately going out in Newport."

"Creepy? What do you mean?"

"Man, you know creepy. Guys are always staring at her. Some are following her. She feels creepy."

"So, the big guy just follows her around?"

"He drives her and helps around the house. You know the drill."

Cole was thinking that he did know the drill, and he bet that Heinrich the bodybuilder was doing some other drilling as well.

Benheim put his right arm around Cole's shoulder and walked him into the house.

"Any more calls for showings?"

"I have two possible showings later in the week. I'm waiting to firm up appointments."

"Good boy. Let's get this place sold. We're moving to Palm Springs as soon as possible. Candy won't need Heinrich there; the whole town has gone gay."

"I didn't know that," Cole said, surprised at the reasoning for the move.

"Yeah. All the old stars and business tycoons have died, and the homos have settled in under the sun."

"Really?"

"Oh yeah. And they all love Candy. They idolize her. And guess what, they love me too. I'm Big Daddy."

Big Daddy changed the subject, seeing that Cole appeared uneasy with the homo talk. Walter had suspicions about Cole. He knew he was married, but there was just something off about him. He was too good-looking, too eager, and too polished, and on more than one occasion WB had given Cole a direct stare in the eye, the queer eye, to test him. Benheim figured Candy was safe around Cole.

"Cole, I asked you to come by because I have a guy you need to meet. He is your age, and he is into real estate and wants to raise capital to build an investment business in property development. He's waiting in the den to meet you. Do you mind?"

"No, sir. Who knows, this could be a great opportunity."

"That's the right attitude."

As they entered Benheim's study paneled in bleached gray wood, his real estate mogul friend stood to greet them.

"Hello. My name is Roman Yusapov," he offered in a Russian accent with an outstretched hand. "Please call me Roman. I am from Saint Petersburg."

Roman was better-looking than Cole, which was hard for Cole to grasp since, after all, he was the Cuban Italian stallion. Standing about five feet ten with a flawless olive complexion, piercing aquamarine-blue eyes, and wavy black hair just wild enough to make anyone take notice of him, Roman spoke perfect English with a disarmingly sexy Russian accent. As he shook Cole's hand, his eyes flashed, and the corners of his lips turned up slightly.

Cole was visibly impressed, and Benheim was now certain his impression of Cole was correct. *He's a switch-hitter for sure.* Candy was safe.

"I wanted the two of you to meet because I believe you have much in common. Primarily, you both are ambitious and want to make big money in real estate. Together you have the skills to charm any investor out of their pension," Walter Benheim said, laughing with a deep growl.

Roman had met Benheim several years earlier. Benheim had helped him to raise money from local investors in order to buy land and build a storage facility on a vacant lot near the Costa Mesa Freeway. Storage facilities were beginning to pop up in the changing new world. They were becoming a necessity, and Benheim smelled money. He was right in his assessment. In a little more than three years, working with Roman, he built some twenty storage facilities all over the Southern California region and now was raising capital to move beyond the state into Nevada and Arizona. Roman, just past thirty, was now getting rich himself thanks to Walter, and to his own drive raising multimillions from investors. Cole was tuned in.

"I think you guys can do the same thing developing Society Hill. The formula is similar. The land is still raw; development, just beginning. Overall, the project is banked by one of America's most respected, and most feared, billionaire developers. Guys with money will be standing in line to be a part of this huge project. The two of you could become real players." Benheim was exuberant in his introduction and in his prediction.

"I suggest you guys set up a meeting, get to know one another, and figure this out. If you decide to form a partnership, I'm in with the first five hundred thousand. More will come if things start to pop."

Cole and Roman shook hands again. Candy Benheim arrived on scene, attired in her designer see-through black bathing cover-up, a black microkini underneath. As she darted over to Cole and Roman, her black high-heel mule pool slip-ons clacked on the bleached hardwood flooring, the notes bouncing off the coffered ceiling. Kissing both her boys, on both cheeks each, she then planted a big kiss on her husband's lips. The kissing pair lingered for a long moment. Tongues were surely being exchanged and exercised. In the shadows, Heinrich stood at attention, arms behind his back, hands clasped.

"Darling, I'm jumping in the pool, then it's spa time. Will you join me?" Candy's invitation was clear.

"We are done here with my business proposal. Why not?"

With that, Walter Benheim stripped, leaving his clothes on the study floor in front of Cole and Roman.

The double doors to the study were both wide open, giving a view of the main hallway of the Linda Isle home. On the other side of the hall was the indoor pool. Candy removed her cover-up and handed it to Heinrich, now standing at the pool's edge with her exquisite pink derriere in full view, covered only by the black strip of her microkini. She dove right in, then her butt naked husband kicked of his loafers, calmly and deliberately walked across the hall in full-ass view of Cole and Roman and followed his wife into the pool with a not so graceful dive. The pool water roared like an ocean wave hitting shore.

Roman turned to Cole. "Do you know them well? If so, you know them well," he said with a grin.

Cole answered, "Yes, I do. Our first real estate meeting in this house was in the spa. I get it."

"One piece of advice, Cole," Roman said with a very nasty grin on his face. "When you sell this house, be sure to drain the pool and spa and have them both disinfected."

Cole promised to call Roman and set up a meeting.

CHAPTER FORTY-FOUR

THIS CHANGES EVERYTHING

Cole arranged a showing with a live client interested in the Benheim pool palace, so he apologized to me for not being able to attend my checkup with the beloved Dr. Grimes. This would be the first one he would miss, his having attended all my appointments when I carried Buddy, along with the first several with the new baby Brady. An earlier ultrasound had confirmed that baby number two would be little Buddy's younger brother.

Kissing the Cuban Italian stallion good morning and goodbye, I sent him off into the real estate world with my customary quick blow of air in his left ear and a strong pat on the left cheek of his bottom.

"Really, it's okay if you don't come. It's only the second trimester. You'll get another chance, I promise," I said, handing Buddy off to nanny Bonnie, preparing to leave myself.

"Promise?" Cole replied.

"Yes, promise. I may be late coming home this afternoon. Monsieur Lawrence wants me to stop by. He says he has a brilliant idea."

With Bonnie assuring me that she would keep everything under control, I walked out the half-opened Dutch door of the cottage with Cole, leaving the top half with the paned window open to let in the incredible breeze off the ocean.

As it was only minutes away on the oceanfront peninsula, even with summer beach traffic, I made it to Dr. Grimes's office up on "Pill Hill" across from Hoag Hospital right on time for my nine o'clock appointment.

Dr. Grimes was on schedule, which was especially surprising since it was the first appointment of the morning. I always requested the first appointment. Nurse Patti escorted me into the examining room, followed by Dr. Grimes. It seemed unusual that she had joined so quickly since Nurse Patti always took my vitals before Dr. Grimes came in. Dr. Grimes looked absorbed as she checked test results on the computer while Patti did her preliminary exam.

"I have some news for you, young lady," Patti whispered. "But I can't tell you. Dr. Grimes will murder me, after she fires me, that is."

Turning toward Patti's ear, I whispered, "Really, Patti, you can't be serious. You're not going to tell me the news?"

"Saved by the bell," Patti blurted out as Dr. Grimes left her computer across the examining room and came to life.

"Good morning, Kate." Dr. Grimes extended her hand. "You look wonderful. How are you feeling?"

"Overall, I feel wonderful. A little more tired than I would like. I don't remember feeling tired like this with Buddy, but I am carrying more weight, and the pregnancy seems even lower to me. Is this normal for a second boy?" I asked.

Patti was grinning in the corner. I shot her a look as if to say, *What is so amusing?*

Dr. Grimes began examining me with her stethoscope, then placed both hands on my belly. "Kate, your previous ultrasound was inconclusive. The blood and fluid samples we extracted are telling me that baby boy number two has a friend."

"A friend? Like a twin friend?" I asked nervously.

"We are certain you are having twins; however, we are unable to verify the gender as both fetuses are literally facing one another." Dr. Grimes added, "But I think it's a girl."

"Is that bad? Not that it may be a girl, but that the twins are facing one another?" I blurted out, instantly concerned.

"It is not unusual. No need for concern. We will know much more in a few weeks," the good doctor reassured me.

"Oh boy, this is big news." I looked over at Nurse Patti, who was still grinning. "Or shall I say, 'Oh girl'?"

Having had my mind set on delivering baby boy Brady, Buddy's future little brother, I was taken off guard by the possibility of having a baby girl too. My concern, confusion, and shock quickly turned one hundred eighty degrees and became an overwhelming sense of delight, bordering on euphoria.

"I never imagined," I told Dr. Grimes and Nurse Patti. "How come I never thought about having a girl? How odd."

"Not so odd, Kate. You knew you were having a boy, even naming him Brady. You have everything you need for another boy-child. Just give me a bit of time to confirm my suspicions before you start shopping for everything pink that you can get your hands on."

"I love pink."

"How did I know?"

"Really, this is such outstanding news."

"Keep it under your hat for a while. I'll call you when I get back the results of the additional tests."

Dr. Grimes instructed me to sit on the examining table so she could finish her routine checkup. I was on cloud nine, daydreaming about baby Billie. That was a girl's name I'd always loved. Dr. Grimes had to let me know three times that the exam was complete and that I could dress and be on my way.

"Patti, make a follow-up appointment for Kate with the front desk in two weeks," she said, leaving me in the room and going on her rounds.

Wandering Around Dazed

I had previously arranged a lunch date with my new friend Heather to follow my ob-gyn appointment, having promised to stay in touch before we both slipped out of the charity luncheon. I don't think that Heather expected me to call quite so soon, but she seemed pleased.

Needing a new girlfriend and realizing my life had narrowed to the care of my husband and child, with career dreams—or fantasy, to be honest—on hold, I found myself talking to the walls without at least one close friend. Heather and I clicked. It was that unexplainable *I get you; I like you; I feel as if I know you* feeling.

The baby news had totally undermined my balance, so I canceled lunch with Heather, calling her on my cell as I left Dr. Grimes's office. Hoping she wouldn't answer, I would leave a message. Cowardly, I know. Heather picked up with a big friendly hello, and I canceled practically before saying hi. She was surprised but understood. I promised not to be such a flake the next time.

The second that I hung up my cell phone, I caught my expression in the side view mirror of a random car in the lot as I walked by. *Am I crazy?* That was my look. Now what was I going to do? I could go home and be with Buddy, put him down for his nap after lunch, and give Bonnie the afternoon off.

Wanting to call Nancy and tell her the big news, I was even thinking of getting on the freeway north to LA and showing up at my Beverly Hills front door. There was Conroy's florist on a corner of Sunset Boulevard not far from the house. I could stop and buy two bunches of flowers, one blue, another pink. My mother would love that. She celebrated every bit of good news with style, and I wanted to be like her. Always had.

My strange mental state, half elated, and half dazed, stopped me from doing what I probably should have done. Nancy and Dalt would hear the news a little later. For now, and I wasn't exactly sure why, I was going to the salon to meet with Monsieur and Madame. We had an appointment for later that afternoon. I would just be early.

A plan of action flashed in my brain as I turned the key in the car ignition. *A metaphor for life,* I thought as the engine revved. Always looking for the message in odd circumstances that connect life's dots, I didn't think I was a fatalist, nor did I really believe in the spiritual or religious concept of an ordained path for every soul. Just the same, when foreign elements collided and brought clarity, I couldn't help but believe in something greater than myself—destiny. Of course, I'd been obsessed with all of this ever since meeting Cole and giving birth to Buddy. Now, there were two more lives coming, joining that destiny.

At the salon, the world was as it should be—everything and everyone in place in the boutique called Avenue Foch West, far from the banks of the river Seine, in this rather unique piece of Southern Californian lotusland by the beach. Seeing Honoré and receiving her warm embrace made me feel safe, at home. Indeed, Honoré and Monsieur Lawrence were my friends, true friends—new friends perhaps, but the real thing.

It was no wonder my car was on autopilot going directly to their shop. Yes, I had come with my plan, which was always in my head. I had never felt brave enough to bring it forward, even after Monsieur Lawrence finished the first sample blazer from my design. Today was the day. The news of expecting twins was the catalyst. Fearing I was a derelict mother for planning a career move, rather than basking in the thrill of baby news, I was scared. But I knew I was a good mother. Why not allow myself to also be the person I wanted to be? Never wanting just to fit in, and proud to be different, I said to myself, *I am different, and I like my difference.* Only, I never seriously had exhibited exactly what that difference was, at least beyond my expressed dreams and aspirations.

"We were expecting you today," Madame Honoré said, releasing her embrace and cupping her hands on my cheeks. Her fingers were cold, and I could see the shining red lacquer on her nails in my peripheral vision. It was all familiar. I took a deep breath.

"Are you busy today, Madame? May I have a few minutes with you and Monsieur Lawrence? I know I am very early for our appointment."

"You can see there are no customers. We can always make time, darling. Now is as good a time as any."

Madame called out for Monsieur to enter the showroom.

"Will it be all right to talk here? If a customer enters, we can pause," she said.

"Hello, my sweet girl," Monsieur Lawrence said, giving me a kiss on each cheek. He looked tired. Strands of hair hung over his forehead, rather than his usual impeccably groomed hair pushed back on his head. Signature clear-framed glasses were perched on the end of his nose, a constant sign of his work ethic.

"Monsieur, are you in the midst of designing an incredible outfit? You have that intense look I know well," I said lovingly.

"You know I can never rest," he replied.

Madame jumped in, saying, "He never rests, and one day there will be nothing but rest!"

"Spoken like a true Frenchwoman who made her home in America for most of her life," Monsieur replied. Turning to me, he asked, "I assume we have some unfinished business from our last meeting?"

"I am thinking, it has given me such hope seeing your finished work on my design that I want to propose a plan as follow-up to your unveiling my sample," I said, trying to show confidence, camouflaging my insecurity.

"We are all ears," Monsieur quickly answered.

Taking another breath, I inhaled, then exhaled slowly.

"Are you well?" Madame asked in response to my breathing. "Should you take some water, my dear?"

"Oh no, I'm fine. Before I share my plan, I should say that I just came from my doctor, who informed me that I am having twins."

Both my mentors let out a joyous yelp.

"Such wonderful news!" Madame cried. Monsieur, lifting off his glasses, wiped away a tear.

"Such wonderful news, and you came here to tell us. We are honored," Monsieur went on.

"I have not told Cole or my parents yet. You both are the first, so it is our secret for now. I came here directly from the doctor's office to talk to you both. Does it sound strange to you that I didn't know where else to go? The news of the babies gave me a sense of urgency to follow up on creating the fashion line in total and starting a real business."

Fortunately, there were still no customers in the shop as I continued sharing my strategy. We all sat down on the furniture placed in the center of the showroom, an homage to a petite salon in any Paris shop. Babbling on and on, trying to cover my confusion or guilt about not relishing the baby news, and not calling Cole or my mother, I had set me adrift. Instead, I was worrying about being swept away by the enormous responsibility of raising three babies, thereby leaving no room for my dream. With one baby, even with Bonnie to help, the dream had lost out. Was I not strong enough? Was I too comfortable, too spoiled? Maybe I simply was not motivated enough. When you don't have a burning need to work, to pay the rent, to eat, you cannot climb the mountain, make the impossible a reality.

Creating, building, and launching a clothing line is one big mountain. Famous designers had many failures. Why should I have a better chance? I was the practical rich girl clashing with the girl who had grown up being told and believing that anything was possible. I did know that such philosophy sold self-help books and made great graduation speeches, but in the real world, making an impossible dream come true took killer ambition and "take no prisoners" dedication. That was my fear. Could I rise to that level and, at the same time, not become the worst wife and mother?

Putting It All on the Table

Getting hold of my runaway hormones, calming down, trying to stop talking as if I were on a race to nowhere, I began to broach the subject that I had come to discuss with my mentors. Sharing my family story about my grandfather coming to the United States, meeting my grandmother in a garment factory in New York during the Depression, and the two of them ultimately making a successful life together set the stage perfectly for me to bring my own personal goal front and center.

"I think my connection to design and fashion merchandising is somehow in my DNA," I told Madame and Monsieur. "I only learned of my family history a year ago, just before my grandmother GiGi passed away. It hit me like a bolt of lightning. It was like what they say when a light bulb goes on in your brain. I just knew what I was supposed to do."

Monsieur and Madame stared at me, smiling but still, not saying a word. So, I got to the point. No more setup.

"Monsieur Lawrence, would you be willing to work with me and complete samples of the entire line?" I asked with newfound confidence. There was a moment of awkward silence. Had I overstepped the line?

"Kate, I don't think you realize what you are asking. Such a task would require my full attention. You are very young, but also very bright. I am sure you can see that I must run this business with Honoré. It is our livelihood, our very survival."

That renewed self-confidence deflated faster than a popped balloon. I didn't know how to respond. Foolishly, I had believed Monsieur would love the idea. He had been very supportive and so excited over the first completed design. A second light bulb flashed in my brain: with my rich girl mindset, I was expecting somebody else to tote the barge while I sat back as the "creative" factor. Reality can be harsh.

"If I committed to come to work here at least three days a week to start, taking no salary, concentrating on just following your guidance to construct the remainder of samples for the line, is that arrangement possible? I know it is a lot to ask."

Madame turned to her husband and winked at him discreetly. He hesitated to answer. She then gave him a whack on the arm.

"Yes, my dear girl, it is possible. We can give it a try. One step at a time. Let us see how it goes."

We shared a three-way hug. I promised to put together a formal plan.

"Can I start next week, Monday morning?"

"We will be here waiting."

Recovering from my roller coaster of confidence, or lack of it, I had succeeded taking my first step forward. Now I needed to lay out my long-range plan to further gauge the temperature. It was crucial that Monsieur not see me as a spoiled dilettante playing fashion designer. He knew me better than that. He had explained the process of fashion creation—moving from pen and ink on paper to the cutting board, to manufacturing, and beyond—and had tutored me in the challenges of selling an unknown new line to buyers from retail stores. Monsieur cautioned that with no track record, convincing a buyer to order was just about impossible. I understood. Once again, with as much bravado as I could muster, I confirmed my Monday morning start date and added some aspirational gems. On a roll, I pushed further.

"Our deal to share in profit still remains as we once agreed before, correct? You and Madame own a share of this new line. Previously, you said we would discuss and finalize later, stating that you would take only a 10 percent cut of any profit. I'm not sure you ever believed there would be any profit. You were just being kind. Now I am saying that there will be profit—maybe not much at first, but you will take 25 percent and nothing less," I said, putting up both my hands as if to stop either of them from speaking and objecting.

Deciding to divulge another aspect of my family story, I shared in confidence that GiGi had left me money in her will with an unrestricted clause stating, "Use this money any way you please to make a dream come true."

"I am going to do that. That's what the money is for, and yes, I know how lucky I am to be able to say that, to have these funds at all.

"Once we have the samples done, I can afford to cover the cost of hiring a manufacturing team to duplicate the line in a full range of sizes. Here is my follow-up request. I hope I am not again overstepping my worth in asking?"

Monsieur knew instantly what I was about to ask. He took my hand and guided me to the front display window of Avenue Foch West.

"We shall create a magnificent display taking up the entire window," he said. "And we shall set up a section of the store exclusively featuring the Fair Child inaugural line of 2002 or perhaps 2003. How fast do you think we can make this happen?" he gushed in his sexy Maurice Chevalier–like French accent. I loved the old movie *GiGi*. Such a perfect name. No surprise I liked it since I adored my very own GiGi.

Madame clapped and told me that it would be a market test. She added that we would need to advertise, need to throw an opening event, and need to put to-gether several fashion shows for local charity luncheons, just to get off the ground.

Overcome with premature elation, I knew it was still all talk. There remained so much to do. As I took another deep breath, Madame offered me water once again and told me to sit down.

"Millions of pregnant women work in the fields until they drop their chil-dren," I said.

She replied, "Indeed they do. The only difference for you, my dear, is that you have the distinct benefit of being pregnant and working in your field of dreams." Then she said, "Now you must go and call your husband and then your mother and share the really big news."

"Yes, yes, I will do that right away," I said, giving them both a kiss.

Running out the salon door, nearly tripping but catching myself, attempting to dash and dial the cell at the same time, I made it to my car in one piece. I took one more deep breath and made a mental note recording this extremely happy moment in my life. Perhaps I did have control over my destiny after all. Maybe I was not totally sidetracked by love, sex, marriage, and children after all. Instead, I was blessed at a very early age with the entire spectrum of all that is important in life. Closing in on twenty-two, and for the first time really, I believed that everything that was supposed to happen to me was unfolding. Maybe I was more of a fatalist than I thought. Was there a grand plan for me? If there was, I knew that it was a good one.

There was something else. Up until this moment I had felt like an expatriate from Beverly Hills living at the beach in Newport. Home was still Greater LA with Nancy and Dalt on Lexington Road. The pain of running away from USC and losing David had faded. Marriage to Cole and the birth of Buddy had closed that door, but I still felt like something of an outsider in Newport. That is, until today.

Bringing two more babies into our world and taking concrete steps to follow a career goal finally had ended that doubt. Newport was now my home. My husband's career was here as well, and my children would grow up here. Perhaps one day the Fair Child fashion line might be in stores in Beverly Hills, New York, Dallas, and Chicago too, all originating from design headquarters in Newport Beach, California. My cell began ringing.

"Cole, is that you? The cell is breaking up. Will you be home for dinner tonight? I have news."

"Can't you tell me now?" he asked.

"Only in person," I came back.

"I've got a second showing at the Benheim house later today. We should be done by five or so. Is that okay?"

"I'll be waiting."

Hanging up with Cole, I dialed my mother. She answered right away, and I shared the baby news. Nancy was over the moon and could not stop asking questions. We talked for at least half an hour while I sat in my car in front of the salon.

Sealing the Deal

Cole arrived at the Benheim residence for his three o'clock appointment with a client who had seen his cable TV show featuring a segment on the Linda

Isle house with the indoor pool. This was a second showing, which in real estate psychology was one big step closer to an offer. A potential two-million-dollar sale is serious business, and Cole wanted another check mark on his growing list of sold properties.

The potential new client was an easy credit car dealer who owned a stable of brands in mostly working-class neighborhoods in Southern California's Inland Empire, which translates geographically to towns approaching the desert rim. The guy was barely forty, self-made, and on his third marriage. Cole had gotten the lay of the land at their first showing when the client's young new bride, probably the same age as Cole's twenty-one-year-old wife, began giggling with joy as she slipped off her cork-bottom wedge sandal and dipped her iridescent-orange-painted toes in the indoor pool. Cole could already smell the ink on escrow documents.

The Cuban Italian stallion pulled in through the Linda Isle gate, cleared for entry by two thirty. He had arrived early in order to prepare the house. Walter Benheim had called him back to confirm notice of the second showing, but it didn't matter since Cole had a key and the security code to get in. Getting out of his car, which he had parked curbside, Cole could see that Heinrich the guard, who was often present at the main door, was not at attention. This did not necessarily mean anything; he could be standing poolside holding a towel for Candy Benheim or performing any number of demands for the couple. Cole thought the setup was strange, but he relegated the oddness of the relationship to the lifestyle of the Newport rich. After all, the Carondolet experience was still fresh.

Ringing the buzzer, Cole got no response. Seeing that the security alarm pad at the front door indicated that the alarm was not set by virtue of a small green light, Cole decided to let himself in. He started to use his key, but the door opened without it. Cole entered.

Finding the main level of the residence in darkness, he began to do a fast run-through, turning on lights and performing the real estate fluff in advance of the arrival of the used car salesman-turned-multimillionaire. Cole had also asked his new potential real estate partner Roman Yusapov to show up and help to push the sale since Roman was also a good pal and business partner of Walter Benheim.

Both Roman and the client arrived on time at three o'clock just as Cole finished the main level turn-on. He had had no time to do the second floor but figured that nobody was home, and they could wing it when going upstairs.

Roman and Tyler Brown, the car guy, entered the front door, which Cole had left ajar. They called out for Cole, who was already just around the corner, having heard their voices in the courtyard as the two men approached. Welcoming them both with a strong handshake and a hug, familiar for only a second meeting with both guys, Cole thought it seemed appropriate. Neither one objected. Besides, Cole now understood the whole hug etiquette.

The grand tour of the home proceeded. Cole inquired if Tyler Brown's wife was coming. Brown essentially responded by letting Cole know that the decision was ultimately his, adding that Tiffany shared a strong desire to make the indoor pool her own.

Making their way up the curvilinear staircase constructed of a steel frame supporting three-inch-thick glass steps rising over one end of the glistening cobalt-blue-tiled pool with its ten-foot water depth under the staircase, the three young masters of their respective universes laughed as some old-fashioned male jostling almost sent Cole over the edge for an Olympic swan dive into the deep blue.

They made the journey upstairs, arriving at the entrance to a very unusual zigzagging dimly lit hallway with doors opening in all directions. As they paraded through, Cole quickly flipped light switches as he described the salient points of the property. Roman was his backup man, adding follow-up points on the property replacement value, market trends, and future appreciation given the limited availability of gold coast property in this area of California.

"The Chinese are coming," Roman said. "And it's just the beginning."

"Is that like 'the redcoats are coming'?" Tyler Brown asked, thinking he was smart and funny.

Cole forced a laugh—fake, but obligatory.

Reaching the sitting room adjacent to the master suite, they found that the door was open. They entered. The room was dark. Cole turned on the ceiling spotlights and two lamps on either side of a sofa facing a fireplace. As he pushed another switch, the electric shades rose over French doors leading to a balcony overlooking an inlet of the Newport harbor.

Roman summoned Cole, thinking he heard something coming from behind the doors leading to the master bedroom. The three of them stood together by the doors to the bedroom as Roman told them to shush so they could listen carefully to determine if there was life behind the proverbial curtain.

At first, there was nothing. Seconds later, nothing turned into definite human noises, but they could not make out the sounds. Cole chose to knock and call out to see who, if anyone, was inside the room. Maybe a television had been left on. There was no reply, so he slowly opened the door. The bedroom was pitch-black with the shades fully drawn, so there was no light, either natural or electric. Inside the massive bedroom in complete darkness, it was difficult to make out where the furniture was, including the bed, which was also massive—two queens side by side, creating a superking. Cole remembered the unusual bed from his original tour of the property when he was trying to get the listing. He had made certain to include the superking bed in the video of the property, which he put on his cable TV show *Living the Dream*. In turn, it had become one of the hooks enticing Tyler and Tiffany Brown to check the place out. Ty and Tiff—that's what they wanted to be called—found the pool and the superking bed very sexy. Deal closers for Cole.

Cole called out again, still no answer. He went to the plate by the door to flip on the ceiling spotlights. The bedroom, the size of a football field, lit up like a football stadium.

The three men froze momentarily as the superking bed came into full view. What also came into full view was one stark white ass gyrating up and down, positioned on the knees of a man otherwise camouflaged by rumpled bedcovers. The now clearly audible sounds of sexual pleasure were identifiable.

Still, none of the three voyeurs moved, not even attempting to leave, assuming they were witnessing Walter and Candy sharing a little afternoon delight. And the lovers were seemingly oblivious to their audience; they kept going full-on as the familiar animal moans of passion grew more intense. Climax must have been approaching.

Cole turned to Roman and told him that he didn't think the gyrating guy was Walter.

"His ass is too small," Cole announced. "Walter is a big boy, a three-hundred-pounder."

The guessing had ended practically before it began as the sex reached a crescendo and the woman, whom they could not see, let out a climax scream that should have alerted paramedics.

The jokester Brown quipped, "Boy, good solid wall insulation. That's a plus for the sale."

This time both Cole and Roman howled—real laughs. All of them were still watching, none having the slightest compunction to step out into the sitting room and close the bedroom door.

Maybe it was because it all had happened so fast, in a matter of just a few minutes. They figured the pleasure scream had come from Candy Benheim. Who was the owner of skinny white ass, which remained in view although the gyrating had stopped?

Then came the ultimate shocker. Walter Benheim came prancing out of the master bathroom, naked and erect. The three voyeurs backed up, not sure what to do. They even began apologizing to Walter, explaining the odd circumstances. Walter gave them a high five and jumped on the big bed. The skinny white ass pulled out and moved over as Walter mounted the woman Cole had presumed to be Candy.

The mystery was solved as the skinny guy turned to his side, revealing that he was none other than the private guard Heinrich who had been hired for Candy. Apparently, his duties of service were wide-ranging. Cole and Roman glanced at each other, both surely thinking the same thought: that older Walter needed to keep younger Candy satisfied so that she could also be satisfied with him. Sloppy seconds were better than no sex at all. Heinrich was the warm-up act.

It was time to step outside and close the bedroom door, so Cole, Roman, and Tyler Brown disappeared, shutting the door, as the second act of sexual groaning became discernibly louder.

Tyler Brown was first to announce, "It's three-way time. They are both doing her now."

Roman responded with another *Oh brother* look to Cole.

"I think the guard may be doing the boss while the boss is doing Candy," he said. "Walter is one kinky guy. He is sex crazed. He will do anything with anyone for that rush."

Cole was not surprised, at least until Roman shared that Walter had told him that he had a thing for Cole, and that Cole was "one really handsome fuck." Walter had shared that he and Candy might close another kind of deal with Cole along with the house sale, also confessing that Walter believed Cole may very well be a switch-hitter.

Cole was genuinely caught off guard. Despite his own sexual wanderings, he was not used to having the flip side of his hidden libido thrown into his face.

"So, what do I do about that?" Cole asked Roman, as Tyler wandered off down the hall, back toward the glass steps. Roman had no idea about Cole's private life, only knowing that he was recently married and the father of a young child. They laughed off Walter's sexual wonderings.

"Just keep cool and keep it professional," Roman told Cole. "Sell the fucking house to this clown, and then let's move on to bigger things."

Meeting Tyler Brown downstairs by the main door, Cole joked with his client about the unusual showing.

Tyler Brown responded, "That was really a turn-on. This is one lucky house, if you know what I mean. I'm going to make an offer," he said.

"Fantastic." Cole beamed. "I pride myself on giving clients exceptional showings."

That was over the top even for Cole. Roman shot him a look as if to say, *Cool it, man, Don't press your luck.*

"I'll call you tomorrow morning to write an offer," Tyler Brown said as he walked to his car.

Roman gave a high five to Cole, repeating what he had offered in their previous meeting. "I want to sit down with you and make a business plan. Let's get this going."

"Will tomorrow be soon enough? I'll call right after dealing with Brown on an offer, then we will meet."

"The time to act is now—not a day to waste," said Roman.

"I get it, man. Not a day to waste," the ambitious future Newport real estate mogul wannabe replied, brushing off Roman's comment about Walter's sexual attraction to him.

As Cole reached his BMW on the curb and opened the driver's-side door, a sparking new snow-white Porsche Carrera with the top down roared into the Benheim driveway. Slamming on the brakes, which screeched, just inches from crashing into a garage door, the driver, whose face was not visible beneath the camouflage of a low-riding white baseball cap, let out a feminine scream of relief that echoed across the stone driveway. Exiting the Porsche, the woman noticed Cole and waved.

"Hello, baby doll. It's Candy. Do you love my new car that Walter gave me? I just picked it up. Can you come in and visit?" she called out.

Waving back at Candy, Cole expressed his love of the new car, then told her he was late and would catch up soon. Getting in his BMW, he sat motionless, staring at the steering wheel, thinking, *Who was the woman in the Benheim bed?*

CHAPTER FORTY-FIVE

TIME TO GET SERIOUS

The best time of my day with Buddy was his early dinner hour. Making it back from the salon in perfect time, I found that Buddy was up from his afternoon nap, happily playing with some of his blocks and his ever-present companion, a plush Scottie dog. Nanny Bonnie was sitting with Buddy on a huge multicolored alphabet comforter/blanket spread open on the living room floor that my mother had delivered on one of her many gifting visits. This was my son's safe harbor: his blanket, his dog, his Bonnie, and me—nothing better in his barely one year of life on the planet. Not for him, and certainly not for me.

Taking a moment to solidify this memory of such pure, unspoiled joy, I counted my blessings. I did this often, on some days morning, noon, and night. But really, what an exceptional day it had been: twins coming, career dream back on track, and a loving husband soon coming home for a very special dinner.

The next hour belonged to Buddy as I did my motherly routine of peeling and cutting a banana into bite-sized pieces, slicing strawberries, and making perfect wedges of my son's favorite food, avocado. Bonnie went for a jog on the beach, giving me special time alone. Buddy and I finished his dinner as Bonnie returned, looking energized and refreshed, glowing just slightly from the exercise. Asking her to ready the bath for Buddy, I prepared dinner for Cole. With special news to deliver, I thought something romantic was in order.

Cole came charging through the Dutch door, smiling broadly and calling out for me. I caught the big smile from the sidelines as I set our table for two on the beach patio.

"Kate, I have news," Cole sang out.

Little did he know the news I had to share. As I called back to him, he turned and saw me and began rushing toward me. Before a word could be said, Cole embraced me, kissing me as if it were our wedding night. I knew that passion well. He wanted to make love; dinner could wait.

His kiss became deeper and stronger. I gave in to it. Whether it was instinct or just reflex reaction, I took his suit jacket off his shoulders, letting it fall to the ground. Cole paused the kiss for just a second to undo and drop his tie. I unbuttoned his shirt.

He picked me up, and we were up the stairs and in our bed in what was a speed record for the two of us. Placing me on the bed, my head resting on two feather pillows, Cole undressed me. After he'd removed my loose-fitting dress, there I lay in full-blown pregnancy.

"Are you sure it is safe?" he asked gently.

I nodded and whispered, "Dr. Grimes has given her blessing."

Cole laughed. "Well, at least we know we won't get pregnant with another kid. Only one at a time, right?" He'd made another of his silly jokes.

Hesitantly, I came back, "Well, not exactly true."

Cole was naked and rubbing his incredible male body up and down, side to side, moving against me carefully, refraining from pressing his muscular weight on my stomach. He just teased the surface of my body, his thick, soft body hair brushing my skin, causing it to tingle. With me thinking that he had missed my comment altogether, Cole began running his tongue over my pregnancy and up the center of my torso and onto my breasts, gently taking my ridiculously enlarged nipples into his mouth.

My words must have registered. Pulling back, he asked, "What did you mean? Did I hear you right? It isn't true that a woman can have only one baby at a time?"

Cole then confessed that he was damn basic when it came to understanding the facts of life. Yet he thought he at least understood the concept of one pregnancy at a time.

I smiled at him and ran my hands through his amazing wavy black hair, one portion fully draped over the right side of his forehead.

"Did I ever tell you that you have the sexiest hair?" I asked.

"Yes, you have told me," he answered. He moved his lips off my breasts and up the left side of my neck, ultimately nibbling on my ear and blowing a soft breeze of warm Cole breath into it. This was a wild turn-on for me, the lovely little pregnant wife with her head on feather pillows becoming the tigress of love.

Cole entered me, and we danced the love dance for at least an hour, maybe longer. I think it might have been the best ever. Both of us were spent. Cole had delivered twice, pretty good for just one hour. And I was thrilled over two full-blown O's. Also, amazing for me, pregnant or not. Boy, the hormones were in full-speed-ahead mode.

We lay side by side in our marital bed. The sun set, as it was somewhere between seven thirty and eight o'clock in the evening. Living on the sand, I could tell time by the position of the sun in the sky over the horizon. I even had come to know the difference season to season, a veritable navigator.

Turning to Cole, with both of us satisfied and dazed, I asked, "Would you like dinner, my handsome lover?"

"I don't need food. I need you."

Cole moved over to me, turning on his side and moving up against me. He wanted a third go-round. *Really?* I thought.

"Cole, I have something to share."

"It was the best sex ever? It was for me," he answered instantly.

"Yes, it was the best sex," I said, softly looking at him in the eyes, the two of us only inches apart.

"I have news, Kate," he replied instantly.

"I'll bet it is good news. I saw you grinning from ear to ear when you came in the door tonight."

"It is good news. I sold the Linda Isle home. Had a great showing with the buyer, who told me he would call to make an offer tomorrow. But he called right after the showing, and we made a deal on the phone."

"Congratulations, my wonderful husband," I said, meaning every word. I was truly proud of his success, and I knew it gave him validation, along with a sense of purpose. Even more, it provided a level of worthiness what with his being married to an American rich girl. Not that the fact of my parents' wealth ever mattered to me in my relationship with Cole. But I knew it was important to him, his coming from the other side of the equation. Certain that is why Cole had refused to take investment dollars from Dalt. He would launch his development business with the coastal land being called Society Hill in Newport his way.

"Cole, that extra commission income might just come in handy," I told him. He looked perplexed, furrowing his brow.

"Really? Extra income is always good, right?"

"Especially with three babies to feed," I said, smiling.

"I'm confused. We have Buddy, and you are pregnant with number two. Didn't we just determine that a woman can only be pregnant one nine-month period at a time?"

"One pregnancy at a time, yes. But not one baby."

"Oh my God, you're having triplets?" Cole looked as if he might faint.

"No, no, silly. First, your math needs help. If I were having triplets, we would have four mouths to feed."

"We're not having triplets?"

"No. We're having twins."

"Twins? We're having twins? Why didn't you tell me?"

"I am telling you."

"But I could have hurt them with all of this sex."

"Cole, Dr. Grimes said—"

"I know, but that was for one, not two."

I kissed him on both cheeks and told him to relax—all was well with both babies Baldwin.

"When did you find out?" he asked.

"Just today, baby."

"Are you happy?"

"Delirious."

"What do we do now?"

"Buy two more cribs, give Bonnie a raise, and become one big happy family."

"I love you, Kate. I am so lucky. I do not deserve this happiness."

"Yes, you do. And don't you forget it. I love you, Cole. Maybe even from the first meeting over my crunched car."

"Maybe?"

"Don't press your luck."

"Oh no, don't want to chance that."

"How about going downstairs for some ice cream? I think I have almost all thirty-one flavors in the freezer. It's a pregnant woman's prerogative after all."

Getting Down to Business

Cole had scheduled an early morning video session for his cable television real estate reality show *Living the Dream*. About a year into the project, with the show airing on a local cable outlet in Orange County and directed at high-net-worth residential neighborhoods, some real success, including the Linda Isle sale, had come his way from the marketing exposure. He looked very handsome on camera, and he had that *it* personality factor. Yes, much of the *it* was also bullshit, but wasn't such the case with all marketing? Just about everything, including all the meds now being blasted on the airways, was a marketing tool. I wasn't one for any BS, but I gave Cole some room on that front.

I might have been young, but I knew real estate was one tricky business. It is said that many agents would sell their own mothers for the right deal. Cole, as yet anyway, had not revealed that potential trait. Thank God, since I had planned to marry a doctor who saved lives for a living. Best-laid plans. Being a real estate wife was fine with me. My mother was somewhat defined by being my father's partner. She was the financial investor's wife. Nancy had no problem with that. She loved Dalt and everything about him, even his faults. If you were to ask her what faults, she'd tell you he had none, that he was perfect.

"But, Mom, there's no such thing as perfect," I would protest.

"That's only because no one is like your father," she would say with that knowing smile. I would never say another word.

Cole arranged to feature a new build on Society Hill in the current episode of his show, now in production. The new Italian Mediterranean–influenced architecture of the home caused it to be labeled as another McMansion by the cynics, the critics, and those who found the million-plus-dollar entrance fee for a home buyer in Newport to be outrageous. Cole sensed it was only the beginning of a run to the stars. Frequently he had told me, "In a few years, those homes will be selling in the multimillions." Every time I heard him speak the line, I would kiss him and tell him I supported him 100 percent. Cole needed the affirmation from me. I know that it pumped him up, gave him confidence. It was a lesson I had learned from Nancy. As a child of the new age of independent and equal women, my mother, the ultimate supportive wife, was the most independent and equal woman in the universe, at least to me.

Cole's new buddy—I called him the "add water and stir" business partner—Roman Yusapov had made the arrangements literally overnight with a builder-developer to feature this particular property on the cable television broadcast. Roman had taken the producer reins with great seriousness, relieving Cole of the production details so he could concentrate on his on-air personality and ultimately sell the hell out of the property.

Roman had arranged everything for the morning video tour of the home up on Society Hill. He even brought in a second camera for two angles. Previously there had been only one camera on a shoot. Cole arrived to find a makeup artist and hairstylist on-site as Roman made camera position notes to the small crew and adjusted the lighting with a hired lighting director. Cole basked in the Hollywood treatment.

"We now have two cameras, makeup, and a lighting director?" Cole said, impressed.

Roman responded, "Go big or go home."

"Can we afford to go big?" Cole followed up, somewhat out of character as he always wanted to go big.

"Don't worry. Just do your magic," Roman offered. "Man, we are getting on the fast track to real estate glory."

"That sounds great, I think." Cole added, "What exactly does that mean?"

"It means we will one day very soon have our names on a big office building, and we will control this market, one of the richest in the world."

The shoot was flawless. Cole was at the top of his game. Roman edited the footage that afternoon and finished delivering the half-hour program to the network the following morning. It was up and on the air, playing in the several time slots that *Living the Dream* had previously purchased.

On this day at the close of summer 2002, things changed for Cole. I would always remember because my husband had come home that night and I knew he was not the same guy. On this day, he believed that he really could make his dreams of a big real estate career real. It wasn't just talk anymore.

Days later, Cole shared that the phone was ringing like crazy, his email had crashed, and his office manager wanted to take us out to dinner at the chic new

Society Hill Resort perched high on a cliff over the Newport coast with a view of the vast Pacific Ocean.

"Can you believe it? The manager wants to take us to dinner, and my partner Roman wants me to quit," Cole told me. "I think I'm going to quit," he added.

My practical side immediately kicked in, but I held back. After waiting to come up with the right words—words of support, words of confidence building, words of believing in my husband 100 percent—I finally spoke.

"If you quit, what do you and Roman plan to do?" I said, disguising all hint of fear and trepidation. I practically sang the words in the melody of Disney's "It's a Small World."

"A bunch of the calls and emails coming in were not from people wanting to buy the house. Rather, they were from people wanting to invest in Society Hill development. We had calls from China. Can you believe that? Technology is creating a different world," Cole said, wrapping his arms around my pregnant belly and planting a kiss on my dress at navel level.

"Will we know who is in there before they come to live with us?" he asked sweetly.

"Dr. Grimes said most probably at my next ultrasound visit. She thinks it might be a little girl, but she's not certain."

"That would be the best. Wouldn't you love that, Kate?"

"I will love them both. We will love them all, all three of them, the Baldwin Bunch."

Hearing me use the phrase for the first time, Cole loved it. Neither one of us had grown up in the 1970s with the Bradys, so there was no connection there, even though we had watched reruns on TV. It just sounded happy. Being happy was important to me. Another lesson I had learned from my mother, Nancy. "Happiness is a choice." She had made that crystal clear.

"Bad things happen to everyone. Never dwell. Never talk about bad news to excess. Just push forward. Seek happiness. Live happiness. Be happiness." That was the mantra direct from my mother, speaking about a rapidly changing universe that was starting to classify her version of female strength as irrelevant. Her advice: "Ignore the haters. They are irrelevant. Never allow anyone to pigeonhole you, classify you, or put a label on you," she would say, always ending by quoting a line from the film *Dirty Dancing* when the Johnny Castle character, played by Patrick Swayze, says, "Nobody puts Baby in a corner." That always made me smile.

Nanny Bonnie had finished giving Buddy his dinner. He was starting to be a bit more daring with food. Tonight, buttered noodles were hanging from his lips and dripping down his onesie, some of it now on the snaps. Cole and I came into the kitchen as Buddy raised both arms in joyous recognition of his father. Cole picked him up out of the highchair, thereby adorning himself, or rather his expensive Armani pinstriped suit, with buttered noodles. Giving Bonnie a minute of breathing room, we took Buddy upstairs to give him his nightly bath and prepare him for an early retirement. Cole handled the bath duties as I prepared the boy's bed and his nighttime needs.

To my surprise, Cole removed his buttered noodle clothing and got in the bath with Buddy. My two men came out of the bathroom partially dry, hand in hand, and naked. Buddy was just starting to kind of walk. With Daddy's help, this was the best moment of his almost one-year life. We laughed, and Buddy let out a screech—the happiest kind of baby joy. No doubt this was one of those special happiness moments.

I wrapped towels around my guys. We sat in a circle on the carpeted floor, where I placed a stack of books—animal books, train books, fire truck books, and of course, alphabet books. Buddy turned the pages with urgency, many of them showing signs of tearing. Cole dimmed the light just a touch. We read all of them, Buddy turning or ripping the pages, with good night melodies filtering through the room as the sun setting in the west over the sand faded into China. The three of us fell asleep on the floor, I kept one eye open as best I could watching the baby.

Bonnie came looking for us, finding the three Baldwin bears dozing. She picked up sleeping Buddy, put him in a diaper and nightclothes as he remained totally out to the world, and placed him in his proper bed. Stumbling and rising from the floor, Cole, wearing only a towel, which naturally almost fell to the floor, kissed our son good night and thanked our Bonnie. Then he and I quietly tiptoed out, our arms clasped around each other's waists.

"Cole, do you want to get your suit?" It had been left in a pile on Buddy's floor.

"I'm so happy I think I'll buy a new one tomorrow. I think I've earned two deal-closer suits; don't you think?"

The following morning, Cole resigned. His office manager took the news with something between shock and anger. Cole knew in his gut that it was the right move. With enough savings to cover our living expenses for a year, he figured it was a risk that surely would pay off. Besides, he had told me that he was only twenty-seven years old. There was time to recover from a big mistake. I did my supportive Nancy thing.

"You will make it work. And if there are challenges, you will learn from them and do even better," I said.

"When was the last time I told you how great you are? I don't deserve you, Kate, but I love you."

"Don't you forget, it bud," I said. "Not to change the subject back to business, but what is your first step?"

Cole went into the business mode and explained that their first investor was going to be Walter Benheim, the man whose home he had just sold. Further, Cole planned to open a small office with Roman, find a good lawyer, set up an investment trust, then jump through all the legal hoops, also confessing he knew nothing about them. Assuring me that Roman did, Roman's having been successful with Walter Benheim for the past several years, Cole said that all would be handled professionally.

I asked if we needed to put in a share of money. Cole nodded, replying that we did. He had the initial money saved, and he would share the decision-making with me, keeping me in the loop always. That made me feel like a grown-up and, more important, like an equal partner. Okay, now it seemed I had one foot in Mother Nancy's world and the other in my new age generational world with its views of the modern woman. Some days it all seemed very confusing. Often, I wished that life could be—as indeed I thought it should be—very simple in terms of a woman and a man being equal.

CHAPTER FORTY-SIX

EMOTIONAL HIGHS AND LOWS

First thing Monday morning, I made my way to the salon as promised. Honoring my self-imposed commitment to dedicate three mornings a week to advancing the Fair Child line, I met Monsieur in the workroom and began cutting sample fabric under his tutelage for the next piece, which was to be a sleeveless A-line sheath cut six inches above the knee. Exacting in detail, Monsieur called out minutes into my cutting the neckline of the dress, using the paper forms he had created, "No, no, no! Stop!"

"You are cutting too deep," he advised. How could he possibly have seen this from across the room? Monsieur was right though; the form had slipped, and I hadn't noticed.

The morning flew by. We did not take a break. By noon, all the cuttings were ready to assemble for three additional pieces of the line. I was truly happy, feeling incredibly accomplished. It meant a lot to me. Admitting that I was feeling tired, I gave into my requirement for a break. Hugging my mentor goodbye and promising to return midweek, I blew a kiss to Madame, who was working with a client in the showroom, and left without fanfare.

As I was walking to my car, a familiar face came toward me.

"Kate, it's Heather. I didn't have class today, so I thought I'd take a chance and come by the salon, hoping you might be here." My new girl pal Heather Adamson gave me a big hug hello. I apologized again for having broken our lunch date last minute. She dismissed the cancellation with a wave, saying that she wanted to talk to me. Heather had come with a proposal.

This was certainly the Baldwin week for propositions. Heather asked if I had time for coffee or a quick lunch, and I accepted. There was a little patio cafe near the salon. We took a table for two by the fountain in the center in the awning-covered al fresco dining area.

Heather wasted no time with "How are you?," "How's the family?," and the rest.

"Kate, this will come as a surprise, since we do not know each other well, but I would like to try working with you on your fashion line."

I'm not sure what I had expected her to say, but I knew it wasn't that.

"Go on, please explain more." I stumbled over my words somewhat yet was flattered and interested to know why and how.

"I will be graduating with a business degree from USC in the spring and plan to go to law school. Stanford is my dream school. Lately I feel like I need to dive into a real business first to find out if I really have the right stuff, to find out if I am right for law school."

Heather had gotten my attention. In my own way, I was in the same frame of mind, just with different life circumstances. She continued, "It would be too easy to get a job with the family business. That would not deliver the answers to my questions as I search for self-worth. The fashion business interests me, maybe because my mother is the undisputed fashion queen of Newport. And while I don't follow in her style footsteps, my mother is my best friend and is amazing."

Heather sounded like the sister I never had. Was it possible to have found such a like-minded soul by accident? Was Heather my new best girlfriend out of the blue? At this point I shared with my new BFF that I got it. She smiled, and I asked her to tell me what she had in mind.

It came down to a simple equation. Heather wanted to be the business end of the partnership. I would be the creative; she would be the administration. Someone had to keep the books, file the papers, watch the budget, deal with a lawyer and an accountant, track the details, negotiate contracts with jobbers and distributors, supervise the marketing and advertising, and produce the fashion shoots and shows. Heather went on for ten minutes. She echoed in detail what Monsieur had offered at the start. I got all of that too. It wasn't that I had ignored the reality; I simply wasn't facing it as I started cutting samples. After I shared this with Heather, she replied, "That's exactly why this is perfect. The creative partner in a creative business must have a clear vision uninhibited by all these matters. At least at first. Later, the creator must also learn to be a businessperson too, or else the business could fail miserably. I want to be the businessperson at the ground floor. Let's see what we can do together. Interested?"

Without hesitating or asking to think about the proposal, I answered, "Yes, absolutely. Let's do it." Shocking myself, I realized I was acting like my husband, following a dream with ultimate bravado. Throwing caution to the wind, I was jumping in with both pregnant feet.

"How do we proceed?" I asked with a certain degree of wonder, tempered by shock over my impulsive move.

"Give me a few days to make notes and come up with a business plan. Will you be at the salon Friday morning? I could come by, and we can put our heads together."

"That sounds good. I must also include Monsieur. He is my partner too," I told Heather. "He and Madame will be our partners," I added.

"Is that a problem for us?" she asked.

"Oh no. Monsieur is right on your page," I advised.

"Then it's a date."

We departed the cafe. I headed home for a much-needed afternoon nap, my head literally spinning.

Reality Is a Bitch

The lyrics of Billy Joel's song "Summer, Highland Falls" with the line "From Sadness to Euphoria" echoed my emotional state, but in reverse. September 11, 2002 had arrived, the one-year anniversary, and I went into a major funk. Picking up the phone to call my father numerous times, starting at daybreak, six in the morning, I kept hanging up. By noon, I let the call go through, knowing Nancy would answer, as she was Dalt's sergeant at arms, the protector. My mother was always on duty to screen the expected calls of goodwill about my father and brother's survival that morning in New York. Mine was not just another one of those calls. Mother signaled to my father to pick up the line.

We talked for an hour, the best talk we'd had in a very long time. Dalt was strong and resilient, yet 9/11 had taken, or at least chipped away at, a layer of his granite. Candidly, he shared the depth of his emotional response when witnessing the towers fall, inhaling the toxic dust, and smelling the foulest odors that made him think of what it may have smelled like as the crematoriums took millions of lives in the World War II camps of Auschwitz and Birkenau. I asked why his mind had gone to such a time and place. Dalt responded that humankind never learns the lessons of evil from our history; the cycle repeats, with only the time and place changing. As a member of the boomer generation, he had not lived through the atrocities of World War II, as his generation had reaped the benefits of the sacrifices of their parents, members of the "greatest generation."

Putting geopolitics aside, Dalt was far more direct when it came to talking about my brother, Jamey. Jamey had taken the brunt of the experience, and for him the past year had been rough. For Dalt, "pretty tough" meant seriously tough, as he always put an optimistic spin on the worst of situations. I often thought of my father when listening to Casey Kasem's Top 40 broadcast on the weekends when I was in high school. What was his sign-offline? Something like "Keep your feet on the ground and reach for the stars." Or was it "Keep your head in the stars"? I don't know precisely, but corny or not, that was Dalt.

Today that optimism included some direct talk that made me cry, yet I did not let my father hear the tears in my voice.

"Kate, I go to bed at night worried sick that Jamey will never be okay. What will become of my son? I don't know how else to help him."

"I thought he was doing better?" I responded softly.

"His doctors allowed us to send him to Beverly High under strict supervision so that he would have a chance to 'normalize.' Too much teenage time in one rehab after another can be a trigger for a life of dependency of another sort."

Dalt continued to share all his ideas and all his fears about Jamey. Finally, I just cut to the bottom line.

"So, Father, where does he stand now? And what is the plan?"

"Your mother and I think he's back on drugs, but his recent test proved negative."

"Okay. Well, that should be a relief."

"We wish that it was. Jamey seems more withdrawn every day. He hardly speaks to us. He has no friends that we know of. His special tutors and regular teachers are concerned, but they give him room. I've suggested they not do so, but they refuse."

"Do you think maybe that the whole Beverly Hills rich kid fast lane life could be part of the problem? Jamey is a gentle soul, not into all the hype."

"Just like his big sister."

"That's right, just like me. I was never part of the whole Beverly scene."

By the end of our marathon talk, Dalt finally made his point.

"Kate, Jamey is going to be eighteen next year. I'm afraid he'll just take off and there will be nothing I can do. In fact, I'm afraid he could bolt anytime."

I told my father that I knew Jamey and that he loved his mom and dad and would never do that.

"You know, last year Jamey came down to Newport for a few days, and we went to a Sunday morning service on the beach led by the Surfer Saint. Remember him? He officiated at our wedding. The preacher's real name is Paco, and his preaching is not very religious—more spiritual and feel-good, like our wedding. Jamey liked him. Maybe another visit would be good?"

Dalt hesitated. I knew he was afraid to let my brother loose. Leveraging the excuse that I was pregnant and due to have twins soon, along with having to take care of Buddy, my father said he didn't want to add to my responsibilities. Naturally, I told him he was concerned for no reason. Cole and I would be very happy to have Jamey come down. A weekend visit was nothing and might help him come out of whatever depression he was feeling and not verbalizing.

"I remember how kind Paco was to Jamey. They were even laughing together. Let's give it a try," I said.

"I'll talk to your mother and Jamey and get back to you soon. Oh, and thanks for the 9/11 call. We're doing darn well considering, my darling girl."

As I was about to hang up, I caught Dalt say, "One more thing."

"Sorry, Dad, I thought we were done."

"Sweet girl, your mother and I want to make you and Cole an offer."

"No more offers, Father."

"Soon you will be a family of five. The beach cottage has three small bedrooms. Would you both consider moving into the larger home on Lido Isle? We would be delighted to have your family in that house."

"Wow. Going from fifteen hundred square feet and a bath and a half to eight thousand square feet of Regency architecture on the bayfront seems like a very big step," I replied, being silly but also serious.

Before Dalt could say another word, I made it clear, albeit ever so gently, that Cole would never go for it. He had turned down the investment proposal. And I shared once more that all his self-esteem was presently tied to buying us a house of our own. Dalt said he understood but reiterated that the offer was open.

A Little Ride before Dinner

Cole had spent the entire day with Roman making plans, dreaming big, and scouting land in the Society Hill region of the Newport coast. Major development was still in the early stages, with construction starts in the very high-end estate enclaves, as well as in the more affordable but still upscale semicustom gated communities. The overall development project had been decades in the making, created with considerable political influence, transforming former Mexican land grants serving as ranch property for more than two hundred years into what was destined to become one of the most exclusive and most expensive residential areas of the California Riviera.

The timing was ideal for Cole and his new pal Roman. Money was loose. Banks were lending on futures rather than based on common sense. And Roman knew how to work the system. He had already been at it for several years and had made his own small fortune leveraging loans for real property then flipping those properties for a profit. Walter Benheim was the early catalyst for Roman, and now he was backing Cole as well, with a half-million-dollar fund just to start.

Cole called me to clue me in, telling me that they could purchase three, maybe four lots in a particular division being called Ocean Palisades, a gated community of smaller lots in a range of sizes, up to a maximum of ten thousand square feet. Two builders were presently at work developing lots, and a street of six model homes stood handsomely against a broad hillside and the Pacific Ocean seascape. Prices for the finished homes started at just over half a million dollars and went up to around seven hundred fifty thousand dollars. Cole and Roman had formulated that with a lot cost of one hundred thousand and a construction cost of no more than two hundred fifty thousand to three hundred thousand, each build could deliver a 20 percent to 30 percent profit at closing. That could easily be one hundred fifty thousand to two hundred thousand dollars' profit per deal.

Multiplying that by four lots, they would be approaching one million dollars with the first small development.

Asking Cole a ton of questions, especially the practical ones, I did not want to seem negative or put a damper on his dream. He gave me reasonable responses, so much so that I began feeling the enthusiasm too.

Bonnie and Buddy were in the car with me coming home from the pediatrician when Cole called. It was around three thirty in the afternoon. My car did not have the new thing called Bluetooth, and I had promised I would never again talk on the cell while driving, especially with Buddy in the car. We were on Balboa Boulevard headed toward the cottage, waiting at the red light crossing that led to the Balboa ferry, which took people from the ocean peninsula across the bay to the mainland. I pulled over to finish the conversation.

"Babe, are you in the car?"

"Yes, Cole. I just pulled over. Say hello to Buddy and Bonnie."

Cole obliged and rapidly came back to his mission at hand. "Are you taking the family home?" he asked. I responded. He went on: "Can you spare a couple of hours? I want to take you on a ride to see something."

"Sure. We'll be home in five minutes. When will you come?"

"Be there in fifteen. Love you." Cole hung up before I could love him back.

Leaving his BMW running in the alley in front of the cottage garage, Cole ran in the house, calling for me. Bonnie and Buddy were upstairs, situated, and I was ready for my ride. With Cole's delivering an ultrapassionate kiss hello, I wasn't certain we would make it out the door to the car.

"I am just superpumped. Can't wait to show you what I've done," he said.

The "what I've done" part resonated loud and clear. This was not just a ride; it was going to be a revelation.

"We need to get going. The place closes at five o'clock."

We're going shopping? I thought.

Cole was in a wonderful mood; he did not stop smiling. His voice was hitting upper octaves as he spoke. I kidded him, saying that whatever it was he was going to show me had taken him from a tenor to a soprano. We laughed. I really loved it when we shared laughter together. Laughter was right up there with sex in a good relationship. These were perfect times.

"So, where are we going?" I finally inquired.

"I want to show you some property that Roman, and I are thinking about buying to start our development business together."

"Thinking of buying, or already buying?"

"How do you know me so well? We've been married less than two years!" Cole went on, "This may be the answer for us too, a new home thrown in with the deal."

"I'm a fast learner," I said, again laughing. I was not surprised that Cole would be making a fast move. That's the man I married. I knew that; it was part of the whole package.

As we pulled into the open gates of the Ocean Palisades community, I was impressed by the tall stone pillars fronting either side of the driveway topped with classic Italian urns. The handsome rustic iron gates fashioned in an ornate old-world design of curves and garden patterns of turned iron were wide open, signaling welcome to prospective buyers. The fresh jet-black pavement was laid out ahead of us, bordered by stone pathways that matched the entry pillars. A manicured privet hedge, which I gathered had magically grown into full and perfect shape, was bisected every six or so feet with full blooming rosebushes presenting white blossoms. Entering, I saw that a row of very new and pristine model homes offering a selection of facades, all derivatives of Tuscan Italian Mediterranean architecture, awaited us.

The models were Disney perfect. I thought they looked like little pieces suitable for a Monopoly board. We parked, got out of the car, and walked via directed path into the first model, which was also the sales office, which set up in the home's garage. A handsome guy, fortyish and most probably either a former TV game show host or at least a salesman for a high-end car marque, greeted Cole as if he were his closest friend. Cole introduced me. The guy said nothing other than "So nice to meet you." He was absolutely coached. No doubt Cole had requested silence about any details.

Cole took my hand and offered me the grand tour. I admit this was fun. Seeing a model home was new to me. There weren't any in Beverly Hills.

Everything in each model was perfect: gorgeous new kitchens and bathrooms, big family rooms, and the odor of brand new, untouched by humans other than us wandering through. Perhaps a new semicustom—whatever that meant—home would not be so bad for a young family.

Each model featured a garden with instant grass, trees, and flowers. Patios had outdoor kitchens, views of the ocean, and childproof fences. And then there was gated security and no traffic noise, no airplanes flying over in and out of John Wayne Airport, plenty of guest parking, even a community pool and recreation area. Was I talking myself into Cole's plan? With each new model, I was coming around in a major way.

Finishing touring the six models, Cole and I went outside and sat down on a charming white wicker settee looking out over a deep canyon ravine leading down to an uninhabited white sand beach inlet far below. We could see the white water turning over to become blue and hitting the sand, but from our vantage point up on the hill there was no sound, only the faint squeal coming from a flash of low-flying gulls swooping through the canyon.

"Kate, what do you think of these homes?"

Not hesitating, I answered, "I didn't think I would like them, but I was wrong. They are terrific. If you and Roman are planning to make an investment, I support it. I can see the value and the potential. Yes, Cole, my future real estate mogul husband and love, Ocean Palisades may be your start."

Cole was over the moon with my support and positive encouragement. I believed everything I told him. I would not have lied to boost his ego.

"Roman and I did put several deposits down on vacant lots," he went on. "Did you like any of the models best?"

I replied instantly: "Number three is my favorite." After that confession, I added, "They really are all quite wonderful."

"Could you live here? Could you see yourself living in a number three of your own?"

I knew what was coming next. Cole had hinted at the possibility when we drove in.

"Honestly, I never thought about living in a new house. I love the cottage. But you're right, it could be perfect for us. Cole, I'm surprised to admit this, but I understand your purpose, and I think it works."

Cole put his arms around me and took a small step back, still holding me firmly around the waist.

"Let's pick out a lot. We will make it one of our projects and build a model three. It will take a year. When it's done, if you still love the idea, we can make it ours. If not, we can sell it at a profit. What do you say?"

"I say I love it. And I love you."

Changing the subject abruptly, a pregnant woman's prerogative, I said, "It's early, but how would you feel about Chinese food at the place on Balboa Island?"

"Kung Pao chicken for two on the special dinner?"

"Don't forget the fried wontons and egg rolls," I replied.

We drove out of Ocean Palisades on the spotless black asphalt, going through the gates and down Newport Coast Road to Pacific Coast Highway. Making a mental note of the moment, I mused that this was another exceptionally happy time.

One Heck of a Fortune Cookie

Sitting in the Chinese restaurant at the corner window table, facing the shops on Marine Avenue, the main street on the island known as Balboa, plopped in the middle of Newport Harbor, Cole and I talked nonstop. We rarely communicated like this, covering every from babies, to business, to hopes and dreams. Sharing Dalt's offer of the Lido house had met with zero enthusiasm from Cole. Surprised a bit, I had thought Cole might like the idea. After all, he had sold the house to my parents, and it was a very grand house on the bay, a statement property. Cole knew the power of statement in a world of impression.

Instead, he kept repeating that he needed to do things his way, the right way. We ordered more food, my favorite: sweet and sour chicken. The giant order arrived within minutes, and I helped myself as if Chinese food was leaving the planet tomorrow. Cole cautioned me to take it easy.

One bite into my second portion of the sinful sugar-glazed chicken, I was hit with a lightning bolt of pain in my abdomen. It was getting worse by the second. I doubled over, trying to muffle my screams so as not to put the little Chinese restaurant out of business. It was no use. I let out a whopper as the next bolt came crashing. Cole had jumped up on the first gasp, and now with this big scream I was surrounded by Chinese men in waistcoats who smelled like a combination of hoisin sauce and fried shrimp.

They were babbling in what I assumed was Mandarin, but I intuited what they were saying when I heard someone say "911." Cole wiped my sweating brow with a cloth napkin tinged with soy sauce and told me we were getting out of there and going to Hoag Hospital.

"Did they call 911?" I could barely speak.

All the men nodded in unison just as the sound of sirens came blaring down Marine Avenue. The calendar-quality handsome men of the Newport fire crew rushed in. I was at Hoag's emergency department on a gurney, being attended to by doctors and nurses, in less than ten minutes. Apparently, my water had broken in the ambulance. Cole was at my side, pointing to his soaked pants. "This cannot be happening," I told him, as the doctor advised me to stop talking and breathe. It was too late for an epidural. I was dilated, and the doctor could see the crown.

"But I am not due for another three weeks" were my last words as I was wheeled into delivery.

Screaming through the process, which was fast, thank God, I could not stop apologizing to the doctor and crew as two nurses handed me two small but healthy preemies. Both were boys. So much for intuition by the experts, including me. I was so sure the mystery child would be a girl. Like every decent new parent says, it didn't matter as long as they had ten fingers and ten toes. Cole was with me for the entire delivery, the first to see both his new sons arrive. I hoped that he wasn't disappointed not to have witnessed the birth of a daughter. My worry vanished as the nurse took the boys from me one at a time and put them in Cole's arms.

"Which one is number two?" he asked the nurse.

"He is in your left arm."

"Kate, if he were a she, I'd kind of like the name Blair," Cole said with a wink.

"Guess what, father of twins? Blair is a boy's name too. I like it, so if that's what you want, it's your choice. But I get to pick the name for boy one, in your right arm. Are we sticking with only *B*'s?" Cole nodded. "Then I think I like Baldasario."

"What?"

"Well, it's Latin, your real ethnic heritage before you Waspified yourself. Your mama would love it," I said, laughing.

"How can a girl who was in killer pain fifteen minutes ago be making crazy jokes?"

"Well, they say delivery can cause delirium, you know."

"You got that, babe."

"Okay, if not Baldasario, then how about Barney?"

"Like in Fife, Barney Fife from that old TV show in Mayfield, or was it Madison?"

"It was Mayberry, darling husband. Forget Barney. How do you feel about Brady? Buddy, Brady, and Blair."

"Sounds like a law firm. Strong yet friendly. Brady and Blair have my vote."

That was the extent of my witty and deliriously happy chatter. My ob-gyn Dr. Grimes came bolting in as I faded. Cole helped the nurses take my boys to the ICU for preemies as the good Dr. Grimes apologized for having missed the emergency delivery, assuring me that the newborns would receive all the best care. I asked Cole to call my parents and then fell sound asleep.

CHAPTER FORTY-SEVEN

LIFE IS A JOURNEY

For months I had told myself that missing that first important appointment with Heather scheduled for Friday at the salon Avenue Foch West to discuss a potential fashion partnership was not a setback, not a sign of failure, just part of the path of my life. Instead, Heather had come to the hospital on that Friday. I was still there dealing with a few complications from the unexpected delivery, and also I needed to stay close to the boys, who were both under bili lights, fighting jaundice along with all the complications of birth at less than six pounds each. The good news was that the doctors were superpositive, although they'd made it clear that Brady and Blair might be spending some time in their care.

Heather was amazing. She made me feel very free and easy with no worry about the necessary delay of our big journey.

"Who said we can't work together from home for as long as you need." Heather's words were a gift. Certainly, we could accomplish a lot. We did not have to be in the salon workroom. The salon workroom would come to the beach.

And indeed it did, along with the boys, who were released after some six weeks at Hoag Hospital. Baby nurse Belinda returned, that wonderful woman who had lovingly brought Buddy into full and healthy life, giving me the luxury of rest. Yes, I knew that was one of the benefits of being rich. I didn't take that for granted with Buddy, and I certainly wouldn't with the two new Baldwin boys. What a blessing to have Belinda back.

Bonnie gave up her room for the twins and for baby nurse Belinda, who moved in with Buddy. We became the Baldwin Bunch of seven in the fifteen hundred square feet of pure love nest with almost two baths. The Lido mansion was still available as an option; however, we had not pursued it.

Cole and his new full-fledged Russian American business partner Roman Yusapov were 100 percent moving forward. They had closed the deal on the four lots at Ocean Palisades, and construction had begun. Model three was going up on my favorite lot, which I had selected. It was one of the largest lots, sort of a fan-shaped property with a 180-degree semicircular rear border with views of the coast over the chaparral-covered hillside from Laguna Beach north to the Palos Verdes Peninsula.

The guys had officially opened their real estate investment trust and had rented prime office space for Cole to open his own agency with Roman serving as broker of record. Already some half dozen independent agents had signed on to be a part of Baldwin et Cie. Roman had chosen the French term *et Cie* for the company because he figured it gave them a bit of international status.

Cole, by design, would be the handsome celebrity face of the venture. He was, of course, a natural, and Roman knew it. The television camera knew it as well. Cole's *Living the Dream* on cable TV was now being distributed beyond Newport Beach and playing on TV sets in places like Beverly Hills, Aspen, Scottsdale, Las Vegas, and Palm Beach. Roman was also negotiating in conjunction with Rocco La Penta, owner-producer of the cable network California Lifestyle, seeking new TV channels as national reality platforms focused on luxury real estate.

Everything was working brilliantly as investment money came in and as "the Fund" as was labeled, designed to fund the building cost of home development, was growing with surprising ease. Secure with the investment in the first four lots at Ocean Palisades, Cole and Roman were already seeking the next land purchase.

It seemed very fast to me, almost too good to be true. But who was I to doubt? Dalt confirmed that the economy was inordinately robust post-9/11, with money readily available from banks and private investors. No-money-down loans on real property were common, even granted with little or no financial security other than the property itself. Real estate was strong, in such demand that prices were rising faster than banks could appraise. For a conservative investor such as my father, this raised a red flag, yet it was real. Red flag or not, Dalt was also making considerable money in the stock market, watching his own fortunes rise.

The year ended in the Baldwin home, where we celebrated all the incredible family changes along with the business explosion. We held Buddy's small one-year birthday party on the beach. At first, I was tempted to go crazy with a big production, but the birthday arrived too soon after the twins were born, and a production was not part of my present skill set. Truthfully, even if it had been, we really didn't have many friends, and none with infants or toddlers.

Even so, I did manage to hire a small petting zoo. Buddy loved the big black Rex rabbit, but he cried when the pony arrived. Nancy and Dalt had the best time of any of the other ten partygoers. Cole's parents had come down from Reno, showering their first grandson with love. His mother, Rose, kissed the boys so much that I almost handed nanny Bonnie a towel to wipe their faces. Heather was a miracle worker, as always, taking charge and making everything look special and unique. In a very short time, we had become close. And we had made progress on the Fair Child line. With Monsieur Lawrence at work in the shop, another half dozen samples had been completed. I had chosen to remain home, not going into the salon, instead turning the kitchen table into a cutting room. My ironing board was permanently at the ready to smooth. I'd stretch my cuttings out there prior to shipping them off to my mentor at Avenue Foch West.

Besides my parents, another birthday party attendee enjoyed the best time. My little brother, Jamey, had come down after we talked on the phone several times over the previous weeks. Cole and I invited him to stay with us over the birthday weekend, albeit on the sofa, which he didn't mind at all. In fact, he was totally excited over the prospect.

Dalt remained hesitant about Jamey's weekend visit, but he saw that my advance phone visits with Jamey were positive.

Wasting no time, since Dalt had softened after his initial objection, I stretched the invitation for my little brother, offering that he stay in Newport for a while longer. The timing was perfect. Beverly High would be on holiday break the following week, so Jamey wouldn't miss too much. Being here with us was what he needed; school would still be there.

December in Southern California can be glorious with brisk clear mornings and sun-filtered afternoons, and the beach generally quiet with no crowds. Even traffic seemed more manageable. The best part was that people were in holiday happy mode. Shopping craziness was overshadowed by a sense of joy. Even some of the rock stations on the radio were playing Bing Crosby's "White Christmas" every ten minutes.

Jamey was over the moon with my invitation for an extended stay. He asked Nancy and Dalt for their blessing, which he received without visible anxiety on their part. We all entered a serious group hug.

Revealing my plan to the family, previously shared with just my father, I mentioned that it was Sunday and Reverend Paco would be holding his eleven o'clock morning service on the beach just down the sand. Jamey was most excited over the proposition, and our parents witnessed his dramatic attitude reversal. Their withdrawn and silent son displayed a momentary transformation. He rushed to finish the final bite of warm ham and cheese croissant that I had picked up for Sunday morning breakfast from this odd little doughnut shop over by an arcade just off the beach that generally catered to mobs of tourists. We readied ourselves for a dose of Sunday spiritual impact from the good reverend the Surfer Saint.

Choosing to forgo the car, the family walked from the cottage to the shoreline and made the ten-minute walk to the beach service on the hard wet sand at water's edge. The twins remained at home with Bonnie. Cole took the stroller for Buddy, who was just beginning to walk. The birthday boy wanted his freedom. Cole released him, and Buddy made a direct, somewhat stumbling, beeline right into the water. With the gentle foam of white water slapping the shoreline, Cole, an instant before a total rescue would be necessary, grabbed his drenched son and swung him up and onto his shoulders behind his head. Buddy squealed that baby squeal of ultimate delight over a new experience. Witnessing the wonder of a child's first taste of a food, first rainfall, first pet of a dog, or first run into the ocean gave me such unexplainable pleasure. I was a crier, and these moments delivered a discreet tear.

A large crowd had gathered by the old Newport Pier for Reverend Paco's Sunday spiritual journey. This one was larger than the one at the service we had attended before.

I hadn't attended Paco's service for some time, not since my last visit with Jamey. His message was clearly reaching more people. Of course, it could have been the proximity to the doughnut shop with the to-die-for ham and cheese croissants, which happened to be only one hundred yards from the sand pulpit.

Paco saw me. I waved, making a gesture and pointing to Jamey and the family. The Surfer Saint jumped down off his makeshift stage and came around to us, proceeding to escort the Baldwin, Fairchild, and Costa entourage up toward the front and in the center. People didn't seem to mind. Paco apologized and told them we were very special friends, everyone shaking hands and hugging.

As he leapt back onstage, the music of some six guitars opened the service. Paco motioned for his congregation to stand and pray. For the next hour we were immersed in fellowship. There was no talk of sin or redemption, no choice between heaven and hell. Paco was magical. Granted, his message held plenty of Psych 101 "feel good, be good, love thy neighbor as thy self" stuff, all wrapped up in the Ten Commandments and delivered with an ocean backdrop that could have been created only by the genuine Master of the universe. God was there, in that ocean, on that sand, and in the flawless sky. Pure white feather pillow December clouds punctuated the scene, making their way northeast to deliver snow atop the Sierra Nevada.

How could anyone not be in love with the uncomplicated peace Paco preached? Somehow, he knew that we were there for Jamey. At the end of his sermon, for the closing prayer, Paco asked Jamey to come up next to him on the makeshift pulpit. Placing both hands on Jamey's shoulders, the Surfer Saint, in his signature Hawaiian-print shirt, board shorts, and sandals, bestowed his closing blessing over Jamey. Then Paco whispered in his ear, delivering a private message. We were all transfixed, especially Nancy and Dalt. As I was looking over at them, my mother turned to me and quietly asked what was going on. I told her I had no idea.

The congregation dispersed following a fellowship handshake and a neigh-borly greeting. As I had expected, many of the faithful headed for the doughnut shop. Paco came over to us, and we learned what he had whispered to Jamey.

Putting his arm around my brother yet again, he shared an idea.

"There is a sect of Judaism known as Chabad. It is a very ancient practice, rooted in tradition and Torah teaching. It is also something of a mystic sect inas-much as it is both very orthodox and very modern at the same time. Chabad has a program to help people with drug and alcohol addiction and related life challenges. The program is considered one of the best and most successful in the nation, and they have facilities in LA and the OC. I would like to take Jamey to meet my friend Rabbi Miller, who runs a program here. Would that be possible?"

Nancy and Dalt may have been somewhat surprised earlier. Now they were cautious, but of course they didn't show it. Breaking the awkward silence, I asked Jamey what he thought.

Not sure what Chabad was, not even able to pronounce it correctly, my brother answered intelligently. "I am open to learn more about it," he said.

Paco jumped in to ease the tension he sensed that Jamey and my parents were feeling.

"Can I come by and talk more about this with you when it is a good time? No rush to commit. I believe it is an option to be investigated. They really do work miracles," he said.

Jamey surprised us all.

"I know who they are," he called out as if he had experienced some kind of epiphany. "I've watched the telethon on TV that they do with all the dancing and singing with men in robes with gray beards."

"That's right." Paco smiled.

Nancy and Dalt smiled too. They were familiar with Chabad. It was well-known in LA, especially because of their addiction program. It was one program they had never tried for Jamey, among many that seemed to offer little success.

"Jamey will be staying in Newport with us for a few days. Maybe we could set something up to learn more while he is here?" I asked Paco, although really I was asking my parents and Jamey.

My brother answered. "Yes, I want to learn more. I want to meet the rabbi. I trust Paco," he said firmly.

Paco offered to call me on Monday, then made his exit. My family and I walked back to the shoreline for our return to the cottage. Not a word was spoken. Buddy enjoyed the time of his life with his daddy's full attention—lots of shrieking and giggling. Dalt and Nancy held hands, staring at the vast Pacific. Cole's mom, Rose, and his dad, Joe, took their shoes off, rolled up their pants, and waded in the water the entire trip back. Being by the ocean was a real treat for the in-laws from Reno. Jamey searched for the occasional shell appearing on the surf, and I just walked ahead of the pack thinking how strange and amazing life was. *How did we get to this point? This is not what I expected my life to be like growing up.*

Moving Forward Yet Again

The dawning of 2004 opened the door to radical change in the Baldwin journey. Reality TV, now around for a decade with shows about lifestyles and homes clearly, was still a big factor in the not so traditional new age American dream.

Producer Rocco La Penta had formed a new cable company, making a huge national debut as the American Home Network (AHN), of course financed by a Chinese investor. They were buying everything, it seemed. Rocco originally discovered Cole as the face of TV's *Living the Dream*. The instant local hit had eventually transformed my ambitious husband into both a real estate celebrity and a media darling.

In Newport, Cole had become famous along with a TV network drama called *The O.C.*, which was based in Newport Beach.

All this glory meant something else: there was not much time with my husband. He was wheeling and dealing 24/7, and I was a baby mama work widow. Yes, I had help. I'm not whining. But I think I buried some sadness. Sadder than regular sad. Like the sadness one feels when something bad happens but then the feeling passes, becoming a different kind of sad. Mine was a constant low-dose sad. As a twenty-three-year-old work widow, I didn't like it, but I knew that it was what it was. Did I expect to have a nine-to-five, picket fence marriage, especially with an ambitious husband? I could hear my mother's voice: *Darling, wake up and smell the roses. Young married couples must sacrifice to move ahead. Your father did. For years we did nothing socially week in and week out as your father was up at five in the morning to be ready for the New York market opening on the West Coast.*

Just the same, I was having a rough time. Not enough of a pioneer woman to manage a toddler and two infants, I did my best. Throwing myself more into work with Heather became my escape. Intellectually, I knew this was wrong. Emotionally, it helped. Heather was a champion. She had postponed law school to avoid it getting in the way of our fledgling fashion empire. I so admired her sacrifice and her dedication to the dream.

By the fall, in less than a year, Monsieur Lawrence had finished the last of the initial samples. At the rate of about one sample piece monthly, we had completed a dozen finely tailored interchangeable garments ideal for a resort climate. The concept was to create clothes a woman could wear for any occasion, from casual to work to dressy, depending on how she combined the pieces and accessorized the outfits.

My inspiration had come in part from Halston, and from Courrèges. Monsieur and Madame understood, and the result was stunning. Nancy, my biggest fan and my most direct and honest critic, was floored. She raved endlessly. So did Heather's mother, Mrs. Adamson, whose opinion mattered in the social hierarchy of Orange County. Heather said her mother had offered to invest in the business when she saw the line.

I thought it unbelievable that there were potential investors clamoring to have a piece of me, just like investors seeking Cole. Was this real? Well, clamoring may have been an overstatement. But that was how it felt.

Both Heather and Monsieur warned me that creating the line was only a baby step. Getting it into a store—well, that was another matter. We needed multiple sample lines and sales reps to convince buyers at the big three fashion marts in LA, New York, and Dallas to take a chance on a start-up. There was the big rub. Almost nobody would take a chance on an unknown. It was just too risky. Customers didn't know the product. A new line could go belly-up unable to fill orders. There were so many pitfalls.

Heather and I spent weeks, right up until Buddy's second birthday, again in makeshift business, organizing and working out a plan for the marketing and sale of the Fair Child line. Our respective mothers went to work too. Mrs. A strong-armed the manager at Newport's Neiman Marcus, as she was arguably their best customer. Mother Nancy went after the boss at Saks Fifth Avenue, Beverly Hills. It helped. We were given courtesy appointments with buyers from both major fashion empires set up in Los Angeles.

In advance of the meetings, savvy Heather arranged a photo shoot hiring exquisite fashion models: a tall, willowy Lauren Hutton–like WASP princess; an athletic, chiseled-faced young African American woman with short-short hair and incredible perfect translucent skin; and finally, another exquisite porcelain-faced Asian model with heavily made-up eyes and sharply defined red lips. This cast was perfect for the Fair Child line.

The big shoot would take place using one of the West Coast's preeminent fashion photographers, a petite woman with electric hair that stood out as if it had been shocked, and with huge boobs perched above a torso atop spindly legs covered in ragged torn Levi's. She was known simply as Chatillon.

The site for the fashion shoot was a plateau high atop Society Hill in a very dramatic canyon with cliffs of limestone rising from a creek bed to more than one thousand feet. Along with Chatillon, Heather had hired one of the best fashion directors in LA, Wolfgang Abromovitz, who came with a massive crew of lighting techs, makeup and hair artists, and even a sound engineer. Wolfgang required the music of Queen and David Bowie pounding through Dolby speakers bouncing off the canyon walls as he worked magic.

The Fair Child models were positioned in the most daring poses on boulders: their feet in the creek with water rushing past; peering out from behind an enormous Mexican fan palm; and even perched on the hood of a beautiful white 1956 Cadillac Coupe de Ville convertible with obligatory red leather seats, positioned at the edge of a major drop in the canyon floor as if the car were about to go over the cliff. For special effect, Wolfgang ordered his men to deflate the front tire, adding to the drama.

Grandmother GiGi's career fund was being spent on this impressive artistry. She was smiling in heaven; I was smiling in the canyon.

At the salon, Monsieur kept busy seeking out top-selling fashion reps in New York, Dallas, and Los Angeles. Waiting for the photos, he hoped that interest would rise. Heather and I interviewed numerous PR firms and chose a boutique entity in Newport called the Fabulous Agency. We loved the *fabulous* in the name. After all, we were fabulous. The Fabulous Agency was run by a fashionable, flamboyant ginger-haired thirty-something man named Waldo Newman. There was a picture of him on his desk in a gleaming silver frame taken with Anna Wintour at the Met gala in New York. Heather and I were impressed. I asked him about his friendship with Wintour. "Oh, honey, we are not friends. I've met her many times, but she wouldn't know me from a bowl of corn flakes. I just happened to be standing there when the paparazzi flashed."

Heather and I broke into hysterics.

"It's all marketing, girls. It's just a picture. An image. A subtle message," he said.

"A fake message," I added under my breath.

Wolfgang had heard my snide remark.

"Perhaps, but it caught your attention. Do you think any idea in the fashion world that rises to trend just happens because it's so fucking brilliant?"

We got the message. We liked the brutal honesty. The price was right. We were believers in this guy named Waldo. Where's Waldo, or rather "Who's Waldo"? Well, he was our guy. He made us laugh. He made us think. Mostly he put us at ease.

"Make no mistake, girls: you have no hope of normalcy from now on. You just got on the roller coaster from hell, and you lost your tickets. So, hang on."

On this day at the canyon photo shoot, it hit me that this was finally the real deal. Certain we were destined for the cover of *Vogue*. Hypnotized by the setting, the artistry, and my designs on the models, I was feeling a sense of pride and accomplishment. Not letting the euphoria run away with me, I gave myself a mental pinch to return me to the moment just as one of the models, the Asian dollface, began cursing at Chatillon. Heather ran to the conflict like a general on a battlefield. I remained in the shadows. Realizing I was more comfortable in the balcony of my own life, I valued Heather's leading the orchestra from the front row even more.

Finishing on time, and on budget according to my partner, we wrapped as the sun dropped behind the canyon cliffs. The evanescent light sent the walls of granite into pitch-black darkness, igniting a halo on top of the ridge, with a layer of fire between the blackened cliffs and the vibrant blue sky above. The entire crew stopped breaking down our fashion set to pause and take in the majesty before us. Within minutes, it all vanished. I took it as a sign of promise. There was hope for the Fair Child line, hope against all obstacles, all rejection, all fear of personal failure.

Funny thing, I also thought about Cole in that moment. We had not made love in a couple of weeks. I knew the actual date, time, and place. Specifics mattered. They did to me. Our separation created by circumstance needed to be discussed. Just the same, I was also thinking about how successful he had become in such a short span of time. His dreams were coming true, against all odds and regardless of all obstacles and fears of failure. Was this some sort of revelation? Or was it a warning? What if I could not achieve the same level of achievement? Would it matter? What if our success meant we wouldn't make love for two months, instead of two weeks, two years? Could love last without intimacy, without sex?

On the way home with Heather, I kept these private thoughts private. Instead, we talked business, our next step. How could these photos be used to market Fair Child—raise the attention bar as Monsieur had suggested? Heather did the talking; I did the nodding. As she pulled up to the beach cottage, I gave the final nod. It was a major nod. Heather had no trouble convincing me to spend some significant dollars from the GiGi fund to use the photos and create a dramatic ad campaign placed in all the major fashion and society magazines—double truck spreads in *Vogue*, *Elle*, and *Vanity Fair*, and maybe even a full page in the Sunday *New York Times* and *Los Angeles Times* society pages. I had one question to ask Heather.

"Nobody has even heard of Fair Child. Are you sure this will work? Wouldn't it be best to begin on a smaller local level?"

She simply replied, "They will hear, they will see, and they will want to know where to buy. We must go big." She winked.

Nodding yet again, I jumped out of the car and began running toward my three babies, all of whom were awaiting their work widow mommy to return to the nest.

The old reliable Dutch door was open at a forty-five-degree angle. I darted in literally, crashing into Cole, who was standing in the entry, briefcase in hand, black silk necktie loosened at the collar. Apparently having come home minutes prior, Cole dropped the case and met me at the midpoint of the hallway with an embrace.

I was very happy to see him. It was a Doris Day embrace. I even felt my right leg rise behind me as Cole put his arms around my waist and kissed me with full force, which sent shivers through my body. Two weeks without sex had not gotten in the way of those shivers. Cole could feel the tremble. He responded with heightened passion.

Nanny Bonnie and the supernurse Belinda had the three Baldwin boys lined up in highchairs in the kitchen, sharing an evening meal. The twins were nearly nine months old. We had bribed Belinda to stay, and she committed to a nine-month contract, due to end in a week. I disguised my panic over her impending departure. Cole and I swapped the possibility of instant lovemaking for a loving hallway hello followed by grabbing a little something to eat, joining the boys as they finished before bath and bed. As the boys seemed restless, clearly excited by our entire family's sharing an early dinner, Bonnie and Belinda managed to lower the heightened energy level so the boys could exit without tears and head for their nightly ritual.

Cole invited me on a date in our bedroom. We made love upstairs to the not-too-distant sound of splashing bathwater and squeals of rubber ducky joy. The sex was amazing. My dry spell had ended. I was a work widow no more.

Beware of Left Turns on the Road of Life

The bombshell dropped at the breakfast table instantly neutralized the emotional and sexual heights of the previous night with Cole. I had gotten up early with the boys and fed them along with my team, also making Cole's favorite waffles and crispy bacon for a midweek surprise. Smelling the aroma of bacon throughout the house, he was up and showered, dressed, and in the kitchen with record speed. The boys were finishing, but Bonnie kept them happy and calm so Cole could share some morning time with his three sons at the tiny table in the corner with its windows onto the Pacific. Beyond us was a low-rising dune of white sand with random sprigs of ice plant abloom with tiny shimmering purple flowers delivering another spectacular day on the Newport shoreline.

With both arms full, I delivered a sizzling tray of bacon, extra crispy of course, a stack of waffles so tall I could barely see over them, and melted butter in a bowl. With two fingers, I gripped the handle of a glass pitcher filled with fresh-squeezed orange juice. Cole clapped, the boys squealed, and Bonnie laughed, asking if she could stay on, then excused herself and the boys. I promised bacon and waffles for dinner sometime. Belinda appeared and joined Bonnie and the boys leaving the kitchen, with plenty of hugs. I sat down.

The two of us relished a moment of silence together, something we rarely shared over an early breakfast. It felt right, normal, everyday, like a regular family. Taking a bite of my crispy bacon, I shared with my handsome husband the details of the fashion shoot. The bacon enhanced my enthusiasm as I delivered a blow-by-blow account of my amazing experience. Cole let me go on, genuinely into my excitement. But when I took a breath, he just smiled, saying nothing. I knew that reaction: pure detachment. His mind was on something else.

"I have good news too." Those were Cole's first words.

"Really?" That was all I could say, as I was still somewhat hurt by his lack of attention.

"We received an offer yesterday on the last house under construction at the Society Hill project, and it is twice what we expected. We could make an additional million dollars on the sale."

"So, the only one left now is our house? Will that extra profit help to pay for our house so we have very little debt?"

Cole hesitated. "In a manner of speaking," he finally replied.

"In what sort of manner?" I asked.

Again, he hesitated. "The offer is on our house," he said, coming clean, knowing that the news would be hard for me to take.

I don't think Cole understood how hard such news would come crashing down on me. It always took me time and consideration to face a change that was not in my spectrum. The idea of moving into a tract house in a new community with three babies took some serious adjustment. At this stage I was invested in that house. And just like that, whoosh, it was gone. And I had nothing to say about it.

I didn't cry. Holding back beyond belief, I was ready to gush, but I didn't. Counting to ten in silence, looking down at my plate of bacon and waffles, I poured a crazy amount of butter from the bowl onto the waffles. Taking my fork, I sliced a huge corner piece, crumbled two large strips of bacon on top of it, and literally shoved it in my mouth.

Cole looked at me with a dumbfounded *What the heck are you doing?* expression.

Wanting to speak, obviously unable to form words, my mind spoke internally, *Why the hell didn't you tell me so we could talk about this?* Midthought, still trying to chew the world's largest butter-soaked waffle, I realized it was clear that Cole was doing just that. He was telling me. It was just an offer, not a done deal. This was his business, and it was also our future. Could I be a grown up about the whole thing?

Swallowing the final chunk, my composure intact, I did the mature thing. Yes, I wanted to smack him for even considering doing that, but instead I asked him if it was the right thing to do business-wise.

"Kate, I know this is not fair to you. I know you have your heart set on this house, but it is just a house. There are lots more houses out there. At this point the house is just in the framing stage. You haven't even picked out a toilet."

"Well, as long as you put it that way ..." I cut in with my sarcastic wit.

"I will use the extra profit to buy us a better house," Cole offered, thinking that I wanted a "better" house. That, of course, was his way of thinking. I didn't want or need better. That one was fine.

"What have you got in mind?" I questioned, not expecting much of an answer.

"I have my eye on lots in a new development being called The Summit. The ocean view lots are each an acre minimum, meant for custom homes."

"Rather ambitious, don't you think? Also, a custom home build could take two years. Are you sure that's a good idea? Couldn't we aim a little lower, and build a little faster?"

"You're right, as always. Let me look around and see what might work for us in terms of a finished project that would meet our needs right now. The Summit project is not right for us at this time, but it is right for business. Baby, remember that we talked about having to move a few times to build up equity and make a business plan for the future? We cannot get personally invested in any house. Not yet anyway."

Cole sounded sincere; his tone, apologetic, understanding. I could not help but wonder silently if this pattern of building equity would ever, could ever, come to an end. Was our family destined to endure endless moving and flipping houses? I wanted to pick up the phone and call Dalt and ask if the offer to move to the house on Lido was still an option. I resisted.

Thinking of my dad, I recalled he used to quote J. Paul Getty whenever he dealt with a greedy investor client. Getty's words: "When is enough, enough? There is always a little more." I wasn't sure my husband knew much about Getty, but the consuming pursuit of money didn't motivate me. Maybe it was because I'd always had money. Then I flashed on my own career goal. Wasn't fashion design also about selling clothes, making money? Okay, yes, it was art, but it was really all about business. After all, if nobody buys the clothes, what's the point? The analogy brought me some clarity on Cole's handling of the real estate business. We did not lose a house; we had gained a million dollars. Cole was my own Getty in training.

CHAPTER FORTY-EIGHT

LIFE IN THE FAST LANE ACCELERATES

Cole took the deal on our house, the house I was not supposed to get emotionally attached to. He accepted the offer with my nod. At least he had consulted me, even though I realized it was only a gesture given the forgone conclusion. And he and his partner Roman did make that million-dollar profit on what was an investment made with Walter Benheim's cash infusion. Benheim would get his money back, plus 20 percent. Cole and Roman would each take one hundred thousand dollars on the final sale of their project. In a little more than a year, Cole had made more than a million dollars with his share from all his sales. We had cash to buy just about any house we wanted.

With the finality of the Ocean Palisades sale, I began to research the Newport market. There were nice homes all over town under half a million dollars. Maybe Cole was right. My right brain business mind kicked in, a gift from my family tree. Anyway, with three kids to raise, a fashion line to launch, and a little brother to help get on a healthy life track, I asked myself what twenty-three-year-old faces the good fortune to fret over which half-million-dollar house she gets to buy for a first house. Not many. Almost none. Yet, every girl I'd grown up with had this opportunity. We were all a pimple on the map of privilege, versus the "earn it" reality of life. Sitting at my computer and looking at local real estate for sale, I took a deep breath and began to feel lucky that Cole had provided me a life lesson despite my hurt feelings. It was a lesson I had known intellectually but not emotionally. It's easy to be open-minded when one is not directly hit with a choice one would rather avoid.

My cell phone buzzed as I went deep in philosophical review. Heather had called to tell me that the final fashion photos were fabulous, which was expected since they would be placed in the hands of the Fabulous Agency.

"Monsieur Lawrence is dancing in his salon workroom," Heather conveyed with glee. "I have a feeling the old guy hasn't danced in a while, and he's loving it."

Heather continued to share that my mentor had offered some strategic advice. Agreeing to spend money on advertising, we planned to produce a limited line to place in an undetermined upscale boutique in Newport. Following Monsieur's plan, Heather focused on getting the attention of buyers from major fashion marts potentially selling to the big stores such as Saks, Neiman's, Bloomie's, and Macy's. "We must hold on to a vision of the big prize, the home run," Monsieur said. "But we need to build, perhaps starting locally."

I asked Heather what he meant.

"Fashion Plaza in Newport sells space to small portable pop-up boutiques of all kinds in the massive courtyard between Neiman's and Bloomie's. Monsieur wants us to create a Fair Child pop-up to attract and sell to women coming in and out of the big established stores," Heather explained.

"Wow, that's really interesting. But wait, I've seen those pop-ups. They sell purses, sunglasses, and T-shirts. That's not us. And how would women try on the clothes?" I questioned.

Heather had already figured it out with Monsieur, and she tried to calm me with humor. "We'll set up shop right by the giant reflecting pond. The women can slip on a Fair Child jacket and look in the reflection of the water to judge the fit."

"Really?" was all I could say.

"You're not going to believe this, but Monsieur and I have drawn a basic plan for our portable store that consists of a small white tent striped with black and accented with black tassels on a scalloped flap over the entrance. The Fair Child logo will be prominently placed above. Inside the small, but inviting, space, our line, limited in scope but beautifully displayed, will also have a small dressing area with a curtain and three-way mirrors. How about that that? Sounds stunning to me," she declared.

Heather's description was amazing. I didn't have to think; I knew it was right. A little more of the GiGi fund would make it a reality.

"How fast can we make this happen?" I asked.

Heather replied that with my okay, she would get in contact with the Fashion Plaza shopping center office to make a deal, and we could be up and running really fast.

"First step is to make a budget. Second step would be to make a deal," she continued.

"Third step is to make it happen," I followed. "Will you work the shop with me?"

"Count on it. We both need to be hands-on. It must be us."

"Let's go," I said with sheer joy, then clicked off the cell.

The afternoon was fading fast, and I had promised Cole that I would go with him to a black-tie charity dinner at the Harbor Club. It was a Tuesday night. Only in Newport would there be a black-tie dinner on a Tuesday night.

We were attending at least one black-tie dinner every couple of weeks. After the twins were born and my maternity was no longer a noble motherly excuse, these glitzy celebrations were an essential part of our lives, as they were an essential part of the social fabric of this town. It was important to be seen and heard in the crowd of the rich and influential—especially important for the larger crowd of wannabe rich and wishfully influential comers. Cole fell into the latter group, and I alongside him, regardless of my indifference to all of it.

Perhaps Cole was part of the latter group, but you wouldn't guess it seeing the attention and adulation my husband garnered when we entered yet another ballroom. We were surrounded, make that swarmed, by Cole's fans delivering the warmest greetings. I felt invisible, which was perfect. Cole attempted to compensate by telling me that I am the draw. It's a husband's duty, but we both knew it was just part of the dance. I'd been brought up well. I had the smile and the nod down pat. Funny how that whole television thing was so powerful. None of these people knew much about either of us, especially about Cole. Having his face on that small screen made him a celebrated member of the community family. Sometimes I laughed to myself, thinking about his real birth name, Salvatore Mario Costa, the first-generation American son of a Cuban immigrant father and an Italian immigrant mother. The disconnect between reality and manufactured image flashed in my brain. Then I stopped myself with a mental face-slapping for my own hypocrisy. Was I the wife of the real person or the wife of the created personality? Clearly, I was both, and that was part of what defined Cole in my life.

On this Tuesday evening at the launch of the fall social season 2004, some four hundred members of the black-tie and low-cut-gown crowd gathered to raise big dollars for a very worthy cause, the big C, otherwise known as cancer. Walter and Candy Benheim were hosting. Naturally our presence was required to greet and applaud the guest of honor, a brilliant Indian doctor whose name I could not pronounce after being introduced multiple times. Given his seriously heavy accent, I'll call him Dr. Aram. I think that was his first name.

Dr. Aram, both a research scientist and clinical cancer surgeon, had quietly treated Candy Benheim's breast cancer for several years. She remained in full remission. The party was something of a coming out for Candy. Nobody knew about her cancer, including my husband. He was surprised.

"I saw those giant bolt-on breasts when I found Candy and Walter in their spa, when I toured their house on Linda Isle. Remember I told you?" Cole whispered as the tribute speakers lined up on the dais to salute Dr. Aram. Aram stood next to Candy, who was outfitted in a strapless shimmery silver lamé body-hugging minidress accenting the voluminous expanse of her now healthy décolletage.

"Cole, do you think that her massive breast enlargement may have been a contributing factor to the cancer? Aren't women supposed to remove the implants when problems arise?" I questioned sincerely.

Cole smirked, unable to find words. He was still in a mild state of disbelief, even for a guy who let most everything strange roll off his back. Meanwhile, the adoring crush of Cole admirers kept stepping forward with outstretched hands. Partner Roman, who had come with a date neither of us had ever met, created a buffer, aggressively greeting the onslaught and protecting Cole, and me as well, at least to a degree.

In Newport there are seasons just as there are in the rest of the nation, only Newport seasons were delineated not by weather but, rather, by lifestyle.

The four seasons were winter holiday parties and Aspen ski escapes; spring luncheons and fashion shows; summers on the beach and jaunts to Hawaii and Europe; and full-on social black-tie charity galas in fall.

Along with all this fun, there was always drama. It seemed as if the black-tie gala drama followed me. Often such drama resulted from an overindulgence in lemon drop martinis, cosmos, or whatever libation of choice. Champagne flowed like water. Anything to dull the senses and heighten the libido. Don't get me wrong, I too loved a tall, chilled flute of champagne coming off a silver tray passing by, but I found myself always being the outsider, an observer rather than participant. I was not a snob; it's just that I was not a player. I never had many girl pals, so this was nothing new. Admittedly, I was overly judgmental. Not just of people drinking at parties, but also pretty much about everything. One exception: love. I was never judgmental when it came to love. Love trumps everything, which could be a problem when everything included some really bad stuff. But that's the way it has always been. I knew that because I felt it and lived it.

"So, what do you think?" the young woman Roman had brought as his date asked. She and I had been left alone at our table as Cole and Roman were summoned over to deal with their investor Walter, who was apparently suffering from some considerable overindulgence of his own variety. He was yelling the F-word and flailing his fat arms wildly over his head just two tables in front of us. The ballroom was noticing but ignoring him in favor of the loud orchestra. People were dancing, and the overall noise level from the chatter was near deafening. That was another thing that was curious to me at all the Newport galas. They were always so loud. The music blared, and people laughed so loud that conversation was impossible at a dinner table. Accustomed to just sitting in place, I offered plenty of smiles and nods, and was polite when approached.

Roman's date, who wanted to know what I did, was a tall, skinny, raven-haired woman, thirtyish, with no boobs and no butt, and with long, straight silky hair parted in the middle of her high-brow forehead. She wore a simple spaghetti-strap cocktail dress, rather cheap looking, accented with a choker—a single strand of rhinestones—around her neck. I fixated on her oversized fake red nails as she prodded me for the details of my life. Finally introducing herself as Sierra, she explained that she had met Roman at a local hangout called the Beach Bar on the oceanfront. Sierra worked as a hostess there. Her cocktail dress made sense; it was her uniform. She had just added a rhinestone choker, and bingo—perfectly ready for a Tuesday night cancer fundraiser at the Harbor Club.

"Have you been dating Roman for a while?" I asked.

"Oh no. We're just friends with benefits," Sierra answered coyly. I felt a moment of self-loathing as I passed judgment yet again. This was an affront to me as love was always supposed to be the one exception. *For God's sake, Kate, love and sex are not always the same thing,* I said in my head.

"So, what do you do?" Sierra asked again.

"Me, well, I take care of three babies ages nine months and two." Feeling the need to clarify the math, I added, "Two nine-month-old twin boys and one two-year-old boy."

"That's a lot," she came back. "Is it really hard?"

"Never," I answered, not sharing that I had help from Bonnie the nanny.

"You must be a superwoman. You look so beautiful."

Sierra was winning points. But not many. I was ready to get up and go over to Cole when the commotion at the Benheim table turned from multiple utterances of the F-word to breaking glass.

Sierra and I made a dash over to rescue our guys. We found Walter facedown on the dining table. He had crushed the stemware when he fell and had tipped over a large clear crystal globe centerpiece filled with roses. Water from the vase was streaming downhill, over the side of Walter's left cheek, which was flat on the table, while a bunch of the long-stem roses lay atop his bald head—a crown of thorns. Roman stood by his side, fanning him with a heavy starched white table napkin, hoping the air would revive him.

Funny thing, the orchestra was still playing, with other people still dancing. Nobody seemed to care that Walter lay facedown wearing a rose headdress at his table. I was experiencing déjà vu—another of Cole and Roman's potential investors flat on his face. Different gala, same result. This was getting seriously old. Bad behavior was contagious, spreading from gala to gala like a virus. Even the guest of honor, Dr. Aram, was oblivious, chatting up some seriously gangster-looking men off to the right side of the orchestra. These guys were right out of *The Godfather*— short, bald, mean-looking men, each with a cigar in one hand and a barrel glass of whiskey in the other, attempting to loosen their collars, which were strangling their necks, while still balancing all their tasks.

"Roman, what happened?" Sierra pushed on.

Roman kept fanning, but Walter wasn't showing signs of life. He began explaining the events to us.

"I was talking business with Walter. Cole and I want him to reinvest in a new deal, and I was making the sale. Walter was on his fifth or sixth J&B Mist, feeling no pain and yelling 'Fuck yes!' then 'Fuck no!' I didn't know what the fuck his deal was." Roman stopped explaining as Walter began to rally, partially sitting up, causing the roses to drop off his head. Apparently one of the stems had not been totally stripped of thorns, and Walter got a thorn stuck in his cheek as he rose from the table, again yelling out a very clear "Fuck!" as a stream of blood began to flow south.

As Roman continued offering his version of events, Sierra began acting strange, twitching nervously. I asked her if she was okay. She just shook her head, turning back and forth, rubbing her hands together, and repeatedly patting her brow. Cole simply stood by watching. He didn't know what to do or what to say. Roman was in charge.

Walter still was not coming around, his head back on the table. Minutes passed. Roman's fanning was not helping, and now Walter was not breathing, beginning to turn blue.

"Call 911!" I yelled. I did not have my cell. I never carried it because I hated carrying a purse to dinner parties. I carried only a small clutch filled with absolute essentials. Turning to Sierra, I found her still twitching and standing there staring, immobile.

I practically screamed, "Sierra, do you have a phone in your bag?"

I began thinking that I was living in a *Twilight Zone* rerun. The band played on. People kept dancing, totally oblivious to the drama at my table. Sierra appeared to be in a semicoma. I yelled at her again to call 911. She fumbled with her little black velvet purse, which was slung over one shoulder and attached to long gold chains. Not getting the clasp to release, Sierra yanked and lost her balance, beginning to go down. Catching her before she went over, I stopped her from landing on top of blue- and bloody-faced Walter. The black velvet bag opened, its contents spilling to the floor, including her cell. Sierra did not go for the cell to call 911; rather, she was down on her knees collecting a spread of small clear plastic envelopes filled with white powder. Diving for the cell, I realized Sierra was more concerned about her cocaine stash than about Walter's life. Wanting to scream at her, I realized there was no time and that there would be no purpose to it. Dialing 911, I asked for an ambulance.

At the same time, Cole, who was on the sidelines, also acted, banging on the table to quiet the room and yelling for help. It wasn't working. Making a dash for the orchestra, he jumped onstage, grabbed the microphone from the band singer, and halted the performance.

"We have an emergency. Is there a doctor in the house? Hurry! I need a doctor," Cole called out.

In all the chaos, I thought, *Of course there is a doctor in the house. This is a benefit for doctors, for God's sake.*

Indeed, there were many, including all the gangster-looking men I'd been watching. They were not mobsters. All were physicians, along with Dr. Aram, and all of them were at the table instantly to rescue the blue and bloodied Walter.

Sierra was still down on her knees searching for more missing cocaine packages. Now on all fours, she began crawling under the table. Apparently, she knew the exact count of her merchandise. Literally under the table in front of passed-out Walter, she had her bottom sticking straight up, with the table skirt draped over the rest of her body.

The crush of doctors enlisted Roman and Cole, the latter of whom had returned from the stage, to lift three-hundred-plus-pound Walter off the table and place him flat on the floor. Dr. Aram, the event's guest of honor and the oncologist who had saved Walter's Candy, took the lead. Candy was nowhere in sight—missing in action. Administering CPR without success, Dr. Aram repeated the procedure, then again, and again. Checking vitals, he found that Walter did have a pulse, but it was weak.

Another doctor called out, "This looks like an overdose. Does anyone have Narcan? Has he taken anything?"

Roman answered, revealing Walter's heavy consumption of scotch, claiming no knowledge of anything else.

With the one doctor's observation of possible drug overdose, Sierra's bottom disappeared totally under the table. She came out on the other side, stood up, and remained silent, standing in place.

The Narcan call had resulted in nothing. Fortunately, we could hear sirens blaring in the near distance. The paramedics were on the way.

Dr. Aram kept telling Walter, "Stay with us. Wake up. No sleeping. Wake up!" He instructed Cole and Roman to raise Walter's head slightly. Suddenly, Walter showed some sign of consciousness, and then he threw up in projectile fashion. In the direct line of his expulsion, I thought, *I am one girl who does not throw up on myself. Not ever, at all costs. Never did. Never will.* I was horrified. Cole dashed over to me and attempted to wipe it off. The smell was deadly. The room began to spin, but I did not gag. Cole kept apologizing. He knew how I felt about all of this. And it could not have been any worse.

Four paramedics came rushing through the Harbor Club ballroom doors. Surrounding Walter, they took over, with the fraternity of doctors circling the victim. The lead man immediately gave Walter the shot to revive him. The paramedics' instant diagnosis agreed with the doctor regarding some sort of overdose, probably beyond alcohol poisoning. Walter was loaded onto the gurney, and three of the men raced him out the door to the waiting ambulance to take him to Hoag Hospital. One of the paramedics called out asking if anyone would be accompanying the ambulance. We all looked around for Candy, who was still missing in action. Roman waved them on, saying we would go to Hoag shortly on our own.

The fourth paramedic stayed behind. Since there was possible evidence of an overdose, he was required to make a report of any findings. After questioning all of us and getting no valuable information, he saw Sierra standing nervously across the table and went over to her.

"Miss, I'm Dave DiMeco, reporting from the Newport Beach Fire Department. May I ask you if you have any knowledge of anything that may have contributed to this man's situation?"

Sierra was now convulsing, preshock. DiMeco asked her to take a seat at the table. As Sierra sat, her black velvet bag flew open again, and the contents she had so diligently collected all spilled out. Cocaine packets littered the floor. Some landed on Sierra's lap, and one even fell on DiMeco's leg, sliding into the cuff of his uniform trouser.

Sierra began to weep. "I'm so sorry," she managed to get out while hysterical over having been caught with the drugs.

"Sorry for what exactly, miss?" the paramedic asked.

"Walter and I met during the cocktail reception, and I sort of sold him a little extra octane for the night. I didn't know him, but he seemed very nice," she explained rather lamely, her voice cracking.

I stared at her in disbelief. Then my eyes fixed on Roman. Was my husband's business associate also a cocaine dealer like his date? Oh, terrific, were we in trouble now?

Roman and Cole were both standing in place like stone pillars. Roman did not even attempt to go to Sierra's aid or defense, or even try to offer comfort.

"Please try to calm down, miss. Stay seated. I'm afraid I must notify the police as you have a large amount of controlled substance on you tonight. They will come shortly."

DiMeco notified the Newport Beach Police Department and alerted Harbor Club security. Security arrived quickly, five men and one woman. The drama had extinguished the party mood. Most guests departed. Those remaining stood back, watching the drug bust unfold. A little Tuesday evening intrigue on the Orange Coast. Nothing like a drug overdose and drug bust at a five-hundred-dollar-per-plate cancer fundraiser dinner midweek. This was a gossipmonger's paradise.

Sneaking away after being questioned, I raced to the women's lounge to attempt to literally clear Walter off me. Upon entering, I found Candy primping her makeup and hair.

"You smell disgusting," she blurted, smearing a corner of her blue mascara application. "Oh damn, look what I've done," she exclaimed. "So, what smells so awful?"

"Well, if you really want to know, it's Walter," I told her straightaway.

"Walter? My Walter? He doesn't smell like that. He smells like too much Aramis."

"This ain't Aramis," I answered.

Trying to explain, I realized Candy was only half listening. When I got to the part about Walter being carried off by paramedics to Hoag Hospital, she ran out of the lounge without a word. At least she cared enough to go to him, I thought.

More sirens were now blaring, coming down the Pacific Coast Highway toward the Harbor Club. This time it was certainly the Newport Beach Police Department. Wanting nothing to do with the final act of this Tuesday night drama, I stayed in the women's lounge, removing my dress and washing off the vomit as best as possible. Standing facing the mirror in bra and panties, I was conflicted. Should I scream cry? I did neither. But I was angry. This was not who I wanted to be. These were not people I wanted to be with. I kept thinking about Roman, worried that Cole was in bed with another loser, only worse than Tom Murphy, the ultimate Newport poseur.

Remaining in hiding for what was at least half an hour beyond the time I had heard the last of the sirens approach, I did all I could to partially erase Walter from my dress. I sat on the settee in one corner of the ladies' lounge. This was one time I regretted not having carried my cell in my purse to a black-tie dinner. Not wanting to put the dress back on, and not able to do a partial Lady Godiva exit, I prayed that Cole would come looking.

He did. Prayer answered. The good husband even had brought my coat. Saved. We escaped the ladies' lounge, went directly to the car, and drove back to the cottage.

Sierra somehow managed to slip away, evading arrest. Dr. Aram drove Candy to Hoag to find Walter. Roman snuck out, probably with Sierra, without saying anything. The cops took information from everyone, alerting that a follow-up would be forthcoming.

"I am going to take a two-hour-long hot shower, using Lysol instead of soap," I said to Cole the second we entered the cottage.

"Can I join you?" he inquired.

"After the first hour maybe," I replied. "Give me time to wash this night down the drain. There still might be a chance for a happy ending," I told him, trying to forget the whole thing. "Oh, and by the way, burn that dress and buy me a new one!"

Flexible at All Times

More than a month had passed since the drama on the dance floor, and now Roman was facing the reality that the long stall from Benheim to commit to investing in their next land deal in The Summit development likely meant the deal was dead.

Cole entered escrow on another million-dollar-plus sale in Society Hill, again a buyer who had responded to the cable television exposure. The entire office of agents who had joined the start-up star were all doing well under the Baldwin flagship.

Cole's personal confidence level was seriously on the rise. His demons and his fears of failure, which came from his foundation of limited worldliness coupled with an education of little value, were supplanted by ambition, which was proving to be the answer to all. Along with his expansion in confidence was an expansion of his taste for the perks of success. His wardrobe had expanded from one blue suit off the Nordstrom rack just a few years earlier to a wardrobe suitable for the cover of *GQ*. His suits filled every spare inch of space in any closet available in the beach cottage. Not only were the Baldwins cramped with three kids and a nanny, but also, they were being overrun by a rapidly spreading virus of men's suits.

Cole justified his newly found addiction to bespoke suits by mentioning his ever-increasing events schedule. He was creating an image that was becoming a tool for building his business. And it was the perfect path in Newport Beach, a town like no other, sporting a society divided into two very distinct sectors: invisible old beach money and neon-bright new invaders, some flush and others made of dreams and tissue paper.

The funny thing was that Cole never planned his ascension to glory in this town. He had not analyzed Newport, choosing it as his target base. Rather, he simply landed here in his Toyota because the weather was fine, and the ocean was a nod to freedom after his landlocked life in Reno.

Cole arrived late at the office on this Monday morning, after eleven o'clock, to find his partner Roman pounding on the glass-top table desk recently installed in his office. Closing the door, also glass, Cole inquired about the tantrum. Roman looked up at his celebrity front man, withholding one final pounding of the glass.

"Do you really want to smash that fifteen-hundred-dollar piece of glass?" were Cole's initial words.

Roman took a deep breath and counted to ten out loud in his native Russian.

"Whenever I hear that countdown in Russian, there's trouble. What now?" Cole asked. "I think I had better learn your language so I can be sure I'm getting all the facts right."

"Probably a good idea," Roman retorted.

"So, what's the deal?"

"There is no deal. That's the deal. Benheim is out. We need his million bucks to close The Summit deal."

"Big jerk. He gave me the creeps. So did his blow-up doll of a wife. This is all because of her."

"Maybe so, but so it is."

"You've worked with him for a while. You can change his mind."

"I've tried. For about a month I've tried. He won't move."

"There's got to be more to this."

"Who knows? He's a strange dude. But he smells money, and nothing gets in his way when that happens."

"He's not smelling The Summit?" Cole tried to be clever.

"Funny. I think he's never liked you. I've told you things he has said, including the switch-hitter remark. And this Sierra episode might have been, how do you Americans say, 'the clincher.'"

"Whatever. So, what now, financial Russian wizard? I'm the pretty face, remember. You are the money guy. How do we come up with another million bucks fast?"

"Pretty face needs to put the charm in gear and talk to your rich fans. You're right, I'm the background guy. You're the draw."

"We have until just after Thanksgiving to make the offer."

"That's not much time to court a million-dollar investor."

"We will make it." The Baldwin confidence factor was strong.

Roman calmed down and went back to work at the undamaged fifteen-hundred-dollar glass-top desk. Cole exited for a lunch meeting at Harbor Club with a new client.

Surprised by Benheim's retreat, but not sidetracked, Cole's gift was a barrier of ignorance when it came to harsh reality. The inflated confidence bolstered by the full selection of Armani black suits, tailored to his frame, and the lease on the new black 2004 BMW 7 Series sedan, provided faith like no religion ever could.

At lunch on the waterfront terrace at Harbor Club, adjacent to the "members only" Captain's Cabin Dining Room, Cole sat facing the megayachts berthed at the club docks. Arriving on time, he relished the mild breeze off the water while shaded from the strong fall sun by the club's signature nautical navy-blue scalloped awnings trimmed with white piping and properly spaced white knotted fringe. Sparkling white-painted director's chairs, featuring navy-blue canvas seats, were placed around circular tables. The upholstery of the seats was monogrammed with the Harbor Club name in classic white script on the back panel of every chair. Cole removed the white linen napkin, piped in navy blue and folded in an open fan shape, from the tall goblet at his place setting.

A server appeared, offering a beverage. Cole accepted water and asked the woman server, also in a coordinating navy and white uniform, to return when his guest arrived.

The view directly in front of his table in the harbor was focused on the largest vessel among many that the locals referred to as "Battleship Row." The stunning yacht, christened *Princess Gilda*, was owned by a German industrialist whose pedigree was borne mostly of rumor and innuendo. Cole had heard the rumors but never crossed paths with the man. Until now.

An entourage appeared coming down the gangplank leading from the club toward the yacht. It was an array of uniformed servants in black tie pushing carts festooned with florals, libations, and God knows what else.

Behind the service train, a man of perhaps fifty, sporting long blond hair flowing back over his forehead, oversized black shades, an untucked open-collar white Lacoste polo shirt, white Levi's, and white slip-on tennis shoes with no socks, marched forward with a bikini-clad woman on each arm.

Certain this was the German mystery man, Cole stared at the alternate universe lifestyle parading only fifty yards, yet a solar system away, from his place at the Captain's Cabin table. Then Cole's new client arrived. The man had come as another referral call from the cable show, claiming to be a car dealer looking for a bachelor pad, newly divorced for the third time. Roman had done a bit of a background check on the man, who proved to be legit. He was a dealer not just in Newport, but also in LA. Known as the "Titan of Toyotas," this guy sold more Corollas and Camrys than anyone on the West Coast. As a former Toyota owner, Cole figured he could relate. Cole thought, *Here we go again with another car dealer client.*

Cole stood up to greet the Titan of Toyotas. The new client charged over and threw both arms around Cole, gripping him in a big manly bear hug. He stepped back. "Great to meet you, man. I'm Christian Marlow. Call me Chris. I'm a big fan of *Living the Dream.* I want to live the dream, and I'm here to buy," he said with mucho bravo machismo.

Cole smiled. "I'm here to sell," he answered.

"That's what I expect," Chris came back. "Hey, look over there: it's Richard Hellman with two of his future ex-wives."

"I've heard about him," Cole replied.

"Don't believe most of what you've heard. Newport loves a good story, especially if it's a lie. Remember, buddy, the lie is always preferred."

Cole skipped a beat, taken by surprise with the candor. He said nothing as Chris continued, saying, "I'll bet you've heard all the bull about the big shot German industrialist crap. Have you heard that the next Bond film will be based on an adaption of his life from an unknown Ian Fleming novel? How about the one that all his money comes from the estate of his first wife, twenty years his senior, who mysteriously drowned in the lake in front of her Austrian manor?"

"Really?"

"No, not really. But yes, that's what goes around. The truth is, Hellman is a loan shark. You know his ads on TV. Some of them run on your show, man. Quick cash, no-collateral loans with 40–100 percent interest and a broken leg if you're late. That's the Hellman money, and that's what pays for the famous German *Princess Gilda* yacht. Hell, I'm not even sure Hellman has ever been to Germany. Everyone here has a story. Everyone has a card to play."

Cole was thrown off-balance just a bit. He too believed, to a pretty good extent, that the lie was preferred. He too had a story, a card to play. For him it was true and real, and made sense. He was grounded. He had a wife and three kids, a business, and life goals. His act was justified and legitimate.

Chris, standing up at the table, called out across to the dock, "Hellman! Hey, man, it's me, Marlow." He watched the loan shark and his babes on the gangplank across the narrow passage of Newport harbor, the water dividing them. At first Hellman did not hear the call. Marlow yelled louder, waving his arms. Hellman turned.

"Come over here! I want you to meet someone," Marlow called out.

Cole looked across the water at the mystery man as he turned, along with his bikini-clad companions. Hellman started walking back toward the ramp leading to the Captain's Cabin's outdoor dining terrace.

As the triad passed by the maître d' station at the entrance to the terrace, the companions were asked to cover up before entering. They had nothing to cover up with. A busboy passed by with a cart holding a stack of freshly laundered table-cloths, signaling Hellman to act. Grabbing two starched white cotton tablecloths off the cart, he draped his two armpieces as if the cloths had transformed into couture gowns. Only the women's gold sequin-adorned stiletto heels were visible.

"That should take care of it, don't you agree?" Hellman said to the maître d', who said nothing as they passed by. Cole was amused. Chris Marlow was laughing like a hyena.

"Get over here, you rascal," Chris called out. Hellman and his gal pals sat down and called for a waiter to bring champagne.

"Meet my friend, and new real estate guy, Cole Baldwin," Chris offered. "You probably know him from his TV show *Living the Dream*."

Both women chimed in with instant recognition.

"Gosh, you are better-looking in person," one of them quickly announced. The other one, sitting to the left of Cole at the round table, placed her hand on his knee and gave him a squeeze.

Marlow explained the purpose of the gathering with Cole. Hellman seemed to pay little attention, continuously clicking champagne flutes with either one of his women, who were wrapped in tablecloths. Cole did his best to stay on business track. He did not want to lose a new client looking for a possible multimillion-dollar purchase.

Hellman finally joined in the conversation, dominating it, bragging about his extensive real estate investments. Cole would not be outdone, bringing up his future deal in The Summit land development project with Roman. Hellman showed interest.

"Are you looking for cash?" he inquired.

Cole hesitated, but in need of a million dollars to replace the Benheim pullout, he replied, "My partner and I have raised two-thirds of the investment. We are looking for a one-third infusion of cash."

"How much is one-third?"

"Two million," Cole said, exaggerating.

"I'm interested. I know the land development project. The potential is very good." Hellman continued, "Send me your proposal. I will get back to you."

Instructing his women to finish their champagne, he passed a card to Cole. They all rose, offering salutations to Chris Marlow, and left. Hellman did not pay for, or offer to pay for, the champagne.

"Sorry about all that, man," Chris Marlow offered. "He's a walking circus act, but entertaining, don't you think?"

"Definitely that," Cole responded.

"Do not expect a follow-up. The guy is all about himself, not serious business partner material," Chris Marlow advised.

"Let's talk about your home search," Cole moved on, changing the subject. "Tell me exactly what you want."

For the next hour, Chris Marlow did just that. The two of them discussed every detail discussed over lunch, which included several rounds of drinks, even a fancy dessert. The new client ate as if it were his last meal.

When the check arrived, Cole glanced at the bottom line while appearing nonchalant, finding that lunch had run over three hundred dollars including Hellman's Veuve Clicquot. Good thing he hadn't taken time to review the wine list. Cole told himself that he now needed three million dollars to finalize his potential Summit deal.

"Great meeting you, man." Chris Marlow put out his hand. "Thank you for lunch. Call me with prospects. I'm ready to deal," he said, then bolted up and left the dining terrace. Cole remained. On either chair beside him, a crumpled white tablecloth lay limp. Looking over the water and the *Princess Gilda*, he noticed that rock music blared from its aft deck. With no visible sign of Hellman or the women, the yacht was rocking excessively, which was strange since the water in the harbor was totally flat, not a ripple. There were no waves at all, except those generated by the *Princess Gilda* in the middle of the afternoon.

CHAPTER FORTY-NINE

FOLLOWING THE MONEY

Cole and Roman relentlessly pursued every lead to find the million-dollar investor who would enable them to make The Summit land deal. Cole put his search for a replacement home for me and the boys on hold, knowing that all his funds would be needed to make the land deal work. I was supportive, although I needed space. It was crowded perhaps, but I was still happy in the beach house. The disappointment over the sale of the new home on Society Hill was already off my radar. Besides, as Cole reminded me, not even a toilet had been selected for the house when it was under construction.

Sadly, that fact meant something to me. Hoping that Cole would be more present in our young married life, I wanted him involved in planning and creating the new house. We could pick out the toilet together, or so I wished. That plan was dashed, yet Cole remained my dashing absentee husband, totally consumed in work. Lovemaking was once again on hold, the last time having been more than a month before, after dinner with the boys in the cottage. The dry spells were almost routine, a pattern indicating that our marriage of only a few years was out of balance.

I poured myself into the needs of the boys and into plans with my business partner Heather. Trustworthy nanny Bonnie, the surrogate aunt, made everything work for me. I spent full days, as often as possible, with Heather and my mentor Monsieur Lawrence at the salon, and with the blessing of Madame Honoré, we created a small office space for the Fair Child line in a back corner of the workroom that previously had served as a fabric storage area. Heather used her technical expertise to outfit the "world headquarters" as we attempted to create our dynasty.

Grandmother GiGi's financial largesse paid for a jobber in downtown Los Angeles near the California Mart, the West Coast's fashion headquarters for all the big-name lines and important buyers, to manufacture a full workout of the new finished samples of the Fair Child line created for launch in spring 2005. We partners had decided to go big, being admittedly overzealous and going somewhat against the warning of Monsieur Lawrence. We had ordered a full-size range of the line, totaling more than fifteen hundred pieces covering the eight styles of the first seasonal selection of garments. A major risk.

"GiGi would have told me to go big. I knew this, so I did." Repeatedly I told my true believer partner Heather that I was following GiGi's spirit.

"That may be, my darling girl, but even the House of Chanel is cautious with new designs before producing a mass buy," Monsieur Lawrence said, tempering my enthusiasm.

The big order was clearly an act of unfettered youthful confidence. I knew it, GiGi's voice in my head aside. I also knew it was the same kind of confidence Cole had. Essentially, I had the same core belief in myself that Cole had in himself, regardless of our different foundations. I vacillated on a dime, sometimes going from confident to reluctant, a swing that sometimes got in the way.

All the garments were ready to ship in a matter of weeks. We moved fast on the plan, even though none of the meetings with regional buyers had materialized into sales. Heather's mother Mrs. A's intros in the buying office at Neiman's also failed to result in instant success. They insisted Fair Child do what they called an "off-Broadway" tryout before hitting the big luxury retail market.

Mother Nancy had found a similar response from her Beverly Hills sources. What did help somewhat was the advertising campaign we had shot in Laguna Canyon. Heather placed full-page ads in local and regional fashion magazines and appropriate sections of the newspapers. Phones were ringing with inquires, mostly from small one-off luxury women's ready-to-wear shops in towns such as Beverly Hills, Pasadena, Palm Springs, and yes, Newport Beach. But we'd made no sales—just talk, promises to come see the line, and some appointments for us to take the line to the stores.

Two days a week, we would travel to shops in specific locales with people who could not visit us in Newport at Avenue Foch West. It was a lot, especially for me. It wasn't easy, even with nanny Bonnie. Conflicted over being the perfect mom to three boys under the age of three and a fashion career woman, I realized the perfect wife role was also on hold.

Having been turned down by the big stores, which were unwilling to take a chance on the unknown, I offered to supply them with the line at no cost up front, with the full right to return all unsold products. That resulted in another lesson learned. Monsieur advised his two Carolina Herrera wannabes that the stores had that sort of arrangement with many established lines. "With all the competition, that's the new mode of business," he cautioned.

We protégés took the advice to heart, immediately shifting gears and going full speed ahead with the fall / winter / holiday season pop-up concept, offering the new spring 2005 line of Fair Child.

Again, Mrs. A was enlisted to influence the management company operating Fashion Plaza Newport Beach, a world-class shopping destination designed as an Italian Mediterranean village set on a rise above the Pacific Ocean surrounded by palm trees. It was arguably the United States' most exquisite shopping plaza. Fountains splashed; vibrant annual posies were planted in militarily precise rows and replenished constantly; punctuated stone walkways were adorned with enormous terracotta urns sporting twenty-foot-tall cypress pillars. Classic lanterns flickered beams of light. Fashion Plaza was the shopping destination of the young, the young at heart, and the ever-trendy Newport Riviera set.

Out of nowhere, I let out a controlled yelp.

"What happened?" Heather asked, concerned. Monsieur came over instantly with a cup of water. He was always at the ready with water, tea, or aspirin.

"Gosh, I don't know. Maybe it was the salmon salad we ordered in for lunch?" I said. A second bolt hit me. I doubled over.

"Okay, that's enough. We are taking you to the emergency clinic around the corner," Heather insisted.

"Oh no, not yet. It's nothing. Give me a few minutes. I think I have a bad stomachache."

The third bolt struck. No more waiting.

Ten minutes later, Heather and I were in the clinic. It was late afternoon, with no waiting. I was shown to an examining room, Heather by my side. The bolts of pain stopped. That was what always happened when I went to the emergency clinic with unknown pain. The minute I got into the examining room, it stopped. We future fashion icons were laughing as Dr. Grimes entered.

"What are you doing here?" I asked, moving toward my cherished and devoted ob-gyn.

"I help out here two afternoons a week," Dr. Grimes shared. "I'm a business partner in this clinic. I have a kind of passion for old-fashioned walk-in 'expect everything and anything' kind of doctoring," she told us, sharing hugs. "Why are you here? Or is this visit for your friend?"

Introducing Heather, I didn't need to explain as another bolt of pain struck. Dr. Grimes began a cursory exam, asking the anticipated barrage of questions. Her final inquiry: "Are you regular?" I hesitated, thinking, *No way. It couldn't be.*

"Well, I am late, but that is not it," I said.

"How late?" Dr. Grimes asked.

"Late," I said sheepishly.

"We can do an immediate test," the good doctor offered.

"Really, it could not be."

Dr. Grimes took the blood test and handed it off to her nurse. Within five minutes, the nurse reappeared, handing the results to the doctor. Dr. Grimes glanced at it quickly, looked at me, and said, "Are you ready for number four?"

Looking at Heather with my eyes wide open, the size of planets in an outer solar system, and in shock, I turned to Dr. Grimes, smiling.

"Yes, I am in shock. Yes, this is wonderful news. No, I'm not ready for number four. No, it was not planned. We have not been together in weeks. And how is it even possible that I will have four children in a little more than four years of marriage? This is not part of the big plan for my life." I went on, with great excitement building.

"It's possible because you are making very passionate love with your husband." Dr. Grimes enjoyed being cute. "Even if it not as often as desired."

"I'm not a very good planner when it comes to sex and babies," I replied.

"Oh, I'd say you are an excellent planner," Dr. Grimes said.

"Do you think this child could be my little girl?" I asked with an overwhelming tone of hope in my voice.

"God knows. We'll know a little later," the doctor answered.

"Oh my God. God knows," I repeated, grabbing Heather's hand.

"That's right, partner, God knows," Heather confirmed. "And I know that God knows you have three loving sons, so you should have one loving daughter. After all, somebody in your family will surely want to wear the vintage Fair Child line someday for her seventh-grade costume ball!"

Heather embraced me. We said our farewells to Dr. Grimes and headed back to Avenue Foch West.

Getting into Heather's car, looking at my fashion partner, I asked, "Now what?"

Trouble Back at Real Estate Mogul Central

Roman, the money half of the Roman–Cole equation, had finally come up short.

"How is this possible?" he yelled at Cole. "Money is so loose now that banks are lending to dead people. Why can't I find an investor with an extra million to come in with us on The Summit? This should have been a no-brainer," Roman said, spitting out the last of his frustrated words. *No-brainer* in a heavy Russian accent required a significant release of saliva. Cole stepped back to avoid the spray.

"We are each putting in seven hundred fifty thousand dollars. That's a lot of personal equity. We have a track record. Why can't we borrow from the bank?" Cole asked.

"Because the loose money is not so easily granted for undeveloped land, and we don't have enough of a track record. You have more than me. Remember, I'm not a US citizen. American banks are slightly suspicious of potential clients who list assets in Moscow."

"Yeah, I get it. Are you sure Benheim won't change his mind?"

"Not a chance."

"I could approach my new client Christian Marlow. We just entered escrow on a two-and-a-half-million-dollar estate on Society Hill. Or how about that guy

Richard Hellman whom Marlow introduced me to? I have his card. He told me to reach out."

"Not a chance. Hellman the loan shark? No way!"

Roman wiped the sweat off his forehead, gathering his composure.

"What about your father-in-law?"

"You think I should ask Dalton Fairchild? I told him two years ago that I wanted to build my business on my own. How can I do that?"

"You can do that. He's your wife's daddy. He wants his daughter to be happy and comfortable. He's rich. He offered to help before. And this is a great investment. We will pay him back with a potential 40–50 percent return in less than two years."

"I don't know. How about I go to my TV production company? It's a natural connection. The two guys who own it are also rich. I could do segments on the TV show featuring the development. This could work."

"If you want to try, do it now. We have no time. We will lose the deal to other bidders who can produce the cash."

"I'll call now and move fast."

Leaving Roman, Cole went into his office and shut the door. The Baldwin et Cie office was humming. Agents were on phones; papers were being passed from desk to desk. A receptionist at the front ran back and forth among the staff of agents, delivering messages and files. Everyone in Newport was taking advantage of the loose money, thanks to a wink from Wall Street and the Fed. Homes were a hot commodity, selling sight unseen in many cases. Agents were making hay.

Cole dialed the private number for Rocco La Penta, executive producer and co-owner of American Homes Network, the company behind *Living the Dream*, which had made Cole a local celeb.

La Penta was twenty years Cole's senior at forty-seven. of Italian heritage like Cole, he was handsome but not too handsome; going bald but with a ponytail, and insecure about it; and openly gay. He lived with his partner in business and in the bedroom, but Cole had never met him. It was explained that he was the "silent partner."

"Hello, Rocco, it's Cole."

"Hey, my number one TV star guy. How's it hangin'?"

"Low and loose," Cole answered. He teased La Penta with gay innuendo, which his producer took as a sign of friendship. Cole continued, "Rocco, I need to meet with you on an investment matter. Are you free anytime soon?"

Cole had worked with the producer for almost two years, and the relationship was mutually successful both financially and personally. They were friends, so Cole felt he could approach Rocco with the ask. It made sense. He would not be overstepping any boundary.

"This sounds urgent," Rocco responded.

"It is," Cole answered.

"Give me a heads-up," his producer said, prodding for more information.

"I have an ask, but I'd rather ask in person," Cole came back.

"Do you want to date?" Rocco teased.

Cole laughed. "You're taken," he replied.

"Oh, right, that is the case. Just tell me what you want to ask."

"Rocco, Roman and I need an additional million in cash to make a raw land purchase for developing The Summit. We need a partner. We'll put up one-point-five million, maybe two million if we can stretch, but we still need another million. Any chance you might consider?"

Cole paused. There was a short, uneasy silence.

"How soon do you need an answer?" Rocco inquired in a very businesslike tone, no gay humor this time.

"Yesterday. Last week," Cole answered.

"Then you've been turned down by others?"

Cole decided to be totally up front. "We have. But only by a few."

"I'm here in the Costa Mesa production office on Newport Boulevard. You've been here, I think. It's in the building next door to the Ali Sheba Motel. Come by in an hour. I'll meet you at five."

Cole let out his breath, which he'd been holding, and, hanging up, dashed out of the floor-to-ceiling glass doors of his office, on a race to Roman's sanctuary at the other end of the space, behind matching double floor-to-ceiling glass doors.

Roman was on the phone making yet another pitch to someone else as Cole blew in. The pitch was in Russian, and it was loud and getting louder. Suddenly, Roman slammed down the receiver. "Shit. Bastard asshole Russian prick!" he shouted.

"What?" Cole wasn't sure he wanted to know.

"It was a guy I know. His family comes from Latvia, low class. I found out he is bidding on our land. Can you believe I called him not knowing this to ask him to partner with us?"

"Okay, that explains your frustration."

Cole changed the subject and explained to Roman that he might have a chance getting funds from his TV producer pal Rocco La Penta. He was meeting him in an hour. Roman came around his desk, arms wide open, grabbing Cole and kissing him on both cheeks, and then, catching Cole totally off guard, placing a big one right on his lips.

Roman pulled back.

Cole pulled back as well, reeling just slightly from the momentary sensation of Roman's tongue in his mouth.

"That's a Russian kiss for 'go fucking make a deal.' We'll toast when you return at six o'clock tonight. I'll be waiting for good news." Roman went back to his desk. Cole went back to his own office.

Rocco was at the console, directing his video technician in making edits for the final version of Cole's latest show, when the reality television star arrived for the five o'clock meeting. Cole parked his BMW in the lot directly adjacent to the huge, white-painted Moroccan dome tower of the kitsch 1960s-era Ali Sheba Motel, which was now somewhat less whimsical with rates starting at $19.95 a night. Entering the studio, Cole walked down the long, dimly lit hallway with its walls covered in handsomely framed enlarged photos taken at various locations where *Living the Dream* was shot. His destination was the last door directly at the end of the hallway. Cole could see light flickering from the tiny crack between the bottom of the door and the metal sill.

Knocking twice, he entered the editing suite before being asked in. Standing behind the console, Rocco and the technician had their backs to him. They were all facing a wall of multiple video screens, each one featuring a different angle of Cole on camera. Cole stood there for at least ten minutes, not saying a word, knowing that Rocco was aware of his presence but not acknowledging it. Editing instructions were being hurled at the tech, then Rocco exclaimed, "That's the keeper! Cut."

Moving away from the console, Rocco took Cole by the arm and ushered him out of the editing room, going through a door into a small private windowless room furnished with only a heavily worn cushioned sofa and marred wooden side table supporting a tarnished brass lamp with a ripped shade and a black landline phone. Rocco sat down in the center of the sofa, motioning for Cole to sit as well. Cole obliged.

Sitting next to Rocco, close to him since it would have been awkward to sit at the far end, Cole launched into his request. With barely a sentence having been spoken, Rocco placed his left hand on Cole's right leg. Cole glanced down, looking at Rocco's hand on his leg.

"Cole, you know how much I like you, believe in you, and love working with you. We have simpatico," Rocco said with his customary flourish. "We have the same goals, you and I. We love what we do. We want to be loved, admired, successful, and rich, and we have been achieving all of that and continue to do so together. Would you not agree?" Rocco asked. Cole was caught off guard. He froze, pretending to be cool. He knew what was coming but kept his mission on target.

"Yes, of course, Rocco. I understand." Cole continued, "Shouldn't that mean we could be good investment partners as well?"

"Perhaps so, but I need to know something more about you," Rocco added.

"I don't think I understand," Cole replied, despite knowing fully well what Rocco meant.

Rocco leaned in, took his hand off Cole's leg, placed both his hands on Cole's cheeks, and kissed him on the mouth. Cole accepted the kiss, pulling away as carefully as he could. He said nothing, acting neither angry nor surprised. Rather, he tried to defuse a dangerous situation. A line had been crossed, yet it was not totally unexpected.

"Rocco, I'm your friend. I like you very much, but not this way," Cole finally said, speaking as sincerely as he could. Confused because so much was going on, his mind raced. Cole desperately needed the investment money. Trading sexual favors for business was part of his repertoire. He also needed to keep his TV gig with Rocco, his connection to sales traffic and the vehicle to local celebrity, which he craved. First Roman had kissed him, now Rocco. All this sexual tension within a couple of hours. *Am I sending out signals?*

Rocco moved over on the sofa. "I didn't think you would mind," he uttered. Cole did not answer. "Forgive me if I misunderstood. I thought you might like men and women." Rocco was blunt. Cole still said nothing.

"Cole, this changes nothing. We are still friends. We are still partners in the TV biz. But I think we had best keep it at that. I cannot be your new investor, but I wish you nothing but good luck." Rocco stood up and began walking toward the door, intending to go back into the edit bay, calling out, "Don't forget, we have the next shoot on Friday at the estate in Smithcliffs, Laguna Beach. We start in makeup on-site at eight o'clock."

Cole waved as Rocco went through the door. He fell back on the sofa, his head against the rear cushion, staring up at the dirty sprayed popcorn ceiling, his legs spread apart and his feet dangling above the floor. Looking like he had been sucker-punched, his thoughts raced, his emotions conflicted.

"Who the hell am I? What am I doing?" he said in a whisper, even though no one could hear him. "Now what do I do?" The gay connections were familiar to Cole; he carried several in his memory over his twenty-seven years. At five, a boy buddy on a playdate had pulled down his shorts and told Cole he wanted to see his pee-pee. There was an incident in the high school locker-room shower after football practice, and another in junior college with a horny English teacher. More recently, prior to his marriage to Kate, there was the guy at the Holmby Palms Hotel pool spa. And now his producer, Rocco, was making the moves.

A husband, father, and manly man, Cole had not pursued the gay connections; they found him. Yet, he did not object, although he did bury the feelings. He certainly wasn't going to talk about the experiences. This was not done ever. Besides, it didn't matter. Who cared? Gay was cool now, no big deal. It was just sex. Everybody tried everything, a new generation of people who pursued hookups.

Once he'd received his initiation into hetero sex, Cole hit the ground running. His previously limp device frequently became hard and straight at any given unexpected moment. It appeared daily on the bumpy high school bus ride. The rod surfaced after school, again on the bus, as he sat next to his next-door neighbor, an eighteen-year-old Mormon virgin, the youngest of eight kids in her family, who couldn't take her eyes off it. One afternoon, in the grove of trees behind their two adjacent houses, Cole and the girl next door lost their respective virginities. Moving forward, Cole lost count of his sexual exploits with girls during his senior year in high school. He did know one thing: he had never experienced what he thought was supposed to be love with sex. That had happened only once, when he met Kate.

CHAPTER FIFTY

HETERO SEX TAKES CENTER STAGE

As I'd done with my previous pregnancies, I did not immediately share news of the latest event with Cole, or anyone other than Heather. She had agreed to keep quiet. This time, I really needed time. Time to think, to plan, to be smart. There would be four kids under five years of age. My ambitious husband was a semiabsentee as he built his empire and proved his worthiness to be on the planet. This despite my very constant reminder that there was no need to do so in my eyes. And then there was my dream, a personal goal in its infancy, as Heather and I launched a business with Monsieur Lawrence's tutelage and GiGi's gift. We were right on the cusp of launching from the ground up.

On top of it all, Cole, with my after-the-fact blessing, had sold our potential new house. *Overwhelmed* was becoming my middle name.

In true Kate Fairchild fashion, I pulled myself together. "Everything will work out. All is fine. I am blessed. I can handle anything," I repeated, looking in the mirror in the front entry hall of the beach cottage. After taking the rubber band out of my pulled-back hair, the straight shoulder-length blonde strands fell in my face. Looking darn good for a four-time mommy at not yet twenty-five, I figured I could still pass for sixteen and be carded at the checkout line.

Once the proper time to reveal the new addition to our lives presented itself, I figured the ideal place would be my parents' home in Beverly Hills for Sunday night dinner with the whole family. Things were going well with my baby brother, Jamey, and his program at Chabad. Rabbi Miller here in the O.C. had put him in touch with Rabbi Silverman in LA so he could get involved there and be close to our parents. Over the last several months since our beach visit with Reverend Paco, Jamey was much better and stronger. I heard the improvement in his voice over the phone; he was finally making progress. Thank God for Chabad, which I previously knew very little about.

Sunday dinner was also supposed to deliver a Jamey surprise, but Nancy had spilled the beans. My little brother was bringing a girl to dinner. How had Jamey become almost nineteen? The same way I had become almost twenty-five, soon to be a mom to four. Time moves, and life moves with it. I was beyond happy that my brother was doing okay. Beyond happy.

Cole was acting more agitated than usual, which was alarming and made me nervous, which caused me to hold back the baby news. When I pressed him for details, he said it was nothing. Cole was a champion avoidance artist. "Not to worry. I'll take care of it. You have enough on your plate," he said, and said again.

I stopped asking.

At the end of the week, Cole did open up, explaining that he was under pressure with his partner Roman to raise the extra million to make the land deal. Sharing some of the details, he still followed the optimistic high road. "We'll make it work," he said. "This is a big deal. It will make a difference in our lives."

Sitting on our cherished beachfront terrace at dusk on Friday, I poured Cole a glass of chardonnay in his favorite oversized crystal wineglass. I poured myself a ginger ale. He didn't ask. We toasted to our love, our happiness, and our family. So romantic. It put my husband in a lovemaking frame of mind. Moving closer to me on the settee, he placed his free hand on my leg.

"Why don't you ask Dalt?" I offered in a quiet voice.

"Huh?"

"Why don't you ask Dalt to invest?"

"I can't do that. You know I made a big deal about not taking his help. I need to do it on my own. Two years later with some pretty good success and I come crawling?"

"It's not like that, and you know it. Dalt is proud of you. He sees what you've done. He's your biggest TV fan—never misses an episode and brags to all his friends. Besides, you believe in this deal. Dalt is not stupid. He knows a winner. And he is your father-in-law."

"Kate, you amaze me every day. I know I don't tell you often enough how lucky I am to be with you. Everything you do to support me and raise three beautiful boys—you are my superwoman." Cole took a beat. "Would you like to have Friday night sex?"

"Later. It's only five thirty. Time to feed your sons, then bath time, stories, and bed. That's what Superwoman does."

"That never stopped us before. I think the last time, we started on the steps before making it to the bedroom."

"Yeah, that last time, I must remind you, was a while ago. It was a real whopper."

"Good, yes?"

"Oh yes, very good. I'll remember it forever." I still did not explain. Cole took it as the supreme manly achievement pleasing his woman.

By nine in the evening all was well on the cottage front. We went to bed and made love until *The Tonight Show with Jay Leno* came on television. Falling asleep during the monologue, we held one another through the night, until the Pacific sun landed its rays on our naked bodies stretched out on the bedsheets, the coverings all tossed to the floor.

Sunday Dinner on Lexington Road

Devoted Jefferson, family Fairchild man for all seasons, greeted the Baldwin crew at the Lexington Road front entrance as he had done for the family for more than twenty years.

I adored him. He was a quiet gentleman with layers of hidden soul, sparingly revealed at the appropriate times and places, a reflection of his artistic heart developed in his youth spent playing jazz in salons on New Orleans's Bourbon Street and, later, in the clubs of South-Central LA.

"Come in, Miss Kate, Mr. Cole. We are so pleased to welcome you tonight." Jefferson was the arbiter of graciousness, a learned and rehearsed art. Mother and Dad appeared as soon as our gang crossed the threshold. They were overjoyed to see the boys. It was a love fest, all of us on our knees with the three Baldwin musketeers on the marble floor of the entry. Enjoying the moment with full focus, Dalt was acting silly and was very much at ease and playful.

Cole raised the temperature of merriment, egging the kids on, and soon they were giggling and running in circles. He started the chase around the large antique circular pedestal table in the center of the foyer.

Dalt joined the running around, counterclockwise, and they all met in the middle, crashing to the floor in joyous hysterics. I had dressed all three boys in matching Ralph Lauren toddler boy's blue and white striped shorts, white shirts, and navy-blue bow ties worn under the perfect toddler-size navy blazers with sparking gold buttons and the signature Lauren emblem embroidered on the left breast pocket. Wasn't I the perfect mother after all? Very *Town and Country*, of course. With the second run around the central table, the bow ties were askew, and the boys were ridding themselves of their emblazoned blazers. All thrown on the black and white marble floor, Jefferson was picking them up. I told him to stand down and relax.

"Mother, is Jamey here?" I asked.

"In the living room, darling. He is with a friend he wants you to meet."

Since the news about the girl had been spilled, I felt comfortable asking. "I've talked to Jamey at least once a week over the past month and he never mentioned a friend. Is this new?"

"Yes. They are both in the Chabad program here in Beverlywood. Jamey met Rachel as a freshman at Beverly High. They lost touch, then became reacquainted in the program. He is quite smitten with her. You will see."

"Is this a good thing?" I pursued.

"Darling, it's a fabulous thing. He is a different young man. Just wait."

The opening act of Sunday evening dinner in the foyer moved into cocktails and hors d'oeuvres in the living room, where we all met Rachel. Mother was right.

She was lovely, and my little brother was over the moon. It was a miracle. Total transformation. I prayed it was real, possibly lasting, a turnaround. Rachel was also bright. Opening small talk was followed by smart conversation. Rachel and Jamey shared stories about the goings-on at Chabad and the programs they were both immersed in doing community outreach at a local food pantry and homeless shelter. They were candid about the drug rehab program, saying it had its ups and downs. Mostly, they were just happy teenagers sitting next to one another on Nancy's cream-colored silk sofa, holding hands.

Jefferson announced that dinner was served in the dining room. We all obliged. Marta had prepared a prime filet roast. I could smell its powerful and intoxicating aroma as we neared the double doors to the dining room, which were closed.

Leading the parade toward the Sunday filet roast, again in elegant Jefferson style, the five-foot-six former jazz trumpeter with his slicked-back thinning gray hair and his formal waistcoat, opened the double doors to the dining room. Pure elegance.

My mother loved a reveal. She always said it made the food taste much better. It was ridiculous perhaps, yet I believed her. It did taste better. Nancy's table was set in grand Sunday style, as expected. No cloth, just a gleaming wooden table surface topped with linen place mats, sparkling sterling silver, hand-selected posies from her garden, and of course a sea of flickering votives in tiny cut-crystal cups. We all took our places, even the boys, all in highchairs perfectly spaced apart. They had been supplied bibs and plastic cups and dishes to match. I sarcastically asked my mother why the plastic plates and cups were not monogrammed. She replied that she had not had time. Naturally.

Jamey and Rachel sat together at the far end of the table away from the boys. The two of them just kept talking to one another. This was turning into a special night at home. Planning to do my own reveal and share my pregnancy for the first time with Cole and my parents, I was not feeling totally convinced that it was the right time or place to do so. After all, this was Jamey's night. Dinner with the family had been arranged for my little brother to introduce Rachel. Maybe a pregnancy reveal would be too much. Seeing how close the two of them were, I certainly did not want to give the hormonal eighteen-year-olds any ideas.

Marta served the salad. Jefferson poured the wine. The pungent smell of the filet roast, along with the idyllic scene of my three toddlers in their rumpled Polo outfits sipping apple juice out of their unmonogrammed sippy cups, made me blurt out my news. Taking the silver spoon at my setting and clinking it against my goblet, I called out, "I have amazing news, family," my voice jumping up an octave into soprano range. I cleared my throat. Cole looked over with that *Are you okay?* expression.

"I'm six weeks pregnant with Baldwin number four!"

Everyone at the table froze for a split second, then all let out a shriek. Cole jumped up at his place and knocked over his wine. The boys giggled over all the excitement.

All the expected reactions were followed by all the expected questions. After the initial news, Cole seemed detached. He was happy, but somewhat distant. I think I had hurt him by not sharing with him first privately. Still, he got with the program, putting his arm around my waist as we were seated side by side at the table.

The filet roast was divine. Cole wasn't eating much; I took a bit of the crusty well-done edge of his portion. He smiled, offering another bite.

In the middle of my second bite, Dalt made a fatherly toast to the Baldwin Four. Ending the sentimental speech, he finished with the line, "May our new grandchild be born in perfect health, with ten toes and ten fingers, and be brought home to a nursery of his or her own—pink, blue, yellow, or purple, I don't care."

He followed with an offer: "Your mother and I have been talking about this before your wonderful announcement tonight. Now it seems the timing is appropriate. We would like to again offer you the option of moving into the much larger home on Lido Isle, the house Cole sold us."

"You're funny, my father," I said. Barely skipping a beat, I added, "We'll take it. That is, if Cole agrees?"

I turned to Cole. He nodded his head in the affirmative.

"Then it is settled," Dalt proclaimed.

Things were looking up. I had not planned to request a move into larger quarters, and certainly not at the Lido house. But the universe had spoken, I guess. I was not part of the "things happen for a reason" crowd. Things just happened. It was nice when they happened in such a way to change things for the better.

Cole was surprised too, but I also think he was somewhat relieved. This took the pressure off, neutralizing the sting from having sold my new house out from under me. Even better, I would not have to wait a year or more for space. It was already there and was a pretty darn nice space as well. We could never have such a large home, and certainly not one right on the bay. Cole could use the address to show off to prospective clients and investors. A twenty-something couple with four kids in a multimillion-dollar waterfront home should spell some measure of success. Never mind that we were squatters. Who had to know?

Marta started to clear the table to serve dessert and coffee. Nancy enlisted me to help her with tasks, requesting that Marta serve the chocolate sundaes in the solarium, specially prepared for Sunday dinner. Dalt rose to leave, and Cole caught his attention in the double doorway.

"Dad, can I have a private minute before dessert?" Cole had started calling

Dalt "Dad" at no one's suggestion. It just happened one time a few months ago. I liked it. Dalt liked it too.

"Sure, Cole, come with me into the study."

My two extremely handsome guys crossed over the black and white marble foyer and went through another pair of double doors on the opposite side, entering the classic old-world dark-wood-paneled library. Dalt took his place in the fatherly wing chair, and Cole sat on the adjacent leather sofa, for the talk between father and son-in-law.

"Is this about moving into the Lido house?" Dalt inquired.

Cole jumped in at once. "No, no it isn't. I am very grateful for that opportunity. It will make Kate happy and give us room," he said. "Well, actually, it is sort of about that, in a way."

"How so, Cole?"

"You know that we just sold out our first development on Society Hill, and as part of the project, we sold the lot and house we had hoped would be for us. So, you see, in a way, this is tied to my gratitude for your offer of the Lido house. But here is the bottom line. The money made from the overall project provided us with half a million dollars cash. We have saved another quarter million from my business sales over the past couple of years, again thanks in part to you and Mom letting us live in the cottage rent-free."

Cole continued, "You also know about my partner Roman. Kate has shared his story. Anyway, together the two of us have a total of one-point-five million to invest in a new land development deal in an area called The Summit."

Dalt interrupted Cole. "I am proud of you. Doing that kind of business and saving and making that level of funds at your age is an accomplishment. What is your plan with The Summit? I am aware of it. I know it is prime property."

"We have a chance to buy a parcel that is well located with great views and perfect for building six estate homes, each on more than one acre of land. The entire parcel cost is two and a half million. We need an investor with a million-dollar buy-in, and honestly, we don't have one. The deadline to bid is next week."

"There will be competition," Dalt continued. "Obviously, you need to be certain you have the funds to bid. It might be wise to overbid just slightly."

Cole was surprised. He thought, *How am I going to do that?*

Dalt continued, "Get me your full proposal, and if it looks as good as it sounds, Nancy and I will invest one and a quarter million dollars. Offer two-point-six million on the bid and hold onto one hundred fifty thousand dollars for unforeseen initial expenses as you seek construction loans from the banks. We will sign papers."

Cole rose from the couch to shake Dalt's hand. The handshake was clearly insufficient, so Cole initiated a manly bear hug.

"Oh my God, thank you, thank you," Cole offered genuinely. He knew that this was one amazing opportunity, one in which he did not have to compromise himself, trade sex, or do anything else in order to move ahead in life. It was a shocking counter to all the rules related to survival of the fittest he had learned through observation in his growing-up years.

"Shall we join the family for chocolate sundaes, Cole?" Dalt put his arm on his son-in-law's shoulder. Leaving the library, my husband appeared to be floating across the foyer floor.

CHAPTER FIFTY-ONE

THE RUBBER HITS THE ROAD

Halloween Week presented conflicting challenges for me. I felt a pressing obligation to provide our three toddlers the absolute best celebration possible, or was it their parents' desire to ensure that they would have the best costume-clad romp possible? I didn't know, but I was going all out, rounding up all the children and parents from my Mommy and Me group to come and join in the best Halloween party ever.

Bidding goodbye to our honeymoon beach cottage, Cole and I were now ensconced in Dalt and Nancy's French Regency mansion on the bay. It made for the ideal haunted house. Cole and I went crazy with the phony cobwebs, giant dangling black widow spiders, and the creepiest full-size, white-boned plastic skeletons, which were backlit with portable spotlights and accompanied by CD players sending out the whispering voices of the dead. That was Cole's idea. I thought it would scare the kids, but he insisted. Ultimately, I gave in. Buddy loved it; he was a very mature three-year-old. The twins cried. I gave them each a giant iced pumpkin cookie on a stick. No more tears.

During all the Halloween frenzy, I had left Heather carrying the weight to pull everything together to launch our first fashion presentation. This was the Fair Child debut. Or should I be honest and call it what it was—a pop-up store in a tent, somewhat less grand and less far-reaching than my dreams dictated. The tent was due to rise on the courtyard facing Newport's Neiman Marcus on the first Monday in November following Halloween.

Searching my soul to determine if this date of debut carried mystical, magical, deep universal significance, I came up short. It was just a fall Monday. The black and white tent was darn cute, but it was just a tent rising on the courtyard early that Monday morning before the center opened. Heather and I, along with a small crew, arrived at seven o'clock sharp. The tent was erected and in place by eight in the morning; black and white checkered vinyl flooring had been laid out, inspired by Nancy's entry foyer; the furniture and props had been placed; the electric hookup had been tested; and the lights and music were on by nine o'clock. The guys doing all the heavy lifting were pros, and Heather had every detail covered. Every part of the display was loaded on the truck, with nothing missing. The guys assisted with the final setup of the racks for the clothing and then assembled the corner of the tent with modesty drapes for the pop-up fitting room. Instant showroom.

At nine o'clock sharp, Monsieur and Madame came on the scene with the garment bags. Our devoted mentors each lugged one large heavy bag from their car, making it to the tent with heavy breathing. Heather got our guys to fetch the remainder of the line from the Lawrences' car, and the four of us began placing the clothes on the racks and display props.

I was starting to tear up. Heather noticed immediately and asked me why. Once I told her that I was not crying, just sweating, she laughed, knowing the truth. We hugged, only for a second, then work called; we needed to open at ten o'clock sharp. Our guys came back in no time, all the goods unpacked. Madame arranged wonderful small bouquets of pansies, our signature flower, in small clear vases. Finally, a ladder was positioned next to the entrance of the tent, which enabled our guys to place the canvas banner bearing the Fair Child insignia over the draped front door. In bold, simple, classic yet modern font, with black lettering on white background, it was sparingly punctuated with the black-bordered pale pink pansy blossom, which was used as the tittle over the *i* in both words *Fair* and *Child*. With this, we announced our launch. The four of us fashion royals stood and watched as the banner was put in place. Each of us instructed the guys to move it a little to the left, or maybe just a touch higher, or to fix the crooked right top corner. At last, perfection. At ten minutes past ten, we opened and launched the business.

Bidding farewell and sending love beyond all words to our crew, Heather and I both did a quick change into our Fair Child outfits, utilizing our makeshift fitting room. We adjusted the lighting, turned on the music, and pulled back the curtains bordering the entrance to our tent, tying back the black and white striped canvas with huge pink satin fabric, again bordered in black trim.

As we looked at one another, Heather took both my hands and said, "Girl, aren't we just the chicest fashion icon things in town?"

"Partner, I don't know about that, but I am proud. I owe most of this to you. I would not be here without you," I said with great sincerity.

"Nonsense. This is your creative dream. And it is my business goal. We are an ideal partnership."

"And it's GiGi's money. Thank you, my beloved grandmother. I am thinking about you more than ever today. I miss you so much." Heather took my hand again.

"This is your moment, friend. These are your designs, your talent, your vision. Relish this moment. No longer a dream. It's real," my confident partner advised with authority.

I wiped away another tear, exclaiming, "It's just more sweat. I'm still cooling down."

"Right," Heather replied.

Monday mornings at the fashion center were generally quiet traffic-wise. Our Monday debut was no exception. The fashionable women of Newport did hit the stores on Monday, but generally not until lunchtime or just afterward. Heather and

I had created a marketing plan that kicked off a couple of weeks prior to opening, purchasing ads in the local paper the *Daily Pilot* and a section of the *Los Angeles Times*, Orange County edition. Smart Heather, taking a chance, also placed full-page ads in the regional fashion magazines ninety days prior. There was some positive talk, even inquiries from a couple of reporters and a fashion critic. But would they appear on debut day?

Around eleven o'clock in the morning, we welcomed a handful of curious shoppers, all women of course, but made no sales. We looked at one another, knowing instinctively what the other one was thinking. This was not going to be easy—no trumpets blaring, no klieg lights crossing the sky.

"Do we need two men in uniforms sounding trumpets?" I joked.

"Not allowed, but not a bad idea," Heather replied.

At noon, on the dot, the tide turned. The first one to come through the parted black and white curtains was my mother. Nancy swooped in carrying the most exquisite bouquet of pink and white tuberoses in full bloom. She was dressed to kill; she sure knew how to make an entrance. And on this day, the grand entrance had nothing to do with her; it was all for me. Nancy knew her marketing stuff, and she meant to impress any strangers within or near our makeshift store. But that was not all. Following my mother, in came another ten women she had enlisted to welcome the new fashion line to the world. A chartered luxury bus had delivered the Beverly Hills entourage. Chatter in the tent became almost unbearable, except for the fact that all of it was glowingly positive.

Moments later, entourage two arrived as Heather's mother, the formidable Mrs. A, appeared, also dressed to kill, another marketing maven in her own right, followed by about a dozen of the most socially prominent, best-dressed Newport women, arguably the biggest shoppers on the California Riviera. Fair Child came to life.

Nancy quietly asked where the champagne was. Heather whispered in her ear that the request had been denied—legal reasons. It didn't matter; Nancy made her toast with sparkling water, and the fashionable crowd came to a hush.

"My darling ladies, my friends old and new, with heartfelt thanks I express my fondest appreciation to you all for being here today to welcome the Fair Child line on its debut. I am overwhelmed with joy and pride for what my cherished daughter, Kate, love of my life, and her remarkable partner Heather Adamson, along with the guidance of mentors Monsieur and Madame Lawrence of the Avenue Foch West Salon in Newport, have provided to make this auspicious day come to be."

Nancy went on, "Even more wonderful is seeing two young women pursue a goal and make it happen. The magic of unbridled youth doing the impossible, overcoming obstacles—a new generation forging ahead, making their own path, creating their own destiny.

"As the older generation, the parent, I watch and marvel, reliving my own 'anything was possible' years in my twenties. I wonder if I would have had the guts to accomplish what you girls have done and hope to do.

"I love you, Kate. And I love you, Heather, for all you have done for Kate. May the two of you one day soon be the cover story on *Women's Wear Daily*, *Vogue*, *Elle*, and the rest!"

The crowd cheered. Mrs. A stepped up onto a small round cylinder in the rear center of the tent, placed for modeling an outfit in front of a large three-way mirror. She caught everyone's attention, simply stating, "I could not have said it better than Nancy. Oh, just one thing. Nobody may leave this tent without a garment bag or shopping bag in hand!"

Cole Closes the Deal

Our Monday opening was the bomb. Heather and I accepted the raves with a certain level of expectation. After all, the love fest was coming from our respective mothers, with their personal entourages in captivity. The joy was certainly validated with more than ten thousand dollars in sales. Tuesday, well, it was also the bomb—as if a bomb had dropped. Only three stragglers wandered in all day, with no sales. Heather was totally cool, but I was nervous. Where was my instant overnight success?

The rest of our first week was not much better. By Friday there were sales, only in the hundreds, but the customers who did come in left very pleased. We were getting super reviews and, better yet, promises to spread the word. "We've been in business for one week," Heather continued to remind me. "Magic doesn't happen; it's rehearsed and practiced and created."

I was prepared for the rehearsal and the practice. The pop-up shop was the beginning of a journey, possibly a long one. But I had not been prepared for how long and how tough it would be, or how much sacrifice would be demanded of me in order to make magic. Having these doubts at the onset was not a very good sign. My image and vision of myself was greater than the reality in front of me. Where was my supreme confidence, the unchecked optimism, and the take-no-prisoners attitude inherited from just about everyone in my family?

We closed the black and white curtains at eight o'clock Friday evening as the shopping plaza had remained open late. That day, Heather opened at ten in the morning. I had come at two in the afternoon, giving me time at home with the boys. Following their lunch, and after helping Bonnie put them down for naps, I rushed out of the house to work. Thank goodness for the new house, or rather thank Nancy and Dalt. The boys had separate rooms; Bonnie had her own quarters; and the wonderful space provided a greater sense of calm and order in our lives. I cherished calm and order, which fact merited some introspection, given that I was crazily complicating my life with a fashion career dream, not to mention having chosen a husband fueled by constant unrest in an ever-evolving and often hyperemotional money nuts business. Who was I kidding about calm and order?

The truth was that I felt tired by two o'clock when I got to the pop-up. Still not really feeling the pregnancy, I could not blame any lack of energy on that. I just did not have the 24/7 stamina of Heather. As I followed in her wake, she always gave me superior credit, which was not always deserved. I knew that for certain.

"I'll do the heavy lifting," she would say. "You keep designing. That's your role, and it is the core of the business. You need to be brilliant with each piece so I can sell and market the line. If we work that way, one day customers will be lining up. You are that good. Don't forget it." Heather's pep talks were like a drug: total and instant revival. I needed that because I also knew I could not be 100 percent invested at all times. Heather was alone. Yes, it made a difference, and it mattered to me. Cole and the kids were number one; the line was number two. That would not, could not change. One day, to be truly successful, I thought perhaps it must change.

Finishing the day and the week, I started home in the dark of a fall night. The Newport weather delivered its customary indication that temperatures were dropping from the warmth of late Indian summer to the chill of fall. I could smell the change. It was visceral; a person can taste the weather changing.

Approaching my car in the parking structure, I joined a mass exodus of working women leaving all the stores, presumably returning home to families of their own. This was another reality check. Most women worked and had a family to take care of, a husband to attend to. I was just another one of those women. Perhaps I was luckier, at least in a monetary sense, but really, I was no different emotionally. Walking the Superwoman "do it all" line was the new age zeitgeist of my generation.

Getting in the car, I sat for a few seconds before starting the engine. As I was staring at the concrete wall in front of me, another wave of guilt came over me. I had missed dinner with the boys, and I had missed their baths and bedtime tuck-in. Cole had promised me he would come home early to be there and would share dinner with me when I got home. Cole was not a Mr. Mom husband, not hands-on with the boys, so I knew I was asking a lot. When both parents are consumed with careers, it's obvious that the children often get the short end of the stick. I was determined not to let that happen. Our kids would grow up in a home like mine, with great parents as role models.

Cole was home as promised. I found him outside on the terrace by the swimming pool, perched on a chaise lounge, staring out over the pool, beyond the dock that came with the Lido house, and toward the bay. The sparkling lights on the boats and the homes across the channel, like so many fireflies, dotted the picturesque waterfront. My husband was still in his dark gray suit, sans shoes, socks, and necktie. The outdoor heater on a tall stand next to him blazed red hot, taking away the soft chill in the night air.

"Hey, there you are. Home at last, my talented career woman," Cole called to me as I passed through the ten-foot-tall glass doors leading to the terrace pool. He started to get up, and I waved, letting him know I was coming to him. Looking very relaxed, and very sexy with his white cotton shirt unbuttoned to midchest, my Cuban Italian stallion with the thickest black hair on his head had no chest hair to match, only a very worked-out, firmly defined torso. His body was a definite turn-on, coupled with his broad white toothy smile. He was beaming with the joy of a ten-year-old boy who had just shot the basket of a lifetime.

"Did you and Heather sell out?" Cole continued.

"Not exactly."

"You're kidding. Does this mean we are not celebrating? I am prepared."

Cole had put together a small dinner picnic without any culinary help from Bonnie. He had it presented on the glass patio table under an awning—no champagne tonight, just sparkling apple cider, chilled in a silver ice bucket. There were Cheetos, the crispy kind, along with sliced Fiscalini white cheddar, Genoa salami, some extra-large pimento-stuffed green olives, and sliced green apple wedges.

"This is quite a spread, Cole."

"It's a collection from the kitchen—all your favorite items."

"I am impressed. So many of my favorite treats that I enjoy separately, but now all together. Unbelievable. You've thought of everything." We laughed. I grabbed a coffee cup. Cole had forgotten the flutes, or hadn't been able to find them, supplying coffee cups instead. I poured the sparkling apple juice.

"Care for a cocktail?" I asked.

Cole held up an open bottle of beer that he'd had resting on the floor beside his lounge chair.

In one hand, I held the cider. In the other, I had a fistful of crispy cheesy Cheetos, joining Cole on the chaise.

"Move over, baby. Make room for a woman with child," I told him.

As we sat quietly together, not saying a word, I stroked Cole's bare chest, invited by the open shirt. This was the sort of calm and order I sought. It also filled the bill for proper family time at home on a Friday night, even though I had missed dinner with my kids.

Several weeks had passed since Dalt provided the funding for Cole and Roman to close the land deal for The Summit. As my father had advised, the boys overbid and ended up winning the contract. The legal documents passed through appropriate channels on all ends of the business deal, including with Dalt. He revised his initial offering, giving Cole $1.5 million, making my parents equal partners with Cole and Roman. The boys ended up paying $2.6 million for the land, $100,000 over the asking price as Dalt had advised. The additional $400,000 from Dalt would be allocated to cover living and development expenses to launch the project. My savvy dad had followed up with Cole after the family dinner on Lexington Road, advising him that it was shortsighted to use all the cash, literally all of it, leaving no cushion upon entering this deal. Dalt provided the safety net.

He said, "If you are strapped for cash, you will make poor choices if problems arise. If you have a level of security, you will not make bad situations potentially worse."

Leave it to Dalt. He also made himself clear by saying, "The additional funds are not a gift. They are also to be repaid when the profits are shared."

Cole and Roman were grateful. I was too. It enabled our quick move to the house on Lido to come with, again, some sense of calm and order. It also allowed both of us to take major steps forward with our individual life goals. I was also blessed with time to care for our family.

Cole sat up straight on the chaise. I removed my hand from his chest. "I have a plan, and I need your okay," Cole spoke, with a clear change in tone from one suited to a romantic evening at home cuddling to one indicating, *I want to talk business.* As he went on with his pitch, I think I would have said okay to just about anything he wanted at this moment of pure relaxation.

"Marketing. The key to success with this new development deal is marketing. I've got to get out in front of the norm, do something different." Cole started revving up. Happy sipping my cider and crunching on Cheetos, I knew well enough that my credentials did not include a expertise in fashion marketing.

"What do you think about throwing a big party? I will get Rocco to shoot the event and put it on TV, along with featuring the new lots."

"A big party? I'm not sure I get the connection to real estate sales?" I managed to say with another major crunching sound. My fingers were turning orange. I began licking them.

"That's where marketing comes in. We'll invite super-high-end car brands like Mercedes, maybe even Rolls-Royce, or Ferrari, or Lamborghini. I'll get a liquor brand, or a jewelry store, or a fashion label. How about caviar and champagne companies—all to sponsor the party? It could also be an opportunity for you and Heather to showcase Fair Child. Then, we'll invite the best-looking crowd that can be assembled—female and male model-looking types, you know, the whole California Riviera–Newport fantasy look that the world wants to buy into."

"Cole, I think *fantasy* is the operative word. Come on, you know all those people we see at the never-ending charity black-tie dinners are mostly wannabes. The real Newport rich call them 'the freeloader express.' They go from event to event on the hunt."

"Babe, it doesn't matter. It's all candy. Tempting visuals send a message that plenty of people want to hear. 'You too can live like this when you build your home at The Summit.' That's all I mean."

I did admit, even though the idea revolted me on a certain level, that my husband was not entirely wrong. There was a great deal of flash and a greater degree of dash, as in "run for the hills" when things went south, in a whole array of financial outings in Newport. I didn't have a clue at first, but four years now into my life journey at the beach, the dynamic was crystal clear. So, when my friends in Beverly Hills asked me why I hadn't come back, the answer was simple: The schemers and dreamers in LA are reptiles. In the OC, they are just opossums. I'd take opossums over reptiles any day.

Cole finally got around to asking me the question he had started with, before distracting our romantic moment of calm on the chaise.

"I'd like to have the party here at the Lido house. It would be impressive for TV, and it would help me attract all the right sponsors."

Although I wanted to say no, please no, Cole went on with all his reasons why this would be the best plan for the thing. Then as he turned to me on the chaise, looking directly into my eyes, this strong, self-aware, intelligent mother of almost four said, "Sure. Why not?" Had I really said that? Before I could rewind, Cole was all over me. Giving into the sexual turn-on, I was helpless. So much for strong and self-aware. I wanted him, and I was going to have him.

A prolonged session of passionate kissing on the lounge led to a late evening boat ride in a darling electric-powered boat tied up at the dock, both of which had come with the house. The little boat, known as a Duffy, after its designer, was essentially a silent floating cocktail and hors d'oeuvres lounge on the Newport harbor. Literally hundreds of these boats cruised the majestic harbor waterways, carrying privileged passengers partaking of the best of the best of life's little sensuous travels.

It had been Cole's idea to take the Duffy out, and I found no fault in the plan. There was a chill in the night air, but it wasn't cold, at least not very cold. The sides of the Duffy were open to the sea air; a canvas roof shielded from above. It was equipped with roll-down heavy-duty clear plastic panels hidden in the canvas above. We chose to leave them in place, opting for the night air and a view of the harvest moon that surely was inspiring love song creations somewhere.

As we left the dock and floated out into the main channel of Newport harbor, the view opened to nearly three hundred sixty degrees in the expansive mouth of the waterway leading to the Pacific Ocean. Pure magic, day or night, the scene was supremely beautiful and quintessentially Southern Californian. Every time I came upon the view, I held my breath.

Cole took the helm of the Duffy. The steering wheel was placed at the aft, and there was an upholstered bench to seat the driver and passenger if desired. Passenger number one sat right next to the driver, practically in his lap. Minutes into the mouth of the Newport harbor, we were also into each other's mouths. Cole managed to keep the craft on course. There was very light traffic at nine o'clock at night, but plenty of major yachts were berthed midchannel that we needed to avoid.

Reaching the edge of the breakwater, leading right out into the ocean, we were naked, in each other arms, our clothing strewn about on the deck of the boat and hanging over the gunwale as well.

The smooth bay water gave way to choppy seas as we approached the entrance to the harbor; we were very close to entering the open ocean. As we were rocking and rolling with the moon, a laser beaming and bouncing its light upon us, Cole shut off the electric engine and somehow kept the boat even and straight, yet seemingly not moving farther ahead.

Stretching out on the elongated upholstered bench on the starboard side, we made bigtime love. Once entering me, Cole refused to pull out even after climax. Holding each other very tightly, we moved with the sway of the rippling current, romance heaven.

We were startled out of our perfect love trance by a rogue wave rising over the gunwale of the Duffy and drenching us with sixty-some-degree seawater. And I mean drenching. I let out a scream. Cole pulled out of me very fast, causing me to scream even louder, with pleasure.

"Oh my God," he exclaimed.

"What? What's the matter?" I responded, trying to wipe the seawater off my face and shake it out of my hair.

"We're at sea, my naked lover," he replied, laughing with a decidedly nervous kind of laughter.

Cole darted to the controls, naked, wet, and with a piece of seaweed dangling from his shoulder. The electric motor started, thank goodness, and Captain Cole managed to steer the little boat around and head back in the direction of the harbor entrance. Once we were on course, I moved next to him at the controls, drying us both off, using my hand to wipe off the water. I got his damp shirt on his body, but mine was missing overboard. I did find my bra and panties. Cole's pants were soaked on the deck, so he sat butt naked all the way back to home port at the Lido house. It was after eleven o'clock at night.

Docking the Duffy, Cole, in his dripping wet shirt, with no pants and his privates bouncing, walked me down the dock ramp, holding my hand as his momentary mermaid wife in black bra and panties kissed him on the cheek and said, "Who needs a big party? We are our own big party, and it cannot be topped or marketed in any way."

"I love you, Kate."

"I love you more."

CHAPTER FIFTY-TWO

MONEY IS IN THE BANK

The stress level around the Fairchild–Baldwin homestead having been lowered; we took a collective deep breath as 2004 came to an end. All the funds required to do the land deal were solidly within Cole and partner Roman's control. With financial confidence, they had won the bid. However, as expected, a final signed contract was being held up by lawyers dealing with the California Coastal Commission and the City of Newport Beach. Cole's legal team assured him of a proper conclusion yet cautioned that it was going to take time, perhaps six months. Dalt was right: the extra cushion of cash was a necessity.

In my professional corner, sales at the pop-up were disappointing, which is code for depressing. Heather kicked into high sales gear as the ultimate general in charge. We did our best, selling our hearts out to the trickle of customers over the holidays.

Ramping up advertising, we also took out full-page ads in the local paper. And while we didn't really need the help, as Christmas approached, we hired two young women as holiday sales associates so we could cover the boutique seven days a week.

Heather remained bullish at all times. I remained optimistic; it was easy to be optimistic when I was losing my grandmother's money. Feeling guilty, even ashamed, I plowed forward writing checks.

Things did pick up somewhat. A full-page ad on the back page of a local insert in the *LA Times* started to draw traffic. Customers came in asking to see the outfit in the ad.

"An early Christmas miracle," I said to Heather. We both decided to work that Sunday.

Heather crossed her fingers as two women went behind the drapes of the makeshift dressing room to try on the outfit shown in the ad. It was one of my favorite designs, a coordinated short skirt with a round neck, short cap-sleeve top, and cardigan sweater. We had made it in rich piqué cotton, available in pale pink, ice blue, and white, all interchangeable. It was simple, chic, classic, and supremely wearable for any occasion, and could even be dressed up with the right jewelry and shoes. Monsieur had created a silk scarf, screened, using the Fair Child pansy logo as an accent.

Clearly the pre-Christmas uptick was only a blip. Overall, December sales were anemic. The shopping center was not happy. The big stores around us were not happy. We were supposed to help drive traffic. Of course, our hope was that the big stores would drive traffic to us. Clearly, that didn't work. It was time to regroup and reevaluate since our pop-up contract was approaching its end on January 15.

Despite this apparent failure, we were not thrown off the rails. Instead, Heather and I took a needed breath. The break was in perfect harmony with the lowered stress level at home with Cole. It was something of an ambitious hold for both Cole and me.

Looking back on the holiday season, I recalled we had celebrated a wonderful family Thanksgiving at the Lido house with Nancy, Dalt, Jamey, and Jamey's girl-friend Rachel all at the table. From Thanksgiving, we sequenced into more family memories, lighting birthday candles for the twins' first birthday weeks later. I had invited Cole's parents and his sister, Maria, to come down from Reno to join in all the milestone celebrations.

Cole's mom, Rose, one of the all-time sweetest women, could not accept the invitation fast enough. Hearing her over the phone yelling across the room to Cole's dad, sharing the invitation news, I knew I was doing the right thing. We didn't hear much from Cole's family. It was hard for them to get away. His dad now worked full time for a building contractor, and his parents were essentially homebodies otherwise. They lived in their own comfort zone, and while it was very basic and honestly simple, it was a happy place. At least that was my intuition. Consequently, they didn't venture far. Having a married son with a changed name living a foreign lifestyle some five hundred miles south with a wife from Beverly Hills and almost four kids was, on many levels, unimaginable for Joe and Rose. Yet, they put on a smile and got with the program. Surely, their private conversations included plenty of head-scratching.

Just the same, whenever we did see them, their love for a son they essentially lost and did not fully understand was pure, simple, and ever present.

Rose could not bring herself to call Cole anything but Sal, his given name. She said, "Cole is a character in my soap opera. Oh, it's also the brand of a man's shoe—Cole something, I think."

Showered with the same adoration from Rose, the babies and I were smoth-ered with kisses and total obsessive attention. To a certain degree, it made Cole somewhat anxious, but I encouraged the obsession. It was real.

Making the road trip from Reno down the back route through Nevada into Las Vegas and over to Newport to avoid any winter weather in the Sierra Nevada on the California roads, the family arrived, including Cole's sister, Maria, casino barmaid and part-time dancer, a day before the twins' first birthdays. My invita-tion had come with an insistence that his family stay with us, not in a motel. His dad had put up a reasonable refusal, but his mom and I prevailed. We had a huge house with plenty of guest rooms to accommodate our growing family. What was the point of having all this room if family could not stay with us? Again, Cole was hesitant, but he agreed. If the situation had been reversed, Joe and Rose would have insisted that we all stay with them in the three-bedroom, two-bathroom house at Reno city limits. As Mother Rose often said to me, "Families survive together no matter what. It doesn't take money."

Sister Maria was, shall we say, something special. She was quite beautiful. Maria had height and a showgirl figure. You know, big on top, little on bottom, long legs and elegant shoulders, very thin arms. Her olive complexion glowed, and she had the same thick wavy black hair that made her brother so handsome. One other dominant feature shared with Cole were her spectacular blue eyes. Maria didn't realize the exception of her beauty. What she did know was that she was a working girl needing to make a living. She had no education and no husband currently visible on the Nevada prairie. Like her mother, she was kind and loved being with us and meeting her nephews. Cole was surprised at this, since he thought I would dislike her based on his own preconceived notion of his sister's lack of so-called class. Seeing Maria and me form a friendship helped Cole to let go of some of his embarrassment over his own people. Mama Rose took every opportunity she could to tease him over his phony name. Cole took it well, but it did wear thin. Rose finally let it go, but she never stopped calling him Sal. "I named him after my father after all," she said. A mother's right.

Nancy and Dalt joined the family in Newport with Jamey and Rachel for the twins' birthday party. It was the best time ever. Nancy bonded with Rose on their first meeting, which was our prenuptial dinner. They picked up their friendship instantly and took over in the kitchen. My parents could see how special this time was for Cole's family, so unlike most of our family gatherings that extended way beyond the normal time frame, Nancy and Dalt graciously departed early with Jamey and Rachel after the candles were blown out on the cakes and the presents revealed.

Cole's family was set to leave, driving back to Reno the following day. I complicated the plan.

"The holidays are just days away. Why not stay for Christmas?" I asked boldly. Cole replied that his dad had to get back to work. Joe gave his son one of those looks. Both our families communicated with looks, often without need for words. After some amount of back-and-forth, Joe and Maria explained that they did have to get back, leaving only Mama Rose to accept or decline the invitation. Joe reluctantly agreed to leave her behind, seeing how much his wife wanted this extended stay. It was the ideal time for this visit as the pressure cooker was temporarily off the burner for both Cole and me. The final chapter of 2004 was about family.

Back in Gear

Christmas arrived without fanfare and was special because it wasn't crazy. With no big doings at Lexington Road this year, we stayed home in Newport with the boys and Rose. Cole offered to take his mom to midnight mass at the Catholic church on Balboa Island. She cried. It was the only time I'd ever known Cole to want to go to church.

The day after Christmas, we drove Rose to John Wayne Airport for her flight to Reno, the second time in her life on a plane. A week later, New Year's passed in similar quiet fashion. No black-tie balls at the Harbor Club for us. I made a fabulous family dinner. We ate early and put the boys to bed by seven. Bonnie took a couple of days off. It was TV till nine as we watched the ball drop in New York, and then we made love, firecracker-exploding love, until our own New Year came at midnight. We both had made big plans for 2005.

The New Year started with promise. Cole's real estate business was on fire. More agents were joining Baldwin et Cie. By March, with Roman now the head of business operations, they expanded their office space, taking a larger office in what was considered the premiere tower on tony Newport Center Drive. While other real estate offices were located on local street corners in one-story commercial buildings, Cole, from the start, had chosen to be in a gleaming silver steel tower with Fortune 500 executives working side by side.

He constantly built his brand, and he received notice because he had developed superior marketing talent. Competitors called him brilliant. With no real education or pedigree, he simply had focused instinct and a keen eye. Not everyone, regardless of education or experience, has an eye. It's a gift. Cole had it; he knew it; and he was making the most of it. Choosing to be in that tower was just one example of his unique instinct.

Ongoing, a major part of his marketing package remained tied to the TV show. Producer Rocco ramped up production in January, and they turned out a new half-hour episode each week. With the easy flow of money, homes were selling before they reached the market. It was getting nuts. Cole expressed concern that they would run out of available properties to feature on the show. My husband worked 24/7.

Again, finding myself a work wife widow, I handled it better this time. I knew the drill. Besides, now entering my fourth month of pregnancy, I was really feeling it this time. My energy level was uneven—strange for me. Dr. Grimes ordered more rest and a lighter schedule.

We also learned in January that we were going to have a girl. I was thrilled, as was Cole. It would be an entirely new and wonderful adventure. Maybe that was the reason for my fatigue. Dr. Grimes discounted my reasoning, assuring me that there was nothing to worry about. Accepting her confidence, I was still worried; it was a pregnant woman's prerogative—especially a young mom with three boys who was expecting her one and very probably only girl-child. Which gave rise to the bigger issue: this was going to be the final issue of the Fairchild–Baldwin progeny. Four children would make a perfectly amazing and full family. That discussion with Cole would be forthcoming. Birth control pills did not agree with my body, so Cole would be receiving a beautifully wrapped package of condoms on our next gift exchange. Either that or an appointment with the snip doctor.

Heather and I exhaled during the postholiday fashion hiatus following our disappointing debut over Christmas with Fair Child. The break turned into three months. Heather remained steadfast, ever patient. I was the slug, needing quiet time. As I was taking advantage of my self-induced minor pity party, Monsieur Lawrence gently prodded me to get back up on the horse. I kept asking him where the horse was, teasing my mentor. He was the most charming and understanding man. Still, he was not going to let me wallow. Both Monsieur and Madame believed in my talent. Sure, Nancy and Dalt believed, but they were my ardent unconditional supporters. It was different with my mentors. They did not have to believe.

Giving in to the pressure applied, I arose on a Monday morning in early April. The sun was warm, and the skies were vibrant colbalt blue, dotted with slow-moving white puffy clouds passing from water to land, as they often did, with supreme grace over the Newport harbor. The boys were happy; Bonnie, as always, in full charge. It was time to venture out and get back into the race. Then again, I questioned why I needed to be in a race at all. My life was very full; I was blessed; and I was six months pregnant.

Why wasn't it enough to be so lucky? A husband, children, a home, health, money, a loving family—wasn't that the goal of having a successful career, to one day be able to attain all that I already had in my life?

This was basic truth. I also knew the answer to my query. As a kid I had been the creative one in my class. My drawings were praised by the teachers and envied by friends. My projects were A-plus. At the age of five, I started redesigning clothes for Barbie. Sitting for hours with my nanny or with housekeeper Marta, and sometimes with Nancy, I would sew the creations I fashioned out of any kind of material I could find. Trouble came my way when I took scissors to new drapes in my bedroom, cutting off a bottom section of a panel. I deemed the drapery fabric perfect for a new winter coat for Barbie.

Becoming a serious and real designer was something I felt I must do. It was not about money or recognition. Well, truthfully, it was about recognition, and probably about money too. How about fulfilling my destiny? Boy, that sounded pretentious. Was it possible to feel that I was supposed to follow a path, maybe a

God-given path, or call it a DNA-delivered path passed down from my ancestors? My grandparents were once in the rag business in order to survive, in a very rough time in their youth, which had led to a major business career. This was in my genes.

Whatever the impetus, my inspiration was back. I would not let Heather, Monsieur, or Madame down. I would not let myself down.

The universe spoke, and there were unexpected results. The first week in April not only brought restoration to my design inspiration but also delivered signed documents to Cole and Roman, finalizing their land deal at The Summit. The development process would now begin.

As expected, my marketing guru and lover wanted to throw his lavish party right away. Earlier, in a decidedly weaker moment, I had agreed to throw the bash at our Lido home, but now I feared the project. It just would throw the family, and frankly me, into unwanted overload.

I shared my misgivings, and Cole agreed. He knew I was feeling tired with the pregnancy, and he also knew, although he was not always 100 percent invested in my design corner, that getting back to work with my team was important to me. Cole didn't take my work seriously before, even though he always said he was proud of me. He saw my passion as more of a hobby or a diversion.

Knowing my husband's mantra that a macho man made the money in the family, I was not deterred by his dinosaur attitude. He had too much to do on his own ancestral / God-given path. He also had too much to prove to himself. I knew nothing was going to get in his way, certainly not my career aspirations.

With the final development approval, it took no time for Cole and Roman to create a plan for the land debut. The spring party of the season would be held in a massive white tent on the raw dirt at The Summit, destined to transform into multimillion-dollar estates. Cole shared that he had borrowed the tent concept from my pop-up store. I told him I would pray for him to have better results. We laughed.

It was scheduled for Cinco de Mayo, May 5, just weeks out, a major party date in Southern California. Cole and Roman set about to pulling out all the stops. They invited a who's-who guest list, as well as rallying luxury vendors including car dealers, jewelers, cruise lines, private jet charters, high-end boutique brands of spirits and wine, and best of all, Fair Child fashions, and the event came together with remarkable ease. I was impressed, as was Heather. Altogether, the vendors, paying a fee to display their wares, would cover the entire cost of the production. We were in minor awe. The event, given a bit of advance hype, was now the talk of the town, the A-list ticket.

Strangers were somehow getting my number and calling me to request a favor and receive an invitation. By the end of April, I was scared to answer my phone.

The Big Event

The Baldwin et Cie spring blowout was making news all over Newport. Local paparazzi from the crop of OC society magazines were there in full regalia, shooting like mad and taking names. The crowd adored having their names taken. All the high-end luxury vendors had shown, along with their wares. Amazing cars lined the driveway, perfectly placed, leading to the massive tent erected on the most spectacular ocean-view promontory point on The Summit.

On arrival, some dozen exquisite models, male and female, dressed in label fashion from a dozen distinct design houses, greeted the crush. Klieg lights crossed overhead in the heavens. Waitstaff passed lemon drop martinis created for the occasion and served in oversized half lemons, hollowed, filled with vodka, and rimmed in sugar with floating lemon drop candies. Sweet lemonade-infused clear straws were provided by servers outfitted in neon-yellow waistcoats over white cotton T-shirts, white shorts, and spotless white canvas shoes sans socks. It was a scene.

The extravagance of the party detail, to a degree, paled in comparison to the extravagance of its attendees. I'm guessing, but I'd say that nowhere in the United States, no city or town, regardless of its wealth or prestige, could assemble a crowd like Newport.

Easily four hundred people jammed into the big top. They were young, and they had come to see and be seen. Gorgeous slim women with bodies by top plastic surgeons were attired in superexpensive, superrevealing tiny dresses. Lots of skin, not much material. I was in awe of the makeup—eyelashes so thick and so heavy, I could not imagine how these young women could see. Surely, they needed to see since, I assumed, they were on the hunt. That's the thing: so much hunting and sizing up going on. I took Heather by the arm. We wandered the tent. Heather was my date. Cole was busy. Yes, he had introduced me at first to just about everyone he could, but then I allowed him to do his bidding. He, too, was on the hunt for business.

Oddly, Heather and I found very few couples at the party. Everyone seemed to be there on their own. I thought that strange. Were all the guests single? I assumed the young, sexy, trendy guests were all in some sort of related real estate business. Heather pointed that out—Newport real estate agents representing some of the region's biggest clients. At least that made sense.

"Kate, believe it or not, this is not a bad opportunity to show off Fair Child. Look at all the major labels that have provided their clothes on all the models. We are the unknown, but we are here with the big guys." Heather was always wise.

"Do you think these women will go for our line?" I asked with some reservation.

"Just you wait," Heather said with her usual confidence.

My savvy business partner had coordinated with my savvy marketing husband, allowing us to change the theme from Cinco de Mayo and instead do the whole 1960s retro James Bond thing with models in go-go dancer cages moving to the music of the Stones and the Doors. Cole even had managed to borrow a silver Aston Martin, placing the car in the middle of the tent. It also made perfect sense that the gorgeous gaggle of women in their miniminis were dressed in homage to Pussy Galore from the Bond film *Goldfinger*. There was pussy galore. I shared my observation with Heather. She doubled over in wild laughter.

It was then our time to take center tent. Two hours of lemon drop martinis, and the crowd was ready. Cole and Roman climbed up on a riser next to the Aston Martin. Both were wired with radio microphones, a nod to P. T. Barnum introducing his circus.

"Ladies and Gentlemen. May I have your attention?" Cole took control with his powerful and exceptional voice. "Roman and I thank you for coming tonight to launch Baldwin et Cie Estates at The Summit. We are very excited about the project, which promises to be the premiere estate community on Society Hill. Construction will commence in the fall of this year, with some semicustom homes in the final stages by early 2007. We are taking reservations from your clients now for custom estates." Cole continued on his pitch. Roman stood by, smiling and supportive. Both men were the best-looking in the model-handsome crowd. They made an impression.

Finishing his pitch, Cole introduced Heather and me. We joined the two male gods onstage. Standing beside Cole, I placed my hand on his shoulder, moving in very close by his side. Heather stepped between us and Roman, then said, "Hello, everybody. I'm Heather, and I think you all know Kate, Cole's wife." A bit of applause circulated. Heather continued, saying, "What you probably didn't know is that Kate is an amazing fashion designer. Her new line, called Fair Child—guess where that name came from—made its debut last Christmas at Fashion Plaza. Did you see the amazing tent, kind of like this one tonight, in front of Neiman's? Well, since this night is all about the best of the best in Newport—the best things life has to offer, that is—Kate and I proudly present Fair Child."

As Heather finished, the lights in the tent dimmed on cue, except for spots strategically placed above each of the go-go dance cages set up in a circle around the circumference of the tent, all facing the silver Aston Martin in the center. The cages remained empty and unlit until their cue, the music of the Rolling Stones's "Satisfaction," which came over the sound system at full blast.

Fair Child models, the same crew who had posed for the fashion photo shoot in Laguna Canyon, appeared, showing off the full line of spring prêt-à-porter. Prancing and dancing to "Satisfaction," each one entered her assigned cage as more lights flashed, and the crowd began to cheer. It was pure theater.

I was totally thrilled—not an easy level of excitement often reached by me—that everyone in the crowd was dancing or moving around the cages. Guys were hooting, and I could see the women staring at the clothes on the models.

"Heather, this is working. Unbelievable."

"Was I wrong?" she asked with a grin.

"Now I am surrounded by two marketing masters. Cole and Heather, some pair," I said.

"If this does not get you moving again on the dream, what can I say?" Heather knew how to motivate.

"I know. And I am back. I made that promise to myself just recently. I've got until midsummer to work with Monsieur on a new line, then the baby comes. For now, that's the plan."

"Fight the temptation to deviate. Make it happen. Look at the excitement tonight. If we had a sales booth tonight, the register would be ringing."

My thrilling mood got a big slap in the face as I glanced around the tent and spotted the back of a young woman at the far end of the tent chatting up a group with Roman. Seeing Roman's profile at her side, I also saw the back of the young woman's strapless cocktail dress with the gold chains of an evening bag draped over the right shoulder, signaling the return of Sierra. Clearly, she had avoided trouble when slipping away from the cop at the cancer dinner. I had thought, had hoped, that the drama would have been the last of her. But there was Roman, the guy who had totally ignored her when she was getting busted for cocaine, back in her fold.

I was staring at them with searchlight focus. Heather noticed.

"What are you looking at?"

"It's her, Sierra. The cocaine-carrying cocktail hostess," I blurted.

"What? You mean that girl you told me about at that dinner you attended?"

"That girl."

"Why is she here?"

"Because everyone is here. Maybe they're all her clients," I said, hoping to be wrong. We were now both staring.

"I don't think you're wrong," Heather said. "Did you see what I think I saw?"

"Like, open black velvet bag, take out small item, hand it over to guy on her right?"

"Yes. That's what I saw."

"We have a dealer doing business."

"Do you think we'll be nailed?" Heather asked.

"Of course not. I hope not. That would be horrible for Cole," I said, defending my husband's business dream. Then I flashed on Walter Benheim and his reaction. Was Sierra dealing bad dope? That's all we needed, more of Sierra's clients passing out.

Finding Cole talking with a couple of businessmen in fancy suits just like his, I left Heather and approached.

"Excuse me, darling. Sorry to interrupt. Can I have a word?" I said, holding out a hand to greet the men. "Forgive me. I'm Kate, Cole's wife," I offered. They all politely disbursed, nodding and obliging my request.

"Cole, Sierra is here. Did you know? Is Roman still dating that girl?" My tone was serious.

Cole was slow in responding. Finally, I jabbed him in his side as if to say, *Come clean, buddy.*

"Yes, he is seeing her. I'm staying out of it, Kate. Not my business." Cole was firm.

"You're dead wrong. She is a drug dealer. Can't you see what she is doing here tonight? That girl could destroy everything you have done to land The Summit. Worse, is your partner also a drug dealer? Your partner with whom we have invested all our money, everything you have made and saved, not to mention one and a half million Daddy dollars."

"Roman is not a drug dealer. He does have a habit. Sierra is his contact, and more," Cole said, offering no further explanation.

Clearly, none was needed. It was the ideal modern romance. Unburdened sex and unlimited cocaine. No strings, no commitment, no love, plenty of selfish pleasure. The new American love formula.

"Roman's so-called habit could bring you to your knees and us to our knees. This is not a worry?"

"I am not worried. He's under control. This is nothing new. Not for him, and not for half the people I've met and worked with in town. Alcohol and drugs are just part of the scene. People function: they make money; they dull their pain."

"Pretty cavalier for a small-town kid. Cole, I know you're not into drugs. Tell me I'm not fooling myself."

"Baby, I've never touched the stuff. Don't smoke dope, don't snort coke. Hardly take an aspirin. You know I drink. That is my escape valve, and I've tried to curtail that, as you know."

"Can I talk to Roman about this?"

"Rather you didn't. Need you to trust me."

"I do trust you. But now I don't trust Roman. Please keep your eye on this, Cole. I am asking you for your sake, for mine, and for your children's."

CHAPTER FIFTY-THREE

LIVING THE LIFE

Turning twenty-five, feeling that my life's path was set on course that I had no control over, I was dismayed to discover that depression had set in. Not the kind of depression that was serious, although I guess all kinds can be. It was more of an overwhelming melancholy. How could so many strange events impact my simple little existence in so short a time? Where had the confident prep school teenager gone? Yesterday's innocence was now so far in the past, while at the same time, conflicting thoughts raced in my brain, telling me I was just getting started. So much to try; so many roads to follow.

Cole kept reminding me that I was almost seven months along. I didn't want to be reminded; I understood. Meaning well, my husband was patronizing, dismissive. Not intentionally. Most men, I thought, didn't really understand their pregnant partners. Some were better at it than others. For Cole, he dealt with my pregnancy as he mentally dealt with my work. He cared, supported, and was interested to a degree. Facing that reality now, at this moment, seven months with child number four, with twenty-five feeling more like fifty, I wanted Cole to be 100 percent invested in me. I wanted one of those husbands who smothered his wife with attention.

Since whatever level of depression that had come over me did not seem to be leading me to pills, alcohol, or seriously antisocial behavior of any type, I sucked it up and kept smiling. More importantly, I put on my big girl panties and went back to work with Heather and my mentors at the salon. Determined to take advantage of the time I had left before presenting Baldwin number four to the world, my goal was to pick up where we had left off following our not so auspicious opening last Christmas season.

Heather did not miss a day, or a beat, analyzing our failure. She was into the metrics of everything. Tallying the daily sales during our brief opening stint, she was analyzing what people bought, what they returned, how many mentioned our ads, what colors sold best, and what time of day was prime for sales. Beyond all of that, she'd done research into the ideal price point, what buyers felt about paying too much versus too little. To me, Heather's most interesting research involved a new company called Amazon, which had been around for some five or six years, that was selling clothes online and delivering to customers in a day or two, also granting easy returns. Heather repeatedly told me that Amazon would change retail forever. I really knew nothing about them, but the idea of not actually seeing, touching, and getting up close to an item of clothing before buying seemed counterintuitive.

On our first day back at the salon, all of us debated the concept, almost getting into an argument. Monsieur and Madame were horrified by the idea. They sided with me, at least initially.

"You just don't understand how much the world is changing," Heather pressed on.

"I think online buying can work for established products and brands of items such as toilet paper and toothpaste. But clothes?" Monsieur demanded.

"Clothes are products, and many are brand names," Heather answered. "If you are a regular customer for a certain brand of, let's say, jeans, and you know how they are sized, why would you not order the latest style and have a pair delivered to your door?"

Heather had made a point. We all stepped back, pausing. Monsieur Lawrence was the first to speak.

"Yes, my child, you have a point. And that is fine, I suppose, if you know the brand. But what about Fair Child? Nobody knows Fair Child. How do you get the public to buy an outfit on the 'puter [Monsieur always called it the 'puter] when they have not seen the clothes in person, either in a store or on a body, such as that of a friend?"

Now even Heather agreed, but she had the last word.

"Indeed, you are correct. Mark my words, this is the future. You'll see. It is now our challenge to get this line in stores and on bodies. We are still ahead of the tide that will wash over retail. In four years, if we are in business, we will be in stores, but we will also be on the 'puter. I will bet the 'puter sales will outpace those of the retail stores by a wide percentage."

I was fascinated. Instinctively, I knew my partner was on target, or on trend as they were now saying in the fashion world. Then I worried that Fair Child was not so much on trend as it was simply beautiful.

"Heather, are we on trend?" I asked quietly.

"Partner, we are on the ultimate trend in fashion. We are beautiful, and beautiful sells. It always will."

How did Heather know just what to say?

We stopped discussing market strategy, and I went into the back room with Monsieur and started to show him my most recent drawings. Heather got ready to leave for an appointment with a wholesale sales rep we had been introduced to at the California Mart in downtown Los Angeles. It was a husband-and-wife team, Arnold and Jackie Berg, who had built a major national business representing many fashion lines to buyers at stores large and small all over the country. Their specialty was lesser known but highly desirable lines for younger women and girls.

Heather hoped for a match of our goals. Loading samples into her car, she would have an hour's drive to think and get her pitch in order. Having been advised that the Bergs were bottom liners, she prepared to talk the talk.

By early afternoon, I was going blind looking at the drawings, reworking them repeatedly under the tutelage of Monsieur Lawrence. Snacking constantly to feed my baby-girl-to-be, I was not hungry and did not stop for a lunch break. Instead, calling a truce around one thirty that afternoon, I went for a walk. Avenue Foch West was in the tony retail center right on a prime spot just off the main avenue of Newport Center Drive. A lovely green space of manicured lawn bordered by verdant seasonal blossoms and shaded by enormous Mexican fan palm trees provided the ideal spot for fresh air and a short walk. The parkway directly bordered the main avenue, and a traffic light halted cars at the corner. The light turned red as I approached and was about to cross over into the garden. As I glanced to my left, I saw that the car in first position at the red light was Cole's. Rolling down the electric passenger's-side front window, he called out to me.

"Want a ride, lady?" he shouted.

Not to be outdone, I replied, "Where are you going to take me, big boy?" Turning to my side, I accentuated the baby bump.

"I'll take you to places you have never been," Cole said, having come up with a line.

"I'm not sure I want to go to such places."

"Oh, I think you will. Why don't you hop in?"

So much for the walk. I dashed over and jumped in as gracefully as possible, just before the red light turned green.

Cole's office was just a block up Newport Center Drive. Recently, Roman had convinced Cole to finally launch Baldwin Investment Group (BIG) to bring in more capital on an ongoing basis. Cole shared bits of this venture with me, but not much, as it was only in the start-up stage. As always, my first instinct was to be cautious, even negative. But again, I held back, instead offering praise for the inventiveness and boldness of the potential plan. I did offer my ever-constant soft warning: "Cole, you are doing so well. Take it one step at a time. Do not overload. You have thirty, forty, maybe more, years of a remarkable career in front of you."

Cole replied by telling me he loved me very much. He always said that when I gave him praise and boosted his confidence—part of my job.

On this afternoon, in his car for an unplanned ride on my break, I did not want to talk about work—not his or mine. I wanted to take Cole up on his offer to take me to a place I'd never been. Instead, we drove once around the circle that was the route of Newport Center Drive. I admired the beauty of this center of business and retail in Newport, which was perhaps the most pristine and stunning center of town in modern America. Created with vision, planning, and an architectural eye, the center was an aspirational interpretation of the good life in the United States, the best of the best.

The journey had not taken me to places I'd never been, but it was a nice break just the same. Cole let me out back at my corner by the parkway. After I'd kissed him goodbye, he promised to be home later, but not for dinner. I told him to be safe and to be careful. I always did. It was a habit, and probably overkill since I said it too often. My concept of life had always been that it was as fragile and fleeting as it was strong and everlasting. Being careful was key to staying strong and lasting. Perhaps not everlasting, but at least lasting.

Making Hay

Cole pulled into the parking garage after the unplanned spin around Newport Center Drive. He always experienced a moment of pride upon seeing his name painted on the concrete parking bumper reserving his spot in the line of VIP bumpers in the first row of spaces closest to the executive elevators. The morning agenda featured a meeting with Roman on the concept of starting an investment trust, followed by a luncheon speech to be given at the Newport Ritz, addressing a businessmen's monthly gathering on real estate trends. Cole's appearance had attracted an overflow sellout crowd, the organizers advised.

Entering the high-floor suite midmorning, Cole's pride over his name on the parking bumper rose another notch. The Baldwin et Cie office was on fire. Phones rang in what sounded like musical octaves reaching a crescendo. Agents huddled in confidential financial transaction conversation all across the expansive open-floor bullpen, divided by handsome upholstered cubicles furnished in the latest design for upscale business settings. Floor-to-ceiling glass surrounded the offices on three sides, offering vistas from the mountains to the Pacific, east to west. Cole stopped and took in the energy all around him. It was the buzz of money being made. Roman, having seen him exit the elevator from across the room, stepped out of his glass cage office and waved him over.

"Man, I am on to something here with this investment trust idea," Roman shared enthusiastically.

"Sorry to be a negative voice, but how come only a couple of months ago we couldn't raise a dime and I had to go to Kate's dad for money?" Cole asked, deadly earnest.

"A lot changes in a couple of months."

"Yeah, really? How come?"

"Probably because we got the money from Kate's father, and because we then bought the land. Word travels, partner. We went from wannabes to winners. Get it?"

"Got it. It's all good news. Do you have any solid real investors already?"

"I do. But we have to take care of some legal matters first."

"Roman, I think we need a plan first. Like, what are we going to do with the funds, and how will profit be shared? That's just for starters."

Cole caught himself taking on a serious business role, one that was supposed to belong to his partner.

"Wow, I thought you were the big-picture dreamer, and I was nuts and bolts. Isn't that what you call it in USA?"

"That's what we call it," Cole retorted sarcastically, changing the subject. "Okay, it's not my business, but I've wanted to ask you about Sierra. Are you seeing that girl?"

Roman paused. "Yes. Off and on. Nothing to talk about. She's a great lay, and she really likes the way I do her." Roman was blunt.

"What about the coke?" Cole pushed on.

"What about it?" Roman sounded slightly annoyed.

"Well, I've got to say, I had no idea you were into coke until that fiasco at the Harbor Club cancer dinner with Benheim."

"It's no big deal. I'm no addict. Just another recreational indulgence from time to time. Sierra has a line on the best product, giving her two very attractive attributes—sex and drugs." Roman was trying to connect with his business partner mano a mano. He was flip, and Cole bought into it. "Do you think coke has ever gotten in my way of making money, man?" Roman went on.

"Never," Cole answered obligingly.

"And it never will. Not with Baldwin Investment Group either."

"Do you have a plan in mind?" Cole pressed, changing the subject once again, leaving Sierra and cocaine behind.

"This is what I am thinking, my man. Instead of trying to shop bank construction financing for the development of The Summit, instead we raise all the funds needed to build from investors, and we totally control the project. We offer a rate of return on their money better than what they could get at a bank, and we use the money ourselves to build, rather than sharing with outside builder/contractors, who will enable us to reap much higher margins of profit."

Higher margins of profit was a phrase that resonated with Cole.

"Is this legal?" he asked.

"God yes, perfectly legal."

"I've got to get ready for my speech at the Newport men's luncheon. Can I talk about this idea there, or is it too soon?"

Roman instructed Cole to close the glass door to his office. Sitting down at his glass-topped table desk, Roman pressed a small hidden button positioned on the leg of the chrome frame of his desk. The floor-to-ceiling clear glass turned silver and became opaque. He motioned for Cole to sit across from him at the desk.

"Let me share something with you to help you make your best presentation with the men at the luncheon." Roman proceeded opening his briefcase.

"What should I say about the investment fund?" Cole looked for guidance.

"Just be vague. Tell them it's the land opportunity deal of the decade—total platinum, AAA location, and the rest."

"Okay, yeah, what else?" Cole pressed.

"This is what else," Roman said, taking a small wax paper package the size of a large, wrapped square of chocolate from his case and placing it on the desk. Opening the corners very slowly, Roman flattened out the wax paper, revealing a small mound of white powder.

"What are you doing?" Cole was surprised.

"Don't tell me you've never tried coke?" Roman was direct.

Cole had never tried coke. Pot, yes, but not much. Coke was out of his league. Rich kids did coke, at least in his way of seeing the world.

"Trust me, a snort of this perfect stuff from my little Sierra, and you will conquer the lunch meeting. The guys will line up to sign up."

Roman was loud. Cole stared, his eyes popping.

Roman portioned out two samplings, inhaled his, and pushed the second serving across the glass-top table, still on the wax paper. It had been lined up with skilled perfection. Clearly, Roman knew what he was doing. Cole went for it. Bending down and over the desk, with instructions from his partner, he picked up a rolled-up dollar bill provided by Roman, pushed one nostril closed with one finger, lowered the other one close to the powder, and inhaled. Repeating the motion, but with the other nostril, he felt the drug taking him to a place he'd never been. The room didn't spin and there were no psychedelic colors flashing, just pure orgasmic euphoria. He had a sense of total control, feeling invincible and in charge with an uncompromising power.

"My God. I've never felt like this," Cole said.

"Man, can you imagine adding sex to this?" Roman asked.

"How long will this last?" Cole asked.

"Should be good for a couple of hours."

"Then what? Do I crash?"

"Hell no. You'll just come down gradually, then you'll rest, man."

Cole got up, straightened his jacket, and checked to make sure there was no cocaine dust on his navy-blue pinstripe suit. It was clean.

"I'll let you know how I do, Roman," Cole said just before leaving the office, as the opaque silver glass transformed back to clear.

Roman waved him off with final words: "Now do you see why we must keep Sierra around?"

Cole was so buzzed with his introduction to coke that he went directly to the Newport Ritz after leaving Roman's office, neglecting to gather his notes for the speech he'd prepared, leaving them sitting on his glass-top desk. Not only did he arrive without notes, but also somehow his wallet had slipped out of his pants, probably on the floor of Roman's office, and he had no cash to hand the Ritz valet his customary five-dollar advance tip. The currency guaranteed a parking slot up front suitable for a noticeable departure as the rest of the crowd waited their turn at the valet stand.

Having no money on him presented another challenge. A good forty-five minutes early, Cole realized that the coke had also messed up his timing. He entered the Ritz and sat down at the bar with time to kill, having no cash for a cocktail. Not that he needed one. The barkeep recognized him and offered a complimentary first round, so no explanation of his predicament was necessary. Cole ordered a vodka on the rocks with extra lime, which provided him a glass to play with and nurse until his luncheon crowd descended at noon.

The forty-five-minute wait felt like a life sentence. Cole worried that the out-of-this-world euphoria would begin to fade before he could master the universe with the men. It did not fade. The guys arrived; cocktails were passed around. Cole managed to get another comp vodka on the rocks, then luncheon was served at a long banquet table on the Ritz terrace, which was in front of a stone fireplace and covered overhead with a ceiling of intricate framed lattice panels. Handsome stone pottery and hammered silver utensils atop thick wheat-toned china greeted some twenty high-profile Newport businessmen. Among them were one billionaire, the mayor, two doctors, a credit dentist, four lawyers, a paving contractor, a paper box mogul, one pawnbroker, the owner of a small private bank, a guy who owned storage units, and a well-known used car dealer whose commercials were even more familiar than Cole's TV show *Living the Dream*.

Luncheon was served—Caesar salad prepared at the table, followed by portions of individual rack of lamb, asparagus, and stuffed cheesy baked potatoes, then a decadent caramel chocolate sundae for dessert. The best wine selections flowed like water. Cole favored the Opus. At close to two o'clock, he was higher than he could ever remember. It was time for his address. Surprising himself, even in his state of inebriated glory, he rose with some element of grace, moved to the head of the table, and took a place next to the chairman.

The confidence factor Roman had promised did indeed materialize. Delivering his pitch on the current state of real estate in coastal Orange County, the liquidity of funding, and the cooperation of the Federal Reserve on interest and lending practices, including zero down fully amortized loans on residential property, and more, Cole had the crowd eating out of his palm. He knew it. Which was something because he wasn't entirely certain of his own name. At one point, he slipped and referred to himself by his birth name of Sal Costa. He covered nicely though; none of the men had a clue. "Who is Sal Costa?" the credit dentist at the table asked.

"Oh, Sal, he's a great guy—one of our investment analysts. You will meet him when you join our fund," Cole said.

Talking steadily far more than half an hour, Cole finished to applause and a raising of glasses for one more serving of Opus. The exclusive monthly get-together was just an excuse for a band of rich guys to drink themselves silly on a weekday afternoon. Even so, business did take place. This was a fraternity, and the men supported one another. Cole was a first-time invited guest, but they wanted him in the fold. He won admittance to the society, along with many business cards from guys at the table, following the talk. Wanting more information on the fund, one by one, they offered their farewell handshakes, along with their cards and instructions for Cole to call. He assured each one that follow-up was part of his credo, and he thanked each one with the sincerity due a longtime friend. Pure Baldwin BS. It was his gift, but not his alone, although he was among the best of the best.

Managing to get out of the Ritz in one piece, still feeling like a very high master of the universe, Cole got his car, which had not been parked in the VIP strip. It didn't matter since most of the men had left before him and nobody was looking. Remarkably back in his Newport Center Drive tower office in minutes without incident, the master of the universe went directly to his office. The main floor was pretty much empty by three in the afternoon as the agents had gone out on appointments. No reason to greet anyone—just a straight shot back to his sanctuary. Closing the glass door behind him, removing his suit jacket, pulling off the tie, and yanking hard on his shirt, Cole popped open buttons. He went for the beige leather couch in front of the glass facing the outer office. Throwing himself down on the cushions, propping one of the back cushions up under his head, he realized he had not gone over to his desk to push the magic button to turn the glass opaque. Forcing himself up, he stumbled over to find the button, then practically launched his body in the air to get back to the couch.

The cocaine was fading. Losing his supreme dominance and the euphoria, Cole began feeling somewhat normal, which soon turned into sadness, depression. Roman had not warned him of this unexpected letdown. The drugs, the alcohol, the adrenaline charge from Cole's successful pitch at the lunch had all mixed together and wired him. He was wiped out but wide awake, unable to close his eyes. Desperately, he wanted to sleep, to escape these unfamiliar feelings. After lying there almost motionless for some two hours staring at the ceiling, Cole finally fell asleep. It was after five, and the spring sunlight was also starting to fade. A golden glow off the western horizon over the water enveloped the office, bouncing off the glass. The phones had ceased ringing, all agents and staff gone from the office for the day.

At eight o'clock, Cole's cell phone buzzed. He jerked and turned to his side to find the phone in the left pocket of his suit pants. It was Kate.

"Baby, it's eight o'clock. I know you said you'd not be home for dinner, but I wanted to check on you," she said. "Did you have a dinner meeting, darling? Did it go well? What did they serve you? I'll bet it was better than what the boys and I had. We do love peanut butter and jelly sandwiches, no crust, with sliced banana and fresh avocados."

"I love all that too," Cole managed to spit out.

"Will you be home soon, darling? I miss you," Kate said.

"Yes, I will. It's been a long day. I'm still in the office. See you in less than an hour."

A private gym in the building was open until nine o'clock. Cole pulled himself together and raced down to the gym for a steam and shower. He was not going home without it. The facility appeared empty, other than a male attendant at the reception desk. He handed Cole a locker key, shower shoes, a towel, and a terry robe, advising him of closure in an hour. As Cole opened the door to the locker room, a man with a towel around his waist came out of one of the private massage rooms, followed by a petite young Asian masseuse in a white uniform carrying more towels. The man recognized Cole. In greeting, he said, "Baldwin, I'm Mark Hopkins from the ninth floor. We've met before in the elevator." He offered his right hand.

"Sure," Cole replied. "I recognize you, even in a towel instead of a dark suit."

"Listen, I just had the best rubdown I've ever had from Sue. You've got to try her," he said.

Sue stood by, smiling.

"I can give you a half hour now, if you'd like," Sue offered.

Cole didn't blink, accepting. "It will take me a minute to change and shower. I'll see you shortly. Shall I come here?" he asked.

"Yes, I'll set up the room," Sue said.

Cole made a dash for his locker, where he stripped and showered, and then returned to the massage room. Sue was waiting with fresh sheets and pillows in place on the massage table. Scented candles were flickering, and there was soft jazz trumpet on the audio system.

"Please remove your robe and lie down faceup," she instructed. Cole followed her command.

As Cole lay naked on the table, Sue adjusted his head on the soft pillow, then moved his entire body over just slightly to the center of the table.

"Are you cold?" she inquired. Cole closed his eyes, already fading, oblivious to his full exposure.

"No, no, I'm fine," he managed to offer.

"Shall I cover you?" Sue asked.

"I'm okay. Not necessary."

The petite Asian masseuse began her treatment, applying a coconut-scented lotion to both her hands and beginning to stroke Cole's face, temples, and scalp. Her touch was gentle at first, then became firm as she gave him a deep head massage. Cole was turning on. Sue had magic fingers.

It didn't take long for Cole to regret not having asked for a towel to cover his privates. The natural response to the erotic head rub was a rigid erection. He tried to mentally deflate the flagpole, without luck. It was big and it was bold, and its message was clear. Sue got the message. For the remainder of the half hour, Cole did receive the best rubdown ever given, as promised by Mark Hopkins, who'd been treated before him. The ending was superbly happy.

Cole showered again, dressed, and greeted Sue in the reception room with a hug and a discreet hundred-dollar tip on his way out.

"I'd love to help you again. Anytime," she called out as he left the gym.

"It was the best," he called back, and was gone.

Arriving home at Lido after ten o'clock that evening, Cole found that all was quiet. He made his way silently upstairs to the master suite, finding Kate sound asleep in their bed. She was curled up on her side, still in her robe, wrapped in a comforter, and cradling a stuffed bear that was often her bedtime companion, in addition to Cole. He did not wake her. What would he say if she arose? Kissing Kate on the forehead, Cole slipped into the master bath, where he undressed, before returning to the bedroom and climbing silently into bed beside her.

CHAPTER FIFTY-FOUR

THE BEST GIFT OF ALL

Rising on the morning of August 13 in the hospital, I felt strong. Our daughter had been born at one minute after midnight. Having slept soundly, the special kind of rest that rarely happens, I opened my eyes surrounded by my husband and my parents. Two nurses appeared, ordered by Nancy, my personal general in charge. They went to work checking vitals.

"It is so wonderful to see you all." Those were my first words, sincerely delivered. Cole was sitting in a metal chair beside me, holding my hand. Dalt was resting on a small sofa across from my bed. He stood as I rallied, and came to the other side of my bed, placing his hand on my shoulder. Nancy continued grilling the nurses for updated information.

"Baby, you're back," Cole said in a happy voice. "We were so scared. I was so scared," he continued.

"Nothing to fear," I answered with a forced grin. "I've never felt better. Okay, well, maybe I have felt better, but what a gift. You know, women have been doing this task for a few years. Heck, I've done it twice before."

Baby girl Baldwin remained in the neonatal intensive care unit, her birth having been difficult and complicated. Seeing as she was nearly two weeks late, Dr. Grimes had performed a caesarean when all options for natural birth were determined to be too dangerous for both mother and child. Somehow, in the final hours, baby girl Baldwin turned herself in a twisted position, blocking the birth canal.

"I thought the third delivery was supposed to be a breeze," I said to my mother, who had finished telling my nurses what to do. "I popped the twins right out."

"What matters is that she is alive and doing well and is in good hands. And the same goes for you, my darling girl."

Given the situation, I expected to remain in the hospital for at least five days, not the new norm as most new moms were escorted out the door in a wheelchair, baby in lap, the next day, or at most two postdelivery. Baby girl Baldwin would remain for at least a week, giving me time to heal and to bond. The nurse advised that I would have to hold off on cradling my daughter, but they would put me in a chair right in front of a window looking in on her in the neonatal ICU. I could not wait.

Cole leaned over and kissed my lips gently.

"Should we share our baby's name with the family?" he asked me softly. I hesitated.

"Cole, I know we talked about the name, and we agreed it would be best to choose a *B* name since all the kids would share that in common, but I have a special favor to ask."

"Babe, anything at all," he replied instantly.

"Could we name her after my grandmother?"

"Gertrude? That's really old-fashioned." Cole looked puzzled.

"Not exactly. How about her nickname, GiGi? I would love to name her GiGi Fair Baldwin. Would you agree?"

"GiGi is perfect," Cole offered.

Nancy and Dalt started to cry silently. I saw the tears. My parents were holding one another tightly, standing in front of a large plate glass window in my hospital room with an expansive view of the Pacific framed perfectly, and Catalina Island in the distance. I made a memory of them in front of that window, an indelible mark on my permanent mental record.

"Darling, that is such a wonderful gesture. Family legacy matters. It's who we are, how we got here, and now how we pass on into the future. Your father and I are truly touched. GiGi is sharing the news with your grandfather in heaven." Nancy made me cry.

"There's no crying for postpregnant women in recovery." Cole was sweet. He grabbed a tissue from the box on the side table and dabbed my cheeks.

"Can I share some more wonderful news?" Nancy asked.

"Of course, Mom. What?" I spoke for Cole and me.

"I know you talk to Jamey often, so you are aware that he has been sober for about a year and is doing so well with the Chabad program. But I'll bet he didn't tell you that both he and his friend Rachel will graduate high school with their GED diplomas at the end of the year. Both of them have turned a corner, are sober, healthy, and happy and are planning to enroll at Santa Monica City College in the spring semester." Nancy was glowing with joy.

"He didn't tell me that, Mom."

"It's new news!"

"Hard to believe Jamey is turning twenty. My little brother is a man!"

"There's more," said Nancy.

"They want to share an apartment," Dalt chimed in.

"Isn't Rachel twenty also?" I asked.

"She is. And she is bright, hardworking, and totally in love with your brother," Nancy added.

"Then, why not?" I followed without hesitation.

"That's what I said to your father," Nancy came back.

Dalt nodded his head, then shook his head.

"Daddy, this is good news. Just accept that it is good news. Jamey has had a rotten time, but he is turning his life around. Be happy for him that Rachel is there for him too." This new mother of a daughter and philosopher/therapist kicked in her opinion. Had I become wise at twenty-five? How could Jamey be twenty? He was ten yesterday, but then I was fifteen.

A knock on the door was followed by an orderly bringing breakfast. Cole stayed with me while my parents went to the hospital cafeteria. We were scheduled for a trip to the neonatal ward in an hour.

My stress over getting the new Fair Child line ready had evaporated. Our search to find a fashion rep who would take on the line and sell it to stores was also on hold. Dr. Grimes cautioned me that too much stress could have been a factor in the lateness of the delivery. I had felt I had everything under control. Concentration on work had taken my mind off the normal uncomfortable end-of-pregnancy nervousness. It was meant to be that labor would begin at my design table.

The labor pains had started early in the week while I was working at the salon with Monsieur Lawrence.

"You are pushing yourself too hard to get these samples done," my mentor had cautioned.

"Monsieur, I'm not pushing the work; my baby is pushing me," I explained, out of breath.

"Oh my, what can I do?" he offered, coming to my side at the worktable.

"Call Cole," I told him, handing him my cell, which was already set to call my husband.

Monsieur was correct. I had been pushing myself hard for the previous several months. There was a deadline to meet, the deadline being my baby's due date. I had felt the new samples must be finished and perfect so that Heather could try to close a deal with the Bergs at the LA Mart to represent us. Madame Honoré even told me daily how proud she was of my dedication. Frankly, I had amazed myself.

Finding renewed focus, I had managed work and family without drama or complaint. It did help that Cole had been totally absent most of the time, more so than ever before with the TV show, the real estate office, The Summit development, and now an investment operation. It was nuts, but he seemed happy and supercharged with energy, and his dream was alive and well, and expanding.

Monsieur had stepped in as I was carted off by Cole with premature labor pains. He promised to put the final touches on the new line for spring 2006. We had skipped fall/holiday 2005 since our timing was off, not to mention with the dismal debut the previous year during the holiday season at the Fashion Plaza pop-up.

For the second rollout of Fair Child, I increased the emphasis on trend and let go of my inclination to stay too classic. This line included flowing silk palazzo pants with a high waist and a leotard bodysuit. I did a wonderful shirtmaker top that looked like a man's Brooks Brothers dress shirt that could be worn over pants or even as a dress. The signature Fair Child three-piece ensemble was tweaked with a plunging neckline camisole, a pencil skirt with side slits, and a jacket fashioned after military fatigues. Heather loved it all, as did Madame. Monsieur, well, not so much. Then again, he was a classic himself.

Heather stepped in to supervise the creation of the sample line, coordinating with Monsieur and the fabrication jobbers in downtown LA. The second line featured twenty pieces, a lot for an upstart company, Monsieur had said. He warned again that we were overly ambitious, even overconfident at times. Yet, he was 100 percent behind the plan. Cautious, yes, but he was not afraid to go big.

The jobber estimated that it would take at least a month to roll out a full line of samples, in sample size 4, to show the Bergs. We had completed the task early the day before I went into labor. Heather then set an appointment to do the show-and-tell with the Berg Group at the end of the month. Everything was falling into place.

Unable to Resist

Cole and Roman left an important follow-up meeting with the developers who had sold them The Summit parcel with elevated optimism. Bidders, including Roman's Russian competition, contacted the developers, offering to increase their offers by some 25 percent if the deal with Cole and Roman were to fall apart. It was not going to fall apart; Cole would stake his life on it.

At my urging, and with counsel from my father, Cole insisted that Roman agree to pursue bank construction financing to inaugurate the project and hold off on taking in outside investor dollars. Roman resisted. Money was being thrown at them. Dalt prevailed; he was the major investor. With Dalt's entrée, the partners compared lending offers at three different major banks.

Even with banks bidding, it was far too early to finalize the financing since there were no building plans. The land excavation was not totally completed. The site was home to an armada of bulldozers at work, doing their dance back and forth, rearranging Mother Earth. Cole and I drove up the hill to the site almost every day after I got out of the hospital and took GiGi home. Late in the afternoon and sometimes at sunset, we took a drive to survey the future. This became a special romantic event, a routine cherished in our evolving lives. Baby GiGi was finally home and in the loving care of Nurse Belinda, a gift from God, who had returned to us. It was sheer luck and perfect timing, as Belinda had only days earlier ended a six-month job in New York. We booked her first class on American out of JFK to LA, a perk she deserved.

On one outing up to the site, Cole and I got out of the car, which was covered with the dust from the storm created by one of the final runs of the big-gest earthmover known to humankind, and walked carefully in the rich, dark, luscious-smelling soil over to a promontory on the land. Looking out over the acreage, surrounded by chaparral-covered coastal California hillside, I thought about the magnitude of change we were responsible for in developing this land.

"Cole, did you ever consider that this very land has existed in one natural state for possibly millennia since the ice age?" I asked my husband, watching the bulldozer getting too close to his once shiny black BMW.

"What did you ask? Oh, I got it. Sorry, I was distracted. And no, this is the first time I ever considered that," he came back.

"In a matter of months, this land will be transformed, never again to be the same," I told him. "We're creating a fundamental change on this one tiny piece of the planet."

"Gosh, you make it sound awfully important, almost spiritual," Cole said, looking me right in the eyes. I had his full attention.

"Well, it is kind of spiritual. Don't you feel it? I do. I feel it. I see it, and I smell it too. Breathe in that aroma of newly turned earth."

"I think I'm getting turned on," Cole said, grinning.

"Oh no. Not here. Not now," I returned, laughing.

"How about in the car?" he said. "There is so much dust on the windows, we'd be totally in private. I don't think we've ever done it in this car."

"That's because the car is almost new, and besides, we haven't sealed our agreement on future relations without more planning. I love having three boys and one girl."

"I did buy a whole case of protection like you asked for. I think it's in the trunk. How's that for planning?" Cole was proud of his comeback.

"I am impressed. Just the same, how about a nice dinner for two at the Quiet Woman in Corona del Mar on our way home? It's that cute local bistro bar we love that is named after a headless wench. Maybe we can discuss lovemaking terms over dinner." I ended the train of conversation, leading to an unwanted conclusion in Cole's back seat. A mother of four does not do such things, especially when dinner awaits at a pub named the Quiet Woman—every man's fantasy.

Moving Ahead

Cole and Roman came back to the office after learning of the offers from their former competitors, finding the agents popping open champagne bottles. One of the agents, a rookie, walked in with a signed listing agreement on the most expen-sive waterfront estate in Newport with a meteoric asking price of thirty-five million dollars. The highest waterfront sale ever had not topped the twenty-million-dollar mark. The staff went wild over the news, making the Baldwin office the unofficial leader of a formidable pack of bigtime real estate offices in Newport.

Cole had signed up the guy only a couple of months before. As Cole himself had, his new agent had come from nowhere and knew nobody, but he had the magic. Kit Hamilton, twenty-eight, about the same age as Cole, a southern boy from Fairhope, Alabama, arrived in California with a résumé featuring a year of community college, several jobs selling used cars, and not much else other than exceptional looks and magnetic personal attraction. The six-foot-two, green-eyed, dirty-blond-haired man with a male model physique first landed in where else but Hollywood. Five years, one nonspeaking role in a detergent commercial, a great many failed auditions, and a great many male sexual propositions later, Hamilton pulled out of Hollywood and came south to Newport, where he got a real estate license and walked in for an interview with Cole Baldwin, real estate TV star. It was kismet.

Apparently, Kit Hamilton was also a pro at luxury barstool conversation and happened to be on the stool at the Newport Ritz next to a drop-dead gorgeous middle-aged blonde wearing an off-the-shoulder black top and displaying a major diamond choker, the genuine item. Several hours and many drinks later, Hamilton picked up the tab and then picked up the blonde. She turned out to be a recent widow—childless, friendless, and alone in a landmark mansion. Husband Harry had died in bed with her, his fifth wife of only two years. His kids got all the money; she got the house. Hamilton got the entire story while bedding the sad and lonely widow, who was short on cash but long on mansion. The power company was about to turn off the lights. He provided the solution; she signed the documents.

As Cole and Roman walked into the office party, Hamilton waved the listing agreement over his head. Catching Cole's attention, he made a direct move toward the boss.

"Here it is." Hamilton handed the papers to Cole. Roman stood by, amazed.

"Very cool," Cole told his protégé.

"You're partly the reason," Hamilton responded.

"Really? How's that?"

"My client Vanessa watches your TV show all the time. She told me that since I work with you, I must be all right."

Hamilton's praise made Cole think that somehow he should have landed this big fish. Real estate jealousy kicking in, he noticed a change in temperature in his enthusiasm level for Kit. Kit was now a threat, maybe a little too much like Cole. There was no room for that kind of competition and similarity in Newport real estate. Cole sucked it up for the moment.

"Kit, congratulations. Keep me informed every step of the transaction so we can support you. This is an important transaction for the office as well. We don't want to screw it up. Let's close it and make money," Cole told his new star agent with the largest listing in the history of the town, despite having no prior sales record or experience, just like Cole.

Roman grabbed his partner's arm and led him off toward his glass cage. They high-fived all across the bullpen floor, which was alive with the celebrating sea of masters of the real estate universe.

Roman closed the door behind them, leaving the party behind. As the two men took their respective places across from one another at Roman's desk, Roman pushed the button and the glass panels went opaque.

"Cole, I agreed to fund The Summit through regular banking channels. I had no choice."

"We had no choice," Cole came back.

"Yes, we had no choice. But I do have a choice moving forward with our investment arm raising money for other property deals down the road. I will not miss the timing of this opportunity. Guys want to hand us briefcases of money now. Who knows, in six months or a year?"

"So how do we proceed?" Cole pushed.

"Just as we planned. We form a separate business corporation as an investment fund and we make it all legal, and then we go to work courting investors." Roman was nonchalant.

"I think you've leaving out a few steps," Cole replied. "It can't be that simple."

"It is that simple. Like leading a horse to water."

"I thought horses didn't like water," Cole said, attempting to lighten the exchange.

"Horses love water, and I love money," Roman said.

"That's not all you love," Cole shot back.

"Sierra? Don't worry, she's on her way here now," Roman replied. Cole stared at him.

"Listen, before your coke supply arrives, talk to me straight about this investment business. I get it that there is a lot of money out there right now. But what are we offering? Why would anyone give us money? We have no specific project other than The Summit."

"That's right. No other project now, but we will have one soon. And when we start building at The Summit and guys see what we can do, new projects will be handed to us."

Roman was bullish. That was always Cole's attraction to him. Even if he sounded crazy, somehow, he could convince Cole that it was possible.

"Anything is possible," Roman always said. "Anything."

A tap on the glass signaled the arrival of a much-desired guest. Sierra was right on time, and Roman was anxious. He buzzed her in. She pushed open the opaque glass door and sashayed in.

"Cole, one more thing. Keep your eyes wide open with Kit Hamilton. Watch him like a hawk. I assume you've got a major piece of his business for a while as he earns his stripes, so take charge on this deal. I don't trust this guy—too much of a showboat." Roman turned serious.

Cole was not surprised by Roman's words of caution. He shared the same instinct, even though he had brought the guy in based on the flip side of that same instinct. Sierra cut the business talk short, and Cole rose from the chair at Roman's desk to make his exit. Sierra had her own business to discuss with Roman. Today she carried with her a very large black tote fashioned in faux alligator patent leather, or something like leather. Cole knew exactly what she carried in that tote, and it certainly wasn't real estate contracts.

"Nice to see you, Sierra. Take care." Cole offered Sierra a hug as they crossed paths. She accepted it and snuggled right up to Cole, even giving him a little peck on the right cheek.

The high fiving and the champagne toasts faded, and the agents went back to work on their phones, dialing for dollars. Cole entered his glass cage, having made it across the sales floor without stopping to chat with anyone. His phone was ringing. Normally, the office secretary cleared all his calls, but right now she was nowhere in sight. He picked up the landline on his desk.

"This is Cole Baldwin."

"Cole, it's Bill Sanders. I have something I want to discuss with you."

Sanders was one of the executives with the Newport Land Trust, which Cole and Roman had visited earlier that day to discuss The Summit.

"Did we forget to go over something at the meeting?" Cole asked.

"No, nothing at all. This is something totally separate that I thought you might be interested in."

"Something for Roman and me together?" Cole was curious.

"No, but I guess it could be if you wanted it to be."

"You've got my attention, Bill," Cole answered.

"For the past year or so you have contacted me multiple times looking for a special deal on either a lot or a semicustom home under construction for yourself and your family. Something has come available, something very special, and at a steal price. Cole, we are all fond of you here at the trust, so I am offering this to you if you're interested."

"Now you really have my attention."

"We just did a deal on another parcel of raw undeveloped land on a sector of Society Hill you know that's called The Pinnacle. It's our biggest deal to date. It will eventually become the most exclusive gated private enclave of megamansions on the coast."

"Sounds amazing. Maybe a little out of my range now, but I'm flattered you are sharing this with me." Cole wanted to sound humble yet proud. Did Bill Sanders think he could afford to live at The Pinnacle?

"It will be Billionaires Row. We expect mostly foreign buyers, probably Middle Eastern or Chinese."

"Okay. What do you have in mind?" Cole was getting mixed signals, not grasping what his involvement might be.

"There is a once-in-a-lifetime opportunity to buy a two-acre parcel of land, of which only about one acre of the plot is buildable, adjacent to this new development. The buyers could not use this strip, and it's pretty much not practical for any developer other than for personal use. Amazing location, total coastal view, just outside the gates of what will become Billionaires Row." Sanders had painted an irresistible picture.

"Are you offering to sell this parcel to me?" Cole was direct. He had gotten the message. He was also very excited.

"Yes, yes I am. How does three hundred thousand dollars sound? Total steal," Sanders added. Cole held back an immediate confirmation.

"Two prime acres for one hundred fifty thousand dollars each? Why aren't you buying them?" Cole put his businessman pants on.

"Fair question. The answer is that this site is unusual. It will take some real creativity to turn it into something. Our group just wants to find the right buyer with vision. Is that you, Baldwin?"

"Will you take terms, carry the paper, say, three years?" Cole pushed forward.

"Possible."

"Three hundred thousand dollars firm?"

"Of course."

"Then, 20 percent down, sixty thousand dollars, balloon balance in three years, payments with interest only at 5 percent." Cole made an offer sight unseen, but with one caveat. "I make this offer conditional on inspection."

"Naturally. When do you want to take a tour? I can set it up right away. We'd like to move on this, Baldwin."

"Is tomorrow morning soon enough?"

"Meet me at my office at ten o'clock in the morning," Sanders confirmed. "Please do not discuss this with anyone."

"No problem. And thank you, sir. I am very excited." Cole hung up the phone, leaned back in his chair, and let out a huge yelp.

The missing secretary who had not taken the call originally was now back at her post. She came running in to see if everything was okay.

"Oh boy, everything is just fine. Totally fine," Cole told her.

The young woman exited his office, thinking it must be another big deal for the firm. Heading back to her desk, she said under her breath, "I make nine dollars an hour. In one deal, these guys make five years of my salary. Where did I go wrong?"

CHAPTER FIFTY-FIVE

STRIKE TWO

Not quite a full month after delivery of GiGi, an absolute doll baby if ever one existed, I kept the promise I had made to myself to join Heather at the pitch to the Berg Group held at the LA Fashion Mart. We were scheduled on a Monday morning the week after the Labor Day holiday. Being superstitious, which I would never admit to, I always felt that Monday morning meetings came with a negative vibe. This sense of foreboding stemmed from my having avoided all Monday morning classes during my time at USC. That wasn't such a great plan in hindsight.

Nevertheless, it had to be either Monday morning or nothing. This was the slowest morning of the week at the Mart, and the week after Labor Day promised to be even slower. Heather advised that the slowness would give us a greater share of the Bergs' attention. There would be no buyers walking into the showroom, and the phones would be quiet. I wasn't certain that the slowness would work to our advantage.

"Wouldn't we be better off if some random buyer, say, from Saks Fifth Avenue, wandered in while we were showing the Fair Child line to the Bergs and the buyer showed some enthusiasm or even interest in maybe buying?" I asked Heather.

"Good point," she said. "But it usually doesn't work that way. The buyers come by appointment, especially the ones from the major retailers. They get private, priority treatment, no interruptions. The walk-ins are mostly small shop owners— one-offs as they are called—checking out the new lines all throughout the Mart."

My business-minded partner had learned a great deal about the fashion business in a very short span of time. If we had any chance of convincing the Bergs to take us on, it would be because of Heather Adamson.

Our meeting was set for nine o'clock in the morning in downtown Los Angeles. Traffic north on I-405 from Newport to LA would be rough, so we left at six. Heather picked me up on Lido Isle. The sun was coming up, preparing to deliver a hot summer day, standard fare for September in Southern California. I wanted to wear the line, but Heather said not to: bad form, too aggressive, even amateurish. Understanding the concept, I dressed in what might be termed a complementary wardrobe. Having chosen a crisp white cotton camisole top, tailored khaki slacks, and a matching cream-colored cotton sweater over the shoulder and tied at the neckline, I hopped into Heather's shiny new white Mercedes 500SL, a gift from her mom and dad at her recent college graduation. We were off to LA.

Heather and Monsieur had arranged to have the entire line delivered by van. It would be picked up at the salon at the same six o'clock in the morning start time. The two of us had rehearsed the pitch all week long. I hadn't left the house much since GiGi came into our life, so Heather had practically moved in, and we shared wonderful times that entire week of prep. In between baby time and playing with the boys, we had dreamed and schemed about our future business together. This was going to be the break we needed. As we talked nonstop on the freeway, my Monday morning superstitions vanished, and so did the traffic. We made it into downtown LA in about fifty minutes, exiting the freeway at Olympic Boulevard. At ten minutes to seven, we were two hours early for our meeting.

Olympic Boulevard led directly east just south of the major sections of old downtown LA. A few blocks from the freeway on the corner of Olympic and Figueroa was a diner known as the Pantry. Heather and I both knew the place well from our respective times at USC. Spotting the familiar hangout, we hollered "Breakfast!" in unison, then pulled over and parked.

Thankfully, the line at the front door on the corner of Olympic and Figueroa was only five patrons deep. Sometimes it could stretch around the block. We made it inside in less than ten minutes, not that we were in a hurry, just nervous about our looming fashion pitch. Passing through the old metal turnstile at the door, we felt at ease entering familiar ground. The early twentieth-century working-class ambiance remained untouched. A long counter running along the north wall had it stools mostly occupied. Behind the counter, longtime waiters, middle-aged men sporting thinning slicked-back hair, stood proudly at attention in their starched white shirts topped with shiny black clip-on bow ties. We both waved at the men as the head waiter at the door showed us down the aisle on the opposite end of the restaurant from the counter to a row of basic wooden tables and chairs.

"Will this do?" he asked, pointing to a small table for two adjacent to a wall featuring a mounted chalkboard menu. We nodded, sat, and looked at the daily breakfast special advertised at $5.99.

"Heather, can you believe it? I think it's a sign, an omen," I blurted out.

"Huh?"

"Corned beef hash over crispy hash browns with fried egg on top. It's a sign," I repeated.

"Yes. It's a sign all right, a sign of calories galore, possible indigestion, and worse, potential gas explosion during our meeting." Heather came to the point as always.

I laughed and ordered the special.

"It's my favorite, and I never get this," I shared. "I'll take it as a sign of good luck."

Heather gave me the look, the look that was part *Love you, friend* and part *Some kind of crazy*.

"I'll have two scrambled eggs, no toast, no potatoes," Heather told our waiter.

"Living large on our big day," I snapped back.

The unplanned breakfast interlude passed quickly—too quickly. I wanted to linger over coffee as I reminisced in my mind about my time at USC and the two-o'-clock-in-the-morning breakfasts I had shared with David to break up a night of studying. Well, studying for him, the premed serious guy. Many nights I would just stare at him while pretending to read a book. One night he caught me watching him at his desk. He turned and startled me. I'll never forget what he said.

"Kate, I'm really impressed that you have mastered reading freshman biology upside down. Now that's real talent."

Heather noticed that I had drifted in thought. She inquired, but I just sloughed it off as nothing, because it was nothing: just a fond memory from a time that seemed a lifetime ago. Funny, so much life gets packed into each year of a person's twenties. USC and David in my life had happened only five years ago, yet I rarely went back there. My past was just the past.

Minutes later we pulled into the garage at the California Mart. Still ahead of schedule, with some forty-five minutes until our nine o'clock appointment, we chose to walk the halls and check out some of the design reps' showrooms. The Mart was bustling with morning activity. Deliverymen were pushing racks of clothing covered in navy-blue garment bags. Models, who clearly chose not to order the corned beef hash for breakfast, streamed up the massive lobby escalators to their appointed showroom destinations. It was easy to spot the creative staff. Young, good-looking gay men dressed to impress, from trendy to bespoke, arrived to earn their daily bread. Some were salesmen, I thought, showing the lines to buyers. Others took off their trendy jackets and went to work in back rooms, sewing and fitting models and dressing the windows and the mannequins in the showrooms. Such great energy. I loved all of it.

While I was lost in all the action, Heather spotted Monsieur Lawrence and his two men coming out of a freight elevator with our own rack of dreams covered in navy-blue felt garment bags.

"Monsieur, here we are," Heather called out across the massive granite-floored lobby surrounded by twenty-foot-tall floor-to-ceiling panels of glass. I marveled at the architectural statement since the walls of glass looked out upon gritty, working-class streets and alleys in the gut of urban LA. Maybe that was the architect's concept: armadas of trucks hauling garments off to stores; factory shops and jobbers with workers in small warehouses open and visible, facing the alley; even street vendors peddling knockoff designer goods in carts shaded by rainbow-paneled umbrellas—all part of the glass-encased view from LA's center of fashion.

"Ladies, are you ready for your showing?" Monsieur Lawrence was both mentor and cheer coach.

"We could not be more ready." Heather took charge. I gave Monsieur a hug, saying nothing.

"You are very quiet," Monsieur said, directing the statement toward me.

Not hesitating, I spoke, "Oh no, not quiet. Just introspective. Thinking about the moment. Taking it all in. We've come far in a couple of years, with you at our side."

"You wish to make a middle-aged man cry in the Mart lobby," he said, returning the sentiment with few words.

"No crying," Heather demanded. "Let's find our elevator to the seventh floor."

The Berg suite was dubbed "California Celebration," occupying nearly half a full floor on the seventh level. It too had floor-to-ceiling walls of glass that opened out onto the central corridor traversing the building. In the center of the glass-walled showroom, a double glass door opened on to the suite, were we were met by a classy-looking woman of fifty-something, slightly overweight but beautiful, dressed exquisitely in upscale office-appropriate wardrobe, with perfect makeup and a full-coiffed head of golden-blonde hair fluffed and flowing to her shoulders.

"Welcome. You must be the design team from Fair Child. We're expecting you. Please come in. Antonio will show you to your staging area. My name is Madge, by the way."

Madge extended her hand. I took it and introduced all of us. Antonio appeared out of nowhere.

"Good day," Antonio offered with flourish.

This tall, maybe six feet five, Hispanic young man of considerable girth—three hundred to four hundred pounds worth—wearing wildly patterned mismatched shirt and pants with a flowing waist-length silk scarf tied around his neck, stretched out both arms, embracing the three of us in a group hug.

Monsieur's two helpers stood behind with the rack. Antonio could not get all of us in the embrace. He guided us to a salon in the rear of the showroom divided by drapery from the adjacent workspace. There was a circular riser in the center of the salon, off the floor by just a foot. Plush seating faced the stage on one side. To the left and right, movable drapery on racks served as changing areas for models. We had no models.

Monsieur and his men rolled our rack of samples behind one of the draped areas and began unpacking. Antonio advised us to sit as the Bergs would be forthcoming. He offered us a beverage: water, coffee, tea, or Diet Coke. Antonio pretended to be a stewardess on a plane ready to take off. We laughed. I cringed a bit. Then I asked, "Antonio, what does the name on the showroom stand for?"

"Honey, that's who we are. We are California Celebration. Casual, cheap, cheerful clothing for juniors and misses. Our lines are huge worldwide in all the finest discount stores and malls."

I looked at Heather; my cringing was no longer private. She whispered, "Kate, I was told the Bergs carry lines from discount to upscale, not just cheap and cheerful."

We had no time to dwell on our horror, as Arnold and Jackie Berg made their entrance. The husband–wife team were apparently legends in the LA fashion business. While I didn't know that they were the king and queen of cheap and cheerful, I did learn that they were no-nonsense businesspeople, trustworthy and even visionary. One source confided that they shared the coveted "fashion nose," the ability to judge what would sell in the next season before the designs hit the runways.

Arnold marched in silently and sat down in the center chair facing the riser. Jackie followed close behind, and greeted us. He was in his late fifties, handsome and classically dressed, no suit and tie, only tailored slacks and a monogrammed French-cuffed shirt. She was younger, slim, and elegant in a two-piece lavender and cream knit suit over a cream silk camisole, with large diamond stud earrings, four-inch heels, and a Palm Springs glow on a tanned face that was made up for a camera close-up. Jackie's jet-black hair was pulled back in a CoCo bun and tied with a lavender satin bow bordered in cream to match her outfit.

Thinking to myself that this woman was going to appreciate the Fair Child line, I also thought that maybe everything would be okay. Jackie was polite but direct. Pleasantries were short. She launched in with a barrage of questions: Who were we? Why were we here? What was our background? How long had we been in business? What had we sold? Whom had we sold to? The questions were seemingly endless. Heather and I did our best. Monsieur came out from behind the drapery but did not engage. Jackie gave him the head-to-toe once-over but said nothing. I was seated in the semicircular area in front of the platform, facing the center toward the Bergs, while Monsieur remained to the side and behind.

"Well then, let's see it," Jackie commanded.

I stood up. Monsieur took my arm and guided me to the curtain, where one of his men handed over the first garment. I took the dress, and Monsieur helped me up onto the platform, where I displayed item 1 in the line. Holding it out grace-fully, then turning it side to side, front to back, I explained every detail. Nervous momentarily, I said a silent *God help me* and found the confidence to proudly display and showcase my dress.

"This is the Fair Child dress, the signature garment in my line. From this dress, all else flows and coordinates," I said, beginning my speech, serious yet up-beat and professional, feeling self-assured. The gallery was silent. Not taking too much time, I moved on to the next item in the line. I signaled Monsieur, and he handed me the signature tunic jacket, designed to be worn with the classic A-line dress, or with jeans for a casual yet tailored look.

Explaining all of this, I clumsily dropped the dress when trying to display both garments, one over the other. Heather jumped up from her seat, joined me on the riser, and picked up the dress. We continued as a team. Monsieur proceeded to advance items 3, 4, and 5 from the line. Heather and I were clicking; it felt right. When the sixth item came up for display, my palazzo pants over the body leotard, Jackie spoke.

"Charming. Absolutely lovely." Those were her first and only words before a pregnant pause. Turning, she looked at Arnold, who said nothing. Then she continued.

"Dear girls, I am impressed. But sadly, this is not for us. May I be blunt?"

"Yes, please," I replied.

"I'm not sure your line is for anyone. Not yet anyhow. You are too young, too inexperienced. You have paid no dues. Forgive me, but you seem like very intelligent young women but also, I'm guessing, somewhat privileged young ladies of some means. My advice to you both, if you want a career in design, is that you must get jobs with a recognized design house and work, learn, and grow. Thank you for coming, and all the best of luck."

Heather and I handed our samples to Monsieur and his men. Although I was tempted to introduce Monsieur as our mentor and reveal that my paternal grandparents were immigrants to the United States working in New York garment factories, I did not do so. Stepping off the riser and going over to thank the Bergs, I approached Jackie to shake her hand. She stopped me.

"Darling girl, what is that yellow spot on your blouse?"

Looking down, I found a yellow stain midway and toward the left side of my cream camisole.

"Oh dear, I'm afraid it is a drop of egg from breakfast," I said, blushing considerably.

"Antonio," Jackie called out, "bring me a cup of soda water and a clean wipe."

Antonio moved on demand and returned to the spot with the soda water and wipe. Jackie proceeded to dip the wipe in the soda, then gently tap the wipe on my blouse to remove the stain.

"A young lady with your class must always be stain-free," she offered with a grin. "Oh, one more question. Do either of you sew?"

I looked at Heather. Neither of us responded.

"Before you envision your designs in the Fifth Avenue windows of Bergdorf's, consider becoming an expert seamstress."

Jackie was cold but not mean.

And that was it. We packed up and left. I cried most of the way home to Newport.

Taking Risks

Cole came back to the Newport Center headquarters later than expected on this Friday afternoon. It was closing in on six o'clock, with the BIG Fund—that is, Baldwin Investment Group Fund—cocktail reception scheduled to start at six. Roman was the one to have set the plan in motion to raise real estate investment dollars with a reception in the office when the Lido house had been checked off the list of possible venues. With no tent erected, no caviar served from ice sculptures, and mostly, no beautiful models, this event would be hardcore business, none of the wannabe Newport flash crowd, especially the real estate agents, all not welcome.

In place of the sex-on-a-silver-platter crowd, Roman had invited corporate leaders, investment bankers, stockbrokers, and a carefully vetted list of Newport rich guys, mostly the nonworking kind who fancied themselves masters of their own universe. These men wrote checks, big ones, and bragged about it when the town got news of a big deal on the horizon. It was important to be ahead of the pack.

Cole and Roman were not members of this inner circle. Like a new record on the charts, the pair of developers were rising like a bullet. Outsiders on the inside track, young, good-looking, and charismatic to the tenth degree, they sealed the deal on so many levels. Roman knew this instinctively. Cole knew it too, but he had considerably greater insecurity, regardless of his 24/7 effort to camouflage any fears as he faced the world.

Cole's late appearance at the reception resulted from a longer than expected meeting with Bill Sanders at the Newport Land Trust. Having signed papers for the purchase of the land parcel discreetly offered to him at the substantially under-market value of $300,000, Cole was on cloud nine. In the weeks since the initial offering from Sanders, Cole had done his homework, also discreetly, not discussing the deal with anyone—not Roman and not even Kate.

As expected, he realized that there were no free lunches in life. The two-acre parcel was something of an error. It had come into being, as it were, when the bulldozers were creating this hilltop enclave expected to be known as Billionaires Row. Given all kinds of restrictions, the land could not be included inside the gates of the development, so it was a "leftover."

Consequently, it could be left in its natural state as open land. Not easily accessible, and not large enough or flat enough for parkland, the land had limited value. The trust had offered it confidentially to anyone interested. There were no takers except Cole.

Armed with this information, Cole went ahead with a lower offer of $200,000 cash, a third less than the already giveaway price. By meeting's end, it was agreed. There would be no financing, no terms as originally discussed—a clean cash transaction, with no delay and no publicity. Cole insisted on anonymity. The funds would come from his own real estate account. One small detail: all his funds were committed to the deal on The Summit with Dalt Fairchild. Cole rationalized that a couple of solid home sales would replenish the money needed to move the needle forward on existing business with his partners Roman and Dalt, the latter his father-in-law.

Entering his eighth-floor office suite minutes before the start of the inaugural Baldwin Investment Group cocktail meeting, Cole greeted confident men with their hands up, anticipating high fives. The knot in his stomach created by his bullish move on the land purchase began to ease. With cause to be nervous, he had made a $200,000 investment on his own and on a whim without the cash, which was taking a crazy risk. Cole high-fived the men with a big smile, his machismo and bravado in high gear. He thought, *I bet we raise a million dollars here tonight.*

As the stomach knot faded fast, in came upstart star agent Kit Hamilton. At his side was Richard Hellman, flanked by two serious men in dark black suits. Cole noticed earpieces in each man's left ear with an attached wire over the back of the ear and down into the collar. Recognizing Hellman immediately, he assumed the men to be bodyguards.

Why would he need bodyguards at a business cocktail reception? And what the hell is he doing with Kit Hamilton? Cole's mind raced, but without a beat, he turned to greet the unexpected entourage.

"Hey, Kit, heard you closed that big deal. Congratulations, man. Wow. Amazing," Cole gushed, going overboard. Kit basked in the glory.

"Let me introduce my new client, Cole. This is Richard Hellman."

Cole offered his hand. "Yes, I know who Mr. Hellman is. Welcome, sir. Who are your associates?" Cole tried to be cool.

"First, you can call me Richard," he said. "My friends are with me to learn about real estate investment. This is Mr. Jones, and that is Mr. Smith," he said, pointing to each.

"I see. Welcome, all of you. Please come in and have a drink. Our presentation will begin shortly."

Hellman and his men left Cole with Kit Hamilton at the entry console.

"Man, what are you doing with Richard Hellman?" Cole was direct, his tone changing markedly.

Kit was flip, returning the "man" salutation with plenty of tone.

"He's a new client. Wants to buy a mansion on Society Hill, or perhaps build one from the ground up in some new development that is being referred to as Billionaires Row. I don't think it has a name yet. Have you heard about it?"

"Of course I know about it. The current name of the development is The Pinnacle. Lots start at one million dollars."

"Boy, that's big money," Hamilton said breathlessly.

"Do you know that your new client is a loan shark and is probably involved in a few other business ventures—like drugs, maybe?"

"When did you become afraid of dealing with a devil in a real estate transaction?" Hamilton hit low; Cole was taken off guard.

"What?" Cole came back indignantly.

"What nothing. I've heard about some of your deals; they are legendary in the agent gossip circles. You know what I mean, the 'you didn't hear it from me, but listen to this story' kind of dirt talk."

Cole held his tongue. The golden boy had never been tarnished by tough talk. His transgressions were nobody's business. Where was this underground gossip coming from, and how did this upstart hire come to know all of whatever he claimed to know about him? The knot in Cole's stomach returned.

Kit Hamilton didn't care one way or another. In fact, he did not hold Cole to the wall with something over him. Rather, he was ingratiating himself to the boss. The confession of transgression, alleged or otherwise, was Kit Hamilton's wink of sorts, letting Cole know that they had something in common, namely, the willingness to do whatever it took to make the deal. And that meant whatever.

Cole figured this out, but still he was uncomfortable with the reality. The golden boy, master of the real estate universe, was definitely a preferable reputation to that of a used car salesman sell-your-mother-for-a-deal snake type of real estate agent who would do anything for a closing.

Still, it was a reality check moment. Passing quickly, the moment morphed into full speed with the sales pitch, as it was time to put on the show for investors before they got a third bourbon mist on a Friday night before dinner. Roman had discussed the two-drink rule with Cole when planning the party.

"One is not enough. Three is too many," he had told Cole. "Two cocktails are the perfect relaxer, releasing inhibition and promoting action. And we want these guys to act and impress one another with that action. It's almost too simple and basic to believe." Roman pontificated with authority.

Cole listened and believed. Roman had twenty years' more experience at investment gathering than Cole. He brought all aspects of that experience to bear. The land deal with Cole and Dalt Fairchild would be a platform from which to really move up the ladder. For forty-five-plus-year-old Roman, this was the big chance, the opportunity he had been waiting for, having set his sights on it to cement financial success for the rest of his life. Nothing was going to get in his way.

Standing in front of Roman's glass-enclosed office, Cole tapped the glass with a spoon he had grabbed from one of the servers passing out hors d'oeuvres.

"Hello, gentlemen, and thank you for coming tonight. You are here to learn about a ground-floor opportunity to make an investment in a new trust established to finance and develop real estate land purchased for construction of custom homes on the California Riviera. The property is the most sought after and most excep-tional real estate in America today and, perhaps, the world. Most of you know me. I'm Cole Baldwin, cofounder of the Baldwin Investment Group, which we call BIG. Please welcome my partner Roman Yusapov."

For the next twenty minutes, Roman delivered an address that impressed. He spoke for exactly twenty minutes, another axiom discussed in the planning stages with Cole. Not too short, not too long, the perfect pitch. Get the clients' attention, get them excited, then start the bidding. Roman had followed his plan, and as he concluded his final statement, or rather what might be correctly termed an *ask*, he placed the burden of response upon his crowd, who were now anxious to be part of the initial offering.

"Who among us wants to start the investing at one hundred thousand dol-lars?" Roman called out like some high-energy auctioneer. Cole, still feeling knots in his stomach, gulped silently.

There was only a short silence, then not one, but three men shouted out "I'm in" in unison. Kit Hamilton, stepping in with pen and clipboard in hand, went into the cocktail crowd of some thirty or forty men and started taking names. As the excitement elevated, twenty-two men gave their names to Hamilton, a total of two-point-two million, in hundred-thousand-dollar increments, invested in about twenty minutes.

Roman took charge and asked if there were any others, reminding the rest that this was just the start. "Go home and ponder. Our door is open to you," he told them. "We're in this for the long haul, the big payday. This is a five-year plan with an estimated 100 percent return, or an annual yield of 20 percent on your one-hundred-thousand-dollar initial investment."

He then requested everyone to turn toward video screens set up in the office all around them, which were about to deliver a visual performance of the grand plan in its infancy.

When the video concluded, Roman had a staff of young men from the Bank of the Pacific on hand to distribute documents for review to all the initial inves-tors. The crowd was now on the third drink, and it was only just a bit after seven thirty that evening.

In the middle of the room, amid high-decibel cocktail chatter, the two men

Mr. Smith and Mr. Jones, who had come with Richard Hellman, called for silence and attention. It took them only two shout-outs before the eighth floor was still. Mr. Hellman introduced himself. To Cole's surprise, most in the room did not know who he was, this knowledge based on the fact that Cole was standing in a group of men across the floor and all the men around him asked one another who Hellman was.

"I wish to invest one million dollars," Richard Hellman said loudly, but without emotion or flourish. The room went wild. Raising their tumblers, ice clicking like applause, the guys shouted "Bravo!" and "Hooray!"—and "Fuck!" more than once.

As a result, another six men volunteered to put one hundred thousand dollars each in the fund. So, that was a total of twenty-eight hundred-thousand-dollar investors and one one-million-dollar investor, for a total take of three-point-eight million at one two-drink cocktail event on a Friday night in Newport Beach in 2005.

By eight o'clock, the eighth floor was empty save Cole, Roman, and Kit Hamilton. The three of them sat on the floor in the center of the space, eating leftover canapés and working on their third and fourth drinks. Hamilton was an uninvited third party, but he had brought in the million-dollar man, so neither Cole nor Roman objected. At least not vocally. Hamilton soon became really drunk, passing out on the carpet. The partners left him, managing to make their way into Roman's office.

Roman grabbed Cole in a big Russian bear hug.

"We did it, man. I knew we would," he said proudly.

"You did this, Roman. I wasn't sure, but I believed in you." Cole was sincere, but he also needed to ask Roman for a favor.

"Roman, I wasn't going to ask this tonight. It was not my plan, but with this success, maybe it's the right time," Cole spoke as both men took their places, Roman behind his desk, Cole in front. "I need to borrow two hundred thousand dollars from the fund." Cole was direct.

Roman was taken aback.

"It's personal. I need the money in the next thirty days, and I will pay it back in full with my next few escrow closings. I don't have the cash right now because I've put everything I have into The Summit land fund with you and Dalton Fairchild."

"I don't know, man. This is getting us off on the wrong foot," Roman advised. "We don't even have any of the funds yet, and maybe we won't have the money in thirty days."

"The contracts call for investment dollars deposited in ten business days by wire transfer," Cole reminded his partner.

Roman leaned back in his chair, took another swig, and answered, "Hell yes. Can I ask what for?"

"Yes, you can ask, but I don't want to say. Can we leave it at that?" Cole did not budge.

"I trust you, man. So, the answer is yes. But you must sign an agreement."

"I will do that."

"Settled. I'm meeting Sierra for dinner at the Ritz. Care to join?"

"I think I'd better skip that invite; besides, I've spent zero time with Kate and baby GiGi and the boys this past week. I'm going home."

"Give Kate my love and share the big news of our financial success. She is your biggest supporter. You're a lucky man; she really loves you. I'm not sure what she sees, but that woman is in love. Go home and treat her right."

"If you know so much about true love when you see it, then what the hell are you doing with a girl like Sierra?"

"What do you think I'm doing with a girl like Sierra?" he replied as if to say, *You dumb ass.*

"Didn't mean to be rude, Roman, especially after what you have done for me and for us. I will take your advice and go home to Kate, who I know does love me. I guess I meant to say that I wish it were the same for you and Sierra."

"Maybe someday, man, but I do know it will not be with Sierra. At least I know that much."

After another bear hug, the partners went off in their very different directions.

CHAPTER FIFTY-SIX

THE TRUTH SHALL SET YOU FREE

It took me six months to return to Avenue Foch West. Unable to face the Berg failure, and unable to get Jackie Berg's last words, "Do you sew?," out of my head, I had wallowed. At first, I told myself I'd take a month off to spend more time with the baby and the boys. It was my right, my duty, my privilege. The first month turned into two, and so forth. A half year can disappear in the snap of the finger.

Truthfully, despite a nagging feeling of disappointment given my own procrastination in approaching such a challenging goal, I loved the six months with my kids. In the adage "It was meant to be," I found solace. More significantly, I had shared milestone memories with my young brood. These could never be exchanged for a window in Bergdorf's Fifth Avenue. At least not now.

Another serious change in plans had transpired over these six months. I insisted that my best girlfriend and partner Heather enroll in law school. She had put off her admission to USC Law for a year to join me. It was time for her to pursue that goal. She put up a good fight, but I prevailed. Fair Child was not dead; the dream was on hold. While law school was a major commitment, Heather claimed she wanted to stay closely involved, even with a greatly reduced schedule. I assured her this would be the case. Honestly, relaunching the dream might now be a two-to-three-year plan. I would need a good lawyer as my partner.

While it had taken me six months to return to my dear Monsieur, we had talked often. On the afternoon of that dreadful Monday morning pitch at the Cal Mart, Monsieur had called to tell me that a talented designer did not have to be a master seamstress. In fact, he advised that often the two did not go together. "This was not the case a hundred years ago," Monsieur said. "But today, the young designers take a different path. You will be just fine."

Holding back my tears long enough to tell him how much I loved him, I asked for his patience. "I will be back. I have so much to learn and so much to prove to myself," I said, a message delivered many times over in recent years.

"I know that but be easy on yourself. The world is in the palm of your hand. You are so young, so blessed. If this career in fashion design is truly your life's goal, you will find a way."

As I pulled into the same open parking space, I had found on my first meeting with Monsieur and Madame, any trepidation I had felt about walking in eased. Planning to surprise my mentors, I thought better of it, instead calling to make an afternoon appointment. We had agreed on a four o'clock gathering, when business would be slow in the salon as the day ended.

"Oh, my darling girl, I missed you so much," Madame Honoré gushed as I entered the door, jingling the welcome bells. She rushed to me, kissing me on both cheeks, the showroom of the salon free of customers. A new salesgirl, one I did not know, was busy arranging clothes and placing discarded try-ons back on the racks. Madame introduced me. She was a young woman about my age, and she even looked a bit like me. That sinking feeling returned as I faced the reality that I had never worked as a shopgirl for longer than a nanosecond. What dues had I really paid on this journey? Jackie Berg was haunting me.

Monsieur came in from the back room, bounded across the sales floor, and landed on me with an embrace and a double-cheek French welcome. The three of us returned to the workroom, sitting on the timeworn settee and timeworn slipper chairs, and talked.

"Teach me how to sew. I want to be a master seamstress. I'm late. Should have started sewing as a child, but that was not my path," I blurted out.

My mentors stared at me.

"Are you certain?" Madame spoke first.

"I am," I replied matter-of-factly. "Jackie Berg was right. I have not paid dues. I did not attend a fashion institute or college. I have not worked as a shopgirl, except for here briefly. I have never taken any design courses, and I have never studied the history of design. My total immersion in the field is attendance at many fashion shows and shopping at both fine and discount stores. I no longer wish to be a dilettante. I will earn the right to call myself a designer. This may take ten years, perhaps more, but the right road begins now."

"Quite an impressive speech, my young designer-to-be," Monsieur said, looking at his wife.

"Will you teach me to sew?" I asked again.

Silence followed.

"Will you teach me, and will you hire me to sew when I am capable?" I asked for more.

Monsieur looked at Madame once again. They both turned to me and answered in unison, "Absolutely."

Over the moon, feeling confident, I pushed ahead. "Can we set a teaching schedule?"

"Will twice a week suffice?"

Monsieur followed with, "How about two-hour sessions at the end of the day?"

"Great. We shall figure out a schedule."

We did another hug, a three-way. There were never enough hugs with my French mentors. Indeed, they were family. Dashing out to make it home by five to be at dinner with the children, I was thankful that Bonnie was in full charge. She was my shortstop, my first baseman, and my outfielder. Yet another flash of irony hit me driving back to Lido Isle. As a mother of four with a full-time nanny, Bonnie, who also had had the luxury of a full-time nurse, Belinda, for almost six months, I realized that having the time to take classes was a privilege. Just signing up for a couple of hours of sewing lessons—what mother of four without a Bonnie or a Belinda could do such a thing? This was not lost on one American rich girl.

Pushing Limits

Bulldozers were finally moving the rich reddish-brown soil on top of the Newport plateau named The Summit, making way for the luxury housing development of Baldwin et Cie, LLC. The limited liability following the name came with a double meaning. It was a limited partnership according to IRS guidelines, and one of its principal partners had limited expertise. Cole knew it, but lack of expertise had never gotten in his way and certainly was never an impediment to his dream. Besides, with Roman's boldness and Dalt's considerable expertise, Cole was protected.

The same six months passed for the partners since the agreements had been inked. The process was long, complicated, and unexpectedly challenging. The additional funds put forth by my father were used in considerable part on architectural designers, urban planners, attorney fees, and public relations expenses, which were needed to quell growing public outcry over expanding development in the coastal canyons, which had been untouched by humankind since the time of creation.

In the end, the bulldozers came. One of the architects hired was charged with creating a design for an iconic entry portal. He followed a similar design from Cole's previous project at Ocean Palisades, only grander, a Roman-era Italianesque stone arch gracefully curved above the driveway, bordered on either side by twenty-foot-tall, polished stone obelisks. Mature cypress trees lined the curvilineal drive, which was also paved in stone, rising to the ocean-view land destined to become one hundred twenty multimillion-dollar residences, all designed to reflect the architectural heritage of the Amalfi Coast as translated in California.

Dalt calmed the anxiety of his ambitious son-in-law at each hiccup.

"Cole, this is a process that requires all our skill and patience," he reminded.

On the day the bulldozers began rolling, Cole called Dalt to share the news.

"Let me tell you, son, six months is remarkably fast for the scope of this project. I was expecting it to take a year." Dalt expressed pride in Cole.

The half year spent wrangling all obstacles had not gone to waste. Another three top architects had been selected to create potential estate designs. Lot lines were laid out carefully; the underground utilities were ready to move forward; and hardscape and softscape designs had been finalized. The Summit was a reality.

A more important decision had been made during the development months. Initially, Cole and Roman wanted to control everything: designing, building, and selling the homes. Dalt had convinced them to be just developers, not builders, and sell the lots to others. Word was out that 120 of the finest view estate lots would be on the market shortly. Top builders were jockeying for the best of the best. In the shadows, Roman continued planning to use the BIG Fund to also build their own homes—a betrayal of the agreement with Dalt at the onset. Roman's plan was to wait until the right time to move forward and then get Dalt on board.

At the same time, Cole's reputation as a local celebrity continued to rise. The TV show remained a topic of considerable gossip and interest. Producer Rocco had expanded Cole's reach, featuring properties owned by movie and TV stars in LA, along with showing off the inner world of the Newport rich. Cole had become a better-looking latter-day Robin Leach, host of the 1980s' *Lifestyles of the Rich and Famous*. Cole basked in the complimentary attention, but he was working 24/7, casting too wide a net. It was taking a toll on me and our family.

At a rare evening at home sharing dinner with me, Cole did his best to renew the spark. Resigned to facing the reality that my fashion career was going to be a long and dedicated process; I knew my situation was similar to Cole's and his real estate development. Dalt had also counseled me, following the wake-up call after the Berg experience displaying my fledgling line. With the serious reality check, I no longer dreamt of fashion magazine covers and Paris runway shows. Instead, I was paying dues. It felt good.

The dues paying was sincere but part time. With four children to raise, I knew it would certainly be a full-time job. Even being blessed to have nanny Bonnie, I was a serious mom, fully involved and totally available. The Baldwin brood were unquestionably my priority. As expected, I had become extremely emotionally close to infant GiGi. My marriage to Cole was strong and intact but had changed radically. I was in love, but our intimacy was now redefined. Making love was sporadic, often awkward. Cole was often conflicted, rushing, worrying, juggling. With all his success, I excused his behavior. Having grown up with a very successful and driven father and with a mother who also dealt with the conditions that came along with a man on the rise in the business and financial world, I knew that sacrifices were made. Exceptions were understood, and absence was tolerated.

Cole arrived late, having missed five o'clock dinner with his children. He had made a serious effort but got trapped in the office by Kit Hamilton, who needed help with a real estate deal about to implode. In the year since joining Baldwin et Cie, Kit had closed major business, even outpacing Cole at times as Cole concentrated on the development projects, the TV show, the investment fund, and God knows what else.

Confiding that he remained uneasy around Kit, Cole felt that his suspicions were proving found. Questioning Kit's hidden motivations, Cole could not grasp the meaning or message. Roman repeatedly warned him, saying he smelled a rat. Yet, as long as the dollars flowed into the business, including major investment funds initially brought in by Kit from Richard Hellman, the principal stockholder, with now more than ten million in cash in their account, neither Roman nor Cole said a word about Kit. At least not to his face.

The big crisis on this occasion was a failure to close a Hellman deal, the purchase of a large storefront commercial building on Pacific Coast Highway in Corona del Mar just south of Newport. The funds coming in from an offshore account could not be traced and verified as noncontraband, non-drug-related, and nonterrorist-connected. Richard Hellman was screaming bloody murder, dropping F-bombs like rain. Kit had come to Cole to make things right. Two hours on the phone with some half dozen bankers, and Cole convinced the team on the method to receive the funds and close the deal. The nine-million-dollar deal would close.

"How did you do it?" Kit asked, coming back into Cole's office after having been asked to wait outside while Cole did his final bidding.

Cole hesitated. He did not want to explain, but his ego got the better of him.

"They weren't going to do it," Cole said to Kit.

"What changed?" he came back.

"I guaranteed that the funds are legitimate and offered to back up the guarantee by replacing the money with funds from our trust fund," he shared with his protégé, who had become, in Cole's mind, a rival.

"You did that for me?" Kit asked, surprised.

"I did that for the team," Cole shot back.

"What if—"? Kit followed.

"What if nothing. Money is money. Richard Hellman's funds are real. We're not asking more questions. They took the arrangement. Keep quiet, keep your head down, and this will pass." This from the almost thirty-year-old self-proclaimed master of the Newport real estate universe.

The children had finished dinner and were gone from the table, now upstairs with nanny Bonnie, winding down the day before bath and bed. Cole ran up the grand helical staircase to the second floor, where he found his offspring happily looking at books and playing with toys on the carpeted floor of a playroom adjacent to their bedrooms.

He greeted Bonnie with a warm, over-the-top Cole salutation. Bonnie smiled, knowing well in her superpractical midwestern brain that his affection was not 100 percent the real deal. Then Cole went to embrace his babies. Getting down on the floor, he cuddled up next to each one. They cooed some, and giggled as he tickled him, but they seemed detached from the absentee man of the house, their father.

Hearing all the happy sounds, I entered the playroom, finding my husband on the floor with his son Buddy, who was pulling on his tie as if it were a dog leash. Cole obliged, barking on all fours as Buddy led him around, his twin brothers gleeful and baby GiGi bouncing in her infant seat, waving her little hands at the big funny doggy. For me, this was another small, insignificant moment of incomparable happiness. Cole's usual distraction vanished for these few moments. Perfection of the moment, I called these tiny slices of life. I cherished them. I wanted more but took what came.

Buddy gave his dog a major tug on the leash, and Cole landed flat on the carpet. Standing beside him, he turned his head.

"Kate, I have a crazy idea. Are you game?"

"I suppose you'd like me to play doggie with you?"

"Now that's a wonderful plan, but maybe later."

"So, what is the idea?"

"Remember when we took drives together up to the first land development before all the kids came?"

"That comes with wonderful and not so wonderful memories."

"Fair enough. But how about trying to recapture just the good part, the excitement of the project, the realization of a dream?"

"Yes, I'd like that."

"Would it be okay to put the kids to bed late tonight?"

"I'm not following."

"I want you to see the progress at The Summit. The dozers are finally breaking ground. I want to take you, all the kids, and Bonnie too up the hill to watch the sunset and see our future."

Cole's plan caught me off guard. It would upset our bedtime routine, which every parent knows can spell disaster, but I went for it completely.

"I love it. Let's do it," I said, grabbing my husband by the arm to help him up off the floor.

"Bonnie, are you game?" I asked.

"Give me fifteen minutes. I'll skip the baths and put them all in their jammies, and we'll be ready with bottles and snacks if needed. It will be a twilight road trip for the Baldwins."

Cole went to get my Tahoe as I joined Bonnie in the preparations. Nancy and Dalt had gifted us a Chevy Tahoe, with three rows of seats, following the birth of GiGi. Cole wanted me to get either a BMW or Mercedes wagon, but I opted for big, bold, and indestructible. I also chose white subconsciously, I think, because every big mommy car in Newport seemed to be black. We had four semipermanent car seats professionally installed in the middle row of the Tahoe for the menagerie.

Sergeant Bonnie, General Bonnie, deserving of major promotion in rank, got all in order in the prescribed fifteen minutes. The children were lined up in their seats. Bonnie got in the back; I jumped in the front; and we left Lido Isle at dusk, on our way to Oz, my magic moment of perfection extended.

Passing through the impressive stone arch entryway at The Summit, I glanced back to find the four Baldwin heirs fast asleep.

"Cole, your babies have lost interest in their land legacy. We need to speak softly," I told him, placing my hand on his arm across the center console of the Tahoe.

Driving on a packed dirt road off the main stone driveway, the car was basically smooth, except for a few significant bumps. The kids slept through them all as we reached the top of the hill.

Falling into the western horizon, the always spectacular Newport sun faded, illuminating so many silver glass panels reflecting off the homes and office towers to the west. The flashing light show transfixed both Cole and me, with Bonnie catching it all as well from the back window of the Tahoe.

"So, this is the big dream?" I asked quietly but sincerely.

"It is, my wonderful bride and mother of our special passengers." Cole could be very romantic.

"My father believes in what you are doing, so I know it must be right."

"Your father is amazing. Without him, this would not be happening."

"Have you been up here with him?"

"Several times when we made the deal, but not since groundbreaking. You are the first."

"That feels special, Cole. I appreciate that."

"You deserve it. You put up with a lot."

I did not respond.

Cole continued to point out everything that was going to happen, including showing me the new adjacent development, The Pinnacle, expected to be the most exclusive residential property on the West Coast. The Pinnacle occupied the ridge just south of The Summit. I noticed a very long and narrow piece of land on the southwestern edge of the property, with a green construction fence surrounding the parcel. Because of its shape, I just had to inquire.

"Cole, what is that land down there surrounded by a fence? It is so skinny but also so long. Looks like multiple acres. What could it possibly be used for?"

Cole responded quickly: "Every piece of land up here that is not being designated a natural habitat has a purpose. I'm sure that land will have some sort of house on it too."

"A very long and thin one, I suspect," I followed up, changing the subject, as it really didn't matter to me. Just my curious eye. Cole stared at me intently, turned the car around, and headed back down the dirt road. Driving through the arch, he began making his way back to Baldwin world headquarters on Lido Isle. We talked all about The Summit development, more than we ever had before. Cole explained that my father had influenced him and Roman not to be builders, just land developers selling the lots to other builders. This came as good news to me. It sounded sensible, less stress-inducing. Money would be made on the land. The builders would make their money on the product. Building the first project at Ocean Palisades really had done Cole in, and me as well. This was progress.

CHAPTER FIFTY-SEVEN

GROWING ON TREES

Another six months passed as the dozers carved out the lots and set the infrastructure in place at The Summit. The dirt roads were now lovely stone-clad drives lined with sidewalks and old-world streetlamps. Olive and Italian cypress trees, mature and manicured, dotted the hillside landscape. Cole and I, with and without our entourage, savored several outings to the site since that first trip. They were good times, but not as special as the first, as lately Cole had become more distracted than ever.

By the winter of 2007, cash was being distributed by banks like paper napkins at a carnival hot dog booth. Dalt warned that the free-for-all was an aberration, and that the no-collateral real estate lending would lead to a serious market correction eventually. My father quoted nineteenth-century financier Bernard Baruch: "The tree does not grow to the sky," cautioning Cole and me as well. I listened to my father. Cole did not heed the warning. His office kept making deals because the tree had not only grown to the sky but also had gone through the clouds and was nearing heaven. Money was literally free. Zero-down real estate was the norm.

Cole shared with me, on occasion, rare but vocal occasions, his frustration with agent Kit Hamilton. As 2007 dawned, Kit was coming close to equaling Cole's million-dollar received commission sales record. Professional competitive friction and a dose of the green monster at play. I sensed there was more, but Cole was not forthcoming.

I did manage to secure some of the insiders' office politics intrigue, seducing Cole's partner Roman to divulge information at one of the many cocktail parties and dinners we were attending. Being the good wife, I filled the duty as supportive armpiece and charmer as often as possible and on demand. This event, I had been summoned. The president of the Bank of the Pacific was hosting a Thursday night invitation-only black-tie dinner for twenty of the top under-forty-year-old entrepreneurs and their spouses, partners, or dates. A celebrity chef had been flown in from New York's Le Circ to create "the dinner of the decade." For this night of power networking among the young and rich, the dinner unfolded at a newly constructed mansion on the Newport coast, build by the Newport Land Trust to be used as a model, erected on The Pinnacle, perched across the ridge from Cole's The Summit.

Admitting my excitement to sample the cuisine prepared by the New York chef, I confessed that attending this night event held some promise. Cole knew that the big smiles and air-kissing at such gatherings had lost its appeal to me four kids and four years earlier. Just the same, whenever I did escort my handsome star mate, I was always welcomed with great sincerity and generosity. Well, I did generally look better than most of the women, which sounds bitchy and rather egotistical. Okay, I did look better—that's the bottom line.

Directed by a maître d' attired in a formal English waistcoat to a baronial table centered on a white Carrera-marble-floored dining hall, I was impressed by the spectacular ocean view through floor-to-ceiling open doors lining the south wall. A soft breeze at sunset made the pure white silk sheers sway. They were pushed to the side of each panel of all the doors, fastened to the walls by bouquets of white gardenias. The floral effect was duplicated by low crystal bowls placed down the center of the dining table, intersected by three-armed silver candelabras with twelve-inch white toppers ablaze.

My jaded attitude vanished as I took in this sensuous backdrop. The scent of the gardenias and a faint spray of Pacific Ocean aroma was totally intoxicating. Prior to taking our places at the table, Cole and I were offered champagne. Another server delivered bites of Petrossian caviar on small toast points garnished with crème fraîche and a touch of onion. Cole noticed my pleasure.

"See how much fun we would have together if you came out more often?" he said softly as we walked through a set of tall doors and out onto a terrace with a full ocean view.

"This has the feel of an ocean liner deck," I said. Cole temporarily halted my speech, placing his caviar at my lips. Accepting, I savored the exceptional flavor, hesitating, not wanting to destroy a second of the sensation. "What a wonderful treat," I gushed, leaning in to kiss Cole, delivering just a brush across the lips.

The romantic mood ended abruptly. I saw my husband tense up, his smiling handsome self stiffening as I turned to see his partner Roman coming our way with his date, Sierra. I hadn't forgotten my former experience with Sierra in the tacky, slinky low-cut black spaghetti-strap dress clearly worn too many times and slept in more than once or twice. Cole was not happy. I expected some sort of drama to follow this young woman. Turning back to Cole before their pending arrival at our balcony perch, I said, "Oh boy, here comes Sierra. Didn't you tell me Roman was cooling off on her? Sure doesn't look that way." The two came closer, arm in arm, Sierra's head leaning slightly toward Roman's shoulder.

"He's been seeing her more. I didn't tell you because I know how you feel."

"It's not just my feelings that matter. I think she's dangerous. Her drug habit is obvious. You and Roman are in a business of trust with clients. Drugs and trust are not good partners. If Roman goes down, we go down."

"That will never happen," Cole responded emphatically just as they arrived, finding us looking out over a balustrade at the Pacific. Sierra moved in to hug me. I fumbled with my champagne flute, distracting her phony affection. In return, I delivered my own brand of phony affection with a big smiling "hello" and "great to see you again." She believed me. Cole took Roman aside, leaving us girls to chitchat. I sent Cole a secret look meaning *Thanks a bunch.* He stepped aside with his partner.

"Roman, you didn't mention that you were bringing Sierra here tonight." Cole was serious.

"You didn't ask, partner."

"Did you tell her to behave?"

"Do you tell Kate to behave?" he countered.

"That's different."

"Really? How so?"

"Kate is not on drugs. Kate is my wife. Kate has four kids. Kate comes from a nice family. Kate—"

"Yeah, yeah, I get it." Roman stopped the discussion.

"Sierra just better not repeat the performance she gave a year ago with Walter Benheim."

"Look, I don't control Sierra. It will be fine."

Cole dropped the subject, returning to me.

Having watched the interchange out of the corner of my eye, I knew what was being discussed without hearing a word. Sierra continued blabbing to me about all the rich people coming to dinner. "So many important men, all movers and shakers," she gushed.

"Oh yes, lots of those," I told her. "Lots of those."

The waistcoated maître d' began circling the terrace, ringing a little dinner bell, which meant it was time to sit for the program. Of course, nobody paid much attention. Twenty young rich men and their plus-ones were above taking such mundane instructions. They would sit when they felt like it. Another twenty or so minutes would pass. The bell ringing was getting louder with each pass.

Meanwhile, Sierra left her plus-one to go talk with Cole, also leaving me, our little talk done. She began working the room, as they say. Fearless, the skinny chick in the little black dress inserted herself in every conversation with every person she approached, mostly men talking to men. She avoided couples. From where I stood watching, many of the guys seemed to know her. Maybe they were just being strutting vessels of masculinity cozying up to the female species. It was all a dance anyway. Life was a dance. Life was a sexual dance. I believed that. My young life had been determined by hormones. That reality I accepted. And at twenty-five, I was facing that reality head-on. My attraction to Cole was ever present, overshadowing all negatives, all questions, all doubts. The physical attraction fueled and joined with the mental and emotional attraction. I knew that if I were to lose the sexual desire to be with Cole, the emotional love connection would fade as well.

Seeing Sierra at work made my mind race into personal territory I'd explored on many, too many, occasions.

I was still standing at the stone balustrade at the edge of the terrace, watching all the people mingle and keeping an eye on the mingling Sierra. Cole rejoined me as Roman went looking for his date. Peering over the ridge, focusing on the narrow strip of land that I had asked Cole about some weeks before on our last visit to The Summit, I noticed that construction appeared to be under way.

"Cole, remember I asked you if you knew anything about that long and narrow strip of land at the edge of the hill below? Last time I mentioned it to you, there was nothing much going on there except a construction fence around the property. Now it looks like there is grading going on."

"Getting ready to build, I would say," Cole responded.

"I don't know why I am so curious; it is just such an unusual parcel. The view from there must be jaw-dropping. I'll bet someone is creating their dream home. Maybe you could find out and do a segment on the TV show?" I inquired.

"Great idea," Cole answered.

The maître d' passed by once again, giving up on the tinkling bell, having replaced it with a spoon pounding on an empty glass goblet. The rich, locally famous, and self-involved were ready to sit at the twenty-foot-long tables arranged together in one extended rectangle, serving as seating for forty guests and the two hosts of the evening.

Taking Cole by one hand, I had my champagne flute in the other as we were among the first to take our places. Roman came soon after, seated next to us with Sierra in boy–girl fashion. Cole had changed the seating cards before Roman arrived, placing Roman next to him and Sierra on his right. So much for formal boy–girl seating.

As Roman took his new position next to Cole, I glanced across the table, catching Sierra up close and very personal with a handsome blond man in a gray suit, white shirt, and dark gray tie. She leaned in between his plus-one, a Newport Beach blue-eyed blonde with pale pink lipstick, her pale pink décolletage appropriately displayed. Not too little, not too much, the perfect formula. I hadn't mastered that act, so I avoided the temptation to try. Reserving the right to do so remained on my palette of future options.

The momentary focus on the good-looking blonde woman and her handsome blond date with the elegant gray suit required much more serious observation. Seeing Sierra slip one of her small white packets into the breast pocket of the gray suit the gentleman was wearing, placing it directly behind his perfectly folded white handkerchief, I elbowed Cole.

"She's at it, Cole," I whispered in a strong hush.

"What?" he asked, not paying attention to me.

The hosts of the evening began introductions. Behind them at the head of the table a large screen was erected, and on the screen there was Cole, introducing his latest episode of *Living the Dream*. Applause rang out at the table. Cole stood to take in the adulation. Failing to get my husband's attention at this crucial moment, I looked back at Sierra from across the table. Standing behind the man in the gray suit, applauding Cole vigorously, she even blew him an air-kiss from across the table.

The video of Cole on *Living the Dream* ended. The hosts introduced him as the applause faded. He was standing at the table, beaming in his glory, and in his element. I was proud of him, discreetly patting his behind. As Cole poured on the Baldwin charm, the top twenty under-forty moguls took in every word. Explaining the launch of The Summit development, Cole moved into the pitch for investment dollars in the BIG Fund, telling the table that the BIG Fund was a real estate investment trust with plans to purchase major tracts of undeveloped land in both coastal and inland Southern California.

That always made me nervous. Dalt's cautionary words rang loudly in my brain. My father did not want us forming such a fund, but Cole insisted, going along with Roman. Not sharing this with my father, I was feeling guilty, even disloyal. Worse yet, I was feeling like a sneak, having gone behind Dalt's back. I rationalized my guilt by figuring it was our decision, even though it was Cole's decision, and I was standing by him.

Cole fielded questions from the crowd about the BIG Fund. The handsome blond guy with the special packet in his pocket raised a hand.

"Cole, will this fund be buying open land out in the Moreno Valley area? I hear it could be booming with warehouse and industrial development."

Cole nodded his head and replied, "Definitely, yes. We are looking at two large tracts of land, both larger than five hundred acres."

The blond man said he would call next week to come in and discuss an investment. Cole had never mentioned anything about two five-hundred-acre parcels in the Moreno Valley, or any valley.

The answer about the five hundred acres generated more questions. Looking over at Roman, I saw that he was totally surprised. Then again, he was the mentor, the teacher, and Cole was just following his lead.

Sierra made her way back over to Roman, leaving her blond client with his packet and his blonde plus-one. As she crossed the room, my eyes followed, interrupted by a presumably late entry to the party. Another well-dressed man came in flanked by two men who looked like Secret Service agents. Moving alongside the threesome was Cole's agent Kit Hamilton, whom I had met. The others were unfamiliar. The one man, seemingly in charge, sucked the air out of the room.

Questions to Cole on the BIG Fund ceased. My husband paused, laying eyes on the entourage.

"For those who have not had the pleasure, allow me to introduce Mr. Richard Hellman. He is the principal investor in the BIG Fund, which we are speaking about. With him is our top-selling Baldwin agent Mr. Kit Hamilton." Cole did not introduce Mr. Smith and Mr. Jones. Whispers flew across the table. "Gentlemen, please come in and take your seats at the center of the table."

While Richard Hellman and Kit took the two empty seats at the center of the table, Smith and Jones stepped back and stood erect and at the ready against the back wall behind Hellman. I turned to Roman.

"Okay, I need to be filled in," I told Roman in a hushed but serious voice. "Who are these guys? How do you spell *mafia*?" I continued.

"Kate, you've seen *The Godfather* too many times. Hellman is not mafia."

"Okay, then what is he?"

"He's a very successful businessman in the finance business. I'm sure you've seen commercials on TV for his loan company QuickBucks4You, the no-collateral lender. He advertises constantly."

"Sure, many people are in need of a quick buck, but can they repay it, or will they get a broken leg?" I offered with a chuckle, trying to be cute and attempting to minimize my personal worry.

"He doesn't break legs for nonpayment; he just charges serious interest rates to compensate for the losses from those who do not pay," Roman said.

"How did he get involved with you and Cole?"

"Kit Hamilton sold him a big house, which brought in a huge commission for the office, and later Hellman wanted to invest in the BIG Fund."

"Is he really the biggest investor?"

"He is."

"How big?"

"Ten million big."

"Oh my gosh."

"Not to worry."

"Are you guys looking at five-hundred-acre plots of land in Moreno Valley?"

"First I've heard of that tonight."

"I think I'm worried."

"Not to worry," Roman repeated.

"Can I ask another question?"

"Sure. Anything."

"Are you paying interest to investors? How much? How often? What is the plan?"

"Let me see, that's four questions, I think." Roman was now being coy.

"Seriously, Roman, what is the plan?" I pushed him as Sierra was doing her best to distract him with a soft message, stroking the back of his neck and shoulders.

"Kate, yes, we have a plan, and it does involve interest and a sizable return on investment for our clients. Everything is legal, moral, and disclosed. Your husband is going to become a wealthy man like your father. You'll see." Those were Roman's final words on the subject.

My attention shifted back to Cole. The Hellman introduction had put an end to his being in the spotlight. Dinner was being served. Cole departed the front of the table, center stage position, and walked back toward me, circling past Richard Hellman and Kit Hamilton on the opposite side. As he stopped to personally greet his investor and his fellow agent, I watched them exchange customary greetings. As Cole began to walk away, coming back toward me, Kit rose from his seat, grabbed Cole, placing one arm around his neck, and said something to him in one ear. Cole pulled back and continued.

"What was that all about with Kit?" I asked as Cole took his seat beside me. The staff were serving our first course, an individual crystal bowl with a large mound of crushed ice adorned with chilled shrimp in the center.

The delicious dish distracted me from my inquiry into the Kit moment, which was meant to be followed by my inquiry into business dealings with Richard Hellman. The table chatter grew louder, and Cole dismissed my queries. I'm sure he knew what was on my mind. All he said was that the Kit exchange was nothing. "He told me again for the hundredth time how much he appreciated me," Cole said. "I think if I hear that one more time, I might lean over and smack him."

"Cole, just let him go. Tell him to go to another office if he gets on your nerves that much."

"I probably should. But now with Hellman as his big client and our big investor, I need to control my personal suspicions."

"You know my motto: listen to your gut. Follow your instincts on work-related matters. Remember what Dalt says about work relationships. If they seem bad, they will most likely get worse. End a bad situation immediately and move forward."

"Do you know how lucky you are to have grown up with a dad like that?"

"Cole, you grew up with a great dad too."

"Yes, I did. But a different kind of great."

"Think about making a change, will you?" I asked sincerely. "I think you'd be so much less stressed. I worry about you."

Before we could settle down and dive into the seafood cocktail, Cole asked me to leave.

"Let's get out of here," he said, rising from the table, pulling back my chair, and putting out his hand to assist my departure.

"Did I upset you?" I followed.

"Not even close," Cole answered.

Driving down Newport Coast Drive, Cole advised that he needed to make a stop in Newport Center on the way home.

"Did you forget something at the office?"

"Not going to the office" were his only words.

I said nothing. Several minutes later we drove up the slight incline of the driveway in front the Four Seasons Hotel, Newport, and pulled up to the valet.

Cole's door was opened at once, and the valet greeted him by name. This was one of Cole's regular lunch meeting hotels.

"Here for dinner, Mr. Baldwin?" the valet inquired.

"No, Woody. We're overnight guests," Cole told him.

Another man opened my door and I got out, staring at Cole over the top of the car.

"Is there luggage, sir?" James asked.

"No luggage," Cole replied, coming around and taking my hand.

"Don't say a word. I planned this. Bonnie is in on the plan. All is safe at home. We're going to have a romantic refresher in the Honeymoon Suite."

I said nothing, as requested.

Perhaps I was about to have one of those amazing life moments that I longed for on a regular basis and accepted whenever they happened to come along.

A Very Sweet Night in the Suite

"Is this really the so-called Honeymoon Suite?" I asked Cole as we entered a penthouse-level hotel room at the Four Seasons, Newport.

"Well, not really. They don't have a Honeymoon Suite, but I did ask. Apparently, that's too old-fashioned. They do have a Presidential Suite, and this is it. I just renamed it for this one night. But don't worry, I didn't have red rose petals placed on the bed in the shape of a heart."

"That's too bad. I would have loved that, corny or not."

"I thought you were more of a modern woman," Cole shot back.

"When I want to be," I said, returning the shot.

"How about now? Are you a modern woman or a traditional one?" Cole pressed on.

"Boy, that is a loaded question out of the blue."

"I guess so, but I'd like an answer."

"If you insist, then tonight I'd like to be a traditional wife whom you slowly undress then take in your strong masculine arms and lay gently on the bed. With perfect timing, while our bodies are so close that there is not even air between us,

I want to make love to you for hours, only pausing to breathe, climaxing over and over until we are spent, falling asleep naked and face-to-face as the sun begins to pierce the opening in the hotel drapes."

Cole was undressed before I had finished my invitation. His white jockey shorts remained at his ankles as he fumbled to step out of them. I stood beside the bed, still dressed for dinner, as my gorgeous naked man approached. Following my direction, Cole gently removed my blazer and began unbuttoning my blouse. Funny, he began at the waist button and worked his way up to the breasts. As he was kissing my stomach with each opened button, I felt that magic love shiver and began to respond to his touch. Grabbing his head at the neck with both hands, I drew Cole toward me, and we kissed endlessly.

"I love you so much, Kate," he said as our lovemaking continued.

"I tried not to fall in love with you, Cole, but I think I loved you the first day we met, when you came to my aid when the guy dented my car in the parking lot in front of Avenue Foch West."

"It was love at first sight for me. I had never seen a more beautiful girl."

"So much has happened since we met, so much in such a short amount of time, not to mention four kids," I said, becoming very sentimental.

"Four amazing kids, just like their mom."

"Cole, they're just like their dad too, and they need their dad."

"I'm trying, Kate, but you know I'm on a fast track and I'm feeling like I matter, which was never the case for me growing up."

"I know, but maybe we could have more nights like this, and you would still feel successful," I joked.

"If we had more nights like this, we'd have five, six, seven kids."

"At a moment like this, I'm inclined to say wonderful."

"What about at a later moment?" Cole was cute.

"At a later moment, well, four wonderful children is perfect."

Changing his tone, becoming more serious, Cole continued, "I arranged this tonight because I know I have not been a perfect husband, and I wanted you to know that I am sorry."

"It's okay, Cole. I don't expect perfect."

"You deserve perfect."

"We both know there is no such thing."

"Yes, I get it. But I've made some terrible mistakes. I will never forgive myself for my drunken attack on you the night in Hawaii when you introduced me to your grandmother."

"Neither of us can forget that night. I hated you, but I loved you. We made Buddy that night, unplanned, even unwanted then, but today he is our son, our firstborn, our love child."

"Will you ever forgive me?"

"You ask me that again five years later? You asked me then, and I told you it was forgiven and past. Is something else wrong?"

"I just feel that I'm losing you. We're not as close. You give me a hard time over business, and I feel that I cannot please you. We're not on the same page. Since you put your fashion career dream on hold and became a full-time mom, the kids are your full-time focus."

"Cole, it's called life. Kids come first in a marriage. The romance takes on a new role. I believe we just proved that here and now. We're not on different pages. We are a family. We take care of each other. We come first in our lives always, in times good, bad, and otherwise. I love you. I will be your partner supporting you, proud of you always. Guess what? We are just growing up like adults. By the way, you will be turning thirty next year."

"Oh God, not thirty. My life is half over," Cole shouted.

"I sure hope not, my love. We've got kids to put through college."

Cole rose from our latter-day honeymoon bed.

"You know, we never had a honeymoon. Does this count?"

"The best honeymoon ever," I said. Cole went into the bath to fetch a pair of white terry robes, then returned to the bed.

"I know you requested lovemaking nonstop until the sun breaks through the drapes, but would you consider a halftime break?"

"Dinner. We didn't stay for dinner at the party. Let's do room service."

"Fantastic plan. It's midnight, so we'll call it the midnight buffet!" I joked.

"What's that?" Cole asked.

"One day we'll take a cruise vacation and I'll introduce you to the midnight buffet," I explained.

"Can't wait. Will we be old people on the cruise?"

"No way. We're going much sooner than that. How about for your thirtieth?" I said.

"Wow. That's neat. I guess it depends on business. Can we afford such a vacation?" Cole asked sincerely.

"Cole, we can afford it. And you know what, I don't care if you're the most successful real estate developer in history or if your business goes under. If we love each other, remain a family, and stay true to each other, I can't think of anything that could destroy us. Nothing, absolutely nothing, in business matters."

CHAPTER FIFTY-EIGHT

AN EXPANDING EMPIRE

With the unbridled money flow in 2007, Cole and Roman took full advantage, holding the Newport Men's BIG Fund Luncheon, inviting committed investors to join prospective ones for a private monthly gathering in the executive dining room at the Harbor Club. They were getting it started late in the year, with the first gathering set for the first Friday in April. With only word of mouth, the confab was sold out with a waiting list. The minimum investment buy-in was set at one hundred thousand dollars.

The BIG luncheon, over a period of ensuing months, became more of a men's Friday afternoon drinking club. All members of this fraternity of investors had money to burn. Stock market excess blended so nicely with family trusts. Month after month, new money came in. And the luncheons always began with a report from Cole and Roman on acquisitions.

Funny thing, the fantasy five-hundred-acre land tracts in the inland Moreno Valley had come to fruition. The fund owned two such parcels of undeveloped dirt. In addition, they were negotiating on major open land in the community of Adelanto, a small dusty desert town on the way to Vegas or the mountain resort of Mammoth. Adelanto's major industry was a federal prison in the middle of nowhere. Investor Richard Hellman was steering Cole and Roman to buy. Land was cheap, available, and ideal for warehouse properties. Under the radar, these warehouses were also ideal indoor marijuana growing operations. My husband had figured this out quickly, sharing the information with me.

"Cole, you know how much I value openness and honesty. But I wish you had kept that a secret. What am I supposed to do now except worry?"

The response I had expected from Cole followed: "Baby, we're just buying the land and the warehouse, not running the business or renting the warehouse." That did not make me feel better, especially when Cole added, "Don't forget, the Kennedy family fortune is based on bootlegged liquor."

"Oh well, I guess that makes it all just fine," I said, grabbing Cole and kissing him. "Cole, you don't look good in orange, and I do not want to raise four children with prison visitation," I warned him.

"How do you feel about conjugal visits? I hear they have rubber covers on the mattresses." Cole was good at replacing the serious with the sublime. I laughed. I ughed. I gave in and shut up.

By late 2007 the BIG Fund had reached eighty million dollars in investments.

At the same time on the Newport coast, the infrastructure was complete at The Summit; power, water, streets, and landscaping had all been finished, all meticulously designed and sparkling new. Individual lots were on the market to contractor/developers, with about twenty in escrow on opening day.

Being the conservative and worrying wife, I did not let up on Cole regarding the business expansion. The proverbial "little birdy in my ear," no doubt placed there by Dalt, repeatedly told me to ask questions, advising me not to close my eyes and pretend everything was just fine. I was still worried about Roman's girlfriend Sierra, although we had not had social contact with either Roman or Sierra for weeks. Sierra's drug connection, along with the marijuana warehouse investment, weighed on me.

Over dinner, after putting the kids to bed on one of those special evenings with Daddy at home, I asked Cole another question about something related to the BIG Fund that worried me.

"You explained that the investors have put their money in the BIG Fund with the contractual promise of a 20 percent return annually, payable in a final payout of a 100 percent profit after five years, on top of the return of initial investment dollars. What assurance do you have that the promise will be fulfilled? What if the market changes? This seems overly ambitious and overly generous." I was serious. Cole was in a relaxed mood, feeling good, and was clearly more interested in sex than justifying return-on-investment dollars.

After laying this heavy question on him, I regretted my inquiry. Was I nuts? What wife ruins her husband's lovemaking mood with a business question? Mother Nancy would be ashamed. Yes, she would be the first to ask a tough business question, but never just before lovemaking. I guess I was becoming my father.

We managed to get past my roadblock, ending up in bed together for a night of love. Over an early breakfast, I was unable to let it go, asking more questions.

"Cole, can I ask how you and Roman get paid from the BIG Fund? And where is all of this money?" Never had I been so direct.

"Are you worried about income?" Cole was surprised by my directness over money. He knew it wasn't my style.

"Clearly not so," I replied, giving it back to him.

"Per contract, Roman and I will have a guaranteed minimum annual management fee of 3 percent divided between us. The fee can be larger depending on the success of the BIG Fund investments." Cole was forthcoming.

I refilled Cole's coffee, giving him a hug, and thanking him for sharing.

"How are the funds invested?" I continued.

"I'm glad you are asking," he said. "You should know. We need to share more," he said affectionately. "Roman is in charge of investing. He is the expert, but he does everything with me informed. You know I have no financial market experience. I'm the sales guy."

Cole put his hands on top of mine on the table. It was almost six o'clock in the morning. We had managed an early rising after making love, starting the new day before the children awoke and the noise of the day ensued.

"Basically, the BIG Fund is divided into three parts: cash, stocks and mutual funds, and land purchase dollars. All of it is managed by Roman and me, but everything is held in a portfolio at Lehman Brothers in New York, overseen by Roman's close friend from his childhood growing up in Saint Petersburg. So that's the deal, my love. You have the whole enchilada," Cole said, looking me in the eyes. "Last night was the best sex ever," he finished, changing the subject.

"Not bad," I replied. "Want to try again to see if we can improve?"

My offer was followed by the arrival of the Baldwin brood and General Bonnie. "How about a raincheck?" Cole asked, rising to dress and head for the office. As he left the breakfast table, he called out, "What does your day hold, Kate?"

This was my day to spend time with Monsieur Lawrence, which I thought Cole knew. I had been religious about the two-day-per-week tutoring scheduling for nearly a year. Sewing was now mastered, maybe not professionally, but mastered. Monsieur had me making patterns and sewing samples. Able to describe in detail various stitch techniques, I understood sizing, almost like learning anatomy. Best of all, I used to simply know what I liked, what I thought was quality fabric and expert tailoring, but now I knew the difference and why there was a difference. I could spot sloppy workmanship. Monsieur had delivered a graduate course in fabric as well as sewing.

Everyone thinks they know that every fabric from Italy and France is superior. My mentor taught me to recognize why they may be superior and, more importantly, why they are not always superior. On this day, my plan was to begin to fabricate a design of my own creation and make an elegant dress for a family party that my parents were planning to throw in honor of GiGi's first birthday and Cole's thirtieth. A fall dinner was set for the first Saturday evening in November at the Lexington Road residence, giving me about six weeks to create my design. Monsieur and Madame called it my graduation, my reveal, which sounds quite impressive in French: *ma révélation*.

Over the previous nine months, I had quietly pursued my goal, not much into sharing my progress. Not looking for support or praise, I was just trying to move forward, to accomplish something authentic. Never would I be called a dilettante again, or a dreamer, but rather a doer. Cole knew I was dedicated. Monsieur certainly did as well, yet I was not so seriously dedicated that I neglected my family. I do confess that Cole's work obsession made my duties as wife less demanding. While I missed the regular and consistent attention from my husband, the lack of it gave me a certain freedom. Proudly, I maximized that freedom, coming into my own, becoming the person I thought I was, the person I wanted to be.

Oh, one other thing I was mastering, thanks to the blessing of my tutor, was the vastly important art of the sketch. Again, from the beginning, I thought I could draw. Ha. Little did I realize how vital the sketch was in the creative process. Monsieur had taught me technique. He explained all the elements of form, position, height, angle, and proportion. Along with such teaching, and followed with hours of drawing practice, I both learned and followed standard practice, and found a signature drawing style all my own, which produced results. With more than one hundred sketches completed, we were finally satisfied with my design concept for my dress as drawn on paper in pen and ink.

On this day at the salon, I would build that special dress for the reveal. Answering my husband's query about my day's plans, I called out to him as he left the kitchen.

"Today I will make magic," I projected across the room.

He called back, "Baby, we made magic last night. That was good enough for me."

Kissing the kid's good morning, I joined them for breakfast at the table. They were in their highchairs. Bonnie did her own magic, preparing their morning serving of healthy energy. A half hour later, as we finished cleaning the last of the Cheerios off the table, Cole passed through. He had showered and shaved and looked as handsome as was humanly possible for the male species. Each of us, including Bonnie, got a kiss. Bonnie made her usual grimace. She wasn't taken by Cole, but she knew I loved him, so it was never an issue. I figured it was friction between one poor kid watching another poor kid rise from the ashes, the latter being perhaps a little too full of himself. Cole offered one more final air-hug and he was out the door. Mastering the real estate universe took plenty of dedication. I was due at the salon by ten to master my design. There was still an entire morning left to spend with my children. How lucky was I?

Pushing the Envelope

Richard Hellman's voice reverberated throughout the office, even with a full staff of agents on their phones making morning calls. Cole entered just past eight thirty, following his morning gym and spa routine at the Harbor Club. As he passed by Kit Hamilton's desk, Kit saluted him while on the phone, then covered his free ear to drown out Hellman.

Standing at attention on either side of the closed glass office door, Smith and Jones did not attempt to stop Cole from entering.

"I expect movement on my cash investment, and you have until the end of the month," the BIG Fund's principal investor demanded. Cole, coming late to the party, requested explanation.

"Roman, what's up with this?"

"Mr. Hellman thinks we are moving too slowly and are too cautiously investing his money, and he feels we are missing optimum market conditions," Roman answered succinctly, without emotion.

"Have you gone over the figures on the land purchase in Moreno Valley?" Cole pressed on.

"We financed that land with zero down, Cole," Roman advised.

"That's a good thing, right?" Cole displayed his lack of savvy in handling investor funds. Roman tried to cover.

"Yes, partner, that is a good thing, but it is not what Mr. Hellman requires. He is insisting that we buy property with his cash, then turn around and sell it, or flip it, for a profit. He then wants to be repaid with a portion of the profit, with our share coming to us."

"That sounds fine too, just a different plan, Roman. Should we flip the Moreno Valley land? We bought it at a great price," Cole suggested.

"We could do that. There are buyers lined up doing just what we are doing. Only thing is, we only closed on this deal weeks ago. The profit may not be worth the trouble."

Hellman cut in. "Sell the damn property. And do it by month's end."

With his final instruction, Richard Hellman left the office, Smith and Jones behind him. As the triad marched down the center aisle of the agent bullpen, all heads turned, and all eyes followed them. The phones were silenced, as if it were a moment of respect, until the elevator door closed, and they were gone. The din of noise then accelerated to its former pitch.

Remaining in Roman's office, seeking a clear understanding of what had just transpired, Cole asked Roman to push the button and close his door.

"Okay, I know I looked stupid, and I know you covered me, but what the fuck is going on?"

"It's better you don't know," Roman responded quickly.

"What's that supposed to mean? I need to know. I must know. I'm not that stupid, man."

"Our big investor, owner of QuickBucks4You, is not just a loan shark raping the poor with usurious but legal interest rates on noncollateralized fast money loans. Hellman is laundering large blocks of cash from sources not disclosed."

"So, our biggest investor is feeding our fund with money that needs to be spent?" Cole was direct. "Why is this coming up now? He's been putting funds in for more than a year and has never demanded that they be turned."

"That's an answer neither of us needs to know, nor do we want to know." Roman was cool, but Cole was getting hot.

"Look, this is really bad news. We are potentially involved at only an arm's length away from whatever criminal source is funneling this cash. I say we need to know, and we need to get out. Give him back all his money." Cole was firm.

"We can't do that," Roman answered.

"Why the hell not?"

"Because we can't. At least not right now. You'll have to trust me and say no more."

"I have always trusted you, until now." Cole's message drew the ire of his partner.

"Let me put it this way, partner: you know the advances, all seven of them, you have taken out of the so-called Baldwin corporate account over the past nine or so months for whatever your 'secret project' is? The money comes out of the BIG Fund, not the Baldwin operating account. You have borrowed, not entirely legally, for your own personal use."

"You never told me that." Cole demanded further explanation.

"You never asked. You just wanted the cash, and you wanted it kept quiet. There's more. I have been cooperating with Hellman all along, buying and then selling property, using the BIG Fund to do his bidding. You never knew about it because I protected you, and until today, Hellman kept his mouth shut about it since it was all working fine. Now, there must be a problem and the pressure is on for him to move some big money all at once."

Regaining his cool, fully realizing the mess he was now in, Cole asked for a plan. "How much can we flip the Moreno land for? We did a deal on the total one thousand acres for just over two million dollars."

"We can get two and a half, maybe two-point-eight, million. There is already an assumable loan in place. We could make between a quarter million and a half million."

"This does not sound like that much of a problem." Cole was acquiescing.

"There's more, partner." Roman now was in full confession mode. "The million-dollar loan to you? Add that to one million I've loaned Sierra."

"Oh my God. What do you mean you've loaned one million to Sierra?" Cole lost the cool demeanor.

"Will you shut up, man?! You just broadcast that news through the glass to the entire office."

"Shit." Cole lowered the decibel level. "Start explaining."

"I admit it, I've been financing Sierra's drug dealing for several years, before you and I became partners and before we created the BIG Fund. It has gone out of control over the last year, and frankly and honestly, I've lost my sanity. Haven't kept track of how deep I've gotten."

"Can she repay this money?" Cole was now seriously worried but still not fully grasping just how dangerous the situation had become. "We can fix all of this, Roman. I can repay my loan, and you can repay Sierra's if she flakes."

"Yes, we can. I agree. And I have a plan," Roman followed.

"A minute ago, I didn't think you had a plan," Cole replied with a strong tone of irony in his voice.

"We are now selling the lots at The Summit, right? Let's keep twenty of the lots out of the total and develop, build, and sell them ourselves. The profit potential as builder/developer of these parcels can be a million dollars or more for each one."

Cole nodded in agreement.

"For now, we keep all this quiet. We deal with Hellman and keep him happy, along with all the other investors. It just might be a good thing to flip some properties, show some profit, and pay a dividend to our group," Roman added.

Cole again nodded in agreement.

"Roman, I thought I was borrowing money from our operating funds, not the investment trust. Over the next six more months, I'm going to need another two to three million dollars."

"As long as we're cool, you can take it out of the BIG Fund, if you will eventually repay. I think you'd better tell me what all the money is for, partner."

Cole hesitated, but realized he had no choice but to share.

"Last year I made an amazing deal with the Newport Land Trust and bought a two-acre lot on an ocean-view hillside south of The Summit. You can see the lot from our development. I am building a dream house for Kate and me. It's a surprise." Cole laid it out simply and directly.

"Kate does not know?" Roman followed.

"No, she doesn't know."

"Is that smart?"

"Probably not, but it's my plan, and I will make it a reality and cover all the cost."

"Trying to impress the old man?"

"No, that's not it at all."

"Since you have already dug your hole, you'd better stay the course, I guess. At least there is value in the land and construction. You can always sell."

"Never. This will be our forever house."

"Never say never, my partner."

Cole left Roman, heading back into the agent bullpen. If the agents had heard him yelling about the million-dollar loan to Sierra, nobody let on. The entire group were masters of their own real estate universes, dealing and negotiating, compromising, fabricating, selling their mothers' wedding rings when necessary to seal the deal. And there were so many deals. Deals on top of deals. Buyers were offering bribes to be first in line amid multiple offers. These were shady transactions of no consequence since everything was based on the current land value, which was on a daily meteoric rise in terms of dollars. That was the only security of consequence. Who was buying did not matter, only the appraisal. The entire nation was drunk on real estate, and it was a high with no hangover.

As Cole passed by Kit Hamilton again, Kit hung up his phone and reached out for Cole.

"I've got two deals going into escrow late today. One sale is lot number eight at The Summit," Kit offered, looking for praise.

Cole did not offer his usual upbeat team captain response. "Good job. Share the news in the staff meeting tomorrow" was all he said, moving by.

Kit was deflated. Cole's approval was the air Kit Hamilton breathed.

Covering Tracks

In less than one week, Roman had fielded three offers on the Moreno Valley land. He took the middle bidder, a cash offer, no terms, and reaped a half million in profit. The entire sum was wired into Richard Hellman's designated account, then was adjusted, reducing the BIG Fund balance sheet by two and a half million dollars and reducing Hellman's stake by the same amount. The first batch of laundry had been fluffed and folded.

Roman was on a roll, with Cole fully engaged. The following week the BIG Fund purchased one hundred flat acres of chaparral within view of the Adelanto prison in the desolate High Desert region of California. A local contractor was hired to erect a row of large metal warehouse buildings on a five-acre campus at one edge of the property. At the bargain price of one hundred thousand dollars per acre, plus the building expense, a total investment of eleven and a half million was funded. Construction would commence immediately after the permit was approved. Along with the two-and-half-million-dollar Moreno Valley sale, the BIG Fund recorded a total of fourteen million Hellman dollars in the laundry machine.

Wasting no time, the partners then turned their Adelanto tract on the market preconstruction, looking for another flip. There were high fives galore when, in another week, a very good offer arrived on Roman's desk via courier from an unknown corporation in the Cayman Islands. "Could it be this easy?" Cole questioned his partner. The cash offer for the desert parcel was a cool twelve and a half million, or a one-million-dollar profit in a week.

"We will use the profit to pay down our individual current draws on the BIG

Fund," Roman advised. "Five hundred thousand dollars for you, and the same for me."

"What about reserving a portion of the profit for eventual investor payment?" Cole asked.

"*Eventual* is the operative word," responded Roman.

"Okay then," Cole followed, "where does that leave us with Hellman?"

"His current total stake in the BIG Fund is forty million and change, less the fourteen million we have just used and will be returning. So that leaves about twenty-six million."

"How fast does he want the rest moved?" Cole pressed on.

"We can't move too fast; it will create suspicion. I'd say we need to move his remainder over the next year and be out of partnership by Christmas 2008."

"What about the other forty million from all the other investors? They expect a profit and return as promised."

"We have time. They all signed five-year terms," Roman reminded Cole. "Besides, we should begin the plan to build out the lots at The Summit. If I'm right, we stand to profit at least twenty million on that one plan."

"That's not enough to cover our promised return." Cole's comfort level dropped.

"Of course not. It's just a piece of the pie," Roman returned. "A nice piece, I might add. Much more to come, buddy boy. We are in this for the long race, not the fifty-yard sprint."

"I agree. For now, let's just keep Hellman happy and then part company with him, okay?" Cole was serious.

"Sounds like a plan, partner."

"One more thing: I want to return Kate's father's investment. This is not what he signed up for." Cole was direct.

Roman hesitated, then replied, "Yes, okay, I agree. You've got that thirtieth-birthday dinner at your in-laws' house coming up. I'm still invited, yes?"

"Yes, you are invited, but solo—and you know why."

"We will hand Dalton Fairchild a check for his original one-and-a-half-million-dollar investment plus three hundred thousand dollars as a 20 percent return, as promised, on one year's interest."

"Roman, we have not made any interest or profit yet other than payment given to Hellman and ourselves."

"We will cover it, buddy. Don't you want to impress your father-in-law and your wife?"

Now Cole hesitated, but not long, before answering, "I do. I trust you, Roman. Things will balance out with profits we made this year, right?"

"They will. No doubt about it."

Taming the Green-Eyed Devil

Unchecked ambition and inexperienced youth can be a recipe for either brilliant discovery or serious failure. Approaching the significant transitional age of thirty, despite a few serious past transgressions, as well as current revelations of business complications, the boy from Reno with no education, no pedigree, and no talent other than exceptional looks and killer salesmanship was doing just fine. Living the dream, Cole was a twenty-first-century Jay Gatsby building his own mansion to impress his bride.

Bulldozers Cole had reassigned from The Summit development were now grading and leveling the narrow land. He also had engaged an architect and designer, having them sign contracts including nondisclosure clauses forbidding any revelation of client information. An engineering firm, a supervising building contractor, a landscape designer, and other essential components were in place. Further, early permits were in order, the fees having been paid and the deposits made. For weeks Cole pored through design magazines, making his own sketches, then met with his architect and design team to finalize the concept.

Ignoring protests from the hired experts telling him that he was pushing too hard and rushing unnecessarily, Cole was adamant to finish the design and break ground on construction.

"We should be spending a good nine months on the design phase for a project of this importance," the architect insisted. "And then at least eighteen to twenty-four months to build."

Making it clear that he would approve the design in three months tops, Cole demanded that the build be complete in one year—fourteen months maximum.

The dominant architectural style on the coast was Italian Mediterranean design. Cole's architect built many of the fine homes as modern twenty-first-century adaptions of Old-World Italian structures. He knew the drill, making the fast-track approach somewhat palatable.

"Cole, under normal circumstances I would request that my client fly to Europe with me for an architectural tour as part of the process," he advised.

"I've never been to Europe. Don't have time for that. Besides, when I go, I want to go with Kate. No offense," he shared boldly.

Cole delivered pages and pages of ripped magazine pages featuring everything from an English Tudor mansion to George and Martha Washington's Mount Vernon, along with a selection of Italian villa architecture, from a Roman palazzo to a Venetian canal house, to a Tuscan stone farmhouse. The pièce de résistance came on the architect's desk in a folder of clippings relating to the design of the Vatican.

"Are you requesting a home design to replicate the Vatican?" he asked. "Will there be a chapel with ceiling art?"

Cole managed to laugh, then replied, "Yes, a chapel would be nice for my mother. Maybe an artist could replicate a version of that ceiling."

"You mean in the Sistine Chapel by Michelangelo?"

"That's the one," Cole answered.

As Cole had insisted on a concept that reflected the architecture of the Vatican, his architect threatened to quit twice. Cole promised to behave, keeping a more open mind.

On a final meeting before a third resignation from the architect, the man produced photographs and blueprints of an estate, not in Italy, but rather in France—Provence to be exact. This was a project he had championed some twenty years earlier when he was first breaking out. A relative of his inherited the property from a distant and long-disconnected grandparent living on this vineyard estate in Provence.

The manor house was seventeenth-century Florentine in style, classic and elegant, but not ostentatious. After the architect had laid out all the photos and drawings on his large design table in the studio, Cole tuned to the romance in front of him. The Vatican re-creation faded in favor of a desire to build a stately three-story Florentine manor with a tiled hip roof accented on all corners with stone statuary, and with a grand carved stone pediment above the main entrance door flanked by enormous stone urns planted with Italian cypress trees trimmed in topiary fashion, all facing a classic formal garden with boxwood hedges surrounding roses, stone paths adjacent to green grass, and rows of symmetrical palms facing the Pacific Ocean.

The architect placed the manor house in the center of the long narrow lot, with a pool, a pool house, a guesthouse, the chapel for Cole's mother, and garages all incorporated into the landscape plans, which also featured a small vineyard on the sloping hillside portion of the property encompassing almost an acre of the parcel.

Cole was sold. He grabbed his architect and hugged him, not letting go.

"This is so amazing. I've never been to Europe, but I'll bet there is nothing there more beautiful than what you are proposing. How long to finish drawings, do the engineering, receive final permits, and break ground?" Cole asked with exuberance. Christmas was two months away, but he had just received the gift of his lifetime.

"At least ninety to one hundred twenty days, and that's pushing it," the architect replied. "But I will make this happen for you."

Before leaving the studio, Cole delivered another check for one hundred thousand dollars at the architect's request. He gave him another major hug and repeated that the project must remain a secret between them.

"Please, make sure none of your staff speaks a word. As soon as construction starts, people will be asking lots of questions." Cole was clear and direct.

"Not a word. We signed the same contract. No worries," the architect promised, accepting the additional payment.

Cole nervously asked, "Any idea of a final cost estimate?"

"Impossible to give a solid number. Too many unknowns. Based on what we know today, I'll venture a guess of under three million, if we are conservative."

Cole left the meeting feeling uneasy. He had already advanced $1,100,000, and all he had accomplished was the erection of a construction fence, the movement of some dirt, and a big dream drawn and assembled on many pages of paper. Worse, he knew that the money had come from the BIG Fund, unearned, with only a promise to repay. Yet, Cole still believed. He believed in his ambition, his destiny, and the creation of his family home.

CHAPTER FIFTY-NINE

THE FAMILY DINNER

Spending the week before the family celebration marking GiGi's first birthday and my husband's thirtieth working closely with my mentors at the salon, I watched as my design started to become a real dress. Avenue Foch West was a small and strange place filled with every imaginable sort of fabric fashioned into garments meant to exhibit and exude the most personal expressions of women choosing to place such fabrics on their bodies. Never taking images of the salon for granted, despite gazing upon the same scenery time after time for days, months, and now years, I knew how much satisfaction the salon brought to my life.

The aroma of the salon was a perfume like no other. I could taste the scent in the thick, rich air of the darkened space, illuminated principally by a glorious old-world crystal chandelier, its lights topped by age-yellowed miniature pleated silk shades. Monsieur had placed spotlights strategically in the cloth-upholstered ceiling, directing them at the displayed garments. Pure theatrics.

Each time I entered, I made a point to check what clothing had changed, moved, and sold. I watched, I learned, and I grew in my own way. I had the education of a college dropout, having run from lost love in search of a new life, a life in which I discovered a new love, married a husband, then had four babies, all born in a speck of time.

Baby GiGi would be turning one. She was beginning to talk and use words in broken sentences, taking her first stumbling steps in her tiny white Mary Janes. Just last week she had attempted a run and then fell; I held back a scream. GiGi rose and ran farther, into the arms of her daddy, Cole. He picked her up and swung her around, turning like a ballet dancer, arms outstretched like ribbons on a maypole. Flying through the air, GiGi squealed joyously, held in her father's firm grip, as the merry-go-round slowly came to an end with applause all around.

This was another image that would remain ingrained in my mind forever, the experience having been just a week ago on a special quiet Saturday afternoon at home with Cole and all the children. The magic flight on the Cole carousel was now the silly catalyst of joy for my almost one-year-old. Every time she found her daddy within sight, GiGi would stumble to him, a small plane barely on takeoff down the runway, and dive into his arms. No doubt at her upcoming birthday party, a moment of flight would be her one birthday wish.

With last-minute inspiration, which was also why I had been working at the salon all week, was that I had fashioned a one-year-old version of my dress for the baby. With Monsieur's brilliant help, we finished everything.

My dress fit perfectly on the body mannequin in Monsieur's workroom. I chose a very pale pink raw silk. The neckline was cut straight across, shoulder to shoulder, meeting a very tailored three-quarter-length sleeve. The dress had no back. Fabric from the shoulder connected to the bodice, then cut across the base of the spine. In front, the raw silk fell straight down, very fitted, to just below the knee. The back was straight and fitted with a deep center slit to the spot just below my bottom. I had lined the revealing edge portions of the dress with contrasting pale pink silk imprinted with the Fair Child pansy, pink and cream bordered in black. The lining showed ever so slightly at the base of the sleeve and the back slit.

Using the same pansy-imprinted silk, I created a wrap, my version of the pashmina. Monsieur called upon his shoemaker to execute my wish to use the printed pansy silk as the replacement insole on a pair of extremely pointed low black patent sling-back heels I had found at Neiman's, reduced more than six hundred dollars to one hundred twenty-five dollars. I couldn't resist. Doing the same customization on an old Chanel diamond-stitched black leather clutch, passed down from my mother, I had the bag lined in the pansy print. Naturally, we did the same for GiGi—all of it, even the Mary Janes with custom lining. Well, practically the same. Her dress was cut way above the knee with plenty of flair.

Dinner on Lexington Road was planned for the first Saturday night in November, which was not the exact birthday for either GiGi or Cole, but it was the best date to gather family before the year-end holiday crazies. We did not want a big party, just family and a few close friends. That's the way we'd always wanted things.

In addition, my brother, Jamey, and his live-in fiancée Rachel, we invited Cole's family from Reno. Rose and Joe accepted with great enthusiasm; Cole's sister and brother both declined, saying they could get no time off work. Of course, Heather was coming; I was thrilled that she was able to take a night off from studying as her law school finals approached. Cole had invited Roman, but I asked Cole not to include Sierra. He agreed.

A table for ten was set, plus a second table for Bonnie and the four kids. The perfect party. My mother was in full prep mode for the big night. I hadn't mentioned that I was also planning to use the occasion to reveal my first handmade design. Surprise was my method of choice.

My parents had asked Cole and me, the kids, and Bonnie to stay the night. There was plenty of room, even a nursery with multiple cribs set up by Nancy and never used. Staying over was a big deal for her. I could tell it meant a great deal. Nancy and Dalt offered to put up Cole's mom and dad at the Holmby Palms, just two blocks from the Lexington house. They were grateful but declined, instead making a reservation at the Holiday Inn, several miles west down Sunset Boulevard right off the 405 San Diego Freeway, only a ten-minute drive away. Cole told me that they had called the Holmby Palms to check room rates because they wanted to pay their own way. Finding out the least expensive room at the Holmby went for around seven hundred dollars a night plus fees, they thanked my parents and booked the Holiday Inn.

The Holmby did get one booking. Cole shared that Roman was going to spend the night there with Sierra after our dinner. For about a second, I felt a small touch of guilt for having insisted she not come, but it passed very quickly. I did not want her around my children, my brother and Rachel, or my parents. It was bad enough she was around my husband and that he refused to recognize, never mind admit, the danger. I said my peace, then let it go. Nagging was not among my least desirable traits. I did not accept negative instruction, nor did I deliver it. This I had learned from both my grandmother and my mother.

Saturday arrived in glorious fall fashion—brilliant blue sky, crisp crackle in the air, the aroma of newly seeded and fertilized lawns, all part of the transition from summer into California winter. For me, fall was special. Like spring, it was a chance for renewal. Change brought new energy in my life. Returning to the salon and working with Monsieur gave me hope that I still had my dream. I was revised and energized and placed on a new and different path. My work was better for it. Best of all, I was more secure with the feeling of change, which had given a different level of confidence that was based on progress, not on the dream.

It turned out that Cole had an important television shoot that was set to take place in Beverly Hills only blocks from my parents' house. We had planned to take off the entire weekend together with the kids, but this shoot was a big deal. Cole apologized ten times, explaining that it was going to be used as a pilot demo to attract investors to launch a new national series, expanding *Living the Dream* into *American Dream Homes*. The only day the production company could obtain access to the Beverly Hills estate of the late silent film star Harold Lloyd, known as Green Acres, was on this day. Cole promised to be finished by dinnertime. I kissed him goodbye and wished him good luck. Bonnie and I then strapped all four Baldwins in the big white Tahoe, loaded in all the supplies for our big family weekend in Beverly Hills, and headed for the freeway.

As we turned into the driveway on Lexington, Buddy was the first to yell out.

"Look, Mom. Look at all the punkins. Does Grammy have a punkin patch of her own?" he squealed.

The twins then joined the squeal of excitement as their older brother Buddy called out for me to stop the car.

Mother, in her inimitable fashion, had lined the driveway, or somebody had, with at least one hundred "punkins" of all shapes, sizes, and colors. No doubt this amounted to a run-on pumpkins, with none left in Beverly Hills, perhaps all of LA.

Once I had stopped the car as ordered, we all got out. The boys went wild, running up and down the drive and the adjacent lawn on both sides, examining every pumpkin they could touch. Some were so large they required a joint effort to lift them. Bonnie held GiGi, who watched all the action with serious intensity. I was taking pictures.

Hearing all the excitement, Dalt and Nancy came out the front door to find their grandchildren in punkin heaven. This was a special start to our birthday weekend and to *ma révélation*, which was still an unknown surprise. I felt a tinge of melancholy that Cole was missing this moment. He would have been the biggest kid in the punkin patch. Buddy and the twins would have relished the memory of their dad playing with them surrounded by a sea of gourds, never to be duplicated.

After we had spent a lovely afternoon together following the perfect light Saturday brunch as only Nancy could create, Nancy joined Bonnie in putting the four kids down in their grandparents' nursery for their afternoon naps. I joined my father on a pair of lounge chairs by the pool. The warm fall sun had faded early and was now descending amid the afternoon chill as dusk arrived. We had at least an hour left of the sun for our father–daughter reunion, just the two of us.

Dalt delivered considerable praise upon me and Cole, saying he was impressed and proud of our family, Cole's growing success, and our adjustment to life in Newport. The praise turned more serious, in typical Dalt fashion. My father liked to begin his conversations with positive spin, then digress to his point. This no longer caught me off guard.

"My darling girl, can I ask you a question?" Dalt headed down his path to the truth.

"Of course, Daddy," I answered, calling him "Daddy" whenever I knew these questions were coming.

"Are you happy? You seem happy, yet I detect undercurrent."

"You just described my pretty perfect amazing life. I have so much to be grateful for," I told him, putting on my own positive spin.

"I'm glad to hear that, Kate. You know you can always come to me—always."

"I do know that. We are all doing just fine. The kids are thriving; that's the most important thing. Cole works too much; I worry about that. But it is what it is. And I, well, I have been trying to study and grow as I pursue my design career."

"Your mother shared that with me. She tells me you have been learning to sew and concentrating on the basics to build a foundation on which to pursue this career dream. I must ask another tough question."

I knew instinctively what was coming.

"Can you balance the duties of a mother of four, wife, and career woman?"

Even though I had known this was coming, I hesitated.

"I'm not sure, Daddy. That question scares me. I only know that I can't give up my career goal. Not yet. Maybe not ever. I haven't tried hard enough."

"The kids are certainly not suffering for it, and it sounds like Cole is too busy to be suffering from it either. Please take some fatherly loving advice and place it in the back of your mind."

"I will not get lost in the dream, if that's your caution," I said before Dalt could advise.

"No, no, that's not it. Just the opposite. On a certain level you must get lost in the dream, especially if it is a creative passion, or else you'll have very little chance of realization. The key is, keep your heart invested in the dream and keep your mind focused on your reality."

I smiled an impish grin, having gotten the message. I had heard it before, often. Questions remained: Could I do it? Was I smart enough, talented enough, brave enough, hungry enough? Being a rich girl could take away the edge. Hunger propelled creative people to fight for their place. Comfort in life was a great big safety net.

I was wanting to continue to talk with my father and was tempted to spoil my reveal, set for later, before dinner, and tell Dalt of my design work, but Marta interrupted. She came out with iced tea and cookies. Following right behind was Cole.

"Look who's here, my TV star husband," I called out.

Cole, my lady charmer Cuban Italian stallion, first put an arm around Marta for a quick hello hug, then came over to me. I rose. We kissed hello.

"I'm happy you are here. I was afraid the TV shoot would make you late, as it often does. It's barely four o'clock. How did you finish so fast?"

"I told them I had more important matters to attend to." Cole was on his best behavior around Dalt.

"Really, how did you get off early?" I pressed.

"Would you believe that I am a one-take wonder? That's what this new director said."

I leaned in and whispered in Cole's ear that I believed that statement in matters of lovemaking. He burst out in a laugh. Dalt inquired. We changed the subject.

"Marta, I think it may be about time to switch from iced tea to something a bit stronger. Can you see if Jefferson is available to take a drink order?" Dalt offered a seat to Cole, and the three of us kept our afternoon confab going. Cole's arrival had taken the pressure off me, at least somewhat.

"It's great to see you, Dalt," Cole offered.

"Likewise, son. You know you can call me Dad."

"Can I say that I am so impressed by you that it feels strange calling you Dad?" Cole was impressively forthright.

"Call me whatever makes you comfortable, Cole. I want you to feel like part of this family, that's all."

Score one for Dalt. My father was smooth.

"Sir, I mean Dad, I am indebted to you. You have been my mentor. The catalyst for my success is real estate. You also have entrusted me with one and a half million dollars to invest. So, you see, I want you to know how seriously I take all of this."

"I wouldn't do this if I didn't believe in you, trust you, and want to do whatever I could to support you, my daughter, and my grandchildren."

Cole stood up, reached into the inside breast pocket of his blazer, and took out an envelope, handing it to Dalt.

"What is this?" Dalt asked.

"Please open it," Cole responded.

Dalt followed the instruction and pulled out a check made out to him for $1.8 million.

"I don't understand," he said, looking at Cole.

"Dad, it has been a year since you invested with Roman and me to make it possible to launch the development buy at The Summit. We decided we wanted to repay you, with 20 percent interest as promised."

Dalt said nothing. He stared at the check, then at me. Finally looking back at Cole, he said, "This is very surprising. Are you certain this is a good move? It seems very soon, even premature."

"Yes, sir. I'm sure, Dad. We are doing so well, money is coming in from developers buying lots. Our final homes sold out at the first development, Ocean Palisades, making us a handsome profit. I wanted to prove to you how thankful we are by paying you back."

Cole was sincere. Dalt seemed pleased with the explanation, although he was still hesitant.

"I believe you should hold on to this, Cole. It is early in the game. Real estate has its peaks and valleys. You have never experienced a valley. Not yet anyway. Are you sure you want to repay this investment?"

"I am sure. We are sure, Roman and me."

Dalt turned to me.

"Kate, did you know about this?"

I paused, not sure what to do. Lie for my husband?

"Daddy, this is Cole's business," I said, attempting to remain neutral. I knew Dalt would be displeased if I said I had no idea, and then Cole would be put on the hot seat for not having shared his major business decisions with me, which was the method and manner of my parents' success.

"Okay then, I will accept the repayment and thank you for the honorable action. However, I will not accept the interest."

Dalt put the check back in the envelope and handed it back to Cole.

"You may redraft a check for the principal only and send it to me at your convenience," Dalt said with no further explanation. It was clear the topic was closed.

Cole put the envelope back in his inside pocket and sat down. I could tell he was disappointed, maybe a little humiliated. My father gave me a stern look when Cole was unaware, while sidelined by Jefferson's entering to take the afternoon cocktail order.

"Mr. Dalt, wouldn't you rather have your cocktail inside? It is starting to chill this late in the afternoon." Jefferson always called my father Mr. Dalt, formal yet familiar.

"Good idea, my friend. Let's all head inside. Jefferson, we'll meet at the bar in the library."

The kind and dignified former jazz musician-turned-majordomo of the Fairchild homestead tucked the silver tray he carried under the arm of his superstarched white uniform jacket and led the charge from poolside inside to the library.

Afternoon Arrivals

Jefferson served Cole a second bourbon and Seven within the first twenty minutes of family talk in the library. Cole had sworn to control the demon of alcohol. Maybe it was the pressure of facing Dalt and seeing the money returned. Cole had not received the adulation he expected from my father. Instead, there was a discernible mood of uncomfortable pullback, and Cole's response to Dalt's questioning was lame. And he knew it.

Across the library, I watched my husband sit silently, swallowed by the oversized tufted leather wing chair. It jarred me. My proud man never faded, at least not into furniture. Clearly, I was the only one in the room tuned in to the image. The boys played with total glee, jumping and rolling over one another on the oriental carpet in front of the fireplace, with Nancy and Dalt instigating the laughter that filled the library.

Marta arrived with several trays of afternoon treats, all prepared in advance by my "hostess with the mostest" mother. My boys rose from the rug and made a beeline for the pigs in a blanket. Why did those little hot dogs always smell so amazing? Make no mistake, there was also caviar and toast points for the big kids. Cole stood up, returning to impressive stature. He was also headed for the mini hot dogs. With two in hand, he walked over to the bar, where Jefferson stood at attention. Cole said nothing, handing his crystal tumbler to Jefferson. His drink was refreshed with a nod and smile.

The doorbell sounded. Jefferson left his bar to answer. Seeing me coming over to him, Cole put his third bourbon down on the side table beside the enveloping wing chair and jumped into the kids' play on the carpet. Marta placed her tray of pigs in the blanket down on an ottoman facing the fireplace so the children could snack and play. Cole helped himself again, avoiding me. Getting the message, I backed off.

The first doorbell chime had come from Roman, who was awaiting entry. Minutes later, a second ring: Heather. The late afternoon family dynamic had been altered with both their arrivals. Roman was a larger-than-life personality, and his presence brought Cole out of his apparent funk. Funny thing, the Russian bachelor playboy was also fantastic around kids. Within minutes, Roman had Cole and the boys lined up and arm wrestling over the ottoman, with the mini hot dogs offered as a prize for the champions.

Heather was also in wonderful spirits. She looked sensational, having dropped a few pounds, showing off a new dress. Heather never wore dresses, just tailored pants, with blouse and jacket for all occasions. It was her thing, so welcoming her in a dress was special. She shared that law school was treating her well and that she was loving all of it, including one of her teaching assistants. Love can change a wardrobe; I made a mental note.

By five thirty the fall sun signaled that man-made lights were to be turned on around the home. Hors d'oeuvres gone, cocktails consumed, and playtime ended, it was time to dress for dinner, called for seven. It was also time for me to prepare for my fashion reveal—*ma révélation*. Heather was in on the surprise, as was Bonnie of course. We departed the library for my upstairs childhood bedroom with the children. Dalt and Nancy followed. This left Cole and Roman behind, both men seated in facing enveloping leather chairs, both nursing drinks in crystal tumblers.

Bonnie put the boys down for an hour nap before dinner, then joined Heather and me with GiGi as we dressed for the reveal. Very strange. I felt like a teenager dressing for cotillion at the same time as I felt like a confident woman proud of accomplishment. GiGi smiled continuously, watching her mother with laser-like intensity prepare the wardrobe we were both about to display.

Bonnie began dressing GiGi. Heather convinced me to sit in front of the mirror so she could restyle my hair.

"I have an idea," Heather began, pulling my straight blonde shoulder-length hair back into a severe over-the-forehead style—part female goddess, part rock star, part ultimate temptress look. I howled as she explained.

"This is your idea to complement my fashion debut?" I chided her.

"Yes. You've designed a contemporary but also classic dress. We need to go against type with the hair and makeup. You'll see," she said with total control. "But the hair is not the idea I want to share. You've heard of the new shopping network Amazon. They started a few years ago selling books online and shipping them. Now they are doing fashion, and it is starting to really take off. People are loving avoiding the store—buy online, have it delivered to the door the next day."

"I don't know much about it," I confessed.

"You will, trust me," Heather replied.

"So, what's the idea?" I asked, still not getting it.

"The idea is that we forget about trying to get stores to buy Fair Child. We go straight to the consumer online, on Amazon."

"Will women buy what they can't see or touch?" I asked seriously.

"Woman have been ordering from catalogs for one hundred years. What do you think?"

"You're right. But what if it doesn't fit or they don't like it?"

"Just send it back. That's the new way. That's the Amazon way."

"I'm telling you, we are doing this. We'll figure it all out somehow. For now, let's get you dressed and ready."

"Are you sure this hairstyle works?" I was feeling a little weird.

"You are a knockout, friend."

The Big Reveal

At a quarter to seven o'clock in the evening, I was ready. Embracing Heather, I kissed her on both cheeks and told her how much I loved her. So many thoughts raced through my mind. What if David had not left me? What if I had not fled to Newport? I would never have met Heather, never would have met Monsieur and Madame, and never would have met and married Cole. And I wouldn't have four blessed children. So many what-ifs, so few explanations.

Bonnie came in with the boys, who were all dressed to impress their loving grandparents. Ralph Lauren would be very proud. They were wearing crested navy-blue blazers over charcoal short wool pants, blue and white striped button-down shirts, and no ties. Heather and I started to cry when we saw baby GiGi in her pink silk dress made in the image of my own. Bonnie cautioned us to control ourselves, or we would scare the baby to tears.

"Besides, all the black mascara you are wearing will run streaks down your cheeks," Bonnie added, staring at Heather's makeup job. "Kate, you look like something between a princess and a prostitute," Bonnie said, then immediately apologized for blurting out her opinion. She was, after all, born and raised outside

Des Moines, so she really didn't know too much about princesses or prostitutes other than images on TV. I laughed, telling her no apology was necessary.

"You can blame Heather for this," I added, joking.

Heather went ahead downstairs to see if anyone had gathered in the foyer. We were awaiting the dinner bell. The party would follow with Jefferson's ceremonial opening of the double doors to the main dining room. When Heather did not return, I knew it was time for the reveal.

Appearing first at the top of the helical staircase with the three boys was Bonnie. The family, along with Roman and Heather, were all gathered, looking up at the children. We had coached the boys to take Bonnie's direction. In perfect unison, at Bonnie's command, and at full volume, they called out, "Nana and Daddy D, we are ready for dinner!"

The salutation echoed off the marble floor below.

Nancy, standing next to Dalt, replied, "Dinner is ready. Please come down!"

Bonnie began the procession, carefully descending the stairs with three hyperenergetic young males in their Polo duds. Just as they reached the three-quarter point on the staircase, I appeared at the upper landing holding GiGi. Hearing Cole gasp first, I felt that was a good sign, or at least I hoped; it could have meant that he was drunk. My parents applauded. Dalt even whistled. I'd never heard my father whistle. Heather clapped. Roman hooted and joined Dalt whistling.

Jefferson came up the stairs and met me halfway, taking my arm to steady me and the baby, then escorting us down the remainder of the stairs. In this way, I made my entrance.

Nancy ran to me and took GiGi as we entered the foyer. Congratulations flowed. There was love in the air. Cole rushed to my side and held me at the waist, looking into my eyes.

"You are so lovely. I love you so much," he said quietly, releasing me to the adoration of my parents, my brother, his fiancée Rachel, and Heather. Cole smelled of bourbon, but it was not the time to be afraid. This was my time, my moment, my reveal. It was my chance to be proud of having learned to sew, for having started over after failure, for having stuck to the dream. Whether Cole was drunk or not, I knew I was surrounded by the love and support of my husband and the family and friends I cherished most in life.

My mother paid me a great compliment that only I understood.

"Darling, you have created a modern masterpiece with a hint of the design of one of my favorite couturiers from the past, David Hayes."

Nancy had noticed the touch of silk lining showing with the Fair Child logo. Elegant lining was a Hayes trademark on the clothes he had made for so many of the grand women of the society crowd during the 1970s, '80s and '90s, including First Lady Nancy Reagan. I was only a child at the time, but I remember my mother in those beautiful clothes—a lasting memory, an indelible impression. I had adapted the concept, making it my own.

The Dinner Bell Sounds

The double doors to the formal dining room were opened by Jefferson. From the foyer, we could all see a dinner setting made with exquisite care. Candles flickered in tall glass hurricanes that lined the table, and white orchids blended with white hydrangeas and roses surrounded by mini orange pumpkins. Dionne Warwick recordings of Bacharach and David hits played in the background at the ideal dinner volume.

We followed Nancy and Dalt into the dining room as sirens sounded outside. At first, they were unobtrusive, overshadowed by the Warwick recording, but then they grew louder—and then even louder, deafeningly so. Dalt turned around first and made his way through all of us to the front door. Jefferson was right behind him.

As he opened the door, we saw red lights in all directions. The noise from the sirens made us cover our ears. GiGi and the boys began to cry. Bonnie rushed them out of the foyer and into the kitchen with Marta.

The driveway, a half circle up from Lexington and coming right in front of the house before turning back to Lexington, was filled with a dozen Beverly Hills police vehicles, a SWAT truck, even a fire truck. At the front of the parade of police was a silver convertible Porsche with flat front tires and a big dent on the front right, the headlight knocked out. The Porsche was surrounded by police, who were barking directions at the driver to put both hands on the steering wheel before getting out. Sidearms were drawn.

Nancy and I were the first to follow Dalt, the rest standing back behind us on the landing. It was impossible to hear much, and we could see even less. I did see that the Porsche had run off the driveway and onto the lawn, smashing many of Nancy's pumpkins, before coming to a stop at the front door. Fortunately, the kids were sheltered in the house. Besides being frightened by the police, they would have been traumatized by the smashed pumpkins. Those pumpkins belonged to them.

At that moment I heard an "Oh my God" coming from behind me. It was Roman. Then I looked forward and saw Sierra being pulled from the Porsche. I realized then that it was Roman's car, which I should have recognized; the drama took on a very serious personal implication. This was not some random Beverly Hills police chase that had happened to end up in my parents' driveway. It was Sierra, and she was in Roman's car. Surely, there was a drug connection.

One of the officers approached us. I felt very ridiculous standing there in my reveal as everything unfolded, but I did not budge.

"Sir, I'm Officer Barton, lead drug enforcement detective with the Beverly Hills Police Department. Are you the homeowner Mr. Dalton Fairchild?"

"Yes, officer. What is happening?"

"I am very sorry for this disturbance, sir, but we were making a drug arrest at a bungalow suite at the Holmby Palms Hotel down the street when the suspect evaded arrest, managing to run and jump into a parked Porsche on Crescent Drive before taking off. We pursued at once. The suspect only made it two blocks into your driveway. Do you recognize the car?" the detective asked.

"Are you asking if I know this person?" Dalt answered. "I do not know the car, and I am unable to see the person."

Detective Barton called out for one of his men to shine a light on the suspect, a tall thin woman now in handcuffs beside the Porsche.

"Do you recognize this woman?" the detective asked again.

Before Dalt could answer no, the woman yelled out, "Roman, help me! Please save me, Roman."

Coming forward from behind, Roman explained that Sierra was his friend, adding that she was in his car.

She had dropped Roman off earlier for dinner at the Fairchild home and then had gone back to the hotel, where they were staying the night. Roman went on to tell the cop that the Fairchilds had nothing to do with whatever had transpired leading to the incident.

"We are taking the suspect into custody and transporting her to the main Beverly Hills jail at Civic Center. She will be processed," Detective Barton said.

"Can you transport me as well?" Roman asked.

"Are you involved in the sale of drugs with your friend?" Barton responded sarcastically.

"No, sir. No, I am not." Roman was clearly afraid.

"Then I suggest you wait. Your car will be impounded; a tow is coming now. You can call this number for information or call your attorney."

Barton handed Roman a card, then turned and rejoined his squad. As Sierra was placed in the rear seat of a black-and-white, Barton again turned toward all of us.

"We are done here, folks, for now. Please go back inside. There is no danger. The city will be in touch concerning any damage to your property resulting from this chase and arrest. We may have further questions later."

In less than a couple of minutes, the armada of police, SWAT, and fire vehicles rounded the circular drive in silent orderly fashion, no lights glaring, ending up back on Lexington and beginning down the road. We all stood staring in a semi-hypnotic state. What had just happened to our perfect family gathering? What had just thrown my proud moment of fashion reveal under the bus, or rather the SWAT van?

Jamey and Rachel were the first to go back into the house. Dalt followed them to see if they were okay. Jamey apologized but said they needed to leave and go home. Rachel was really upset. Jamey told Dalt that she was crying, saying that it could have been either of them in the situation if things were not different. My father assured them that things were very different. They had crossed that bridge. Their lives were now drug-free. They were sober and strong, planning a great future together.

Coming back inside with Nancy, we heard Dalt's final words to Jamey.

"No matter what, Son, we are here for you and for Rachel. No matter what. I'm sorry for this, but I understand your skipping dinner. We'll arrange for a carryout. Your mother made a wonderful meal."

"Dad, that's okay. We need to go. I love you, Dad."

Nancy ran over to join my father in a group hug with Jamey and Rachel. They exchanged goodbyes, promising to talk tomorrow.

Dashing into the kitchen, I found Bonnie and the children calm, happy, and eating dinner. Marta was singing to them in Spanish, and the boys shouted out "Olé!" every time Marta sang the word. Turning and leaving without interrupting, I rejoined my parents in the foyer. They were just standing there with Jefferson.

"Darling, I think I need a drink," Nancy said, the first to speak. Dalt nodded, then they headed back into the library.

"Will you join us, Kate?" Dalt put out an arm. "Where is your husband and his partner?" Dalt's tone was serious.

Realizing Cole and Roman were still out front, I declined the drink and went to check on them. Opening the door, I found Cole yelling at Roman, who stood stoically taking the abuse. Cole was drunk, making matters worse.

Roman made him angrier by not responding. Then, Cole lunged at Roman, clamping both hands around his neck. A momentary strangulation was fended off by Roman, who was sober, stronger, and built like a Russian tank. Pulling away, he threw Cole off-balance, causing him to fall on the brick steps.

Jumping in, I helped Cole up. He stumbled again, and I braced him so he could remain upright. Then I let Roman have it.

"This is your fault. How could you let this happen? More importantly, what are you going to do to make this right? You have put our very lives in jeopardy—everything! Everything you and Cole have worked for, my relationship with Cole, my family. I don't think you can fix this. How will I forgive you?"

I didn't scream; I didn't cry. I just let him have it the best I could without losing it completely. Cole's final inebriated words were, "Take that," as if to second my rebuke.

Roman laughed at Cole, instigating yet another feeble attempt by Cole to prove his manhood. Roman began walking past us, then went down the steps and onto the driveway.

"Where the hell do you think you're going, man?" Cole blurted out. "Your car ain't going anywhere."

Poetically, at that moment, the police tow truck pulled into the drive. Cole shouted out further expletives in a loud drunken voice. "Your fucking car is going somewhere, but not you, you stupid asshole."

As the tow rounded the drive at the top of the circle, another car followed closely behind. As it was blocked by the tow, which stopped right behind the damaged silver Porsche, front and center below the main entrance, I could not make out the car or its driver. What I could see was Roman heading down the other side of the drive, leaving the house on foot. He called back to us.

"I'm walking to the hotel. I will make this right. I am sorry." Roman disappeared into the shadows.

Helping my husband get himself together to go back in so we could face my parents together, I heard another voice rang out, this one a female voice.

"Sal, Sal, is that you?" Cole didn't hear the call, but I did.

"Rose, is that you?" I returned the call.

"Yes, dear, it's Rose and Joe. We got very lost. I am so sorry to be so late." Another car door closed, and Joe joined Rose walking past the tow truck and up the drive. I grabbed Cole to try to sober him up to greet his parents. With all the drama, we'd forgotten they had not arrived on time for dinner.

"Sal, it's your long-lost pop," Joe called out. "How are you doing, beautiful Kate?"

We didn't answer. Rose and Joe were now right in front of us. Rose went to hug her son first, and Joe politely put out his hand and offered me a brush on the cheek.

"Sal, your aftershave smells like liquor," Rose said with conviction.

"Oh, Mama, I've had a couple of drinks tonight celebrating my birthday." Cole managed to sound reasonable enough.

"Oh gosh, such a wonderful family time to celebrate your birthday and baby GiGi's first birthday—all together—and we've missed so much. Where is that baby girl? Can you take me to her? I am just dying to hold my granddaughter for the first time."

We all entered the house as the tow truck began pulling the Porsche out of the driveway. Joe inquired, "What happened to that sports car with the flat tires and smashed front end?"

"Oh, it's a long story. Cole's partner Roman had a little girlfriend trouble, Joe."

"My oh my. This younger generation sure is different. In my day we took extra care of a car, if we were lucky enough to have one. And they weren't fancy ones like that either," Joe said with a sigh.

Joe and Rose stopped and stared as they entered the two-story foyer.

"I've never seen such a magnificent house, except maybe on TV. I loved that TV show *Dynasty*. Kate, did you ever watch that?"

Distracted by my brother and Rachel coming down the stairs with their overnight bags, preparing to leave, I did not answer Rose.

"Jamey, please don't leave," I called out to him.

They stopped at the bottom of the stairs. I ran over to hug him.

"This is my fault. None of this would have happened if I had not made such a big production out of showing off my dress." I began to cry. Bonnie's warning had materialized. All of Heather's excessive mascara began running.

"I don't understand, Kate. Why is this your fault?" Jamey asked sincerely.

"This night was supposed to be a family gathering in celebration of baby GiGi's first birthday and Cole's thirtieth. I turned it into selfish 'look at me' drama over making a dress. I am truly sorry," I said, crying more but getting out my apology.

"If I had just let this be what it was supposed to be, I could have still shown off my work, and Cole could have invited Roman and his girlfriend for dinner, and she wouldn't have been arrested at the hotel and all the rest."

"Don't be crazy. You could not have prevented this by having that girl come to dinner instead of being at the hotel. In fact, if the cops were after her for drug sales, they might have busted down the door and come in here to find her." Jamey was calm yet serious and to the point. My baby brother who had been through so much was calming me, the "in control" big sister.

I turned to Rachel.

"I love you both so much. Please don't go. We need to have a family birthday party."

Jamey dropped their overnight bag to the floor; looked at Rachel, who nodded affirmatively; and said, "We love you so much back. Of course, we want to stay. I can't wait to see the cake!"

"Two cakes. And they are special," I replied.

Jamey and Rachel picked up their bag, went back upstairs, and removed their coats, getting comfortable for the renewed evening celebration.

Joe and Rose were still standing in the entry foyer. Cole was still outside on the front steps, and my parents had not come out of the library. I needed to get into high gear to revive the situation, which had turned in to a disaster, in front of me.

"Rose, I'm so sorry I did not respond to you about *Dynasty*," I began with superficial talk. "I'm afraid it was on TV before I was born, but I've heard of it,"

I said, giving my mother-in-law a big kiss on her cheek. "Rose and Joe, come into the library and join my parents. I'll go get Cole."

"Honey, where's the baby? I've just got to see her," Rose said.

"What was I thinking? Of course, you do. Hold on one second."

Leaving Rose and Joe, I ran to the front door. Grabbing Cole, I begged him to wrest himself away from whatever demons were controlling him, including the bourbon, and come in the house. He needed to be with his dad while I took Rose to the baby. I practically yanked him. He obliged.

Like the angel from heaven that she was, Heather appeared in the foyer, having come from checking on the kids.

"Kate, your makeup! What did you do?" she said, looking at me and holding back laughter.

"I cried—a lot."

"That will do it."

"Heather, could you take Rose into the kitchen to meet GiGi and see the boys? I'll be in to join right away. By the by, please say hello to Cole's parents from Reno. Rose and Joe, this is my best friend, Heather."

Rose was whisked away to meet her only granddaughter and to see the three grandsons, while Cole and I put our arms around one another and Joe, leading him into the library.

Smelling the bourbon coming from his son, Joe remarked, "I guess you're having plenty of fun on your thirtieth, Son, even though it isn't the date."

"Oh yeah, Dad, it's a banner day." After I jabbed him in the side, Cole changed his tone. "Dad, it is great to see you. It's been too long. Let's catch up, then say hello to Dalt and Nancy."

I was amazed that Cole sounded almost sober and thoughtful. He had pulled it together.

Excusing myself at the entry to the library, I went upstairs to remove *ma révélation*, wash my face, and dry my hair. Cleaning up in record time, I returned to the library, scared to death of what I would find. This could require a type of damage control beyond my capability.

Instead, I found the entire family, plus Rose and Joe, including all the children, Heather, Bonnie, Marta, and Jefferson, engaged in conversation in a relaxed and loving family way. Was this possible? A half hour before, the police were taking Sierra away, Jamey and Rachel were bailing, and Cole was drunk on the stoop, watching Roman walk off into the dark of the Beverly Hills night. And I, well, I was having a minor breakdown and my face was turning striped.

The whole group began laughing with hysterics as Rose told the story of Joe getting lost on Sunset Boulevard, totally missing Beverly Hills and ending up almost in downtown Los Angeles.

"We went through a Mexican section, then a Korean section, then a black section, then a section I couldn't pronounce." Rose went on as Joe kept interrupting, creating more laughter. "Yeah, when we got to a lake near downtown that had so many poor and homeless people living under sheets around one side, Joe finally said to me, 'Honey, we've gone too far!'"

Jefferson, standing at the bar, rang his dinner bell. "Family, it is getting late. The children will have to go to bed soon. I suggest we all have the birthday dinner."

Marta then rose and spoke. Her thick Spanish accent seemed to vanish in her excitement, rather than the opposite.

"I made a decision," she offered. "With all the goings-on, I put the dinner buffet style on the counter in the butler's pantry so everyone could help themselves. Just in case we were not sitting down tonight as planned."

"You are brilliant, Marta," Nancy offered.

With that, birthday dinner ensued—casual, family style. Rose chose to sit at the children's table with GiGi, Bonnie, and the boys. Cole miraculously had come out of his stupor and returned to his charming self. Dalt warmed up to him, which was a good sign. It made me happy, less tense.

Out came the birthday cakes, held by Jefferson and Marta. Candles blazed, thirty in number for Cole, and a single tall pink one on the cake for GiGi. Singing off-key, Rose joined GiGi in the first blow and first wish. We applauded with glee. Then Cole sucked in a hurricane of air in order to extinguish all thirty candles, letting go and sending out a bourbon glaze over the top of the cake covered with white and dark chocolate fondant. Nobody said a word, except Joe.

"I always like a little hint of liquor flavor in my chocolate frosting."

More roaring laughter. All kinds of loving, sentimental toasts and tales followed. GiGi was adorable, neither fussing nor crying. Even the boys sat pretty much still. Dalt delivered one of his superdad speeches. We loved them, and we loved him for each talk he made at every major family occasion. Not to try to top him, I stood up at my place at the table and followed.

"First, all my love to my baby GiGi on her first. At least ninety-nine more to go. To Cole, my husband, my love, thirty is only the beginning. You are, next to my dad, the most hardworking and interesting man I know, and our journey is just taking off together. And together we will achieve all our dreams. We are lucky. We are blessed."

Pausing, I looked around at each person around the dining room, making eye contact.

"I want to apologize for my selfish behavior and my obsession over revealing my fashion creation earlier tonight. It was not my intention to steal the thunder away from the birthday party. Nevertheless, it turned out that way. The whole entrance down the stairs was over the top. I am sorry. It is just a dress—a dress that I made, but just a dress. I did not create world peace. I did not cure cancer. Because I was so focused on me, I told my husband that his partner Roman could not invite his girlfriend to my party because I do not like her. It was 'my' party. Look what happened."

"Kate, honey, Joe and I came late, so we don't exactly know what happened before, but we both are having the most wonderful night with you, Sal, and your family. Thank you from the bottom of my heart for including us."

Dalt said, "Who's Sal?" Then he remembered Cole's real name.

"Mom and Pop, you are always welcome. We love you," Cole called out to Rose, going over to her and GiGi, planting a big birthday kiss on his daughter, then a kiss on his mom.

Bonnie moved to take GiGi to prepare for bedtime. Rose handed her most precious child over. I took the boys, and we left the dining room for baths and bedtime—the first time the entire family was staying overnight on Lexington Road. Heather joined Jamey and Rachel, offering good night kisses, ready to depart. My brother and Rachel had decided after all to go home to their apartment in Santa Monica rather than do the whole overnight thing. I called out to them from the stairs.

"You're going to miss waffles, bacon, lox, bagels, and all the rest at brunch Sunday morning," I said, hoping to induce a final change of heart.

"We can always come back," my wise younger brother responded.

"I love you both so much. Drive carefully."

The three boys waved at their uncle, calling out, "Good night, Uncle J." That's what they called him.

Dalt offered a nightcap to Rose and Joe, which they declined. Rose asked Cole if he wouldn't mind leading them back down Sunset Boulevard to the Holiday Inn.

"Oh my God, in the pitch-black, who knows where Joe will end up? I guess we could only go as far as the ocean. Is there a bridge to Hawaii?" Rose asked jokingly, although she was serious.

"Mom, I will drive my car. You both follow. The hotel is a ten-to-fifteen-minute drive, and I promise I'll have you safely tucked in. Better yet, I will pick you up in the morning to return for brunch. How about that?"

Joe was about to decline the offer, being ever so proud. Rose made sure he kept quiet.

Cole, now mostly sober, escorted his parents to their car, promising not to drive too fast, saying he'd be in front of them and wouldn't lose them on Sunset Boulevard on the journey back to the Holiday Inn.

I accepted my father's offer for a nightcap in the library before going upstairs to the children.

The house was quiet; it had been quite the night. Nancy kicked off her heels and curled up on the tufted leather sofa next to my father. Her head rested ever so gently on his left shoulder. Dalt sipped on a liqueur he preferred called Goldschläger. I could smell its sweet cinnamon aroma from across the room. Just as I was beginning to repeat my apology to my parents for all the drama, Nancy sat up and halted me.

"You need not apologize, darling. Shining a light on yourself and your dress tonight did not cause the drama, nor did it take away from the family birthday celebration. It was just one part of the night. Don't be ridiculous. Not inviting Roman's girlfriend to dinner has nothing to do with her personal troubles that landed on our front drive. We could dissect this all night to no avail. Just know one thing: I am damn proud of you. You deserve to grab the spotlight now and again."

Dalt jumped in, saying, "Your mother is right. Keep up your work. Live your dream. You will succeed, and you will handle it all—husband, children, career. And you will do it your own way, in your own time. We will always be proud, just as we were tonight as you descended the stairs."

Nancy added, "But maybe less makeup on your next grand entrance." We laughed. I came across the room, joining my parents on the big leather couch. We were like three human dominoes tilting to the right, Dalt holding my mother and me upright.

"Kate, I am worried about Cole," Dalt confided. "What's with the excessive drinking all of a sudden? Why did he feel he needed to return our investment so suddenly without discussion? And most seriously, his partner is involved with an alleged drug-dealing girlfriend. This, I'm afraid, could spell disaster."

Before I could comment, Dalt went further: "Mostly this worries me for your sake and for the children. We need a private family talk with Cole. Will you see if he is willing to meet?"

Dalt was right. The potential trouble could not be ignored. I was fooling myself, having experienced the drug thing first with Sierra more than a year before. Cole was going to resist a family talk. I shared this with my father, asking that he let me handle the situation, at least for now, and keep it between the two of us. Nancy and Dalt reluctantly agreed.

After sharing good night hugs, I left my parents on their couch. Nancy turned on a Tony Bennett recording. They snuggled with a cashmere throw, and I went to check on my children.

CHAPTER SIXTY

A TURNING POINT

My fashion career was still on hold after the reveal. Looking back, I realized that the serious and overwhelming sense of foolishness remained. It was as if I had reverted to someplace from a childhood fantasy. Really, a grand entrance down the helical staircase? Who was I kidding? Scarlett flipping O'Hara had returned without the green drapery.

So it was. Trying to let go, I remained haunted by my inexperience, despite the gallant effort in learning to sew and construct a garment. Previously blinded perhaps by a privileged life, by the brainwashing since birth that the world was at my beck and call, I faced reality. And that reality was simply that I didn't have a clue about fashion design, or the industry, or how to navigate the path.

The reality did not deny my progress. Thanks to my dear mentors and my best friend, I had the support to figure it out, to reset, to focus, and to start over once again. How many times in life must one start over?

Taking care of the children remained my full-time job, and it made me happy every day. The boys were thriving, with Buddy starting preschool. Adorable GiGi was the light of my life. She was beginning to walk, starting ever so carefully around her first birthday. In the ensuing months she had become fully mobile and enchantingly verbal, speaking not just words, but also sentences. They were short sentences but were sentences just the same, my little genius.

Cole was not around much to share in this joy. Sadly, I had expected as much. It had always been part of the equation, a factor in our relationship. In the first years, the mind-blowing sex had made up for his long absences. Almost five years into our marriage, sex was not the bond, but the addiction. Yes, my husband re-mained a spectacular partner, the feelings of ecstasy not having diminished. But we rarely talked these days—about anything at all. I needed to talk to my husband, but he had become more emotionally and verbally distant. Whenever I tried to break the silence, I was told that everything was perfect—our lives were perfect, our children were perfect, and business was perfect with money growing on trees. Maybe I was suspicious, just a bit cynical. City girls who grow up in rich towns observe plenty of life, from the worst to the best. We develop radar, keener than that of the average woman from less competitive circumstances. My radar told me that things were not perfect as Cole assured me they were.

On the surface, I saw no evidence to the contrary. Business was strong. Construction starts were still rising everywhere. Cole and Roman and their BIG

Fund had raised millions in the first six months of the year, while all the plans, permits, and legal and coastal issues were resolved, with building about to start on their twenty lots at The Summit. The remainder of lots were all sold to outside contractors and developers with most escrows closed.

With all the lofty success, I managed to stall my father in terms of his request for a family meeting with me and Cole. The drug drama that had derailed our family gathering had somewhat faded into the background. Dalt did keep asking, and I kept reassuring him that things were under control. Cole and Roman were on good terms. Sierra was still in Roman's life, but there was no further police involvement. Dalt wanted to know what happened following the Beverly Hills police arrest in his driveway. They never followed up with him. I shared that Sierra had managed to avoid serious trouble. Roman had hired a top attorney, and Sierra did no jail time since she did not have a prior record, having avoided previous consequences with the law. Currently, she was in court-ordered rehab. After I'd shared this much information with my concerned father, he said no more, but he clearly wasn't happy about any of it.

At least Dalt no longer questioned Cole about returning his investment money. With the millions coming in from outside investors, my father took the high road with Cole, as he did admire his business drive and his insistence to make it on his own. Figuring that the return of the money was Cole's way of saying *Thank you. I can take it from here,* Dalt let it go. Cole did send Dalt a new check, less the interest.

Cole never explained to me why he had given back the money, even though I had asked multiple times for weeks after the family dinner. I also asked him multiple times why he had found it necessary to drink himself into a semiconscious stupor that night. Again, no explanation, just an apology and a renewed promise to remain in control when under pressure.

There was more than enough pressure. With all the demands of the BIG Fund and the land development, which was ten times more than enough for any superman, Cole was traveling the nation, shooting episodes of *American Dream Homes.* Producer La Penta had made the deal for the expanded show, which was now on national cable television. The scheduling demands were pulling Cole in multiple directions. He loved the fame and the glory, and he was addicted to the money. He confessed to me in one rare moment of intimacy that he was relying exclusively on Roman to carry the weight on the development project. Pressed to consider if this was wise, Cole was blinded by the TV fame, sharing that being famous was his destiny. I was shocked by the admission. Had he just said those words to me, words that surfaced while we made love, just seconds before climax? Oh my God. Yet again, overcome by my sexual addition to Cole, I let it pass.

The confession had come the evening before Cole was to leave for the East Coast to shoot a series of episodes over the following week in Palm Beach, Chevy

Chase, Bryn Mawr, and Rye. From Florida to New York, he was making another run at chasing fame. Never having considered such a thing before, I asked myself now if my husband was faithful on these TV trips. He wanted sex—needed sex. Was he faithful on the road?

Anyway, as was the case with my concerns over the business, there was no evidence to indicate Cole was cheating. I didn't want to consider the possibility anyhow. When he made love to me, it was true and real. There was no way he could share such passion with anyone else.

A Rough Night

On Friday night the week Cole went east, I put all the kids to bed, giving Bonnie a break. The house was quiet by eight thirty. GiGi was usually the first to go down, but on this night, she was fussing. The fussing turned to tears, and I spent a good half hour soothing my child into sleep. Ready for a glass of chilled rosé and a nibble of something delicious, I did not eat my share of the healthy noodles, fruit, and bites of boiled chicken placed before my children hours earlier. GiGi had not touched her dinner; maybe that was the reason for her discomfort.

Midpour of the wine, I heard the crying. Returning upstairs to GiGi's nursery, I found her sitting up in her crib, clutching a yellow bunny she called Sunny, her fair little face flushed. Putting my hand on her forehead, I felt she had a temperature, and touching her neck and cheek, I thought I was feeling swollen glands. My baby was coming down with the flu. Locating the baby thermometer, I took her temperature: 101°. Placing a cool washrag on her forehead, I picked her up out of the crib and sat in the adjacent rocker, dimmed the lamp by my side on the table, and turned on a bedtime lullaby soundtrack in the CD player behind the lamp.

My child was miserable. Nothing was calming her. I rose and took her with me downstairs to prepare a bottle of juice, the last resort, which generally helped in such situations. GiGi reached out and grabbed it from me and drank the liquid as if she had been stranded in the Mojave Desert. With her seeming to be doing a little better, we returned upstairs, and I put her in bed with me. Wasting no time changing into a nightgown and jumping into bed, I cuddled with my child, holding her close, keeping the blankets off since she was burning up. I continued to stroke her back to relax her. The process worked off and on. GiGi fell asleep after another hour. I remained awake, watching her to be sure things did not deteriorate.

At eleven thirty, my child awoke with screams. I had dozed, so this was a scare. GiGi was inconsolable. The fever was now 102°; her face, tomato red. She kept telling me, "Mommy, I hurt. Arm hurt. Leg hurt. All hurt." Ten minutes later we were in the car going to Hoag Hospital.

I had been unable to reach GiGi's pediatrician on my cell and had left a semifrantic message. My tires screeched upon entering the hospital's emergency porte cochere. I hit the brakes. The midnight valet, whose chin was down on his chest, his body braced on a stool behind a podium, jumped as the car came to a stop. He ran to open the driver's-side door. Getting out and running around to the other side, I picked up my daughter, removing her from the strapped-in car seat. She was asleep and more at ease thanks to the car ride, in spite of my wild driving. Maybe she was just fighting a flu or some stomach infection, and I was turning into the crazy mother.

Luckily the emergency department was slow, a miniature miracle for a Friday night. GiGi remained sleeping in my arms, wrapped in a soft blanket and clinging to her yellow stuffed Sunny bunny. The hospital staff was very kind. We were shown to an exam room within minutes, followed by a nurse and a doctor on call. The nurse asked to hold GiGi for the doctor's examination, and I offered to fill in instead. GiGi was slow to rally, sleeping soundly. The doctor was very gentle with her, checking her vitals. Her temperature had fallen to just under one hundred degrees, a good sign, and the redness in her face had also diminished. The diagnosis was flu. The usual remedies were suggested, and the emergency room doctor advised that we check in with our primary pediatrician in a day or so if symptoms worsened. Otherwise, it was rest, fluids, and baby Tylenol. GiGi was half awake and calm, smiling at me and the doctor. The overprotective wild-driving mom carried her baby girl back to the valet station, finding the attendant sitting on his stool with his head down, half asleep. He managed to retrieve the car, and we were home in fifteen minutes.

Meanwhile in New York

It was five o'clock in the morning in New York. Cole was being interviewed by hotel security at the Gotham Regent Hotel on Central Park West. The *American Dream Homes* crew was overnighting in the city following the daylong shoot at an estate in Rye, New York, a particularly exclusive Long Island domain of old money. It was the last day of shooting following an arduous five shoots that had begun at the Flagler mansion on the grounds of the Breakers Hotel in Palm Beach. Producer Rocco insisted on staying at the Gotham Regent when in New York; the turn-of-the-century hotel designed and built in European chateau style was always his first choice.

Cole had never been to the Gotham Regent. He had never been to New York City. The Big Apple was a sensory explosion for this now thirty-year-old real estate mogul, almost, from his new hometown of Newport Beach. Sure, Newport was ritzy in a Southern California beach kind of way, but New York was the prize.

Dinner with Rocco and several of his East Coast investors was set for eight o'clock in the Grand Pavilion dining room in the hotel. Checking in at five, Cole got to his room and immediately stripped off his suit. July in New York was fiercely warm, with humidity levels approaching what normally accompanied a rain squall. The collar of Cole's white dress shirt was gray with moisture, and its edge was pinkish tan from the makeup required for the cameras. With his clothes piled on the floor by the door, the naked reality TV star, glowing with sweat, made a dash for the shower. Languishing for a good twenty minutes under the rain showerhead pouring water above, running down over his head like some drug rinsing away all the craziness of life, Cole turned the large chrome lever off and stepped out.

Dressed in his Calvin jeans and white piqué cotton pullover polo shirt, Cole slipped on his navy-blue Gucci loafers with the gold buckles, no socks, and headed for Fifth Avenue. There was time to explore. The warm July night had brought out the tourists. Fifth Avenue was busy. With sunlight until well past eight o'clock, and clear skies, no rain in the forecast, the air was cooler, the heaviness of the humidity having lifted. Cole passed by Bergdorf's and stopped to look in the windows facing Fifth Avenue. Every store, each building, held another visual surprise.

Within minutes, he had traveled ten blocks, and the visual map began to change. Landing in the jewelry district at closing time, he watched Hassidic Jewish dealers removing a sea of diamonds and gemstones from storefront windows. Who were these bearded men in black placing diamonds into velvet pouches? Cole had never purchased a significant ring for Kate; somehow it had fallen through the cracks.

Cole thought about not having the money to buy Kate a ring when they first met. She had told him she didn't care—it wasn't important. Then a feeling of guilt hit him as he was window-shopping on Forty-Second Street, looking in one window as a bearded man in black Hassidic garb removed the final sparkling diamond ring. It was a large round stone mounted in a classic engagement setting with baguette-cut diamonds on each side. Cole figured it had to be a least a couple of carats. He knocked on the glass and yelled, "How much is that, and what size stone?"

The bearded jeweler could not hear Cole through the bulletproof, soundproof glass, but he knew what he had asked. The man held the ring up closer to the window for Cole to examine. On a card he wrote, "Five carats, VVSI center: two one-carat baguettes, also VVSI. Sixty thousand dollars."

Cole shouted, "I'll be back," then waved and moved on down the avenue. The guilty feeling subsided, yet he wondered why he hadn't bought Kate a ring after his first big escrow closing that was due to her father. This made it worse. He told himself he would make good. Having seen the perfect ring, the last one in the window, he felt it was a good sign. He would return in the morning to make things right.

Cole liked to think of himself as sophisticated, but when he had moments of raw honesty, he knew better. Leaving the diamond district, he encountered a couple of women on Fifth Avenue who recognized him from *America Dream Homes*. They gushed. He puffed up and signed autographs on receipts they had pulled out of their respective shopping bags. Cole's night was made; it was another sign.

Arriving back at the Gotham Regent, he ran into Rocco La Penta and his investor friends in the lobby. It was early for dinner; Rocco suggested a cocktail in the hotel lounge. The men found an open booth in the Vanderbilt Bar, a richly paneled room fashioned of time-aged mahogany, oriental carpets, and dark red leather booths. The drinks started coming in waves, punctuated by the high-flying stories of business dealings and killings made in the conquest of a dollar. After three J&B Mists in barrel glasses, per his request, Cole joined the talk about success, bragging to the fellowship and sharing details on The Summit development and the twenty building starts he and Roman were about to embark upon.

After a fourth J&B Mist in a barrel glass, Cole told the crew about his secret mansion rising on the Newport coast. He alone was building his dream home, never mentioning Kate. The investors asked bluntly how Cole was financing all this luxury real estate.

"Surely Rocco isn't paying you that kind of money for hosting his TV show," one of them said sarcastically but directly. Howling with liquor-induced laughter, Rocco joined in the sarcasm. Cole was oblivious to the undertone. He went on bragging about the millions in the BIG Fund.

The men pressed on. They were less liquored than the TV star.

"How are you finding investors?" the first man asked.

"What guarantee are you offering?" the second man inquired.

"Are you paying interest, dividends, or what?" the first man followed up.

"Did you sign a personal guarantee?" the second man blurted.

"Just how much have you raised from investors, and how much funding is coming from banks?" man one asked.

The machine-gun barrage of questions continued. Cole smiled, listened, and sipped his J&B Mist, ever so cool.

Finally, the interrogation halted. Cole said nothing. There were more smiles, then he answered with a lie and slurred speech.

"We are at one hundred investors, and the fund is closed. Total capital in the fund is eighty million dollars. Our bank loan is secured with a line of credit for one hundred fifty million dollars at 5.95 percent up to fifty million dollars, and then it accelerates."

His explanation was pure liquor-induced fiction. Cole had no idea about the terms of bank financing. That was Roman's job.

The hour of boozing and bragging was past. Rocco broke up the party, instructing all to meet at eight o'clock in the dining room. Cole stayed behind, nursing the scotch remaining in his oversized barrel glass, leaning back against the red leather upholstery in the old-world New York bar. The after-work business crowd was flowing in for their ritual end-of-day toot before catching the seven o'clock train out of Manhattan. Coming through the main door, surrounded by gray business suits, was Rocco's main man investor coming back. Cole called him simply "number one" since he wasn't sure of the pronunciation of the guy's name, even though it was an Italian name. Cole Baldwin once had an ethnic name, he reminded himself, despite the brain fog brought on by a long day of shooting in New York and three too many scotch cocktails.

Number One approached Cole in the booth.

"Did you forget something?" Cole asked.

"No, no, just wasn't ready to go back to my room," the man replied. Cole was confused.

"You have a room? I thought you lived in New York," Cole said.

"I live in Princeton, New Jersey, across the river. When I'm in the city for business, I often stay over, especially after late-night dinner meetings."

"I'm sorry, but do you mind if I ask your name again?" Cole was up front.

"Jerome Marinello. Call me Jerry."

"Jerry, Rocco shared that you are his main investor in the series. Are you a TV producer of other shows too?"

Cole was staring at Jerry, primarily because he was buzzed, but also because he wanted to size up the guy responsible for his TV job. At about forty-five years of age, maybe older, Jerry was a stereotype Italian stallion, a kindred physical specimen to Cole. He was older than Cole, but young-looking, and tall and blue-eyed with wavy black hair—a superbuff, great-looking man, muscular and studly Cole switched into male competition mode.

"I'm not a producer, I'm an investor. Rocco is a longtime friend. We grew up together in Jersey. We're like brothers."

Jerry explained that he was in the stock market, which Cole had a clue about, given all of Jerry's business bragging earlier. A waitress appeared offering service. Jerry ordered a beer. Cole pointed at his glass. The waitress got the message; another scotch would be on its way.

"So, tell me about how you got involved investing with Rocco?" Cole was blunt.

"Simple. He asked; I wrote a check," Jerry answered without hesitation. "In the interest of full disclosure, Rocco and I, along with Martin, the other guy you met tonight, all belong to a Hollywood club."

"You mean like one of the guilds, the writers, directors, or actors?" Cole replied clumsily.

"Not exactly. Our club has no walls, no dues, no formal member roster. But we know who belongs."

Even in his inebriated state, Cole's curiosity was piqued. Mafia perhaps? "I don't think I get it," he said, looking puzzled.

Jerry lifted his glass, signaling Cole to do the same in a toast.

"Here's to the Velvet Mafia," Jerry announced.

Cole knew the term. It was the control in Hollywood held by gay power players. Jerry Marinello, "Mr. Studly," was gay.

"Are you and Rocco together?" Cole asked, again clumsily.

"Do you mean lovers? No. Not since we were kids, that is. We were both closet jocks in high school, until we were not."

Jerry was open and direct. Cole tried to be cool but was uncomfortable. The waitress delivered the round of drinks. Cole grabbed his barrel and took a large gulp. Jerry laughed.

"I guess I've made you uncomfortable. I wanted to share with you. I thought you might be interested."

Cole took another large sip.

"Did Rocco tell you anything about me?" Cole got out the words, avoiding choking.

"He did. He said he came on to you, but you refused. He also said he didn't believe your refusal but, in the interest of your business relationship, dropped it."

"Rocco said that?" Cole was nervous.

"Yes. He said that exactly."

"I'm still refusing," Cole managed to spit out. "It's not that I'm not flattered and all. No hard feelings, but it's just not my thing. Are you okay?" Cole was drunk, but not drunk enough to risk the ire of the man paying his TV salary and making him famous.

Jerry was okay, watching Cole staring at him, eye to eye, seeking the queer eye connection. There was always hope for a change of heart, a liquor liberation.

Approaching the eight o'clock dinner hour, Jerry suggested breaking up the cocktail conversation and going to their rooms to change for dinner with Rocco and Martin as planned. Cole gulped the last of his scotch as the two men slid out of the booth, Jerry first, then Cole, who lost his balance and fell to the floor. Jerry reacted quickly, picking him up, holding him, and guiding Cole to the lobby elevators. The whole crew had rooms on the same floor.

Cole was out of it by the time the elevator doors opened on the tenth floor. Jerry carried him down the hall to his room, putting him down on the carpet beside his door, then fishing in Cole's jeans for a room key card. The fishing including fondling. Cole was oblivious. Upon entering the room, Cole was laid on the bed, and Jerry called Rocco to cancel dinner plans on behalf of himself and Cole. Rocco knew the reason without a word spoken.

Semicomatose, frozen, unable to move an arm or leg, Cole lay still on the bed as Jerry undressed him, his head spinning yet not moving as he stared up at the hotel room ceiling, mentally counting hairline cracks and noticing the small imperfections in the plaster. Jerry was naked and on him, in him, and in control of him. Cole was being raped. He could not talk; not a word would form. He tried to move but found it impossible. Useless, he gave in and let it happen.

The assault would continue off and on well past midnight. Jerry was spent by one o'clock in the morning, and the alcoholic coma was pulling back on Cole. He was regaining consciousness and some control. He had never totally blacked out, remaining aware of what was happening. He was finally able to move his body to the side of the bed, roll over, and make it off and onto the floor, where he was on his knees.

Crawling to the bathroom, still on all fours, he managed to turn on the warm water and fill the bathtub. He slithered over the edge, a python slipping into a river. Cole returned to the warm water where he had begun this now fateful evening, but the water was not washing away all the dirtiness of life this time.

Managing to exit the tub, standing now, feeling stronger, Cole grabbed the white terry robe hanging on the door back, courtesy of the hotel, and went to face his rapist.

The slamming of the bathroom door as he left jarred the sleeping predator investor. Jerry turned to face Cole, smiling a huge grin of satisfaction and speaking in a low and sexy voice as if to say that their sex was the best and maybe it was time for some more.

"How you doin', dude? Did anyone ever tell you that you have the finest body in all of New York?"

Cole did not answer. Looking at Jerry with a blank expression, he moved over to him on the bed, reached over, and yanked him up by his dried-sex-sweat wavy black mane, pulling him off the bed. Jerry was now on the floor.

"Shit. What the fuck are you doing?" he yelled, screaming out.

"Get up, asshole," Cole said, having managed to find his voice.

Jerry got up, bouncing up with athletic grace under challenging direction.

"What the fuck, man? So we had sex. Get over it. You wanted it. I know you wanted it. Be a man. Be honest. Stop fucking fooling yourself and everyone else." Jerry was still screaming.

Cole's voice raised. "We did not have sex. You had sex. I knew it, but I couldn't move."

"Bullshit, man. Don't give me that. You didn't resist. No fight. No words. You even got so damn hard, I thought you would explode. And then you did explode. So cut the crap."

Cole lunged at Jerry, throwing a first right hook to his chin, followed by a left to the abdomen. In rapid succession, Cole put a forceful knee to Jerry's naked groin, which sent him bending over in pain and screaming at the top of his lungs. Not stopping long enough to recover from the ball-busting blow, Jerry went after Cole with his full might, pounding on him. Cole managed to escape, and Jerry began throwing objects—lamps, the desk chair, the luggage rack, a painting he had ripped off the wall—all aimed at Cole, and all crashing to the floor. He ripped a panel of the sheer curtains off the rod and cornered Cole against the wall, strangling him with the fabric. Cole tried a second knee to his balls. This time Jerry blocked it to protect himself, pulling Cole away from the wall with the end of the fabric that was wrapped around his neck.

Cole went flying and landed against a large wardrobe mirror on a stand, which also flew over, smashing with a crash that finally summoned help.

Rocco was the first on the scene, banging on the door, demanding entry. Jerry let him in. Cole was on the floor surrounded by shards of broken glass; he was bleeding on his forehead. The flow of red staining the white robe created a dramatic first glimpse of the situation. Rocco demanded explanation, but before any could be given, louder knocks on the door followed. Hotel security had been summoned by others on the floor who had heard the commotion.

After threatening police action, security agreed to leave the incident alone, considering it a matter of a personal domestic disagreement. The decision-making process had been lubricated by a handful of hundred-dollar bills Rocco demanded Jerry take from his wallet to ensure discretion. Cole was asked if he wanted to file a report and contact the police. He declined, dabbing at the cut on his forehead to stop the bleeding.

"I will take care of any room repair charges," Rocco told the men as they departed. The men gave him a stern look. Rocco ignored them, and took his old friend Jerry by the arm, gathered his clothes, and went into the bathroom to clean him up and get him dressed and out of there.

Calling out to Cole, Rocco asked, "Are you okay?" Cole did not answer. The bleeding had stopped; it was only a small scrape that had let out a lot of blood. Cole also found his clothes. He got dressed and packed up the rest of his things to leave. It was just six o'clock in the morning. He had a noon flight to Los Angeles out of JFK, but he could not spend another minute in that room.

Jerry and Rocco came out of the bathroom as Cole was picking up his suitcase to leave. The tension was extreme, yet nothing was said. Horrible, scary, unresolved demons filled the hotel room, the three of men silent. Cole looked back at his rapist/investor and at his producer, boss, and best pal. He waited for one of them to say something. Still there was silence until Cole reached the hotel door, suitcase in hand. Jerry spoke.

"You're fired" was all he said. Rocco said nothing. Cole turned and left.

CHAPTER SIXTY-ONE

THE LIE WAS PREFERRED

Cole arrived home from his East Coast TV shoot exhausted, emotionally distant, and nonverbal, despite my repeated attempts to have him open up. The more successful he had become, the more often I faced his highs and lows. The man I had married who once wanted to talk about everything now wanted to avoid talking about anything. This was hard for me—a lonely place. Now lonelier than ever, I was finding the silence and the absences increasingly indefensible. No longer could I explain it all away with a nod to the sacrifice necessary to build a career and move up the ladder financially and professionally. Yes, this was Dalt and Nancy's model, and I wanted it to be mine, but the model was cracking, breaking down.

Nearly a month had passed before Cole shared that he had parted ways with Rocco La Penta and *American Dream Homes*. We met for lunch at the Harbor Club, the last-minute invitation coming from my husband on a Wednesday mid-morning call. I was happy to get that call as we had barely talked much in weeks, with no intimacy. In the rocky moments of our life, our romance withstood the ills every time.

While we were seated at our harborside table, a continuous stream of Cole's fans and business contacts stopped by to make their presence known. Cole was up and down from his director's chair in yo-yo form. I remained seated, putting out a hand, offering a cheery smile, always the supportive wife, as the parade of social climbers, connection seekers, and casual friends finally dwindled, and Cole confessed.

"I've wanted to tell you, but I wasn't ready," he began, reaching across the glass-topped patio table, taking my hand. "I quit the TV show," he said. "I got into a fight with Rocco's main investor, and it led to fists. Rocco sided with his money guy. I had no choice but to resign."

I sat in a state of semishock, my mind racing.

"Cole, baby, you loved doing the show. How could this happen?" My thoughts translated into words.

"He kept criticizing me and demanding that I do things differently with my on-camera stand-ups that were not funny—at least to him. The guy ridiculed me, and he would not stop. It just kept getting worse, until I leaned over the bar at the hotel and punched him in the nose."

"Oh my God, you punched him? How could you lose control?" I said next, stopping as I realized the word *bar* was the operative term. "You were in the bar at the hotel when this happened? How many drinks passed before this punch?" I asked as kindly, yet as directly, as I could.

"Too many."

"Oh, Cole, what are we going to do? I want to help you. The drinking is short-circuiting your life. Darling husband, if the stress factor of your work is turning you into a drunk, I'd rather have a plain old hardworking guy with a good job, a simple house, an American car, and a wife and kids at home for dinner with him every night."

"You don't mean that. It's not who you are. It's not where you came from. You need and expect the best. I know that." Cole was rarely so honest, yet this time he was very wrong.

"How can I convince you that all I want is for us to be happy?" I asked, holding back tears.

At that moment, I got the terrible feeling that I was losing Cole. We were mismatched. We didn't really know or, worse, understand one another at all. What relationship we did have had begun with intense sexual attraction, which is what had sustained it. Suddenly, I feared, it would not be enough for the long-distance journey. If at this stage in our life, with four kids in tow, Cole believed that my happiness was dependent on wealth, especially since I demanded nothing special, I was at a loss for how to reach him.

My mind was racing. I was fearful and confused. Our lunch arrived, placed before us, as another well-wisher walked up to the table. Cole snapped back into "master of the universe" mode, greeting the guy with generous praise for his healthy good looks and finely tailored blazer. Was I having lunch with Dr. Jekyll? I quickly dismissed the mean-spirited reflection on my troubled husband's phony behavior.

When the man departed, Cole reached into his briefcase, which was sitting on the floor beside his chair, and pulled out a small wrapped box topped with a lovely pink satin bow. Handing me the box nervously, Cole let go before I could grasp it, and the box landed in my grilled salmon salad. The fumble broke the considerably thick ice. We laughed. Picking it out of the salad, I wiped the sides of the box with my napkin.

"What is this?" I asked, totally surprised.

"Not everything bad happened in New York," Cole replied. "Please open it. I wanted to give this to you right when I returned, but I couldn't find the right moment."

Carefully, I untied the pink ribbon and peeled back the silver foil paper wrapping the box. Opening the lid, I found a black velvet inner box. Realizing that it had to be jewelry, I pulled the velvet box out and popped opened the lid. A magnificent diamond ring flashed in the midday sunlight. I was speechless, frozen.

"Do you like the ring?" Cole asked, sounding more like a lovestruck teenager than a thirty-year-old father of four. He rose, came around to me, removed the ring from its box, and placed it on my wedding ring finger, sliding it down just above the simple gold band set with tiny diamonds he had given me in honor of our union.

"It's amazing, exquisite, in perfect taste. I love it," I managed to say with sincerity.

I did love it. It was exquisite and totally shocking—unexpected and unnecessary—a gesture that made my fears more real than ever. Cole was proving his worth to me, proving that he could deliver the wealthy life he believed I demanded, needed, could not live without.

"I never bought you a proper ring. I saw this ring in the window of a jewelry store in New York and knew it had to be yours. After I quit the TV job, I left the hotel and, on the way to JFK, stopped back at the store and bought this for you," he explained with exuberance.

Cole leaned down and kissed me. The kiss lingered. I felt the passion, only it just wasn't quite the same this time.

"Will you marry me again?" Cole asked as we broke the kiss. "I love you so much," he added.

"I love you too, Cole," I answered. "I will wear your ring with pride."

It was the right thing to say, even though I had not answered his question. I honored my husband and made him very happy. His face beamed with excitement; Cole came to life. We talked continuously through lunch. He did most of the talking about The Summit construction and the BIG Fund. I talked about our children.

The Mansion Rises

Cole excused himself as he was heading out to meet a builder for an afternoon meeting. Promising to be home for dinner, he requested a night of lovemaking to mark the presentation of the ring. The dark mood had lifted; intimacy in its most primal form was on the horizon of return.

The building contractor awaiting Cole was not one of the men hired at The Summit, but rather Cole's personal contractor overseeing the dream home on the hill. Cole no longer had his television dream home gig, but he certainly had his actual dream home project. Foundations had been poured and the framing was in progress. Over a period of months, with considerable cost overruns, Cole had modified the plans three times, each time enlarging the footprint. What had begun as a respectably modest mansion was now not modest at all.

The house was three floors high with more than eighteen thousand square feet and a subterranean garage capable of housing a dozen vehicles. The property featured a separate two-story guesthouse, a tennis court, an outdoor kitchen/dining pavilion, an infinity-edged pool on the hillside over the ocean, and a vineyard set to be planted on another slope of the hillside. Cole was living his most incredible fantasy. All of it was financed by investors in the BIG Fund. To date, more than two and a half million dollars had been borrowed, only about half of which had been paid back.

Assuring Cole that everything was on track, the contractor estimated finishing by Christmas 2008 with a move-in date during the holidays. A massive landscaping design was under way simultaneously, with specimen trees due to be planted in the coming months, during construction, so that they would be fully mature by finish. The contractor concluded their meeting by promising to have his crew adorn the Baldwin forest with twinkling white lights upon move-in. Cole handed him a monthly check for another quarter million dollars and departed to return to his office.

Thinking about Joe and Rose during the short ride down the hill, Cole envisioned the look on his parents' faces when they arrived for Christmas at the new residence. This had already been quite the day with the diamond presented to Kate, then seeing the framework of the house. He was excited to get back to the office and share news of this great progress with Roman, his sole coconspirator and confidant.

Getting off the elevator in the tower and entering directly into Baldwin headquarters, Cole saw his secretary waving at him as he was headed toward his office. He had advised the assistant earlier that morning that his doctor would be calling him at some point, asking the secretary to make sure he got the call, preferably not a message. She obliged. The call was on hold. Cole darted into the office and pushed the magic button under his desk to shut the glass cage door.

"Dr. Loebman, thanks for calling. Did the test results come in?" Cole questioned with purpose.

"Mr. Baldwin, all of the tests are clear. The first round we tested a month ago was clear, and this second round, which I deemed necessary, is also all clear. No hepatitis, no herpes infection, no syphilis or gonorrhea—all clear."

"HIV?" Cole asked directly.

"No HIV, Mr. Baldwin," the doctor answered.

"And these tests, and the records, are confidential, Dr. Loebman?"

"Indeed. They are your business only."

Cole hung up and jumped up out of his chair, pushing the button once again and dashing out of the office to find Roman. He was safe to have sex with Kate, the true love of his life, if not the only love of his life. It was a separation of values Cole still had great difficulty coming to terms with. He thought that he was at least a decent guy who would not endanger his wife, waiting for sex until he'd been cleared. There would never need to be any confession or explanation. Never would he have to tell the truth about what had happened in New York. It was ancient history, over and done with, forgotten. It was time now to move on and move ahead, full throttle.

From across the office floor, Cole could see that Roman's office was busy. Richard Hellman was in conference with him, while Mr. Smith and Mr. Jones were standing outside against the glass. Kit Hamilton stopped Cole midway across the open agent bullpen, requesting a meeting to discuss a deal. Cole acknowledged the request with a promise to call and catch up later. The promise was a hollow one, as Hamilton made such a request almost daily and Cole rarely responded unless forced. Hamilton remained on the radar of suspicion especially since he was responsible in part for having landed Hellman as both a client and an investor in the BIG Fund. They called that job security. Cole was not alone in finding Hamilton strange. Many of the agents expressed similar doubts about him. Part of this was real estate envy, a common thread in the ranks of competitive, "sell your mother for a commission" residential real estate wars. And part of it was the suck-up factor, which repulsed many on the floor. Hamilton was proverbially on his knees at the sight of his idol and mentor Cole.

Fully aware of the idolization, Cole could have used it to his advantage but saw no purpose, no need. Hamilton brought in business; that was the extent of it. Cole figured he did not need—and nor did he want—a slave following him around. Certainly not Kit Hamilton.

Not bothering to knock, Cole entered Roman's office. Greetings were curt, Hellman barely acknowledging him.

"What's up, guys?" Cole inquired.

Roman spoke first. "Mr. Hellman requires another payment, a rather large payment. We are attempting to find a path to making his happen," Roman said.

"You damn well better find a path," Hellman added in a low, nasty growl.

"What are we talking about here?" Cole pushed on.

"Like the last deal we did, Hellman wants to invest ten million dollars, this time in property that we can turn around fast and sell at a profit and repay him through his private sources."

"More land tracts in the Inland Empire like before?" Cole thought he was being helpful.

Hellman slammed his fist on Roman's glass-top bureau. It didn't break, but both Roman and Cole jumped back, fearing flying glass shards.

"We will need to do something different," Roman spoke up. "And we need to do it now."

"How fast?" Cole asked.

"Yesterday," Hellman answered, turning to leave through the glass office door. Smith and Jones, previously in standby formation, marched behind Hellman through the bullpen, all eyes on the triad of questionable influence. Kit Hamilton rose from his desk and joined the procession, following them into the elevator. Cole and Roman watched.

"I really don't like that Hamilton," Roman said, repeating it twice.

Making Amends

I did not remove the diamond ring from my finger, not even for a day. Everyone noticed. The compliments were endless, with credit going to my husband with each remark. Cole loved the attention, and I loved his receiving it. The accolades mellowed the recent anxiety that had dominated our relationship. No words were exchanged, and we had no conversations about how we might improve our communication or return to a happier family with all of us on the same bus, going in the same direction. Yet, life was calmer. We were closer. If not intellectually or emotionally, at least physically. Cole came home nightly—no late meetings. We shared our bed with considerable return of the spark, which I feared had diminished or, worse, was gone. It was not.

On this Sunday night following a wonderful day at home on the beach with all the kids playing in the sand from morning till dusk, Cole and I went to bed early after all the children were asleep. He began to make advances. We were both beat. Despite my serious attempt to come around and respond to the moment, our heads came together for a kiss, then we landed softly back on the pillows, side by side, and drifted off into that special deep and restful kind of sleep.

Startled awake by cries of pain coming from what we knew immediately was the baby's room, both Cole and I jumped as if we'd been smacked across the face, jolted out of the dream sleep. Instant hangover. Doing our best to slip out of bed, putting on robes, we ran to baby GiGi's room. Finding her bent over the railing of the crib, crying hysterically, I picked my baby up. She was very warm, burning up with fever. I felt her stomach, which was bloated and swollen, as were her lymph glands. Then she threw up over my shoulder, spraying her father, who was standing behind us. Cole was calm for Cole, only managing to say that the baby must have the flu.

Bonnie had the day and night off, so we both could not leave and take GiGi to the emergency department at Hoag Hospital. Cole tried to convince me that such a trip on a Sunday night was not a good idea for what was probably just the flu. He knew I had been down this road before, with the same result. Instinct told me to go, however. I asked Cole to hold down the family fort. Hopefully, the emergency department on a Sunday night would be quiet and we'd get in and out fast.

I was correct. The emergency room was wide open. We were seen at once. A very sincere fifty-something female doctor attended to GiGi. She was very kind and loving, holding my daughter so tenderly that I knew she was in good hands. GiGi began to calm down, closing her eyes. Her crying at first did not upset the doctor as she examined her without hesitation. Given the obvious symptoms, her first diagnosis was of course some sort of infection or flu. I explained that these same symptoms had occurred weeks prior, then subsided. I told her we had come to the emergency department then as well, then went home and administered the usual treatments for flu, with the baby had having responded appropriately. Since then, however, GiGi's overall alertness and energy level seemed diminished to me. I was concerned because her eating habits had also changed. Perhaps it was just the slow recovery from some flu or infection, but then tonight, there was this repeat performance. I went on to say that my child never cried with such painful outbursts. I was worried.

Examining GiGi further, the physician pointed out that splotches of rash were forming in several sections on her back, her legs, and the sides of her abdomen. They had not appeared before. Of course, I asked what would cause a rash like that, and the doctor offered that it could be nothing of concern or possibly a warning sign of a problem. She asked if she could take a small blood sample to send to the lab. I agreed immediately. A nurse was called in to administer the blood draw while GiGi was contented with a bottle of Pedialyte. The gentle doctor stroked her forehead as the blood was taken.

We were discharged with instructions to lower the fever, keep GiGi hydrated, and call the hospital Monday with an update. The doctor gave me her private cell number as well and told me to call her Monday afternoon as the results of the tests would be in. She assured me that no matter the results, the child would receive proper care, adding that I was not to worry, as it probably was just the flu bug. I took comfort in those words. While I had just met the doctor, I trusted her given the care she had shown with my baby.

Home by eleven thirty, I found that all was quiet in the house. Cole was half awake, which surprised me, watching TV and sitting up in our bed. He hopped up out of bed naked as I entered with GiGi asleep in my arms. I joked with him in a whisper, "If your daughter could see her daddy now!"

Cole pulled his robe on and joined me putting GiGi back in her room. About to place my child in her crib, I stopped.

"Cole, I want GiGi to sleep in our bed tonight. I don't want to leave her in here alone. If that bothers you, I can stay in here and sleep on the daybed," I said.

Cole insisted that the three of us stay together. We returned to our bed.

Placing GiGi between us, I propped up pillows all around her to box her in. The baby Tylenol was taking effect; she was peaceful. Cole and I cuddled in around our baby, lying half awake for quite some time to be sure GiGi was okay, then eventually falling asleep. It was not that special deep sleep that had marked the start of this Sunday night in bed together.

Life Changer

The good doctor delivered bad news Monday afternoon. Devastating news. More tests needed to be run for a secure diagnosis, but signs were leading toward childhood leukemia. At eighteen months of age, this was serious. We were referred to Children's Hospital of Orange County for treatment, the local resource dealing most significantly with childhood cancer.

Unable to get through the phone call, I began weeping and convulsing. The doctor on the line was shaken, offering to contact 911. I got it together, enough at least to tell her that I would survive the shocking news.

I realized that my life's purpose was now the full-time pursuit of care and recovery for my child. The doctor provided referrals at Children's Hospital for me to contact at my earliest convenience. I obliged. Hanging up, I called right then, making initial contact. An appointment was scheduled for Thursday, the first available, despite my insistence on seeing a doctor at once. Assured that a two-day delay would not cause further harm to the child, I reluctantly backed off and started doing my own research on the computer.

After downloading documents on childhood cancer, the symptoms of leukemia, the treatments, the survival rates, the long-term side effects, the best hospitals in the nation, the top doctors, and everything else relevant I could find, I started calling people. My mother was first. She screamed into the phone, as I had done. We cried. She said she was getting in the car and coming to Newport. I advised her to remain home.

The second call went to Heather. My rock told me we'd get through it and GiGi would be fine. Heather shared all the positive statistics, probably some she had just created to reinforce her solid and steady positive approach to all of life's challenges. Like Nancy, she offered to come down from school in LA, but I advised her to stay put as well.

The third call went to Cole. He was not in the office. His secretary told me he was on a jobsite. I called his cell. He didn't answer. I left a single message asking him to call me, not mentioning my fears.

Fortunately, Bonnie was at my side. I needed the support. The boys were all playing, oblivious and innocent. Bonnie had GiGi calm and occupied. The pain had once again subsided; there were no tears. She was still somewhat swollen but had no fever. The rash the doctor found had become more widespread, yet apparently did not itch. GiGi was not scratching or troubled by the redness.

The feeding hour arrived, as it always did, at five o'clock. I managed to prepare a fun dinner for the children. Fun meant things they loved, such as crispy little tater tots, blueberries, scrambled eggs, and juice. We sat down with Bonnie as Cole entered.

"How's everybody doing?" Father Cole burst in with high fives for his boys, Bonnie, and finally me. The boys responded with their best power fives, but there was no such response from Bonnie or me. Realizing his mood did not match ours, he asked, "Have I missed something?"

Bonnie said nothing, passing the tots to Buddy, who reached across the table, almost toppling the water pitcher. I signaled Cole to follow me out of the breakfast room, then took him by the hand and went out on the terrace.

Cole knew something serious was up. Before I could tell him the news, he said he had never seen me look so pale and so tight faced. Once I told him what was happening, the news hit him hard, harder than I'd expected.

"So, what do we do?" He was at a loss for words or ideas.

"We have an appointment with a children's cancer specialist on Thursday. It is our first step. I'm scared, Cole. Please hug me."

Returning to the children's dinner table, I found GiGi giggling with her brothers as they lined up blueberries on each of the plates, feeding one another one berry at a time. Mostly, the berries missed their targets, leading to joyous outbursts of laughter. Cole and I sat down at the table on either side of GiGi. Bonnie moved over one seat to allow us to surround our girl. The baby seemed happy and fine at that moment. She picked up a blueberry and offered to feed it to her daddy. He accepted, then kissed her on the forehead.

Our daily routine progressed as usual following dinner, with playtime and a bit of Disney Channel viewing prior to bath and bed. All seemed normal. Bonnie offered to sleep on the daybed in GiGi's room. Cole and I spent the evening reading all the literature I had pulled off the internet. There were multiple calls from Dalt and Nancy. They offered to step into action and find the best cancer specialist possible. I was grateful for the support, yet I'd found the strength not to panic, sharing that we would begin the process with Children's Hospital later in the week. After getting as much information as possible, we would plan. They wanted to be involved, and I wanted them involved. Cole agreed, admitting he was clueless and had no idea what to do. He promised to be as supportive as possible, and the two of us went to bed in silence. There would be no sex tonight. For me, there would be very little sleep, for I feared another relapse, another night of torturous pain for my child. Expecting to hear the cries at any moment, I forced my eyes open as I tried to read a book, propped up against the upholstered headboard with a pile of stacked firm feather pillows keeping me upright. Cole turned to his left side, facing away from the light of my bedside lamp, and fell asleep.

The rustling of early morning children's activity meant we had made it through. I had remained leaning against the headboard all night with my open book in my hands. At some point my forced and frozen open eyes had given up the fight in the early morning hours, as there were no cries to upset me in my ready and waiting position. I had never been so tired beginning a new day. Besides worrying for the next two days before the Thursday appointment, how was I going to carry on the routine without scaring my kids? Boy, this was a test. Talk about finding inner strength. I knew I was up to it. There was no other choice.

CHAPTER SIXTY-TWO

THE BIG DEAL

By the fourth quarter of 2007, the real estate buying frenzy had reached its peak. More than a year of loose lending, fueled by insanely rapid price increases and ubercompetitive demand, had exhausted an overheated market. For months, any property, regardless of price, condition, or location, that came on market sold after receiving multiple offers, often over asking price. A listing to a broker was money in the bank.

Consequently, good deals that made sense were now nonexistent. Deals of any kind, even those not making sense in this crazy inflated world order, were not existent. Roman was in trouble. He could not find anywhere to place Hellman's ten-million-dollar exchange. Worse, even if he could find the right property, Roman feared he could not flip a sale so easily at a profit—especially for a cash buy, and most probably even more difficult for any kind of financed sale.

The soft lending was beginning to harden. Those in the know were betting on a Wall Street correction—maybe not right away but coming up soon on the horizon. That temperature had not been picked up by media, and it surely was not touted by the Bush administration in Washington. Nobody was questioning the strength of US banking, the core foundation of the housing market and every aspect of the US economy that its tentacles touched—nobody with anything to lose, that is. The whispers of impending doom were spreading—slowly, but they were spreading.

Roman was one who had heard the whispers, but he did not share his fear with Cole or anyone else. After all, they had twenty housing starts in progress and another twenty in various stages with outside investors. Many of Newport's blue blood business guys had considerable money in the BIG Fund. Besides, the monthly luncheons and cocktail parties with the investors continued uninterruptedly on the first Friday of every month. The confidence building and the backslapping good-old-boy camaraderie instigated further investment and the induction of new members into the BIG Fund and its exclusive society. None of these men had awakened yet to smell the coffee. Their stock portfolios were percolating with unheard of growth. Their bankers remained bullish. Their own homes had doubled or tripled in value.

Up on Society Hill, Cole had borrowed another three-quarters of a million dollars from the BIG Fund, making installment payments on the mansion. Roman did not protest despite the crystal ball messages he sensed were coming. Perhaps there would be correction, but still, there was such demand for property on the California coast. That surely would never change. Their homes would all sell, and they would make their money and be whole. Another project would follow. Cole would repay his loans to the BIG Fund with his share of the profits from The Summit.

The job at hand was to move Hellman's money, share in that profit, and take a deep breath. Roman wanted to end the Hellman connection, but he knew they were in too deep. For the same reason, he needed to end the relationship with Sierra: he was in too deep. He was sexually addicted to Sierra, but Sierra was also Hellman's addiction, sexually as well, unbeknownst to Roman. But more seriously, Sierra was a Hellman go-between with the Boreanaz brothers out of Bogotá, where Sierra was born and had been raised before coming to Los Angeles as a teenager, the circumstances of which move remaining unknown and unexplained. The brothers were Hellman's main cocaine connection, and cocaine was Hellman's lifeblood business. Sexual addictive blindness had brought down empires. If Roman had a blindfold on, then Cole might as well have been in full body armor. They were both far below their pay grade, having underestimated Hellman.

Marching ahead in full fantasy mode, Cole presented his ever-perfect "master of the real estate universe" front. Never mind that he had lost his job hosting *American Dream Homes*. Most of his adoring fans still had no idea he was off-air; it was too soon, and reruns of shows kept playing. Never mind that he had made no real estate sales in six months while trying to become a TV star. He had generated no cash flow. And let's not forget that his baby daughter was about to enter serious treatment at Children's Hospital, seeking a cure for childhood leukemia.

Beyond the business bravado, Cole did attempt to support Kate. She turned her life upside down to dedicate all her efforts toward seeking a cure for GiGi. Their married life was on hold. The stress at home became overwhelming at times. When that happened, despite his promise, Cole could not rise to the level of support needed and backed away. Business became the excuse, and the construction on the hill was part of his escape. Cole rationalized that he was doing his part. He would earn the money to build a beautiful home for Kate and GiGi to live in with her brothers when she recovered. The Baldwins would live happily ever after in their villa overlooking the ocean.

Roman pressured his partner to get seriously involved in finding a property in which to invest the Hellman ten million. At first Cole figured it would be no challenge at all. In short order he found out he was wrong. "This is nuts," he told Roman. "There was always something to buy. How can this be possible?" Cole suggested that if they could not locate the right purchase, then they could sell a major interest in their development, or perhaps have Hellman's funds purchase several of the projects they had sold to other investors in The Summit. Roman was quick to advise Cole that the transfer of the ten million had to be hands-off, at arm's length, with no direct connection to them. Besides, Hellman was the main investor in the BIG Fund with another ten million used to finance part of the entire project.

"Man, use your brain, Cole," Roman demanded.

Sitting silently in the chair opposite Roman's desk, Cole absorbed the semi-insulting directive before responding.

"I've got an idea. I was at lunch last week at the Harbor Club. One of my pals told me that the biggest yacht in the marina is quietly on the market. The owner is out of the country. I think he said the guy lives in Slovakia. Where is that?"

Roman explained that it was a nation in the Balkans near Poland and Hungary.

Cole continued, "They are asking twenty-five million for the yacht, but my buddy told me it is a bargain-basement sale. The yacht cost like forty million to build, and to replace it would be over a hundred million."

This piqued Roman's interest. Cole was on a roll. He went on.

"Let's take five or ten million out of the Baldwin Fund, add it to the Hellman money—it could even be Hellman's money from the fund—make a lowball offer on the yacht, close the deal, then turn around and put it on the worldwide market at retail. Maybe we ship the yacht to Florida, where the big money yachts are bought and sold."

Cole went on to explain his knowledge of yacht sales in Florida from having seen the real deal while in Palm Beach and Fort Lauderdale on his last TV shoot. He sounded as if he knew what he was talking about. Roman stared at him, wondering who between them was the biggest bullshit artist.

Just the same, Roman now sat silently, considering the audacious plan.

"You know, it just might work. It's a risk, but we could make big money if this deal is what you say it is."

Doing the Deal

The end of the year came with no celebration. I spent every day, at least part of every day, at Children's Hospital with GiGi. The baby was in full-time residency. She was stable, but seriously ill. The final diagnosis was that our child suffered from acute lymphoblastic leukemia, both B cell and T cell. Doctors cautioned that GiGi's white blood cells were experiencing uncontrollable growth. Chemotherapy was keeping GiGi alive, but the side effects were challenging. I watched, horrified, as she suffered, tortured by a blood cancer she could not possibly understand. A bone marrow transplant was on the table for consideration.

Cole did show up at the hospital, unpredictably and at unannounced intervals. Mostly, he stood outside the sliding glass door to his daughter's room, watching me at her bedside. When he did enter, generally following a nurse making her rounds, he would stand at a distance in a corner of the room, which was buzzing, beeping, and pulsating with the electronic vibrations of so many machines hooked up to his eighteen-month-old child. His baby girl had lost all her thick curly raven-colored toddler hair inherited from her father, a consequence of the chemo. Cole would look over at me and see the sadness in my eyes yet was unable to comfort me. Several attempts at an embrace met with a stiff response. My message was clear: I needed space to focus on GiGi, and Cole's role was as subordinate given his erratic presence. I wanted him there with me. Cole could not, would not, deliver.

His mind, his attention, was absorbed in what had become two months of negotiations with lawyers in New York who were handling the bankruptcy case of one Slovenian precious metals trader, now back in his homeland and in hiding, about to lose his multimillion-dollar yacht berthed at the Harbor Club marina in Newport Beach. The BIG Fund negotiations to buy the yacht had failed after several attempts, forcing the partners to hire a high-priced legal team to do their bidding.

Finally, a deal was reached at the end of March 2008 as April's tax deadline loomed. "Timing is our friend," Roman repeatedly advised. The title to the yacht, christened *Xania II*, had been transferred to Cole Baldwin in a sale closing at nineteen million dollars. All the money had come from the BIG Fund, including Hellman's recently deposited ten million, plus another nine million of his original investment. Hellman was consulted and had agreed to the plan. He too saw the potential for a large profit after turnaround. He also saw something potentially even more lucrative.

Immediately after the closing, the partners went to work making connections to display and sell the yacht. More dollars were required for sprucing it up, as the vessel had been sitting unattended for more than a year. The surveys performed prior to the sale ended up in another cool million in repairs. This too came out of Hellman's funds, what was left in the BIG Fund account.

Once again, Cole Baldwin was the talk of Newport Beach. TV star, luxury developer, and sexiest man profiled in countless local glitzy tabloids touting the lifestyle of the nouveau riche, Cole was now owner of one of the California Riviera's most incredible yachts. The gossip traveled.

This was the perfect opportunity for promotion. Parties followed. Big, brash, wild parties attended by loose women with tight assets. Lots of them. Sierra made sure to include a tribe of her single LA friends, who mingled with the distinctly Newport blondes either on the arms of young handsome wannabe up-and-comers more interested in the overall geography than their respective dates, or the side-pieces of their older, more seasoned "uncles." It was all more of the same crowd for Cole and Roman, mostly hangers-on. Some called them sideliners because they were just that, on the outside of the connected real players—the "all hat, no cattle" crowd. Cole knew most of them. After all, he had hosted dozens of flashy real estate open house cocktail parties on land. Now the circus had simply moved from land to sea on the *Xania II*.

The grand party vessel was a favorite sight on the broad channels of the Newport Harbor. Its sleek elegant European-designed hull glided around Lido Isle, past Balboa Island, and out the main channel to the Pacific Ocean for regular Saturday night soirees. Music blared and lights flashed, reflecting off the moving current created by *Xania II*. Gawkers on balconies protruding from the Harbor Club hotel rooms peered through binoculars at the silhouette of party girls moving to the rhythm of the night on all decks as the yacht passed by.

With so much attention directed toward showing off the yacht, certain natives were getting restless back on shore. Cole and Roman had canceled their monthly BIG Fund luncheon two months in a row while dealing with the yacht negotiations, the launch, and the promotion. Their investors were beginning to wonder what was going on. Cole suggested inviting them all to an investors' party on board. Roman rebuked the idea with his customary directness.

"Are you crazy, man? What do you think will happen when you bring all these guys on board for one of these parties?" Roman demanded a response.

Cole tried to be funny. "They'll have a great time," he answered.

"Oh sure, they'll have a great time and want to know if their money is tied up in this yacht," Roman replied.

"Well, that's easy. Their money is not tied up in this yacht. We can tell them that."

"Then they'll ask whose money is tied up and where it came from." Roman was now yelling. Cole retained his cool, adding insult to his inappropriate humor.

"The guys will love all the girls Sierra shows up with. It'll be the ultimate bachelor party," Cole offered with a stupid grin.

"Oh yeah, all of our married investors' wives will love that idea, won't they?" Roman had had enough of the sophomoric plan. He needed to deal with the surge of unrest among the men who were becoming less secure because their money was bringing in no return. Something had to be done. Nothing was coming in; everything was going out. Construction starts were in early phases on the lots they controlled at The Summit. There was money in the bank from the sale of the other lots to outside contractors, but most of that money was spoken for, on paper at least, to cover the overall land buy and the improvements required to create the parcel and the infrastructure for the development. And a million and a half of the profit had been prematurely returned to Kate's father with Cole's attempt to impress his father-in-law.

The only option was to find a legit buyer for the yacht and flip it fast at a profit. Roman found a broker in Fort Lauderdale who was willing to take on the project.

Believing he could move it quickly, he determined that the ship needed to cruise from Newport Beach to Florida. The broker located a captain and a crew for hire, and Roman flew them out to Orange County.

The boat was set to depart the dock at the Harbor Club on the first of May. All the requirements for the journey had been secured. The ship passed all safety tests, and provisions were loaded aboard. Roman and Cole met the captain at eight o'clock that morning to have coffee and finalize all the details. As they were sitting at one of the Harbor Club tables on the terrace overlooking the docks, Hellman appeared, Smith and Jones trailing along, pushing dock carts filled with cases of what appeared to be champagne. Lagging behind was Sierra and two of her friends, all toting Louis Vuitton travel bags and giggling as they attempted to walk the floating planks toward the yacht in five-inch heels, hoping not to get stuck or, worse, fall over into the bay.

The captain looked at Roman and asked what was going on; there were not supposed to be any passengers on board for the voyage.

Roman looked at Cole.

"Don't ask me!" Cole blurted back.

Coffee time ended abruptly as the three men headed for the yacht. One of the crew was helping the Hellman entourage to board as the captain arrived, questioning the embarkation. Hellman introduced himself, letting his captain know that he was the owner and that he was boarding the cruise with his bodyguards and three of his female associates.

"The tall thin brunette is my secretary, and the other two are office clerks," he stated matter-of-factly. "I need their assistance on this voyage to complete my ongoing work," Hellman added.

The captain said nothing. Once again, he looked at Roman and Cole. They said nothing, only nodded in futilely in agreement.

"Sir, I don't believe we have enough food for all of you for the eight-to-ten-day trip," the captain said.

"If needed, we can add supplies at the canal," Hellman stated without blinking. "We may disembark in Panama anyway. I have business there. You will go on to Florida. We will fly back to the United States," Hellman advised loud and clear.

At noon the *Xania II* left her Harbor Club berth and cruised south out of Newport Harbor. The news of the exit was widespread, having been promoted by a mention in the society column in a section of the local edition of the newspaper. Residents turned out in the park at the top of oceanfront cliffs in Corona del Mar to see the yacht leave the harbor. Big ships coming and going from Newport always drew a crowd; this was a yachting tradition unique to a relatively small city on the West Coast of the American frontier. Citizens waved flags and shouted bon voyage; bullhorns sounded from the cliffs, as smaller vessels crossed and cruised alongside the mother ship, blasting their foghorns as *Xania II* left the mouth of the bay and entered the choppy open waters of the Pacific. Even the local harbor patrol had sent two vessels, one on the starboard and the other on the port side of the yacht, sending water spray high into the sky above, bidding farewell and a safe crossing to *Xania II*'s new berth on the opposite coast. Cole and Roman followed the parade on the bay, having borrowed an electric Duffy harbor boat at the Harbor Club dock to witness their twenty-plus-million-dollar investment cruise off into the choppy ocean waters.

With the final turn of *Xania II*, which was now in the Pacific, south toward Mexico, Roman and Cole got a final glimpse as Roman turned the Duffy around, just before it could leave the bay meet the ocean, heading back to the Harbor Club dock.

"I guess we did it," Cole said, speaking first.

"Not so fast, buddy boy. This rig isn't sold yet. We've got a way to go," Roman replied with caution, and for good reason: Sierra was on board. Sierra spelled trouble.

Cole got the message. "You're not worried about her, are you?" he asked.

"I'm always worried about her," Roman answered.

CHAPTER SIXTY-THREE

A NEW DAY

GiGi's white blood cell count began to normalize; the chemo was fighting the cancer, and she had responded, showing a glimmer of the innocent joy found in a little girl. After several months of touch-and-go, there was finally a pause, a momentary "stop the world and allow us to breathe" respite from the daily emotional roller coaster. GiGi's brief life so far had known much pain and little freedom. With the news of a turnaround, even a temporary one, I felt as if I were surrounded by the ghostly embrace of my grandmother telling me the baby would survive. GiGi was strong, a fighter, just like the woman who once shared her name.

The doctor advised that I could take GiGi home under strict supervision, having to return to the hospital for weekly examinations and tests. The chemo was put on a temporary hold, allowing the doctor to evaluate its lasting effect and plan the next phase of treatment. This break would allow the child to regain some strength, permit certain foods, and allow for more movement and play. This was a big change from weeks of confinement to bed.

Cole arrived, having received my phone message of hope, shortly before GiGi was discharged. It was midafternoon on possibly the hottest day in late spring on record in Southern California. I had not seen Cole that week, as I'd chosen to sleep in the hospital room with GiGi, monitoring her turnaround. With few hours of sleep over several days, I was fried, but exuberantly fried. Cole charged into the room, embracing me. He smelled like scotch, his beverage of choice. I chose not to question the scent of his afternoon cologne. Instead, I shared more of what I knew about our child's condition, while the nursing staff prepared us to depart with all the apparatuses required for home care.

When we got to the parking garage, I realized my Tahoe was in long-term parking, which was a blessing of sorts. I was preparing to go home with GiGi and Cole in his car, but I insisted on driving GiGi in my car, despite being exhausted. A tired driver is only a notch above a drunk one. This was not what I had planned for my baby's homecoming. The two-car situation saved us from confrontation, as I cautioned Cole to please be extra careful because we needed him at home safe with us. He got the message.

My husband's drinking was clearly a serious problem—one problem too many at a time when problems had to be prioritized. His substance abuse challenge was not number one on the list. Not for me, anyway, and not for GiGi. Unfortunately, not for Cole either. He was in denial. I finally realized that he was always in denial, having a proverbial awakening slap across my face. I too had shared in the denial. Alcohol had nearly ruined our lives in the beginning. Only Buddy saved us. Cole's promise to control the drinking failed, and I was weak in confronting him. How many bad experiences would it take? What if I hadn't had my car in the lot? What if he didn't make it home from the hospital on his own?

There were too many what-ifs. But I could not face this reality—not now. I would face it later; I knew that. I also knew that I alone could not help him. We were in a bad period in our marriage, yet I was not giving up without doing the work. My first duty was to GiGi, then to Cole.

Thankfully, both cars with precious cargo arrived safely back at the Lido house. Our arrival was welcomed; Bonnie made certain of that. The three boys were charged with energy seeing their mother and baby sister home again, and even dad was there too—everyone home together at the same time. Bonnie shared that my parents had called to check on us and that Heather was in Newport today and wanted to come by if it was all right. I had received the same message on my phone but had not responded to my best friend. At first I thought it would be best to have no company, but now I was having second thoughts. Heather always made everything better.

Cole spent some good dad time with his boys, even taking them all on a bike ride around the island. Bonnie and I set up all the necessary tools in GiGi's nursery while she sat quietly in her crib, holding her Sunny bunny and following our every move. I turned on music.

As I was administering a late afternoon dose of the meds prescribed, Bonnie was at the ready with a juice box and straw, along with two small vanilla cookies. GiGi had had no appetite in the hospital, but she reached for a cookie on the plate offered by Bonnie. Her reaching for that cookie was the most amazing and wonderful moment I had experienced in days. The ghostly embrace of my grand-mother came to my mind yet again; GiGi was going to survive. After I asked Bonnie to confirm my sighting of small strands of hair returning on GiGi's head, she looked very carefully, not seeing anything, yet telling me that she had indeed seen the beginning of growth. Looking again, I saw nothing, loving the lie. It was preferred indeed.

An early dinner was my next task. I called Heather and asked her to come. She was very happy to have gotten the call. Her joyous response at being invited to a simple dinner, a quick, last-minute gathering at the kitchen table with a baby bat-tling cancer, was another proverbial awakening slap across my tired face. Having a real true friend was one of the most important things in my life. I always called Heather "the rock." She was so much more; she was the entire mountain. Every woman must have a best friend; this was essential. Heather was essential in my life.

Cole and the boys returned from their bike ride, and Heather showed up with a bundle of glorious flowers from her mother's garden, plus several grocery bags filled with supplies and plenty of treats from my favorite, Gelson's Market. We were having breakfast for dinner—all I could pull together fast given what was fresh in the fridge. It would be scrambled eggs, precooked bacon from the freezer, buttered sourdough toast, and Welch's grape jelly to the boys' delight. Cole headed for the bar. I followed him and asked him to turn back. Fearing a confrontation, he obliged. I took his hand, and we joined the kitchen table for a family dinner of scrambled eggs. Cole asked for ketchup or Tabasco. I couldn't deny him that request.

"Have you talked to Monsieur or Madame lately?" Heather asked.

"Not in weeks, I'm afraid. I feel terrible about that," I answered.

"Give them a call. They are worried. I was in the salon with Mom a few days ago and they wanted to know about you and GiGi. I told them things were looking better, and I promised I would reach out to you on their behalf."

"I truly am sorry not to have called. I think I will stop by the salon instead of calling. And I will do it as soon as possible."

"Monsieur thinks my idea to place one of your designs on Amazon is a good one."

"I did not forget about that. It is filed away for now. What did he say?"

"Both he and Madame think you should design one signature item, such as the Fair Child blazer or maybe your one-size-fits-all wrap dress that everyone loves and put it on the Amazon website for sale. Just one item, specifically targeted and branded, and we can support driving sales on social media. I think we could reach thousands of young women on Facebook."

"Heather, I love this plan, but you are in law school and I am on cancer patrol. We both have full-time jobs that come first."

"Are you saying I can't multitask? Pass the eggs, please."

"You are the best multitasker in the whole world," I answered.

"And so are you, my dear friend. Besides, getting back on track with your dream is a needed distraction. Believe me, you will be a better caregiver for GiGi if you have a positive goal in your life, something to work toward, something to bring you some happiness, some escape. Please think about this and go see your champions. They miss you very much."

I passed the eggs, now cold, and asked Heather if she desired another piece of freezer bacon. She waved a *No, thanks,* instead instructing me to go into one of the Gelson's bags she had brought containing a large selection of fresh bakery goods, including the richest apple fritters available on the planet. Cole loved that news. He jumped up from his place to follow Heather's instructions. One of the apple fritters had his name on it.

Any fears of a traumatic bedtime for GiGi vanished in the arms of Bonnie.

My child was bathed peacefully and dressed in her onesie pajamas and was being rocked to sleep by her second mommy. Cole and I got the boys ready for the night, reading with them. I don't think Cole had ever read to them. Turned out to have been a rather special afternoon biking with their father, followed by my breakfast for dinner, with dessert courtesy of Heather, then an old-fashioned cowboy story read aloud at bedtime.

Cole and I checked in on GiGi before heading back downstairs. Bonnie had her asleep in the crib, cautioning us both to tread gently so as not to disturb.

"I know it's early, but how about a little cuddling in our room with the French doors open so we can watch the sun going down over the water?" Cole was getting friendly at the top of the stairs.

I thought about the proposition, wanting to accept.

"That's the best offer I've had in a long time." I spoke the words but hesitated to pursue the plan.

"Cole, I really need to talk to you. As much as I love your proposition, could we just go downstairs and sit in the living room like grown-ups and talk?"

"The living room? We never sit in the living room," Cole responded. "This must be a serious talk in a serious room."

"I didn't think of it that way, but you're correct," I said. "It's important. Really, do you mind? I promise to go easy. Let me call it 'good serious.'"

Cole was right, we never used the living room in this beautiful home made possible by Dalt and Nancy. So formal and old-world classic, the very large room spanned the entire width of the back of the Lido house facing the water. It had twelve-foot ceilings, walls of superb handset boiserie, and four matching sets of tall French doors topped by half-round clerestory windows fitted with fine beveled glass panels, with all the doors opening toward the herringbone brick terrace over the south channel of the harbor. On this very warm evening, I took Cole's lead and opened all four sets of doors wise, letting the glorious end-of-day light flow into the cavernous space. A pair of pale celadon settees flanked a Regency marble mantel surrounding a major fireplace at the west end of the living room. Taking my place facing the light, I invited Cole to sit next to me. A small bar resting on a gold-toned metal cart at one corner of the room drew his attention. He poured a drink, asking if I cared for one too. I didn't need to answer; he knew I didn't want to drink.

"Do you object to my having a shot?" he asked politely.

"I do not. Just come sit by me," I replied.

My husband joined me on the small plush sofa, sitting right next to me.

"This is almost as good as cuddling in our bed," he offered, raising his glass in a one-way toast.

"A shame we don't spend more time in this room," I told him.

"It's lovely," he agreed. "Look, I know it's been rough for a long time. What can I say? I'm sorry, Kate. Really, I am sorry."

"I'm not looking for an apology, Cole. I need more than that. Please try to understand. I feel like we are coming apart at our core. It's like I sometimes think that I don't totally know you. While I always have appreciated your unbelievable work ethic, I've made excuses for our lack of real communication because of it. Then again, those same excuses run cold when things happen that I don't fully understand." I looked at Cole, focusing on his drink.

"Like my drinking?" He was quick to get the point, at least the obvious one.

"Cole, the only times I've seen you—and they've been very brief over the last weeks—you have been partially drunk or fully sloshed. What happened to that promise made and kept for the past years?"

"You don't know what I'm basically up against." Cole raised his voice, his speech rapid and staccato.

"Of course, I know. I'm not blind. Maybe I don't know the details, but I know. Trust me, I know. But all the money pressure in the world should not be standing between us and, more importantly, between us and our GiGi at this very serious moment. I need you, Cole, to be there with me, for me, and for GiGi. I need to be we—simple. Can you be a we?" I asked, turning and facing Cole on the settee. The golden-orange ball of fire in the western sky was sinking toward the horizon far beyond our French windows, transforming the cream-colored silk-upholstered walls of the living room into a warm orange like a campfire glow. The mood was ideal for direct conversation, so I went for it.

"Can you be we?" I asked again.

Cole didn't respond. He stared back at me and tried to kiss me. I pulled back, putting both my hands on his chest.

"I can't be a we in the way you want it," he said honestly. "I did promise that before when GiGi first got sick. I failed. I know it. It's not an excuse, but I am wiped out by a deal Roman and I have put together."

Not what I wanted to hear, but I pushed ahead.

"Share with me. Talk to me about the deal. I'd like to know what's taking my husband over like some demon unable to be controlled."

"The demon is our client, the investor Richard Hellman. We are involved in a twenty-million-dollar yacht buy for Hellman, a yacht that we are presently moving from Newport to Fort Lauderdale for resale at a much greater price. It's kind of a live-or-die deal. To make matters worse, our other investors are restless for progress and some sort of dividend payment on their money used to develop The Summit. Kate, I have not had a commission sale in some six months. I got fired from the TV show. Money is tight. I need to make things happen."

I took a beat.

"Cole, you know I have money and can help if you can't provide for any reason. We are not just regular working people. You earn seven figures at thirty, with no education and no leg up from anyone except Dalt in the beginning. Your success is the stuff of legend around this town. Who else has fans stopping them on the street?"

Cole smiled, trying to kiss me again. My hands remained on his chest.

"Are you out of love with me, Kate?" he questioned, noting my resistance to his passion.

"I want to love you," I said. Strange words.

"What does that mean?" Cole's voice raised once again.

"I fell in love with you because you have such a strong sense of self-worth. You know who you want to be and what you want to do with your life, and your confidence is so sexy. We make love with passion that takes my heart where it had only been one other brief time before in my life. It is a rare emotional place I was bound to find again, and it came with you. You make me laugh. You let me pursue my dream career, placing no demands on me for my time. And when you needed me to be front and center to promote the Baldwin dream for you, I did so with pride. I was not always proud of the scene or the platform, but I was still proud of you."

Taking my hands off Cole's chest, I kissed him. The daylight was gone, the grand living room pitch-dark. We had not turned on a single light. His kiss was long and deep. The feeling was there again, not lost as I feared. I still was cautious, breaking the moment a bit sooner than my husband would have liked.

"Where do we go from here, from this moment?" Cole spoke softly.

"We join forces as a real loving team to do everything we can to save our child. We stay close through this challenge, the greatest challenge a parent can face with a child. With God's help, we will all come through better, stronger, loving, safe, and well. That's what I need from you, Cole."

"I need to ask again. You did not answer before. Do you still love me?" he asked.

"I do. We promised to stick together no matter what."

A Much-Needed Break

GiGi made it through the night with relative calm. I heard her cry around midnight, at which point I left our bed and relieved Bonnie. The baby took a bottle as I rocked her back to sleep, then returned her to her crib. Lying down with a pillow and blanket on the carpet next to her crib, I looked up at her through the shiny white rails. For that brief moment, there was no cancer. If only it were so.

Our first day home had gone remarkably smoothly. It was almost normal, if it hadn't been for the routine of treatment and meds required by the strict regimen. Following lunch, Bonnie pushed me to get out of the house for a break.

"Heather told you to reach out to Monsieur and Madame. Why not visit rather than call?" she proposed. "It will do you a lot of good."

Accepting the offer, I told her that I would be gone only an hour. She said to take two or three or whatever time I needed; she'd be just a phone call away.

Entering the salon was a gift from God. I was overcome by a jolt of renewal and relief. Bonnie and Heather were so right. I needed a break. And seeing my loving mentors and second family made so much difference. Feeling guilty about leaving GiGi, and the boys too—I had basically ignored the three boys for the past weeks—I did my best to let the bad feelings go and take in the escape at the salon.

My cell rang just as I entered, before I could greet Monsieur and Madame. It was Heather. She was still in Newport with her mom—a day of no classes at the law school. Once I shared that I had taken her advice and was just arriving at the salon, she told me that she was on her way. Madame heard my voice on the cell and was first to come with outstretched arms, then a kiss on both cheeks. I was home. The salon was empty, so it was time to visit, catch up, and share a little kindness. Taking my hand, as she always did, Madame led me to the workroom, where we found Monsieur.

"*Bonjour, mom amie!*" he shouted with glee. "*Tellement génial de te voir mon ami.*"

"I have missed you both so much."

"And we have missed you. We have been so worried."

"I have felt your support and your prayers. GiGi is getting better. She is now home," I shared, keeping the sad talk brief.

"You are brave as well, dear Kate. Are you handling the stress? You look tired, if I may say." Madame was sincere, nonjudgmental.

"We are doing well," I replied with too little explanation, which they both picked up on.

"And how is your handsome husband?" Monsieur inquired. "We watch his TV show often. You must be proud."

"Cole is well too. Very busy—too busy—but just fine."

Again, I did not go into detail. My closest and most intuitive friends politely did not push, yet their French eyes said what their French voices would not speak. We smiled at one another, accepting the silence and knowing that it was good to be together again.

"This might sound crazy given all that is happening with GiGi, but do you think I might be able to resume working with you, even randomly, schedule permitting? Coming here makes me miss this more. Heather has an idea involving this new online shopping service Amazon. Do you know about it, Monsieur?"

"In fact, I do. A young man from Seattle got the idea a few years ago to create a way to sell books on the internet. As the story goes, his parents gave him money to launch, and he created his business in the family garage. It seems garage start-ups are the foundation of the electronic age, with so many of our now famous tech wizards beginning that way." Monsieur had the story down.

Responding that I was behind the times somewhat, unaware of Amazon for the most part, I confessed that I especially unaware of the fact that the site sold clothing.

"They have been selling fashion for a few years now. They are selling everything. You can buy a tire for a car, or a new mattress," Madame chimed in. "We have even considered trying to sell on the site, but I don't think the mass public will buy original couture online, at least not yet. Perhaps one day. Who knows with the way the world is moving forward in so many unimagined forms."

"Heather believes we could put a Fair Child product for sale on Amazon. Do you think that it would sell?" I followed.

Pure kismet: Heather walked in the salon, the bells over the door announcing her arrival.

"We're in the back," I called out. She found us all talking Amazon.

"Not a bad idea, right?" Heather jumped in right away.

Monsieur was the first to add his voice to the train of thought.

"A very good idea, Miss Heather. We must convince our young protégé to return to the design table, even very part time, so we can create a perfect product for Amazon. We should take this seriously," he said, with Madame nodding in agreement.

"Kate, are you ready for this? Is the timing all wrong? If you can do this, I can be there to handle all the mechanics of getting your design on the site. No sacrifice of time away from GiGi, the boys, or Cole. What do you think, my best friend? Are we back?"

Impetuous and foolish, I leaped at the chance to get back to work. Knowing it was selfish of me, I still needed to try. I also knew the dream would never rise in importance above caring for my sick child. As my father said, I could do it all. Indoctrinated with those words, I had to try my best.

The afternoon customers began entering the shop. Madame went to work. For the next couple of hours, following a check-in call to Bonnie, Heather and I worked on concepts at the table. Under the nose of Monsieur, who was interjecting with comments and critiques at appropriate intervals, we forged ahead.

It was the best afternoon ever. We were back, at least on this one day. It was a blessing. I returned home midafternoon to find all my children were rising from afternoon naps. Life was good again.

CHAPTER SIXTY-FOUR

WHAT COMES AROUND

GiGi's week back at home was a small blessing. She appeared to be thriving for the most part. She was due back at Children's Hospital on Friday for a round of chemo. I was dreading the day, wishing this would all vanish. Why had this happened to my baby? To be honest, I also wanted to know why it was happening to me. I was being tested like never before in my life.

Cole came home every night, leaving his stress at the office, or so it seemed. He also left the scotch at the bar, for the most part—another small blessing. The boys loved having him around, and he spent more time with them than ever. We did talk more, which was good for me. Bedtime talk, quiet time talk. There was no sex, and that was okay. Pleasures of the flesh seemed so wrong when my child lay in her crib down the hall fighting for her life, which our union had created.

We didn't talk about that. Instead, we talked about plans for the future once GiGi would be cancer-free; schools to enroll the children in; a family trip to Hawaii; and finally finding and moving into a home of our own one day. We talked about gratitude, my going back to work, and Heather's plan to put my designs on the internet. I still wore my ring, night and day. Cole stared at it off and on. It was a source of pride for him, an accomplishment of sorts, a symbol of his success to have been able to provide his wife with a significant gift representing our bond—traditional, corny, superficial, and even misogynist, I guess, if one were to analyze the custom. I still loved the ring, a woman's prerogative.

On Friday morning, we needed to rise at five o'clock in the morning in order to be at the hospital by six to check in for the morning chemo procedure. Cole was going to come with me. Bonnie would remain at home with the boys. Cole's support took away some of my dread. When I was smiling at him as we got GiGi prepared to go, he gave me a funny look.

"This is the 'we moment' I've been talking about and asking for," I told him.

"I get it." He nodded. "And we'd better move it so *we* will get there on time."

Cole was nervous; this was new territory for him. This time he would not be standing in the corner of the hospital room for ten minutes before leaving.

I was relieved to have his full presence, but then again, one doesn't always get what one hopes for. The doctor was just starting the procedure; Cole was in his corner, and his cell phone started beeping without pause. He didn't pick up until I told him to do so. Leaving the treatment room, closing the sliding door behind him, Cole answered as I watched him. Instantly, he was clearly upset, appearing to be shaking. His arms flew up and down, his cell phone in his palm, a potential projectile. I expected to see him throw it down the hospital corridor.

Rushing back into the treatment room, accidently slamming the glass door as he threw it back open, Cole met me body to body as I came toward him.

"Forgive me, Kate. I am so sorry once again. I must go. Forgive me, please. I'll explain later." And he was gone.

Karma

As Cole exited the elevator and entered the Baldwin office, turmoil greeted the former TV star. Cubicles were abuzz with the news just breaking, the agents thriving on the gossip. Roman was visibly apoplectic, screaming in Russian and English, mixing the two languages. Cole darted through the bullpen and was avoided by all the agents, even his sycophant follower Kit Hamilton, who was under his desk pretending to pick up some paper on the floor. This did not escape Cole's notice as he rushed by. Roman was down on all fours, pounding the floor.

The big news brought Cole down on that floor too. He attempted to lift his partner, who was now hyperventilating, in prestroke mode. Roman shouted out, and the entire office listened.

"You are fucking kidding me! The yacht was seized by the Organized Crime Drug Enforcement Task Force in the Gulf of Mexico! We are so fucked, fucked, fucked!" Cole was screaming along with his partner.

The "we are so fucked" echoed through the bullpen. Agents were repeating the words and passing the news along. Not that they grasped the situation, since none of them, except Kit Hamilton, knew what the hell they were referring to. The assumption was that some real estate deal had gotten sidetracked and maybe it would have some effect on all their jobs at Baldwin et Cie.

Cole finally got off the floor. He lifted Roman into his chair, pushed the button turning the glass walls opaque, and shut the office door.

He poured water from a crystal decanter into two cut-crystal tumblers.

"Fuck the water!" Roman shouted. "Where's the coke?" he demanded. Cole put the water glass in Roman's hand and forced him to drink.

The redness in Roman's face faded. He wiped the sweat from his forehead with the sleeve of his white shirt with French cuffs and began to share what he knew.

Both Hellman and Sierra were on Organized Crime Drug Enforcement Task Force watch lists, apparently having been so for more than a year. Roman didn't know how deep it went. Sierra had been arrested twice before and then released, including the instance in Beverly Hills at the Holmby Palms Hotel. The charges were small time, with no jail, just court-ordered rehab. Hellman seemed untouchable.

When they boarded the *Xania II* in Newport for the yacht transfer to Fort

Lauderdale, all the cases of champagne were filled with cocaine, the champagne on top. That was millions of dollars' worth of powder on the street market. The DEA had been tipped off and were watching for the Newport launch but apparently chose to wait on enforcement, looking for a bigger catch.

Hellman and Sierra, along with Smith and Jones, disembarked unexpectedly in Panama, and *Xania II* cruised on its course into the Gulf of Mexico, headed for Fort Lauderdale. For some reason the young women remained on board. The US DEA, joining forces with the Mexican government and with assistance from the Colombian government, followed *Xania II* on its course as it sailed out of sight of land.

South of New Orleans, the yacht had drifted just inside US waters, skirting international boundaries, and the government forces watched as another luxury yacht appeared, moving in toward *Xania II*, the two of them anchoring together at sea. Armed traffickers boarded with high-powered guns and took over the *Xania II*.

The captain and crew were subdued, bound and gagged, taken off the yacht, and put on board the attacking vessel. The young women were left alone on the main deck, oblivious, drinking champagne and waving at the invaders. Then, a new captain and crew boarded, along with an additional entourage of models, four more women. Along with the exchange of personnel, the crew from the invading yacht loaded cargo on board *Xania II*, lots of cargo, more containers topped with bottles of champagne.

Cole interrupted Roman's detailed account, incredulous over the explanation.

"How did you get all of this information?" Cole insisted.

"Man, it's all over the news this morning on every channel. It's coming over my cell phone. It's on the computer. Where the hell have you been?" Roman was spitting.

"I've been at the hospital, Roman," was Cole's only response.

"Man, this went down last night in the Gulf. I turned on the morning news while getting dressed and went into shock."

Roman finished telling what he knew, relating that all three different government forces had closed in and captured the drug smugglers, apparently with no loss of life. All were arrested and taken into custody; both yachts were seized. The news was reporting more than one hundred eighty million dollars' worth of cocaine and fentanyl was captured.

"Joseph, Mary, and Jesus," Cole spoke with scary reserve. "We are fucked," he said.

Roman told Cole to sit.

"It's worse, buddy boy. You are the legal registered owner of *Xania II*. The news is also reporting that Cole Baldwin, the host of TV's *American Dream Homes*, is connected to the story. Your picture is front-page news." Changing his tone to one of sarcasm, he said, "And by the way, your mug looks darn handsome on every TV news channel."

"Shit! Fuck! Shit again!" Cole yelled out. The opaque glass panels reverberated, and the office chatter halted. The agents had turned on the morning news broadcasts in the office.

"What do we do now?" Cole could barely talk; he was choking.

Realizing that Kate must also know, he panicked.

"Oh my God, this will kill Kate. With GiGi sick, and now this, I am toast," Cole said, having managed to get out the words. "Then again, Kate turns off her cell when she is at the hospital or any time she is with GiGi. Of course, her parents are calling. Everyone she knows is calling, leaving voice mails, or she would have called me." Cole continued in panic mode.

"Why hasn't anyone called me? I don't have messages," he said to Roman, who was sitting in a semicoma.

"Buddy, it amazes me how little you know about human nature. Dude, when you are the king, the TV star, the real estate baron of bullshit, they want your autograph. They want to sit at your table and be photographed with you for the society column. Many of them want your studly body. But when you are involved in one of the biggest drug busts in the Western Hemisphere, can you spell pariah? Cole, you are now an untouchable." Roman finished his speech, put both hands over his face, and put his head down on the glass-top *bureau plat*.

"What about you?" Cole realized he might be out on the edge of the cliff by himself.

"Oh, don't worry, I'm in just as much shit. Only my picture is not out there. Not yet, anyway."

Roman pulled it together enough to get out of his pity party and pick up the phone to call his lawyer. He told Cole he needed an attorney separate and apart from his and that they would also need another attorney together to defend against any charges potentially leveled at the business.

Cole ran out of Roman's office, across the bullpen, and directly to the elevator, shouting that he had to go to Kate at the hospital. Kit Hamilton jumped up and got in the elevator with him, insisting on driving him. Cole ignored Hamilton, looking straight ahead at the doors as if Hamilton were invisible.

As the elevator doors parted at lobby level, Cole and his sidekick were mobbed by waiting press with flashing cameras and videographers. They were being held at bay by two building security guards and a red velvet rope stanchion—of no real value if a stampede were to unfold.

Hamilton grabbed Cole, yanking him from exiting to the executive parking lot, instead pulling him in through the lobby-level door leading to the garage parking area underground. Hamilton got Cole in his car and found a way to avoid the press, then drove him to the hospital. The media did not know Hamilton, and they certainly would not be looking for his car.

CHAPTER SIXTY-FIVE

HOLDING ON

Two stressful months had passed since that infamous Friday at the hospital with GiGi. Cole's fall from grace was thrust upon me by a nurse who had stopped me in the hallway outside GiGi's treatment room to ask me if I was doing all right. Naturally, I assumed she was referring to a mother's fear over her child's serious illness. I responded appropriately that GiGi was improving and that I was doing better as well. The nurse paused, then said she was pleased to hear GiGi was doing better, but she meant the news about my husband.

It is said that timing is everything. Cole came running down the hospital corridor as doctors, nurses, and staff surrounded me in the hall, offering support. In a state of confusion, almost an out-of-body fog, I began checking the messages on my cell. The second I flipped it on, it began to ring and ring. Refusing to answer, I turned it off and handed the phone to my doctor.

The huddle of medical staff spread wide around me, a chorus line of sympathy, allowing Cole to enter. We looked at one another.

"You know," he said in a low, deliberate voice.

"I do. Just found out."

"I didn't know about the drugs, Kate."

"This is serious, Cole. I think you will be charged."

"I know. We've called lawyers."

"Are you okay?" I asked stupidly. Of course, Cole was not okay. He looked terrible, ready to fall over. At a loss for more intelligent words, I continued: "We will get through this, Cole. Remember, I told you we will get through what life throws at us. GiGi will be cured. And this too will go away if you are innocent of involvement with the drugs."

We came together in an embrace. The medical staff applauded. One nurse even cheered. At that point I knew I was having an out-of-body experience. People were clapping for us as my husband told me of his involvement in the biggest drug bust of the year, while my baby was receiving chemotherapy across the hall. Was I in a bad movie? Would I awake from this dream to find everything just as it had been before?

The initial shock and drama of the news of the seizure of *Xania II* faded somewhat in a week with the ever-fickle news cycle. A tornado in the Philippines, then a terrorist bombing in Jerusalem, and closer to home, jitters in the US stock market and reports of the banks' problematic lending practices, came out of the shadows and into the forefront.

While local gossip had subsided to a degree, the newshounds and paparazzi no longer waited at the front door of Cole's building or, worse, at the front door of our Lido home, which for a few days had created havoc on the island, forcing us to flee north to Beverly Hills with Dalt and Nancy. All of us went except Cole, who was too mortified to face my father, even though Dalt had reached out to him, offering his backing as well as a referral to top legal counsel in Los Angeles. Insisting to stay close, Cole told Dalt he needed to deal with Roman and all the issues. I did not push it.

As soon as the cameras left to follow the next scandal, we returned to Newport. Dalt wanted me to stay with the children. Nancy was the one who said I needed to go home and be there for Cole. It was the right thing to do for him, for our marriage, and for the long-term benefit of the kids. Most importantly, with GiGi in cancer treatment, a routine was imperative. The child was due for her next chemo infusion at Children's Hospital of Orange County. Dalt tried to override my mother, a rarity, telling me we could have the same treatment at Children's Hospital in Los Angeles. He had a very good client whose financial portfolio he managed who was the lead pediatric cancer specialist in LA. I took Nancy's advice, though. Bonnie and I packed up the four kids and went home.

The calendar turned to August, with my birthday coming and going. There were no carefree beach days on the sand with the children. None of that mattered as much as the improvement in GiGi. The chemo was working; the doctors were optimistic. A need for a bone marrow transplant was on hold and, with some luck, off the table.

Cole was home with me and the family a great deal of the time. Always on the phone or computer in the den, with the drapes always pulled closed, he pursued retaining his freedom and trying to maintain confidence. Still managing basic living expenses, Cole's dignity was spared with funds spirited away by Roman immediately after news of the yacht seizure had broken. These were misused funds, presumably the property of the investors in the BIG Fund. Cole did not ask for my financial help and refused despite my repeated insistence. He didn't share the details about where his money had come from, but I knew. That too would get sorted out.

Things were as stable as possible under the dreadful circumstances. We maintained a low profile. People were unusually kind. In the grocery store, I heard only positive words, wishes for the best of luck and continued improvement for GiGi, and prayers for Cole and me.

Cole needed the prayers. With a few exceptions, the agents made a mass exodus from Baldwin et Cie. The bullpen was empty. Two agents who remained had deals closing. Kit Hamilton, loyal lapdog, had stayed at Cole's side, helping him over the past weeks of trouble. Funny how people in one's life alter their roles, their importance changing dramatically.

Seeing as he was now a regular presence in our home, I grew fond of Hamilton. He made life easier for Cole, driving him when necessary, running errands; working on the computer; functioning as a buffer with all of calls from lawyers and investigators, angry investors, agents in the office looking for unpaid commissions, bill collectors, and contractors at The Summit; and managing the continuing press follow-up, which seemed to explode in spurts as more information surfaced on the seizure. Hamilton even helped with Bonnie and the kids. It was clear he was taken with Cole and idolized him. At times it was too much, yet I took it all in stride, figuring he was now our devoted younger brother. I assumed he was gay, though the matter was never discussed. Perhaps he had not come to terms with his own reality.

Anyway, the young upstart agent Cole always called a pain or the nerd, and even labeled as the mosquito since Hamilton seemed to be buzzing around him, annoying and intrusive, was now his right arm. Cole especially relied on his role as a buffer. The mosquito had real value; he knew how to sting.

Hope Springs

Cole's issues aside, GiGi's weekly blood tests continued to deliver positive results. Her young life celebrated more days of normalcy; the progress was evident to all of us. Our hope was restored; a corner had been turned. With this came a degree of freedom, mental and physical, for me, enabling more afternoon sessions at the salon. I dove back into designing new patterns, working with concepts and ideas for a potential internet platform to fulfill Heather's new business goal. There were so many options online, so many products, including every famous fashion label. I had no idea about the power of this new world of shopping. Stores were heaven to me; this was a reality I had not fully grasped.

The new age trend of selling fashion online eventually became crystal clear. On a late midweek August afternoon at the salon, with Heather present, we examined a dozen different new designs that I had worked on over the several months with Monsieur. Methodically, we dissected the pros and cons of my bomber jacket, the perfect boyfriend shirt in white, my wrap dress, the Fair Child women's muscle shirt modeled after a man's white ribbed sleeveless undershirt, and others.

Heather wasn't going wild over any of them.

"What's this?" she asked, holding a baseball cap retrieved from a box under my worktable.

"That's my Fair Child baseball cap, Kate style," I said proudly as Heather checked out the cap. I had used a very soft yet tightly woven Italian cotton in pure white, extended the brim beyond a normal cap size, and used pink satin lining. The ribbon was edged with a black and white stripe and embossed with "Fair Child" in black signature script, to be used as a bow tie to fasten the cap at the back of the head, instead of the usual Velcro or a clasp. Front and center on the cap, I had placed my appliqué signature pink pansy, also edged in black and white.

"This is it," claimed Heather. "This hat will be the foundation of Fair Child online. I will find some influencer or, if I get lucky, a celeb of some sort to wear your cap and post a picture on social media. If it trends and she gets followers who love the hat and want to have one, we'll have the platform."

My best pal grabbed me. I was laughing out loud, the first time in months I had felt totally free from worry. It was only for a moment, but I knew how to recognize and cherish the good moments.

"That sounds great, assuming you can pull it off. What if it works? We don't have any hats except this one," I said, still laughing.

"No problem. We can find a hat jobber who does regular baseball caps and have him get to work. We could have hundreds, thousands if we need them." Heather was positive, bullish as ever.

I was totally jazzed, even jumping up and down.

"That will be all," Heather chided.

Monsieur entered the planning party with his total agreement. Even better, he had the perfect hat jobber in downtown LA. Heather said she'd go to work finding the ideal young woman to launch the hat on social media, advising we should all stand by for our next phase of instructions.

Heather Delivers

On Thursday before the Labor Day weekend holiday, Heather rang my cell at seven in the morning. Not too early these days around the Baldwin fort. Holding the cell in my left hand at my ear, feeding GiGi in her highchair with my right hand, I received news.

"Have you heard of this new hot singer from Spain, Mia Luna? She has a record on the Top 100 chart that's getting lots of attention. Kind of a unique sound, a blend of Abba and Gloria Estefan," Heather went on. I cut her off.

"And this is important why? Abba and Estefan—sounds strange."

"Only because she is wearing your Fair Child baseball cap on a new music video being released this weekend on social media, that's why."

"OMG. That's amazing. How did you pull this off?"

"Sparing you all details, I'll cut to the chase. A friend of a friend of a friend works for her record producer, and I got the cap to her, asking a huge favor. Mia

Luna loved the cap, so no favor required. She put it on and flipped over it. In fact, it is darling on her; she is very tall, slender, and exotic looking with fair skin; long, dark wavy hair; and enormous, big brown cow eyes—and she wears tons of mascara and false lashes. Picture a close-up of those eyes peering out from under the brim of your hat. I'm talking hat sales, girl."

"I had better call Monsieur and have him reach out to the hat jobber in LA," I said, speaking my first thoughts.

"Done. I spoke to him already." Heather was in charge. "Let's just see what happens this weekend on social media. If the likes are as good as I think, then we will be back in business. Kate, get ready for our third try at this; they say the third time can be the charm."

The three-day holiday passed with Heather and me watching the Mia Luna media posts, glued to our phones and laptops. Her record was smashing the charts, and so were the likes on her look—especially that hat. By Monday morning, Mia Luna had more than half a million hits on her site, and Heather, thinking ahead, had also created a site just for the Fair Child cap with ordering instructions and everything. The numbers began in the hundreds, and by eight that evening we had some five thousand orders for the Fair Child cap.

This was a most unexpected turn of events at the most difficult time in my life.

CHAPTER SIXTY-SIX

THE RECKONING

It was ironic having discovered unexpected career promise over the internet fate of a baseball cap. The success was hard to celebrate as I was witnessing the equally unexpected failure of my husband's career and its effect on our relationship. My life focus remained on GiGi. Even with her improvement, that focus was a 24/7 obsession. I was not jumping with joy and planning my next big fashion career move just because we had sold a ridiculous number of hats in a day. By the way, sales had continued to climb every day since. Horrified, I was frankly scared over Cole's situation, which also was second to GiGi. Cole's crisis involved legal problems, not life and death, and would work out in some fashion. Perhaps the best resolution wouldn't be the best, but they would work out. Time would tell. I believed he had no connection to the drugs.

The seizure of *Xania II* in May had triggered a domino slide that would be better labeled as an avalanche. Within days of the news reports, the first domino to fall was a freezing of credit by Roman's bank Lehman Brothers. Construction on the Baldwin projects at The Summit, ten houses in stages of completion and another ten in early phase construction starts, was entirely in jeopardy. Roman kept things going despite the hold on credit, advancing funds from the investor portfolio. It was unethical, a big risk, shining a very bright spotlight on the overall condition of the BIG Fund. With multiple millions withdrawn for personal use by the partners, shared with me by Roman in confidence, my fears grew. We were living on borrowed financial time.

"Taking from Peter to pay Paul is common practice in construction. It doesn't make it right, and it can spell trouble, but it's reality, Kate," Roman told me. "Cole and I will get through this. It will take some time and some manipulating, but we are not dirty dealers," he added.

I refused to fully accept his explanation.

"Not directly, anyway. Are you telling me you had no idea that your client Hellman was involved in drugs? What about Sierra? Roman, I'm not blind. This has been in my face and fell at the doorstep of my parents' home as well."

Roman confessed to having known about Hellman. He told me that Cole knew but had nothing to do with any of it. Knowing and keeping silent did not constitute innocence. At this point I fully realized that both Cole and Roman were facing serious trouble ahead, as was our family.

"Roman, why is Cole's name the only one on the yacht ownership papers?" I wanted answers.

"We had to make this buy a private investment, unrelated to the BIG Fund. Cole found the deal, and he is the one who stood to make the largest share of the resale commission, so his name is on title."

"I guess that means he will also receive the largest share of the trouble," I said, leaving Roman in the empty office, where I had gone without telling Cole, in an effort to understand what was happening.

Finding out had made matters worse.

With their construction credit frozen and with the departure of all the agents working under the celebrity Baldwin et Cie brokerage, Cole continued to spend his days mostly isolated at home, sleeping beyond noon, and working out all afternoon on the beach or at the gym at the Harbor Club. He also devoted a great deal of the day to his scotch. The drinking was out of control. There was no anger and no threatening behavior; he just tried to keep things civil. I confessed to him that I had met with Roman, and he said he was glad I knew more and that he would never forgive himself for having done this to me. Cole thanked me for taking care of his baby daughter, then began to cry over his own failure to step up. Deeply touched by his emotion, I consoled my husband, unsure about the sincerity of my own words.

"We will all get through this. We must be strong. You're a fighter. I'm a fighter. Our child is a fighter. One day we will be healthy and happy again."

That day was not in sight. On this day, it was another appointment with a children's cancer specialist, not associated with Children's Hospital. My mission to save GiGi had turned me into a research intern. I read every bit of information on leukemia I could get my hands on. Cole said he was going into the office to meet with Roman, as they were scheduled to have a phone conference with a lawyer late that afternoon. We kissed goodbye and wished each other good luck.

The closing and tightening of the financial market was now widely felt, no longer simply evident to those with the proper crystal ball. Media were all over the crisis at the Federal Reserve Bank, and major financial institutions were running for cover.

With Wild West lending at the nation's banks in laser focus, chips were falling. Zero-down lending on real estate had come to a halt like a train's brakes failing, slamming the train into a wall at the end of the line. This was a genuine double whammy for Cole and Roman. Even if they had never involved themselves with the *Xania II* fiasco, the market correction would have triggered a landslide. Before the seizure of *Xania II*, they were both so drunk with their own success that they had missed the signs.

All the investors in the BIG Fund were also too drunk with their own success—and a healthy dose of greed. With the *Xania II* disaster, another example of the proverbial train slamming into the wall, in conjunction with the market flattening in real estate, the investor guys who could not wait for their monthly cocktail conferences to brag about their much-deserved good fortune given their exceptional business acumen, were all smacked with the reality. The next move was to blame Cole and Roman. Lawyers were put on retainer. The federal authorities were contacted with claims of fraud, namely, a potential Ponzi operation with serious misuse of investor money. Fear among the investors grew as lawyers advised that there existed a real possibility that they all could be involved in the *Xania II* scandal, even indirectly, if their funds had been used as part of the scheme.

Natives were circling the campfire and preparing for war, demanding a return of their investments. The remaining BIG Fund money was in a separate account, also frozen, an immediate action taken in line with the opening of an FBI fraud investigation instigated by both the *Xania II* case and the BIG Fund investors' accusations.

While the money flow had dried up instantly, the legal troubles did not turn into action as quickly. Investigations were complicated; they took time. The summer months of 2008 passed with threats but without charges of any kind. Cole was in seclusion with Roman, floundering, attempting to pinpoint an angle to get them out of the mess. They both treaded treacherous waters.

Then September 15 arrived. A one-day five-hundred-point drop in the Dow Jones opened the door to the Great Recession, with bank failures and with Roman's Baldwin account with Lehman Brothers being wiped out. Corporate collapse and political upheaval followed. Real estate lost 20 percent in value in a matter of days, heading toward as much as a 50 percent loss in some cases. All development ceased. Home buyers vanished the next day. Home sellers lost their minds, and in some cases, their life fortunes evaporated. In more dramatic cases, lives were lost.

Ironically, September 15 was the day Cole chose to return to his office to meet with Roman. The pair of former masters of the real estate universe sat in disbelief while watching the television news in Roman's glass-enclosed throne room. In the bullpen, a crew of men in white overalls were systematically removing all the office furniture, breaking down the modular cubicle partitions, and removing the assets, which were being repossessed by the furniture supplier. Already months behind in payment, they acknowledged that losing the furniture on September 15 came with a sense of poetic justice.

Two movers came into Roman's office and began to take everything. The movers nodded, not saying anything, as the couch, coffee table, side chairs, credenza, bookcase, and lamp went out the door.

Returning for the next load, the men surrounded Roman's glass-topped *bureau plat*, then lifted it and took it away. Roman grabbed the phone and some papers before the desk was gone. They came back for the third removal, the chairs

Roman and Cole were sitting in. Still no words. The partners stood up; the chairs, on wheels, were rolled off. Roman and Cole sat on the floor, legs crossed like boys obeying the kindergarten teacher, watching the Dow drop on the TV that was mounted on the wall above the now missing custom credenza. At least the TV was paid for, not rented. The power remained on—Roman had paid the electric bill, but not the office rent. Eviction was to happen at month's end. On the afternoon of September 15, somehow it didn't matter so much.

The phone rang on the floor at exactly three as scheduled by the corporate attorney hired to represent both. Pleasantries were short, the attorney cautioning that the call might end abruptly as clients were reaching out given the market collapse. The big fish clients might need his backup assistance more.

"Here's what I know as of close of business yesterday," he began. "The Drug Enforcement Agency, LA office, is working with the LA office of the FBI investigating your connection to the yacht *Xania II* and the Boreanaz cartel out of Colombia, and a new investigation is being discussed in the Orange County District Attorney's Office into fraud and misuse of investor funds vis-à-vis a possible Ponzi scheme under your control."

Cole was already lying flat on his back on the floor of the office. Roman fell backward next to him as the attorney kept talking on the speakerphone.

"There is more bad news. What I've learned is that Hellman is not the focus of this problem regarding the yacht. Yes, he was on board with the woman Sierra and others. Yes, both had been on the FBI and DEA radar for more than a year. However, there is no financial or legal paper trail of any kind linking Hellman—or Sierra, for that matter—to the yacht or the drugs. So far, the FBI knows that they were involved, but they have no direct evidence to pursue prosecution."

Cole interrupted the attorney. "Where are they?"

The attorney replied, "Hellman and Sierra have not been heard from since May."

Cole was desperate. Roman already knew where they were, or at least he had good reason to believe he knew.

"From what I've been able to gather, the FBI believes that Hellman is still in Panama City, apparently living the good life at all the clubs. He's been spotted and tracked, as have his bodyguards. He has not tried to leave Panama and, again, remains untouchable at this time."

Roman followed up asking about Sierra.

"Sierra is another story," the attorney said. "She has flown. There is no sign of her, no record of travel. It is assumed she made her way to Bogotá, Colombia, to join the Boreanaz family. She is not being charged with any crimes by US authorities at this time. They have little interest in her."

Roman looked as if he had just swallowed hemlock and was waiting for a deadly reaction.

"Sorry, men, I have to go for now. Here's the bottom line: Each of you must lie low, below radar. Stay out of the public. Get in touch with your individual attorneys as you will need separate representation. If this comes to an arrest and an indictment, the feds will pit you one against the other. Likelihood is that one will take the big fall, and the other will get reduced time for throwing the other under the big bus. I'd advise that you part ways now, end your relationship, take cover, prepare, and get ready. I'm sorry to end with this, but there is no way you can afford my service or that of my firm to defend your business. There is currently a near-fifty-thousand-dollar balance due on your statement that I am going to forgive. Best of luck."

He hung up. A ten-minute call and that was that. Over and out. His best advice was to end the friendship and duke it out to save at least one of their asses.

Semicomatose, both still lay on the floor, staring up at the ceiling, when in walked Kit Hamilton.

"Why are you on the floor? Where's the furniture? Cole, I went to your home to find you. I have information on Hellman and Sierra. Bonnie said you were here, which I took as a good sign. Maybe it's not so good?"

Roman looked at Cole, then at Hamilton. "Get the fuck out of here, you measly weasel."

Cole stopped his partner from getting up and slugging the little mosquito.

"Okay, enough. Hamilton is here to help me get through all of this. He's not a bad guy."

Cole's praise surprised Roman. "I thought I'd heard it all today" was his only response.

Cole got up off the floor and asked what Hamilton knew about the missing client and the party girl. Hamilton delivered a scenario matching the attorney's information.

"How the fuck did you know this?" Roman demanded.

"I started working in Hellman's office in Newport when I gave up Hollywood. He was a mentor, and the office staff are friends. And you also know that is how you got him as a client and investor—because of me."

"Shut up before I pound the life out of you. You're bragging about bringing Hellman in, the guy who has ruined us?" Roman had to be restrained by Cole. He lunged at Hamilton, Cole yanking him back.

"Hellman is in Panama City and won't be back for some time," Hamilton continued. "He's really upset about Sierra leaving him too."

Cole could restrain Roman no longer. He jumped on top of Hamilton, the latter of whom was half his size in stature and began pounding him. Blood gushed from Hamilton's nose and under his chin. Hamilton screamed for Roman to stop. Cole got on the floor to pull Roman off, his soon-to-be former friend and former business partner. Roman turned his rage on Cole. There were two bloody faces now, and it took both men to pull Roman down to the floor and stop the fight.

"Let's get out of here," Hamilton said, imploring Cole to leave. Cole obliged, saying nothing to Roman, leaving him behind on the floor.

"Fuck both of you weasels." Roman gasped for air as they made it to the elevator.

"I'm okay to drive," Cole instructed. "We'll take my car and get a drink at the Harbor Club. Then I'll need your help with an errand."

"Let me drive, Cole. I can tell you've been drinking today. I'll drive your car," Hamilton protested.

Happy hour at the Harbor Club was packed. The valets were dealing with a line out to the Pacific Coast Highway. Cole was blind and clueless about the overflow, having been advised by Hamilton that it was certainly a reaction to the market disaster and that members were feeling the pain, which they were drowning in alcohol.

"Don't get in this valet line," Cole told him. "Go around to the back, where the loading dock entrance is, and park in the employee lot. Give me the key and go get us a table on the bar terrace. They know you. Remember, my member number is BXX-68. Order a drink. I'll be there in a minute." Hamilton followed orders.

With no one else in sight, Cole made his way into the storage area used by the ground maintenance crew. Locating what he sought, he picked up two large metal containers stacked beside the lawn mowers, then returned to his car, where he popped the trunk and placed the containers inside. Minutes later he was on the waterfront terrace drinking his scotch with Hamilton, who was partaking in a frozen margarita.

As Hamilton had predicted, the club was jammed with members crying over the market, drinking heavily, and ignoring the very recently famous local celeb golden boy Cole Baldwin at his table. Today there were no well-wishers, no stoppers-by, no hot women touching the back of his suit collar as they passed.

Cole had little to share with Hamilton. Instead, the Cole worshipper did all the jabbering. Joking about the fight scene they had come from, each of them dabbed at their wounds as trickles of red liquid oozed. Some thirty minutes later, and at least a couple of more drinks each, Cole rose without explanation and began to exit. Hamilton followed.

"You need to drive." Cole handed the key to Hamilton as they reached the parking lot.

"Where are we going on your errand?" Hamilton asked, pulling the black BMW 7 Series out of the Harbor Club then turning onto Pacific Coast Highway.

"Turn right. Head south up to Society Hill," Cole directed. "We're going to One Society Hill Road off Newport Coast Drive."

"I think I know where that is," the obedient driver remarked. "Isn't that the short street that dead-ends into this major estate under construction? I've been watching the progress. That place is amazing. Is that where we are going?" The mosquito knew everyone's business, or so he liked to believe.

"Just keep driving," Cole said, ending the talk.

Hamilton pulled the BMW up to the construction fence gate at One Society Hill Road and stopped the car. Cole got out, opened the combo lock with his code, and pulled back the gate. He returned to the car and instructed Hamilton to drive to the property under construction. Hamilton stopped talking, a minor miracle. He could tell that his mentor was at odds as his hands were shaking and there was sweat on his brow.

Pulling up to the circular drive fronting the fully framed and partially finished exterior of what would eventually be a very grand villa on the ocean promontory, Cole asked if Hamilton wanted a tour. There was no need for a response.

"Follow me. I need you to help me bringing something in the house." Cole went to open his car trunk, Hamilton beside him. "Take one of these cans. It's heavy," Cole said.

Each of them took one and went into the property. There were no finished interior walls, just wood framing, plywood flooring, and bracing throughout. Cole opened the spout on his can and began to spread the gasoline as fast as he could given the weight of the vessel.

"Hamilton, go up those wooden stairs and spread the liquid," Cole demanded.

"What are you doing?" Hamilton begged for an explanation.

"I'm burning down my house, and I need your help. Go up there and spread the juice. When you come down, I will light the match." Cole spoke quietly, without anger, being strangely reserved and matter of fact.

Hamilton stood in shock, then did as his idol had asked him to do. The odor of the gas was intense, beginning to overwhelm the senses. Both men emptied their cans of liquid poison as quickly as possible. Hamilton raced down the stairs, leaving the can behind.

Standing in the entryway of what would never be the villa Cole dreamed of surprising Kate with one day, he lit the match and ignited the trail of gasoline he had created, leading to larger pools of accelerant around the ground floor. The main stairs ignited simultaneously.

The property went up in flames fast. Hamilton begged Cole to leave at once. Cole refused, instead standing in the circular drive as the growing inferno of raw timbers collapsed, taking the partially tiled roof structure with it. Facing the end of his dream, a final failure never to be recovered from, Cole stood frozen and silent.

The smoke was so thick that it became hard to breathe. With the flames reaching thirty to as much as fifty feet in the sky over Society Hill, Hamilton attempted to grab the car key from Cole to escape. Cole relented, and both men ran for the car. They got it sped off, going out through the construction fence and racing down Society Hill Road toward Newport Coast Drive.

Fire engines and Newport police were on the way, the sirens approaching. As Hamilton and Cole reached Newport Center Drive, heading for Pacific Coast Highway, a flash of police cars raced by them. An open bottle of J&B rested on the console between Cole and Hamilton. Unscrewing the top while driving way too fast, Cole took a swig, then handed the bottle to Hamilton, who did the same. They made it back to the office, another small miracle, and went up the empty elevator to the empty office and returned to sitting on the floor, this time in Cole's former domain, where there was one remaining bottle of scotch.

As they drank themselves crazy, Cole more so than Hamilton, Society Hill burned to the ground on the night the stock market did the same. Newport was mesmerized. The flames burned for hours and were seen not only across town, but also throughout much of Orange County. An armada of boats left the Newport Harbor and cruised out to sea to view the inferno from the water.

CHAPTER SIXTY-SEVEN

THROWING IT ALL AWAY

The fire sirens began to fade into the distance. Cole and Hamilton lay down on the carpeted floor of the empty office, drunk and dazed, alone, with the daylight nearly gone. Turning toward his loyal subordinate, body to body, face-to-face, Cole reached around Hamilton, pulling him closer, embracing him with all his alcohol-enhanced strength. Placing his hand on Hamilton's shoulder, Cole pressed his face against the man who had just helped him destroy his dream. He felt the sweat on Hamilton's cheek and the stubble of his shaven face. He whispered in Hamilton's ear, "You backed me up, man. You took care of me. You were there for me 100 percent."

Hamilton took no time to respond, turning to face Cole eye to eye.

"I worship the ground you walk on, Cole," he said. "I always have, since the first time I met you."

Cole stared at Hamilton and moved in with another embrace. And then there was a forceful coming together of their mouths, a lasting exchange, latent sexual curiosity unleashed. Clothing clumsily discarded, sexual exploration fulfilled, Cole and Hamilton fell into a deep sleep side by side, half naked, with pants around their ankles and shirts with one sleeve off and the other still in place.

By nightfall, the flames on Society Hill had been reduced to smoldering embers. The mansion under construction that had been the subject of gossip and conjecture as to its ownership for more than a year was now ash. Police and fire investigators converged on the scene, immediately determining that this was a case of arson as the odor of gasoline remained pungent over the ruins. Detectives on the road leading to the property interviewed neighbors who came forward with clues. Multiple sources reported having witnessed a black BMW with two men driving at high speed coming from the mansion. Police on the scene concurred, saying they had passed the same car at the corner of Society Hill Road. Some of the neighbors told police that they had seen that car in the area many times and noticed that a personalized license plate bore the initials CB.

With that lead, in no time the car was traced to Cole, as was ownership of the Society Hill property. Officers were dispatched to the Lido Isle residence and to the Newport Center offices of Baldwin et Cie.

It was just after six, and I was coming home from an afternoon at the salon working with Monsieur. The cap sales were phenomenal. Fortunately, our jobber was keeping up with demand and shipping out batches daily. It seemed that every teenage girl in the United States wanted my cap. We were even getting sales outside the United States, and they too were growing, especially in Asia.

Heather advised me to start working on a follow-up item to put up for sale online and on social media. Deciding to do a T-shirt, I created a simple fitted feminine white T-shirt with little cap sleeves and the appliqué pink pansy logo centered on the chest. Monsieur located the ideal fabric: a very soft but strong body-hugging Italian cotton, ultrawhite with no color whatsoever. We were making samples, playing with the lines and the fit of the T-shirt. It was coming together. I was thrilled, and Heather was certain it would be a killer partner to the cap. "We are really in business," she repeated often.

Elated from my afternoon session at the salon, I arrived home on Lido Isle, having driven behind several police cars on the main boulevard Via Lido Soud. Naturally I had wondered where they were going. It never crossed my mind that they could possibly be going to my home. That is, until they were.

I pulled up right behind them. The police cars blocked my driveway, so I left my Tahoe at the curb, got out, and asked what was going on. Since I had not heard from Bonnie, I knew it could not have been an emergency with the children, so I did not panic.

"Is this your residence, ma'am?" one officer questioned.

"Yes. I'm Kate Baldwin."

"Is your husband Cole Baldwin?" he continued.

"Yes. Is everything okay?"

The officer did not answer. "Is your husband home?" he asked.

"I don't think so. He usually works late at his office," I replied. "Do you want to come in? Is Cole all right? Did something happen?"

Still no reply. I walked hastily to the front door, the police in tow. As I called out to Bonnie, we entered. The Newport Beach officers stood in the entryway. Bonnie appeared.

"What's the matter?" she asked, concerned upon seeing all the police.

"Is Cole home?" I asked.

"No, Kate, he's not here. Hasn't been here all day since leaving this morning for the office before you left," she reported.

The lead officer went on his radio and reported that Baldwin was not on Lido and that they were leaving. He handed me a card, instructing me to call and to have my husband call immediately when I saw him.

"Can you please tell me what this is about?" I asked again.

The police officer finally answered. "We are investigating a fire, and we need to speak to your husband."

"A fire? Was that why I heard so many fire sirens this afternoon?" I questioned.

"We must go now. Thank you for your cooperation."

The police were gone in seconds.

"Bonnie, are the kids okay?"

"Kate, they are all in the kitchen having their dinner."

"Go back to them. I'm turning on the TV in the den to see if there is any news about a fire."

The mansion blaze on Society Hill was on all channels. Sloppy local news coverage was not specific about location, cause, or any pertinent facts. I assumed it was one of the homes under construction at Cole's development The Summit. I called his office. The phone line kept clicking off. He did not answer his cell. Running into the kitchen, I kissed the children and told Bonnie I was heading to Cole's office, saying I'd be in touch when I knew more.

From a block away I could see the police cars in front of Cole's building. Red lights flashed in a disjointed drumbeat of alarm. There had been no flashing lights in front of our home. The Newport Beach police had made it to the office before me.

Leaving my car as close to the building as I could, I dashed into the lobby. Sam the building concierge knew me, and he got me into a service elevator, away from the police standing guard. Sam told me they had not yet gone upstairs. He heard one of them saying they were waiting for confirmation of an arrest warrant.

Racing out of the slow-opening doors of the elevator once it reached the office floor, I saw the main double doors to Baldwin et Cie were ajar. Pushing them open, I saw that the office was bare—my first shock. There was nobody there; lights were off; it was dark and quiet. Cole's private office was only steps away from the main reception area. There was enough light from the surrounding tall buildings to illuminate the hallway through the office windows. Entering Cole's office, I saw him there asleep, undressed, lying on the floor with Hamilton, who had his arm over Cole's bare chest.

Frozen, I stared, saying nothing, trying to make sense of it. My head was spinning; my hands were shaking. Holding back tears, I turned to leave, wanting to walk away and get out. It was no use. The police arrived en masse, asking me to step aside and taking charge.

Demanding that the men wake up, get up, and get dressed, the police shouted orders. Standing outside the glass partition separating the office from the hall, I looked in at my life falling totally apart through the glass.

Startled, both Cole and Hamilton rose from the floor, sitting up. Still on an alcohol comedown following floor sex, the pair of odd lovers and arsonists were without coherent words. The police looked at one another, exchanging grunts as they arrested the two men before them with their privates hanging down and their jockey shorts and pants at their feet. Neither one could stand up straight given the position of the pants dragging their ankles together.

As they were read their rights, Cole and Hamilton fumbled to pull up their pants. Assisting each other, they finally stood, leaning against the office wall, unsteady and half-conscious as the officers proceeded.

"Cole Baldwin, you are being arrested on suspicion of arson for igniting a fire at the property located at One Society Hill Road. You have the right to remain silent … the right to an attorney …" Another officer did the same recitation for Kit Hamilton. Cole and Hamilton faced the wall, remaining silent.

As the legal process was completed, the rest of their respective clothing was fetched. I watched Cole try to button his rumpled white dress shirt and put his suit jacket back on. He did not see me. Running his hand through his tousled hair, he retained some vanity and a state of self-awareness as he and Hamilton were led out of the office. Then Cole saw me standing there crying. The police ordered Cole and Hamilton to turn around and be handcuffed.

"Oh my God, Kate, it's you. What are you doing here?" He sounded like a wounded animal.

"I'm here to find you, to find out what happened with a fire, to see if you are okay, and to be your wife and the mother of your four children coming to help."

"Kate, I've messed up worse than ever."

The police pulled Cole and Hamilton away.

I could barely get a word out. Feelings of betrayal, shame, and a total loss of self overcame me. The police were not willing to wait for further explanations and apologies between husband and wife.

"I'm sorry, Kate. I love you so much, Kate. I'm sorry."

Cole kept repeating his words as he was taken away. Hamilton looked at his idol with profound sadness each time he called out "I love you, Kate."

The elevator doors closed. I broke down, sobbing on my knees in the cavernous vacant office. For the first time in my life, I was afraid.

CHAPTER SIXTY-EIGHT

PICKING UP THE PIECES

Surrendering to the loneliness of the office floor, I remained there without moving for half an hour, on my knees, out of my mind. I was questioning everything in my life, even my husband's declaring his love for me, although he had proved it countless times in our bed over years of marriage. Now he had just been arrested for arson after being found naked, presumably following a sexual encounter with a man he once claimed to dislike. Why had Cole been arrested for arson, and what was happening with the drug seizure and the confiscation of the yacht *Xania II*? Was all of this connected?

Managing to find some strength to calm down and pull myself together, I rose and left the office to go home. Although I was tempted to pack everyone in the car and head to Dalt and Nancy's, what little sanity I had left stopped me from reacting in such a way. I was confused, embarrassed, and scared. It was bedtime for the children. I would have to be a big girl and remain in the Lido house, in our bed alone, through the night. Reality would be faced in the morning.

Not wanting to scare my kids by having them see me crying, I let Bonnie handle the evening routine, offering to explain later. When they were all bathed and in bed, she came to my room and found me curled in a ball surrounded by pillows and hiding under the duvet. Sitting beside me on the bed, she listened as I shared what I knew. The facts made even less sense to her since I didn't have all the pieces of the story. What I had seen was enough. Deep down I was sure my marriage was over. Words I had shared with Cole haunted me: "We will get through anything together." Really? I could not get through this. Telling myself that I did love Cole, I also told myself that I could no longer be in love with him.

Choosing not to call my parents, Heather, or anyone, I asked Bonnie to pack up the necessary things for the kids in the morning. Not sleeping at all, I went over and over every crazy detail, every possibility, every scenario, and every possible reason for what had happened. I also made a plan.

Getting Nancy on the phone at eight o'clock in the morning, which was always okay with her, I asked if we could come for a couple of days' visit. She pressed for explanation. I hedged, telling her we just wanted to spend some time. She didn't believe me but didn't press. "Sure, come on. Can't wait to see you all. Anytime," Nancy told me sincerely. She added, "Did you hear about the big fire on the Newport coast? It's all over the news. Is everything okay with Cole's project up there?" Nancy did not mention her serious concern over the earlier news of Cole's involvement in the drug seizure. She was nothing but cool under pressure.

I told her I didn't know much about the fire, specifically leaving out the fact that Cole was the one accused of starting it.

"We'll be there by noon," I said. "I love you."

"Darling, I love you more. I love you always," my mother said. A twenty-six-year-old woman with four kids still needed her mother and her mother's love.

Again, Bonnie saved the day. The children were all excited for a road trip to see their grandparents. Baby GiGi was doing exceptionally well—feeling good and looking healthier each day.

We were met at the door on Lexington Road by Nancy and Dalt, their arms wide open. There was no explaining necessary. Cole's picture was once again on the news channels, with the visuals of the fire pushing my cool and calm parents into major damage control in terms of both the fire and the alleged involvement in the seizure of the yacht. With the fire news, they intended to take charge. I welcomed it.

Moving in, settling down, I took less time than I thought I needed to regain a semblance of security. So many questions, so few answers. For the next two days, through the weekend, I did nothing but exist and tend to the children. Dalt was burdened more than I had ever witnessed. My star father was dealing with the market and banking collapse, along with taking calls at home nonstop, assuring clients who were coming unglued in the financial crisis. My cell phone was switched off. I had texted Heather, and she arrived at the house to stay by my side day and night.

By Monday morning, hiding was no longer possible. The FBI was at our door. Dalt had reached out to criminal defense lawyers, and meetings were taking place in closed-door sessions in the library. Cole was behind bars in Orange County with bail set at one million dollars. According to the lawyers, the FBI was about to issue a second arrest warrant with charges of drug smuggling, money laundering, and fraud vis-à-vis illegal use of BIG Fund investor dollars on personal lifestyle expenditures. Dalt told me, "They are throwing the book at him."

I offered to put up the 10 percent of the bond money, $100,000, from my grandmother's funds. Dalt said it would be unwise. Cole would just be arrested again in a matter of hours when the more serious drug warrant was issued, likely with no bail, only to be remanded into custody. Lawyers also told Dalt that a similar warrant was being issued for Roman, but he was in the wind, unable to be located. Cole was taking the fall for everything.

For days I did not share with my parents what I had seen in the office when Cole was arrested. Heartbroken, ashamed, embarrassed, and confused, I wasn't ready or able to talk about his betrayal. Part of me still wanted to believe that he loved me, that it wasn't a betrayal, just something else. But what?

Toward the end of the week, after dinner when all was quiet in the house, it was time to tell. In the library, on that same leather couch where Cole had sat with Dalt on many occasions over years, impressing my dad with his work ethic and his ambition, I told Nancy and Dalt that I had found my husband naked on the floor of his empty office, drunk and in the arms of his associate.

With my final words, I felt I'd made a mistake. Both looked as if they were facing a firing squad. Dalt's face lost all color. Nancy came and sat next to me on the couch, putting her arms tight around me. They didn't speak; there were no words of consolation or explanation.

Finally breaking the silence, Dalt asked, "How can we help? What can we do for you? Would it help to talk to a doctor? Do you want to see how we can help Cole, or do we need to back away for now? Anything you want. Let us help." He said these things in love. Given the financial stress he was under, I feared that adding my problems to his would give him a heart attack. Even so, Dalt repeatedly expressed his willingness to hire a strong attorney to help Cole.

Cole was going to have to fend for himself for the time being. Telling Dalt to back away, and refusing professional help for myself, I said I would handle the situation day by day. After all, the pattern of day-by-day survival was the norm with GiGi's care and recovery. I knew how to do that. I could also come to terms with my marriage falling apart.

Cole's lawyer reached out, contacting me on behalf of Cole. He told me how sorry Cole was and how much he wanted to talk to me. I asked the lawyer to relay my love. Part of me would always love Cole; I told the lawyer to tell him that. I also asked him to share that I needed time to think, as I was still unable to talk to Cole and unable to see him just now. I was thinking about him, about us, every day. Keeping the kids away from the news, my heart hurt for Cole, for all of us. I only wished him well, despite everything.

I was not ready to go home to Newport. An unlimited stay was offered and accepted. After I sent for more necessities, we hunkered down. Buddy and the twins would miss school, and I would need to figure out GiGi's visits to Children's Hospital Orange County. She was due for a checkup in a few days and then had another possible chemo treatment the following week. I would just make the drive down to the OC as needed.

Dalt took over that dilemma, setting up an appointment at Children's Hospital Los Angeles with the client he had mentioned to me before when discussing obtaining a second opinion on bone marrow transplantation for infant children. His client Dr. Wechsler, who was considered a national authority on the subject, made an appointment with GiGi the following week.

Attempting to find some level of normality amid the chaos created by lawyers and investigators, coupled with all the terrible unraveling of the financial markets, which was bearing down on Dalt and his business, we avoided TV news as much as possible. This was especially the case when the children were with us. One morning Bonnie had the kids in the den watching the Disney Channel. She flipped the channel, looking for another show, and accidentally landed on a news station displaying a full screenshot of Cole. "Look, there's Daddy," shouted Buddy.

Heather stayed with me every free moment she had away from law school, practically moving in. This was a blessing. We worked on the T-shirt design and kept Monsieur in the loop via phone and Federal Express, sending our design changes back and forth overnight. Seeing that big white FedEx truck pull into my parents' driveway in the morning was reassurance that there might be some sort of life after all in the future.

Nancy instructed us to open a little studio in the unused chauffer's quarters adjacent to the garage at the back of the property. Heather took charge and set up a complete studio with worktables, sewing machine, tools, fabrics sent by Monsieur, and just about everything else. From the new pop-up fashion headquarters, she also managed the growing sales of the cap, all the business with our manufacturing partners, the shipping, the social media, and the banking. I did as much as I could to help. Despite everything else, the Fair Child line was growing, and we were weeks away from unveiling the second item—the amazing T-shirt to go with the cap.

Working with Heather took my mind off Cole, at least at moments. The days passed with some laughter, which was healing elixir. Nancy and Dalt loved having the children, and the children loved being with their grandparents. The house was big enough that overcrowding never became an issue.

GiGi's appointment day arrived, and I set out for Children's Hospital LA to meet Dr. Wechsler. With the exam scheduled for ten o'clock, we arrived by nine thirty to fill out forms and get acclimated. At ten thirty a nurse escorted us into an examination room, apologizing for the delay. Dr. Wechsler had been detained with a patient in the hospital and was sending a fellow physician in to start the exam. The nurse also explained that Dr. Wechsler would join us as soon as possible. He had advised his nurse that we were special patients because of a family connection, she shared.

I was relieved. The nurse took the vitals of my toddler, who was perfectly at ease and calm. She smiled at the nurse and spoke to her in remarkably clear words and relatively coherent sentences.

After a polite knock at the door, a handsome young doctor came in. With a full beard, nicely trimmed, and a short military-style haircut showing premature gray, the doctor entered. Burying his head in files, peering through tortoiseshell-rimmed glasses, he studied GiGi's health records, presumably sent from Children's Hospital of Orange County at Dr. Wechsler's request. Not looking up, he walked past me and sat in the chair beside the exam table, going straight to GiGi.

Putting down the files, the doctor attended to GiGi with extreme care. I watched intently, amazed at his bedside manner. This young doctor was sincerely loving and invested in this toddler he'd never treated before. Taking both of GiGi's little hands in his, the doctor turned to me. "Oh, I apologize if I did not introduce myself when I came in. I'm Doctor David Morgan, a pediatric cancer doctor here at Children's Hospital. Infant leukemia is my specialty."

Knowing the voice at once, and then the name, my heart sank. David did not recognize me.

"David, it's Kate." I put my hand out to take his, holding back the urge to embrace him.

"Kate Fairchild. Is it really you?"

"It is really me, David," I answered, looking at him directly in the eyes. David took my hand and placed it upon his heart.

The End—and a New Beginning

In the final days of the golden era of television, before the thirty somethings suits with business degrees from the Iveys invaded Hollywood and turned television into 382 channels of reality, shopping, talk and dribble, three young men would meet at the University of Southern California film school setting their individual and collective sights on careers in the world of the small screen. This is their story.

One had looks, another had talent and the third had connections. Starting at the bottom of the ladder, the way success in Hollywood used to begin with a more sensible predictability, each set out to "make it". Set against a backdrop of the major networks still controlled by the pioneering genius of the big three: Paley of CBS, Goldenson of ABC and Sarnoff of NBC, the three young protagonists, allegorically mirroring the mystical and magical three kings and three networks of television will sacrifice everything to make their dreams a reality. Unbridled ambition trumps honor, humanity and love. Only one man will survive the climb to the top.

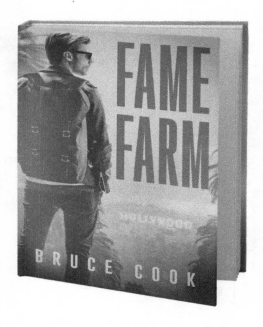

CPSIA information can be obtained
at www.ICGtesting.com
Printed in the USA
JSHW022054230723
45181JS00001B/1